# TEXAS DREAMS

*One Family Struggles to Tame the West*

# LINDA HERRING

BARBOUR
PUBLISHING

Scripture quotations are taken from the King James Version of the Bible.

Published by Barbour Publishing, Inc., P.O. Box 719, Uhrichsville, Ohio 44683, www.barbourbooks.com

*Our mission is to publish and distribute inspirational products offering exceptional value and biblical encouragement to the masses.*

 Member of the
Evangelical Christian
Publishers Association

Printed in the United States of America.
5 4 3 2

**LINDA TIMIAN HERRING** was born in Texas and remains a tried and true Texan. She married a Lutheran minister, had four children, then began teaching. She is very musical, having played the violin, the piano, the guitar, and the organ. She is also a member of the Lutheran Houston Chorale. She began writing in her middle-age years, and sold her first book three weeks after submitting it. Thus began a ministry whereby she could share her down-to-earth faith. She has published seven Christian romances, and is working on more. She and her husband, Mel, have ten grandchildren that they see often. Since moving to Houston several years ago, they are thrilled at being able to participate in the many cultural events that are offered. Her mother, Fern, who is ninety-two is still living, and Linda has a sister, Janice, who lives in Galveston.

# Dreams of the Pioneers

*For Mary Anna Thornton Smith*
*who started the wheels turning.*

# Chapter 1

The Texas air blew cool, but Daniel Thornton's shirt was soaked with sweat born of fear as he hunkered down in the dense plum thicket. *Where are they?* he worried. He strained his ears for the slightest sounds that might give them away.

With a venomous whistle, an arrow sliced through the branches, just missing Daniel. *Over there.* He squinted, trying to pierce the thicket with his gaze.

"Hey! Come out, John. Come out. We won't hurt you," an Indian called, using the name they gave all white men.

Daniel knew that was a lie. Especially now. Now that he had done such a horrible thing to gain revenge from the Indians. The taste of bile rose in his throat at the thought of the atrocities committed by the Indians against white people.

He turned toward the voice and took careful aim with his Sharp's rifle. The gurgling scream that followed his shot told Daniel he had hit his target. *One down,* he thought. *But where are the other two?*

With the same deadly whistle, a second arrow flew from the opposite side, thudding into Daniel's elbow and laying the flesh open to his wrist. He ground his teeth to keep from screaming. He dared not move an eyelash. Two more exploratory arrows skimmed through the bushes at different angles, and then Daniel heard the welcome sound of unshod ponies riding off in the early twilight.

Daniel took off his bandanna and wrapped it tightly around his forearm, just above the entry wound. Then he waited to be sure the horses had ridden away. One thought kept him from passing out with pain and loss of blood: He must get back to Mary Anna.

When he was sure he was alone, Daniel crawled out of the thicket and signaled to his horse. "Take me to town, boy. Home to Mary Anna." He slumped over in the saddle, holding on to the horse's mane. "Mary Anna, Mary Anna," he whispered. "Forgive me, Mary Anna."

~⊷~

In the town of Stephenville, Mary Anna stirred a large kettle of stew over the hot coals of the fireplace. It was a worry to be cooking in someone else's kitchen, taking advantage of Frances Gerald's hospitality this way.

Mary Anna's blue eyes had been haunted with concern for three days now, ever since she and Daniel had lost everything they'd owned to a renegade Indian's torch. It was a mercy this good soul had taken them in. And she was worried, too, about Daniel and her father. There was a rumor about town that some of the men had banded together to raid the reservation in retaliation for all the attacks the Comanche had made on the white settlers.

Had Daniel and her father joined up with these raiders? Surely not. Daniel was an honorable man. Her father, too. No, she was sure they were just out hunting.

She put on a bright smile as she heard the hoofbeats of an approaching horse. "Boys, I think your father is coming in. Tump, help T.P. get washed up for supper." She wiped her hands on her apron and smoothed her hair as she opened the door. Her smile froze on her face. The incoming rider was slumped over his horse.

At twenty-two, Mary Anna had lived on the Brazos River frontier for two years, long enough to learn that she'd best be prepared for anything. Now she straightened to her full five feet two inches and did what had to be done. She ran out and grabbed the reins of her husband's horse, bringing horse and rider to a stop in front of the door.

Daniel's face was gray; he was unconscious. An arrow stuck out of his arm, and a blood-stained bandanna was wrapped tightly around his forearm.

"Whoa, boy. Daniel! Can you hear me?" Frantically she looked for signs of life. Daniel's eyelids flickered, raising Mary Anna's hopes. "Hold on to me. I'll help you into the house." *Thank You, Lord, for bringing him back to me.* Then she turned toward the house and shouted, "Frances, help me!"

A handsome, grandmotherly woman came hurrying out, a frown of concern on her face. "Is he alive?"

"Barely."

Between them they dragged, supported, and carried Daniel into the house and got him to bed. Neither woman thought to worry about the precious quilt under his bloody arm and muddy boots.

Frances hurried off to get some hot water.

Mary Anna carefully moved Daniel's arm and used her scissors to cut away the crimson sleeve of his shirt. She studied the arrow still protruding out of his arm. "Tump, go tell Mrs. Gerald to bring a very sharp knife." The wide-eyed little boy sprinted for the kitchen.

As she worked, Mary Anna asked Daniel, "Where have you and Papa been? What happened?" Indistinguishable murmurs answered her.

Frances came in with the water and knife and gave a sharp glance at the arrow. She looked over to Mary Anna. "You know what to do?"

Mary Anna nodded and Frances stood by to help.

With swift movements, Mary Anna used the knife to cut off the tip of the arrow. She was grateful Daniel was unconscious as she struggled to pull the arrow through to the other side of his arm. Two yellow circles and a red line on the arrow would have told her who owned it had she known how the Comanche marked their arrows.

Fear helped her complete the grisly job of doctoring the man she loved. But would he survive the loss of blood and the infection that was bound to come?

"I'll go make willow bark tea," Frances offered. "Tump, you come with me and bring back the herbs your mama will need to put a poultice on that wound."

While their two little boys watched, huddled in silence, Mary Anna mopped Daniel's feverish brow with a cool rag and applied herbs to cleanse the wound and ease the pain. She eased sips of willow bark tea between his lips to take down the fever.

The fever seemed to make Daniel delirious. He sobbed and kept repeating how sorry he was. Mary Anna was shocked by the intensity of his painful words. She tried to shush him and calm him. "It's all right. It's all right. I'm here." What could have happened to wrench the heart of her brave, young husband?

Daniel heard her voice and understood what she was saying, but he couldn't make her understand what was wrong. He was certain Mary Anna would never love him again. He listened to her comfort, but as the medicine began to ease his pain, he began to drift. Back to the happy times when they weren't in this house on the raw Texas frontier of Erath County.

He floated back to 1853 when he had first come to Texas, to Tennessee Colony in Anderson County.

～

Daniel had just ridden in from his newly rented land to buy supplies at the mercantile store when he saw Mary Anna at the dry goods counter buying thread. She was the prettiest thing he'd ever seen. So tiny. So dainty, with her light brown hair piled up high to make her look taller. Her cornflower blue eyes were demure, and her manners genteel.

They hadn't been properly introduced, and even in the new settlement of Tennessee Colony in East Texas, a man couldn't expect a lady to talk with him. He wished she'd drop something so he could pick it up, for then it would be all right to speak a little. Her voice wasn't as tiny as her frame, but it was pitched in a pleasing tone as she talked with the clerk. She was almost through with her purchases. She was going to leave.

Throwing away the restrictions of good manners, Daniel stepped forward and tipped his gray hat to her.

"Pardon me, ma'am, but I'd be honored if you'd accept a piece of peppermint."

She regarded him with those blue eyes, and her cheeks pinked at his brashness. She was about to say no thank you, but she saw he had almost the same color eyes as she did, and he was a very handsome man. He looked the picture of Southern gallantry standing there with his hand at the brim of his hat, waiting.

"It really isn't proper, sir." But the light in her eyes told him she was going to accept his gift.

It wasn't that Mary Anna was improper. It was more that she was daring and resourceful. And as her eyes refused to pull away from the blue depths of his, she wondered why a simple offer of a piece of peppermint was making her heart beat so fast.

# Chapter 2

Tennessee Colony had the same unfinished look of the many other towns that were like fingers of civilization inching west across Texas in 1853.

Peter Garland, Mary Anna's father, was busy behind the desk of his hotel talking to a robust woman with hair the color of bad ginger.

"Please see that my bags git upstairs real fast," she said in the nasal tone of the unlettered.

"Yes, ma'am," he said without enthusiasm and signaled a small black boy to fetch the carpetbags.

His wife, Louisa, sidled up to him from the hot kitchen. "That daughter of yours is cooking like she's some kind of artist or something," she complained. "Go tell her to work faster and not try to be so fancy."

Peter, being a former military man and accustomed to war, was nevertheless irritated at the constant battles in his own household between his second wife and his pretty, sixteen-year-old daughter, Mary Anna.

Captain Peter Garland stood up straighter and said with quiet intensity, "Louisa, this has got to stop. I can't stand this constant yapping about Mary Anna." His eyes narrowed with anger, and he warned, "If you're not careful, you'll be the one in that hot kitchen."

Louisa was totally unimpressed. "You think doing the laundry and cleaning this place is a lot of fun? Don't threaten me. Go talk to your daughter." She turned and walked away unhurriedly.

Having failed to quash his wife's agitation, Peter Garland retreated to the sultry kitchen where his daughter turned out the food that brought people to his dining room.

Mary Anna was frying large steaks that had been pounded thin and tender, then dipped in a batter of flour, egg, and milk. The browned pieces of meat gave off a mouth-watering smell. It was their most popular dish, served with mounds of whipped, light-as-air potatoes and snowy white gravy with crisp bits of the crust hidden in each bite. When it came to cooking, his daughter *was* an artist. But how to bridge a compromise between wife and daughter?

Mary Anna wiped her hands on the apron around her tiny waist. "Did you want something, Papa?" she asked as she concentrated on thickening the gravy.

Peter's heart grew wobbly at the sight of his favorite child, the image of his dead wife. "No," he said, accepting total defeat at the sight of her. "Just be sure and save me a plate for dinner." He kissed her damp forehead and smiled.

When he returned to the desk, Louisa was waiting for her triumph. "Well?" she demanded. "Did you speak to her?"

"Yes, dear, I spoke to her," he said truthfully. Providence was on his side, for at that moment a young man walked in and strode up to the desk, ending the discussion.

"Good day to you, sir. Glad to have you with us. How long will you be staying?" Peter's greeting may have been a bit too friendly, but he was so glad to see his chance for ending his talk with his wife that he overplayed his hand.

"I'll be here awhile," the young man said noncommittally. As he signed the register, he commented, "Something sure smells good." He glanced toward the rough room that served as the dining room.

"Dinner is about ready. . ." Peter glanced at the name written on the register, "Mr. Thornton. My daughter is the best cook in Texas," he bragged, then quickly looked around to see if Louisa had heard him. "By the time you take your bags upstairs and clean up a bit, she'll be serving."

"Thank you," Thornton replied and got the key to his room.

Peter watched him as he walked up the staircase. Thornton was a good-looking man, and Peter tried to assess his wealth by what he was wearing. Gray cowboy hat, expensive boots. No jewelry. It was a father's duty to check out all the new men in town. He had a marriageable daughter, and he wanted to pick out just the right man for his beloved Mary Anna. *Hmmmm, a maybe*, he decided.

~

Daniel Thornton walked into the hotel room and set his leather bag on the floor at the end of the brass bed. He hung his hat on a wooden peg in the wall and poured some cool water from the china pitcher into the matching bowl. Carefully he rolled up the sleeves of his starched white shirt and leaned over the bowl, splashing the deliciously refreshing water on his tired, hot face. His stomach growled, reminding him it had been a long time since he'd had an unsatisfactory campfire breakfast on his newly leased farmland outside of town.

He checked his blue-black hair in the mirror and saw in its wavy reflection a man of twenty, but the eyes told of experiences older than that. For an instant he was startled to realize that his eyes were the same color as those of the comely young woman he had met at the mercantile store. Something about her had attracted him immediately. "Maybe it's the eyes," he grinned.

He was still tired from the hard labor of the past few days. He had cut timber and begun building a rude cabin. He planned to put in the crops as soon as that was done, but he hated sleeping on the ground.

When he had so adventurously left the Big House on the plantation in Mississippi to make his fortune in this new place called Texas, he'd never dreamed he'd miss his bed more than his family.

Even though this bed looked well used, he couldn't resist stretching out on its colorful quilt. As the springs complained, he sighed and sank his head into the downy pillow. Absolutely anything was better than sleeping on the hard ground, using his saddle as a pillow. He dozed with a slight smile on his face, listening to the hallway sounds outside his room. With the window open, he could hear the busyness of the town and smell that delicious food cooking somewhere down below him. It was a lot like being home again. He half expected the thin, black frame of his old mammy to come in, fussing at him about having his boots on the good bedspread. She had always been there for him through those growing up years, and he loved her as well as he did his own mother. He certainly knew her better.

His stomach registered a louder complaint, and the smell of the food propelled him downstairs to the dining room.

He saw her in an instant, placing hot food on the common table, bustling around like a mother at the head of a family. He tried to catch her eye, but she was too busy to notice.

He sat down next to a large woman with hair too red to believe and smiled his best smile at the comely young woman pouring hot coffee across the table.

She must have felt the smile, for she looked up at him and stopped in midpouring, a blush from the heat already highlighting her soft skin. She returned his smile briefly and then dropped her eyes to finish her job.

He waited patiently for her to come to his side of the table and pour his coffee. She smelled of good food and sweet soap, and though her hands were very small, they looked strong and attractive as they poured the black liquid into his cup. He looked up into her face and saw those eyes again. Twin to his own. Something deep inside him reached for her, and he wondered if she felt it, too. There was nothing in her face to tell him. He had given her peppermint earlier, but now he felt he had given her his heart without knowing her. He tried to think of something to say.

"Your father says you're the best cook in Texas," he offered with a genuine smile. "I know it smells better than anything I've had since I left home." His voice had a pleasingly long Southern drawl.

"You're Irish, aren't you?" she countered.

"Irish by heritage, Southern by birth," he corrected her. "How can you tell?"

"First by your eyes and hair and second by your blarney."

"And you know because you're Irish, too. Right?"

"Yes." Her eyes danced with mischief. Never before had she felt so bold with

13

a young man. First she had accepted candy from him, and now he was plying her with compliments and she was bantering with him like a coy debutante. This was not the way she had been brought up. And it felt wonderful.

"As one countryman to another, let me introduce myself." He rose and formally bowed. "I am Daniel Robert Thornton." He looked expectantly at her.

She curtsied and said, "I'm Mary Anna Garland, sir."

The people sitting around the table had all stopped eating and were gawking with mouths open at the little drama going on at their dinner table. The lady with the red hair had suspiciously watery eyes, which she dabbed at with her napkin. "Ain't that sweet?" she said to her dinner partner. He looked at her as if she had lost her mind and took a large bite of a pickled egg.

Daniel took the hand Mary Anna extended and lightly kissed it. He wanted to put it in his shirt next to his heart. He wanted to wrap his arms around this extraordinary woman and carry her off to a castle. But he stood there holding her hand as if it were the crown jewels.

Mary Anna felt a little faint and realized it was from holding her breath. She exhaled and tried to break his gaze. She knew the entire room was watching, but she didn't care. There was electricity in the air, and it was coming from the touch of his hand on hers.

"Miss," whined an old geezer who had never known love, "could I have my coffee, please?"

The spell was broken, but Mary Anna walked inside a rainbow as she carried out her duties at the table. She knew Daniel had not taken his eyes off her, and the realization made her giddy.

Finally, she retreated to the kitchen, taking in big gulps of air to clear her head. She had so often prayed for a fine Christian man with whom she could share her life. Had he walked in, just like that? *Lord, what's going on? Is this the man for me? I feel something strong about him. I'm excited and I feel silly.* She was standing at the stove stirring the vegetables as she prayed.

"What's wrong with you?" grumbled Louisa as she swished into the kitchen. She picked a small piece of the browned crust of an apple pie and studied her stepdaughter's glowing face for a second time.

Mary Anna was immediately on guard. "Nothing. I'm hot. Do you want plates for you and Pa?" she asked in an effort to redirect Louisa's thoughts.

"No, not yet. You know we always eat after all the guests are finished. Are you sure there's nothing wrong with you?" She stared hard at the young girl's face. Mary Anna was even more beautiful, her face radiating some sort of inner glow. Louisa took one last little pinch from the pie and left, still wondering what had gotten into the girl.

Daniel lingered as long as he dared at the table, but Miss Garland didn't come back. Reluctantly he paid the bill and left the hotel to take care of his business. There was no doubt in his mind where he would be taking supper that night.

Louisa watched the young man hang around the dining room, remembered the look on Mary Anna's face, and quickly put two and two together. What a stroke of luck! They were obviously taken with each other. All she had to do was make sure they spent some time together, and soon there would be a wedding. The problems of her life would be solved. Peter would concentrate on *her* once Mary Anna was married. She smiled broadly and began planning. *Sunday,* she decided. *There's a dinner on the ground after church.* Her smile broadened even more.

Louisa tried not to be jealous of the time her husband spent doting on Mary Anna. Louisa had seen the small locket with Mary Anna's mother's picture in it, and she was well aware that Mary Anna was a constant reminder to her husband of his dead wife. She hated that. She wanted to be his only love. Peter was kind and loving to her, but she never felt he loved her as much as he had his first wife.

She could make him love her that much or more if Mary Anna wasn't there to constantly remind him of his loss. The sooner she was gone, the sooner Louisa could begin to permanently erase the other woman from his life. Now that Mary Anna was of marriageable age, Louisa could find a husband for her. Louisa smiled in happiness. *This one looks like he could be the one.*

# Chapter 3

It was a perfect Sunday afternoon, and Louisa's plan was in full flower. Peter had invited Daniel to church and to the meal afterward, and he had eagerly accepted.

Now Daniel and Mary Anna sat underneath an umbrella of green leaves swishing the air beneath them like a thousand tiny servants moving fans to cool them.

Daniel groaned appreciatively and tried to ease his long frame into a more comfortable position on the patchwork quilt. "That's the best apple pie I've ever had." He washed the last of it down with a gulp of cold lemonade.

His heart rate had steadied since its first wild gallop at the sight of her at church. He had endured the eternal sermon and sung the hymns with a fair baritone, and when it had come time to pray, had he still believed that God was personally involved in his life, he would have had only one prayer—that she would love him as much as he loved her. And then it was time for the meal.

The Garlands had invited Daniel to sit with them, but they couldn't all sit on the same blanket, so he and Mary Anna had a blanket to themselves now that her younger brothers and sisters had run off to play.

Mary Anna's voice was as clear and sweet sounding as water to a thirsty man. "How long has it been since you've been home?" She was tidying up, putting things in the big hamper.

"About a year." He tipped the soft brim of his hat up a little higher on his forehead and watched her.

"Don't you miss your family terribly?"

"Yes. But coming out west was something I had to do." He smiled an embarrassed smile. "I needed to make some money of my own. I got tired of being obliged to my father." Idly he picked a piece of grass to chew on. "Pretty country, Texas."

She leaned against the big, shady old oak and laughed softly. "I remember the day we crossed the border into Texas. It took us a month to come from Tennessee. There were thirty covered wagons in our train, but they were so heavily loaded that all the older children had to walk. I was twelve. Then one day someone shouted, 'We made it! This here is Texas!' I was so disappointed. It looked just like all the country we'd covered. I couldn't understand how they knew we were in Texas. All I wanted to do was to stop walking and sit."

Daniel laughed delightedly. "So you walked to Texas! I walked a lot of the way from Mississippi. We have a lot in common." His eyes sparkled with an intimacy that stirred Mary Anna's senses in a most disturbing way.

She smiled at his enjoyment of her story and took in the handsome face so open before her. A crowd of people was busy eating and laughing all around them, but they were in a private world of their own.

"Some day," he told her, "I'm going to own so many horses and cows that I'll be able to ride from my table to my bed if I've a mind to."

"Richer than your father," she laughed.

"Texas is the land of milk and honey, so the tale goes." His smile was pragmatic. "So far all I've seen is a lot of milk, but the time will come." He left the thought full of promise and adventure, and she could feel his unrestrained excitement. "I want to build my own kingdom. There's so much land out there just waiting to be used. Why, a man could have a ranch of thousands and thousands of acres." He gave a crooked grin. "Maybe I'm just trying to do better than my father. I want him to be proud of me."

Mary Anna felt her heart quicken at the thought of what this man planned to accomplish. It matched her own dreams of being her own person. She wrinkled her forehead in puzzlement. "But why have you stopped to farm in Tennessee Colony if you plan to go farther west?"

"I'm a greenhorn when it comes to pioneering. I've been learning all the things I'll need to know when there's no one around to ask." He leaned forward in his earnestness. "I need to know how to build a cabin, how to plant crops, and which ones I'll need. I'm already a good shot, but I don't know how to skin deer or buffalo. There's an awful lot to learn," he conceded. "And I'll need money."

Mary Anna wanted to memorize the picture of this tall, well-muscled man. His sun-bronzed face was young and strong, full of dreams and plans. With his hat tipped back, a small band of skin that had been shaded from the Texas sun was exposed, and the sight of that pale streak below his hairline seemed a most intimate sight. She wanted to reach out and stroke the well-defined chin, the strong jawline, the mobile mouth. It was on his mouth that her eyes lingered. "How long will you stay here?"

His eyes met hers. "Awhile. 'Til I make enough money to keep going. I want to keep moving west. There are millions of acres just waiting to be tamed." His face hardened. "Now that the murdering Comanche have been taken care of, it should be safe for a man to make his fortune."

"But we have reports all the time that there are still bands of them wandering wherever they please," she contradicted him. Hatred marbleized his face.

"It won't be too long 'til the government has them all locked up where they belong. Reservation life is the best thing for them. It keeps us peaceful people safe."

The injustice of his statement hit Mary Anna like a hammer. She took a deep breath and plunged in, fearless to speak her mind. "They were here long before us. We're the intruders. And they're only fighting to protect what rightfully belongs to them." Her quick temper and sharp tongue had earned her a reputation of some note in the community.

Daniel's face darkened with suppressed rage. "There's enough land for everybody. No need to be killing white people just so they can protect land they're wasting. They don't do anything but ride around all over it."

Mary Anna liked this young man, and as his rage increased, hers lessened. She quietly asked, "What happened to make you hate the Indians so much?"

Daniel's teeth ground together tightly. "When my grandfather was clearing his land in Virginia, the Indians captured him. They tortured him before they took his scalp for the tent pole. I was the one who found him." The horror of that day was reflected in the haunted eyes that stared out into the far-too-recent past. " 'Course my father killed two of them later for revenge, but that didn't erase what they did to Grandpa."

Mary Anna sat paralyzed with the horror of the story and the depths of bitterness revealed by a man she had admired from the moment she had first seen him.

"Are you shocked?" At the dumb nodding of her head, he went on defiantly. "You don't live in the real world here, Miss Garland. Out there it's just you against everything else, and I do mean everything." He pulled the brim of his hat down until it shaded his eyes—and perhaps some of his feelings. "If it makes you feel any better, I have no intention of killing any more Indians for my grandpa. That's over and done. But if I ever had to kill to protect myself or my loved ones, I'd never stop to think about it. That rich land out there was made for ranching and farming, and I intend to work for my fair share. No murdering savages are going to keep me from earning it."

A thousand words of protest rushed to Mary Anna's lips, but the firm set of Daniel's jaw and the resolute look in his eyes broke her desperate desire to argue with him.

The goldenness of the day was tarnished. The conversations that had flowed so freely were now swollen into hidden cataracts that tossed their struggling participants into dangerous areas.

Daniel and Mary Anna limped through the rest of their time together, pretending nothing had happened, and the farewell that they bade when he walked her home was equally strained.

Mary Anna slammed the door to the bedroom she shared with her three younger half sisters and threw herself across the bed, heartsick with her new knowledge. How could she possibly respect a man with so large a blind spot and so much hatred in his heart?

Almost everyone she knew had been troubled by the Indians. Many had had relatives killed by them, too.

No one had forgotten the raid on Fort Parker only thirteen years earlier and the kidnapping of Cynthia Ann, her brother, and several other whites by the Comanche. Fort Parker was only fifty miles southwest of Tennessee Colony. No one had found or accounted for Cynthia Ann and her brother yet. The grisly affair was still retold when people wanted to cite the cruelty of the Indians. It was rumored that Cynthia Ann was living with an Indian man and riding with him as he raided with his band of warriors, killing more whites and stealing their horses. Mothers warned disobedient children of "what happened to Cynthia Ann."

But Mary Anna had a strong sense of fair play that caused her to question the white man's right to simply take land away from anyone. The contradictory nature of her feelings made her wish sometimes that her family had never left Tennessee.

She tried to recapture the goodness of the time she and Daniel had spent together before his awful revelation of his feelings. The pleasant memories wouldn't come.

That night as she tossed and turned in her bed, she realized that she could never share her life with a man who had such hatred burning in him. She prayed her nightly prayers, adding, *And Lord, would You please change his heart? He seems like a good man. Someone I could love. Melt the hatred and clear out the anger.*

She knew the Lord could do this, but would He? She would wait to see if the Lord would give her any signs of change in Daniel's heart. Meanwhile, she would try to keep her distance. She was heartsick at the sudden demise of her dream.

At mealtimes when Daniel came into the hotel, she stayed in the kitchen as much as possible. And when she served the table, she did it quickly and without friendly conversation. She was civil to Daniel at church, but distant and formal.

It was fairly easy to dismiss him socially, but it was almost impossible to banish him completely from her thoughts. He had been so gallant, so easy to talk with, so handsome.

She smiled ruefully as she remembered it had been the easy talking that had caused the problem. She longed to see him, but the naked hatred she had seen in his face frightened her. There was no reason to allow him into her life. It just couldn't work. Mr. Daniel Thornton could go west to follow his dream. She hoped it would be very soon.

❧

Peter Garland knew something was very wrong with his girl, but he hadn't been sharp enough to see it, so Louisa told him what she thought had happened. "It's obvious they've had some sort of quarrel. I can't understand what it could be about, though. They hardly know one another."

So he waited until he could be alone with Mary Anna in the kitchen.

"Darlin'," he said softly. "I can see things have not gone right between you and young Mr. Thornton. What happened?"

The pent-up tears broke over the levee Mary Anna had carefully constructed around her heart, and she wept all over the front of her father's freshly pressed shirt, pouring out her sad story. He held her and patted her shoulder awkwardly, nodding his head and trying to make sense out of the tear-garbled words. When he was fairly sure he understood the problem, he had no answer for it, so he held her and let her cry.

"And every time I turn around he's there," she finished with a wail.

Ah, there was something he might be able to do after all. "They're needing a schoolteacher. He wouldn't be coming to the school bothering you. Maybe you should work there until he's gone. We can get along here without you for a while." It was the only solution Peter could think of on the spur of the moment, and he knew there would be a heavy price to pay when Louisa learned he had let his daughter out of the kitchen. Boldly he went with Mary Anna down to the mayor's store to apply for the job.

Mary Anna had no doubt she could teach school. She had read every book she could get her hands on and was good in math. With the help of books and maps and a chalkboard, she could do a good job. She was concerned that there wasn't a schoolhouse yet, but in her haste to get away from the handsome Mr. Thornton, she accepted the monthly salary of fifteen dollars and walked to the brush arbor where logs were split and pegged and set in rows.

It was worse than disheartening that the books were old and ragged and few. There were a few broken slates and pieces of chalk. But the worst was yet to come.

Mary Anna had students ranging from the first to the ninth grades. Sometimes there was one pupil in each grade; sometimes there were several. But the older boys were twice as big as she was, and she was hard put to make them behave. They kept nudging one another and whispering and smiling at her. It took all her skills to get through the morning as the sun and the temperature climbed higher and the shade from the arbor got smaller. This wasn't what she'd had in mind when she'd accepted the job, but it was hers and she wasn't a quitter.

At least her new job kept her from seeing Daniel except occasionally at church. She continued to pray for him—mostly that he would go away because she couldn't imagine even the Lord melting his hatred away quickly.

The week dragged to a limp conclusion, and when Mary Anna awakened Saturday, she smiled with relief. This was one of the busiest days at the hotel, and she could stay home and would only have to keep up with the youngest of the children. The rest would be working in the hotel.

Louisa had raged when she'd learned that Peter had excused Mary Anna from working at the hotel, but to make peace, Mary Anna had agreed to do the family wash and baking.

She was in the middle of baking the bread while the wash soaked in the big black pot out in the yard when she heard someone approaching the cabin. She wiped her hands on her apron and covered up the rising dough with a towel. By the time the knock sounded, she was ready to answer the door.

He was standing in the open door, silhouetted by the brightness of the sun. Her heart leaped at the sight of him yet was instantly on guard. Her hands trembled, and she gathered up her apron to hide them.

"My father isn't here."

Daniel stepped inside and took off his hat. His blue eyes bore into hers as though to hypnotize her. "You know I didn't come to see your father." He stood quietly, waiting for her to say something.

She saw the loneliness and hurt in his eyes. Unbidden love flooded her heart and made it ache. Dazedly she motioned him to come in. She was having a hard time breathing, and the cabin seemed to be shrinking.

"You knew I'd come," he said softly.

"Yes," and suddenly she did know it.

"I've missed you."

She wasn't ready to concede that she had missed him, too.

He went on in his soft Southern drawl. "You were upset after I told you about my grandpa."

"No," she corrected him, "I was upset after you told me how you feel about Indians."

He walked away from her, pausing before the unlit fireplace with his back to her. Mary Anna followed and stood beside her mother's rocking chair, her hand resting on the carved headrest so she wouldn't reach out to him.

With his back still turned, Daniel began to speak. "I don't expect you to understand everything about me or to approve of it." He turned around slowly, his face pleading for a fair hearing. Electricity raced between them, pushing them together and pulling them apart. Mary Anna felt the intensity of his words resonate in her heart.

Daniel stepped forward and put his hand on hers. The rocking chair moved slightly with the added weight.

"No matter what has come between us, I know only one thing. From the moment I saw you in that store, I knew you were special. Even though you're so tiny, you carried yourself with such assurance. I liked the way your chin tipped up, almost defiantly, just the way it is now."

She leveled her head and tried desperately not to be aware of the warm hand holding hers captive.

"When we sat on the quilt at the picnic, I wanted to tell you everything about myself from the time I was born until that day." He raised her chin up with his other hand to look into her eyes. "I even wanted you to know the bad things about me. Somehow I knew you'd understand."

She cried out, "But I don't understand."

"I know that now, but you will. . .eventually."

His face was coming nearer her own, eyes closing and mouth parting. Her arms rose of their own accord to clasp around his neck. His mouth gently touched hers, exploring, softly pressing and releasing, and coming back again. An unnamed longing filled her and spilled out into the kiss that she was now returning with shameless abandon.

His voice rasped words against her mouth. "Come with me, Mary Anna. Marry me and come with me on my great adventure. I don't ever want to be without you again as long as I live." As though to force the answer he wanted from her, he intensified his mouth's searching of hers. "I love you."

All her reservations, all her doubts about him melted in the intense heat of their embrace. "Yes, Daniel, yes." Her entire being reached for him and fused them into one as she said, "I love you, too."

"We'll build an empire together. We'll have sons and daughters and build a new world. You'll be my queen in the wilderness we'll tame together."

"Sounds to me like you have some mighty big plans," Peter's big voice boomed into their private world.

Daniel kept his arm around Mary Anna's waist possessively as he faced Peter, calm and assured. "Yes, Mr. Garland. I want Mary Anna to marry me and come west. I'm asking for your blessing."

Peter's face was stern as he walked toward Daniel. "Before I give you my beloved daughter, I need to know some things." He looked levelly into the waiting blue eyes. "Will you always care for her and never, ever mistreat her?"

Daniel's yes was firm.

"I already heard you say you loved each other, but love is a funny thing. It comes and goes in a marriage. Can you be best friends?"

Daniel laughed. "I'm counting on that, sir."

Peter's eyes dimmed with unshed tears. "He's taking you west, child. Are you sure?"

Unflinchingly she answered, "Yes, Pa." Her face gave off the luminous glow of new love.

"Then I guess we're having us a wedding," Peter said with as much joy as he could muster. "Welcome to the family, son," he said to Daniel as he stuck out his hand.

When Mary Anna went to bed that night, she couldn't sleep for the excitement and joy that raced through her. Long after her half sisters had fallen asleep, she lay thinking of what had happened so suddenly. But in the darkness, she couldn't ignore the one niggling doubt that kept poking a pin into her happiness.

*Lord, there isn't any sign that Daniel has changed his mind about the Indians. But I love him so much, and when he touched me, I thought I would melt like a candle in the wind. I can't live without him, Lord, so I'm assuming that You will change him as time goes by. Help me to soften his heart. I know he will change once we're married. I just know he will change. He's a good man. And thank You for bringing him into my life. Thank You.* She fell asleep with those words on her lips.

⌒⌒

In the weeks that followed, plans for Mary Anna and Daniel's wedding and their life together were made. They wouldn't be going west right away, a relief for Mary Anna and her father. She wanted adventure, but the Lord had given her love and security for a while.

Mary Anna had a new dress for her wedding. She had sent away for the material, and Louisa had happily made it from a picture in the catalog. It was simple, but she looked beautiful in the pale, blue-green material that made her eyes look even bluer. A perky straw hat trimmed with lace sat at a jaunty angle on her pompadour hairdo, making her look older than her sixteen years.

Daniel was the best-looking groom the town had ever seen. His white shirt had extra starch that made it rattle when he bent his elbows. His boots were shined until he could see himself in the glowing toes, and he had gotten a new suit with an appropriate tie. His blue-black hair was combed just so, and the shadow over his mouth where he was growing his mustache was soft and pleasing.

The ceremony was simple. Mary Anna's family and most of the town joined the celebration, and the small church was hard-pressed to hold everyone. It was the hottest July they'd ever had, and everyone felt the effects of the stifling heat in the small building.

The wedding supper was held at the hotel's dining room, and a fiddle and harmonica provided music for dancing in the lobby.

It was late when the newly married couple climbed into a borrowed carriage and rode out to the newly finished cabin on Daniel's rented land.

"We're on our way home," Mary Anna said happily.

Daniel looked up at the moon hanging in the hazy heavens. "Yes, we are." And he kissed his wife gently under the watchful eyes of a million stars.

# Chapter 4

During the four years they lived out on the farm, Daniel and Mary Anna forged their marriage as well as the land. Forged was a good term for it, for Daniel learned that his lovely bride had the temper of a volcano. But her explosions were usually short-lived, and the making up was wonderful.

With great pride Mary Anna presented Daniel a son, Columbus Erastus, two years after they were married. Life wasn't so hard. The small family accumulated and made what they needed and prepared for the day when they would pack up and head west. During the winter of 1856, they made their final plans. They would have to leave well ahead of the spring rains that flooded the Trinity and Brazos rivers.

Mary Anna spoke to her father about the impending trip.

"It's so exciting, Pa. We'll be like a ship out on the ocean."

Peter frowned. "I'd feel better if you were traveling in a wagon train. It'd be so much safer."

"Oh, Pa, where we're going there aren't any Indians." She put a cup of coffee in front of him and added three lumps of sugar, the way he liked it.

He gazed out the cabin window at the neat rows of dirt waiting for spring seed. Daniel was in the shed feeding the cow. "All the bad things out there aren't red." He sighed, knowing the ugliness of the world and wanting to shield his daughter.

She gave the toddling Columbus a helping hand as he tried to walk from his little chair to his grandfather. Having made it, he pulled at Peter's pant leg, trying to get into his lap. "I'm going to miss you, son," he told the blond-haired boy softly. His words were meant for Mary Anna, too.

But the day arrived when there was no time to delay. The wagon was loaded with their household goods, and the chicken coop was strapped on. Every inch of space in the wagon was accounted for, and the family's cattle and horses were herded together.

After the loading, both families joined together for prayer. Peter led them. "Father, these young people are going off to build a new life for themselves, and we ask You to be with them all the way. Keep them safe, give them wisdom and courage. But most of all, Lord, let them always know that You are there with them, no matter what. Amen."

Daniel hoped that the prayer would be effective, though he couldn't believe God would intervene in his family's life. He felt the enormous weight of keeping his little family safe, and it was a somber man who led his family away from the safety of Tennessee Colony toward the dream he had to follow.

It was still bitterly cold, and the breath of both animals and people plumed in the air. Hastily the good-byes were said. It was too hard to prolong the parting.

But as they began their journey with Daniel astride his favorite horse and Mary Anna driving the wagon with Columbus tucked behind her, Mary Anna's heart soared. *It is going to happen. Now. Today. The beginning of the dream starts now.*

After the noon stop, Daniel tied his horse behind the wagon and climbed up beside Mary Anna.

"Westward we go," she said excitedly. "How far? Have you decided?"

"I've heard that the foothills of the Palo Pinto Mountains are so rich with grass that cattle spring up out of the ground by themselves just to eat it," he grinned.

"We talked of stopping between the Brazos and the Trinity. You want to go farther?"

His eyes focused on the horizon. "I have this scene in my mind, dreamed it several times." Confidently he added, "I'll know it when I see it." He looked at her furrowed brow. "Don't worry. We're not on our way to the Pacific Ocean." He saw her relax a little and couldn't resist teasing. "Just to the Rocky Mountains."

"Thank goodness I didn't marry a man with wandering feet," she said wryly.

The days became as rhythmic as the swaying of the wagon, and a familiar pattern developed. Mary Anna felt safe with Daniel beside her. There was time to plan and dream and play with Columbus. He was a bit of a handful and needed constant supervision to keep him out of the things two-year-olds need to explore.

The only time Mary Anna was uneasy was when Daniel rode off to scout up ahead. The sudden absence of her husband left her alert and acutely aware of her sole responsibility for the baby. She had her cap and ball rifle beside her, and she knew how to use it. But they had not seen a single soul since they'd left Tennessee Colony. With Daniel gone, she had the eerie feeling she and the baby were the last two people on the entire earth.

As the hours passed, that feeling eased and she was able to enjoy the countryside. Daniel was up ahead, herding the stock and breaking the trail. She knew they'd be stopping soon to make camp for the night. It was easy to follow the wide swath of crushed grass, and the broken blades gave off a pungent perfume. It was like floating on a sweet, crackling river. The rolling hills took her up and down, always leading to the man she loved.

It had been hard leaving her family. Even Louisa had gotten misty eyed as they'd embraced in farewell. Mary Anna wasn't sure exactly what had happened between them, but Louisa had gone from being a hard woman to treating Mary Anna kindly when Daniel proposed. "I guess it had something to do with jealousy," Mary Anna told Daniel. "Whatever the reason, I'm grateful. I only wish she had been this loving with me before."

When Mary Anna had gone into labor with Columbus, Louisa had helped her deliver the child. Mary Anna smiled, remembering the first cries from that tiny, squirming bundle. Life had been wonderful during these first four years. Now she was twenty years old with a husband and a child, and she was off on a wondrous journey to a new home.

They forded the Trinity River with only a little difficulty, and the Brazos with heady success. "The Lord is surely taking care of us, Daniel," she said as the back wheels of the wagon hit solid ground.

He didn't respond. Daniel's faith in God being personally involved in his life had ended the day he had found his grandfather's mutilated body. So every time Mary Anna spoke of God, he kept quiet.

They made night camp and had a simple hot supper. Daniel poured himself another cup of coffee as Mary Anna tucked Columbus into the wagon bed; then they sat down together by the fire.

"Just look at those stars. Seems a man could almost reach up and pick one," he said.

"And what would you do with a star?" she teased him.

"Why, I'd give it to my best girl." The firelight revealed his love for her in his big blue eyes.

"I believe that some day you will do just that."

Daniel rose and tossed the remains of his coffee on the fire, then carefully banked it. There was no need for more words as they prepared to settle down in the wagon. There would be another night of love out in the grassy sea with only the stars and the moon as observers.

Daniel and Mary Anna had been on the trail for almost three weeks, and still they hadn't met anyone.

"I thought we'd at least see some Indians or bandits or somebody," she said thoughtfully.

"Worried?"

"No."

"Scared?"

"A little," she admitted. She lifted her chin and looked steadily at him. "I believe this is what the Lord wants us to do, and He's led us this far safely. I have a strong, smart husband to take care of me, too. So it's okay for me to be a little scared." She laughed and then looked at him carefully. "Aren't you just a little scared?"

"Not yet. We haven't had anything to be scared of." He looked serious. "Life out here won't be easy, and I know the scary times will come. Let's don't borrow from tomorrow."

The next day Daniel was out ahead, scouting. Mary Anna's eyes scanned the horizon for him. The dried grass was still high from last summer, and there was a promise of spring in the air. Mary Anna was breathing hard with excitement. Daniel was surely going to decide today. Then she saw a rider galloping toward her at full speed. He was waving his hat in the air and shouting.

"We're here! Hurry those oxen along. We're home!"

They topped a small rise. A good-sized spring bubbled and ran off to the right, making a small stream of clear water. A large stand of timber forested the rise behind it like dark green velvet drapery. The wind rubbed the wintery blades of grass together, creating a swishing, whispering symphony that welcomed them to the land of their dreams.

Mary Anna froze with the awesome beauty before her. She could barely whisper, "Daniel, it's perfect."

They stood, arms around each other, looking at the land the Palo Pinto Mountains cradled at their feet.

Mary Anna swept Columbus up out of the wagon. "Look, baby. It's our new home. Your new home." She turned her face up to her husband, radiant with joy, and felt his finger trace one of the tears streaming down her face.

"I haven't seen you cry since you showed me Columbus." His face was soft with love.

"Some people cry when they're sad. I cry only when I'm happy."

"Then I hope there will be many tears for you here." He sighed contentedly and helped Mary Anna and the baby back into the wagon for the short ride down to the spring.

When they reached the water, they held hands and Mary Anna prayed. "Lord, we thank You for the safe trip here. We thank You for this beautiful country. We ask that You would bless the labors of our hands and help us to be worthy of all these blessings. Amen."

Mary Anna's eyes swept the vast countryside. "When we decided to come out here, I was sure I wanted to. Then when we got started, I wondered if we'd done the right thing." She chuckled. "Sort of reminded me of the Bible story of Peter stepping out of the boat in faith and trying to walk to Jesus on the water." She turned to Daniel with earnest eyes. "If we keep our eyes on the Lord, we won't sink," she said with conviction. Daniel nodded his head more in admiration of her faith than belief in her words.

That night, Mary Anna carefully noted in her journal that her family settled in Dripping Springs on February 20, 1857.

Daniel woke the next morning and started marking the outside walls of the cabin before Mary Anna had stirred up the fire and made the coffee.

"You'll be worn out before I get the bacon fried," she teased.

"You just get that meal made and then we'll build our castle."

"Castle?" she grinned.

He scuffed his toe in the dirt and looked sheepishly at her. "Well, maybe it will feel like a castle after living in the wagon for so long."

Over the next weeks, Daniel cut the trees and used the oxen to drag and lift the logs. It was bitterly cold, and the animals' body heat came off in plumes of steam.

After days of helping Daniel where she could and going to the icy river to make caulking from clay, mud, and grass, Mary Anna longed for the house to be built quickly, but she held her tongue around Daniel. They were both so exhausted by the time they had eaten supper that they cuddled up with Columbus between them and slept the sleep of the overly tired.

Daniel had marked off a tiny, one-room cabin. Constructing it was back-breaking work in the bitter cold. "I know it's small," he apologized, "but it's strong. We'll add on as we can."

They covered the roof with split shingles and made a shelf outside the door with a round hole in it for a wash bowl. Mary Anna hugged Daniel hard when she saw he had taken the time to make this extra nicety.

Both their hands were raw and blistered from the hard labor—especially Mary Anna's. She was vain about her looks, and building a cabin in the middle of the frontier in late February was not a ladylike job. But she gritted her teeth and tried to work as hard as Daniel. Pride was another of her faults, but she wasn't about to let Daniel think he had married a weak, helpless woman. Each night she put salve on her wounded hands, as well as on his.

"I was thinking we'll probably be able to move everything into the cabin tomorrow," he said as they sat by the supper fire. Mary Anna was busy doctoring his hands. He looked at her with great love. "I know this hasn't been as much fun as when we all got together and raised a cabin in a day. And there's no one around to have a party with afterwards. I want you to know I'm proud of all your hard work, and I love you all the more for it."

Her eyes met his. "I love you with all my heart, and I'm not one bit sorry we're here." She gave a tiny smile. "It is too bad about not having the people here for a party. I would love to show off our lovely new home." He moved closer to her and lifted her chin with the tip of his finger, moving her mouth to his. The kiss was long and deep and told both of them the things their hearts couldn't say out loud.

⟡

The next day Daniel was wet with hard labor and panting from hefting up the thick door and setting it in place. He stepped back to look at the snug little cabin.

"Good job, don't you think?" he asked proudly.

"I certainly do." Then Mary Anna cocked her head to the side and her eyes crinkled with mischief. "I think the servants' quarters should be over there, and I'll need a summer kitchen, and let's see, don't forget—"

Daniel grabbed her, threw her over his shoulder, and started walking toward the small river while she screamed, "Don't do it, Daniel; I'm warning you, don't do it!" He laughed loudly as he dumped her into the cold water, but she had hooked her hand tightly into the top of his pants, and he lost his balance, following her into the stream.

"Not my hat! Save my hat!" he shouted and threw it toward the bank.

The cold water was shocking, but it felt good to both of them, and they made good use of the short time they stayed there. The cool air made them towel off quickly and change into dry clothing. Daniel was pulling on another pair of boots as he said, "I hadn't planned on a bath today." He added, "You're lucky you didn't get my hat wet, or you'd be a drowned kitten right now."

"That'll teach you to mess around with an Irish girl," Mary Anna said smugly as she struggled with her dry petticoats. Little Columbus looked up in wonder at his playful parents.

"Son," Daniel said with mock sadness, "don't ever marry an Irish girl. All they'll bring you is trouble."

"And the strongest loving you'll ever have in your lifetime," Mary Anna added as she snuggled up against his broad chest.

# Chapter 5

It was dawn, and Mary Anna rested her head against the side of the cow she was milking. Columbus was happily playing inside the little playpen Daniel had built to contain him while Mary Anna did her chores in the cow lot. If she turned her head, she could see Daniel plowing with the oxen. He was using a forked tree for a plow fastened to the double tree from the wagon. It was clumsy but effective.

Steady spurts of warm milk foamed the bucket, and tiny wisps of steam feathered the crispness of the late winter air. Mary Anna smiled as little Columbus happily chirped away. When the babbling stopped, she instinctively looked up. Her heart stopped. Three Indian braves were standing beside her child.

The sheer terror of the moment passed as she tried to take stock of the situation. The men were not holding weapons, but knives were strapped against their waists. They were dressed in an odd assortment of white man's clothing.

Their faces bore no anger, rather a combination of serenity and pride. Mary Anna's cap and ball rifle was leaning against the cow pen's wall, out of her reach. Daniel was out in the fields. What could they want? If only they would move away from Columbus! She had to distract them from the child. Unsteadily, she rose from the milking stool and with deliberate calmness walked toward them.

Hoping her smile looked natural, she took measured steps to the playpen. She nodded politely to the stone-faced men while reaching in and taking the baby in her arms.

"Good day." She looked straight into the eyes of the man she had singled out as the leader, fearlessly holding the look until he spoke.

He looked her over deliberately, stared at the child, and then at the cow. When he again looked at her, he spoke with unconcerned insolence. "You are small."

Was this a challenge? What chance did she have against three men, even if she had been as tall as they? She answered with unhurried coolness. "Yes, I am small in body, but my heart is as large as these lands."

"Yes," he agreed. "It must be for one woman and one man to come so far from their people."

So he knew how many they were and that they were alone. Did he also know how far away Daniel was? Where were the Indians' horses? The thought that there might be many more men holding their horses in the trees around the stream filled her with terror.

To fight the fear, she challenged them, praying she wouldn't make them angry. "What do you want?" Her voice was steady. She waited to see anger but instead saw the tiniest glimmer of amusement.

"You have a sharp tongue. You make good Indian wife." He ignored her question. With a slow movement of his hand, he reached up and touched the blond ringlets of Columbus's head. "Pretty baby."

"A good baby, like his father." She willed herself not to pull back from the frightening hand.

It came back down slowly. "You have meat to give." It was a statement of fact.

Daniel's voice answered the question from behind her. "Yes, we have meat. Come with me to the cabin." He was carrying his rifle loosely in his hand, and he motioned toward the little home with it.

The warrior made a sound of assent and walked toward the cabin. He waited with his two companions outside the door as Mary Anna entered with Daniel.

"Get that turkey you smoked," Daniel ordered quietly.

Mary Anna got the wrapped poultry and gave it to him. She watched from the door as Daniel handed it to the silent men. They turned and walked toward the stand of trees by the stream, and Daniel came back inside.

Daniel continued to watch the men as they strode into the woods. Venomously he spat out, "How dare they come walking in here demanding meat!"

His anger shocked Mary Anna out of her fear, and her face became red with unspent anger. Shaking, she put Columbus down on the floor and then collapsed beside him.

"He touched the baby! I thought I'd die when he touched the baby!"

Daniel's face was twisted in rage. "They're probably renegades from the reservation."

He lost sight of the men and put the gun in its place over the fireplace. He was trembling with anger. The men had caught him off guard, and he had chosen a path of peace rather than standing and fighting them. He was ashamed of his lack of courage. He tried to justify his actions to himself and his wife. "Ugly looking things, weren't they? Pitiful. No horses, so they can't hunt. I felt kind of sorry for them." He avoided looking at Mary Anna.

Now that she was safe, Mary Anna thought of the men differently. She thought they were very regal. Haughty, in spite of their odd clothing. "Do you think they would have harmed us?"

"Yes, if they hadn't known I was nearby—and if they hadn't gotten something to eat. There's a reservation down on the Brazos that they're supposed to stay on, but some of them still run around. Some escape. Don't ever take any chances with them. They'd kill you in a minute if it suited them. I don't want to get in a fight, but I'd never let them hurt you or the baby."

Cautiously she speculated. "Maybe they were just hungry. But don't worry, I won't ever take any chances. Daniel, I couldn't get to the gun. It was propped on the wall away from me. Oh, how could I have been so stupid! From now on I'm taking the pistol with me in my apron pocket."

"Good idea. I'll leave my rifle here with you and get the one from the cow pen." He looked at her sternly. "You know now what we're up against. Don't ever be unprepared." Then he walked over to her and hugged her hard.

She laughed lightly. "Is it all right if I'm scared now?"

He gave her a small grin. "It's all right. It's all over. You did well out there." He shook his head. "You didn't look scared to me. You're some kind of woman, Mary Anna Thornton." There was pride in his voice, and his step was brisk as he went out to continue his plowing.

Mary Anna hurried out to retrieve the milk bucket. It was a very fast trip.

Once she was safely back in the cabin, she gathered Columbus in her arms and sat in her mother's rocking chair, humming and cuddling him. The picture of the Indian man's dark hand touching the towheaded boy's ringlets wouldn't go away. She had no idea what the man had been thinking, but she had heard such horrible tales of scalps on tent poles and of children taken and never heard of again that she began to pray. "Thank You, God, thank You."

Columbus enjoyed her loving for a while, then grew restless to be down playing with his wooden toys on the hard dirt floor.

With a calmer heart, Mary Anna began the noon meal. There was plenty of wild game, and she made a thick soup with some venison.

Before long there would be berries of all sorts, and her vegetable garden would come in, but they were running low on flour. She couldn't ask Daniel to make the twelve-hour trip to Stephenville for that. But what would she do if she ran out of flour? They had to have bread.

She worried the problem around in her head as she finished making dinner. It was as she was buttering a large slice of bread that a possible solution occurred to her. Using one of her large crocks, she set some of the skimmed milk close to the fire and covered it. When Daniel came in, she didn't mention her idea.

"Hmm, it smells good in here." Daniel had washed up and sat at the table with a grin on his face. The plowing had worked off the last of his anger. "It surely was a good day when I saw you in that store. Never have I been sorry I married the best cook in Anderson County."

Mary Anna deliberately pressed close to him and challenged, "So you married me only because I was a good cook?"

He returned her wide smile. "Well, now I know there's more to marriage than good cooking."

The next morning, after she had done her outside chores, Mary Anna took the curdling milk from beside the fire and wrapped it in a cloth to drain off the liquid. She squeezed and pressed until the curds were dry and then rubbed in a little salt. Then she hung it up close to the fire again to completely dry the curds.

There was a lot to do, but Mary Anna had worked out a logical way to accomplish all the work necessary to feed and clothe her family between taking care of Columbus.

She especially enjoyed this time of year when the earth was waking up and shaking all living things out of its covers. Noisy birds filled the air, and fragile spring flowers peeked from under warm patches of earth. Everything smelled so fresh and new and promising. She did as much of her work outdoors as she could, but the rifle was never far from her hand. She had learned her lesson about that carelessness.

She took down the cottage cheese from the fireplace and tested its dryness. It crumbed nicely. With her fingers she made the curds even smaller and put them out in the sun to dry a little more. Finally, she ground the whole batch into a semblance of flour. She made bread with it and put it in the dutch oven in the coals. It wasn't long until it smelled like bread.

When Daniel came in for his noon meal, she sliced up the fresh, hot bread and served it to him without comment.

Carefully she watched his first bite. "What did you do to the bread?" he asked.

"Isn't it all right?" she asked innocently.

"It tastes good, just different. More like sourdough biscuits or something."

With great pride she told him of her idea.

"It worked, but I think I'll plan to make a run for supplies," Daniel said. "I noticed the coffee was getting a little low, and I don't want to think what you might do if we run out of coffee!"

They both put up a brave front when the supply trip was mentioned. Now that they knew Indians were in the area, they dared not leave their place unprotected. Mary Anna would have to stay alone while Daniel got the things they needed.

That night in bed, Daniel confronted her. "Will you be all right?"

"Of course," she said brightly.

He leaned over and laid his head on her pillow. "It'd be all right if you used up some of your scared feelings." He pulled her into his arms. "I'll do everything I can to make it easier for you and to make you safe."

"I know." She looked at him in the dark, barely able to discern his features. "I trust the Lord to take care of us, too."

"You're not sorry we're here, are you?"

"No. Somehow I feel we were meant to be here, and if that's so, then God will take care of the rest of it."

They fell asleep in each other's arms, with Mary Anna silently talking to God.

The next morning Daniel began his preparation for leaving her. The horses were secured in a paddock, the cows were in their pen, and the outbuildings were secured close by. He looked at Mary Anna confidently. "I'm planning to drive into Stephenville. I'll be gone two days at most. It's a small place, but they should have the things we need." As though to make the trip more important, he added, "Someday it will be a big city."

He held her close for a moment, kissed her gently, patted Columbus on the head, and climbed up into the wagon. His mustache was dark and full, and his teeth looked very white underneath it. "I'll bring you some peppermint if they have it," he promised.

He looked back over his shoulder to watch the tiny woman in the big poke bonnet holding his son's hand and waving. How he wished he could trust God to watch over his little family! But all he could do was hurry back as quickly as possible to protect them himself.

❧

Mary Anna was worried about what might happen to Daniel on the trail, and she prayed with all her heart for their safety. She kept herself twice as busy as usual to make the time go faster. She chose one of her day dresses and began to let it out. It wouldn't be too many months before she'd be needing something larger to wear. She smiled secretly. She hadn't told Daniel yet.

She swept the ground around the outside of the cabin, trying to keep the grass and small trees from coming up. A swept yard was less likely to harbor snakes and other dangerous pests. Then she fussed around her rose bushes. There were four of them, given to her by Louisa.

In the springs of her life, Mary Anna always had special feelings that came over her. It was as if God had made promises all winter long, and now He was about to fulfill every one of them.

The spring scent she remembered most from her childhood was the perfume of roses. Her stepmother had kept a flower garden and filled the sides along it with herbs for medicine and healing teas. Mary Anna would plant hers, too, someday soon. But for now, she babied the tender rose bushes, watching for the first buds to open and give off their heady aroma.

Mary Anna's heart swelled with homesickness and regret, for she had not written to her family since they settled. *I'll write to them and let them know how well everything is going, even admitting how much trouble we've had with the Indians.* She wanted her father to know how well Daniel had taken care of her and her family.

Columbus was playing close by in the dirt, digging with a spoon, as she dug around the plants. Something in the distance caught her eye, and with a gasp she recognized a ragged band of Indians crossing the rise not far from the woods. Her gun was handy, but there was no need to get it yet. The band had women and children in it, so it wasn't a raiding party. She glanced down at Columbus, talking to him as she would an adult. "Look, there goes a band of Indians." She shook her head sadly. "I don't know how Daniel can hate them now. They look beaten. Everything they own is gone. Pushed from their lands. Locked up on government reservations."

She thought of the story of Cynthia Ann Parker being kidnapped by the Comanche and raised as one of their own. In some ways it was a romantic tale, for it was rumored Cynthia Ann had married a handsome chief and had borne his children. It was also said she was happy with the Comanche and had hidden for years from those who would come and rescue her. But Mary Anna had heard the other side of the tale, of those who were not adopted by the Comanche but were kept as their slaves. Shivers ran up her spine as some of the awful stories crept into her mind.

The Comanche had been masters of this land only a few years before. Now that the white man had come and killed all the buffalo and broken every promise made to the Indians, the Comanche and the other tribes had been beaten into a subservient feudal system. The government would take care of them from now on. Or so it said.

Mary Anna shook her head and began digging in the dirt. Her feelings were so mixed up. She felt deep sorrow for them when she saw them in rags and destitute, but she was overwhelmed with terrible fear when they were near. She wasn't afraid of the people in this band, but she watched them disappear, just to be sure.

By dusk she was tired and ready to call it a day, but nervous energy kept her moving. She checked the stock and finally pushed the heavy door of the cabin shut and barred it with a thick piece of timber.

Columbus was not a good companion that evening. He fussed and complained with his teething and was generally bad tempered.

"Taking after your mama, huh?" she accused him gently. After being rocked for a long time, he surrendered to sleep, and Mary Anna read her Bible to take the edge off her uneasiness. She started to take off her clothes and put on her long white nightgown.

"No," she said to her mirror, "if I'm to die tonight, I don't want to be in my nightgown. I want to be ready to defend us." She pulled the baby's bed closer to hers, laid the long rifle on the other side of the bed, and propped herself up on the fat, goose down pillows. "I may not be able to stay awake all night, but I'm as ready as I can be."

The baby slept fitfully, and she dozed between his night noises. Her ears were keenly tuned to any outside sounds. She didn't hear a thing and was surprised when she woke close to dawn. She and the baby were fine, but she worried about the stock.

Cautiously she lifted the heavy timber and, gun in hand, peeked out toward the outbuildings. Everything looked fine. She could see her cow, the horses, and cattle out in their pens. She took a deep breath of relief and stepped outside the cabin. The sun was just breaking the dark horizon. *Thank You for our safekeeping through the night, Lord.*

Her courage was growing with one successful night behind her. She only had to make it through one more day and night. Daniel would be home for sure after that. She would feed the animals later when she could take Columbus with her. She took one last deep breath of the invigorating air and turned to step back into the cabin.

Her body froze. A moccasin print sat right at her front door! Hurriedly she scanned the area, but nothing was out of place. With her heart pounding like a baby rabbit caught in a coyote's mouth, she carefully checked for more prints. They went all around the cabin.

# Chapter 6

The sixth legislature of Texas had created the county of Erath in 1856. Stephenville was to be the county seat, named for the man who had proposed it. The town was laid out with the public square in the center and the streets named. It was a town of promise, a wilderness marked from the beginning to be successful for those accepting the promise, as well as the challenges, it offered.

Scattered around it were several small communities, all struggling to become a land of plenty for the hearty.

The county abounded with post oak, Spanish oak, wild plum, pecan, hackberry, and elm trees. Cedar and mesquite were there, both a bane and a blessing for a cattleman. The cedar made good posts, but the mesquite was almost impossible to clear for crop lands.

Daniel was watchful for Indians and saw some tracks of unshod horses that crossed the road. His thoughts went immediately to Mary Anna and the baby. But he had no choice but to go on as planned.

~⁓~

Mary Anna was mad. Raging mad. She stomped around the cabin and threw one of her best tea towels at the wall, but her hand stopped short of the pretty tea cup lying innocently there on the table. Columbus was watching her with deep interest.

"All they're trying to do is scare me," she fumed. "It's probably those same three raggedy men who were here before. If they think they can scare me into giving them more meat, they've got another thought coming!" She kicked at the hapless chair in her way and scarred its leg with her shoe.

"Come on, Columbus; we're going out to work in the garden. I'll be double dipped if they're going to keep me from my vegetables." She grabbed up the baby, the gun, and more ammunition, slammed her poke bonnet on her head, and strode out to her nicely growing garden. Even in her anger she was careful to put on her gloves and pull down the sleeves of her dress to completely cover her from the sun.

Her head was down, but her eyes were like the eyes of a hungry, hunting eagle. Constantly she scanned the horizon and the small buildings around her. Her anger made the weeds fly from her garden, as though she were hacking the Indians out of her life. Her sharp eyes didn't miss Columbus toddling around the edge of the garden, picking up twigs and rocks, and pounding the ground with his

37

wooden spoon. His happy baby talk brought the first smile of the day to her lips. *He's walking so well. Look at him go! He sees something. Look at him go!* She traced his path with her eyes to see what had so attracted him. Her heart stopped.

At the edge of the garden about ten feet from her baby sat a coiled rattler. Columbus was heading straight for it. It never occurred to Mary Anna that she might miss hitting the deadly snake with the gun. She simply cocked it and took very careful aim. Even the beads of sweat that should have clouded her aim were of no consequence. If she didn't hit the snake, it would strike Columbus. She fired, knowing she wouldn't have time to reload. The mangled head of the snake flew off, and Columbus began to cry. Mary Anna sprinted over to him and swept him up with grateful arms.

"Thank You, Lord. Oh, dear God, thank You!" Her heart pounded and her legs turned rubbery. She slumped to the ground with Columbus on her lap and gulped down deep breaths. Was there no end to the dangers that surrounded her? Why had it been so much easier when Daniel was with her? If only he'd come home! She refused to consider what might happen if he didn't. Only God could keep them alive in this suddenly unfriendly place.

She took her crying child into the cabin and sat with him in her lap, rocking him for a long, long time. Finally, they both settled down.

She could hear the pitiful lowing of the cow that hadn't been milked. Much as Mary Anna was tempted to spend the rest of the day in the relative security of her cabin, she had work to do.

Columbus had fallen asleep, and she took her shawl and made a sling across her chest to carry him in. She got the rifle, reloaded it, and put on her bonnet again. She walked out to the cow pen with her back straight and her eyes darting around.

"I'm sorry to be so late, Daisy, but things have been a little busy today," she said as she patted the cow and settled herself down on the milking stool. "I'm asking you very nicely, please don't knock the milk pail over or step in it. I'm not sure what I'd do if one more thing happened today."

Daisy was compliant, but the chickens acted spooked and extra squawky as Mary Anna scattered seed for them. She didn't act hurried, in case someone was watching her, but she worked efficiently so she could get back to the safety of the cabin.

After the quick noon meal, she locked the cabin door and tried to nap with Columbus. She dozed fitfully, waking with a start and then trying to sleep again. It was not restful.

The remainder of the afternoon, Mary Anna stayed inside the cabin, pulling the rocker where she could look out the door and see the woods. She carded wool and spun it into thread for clothes. Columbus woke happy and hungry and played with abandonment on the floor, unaware of his close call with the rattlesnake.

When dusk came, Mary Anna took Columbus out to the cow pen and milked Daisy again, staying as calm as possible so she wouldn't alarm the cow. It would take twice as long to milk a nervous cow, and she didn't have that kind of time.

With a sigh of relief, she finished the chores and dropped the timber across the door of the cabin. Now all she had to do was get through the night.

Much to her chagrin, she woke the next morning without having awakened once during the night. Columbus was still sleeping as she went through the ritual of opening the cabin and checking for tracks. New footprints stood at her door.

She looked toward the cow pen and saw Daisy chewing contentedly. But when she tried to count the horses, it seemed one was missing. She couldn't be sure about the cattle, and she couldn't check unless she went out there. Gingerly she hurried out. Yes, one horse was missing. Her Irish temper fired up full blast. One of the most important things she had been taught as a child was that if it wasn't yours, you didn't even touch it, much less take it.

*It isn't fair!* she shouted internally. But she walked sedately to the cabin. She had done everything in her power to keep the animals safe, but she couldn't sleep with them. "Oh, why didn't we bring a dog with us?" she wailed inside the walls of her safety. "He could have warned me." She laughed sheepishly at herself. "And then what would you have done—gone running out there and blasted the thieves?" She poured a cup of black coffee and added a splash of cream. "At least it would have scared them off," she consoled herself. "Maybe."

Once again the day had gotten off to a bad start. "I'm never going to let Daniel leave again. Next time I'll go and he can stay home," she said flatly.

She was about to leave the cabin to go to the spring for water when two Indian men rode up. They were not the ragged men she had seen before. As they approached, Mary Anna barely had time to whisper, "Dear Lord, in heaven, help me!"

These men were astride beautiful pinto ponies. Her first impression of them was one of complete elegance. They were dressed in fringed buckskin and seemed to be extensions of their horses. Had Mary Anna known about the riding abilities of the Comanche, she could have identified the men at once.

Their braids were astonishingly long and well cared for, each tied off with strips of fur. A single black feather was rakishly stuck in one man's side lock, and both were wearing necklaces of animal claws. The tops of their ears had been pierced in many places, and long, thin shells dangled down, pulling the ears over slightly with their weight.

The center parts of their hair were daubed in red, and their faces had circles and lines of yellow and white. They presented a breathtaking sight—and a fearsome one.

Mary Anna stood rooted in place, quietly watching the men come closer.

There was something odd about their faces. And as they sat arrogantly ten feet away, she realized they had no eyebrows. They had either been plucked or shaved off completely. It gave them a more menacing look.

Her hand was resting lightly on the rifle leaning against the side of the cabin. Columbus was inside.

The silent standoff was broken when one of the men spoke. "I am called Swift-as-the-Antelope." He waited for a counterintroduction.

"I am Mary Anna Garland Thornton." His name was so long, she felt the need to include everything she could in her introduction.

Each was sizing up the other, and Mary Anna showed absolutely no fear.

"I am here to trade with you."

"What did you bring to trade?" Mary Anna could see no goods.

"I will trade you the safety of your horses for sugar and meat."

The audacity of the man almost made Mary Anna gasp audibly.

"I have meat to trade but no sugar." She took a deep breath and added in a clipped tone, "You already owe me for one horse." She didn't know for a fact that these men had taken the horse, but she was so angry, she didn't care.

She waited for him to pull out a tomahawk or bow and arrow and kill her on the spot for the rude charges she had made against them.

Swift-as-the-Antelope considered for a moment and then spoke. "Then I will take only the meat." He made it sound as if he were doing her a favor.

Mary Anna considered her options and decided that under the circumstances she had little choice. "Wait here," she ordered.

She walked casually into the cabin on quivering legs and retrieved a large package containing the smoked antelope haunch they had put up. She took it outside. The Comanche warrior leaned slightly from his horse and took the meat. Without a visible sign from their riders, both horses broke into a trot, heading for the forest.

Mary Anna walked into the cabin and locked the door again. She was exhilarated from a successful encounter with the Indians, weak with relief that she was still alive, and breathless with fear. "I can't live like this, Lord. Give me courage and wisdom. And please keep these people away from my door, no matter how magnificent they look."

She went out only to milk the cow. She didn't count the horses or check on the cattle. It wouldn't do any good. The rest of the time she kept the door locked and worked inside. Then she began to worry about Daniel. He should already be back.

"Be calm," she told herself. "You know how things are out here. He didn't promise to be back today. He said he'd *try* to be back today. You can make it one more night. He'll surely be back in the morning."

The pounding on the door would have made her heart completely stop if it hadn't been accompanied by the shouting of her name.

"Mary Anna, open up, I'm home!"

And then they were in each other's arms, hugging and laughing. Columbus toddled over and grabbed hold of his father's leg, hugging it hard, until an adolescent dog of indeterminable heritage came running in. He immediately began to lick and play with Columbus. The boy was enchanted.

Mary Anna was so happy and relieved to see Daniel that at first she didn't notice the man standing in the doorway, holding his hat in his hand.

She looked at Daniel expectantly.

"Oh, I'm so sorry. Mary Anna this is Otto Lammert. He's going to be working for us."

Otto stepped forward and made a slight bow. "Nice to meet ya, Miz Thornton." He spoke in a heavy Texas twang.

"And I am delighted to meet you, Mr. Lammert." She thought him to be in his late twenties. He was lanky and wiry, long and relaxed, and strong. She liked him immediately. He was shy in front of her and kept twirling his beaten-up hat in his hands.

"Well, come on in, Mr. Lammert." She looked at Daniel. "Have you eaten?"

"Thank you, yes. Otto shot us a fine bird." He smiled at his wife. "He is an excellent shot."

Otto grinned like a kid and kicked his toe in the dirt floor.

But Mary Anna's face began to burn with anger. "Good, we're going to need him. The Indians stole one of the horses, and two more men have been by here for meat."

Daniel looked at her in deadly calm and walked over to the table to sit down. Otto followed him. "Tell me from the beginning."

While Columbus romped with the playful puppy, Mary Anna told her story. "The only satisfaction I got out of giving the meat away was that it was an antelope haunch, and I hope every time Swift-as-the-Antelope takes a bite, he feels a pain in his behind!"

Daniel didn't smile, but she saw an amused glimmer in Otto's eyes.

"Miz Thornton, you were safe at night. Them Comanche are superstitious, and they won't come in on you in the night. But them horses and cows is another thing. They're used to hunting and they feel free to cut out whatever they want. You was prob'ly smart giving them the meat."

"There won't be any more of that, Otto. I'm not going to be blackmailed anymore. I'm not a government agent, and I'm not a store. Let 'em stay on the reservation. They've no right to my possessions." Daniel's face had the dark look Mary Anna had seen when he'd talked about his grandfather. "And there won't be any more missing horses," he promised. He grabbed up his hat. "Come on, Otto, let's check the stock and make sure the horses are up close to the cow pen."

"I'll bunk down there in the shed tonight."

While the men did what they could to ensure the safety of the stock, Mary Anna knelt down to the puppy. "I haven't given you a proper welcome yet, but I am so glad to see you. What shall we name him, Columbus?"

At the sound of her voice, the dog put his front paws up on her lap and gave her a wet welcome with his soft tongue. He was mostly black with white patches here and there. "You're going to be our guard. I think I'll call you Soldier." She hugged him close. "You have your work cut out for you, Soldier."

She heard the men coming back from their inspection. She had been so excited to see Daniel, and then to tell him what had happened, she had forgotten the treasures he was bringing. As they brought in the goods, she stored them.

While Otto was out getting the last of them, Daniel pulled out a brown paper-wrapped package. "This is for you. I know you're going to be needing material to make baby clothes, so I bought the best flannel they had." His face was split with a big grin by the surprise he saw on hers. "Surely you didn't think I wouldn't know?" he teased softly.

Daniel stood there with that silly grin on his face watching her open the package like a kid on Christmas Day. It slipped badly when he saw the disappointed look on her face. "It's the best flannel they had," he said lamely.

She looked at him helplessly. She had a boy already and she was thinking of the sweet little girl things she would make this time, for surely the child would be a girl. "It's the best flannel I ever saw, but Daniel, *red* flannel?"

"It was the only color they had," he shrugged.

She recovered from the shock, appreciated his thoughtfulness, and then began to laugh and hug him. "Thank you, my darling, for bringing me the fabric. We'll have the most cheerful baby in the whole state of Texas!"

He was reassured by her quick recovery. "I might have bought enough for you to make me a new pair of long johns, too," he grinned.

# Chapter 7

**M**ary Anna woke at her usual time and smiled broadly upon finding Daniel watching her from his pillow. "You're sure nicer to sleep with than that big old rifle," she said.

"You have the whitest skin and the softest hair I've ever seen." He brushed her cheek with his fingertip.

"And you look so handsome with your dark mustache. It's getting so thick, but it's soft. My grandfather's was stiff and bristly."

"It's because it's never been shaved." Daniel was just taking her in his arms when Columbus awkwardly climbed into bed with them, and Soldier, hearing the happy noises, jumped in the middle of all of them.

"Get off this bed, you mangy mutt," growled Daniel as he swept Soldier off with his arm. "Today you start learning how to behave." His tone was gruff, but Mary Anna wasn't fooled. He was pleased as punch to have Soldier around, and he'd train the dog to protect them and their animals.

Mary Anna got out of bed and began to dress. The days were getting warmer, and she decided on a whim to leave off one of her petticoats.

She brushed her hair out and twisted it up quickly, securing it with hairpins. Daniel's compliment had made her happy. Even in this wilderness, she went through her usual toilette and was extremely careful never to let the sun touch her skin. She used lard on her hands to keep them soft in spite of the rough work she did.

*Lord,* she prayed, *I know I'm vain, but I thank You for making me attractive. Help me not to care so much about how I look. And help me with my temper.* It was a prayer she prayed frequently. So far the Lord hadn't made her less vain, but she wasn't sure how He'd go about that. She patted her hair smoothly and hurried to her daily chores.

Daniel brought Otto with him for breakfast. Mary Anna served her cottage-cheese flour bread along with a hearty helping of fried meat and all the eggs she had gathered from her small flock of laying hens.

"Nothing like the smell of fresh ground coffee cooking in the morning," Daniel said happily. Mary Anna stood by his side as she said their mealtime prayer. Columbus was sitting in a high chair pushed up to one side of the table, banging his spoon.

"You have a fine-looking son there, Miz Thornton," said Otto politely.

"You get an extra helping of eggs for that kind observation," she chuckled.

He buttered the bread and took a large bite. As he chewed, he got a quizzical look on his face. "This here is a most unusual tasting bread."

Daniel and Mary Anna broke into laughter, and Daniel explained why he had gone on the trip to Stephenville.

"How did you wind up in Stephenville?" asked Mary Anna.

"Well, now, ma'am, Stephenville wasn't my original destination. I was headed for Louzeanna."

Mary Anna laughed, "But that's the other way."

"Yessum, I'm plumb bad about directions." He enjoyed entertaining people with his implausible stories. "My family came from Germany and settled down close to the coast of Texas. Their ship got knocked off course, and they landed in the wrong place. Seems we've been doing it ever since."

He took a big bite of his food, chewed thoughtfully, wiped his mouth, and added, "I heared this part of Texas was the place to ranch now that the Injuns were pretty well taken ker of." He looked solemnly at Mary Anna. "I'm here to tell you it ain't so. You be kerful, little lady. You ain't been out here long enough to know the good Injuns from the bad uns."

Mary Anna was afraid Daniel was going to mouth the old saying about all Indians being bad Indians, but he caught the look in her eye and took another big bite of his food.

"I think it would be a good move to keep trading with them Injuns if all they want is food. You might call it a peace policy, but while I was in Stephenville, I found out half the federal troops left here to guard this part of the frontier is gone, and the Comanche have been pretty well raiding anywhere they please. When those thirty-three hunert men was here to watch them, they didn't dare bother the settlers. Now there's not enough men to keep them under control, and they're like hungry wolves. Long as they're only trading, you'd best do it. We're a mite short-handed out here on your place."

Otto could tell this didn't sit well with his new boss, but he knew the truth and had stayed alive because he was a smart man. Daniel reluctantly shook his head in agreement.

"But trade is what we'll do. No more stealing from us."

"There's jest one other little thing I thought I might mention to ya. The Comanche and Apache go up north on the Llano Estacado for the winter. No one knows exactly where. They jest seem to disappear clean out of sight. Before the white men killed so many of the buffalo, they followed them. And when they felt like doing a little raidin', they rode on down into Mexico. If I took a map and drew a line from the Llano to Mexico, you'd be sitting in the middle of their road."

Mary Anna felt the hair rise on her arms and the back of her neck. Daniel looked grim.

"It's true a lot of 'em are on reservations in the territory north of us, and some on the Brazos. But they ain't nowhere near ready to give up yet. So that's why I say we should try to git along with 'em as best we can. And always be ready to defend ourselves."

"Well, then," said Daniel, "we'd better get to work. We'll be needing more meat, and I want to strengthen our fences." He looked at Otto.

Mary Anna said, "Guess the Lord was the one who got you lost so we could find you."

"Yes, ma'am." He smiled at Mary Anna. "But I've never been knowed to git myself lost on the way to such a good table, ma'am."

Mary Anna hummed happily while the men worked outside. She felt safe and happy. But she continued to be alert, for she took to heart the things Otto had told them.

A week or so passed before they came in contact with the Indians again. It was getting close to dusk, and the men were cleaning up at the basin outside the cabin when a young Indian man dressed only in breechclouts came riding in on a thin pony. A young girl sat behind him. They waited for Daniel to approach them.

Mary Anna was embarrassed by his nakedness yet fascinated with his bronzed skin. She saw that the young girl was in the last months of her pregnancy. She was also shocked when she estimated the girl to be about fourteen years old.

She was wearing a buckskin skirt, a loose-fitting blouse, and moccasins. Her cropped hair gave her the appearance of an adolescent boy rather than a young mother-to-be, but there was no mistaking the familiar bulge in the front of her skirt. She didn't have the same sunburned color skin as her husband, though she was deeply tanned. Mary Anna looked with disbelief into eyes the same color as her own.

Her first thought was that the girl was being held captive, but as she observed the trading going on between the men, Mary Anna detected no sign that the girl was in any way trying to escape the handsome warrior. She sat easily on the pony, waiting patiently.

Mary Anna clenched her teeth in sadness. This could only be a child who had been kidnapped from her family and raised as a Comanche. Somewhere a mother's heart was breaking not knowing the fate of her child. Mary Anna shuddered as she thought about the dark hand that had touched Columbus's hair. The girl was much too young to be Cynthia Ann Parker, but it appeared she was the second chapter of that familiar story of white girls being captured and raised as Comanche.

～

For the next three days, they were cabin-bound by the spring rains that soaked the earth. There was plenty of time for Mary Anna and Daniel to learn more about the Comanche from Otto.

"They ain't nothing without their horses, but you put a horse underneath one of 'em, and they become a thing of beauty." His eyes clouded with memories. "I was in a freight wagon down around Austin once when they hit us. They're fierce fighters, and they use their horses as shields. Come in hangin' off the side and shoot from underneath its neck. Don't give ya much of a target. And I've seen 'em swoop down and pick up their dead or wounded. They never leave any behind." Mary Anna saw goose flesh rise along his arm where his sleeve was rolled up. "The screaming and yelling they do as they come in at ya is enough to scare the hair right off yer head, 'less they lift it first."

"Do they really scalp people?" She couldn't imagine a more grisly activity.

He nodded solemnly. "But it gives 'um more honor to do it when they're in battle. I knew a man that survived it. Had a fearsome bald spot from the front of his head to the back. Ugly scar. They try to git as close to the enemy as possible. If they touch him or kill him, they get to count coup. That's real important to how the other warriors look at him."

"What about captives?" Daniel asked.

"Never keep the men, only women and young'uns. Usually trade the women off and raise the kids. Make Comanche out of 'em. Use the girls quick as they can as breeding stock, beggin' your pardon, ma'am."

Mary Anna felt her own flesh rise in horror.

Ominous thunder rolled across the land and shook the logs of their cabin with its vibrations.

"Them Injuns is all huddled in their tepees today. That's the one thing they're scairt of, thunder and lightning." He took out a pocket knife and began whittling on a piece of firewood. "The government is going to have to do something about 'em before too long. Too many white folks want to get on with their settlin'. They need the protection of the troops."

"You know a lot about the Indians," Mary Anna observed.

"It's the best way to stay alive." He looked steadily at her. "In some ways I admire 'em a bunch. But I just don't understand their minds about killing and tor-turing." He sighed. "The whole thing is a big mess. Seems like growed men could get together and divide up the land in a way to make everybody happy."

Mary Anna asked quietly, "Would you want someone to come to your ranch and divide it up equally for you?"

"I know what yer saying, ma'am. But this land isn't a ranch. It's a big piece of free land, rich for living on and using." Daniel nodded his head in agreement. "Miz Thornton, I hope the day doesn't come when something awful will happen to you or yer loved ones that will make you think like I do. I admire the way you feel about the Injuns, but you're a tenderfoot out here." He looked sympathetically at her. "I hope life doesn't change your mind." He didn't sound optimistic about that.

⁓

April was a sweet month, spent in tending crops, gathering the first tender vegetables, and feeling the fluttering of the child within her. The whole land was bursting with fruitfulness, and Mary Anna felt a part of it.

There had been no sign of Indians for weeks.

"I want to go out into the forest and gather berries," she said offhandedly to Daniel at breakfast.

"I can't go with you today, and neither can Otto."

"If you can keep an eye on Columbus, I can manage the pails and the gun."

He looked at her as if she were crazy. "You know that's where we always see them."

"I don't plan to go in far, and I don't want to live like a scared ninny." Her chin jutted out in that defiant way he knew so well.

"I can work on the fields closest to the woods," he said, "but you better watch what's going on all around you. Be real quiet and listen." His face held a dire warning of what would happen if she didn't follow his orders. She took him seriously, but she was excited to get away from the cabin for a while.

She struck out across the roughly planed log that served as a bridge across the stream and headed into the forest. Instead of the rifle, she was carrying the Colt revolver in her apron pocket.

It was cool in the woods. She was cautious as she headed for the places close by that promised berries. At first she could hear the beating of her own heart at being alone, but the gun gave her confidence.

She walked quickly to a small hollow deep in the trees where red haws were likely to grow. She froze when a movement caught her eye. There in the hollow sat the pregnant young girl with whom they had traded earlier. Mary Anna looked around for her husband, but the girl was alone.

She slipped her hand into her apron pocket and curled her fingers around the revolver as she watched the young girl. Her eyes were glazed with pain. She was in labor and alone. Mary Anna wanted to help her, but something in the girl's manner stopped her.

The girl put a rolled piece of rawhide between her teeth and rocked on her heels silently as a contraction racked her young body. She panted, and her brow broke out in perspiration. Her buckskin skirt was hiked up, and she was squatting over a piece of tanned hide filled with a soft rabbit skin. Stoically she pushed with the next contraction. No sound came from her as she strained with the contractions that rhythmically rocked her body. She grabbed hold of the tree in front of her and gave one last gigantic push, which delivered the head of her child.

The black hair was plastered wetly against its tiny head, and the girl lay down to finish her delivery. With the next contraction she gently pulled the child out and lay the little boy in her lap. He let out a loud squall as she wiped his face clean with a soft rag. Using a piece of rawhide, she tied the umbilical cord and cut it, and delivered the placenta with one final push.

Awestricken, Mary Anna watched the girl clean the baby carefully with oil and wrap him tightly in soft wrappings. Tucking him up under her blouse and securing the bottom in her skirt, she rose and walked to a small pool of water to clean herself. Then she dug a deep hole and dropped in the afterbirth with the birthing mat and covered it. The girl peeked inside her blouse, and the smallest of smiles flitted across her face. Proudly she picked up her small package of things and walked serenely into the deeper woods.

Mary Anna felt weak and exultant at the same time. She leaned against the tree and tried to sort out the dramatic tableau that had unfolded in front of her.

A young child-mother had silently delivered herself in the woods. If Mary Anna had ever worried about what would happen when her own time came, she dismissed such thoughts now. This was her second child, and if there was no one there to deliver her, she, too, would deliver herself.

It was a wiser and older Mary Anna who walked back to the cabin later in the afternoon, her bucket overflowing with rich, red berries and her heart overflowing with respect for a silent, young Comanche girl and her new baby.

She didn't share her experience with Daniel. It was too precious to put into words. She wasn't even sure he would understand what had happened, and he wouldn't be happy to know there were still Indians nearby. Instinctively she knew they were of no threat to their safety. In fact, they were probably miles away by now.

She found herself more tender with Columbus and Daniel. Life was dear, and the life she carried inside her was a real treasure. She longed to be able to hold the child close to her as she had seen the young girl do.

⁓

While Mary Anna concentrated on her garden and Columbus, Daniel decided to add to their poultry supply by capturing some of the numerous wild turkeys in the area. "We'll have so many more eggs," he promised her.

"But how are you going to catch them?"

His smile was sly. "I have a plan. First Otto and I are going to build a coop for them."

Mary Anna had watched the turkeys perch on the low branches of trees, but they were easily alarmed and could fly for short distances. She gave her husband an encouraging smile. "I hope the plan will work."

Otto was silent as they made the coop. He thought it was a foolish thing to try, but Daniel was his boss, so he kept his mouth shut. He didn't like the taste of the turkey meat and was fairly certain he wouldn't like their eggs either.

When the day arrived to capture the birds, Mary Anna took Columbus along and planned to gather any eggs they might find while the men did the hard work.

The plan called for each man to be on opposite sides of a known roosting place. When Otto came in from one way and Daniel the other, they would grab whatever bird came their way and stuff it in a sack. Mary Anna and Columbus hid down low, waiting.

She could see Otto sneaking up from his side and Daniel gliding though the brush from the other side. There were some birds on the ground pecking for food and some roosting on the low branches of several trees. Closer and closer the men came to the unsuspecting turkeys.

All at once the birds began squawking and screaming and flapping their powerful wings. Some flew, and some ran, and all attacked anything that came near them.

Daniel was desperately holding on to the legs of one big male while the turkey beat him with his wings and pecked viciously at his hands. Columbus began to cry at all the cacophony of screaming. Birds flew and ran in all directions. Otto was hot on the trail of a big fat hen. He grabbed for her neck, and she turned and attacked his face with her sharp beak. He was trying to hold on with one hand, stuff her in the sack with the other, and duck his head to protect his face.

At first Mary Anna was frightened for the men and unnerved by the wild fear of the turkeys. Then she began to laugh and couldn't stop herself even when Daniel shot her an angry look.

"Help me," he shouted.

She couldn't have helped if she'd wanted to, for she was holding her sides and laughing helplessly at the flying dirt and feathers.

When the dust settled, Daniel had one turkey in his sack and Otto had two. They fell to the ground in exhaustion and looked foolishly at one another. "I think there's got to be a better way to do this," Daniel said with chagrin.

Otto wiped the blood from his face with a dirty hand. "Let's forget catching them and just shoot them from now on."

Mary Anna came rushing over to the two men. "I had no idea turkeys were so strong and mean. Are you all right?"

"I'd be better if you hadn't laughed at me," grumped Daniel.

"But you should have seen it from my side," she grinned. "You two rest here while I check for nests." There was a cutting edge to her next remarks. "I'll try to keep these eggs warm and hatch them. Domesticated fowl are so much more tender. And safer."

There was no discussion about whether to try the plan again. The little band went home with their small bounty and turned the mad birds into the coop.

Daniel and Otto built a barn for the horses and raised the fences higher around the pasture. They added a room to the cabin for Otto and dug a root cellar close to the house.

Otto chose to sleep in the little lean-to out by the barn when the weather was warmer. Soldier stayed out there, and with them on guard there was no more trouble from marauding Indians.

While the men gathered the crops, Mary Anna put up everything she could for the winter. There was a good harvest, and the family contemplated the long winter stretching out in front of them with satisfaction. Daniel cured meat and carefully wrapped it for storage. He saved seed for next year's crops.

Summer turned to the last hot days of August and then to the crisp mornings of September. The trees started to have a faint yellow tinge as they began their rest from the summer heat. Splashes of orange could be seen in the tops of the trees across the stream, and an occasional deep purple from the maple trees stood out in marked contrast. The seasons were slowing down, and so was Mary Anna.

She spent more time sewing. They had planted cotton, but the bolls wouldn't pop open until there was a good cold snap. Then she would card the seeds from the bolls, twist the fluff into thread, and weave it into cloth on her loom.

She fashioned a shapeless tunic for herself. The loose-fitting, floor-length shift was comfortable and needed no alterations as she grew. Her feet tended to swell toward the end of the day, and she longed for a pair of larger shoes. Rather than bother Daniel with her needs, she cut up some of the tanned hides they had gotten in trade with the last Indian visitors and made soft moccasins for herself. As she worked on the leather, she wondered how the young mother and child were and if they would survive the coming winter.

The moccasins were not the works of art turned out by the true craftsmen of the Plains, but they felt wonderful on her feet.

Daniel was not as pleased as she was. "Where did you get those shoes?" he demanded.

"I made them. My feet are swelling, and I can't bear to wear my shoes anymore."

"They make you look like an Indian squaw. I'll get you another pair of real shoes." His face reflected the displeasure in his voice.

"But there's no need," she protested. "These feel wonderful. They're so soft, and they didn't cost anything but the time I spent making them." She had her chin stuck out slightly in the way that meant she was not ready to back down docilely to what she considered an unreasonable request.

Daniel noted the tilt of her chin and gave the offending shoes a hateful stare. Silently he stalked to the door and slammed it hard behind him.

Mary Anna felt the roots of her hair begin to burn with anger. She walked to the cabin door and opened it wide, giving it a loud slam of her own. She moved heatedly around the small cabin, pacing her anger. "That man! Why should I be uncomfortable because he doesn't like Indians? I can't wear moccasins because his grandfather was killed by an Indian years ago? This makes perfect sense to me," she added sarcastically.

"Here's your dinner," she told her absent husband as she slammed it on the table. "I hope it gives you as much indigestion as it does me."

In the last stages of her pregnancy, everything gave her indigestion, and her anger made things worse, so she drank a little milk, made up a little lunch for Columbus, and said, "Come on, baby, we're going on a picnic." She was especially careful to slam the cabin door again as she left.

Columbus was pleased to be walking alongside his panting mother on an aimless stroll. They walked down by the turkey pen with Soldier trotting along. She had the revolver in her apron pocket. Even the remembered story of the ill-fated turkey hunt failed to make her smile.

She took Columbus down by the stream and let him play at the edge of the water, helping him toss rocks in its shiny face. She stayed away as long as she could, hoping that by the time she got back Daniel would already have eaten and gone back to his work. She didn't want to see him or be near him.

When she finally opened the door to the cabin, she half expected to see the back of her angry husband. The cabin was empty and the food was on the table untouched. *He's really mad.*

She sat down in the rocker while Columbus played. Her unborn child kicked and played, too. She could just see the tips of her feet when she sat in the chair.

*What happened? I was uncomfortable, and I made some shoes. Daniel got mad because they make me look like an Indian. A pair of shoes has come between us.* She sighed. *They aren't worth it. I'll go barefooted. It won't be long until the baby comes. How stupid to fight over something this trivial!* She rose tiredly and made up a picnic basket of the lunch things. She silently laughed when she thought of Otto. *He missed his dinner, and he doesn't even know why.*

She started for the fields and met Daniel coming up to the house.

"I thought you and Otto might be hungry," she began a little nervously. He met her eyes, and she said, "I'm sorry, Daniel."

Her words overlapped his words of apology, and they threw themselves into each other's arms.

"I won't wear the shoes. You're right, I do need new ones. Winter will be here soon."

"I was silly to be so angry over them. Wear them. I know your feet hurt. I'll get you some winter ones."

"We let a pair of shoes come between us," she said softly.

"I know. After I got over my anger, that's all I could think of. A pair of shoes." Their laughter was low and intimate.

"Dinner, Otto," Daniel shouted and waved at the hardworking man. "Thank you for the lunch," he said tenderly. "I'm sure Otto is as hungry as I am, and he didn't even know why he wasn't getting fed."

With a soft kiss, Mary Anna left and smiled her way back to the cabin. Columbus had crawled up into her bed and fallen asleep. Peacefully Mary Anna lay back in the rocker for a catnap, and then she planned to fix Daniel and Otto a special meal. The moccasins had been hidden away in the big trunk. *Thank You, Lord, for giving me such a good husband,* she prayed as she closed her eyes.

Two long, hot days passed, and Mary Anna thought of the family she had left behind. She even missed Louisa. She hadn't heard the voice of another woman in eight months, and the only people she had been with were Daniel and Otto. This was the time of year her family usually had a big get-together to celebrate the gathering of the crops. There would be dancing and laughter and too much to eat and drink. In her mind's eye she could see her sisters talking excitedly as they used rag strips to put up their hair in curls to dry and chose their prettiest dresses. The whole town would be together.

She served supper with many sighs and no smiles. She picked at her food and was short with Columbus. Daniel and Otto exchanged furtive looks.

Otto cleared his throat. "This is a very good supper, Miz Thornton."

She nodded absentmindedly.

Daniel tried. "You should have seen Soldier chasing rabbits this afternoon. He found a whole nest of them, and when they scattered, he couldn't make up his mind which one to chase." He chuckled and Otto chuckled. She sighed.

After supper the two men huddled under the tree in the front yard.

"Is it almost time?" Otto asked.

"Not for more than another month."

He shook his head and chewed on his lip. "She's homesick, sure as shooting."

"I can't do anything about that." This time Daniel sighed.

"The summer work's mostly done. Can you take her into Stephenville?"

"Why would I want to do that? There's nothing there but a store and a few people. I sure don't want to take her to a store when I don't have any money to buy her anything."

"Will he trade?"

"Maybe, but I don't want to drive a day to find out." Daniel took a deep breath and sighed through pursed lips.

Otto interrupted his reverie. "I think she's got cabin fever." He looked a little fearfully at Daniel. "One time I worked for a family where the woman got real bad cabin fever."

"What did they do about it?"

"Didn't. She jest dried up and died."

Daniel thought very hard. "If she's homesick, we should find her someone to talk to besides us. A little visit of sorts. You know of any other settlers around here?"

"I heared there was a family about five miles north of here. Maybe six."

"Wife, too?"

Otto nodded. "Wife, too."

Their eyes met in silent assent. "I'll watch the place while you take her." He grinned a little. "I don't get cabin fever. I think it's jest a woman thing."

Mary Anna grabbed Daniel around the neck and almost squeezed his breath away. "Visiting! Oh, my, what will I wear?" She hurried over to the trunk and began digging around. "I can't wear this old thing. Where's that dress I wore with Columbus? I'm sure I packed it. It's so pretty. It has lace around the collar. I think I can still get into it."

Daniel stood watching her with a satisfied grin on his face. Cabin fever wasn't hard to cure after all.

Early the next morning, Mary Anna was a blur of busyness. She insisted Daniel go with her to the stream where she could bathe. They hung up blankets in the bushes to afford her more privacy. She usually did this once a week by herself, but she was getting ungainly and needed help with Columbus. "Well," she demanded, as she undressed down to her bodice and bloomers and stepped into the water. "Bring the baby and get in here."

Daniel started to protest, but he shucked his clothes to his bright new red long johns and tucked the revolver up under his hat as he jammed it on his head. There was always the chance of water moccasins.

Otto could hear the family scrubbing and laughing and playing. It was a good sound. Even if he didn't get cabin fever, he was happier living with the Thorntons than by himself.

When Daniel got up out of the water, he reached for his clothes.

"Oh, no! Don't put on those dirty things! I have clean ones laid out for you on the bed," Mary Anna said.

"But that's a long way from here," Daniel said reasonably.

"I've already thought of that," Mary Anna replied triumphantly.

Otto thought his eyes were playing tricks on him when he saw Daniel and Mary Anna wrapped in blankets and marching quickly to the cabin. The look Daniel gave him kept Otto from making the comment on the tip of his tongue, but it didn't wipe the huge smile off his face.

So a scrubbed and happy family went calling on their neighbors. Mary Anna was carrying two pies and smoked meat. She had no idea what shape the other family was in, and she didn't want the Thorntons to put a burden on their new friends.

They approached a cabin that looked pretty much like the one they had left behind. A man stood at the front door quieting three alarmed dogs. They sat respectfully at their master's feet as Daniel climbed down from the wagon.

Mary Anna's eyes searched for the man's wife.

"Howdy," said the man. He was older than Daniel and much thinner. "Y'all climb down and come in out of the heat." He came over to help Mary Anna out of the wagon. He put out a wizened hand to Daniel. "Caleb West." He led the way to the door, where Mary Anna could finally see his wife in the dimness. She was wiping her hands on her apron and had a shy smile on her broad face. "Howdy," she said quietly.

The woman was also older than Mary Anna, much taller and a bit stout. Behind her skirts hung a boy about four years old, peeking at the visitors. "I'm Virginia West," she said in a deep Southern drawl. "This is Albert." She hurried to a rocker and indicated it for Mary Anna. "Here, sit, sit. Make yourself comfortable."

The men sat at the table, and Virginia pulled a chair close to Mary Anna. They had cooled sassafras tea and thick slabs of bread with large plops of apple butter on top. Columbus toddled over to Albert and hugged him hard enough to knock him to the floor, and their friendship was established. Albert took Columbus over to his part of the small cabin to play.

There was no awkwardness in their first minutes together. Virginia was an able hostess, and Caleb was completely at ease.

The men drifted outside to look over the property.

"When's your baby due?" asked Virginia.

"About the end of November." Mary Anna watched the little boys play on the floor together, one blond and one a bright redhead. "Your little boy is precious."

"Thank you." Without bitterness she added, "We had a girl. Two she was, like your boy. She died of the fever last winter. I just found out I'm going to have another one in about six months."

Mary Anna saw the mixed pain and happiness in Virginia's eyes.

"I'm sorry about your little girl but happy you're having another one."

"We all know you can never replace a child lost, but I am hoping this one will be a girl for me."

"So am I! Daniel and I both would like this one to be a girl."

Virginia laughed. "I doubt that. Men need sons to help them with their work. The more sons, the more work that gets done without hiring someone."

Mary Anna was offended that Virginia had contradicted her. Daniel had told her he hoped for a girl for her, but she held her tongue. It was true that men needed sons.

"When it comes your time, I'll be glad to come help out," Virginia offered.

"Thank you, and I will do the same for you."

They talked of babies and cooking and recipes, and finally Mary Anna told Virginia the story of the young Comanche girl giving birth in the woods. She watched her new friend's face closely for her reaction.

"There's a lot of folks that hate the Indians for what they've done," Virginia mused. "Personally, I think maybe we're the ones that ought to be saying, 'I'm sorry for messing up your lands.' " She looked directly into Mary Anna's face, trying to read if she had gone too far with this new friend.

Mary Anna grabbed her hands delightedly. "Virginia, I never thought to meet anyone like you in this place. That's how I feel exactly." Softly she asked, "Does your husband feel that way, too?"

Virginia shook her head sadly. "Caleb is the one who wanted to come out here, not me. He seems to think the Indians are wasting the land and the one God Himself has chosen to save it from the loss. But he's my husband, so I agreed to come. The price has been high. We lost our daughter, and Caleb hasn't been too well. He had the fever, too. It took a lot out of him. Guess if I'd had it, we'd all be dead. The Lord spared me."

"Why do the men feel this way?" Mary Anna asked.

Virginia shook her head, and Mary Anna guiltily changed the subject. Perhaps she had been disloyal to Daniel in sharing her feelings so openly with a comparative stranger.

When supper time came, Daniel offered the meat and the pies. The Wests were delighted with the additional food, and the dinner talk was lively.

Daniel watched Mary Anna across the table animatedly talking with Virginia and laughing. And he made a promise to himself that she would never get cabin fever again.

The men went outside for one last check of the place. Caleb was the first to speak. "You had any trouble with the Indians yet?"

"A little. Stole one of my horses. Beg me for meat. You?"

"Mostly the same things. I have to tell you, though, I think there's going to be more. Be extra careful."

Daniel nodded his head. He agreed with Caleb, though he hadn't shared his concerns with Mary Anna. "We'll be sleeping out here in the wagon. I'll sleep with one eye open tonight."

"You won't have to. I'll leave you my three dogs. They'll give you plenty of warning."

The night passed without incident, but Daniel's uneasiness grew, fed by Caleb's. They had a quick breakfast and made their good-byes.

The ride home was a happy one as Mary Anna and Daniel exchanged information they had accrued about the West family.

"It's good to know friends are nearby," Daniel said, as pleased about the visit as Mary Anna.

Mary Anna smiled her agreement. "Virginia said she would come when my time comes." She tried to read Daniel's face and found the relief etched around his lips she expected to find. "Guess you'll have to stick to delivering colts for the mares," she teased.

"Hey, I could do it if I needed to."

"I know that, but I also see the relief on your face."

"Well, you may not be as easy as the mare," he said to provoke her.

"I would hope it was because you were more attached to me," she deftly parried.

# Chapter 8

Mary Anna lived off the happiness of her visit with Virginia for several days. She hoped to see her again before the baby came. And she certainly hoped to see her when the baby was born.

She was spending more time making tiny red flannel garments and salvaging some of Columbus's things from the bottomless trunk. Virginia had laughed hard at Mary Anna's story of the red flannel. "Sounds just like a man," she had grinned knowingly.

Mary Anna was now sleeping a little later than Daniel in the mornings. He was kind to leave her and feed the stock, then come back and have breakfast with her. The air was becoming quite brisk, and the hot breakfasts she prepared were appreciated.

During breakfast they made their plans for the day. Daniel made sure he knew where everyone would be at any given time. He had warned Otto and also told him not to alarm Mary Anna. "Just be on your guard." Otto, too, was growing tense by the absence of the Indians.

"It's jest too quiet," he complained.

Mary Anna was enjoying that quiet in the softness of her bed, dreaming of happy things, when in her dreams she heard Daniel shout something to Otto. She heard shots and angry whoops, and she awoke, not wanting to finish the dream. But when she sat up, she heard gunfire splitting the air. Daniel and Otto were down by the horses fighting off an Indian raid.

Mary Anna jumped out of bed and ran to the fireplace to get the other rifle. When she turned around, she saw that the door to the cabin was open.

Little Columbus was walking as fast as his chubby legs would let him toward his father. And a Comanche warrior was bearing down on him at full gallop.

"Dear God, help me!" screamed Mary Anna as she sprinted clumsily to the boy.

The Indian leaned from his horse and swooped the boy into the air. She grabbed desperately for the small body and succeeded in holding fast to Columbus's rounded middle. The sudden jerk caused the Indian to momentarily loosen his one-handed grip, and Columbus fell from his grasp. The passing pony's flanks smashed into Mary Anna, and she and the child fell heavily to the ground.

A shot sounded, and the Indian slumped across the neck of his pony, still in full gallop.

Mary Anna untangled herself from her skirts and pushed herself into a low run, clutching Columbus tightly with both arms. She slammed the cabin door and dropped the heavy timber across it, sobbing silently with relief. The Colt revolver was on the mantle. She grabbed it, never turning loose of the crying child, and crouched across from the door by the fireplace, ready to kill anyone who entered the door. The hand that held the gun wasn't steady, but it was determined. She could feel her heart leaping around in her chest. She was cornered and ready to defend herself and her two children, even if it meant killing someone else.

The whooping and gunfire stopped, and in the silence she heard Daniel pounding on the door.

"Let me in, Mary Anna! Are you and the baby all right? Let me in!"

"Daniel, we're okay," she shouted as she ran for the door. When she opened the door, she fell into his arms sobbing. "Oh, I was so scared!"

Daniel's face was strained and drawn. "Otto and I were out at the horse pens when they hit." His eyes were still filled with fear. "They came in just the way he said, riding low, hanging off their horses. Nothing to shoot at. They got all the horses, Mary Anna, all of them. There was nothing we could do. They had us pinned down and—"

"It doesn't matter, Daniel. We're alive! Wait, where's Otto?"

"Right here, ma'am," he grinned as he came limping in. "They plumb scairt me, but they didn't get me."

There was a brief moment of laughter as the thick fear dissipated.

The three adults stood motionless, stunned with the suddenness of the attack.

Daniel walked over to Mary Anna. "I saw what you did for our son, the way you rescued him." There was awe in his voice. "You're the bravest woman I ever saw."

She shuddered. "I didn't think. I just ran for him." She looked up into his eyes. "If he'd gotten Columbus, I think I might have died."

"Ma'am, I ain't never seen no one charge a Comanche barehanded afore." The respect in Otto's voice was reflected in his face. "You're such a little bit of a thang. I couldn't believe you jest ran out and grabbed the boy outten that Comanche's hands. Whooeee!" He shook his head.

Her fear easing, Mary Anna shook her finger at both of them. "You just remember that the next time I tell you to do something!"

After the grins faded, problems loomed large. "What are we going to do about the horses?" Daniel asked. His anger and color were returning. "Meat is one thing, but this can't be ignored. We're cleaned out." Bitterness turned his blue eyes a darker color.

"We kin borry a horse from the Wests and go report it to the sheriff. Mebbe they kin git a posse together and track 'em down."

"Oh, Daniel, the Wests! What if they got hit, too!"

"They may not have come out as well as we did," he agreed. "There's only two ways to get there. Walk or ride an ox."

"We got ourselves two oxen. You kin ride over to the West's and I kin ride into town and talk to the sheriff. Iffen the Wests are all right, you kin borry a horse and meet me there." The two men looked at Mary Anna.

"I'll be fine. You do what you have to." With bravado she added, "If the Indians come back, I'll get out my broom and shoo them away."

Otto looked serious. "They won't be back, ma'am. They got what they wanted. It's horses they need, and they got 'em already. You'll be as safe as a gopher in a burrow."

Daniel looked to her for reassurance. "You'll be all right?"

"I'll be all right." Her eyes were very bright.

As Daniel rode down the road on the slow-moving ox, he grumbled to himself. "I could walk faster than this." But he knew the six miles would go faster on the plodding animal. He was humiliated at having to ride an ox. Humiliated by his enemies. They could even be watching now, laughing at him. Humiliation, fear, and anger came together. Daniel wanted to hit something. To smash something. He wanted something to grapple with, but here he was, riding to his new friend and neighbor on a poky ox.

Scalding tears burned their way down his cheeks. It didn't matter what Mary Anna said about God. God shouldn't have let the bad guys win. True, Columbus and the rest of them were all right, but all the hard work of building up the horse herd was wasted. *It isn't fair! They have no right to my animals! This is free land. They've got the reservation to take care of them. It isn't fair!* His hands tightened on the reins until the knuckles were white. One thing he knew for sure. *The Indians won't drive me from the place I've chosen. It's mine because I've worked for it.* And even the shame of sitting on top a wide-backed ox couldn't make him leave.

Daniel was deeply relieved to hear Caleb's dogs barking as Caleb came out the cabin door. He looked calm and then alarmed when he saw Daniel minus a horse.

"They hit us. Got all my horses," Daniel said as he slid off the ox.

"Guess we'll be next," Caleb said matter-of-factly.

Before he could ask, Virginia was out the door. "Is Mary Anna all right?" The fear in her eyes dimmed as Daniel nodded.

"Let's get us some good horses and go to town and report this to the sheriff," said Caleb.

"Otto is on his way," Daniel replied with a smile. "'Course, it may take him a while. He's on the other ox."

"I'll go to your place and stay with Mary Anna," Virginia said. She was gathering up her things and getting her young son ready before Daniel could say thank you.

When the men reached town, they could see a crowd of men standing in front of the courthouse. They found Otto and stood with him.

"Sheriff, this raidin' has got to stop!" shouted one man.

The crowd raised their voices in assent.

"You've got to do something about these varmints. It's not safe out here as long as they think they can get away with stealing anything they want from us," shouted another.

"Now just hold your horses," said Sheriff Maloney. "The chances of catching the ones that done it are slim to none. They're long gone by now." He was calm and tried to reason with the crowd, but he was also a man of the people.

"Sheriff, I'm Joseph Salmon. Those Comanche stole thirty-seven horses from me. I was talking to Otto Lammert. His boss, Daniel Thornton, was wiped out, too. I'm too old to ride now, but you young men had better take care of this problem. Right now they're stealing horses." He looked grim. "I don't want to think about what they might be doing next."

Sheriff Maloney stroked his huge curling mustache. "Anyone who wants to be in the posse, hold up your right hand so I can deputize you. You're official." In his heart he felt this was a waste of time, but maybe they would get lucky.

The men picked up the Indians' trail at Rocky Creek in Hamilton. Then they discovered how true Salmon's prediction had been. They found Mr. Bean and his black laborer killed by arrows. The men were shocked into silence at this sudden escalation from stealing to killing. Four men volunteered to stay behind and bury the bodies.

When they caught up with the posse again, the news was worse.

"We found Johnson."

Chesley Turnbow paled. "I know him. Dead?" The men nodded. "Arrows?" Again they nodded.

"We buried him, too," they assured Turnbow.

The men rode on. The trail was getting farther and farther out, and they were not prepared to stay out for long. But before turning back, they found several of Mr. Salmon's horses dead. The brand was unmistakable.

It was agreed the Indians had indeed gotten away, and the thirteen men rode back to Stephenville.

Daniel purchased three horses from the local livery and headed as fast as he could back to Mary Anna.

~≈~

Mary Anna was completely drained from the terror of the past hour. She pulled

Columbus up with her in bed and sang quietly so he would go to sleep, and then she fell into a much-needed rest.

She was awakened by pain. *Oh, no. Not yet. It's too soon. Maybe I hurt my hip when I fell,* she thought hopefully. But the contractions began to be regular and harder.

*I can do this,* she reminded herself as she got out of bed and collected the things she would need if the contractions led to an early birth. And then there was a blessed sound, the rattling of wheels.

"Open up, Mary Anna. It's me, Virginia." When Mary Anna opened the door, Virginia swept in with Albert in tow. "You look a little peaked."

As Mary Anna bent slightly with a contraction, she said, "Albert, you take Columbus outside the cabin and play. Don't go far," she warned. "I don't want the Indians to get you." Albert nodded and took Columbus by the hand.

"And now, missy, let's get you to bed."

The pain continued to crescendo, and at the top of it, Mary Anna felt the sudden emptying of her womb. She waited for the cry that never came. Virginia worked on the infant, rubbing him and blowing in his face. He was a tiny, tiny baby who needed the safety of his mother's womb to finish growing. Virginia worked diligently but to no avail. Finally, she wrapped him in a clean piece of cloth and laid him in Mary Anna's numb arms. "I'm sorry."

Mary Anna looked at the underdeveloped baby. He already had a little dark fuzz on his head and a tiny pink mouth. He looked for all the world as if he were asleep in her arms. Somewhere in her heart, a hot stone burned. It grew and grew, but there was no way to stop the heat and the size of it. The heat dried her tears before they could flow. Her eyes were like coals in the fireplace, red and smoldering.

"They took my baby from me. The Comanche took my baby. I saved Columbus, but they got this one." She ran her fingers over the baby's soft cheeks and hair, memorizing the features she would have recognized anywhere. "I made you some happy red clothes, little one. I was counting the days until you came. Columbus is looking for you. Your father was so excited. We were all waiting for you. But you came too early."

Virginia waited for the tears, but they didn't come. "Let me have him. You sleep for a while. I'll wake you when Daniel gets here." She gently took the baby from Mary Anna's embrace and laid him in the waiting cradle Columbus had out-grown. Then she sat in the rocker and silently cried for the mother who couldn't.

❧

When Daniel rode up to his home, Virginia was waiting in the doorway. He knew something was wrong by the look on her face. "Mary Anna had her baby. A boy. He was born dead," she said simply.

Daniel slid off his borrowed horse. "Is she all right?"

"I'm worried about her. She hasn't cried."

"I'll take care of the coffin," Otto offered and rode off toward the barn.

Daniel walked slowly into the house, paused at the cradle, and walked to Mary Anna lying in bed. He sat down and gathered her in his arms. "He's beautiful. I'm sorry. I'm sorry I wasn't here for you."

Her smile was tired. "It's not your fault. You did what you had to do. It just happened." She couldn't tell him about the awful feelings she had and her anger at the Comanche who caused her baby to be born too soon. It was too raw and too powerful to turn loose in the small cabin.

The next day the child was laid to rest in the Texas soil. Mary Anna held on to Daniel and felt a part of her was being put down in that hole. She was no stranger to death—it was part of everyone's life. But this was her child.

Caleb read the short service. Daniel clenched his jaws in sorrow and anger as loving words were read from the Bible. Mary Anna carefully felt nothing as the promises meant to comfort washed over her. All she heard was the memory of horses' hooves pounding as she clutched Columbus and the thump from her hard fall when the pony's flanks knocked her down. Her mind echoed with Indians' screams, her own voice calling for God's help, and shots and more shots.

She could see Caleb's lips moving and she knew he was reading from the Bible, but the words couldn't penetrate the sounds in her head. As soon as she saw Caleb stop talking, she walked toward the cabin. Virginia walked with her, and Daniel stayed to help finish with the burial of his son. Mary Anna couldn't bear to see dirt being put on top of the child.

She sat down in the rocker and moved to and fro silently. Virginia prepared a simple meal.

"Do you remember the story in the Bible when Jesus sent His disciples out in the boat?" Mary Anna asked. "He walked on the water and Peter tried to go to Him. As long as he looked at Jesus and trusted Him, Peter stayed on top of the water. But there was that one moment when he looked at the water and his feet, and he doubted. Then he began to sink.

"I'm sinking, Virginia. We don't belong out here where bad things happen. I think maybe we should have stayed in Tennessee Colony. I wouldn't have lost my baby there. I stepped out in faith, just knowing we were supposed to come out here. Now I'm doubting it, and I'm sinking. I can't see the Master's face. It's too dark. All I can see is my feet going into the water. I can't see His face."

"Time is a funny thing," Virginia responded. "It gets bent around and some things seem to last forever when it's really only a short while. And other things seem to pass so quickly you never really get to feel them. Right now you're caught in that strange time. You're in the middle of the story. But the end of the story is yet to come. Jesus reached out His hand and took Peter's. He pulled him back up out of the water. Give it time. Feel the pain. Live through it and let it wash over you. When you've spent the anger and the pain, you'll begin to feel the Master's hand reach for you and pull you up out of the water. I know. I've been in the water, too."

Mary Anna remembered the little girl Virginia had so recently lost.

"I'm listening to you. The words will sink in eventually. Right now I can't seem to feel anything but hatred and anger." Her eyes burned, but still no tears came. "I wanted to change Daniel's mind about the Indians. I felt sorry for them. I admired them. Otto's wish for me not to change my mind isn't going to happen. I understand how Daniel feels now."

"It's all right for you to know how Daniel feels. The important thing is how you will feel when time passes. A person can't live with hatred in her heart. It'll poison her soul. It kills. Give yourself time." Virginia placed a comforting hand on Mary Anna's shoulder. "Just give yourself time."

## Chapter 9

Daniel rode into Stephenville with Caleb to see if there was any chance of buying some horses. They stopped at the mercantile store to pick up supplies and listened to the latest gossip. This same gossip was heard at the livery stable as they bought three horses.

"We need a fort around here," said Mr. Turnbow. Fred Gentry and Dave Roberts nodded their heads in agreement.

"But we can't get any government troops to come stay in it," argued another man.

"But it could be a place of refuge, like if you got caught out in the open, you wouldn't have to ride all the way to town to be safe," argued another man. More heads nodded in agreement.

"It doesn't have to be big. Just strong and safe."

The idea was talked up around town and organized. With many men helping, the small fort was erected as an emergency shelter.

⁂

The trees were donning their fall wardrobes. The last of the garden was put away, and the smokehouse was full of food for the winter. As the first cold snap blew in, Mary Anna began to feel some semblance of normalcy in her life. Columbus was a handful to keep up with, and Mary Anna had stopped putting wildflowers on the baby's grave each day. She had come to terms with death. The red flannel baby clothes had been stored away. Someday there would be another child. Never for a moment did she think to replace the baby, but she yearned for another child to hold and love.

Daniel, Caleb, and Otto built a strong barn for the winter. It had been an enormous undertaking, and when it was finished Daniel decided to have a celebration. Caleb was to bring Virginia and Albert, and Otto asked a young woman he was courting in town.

Mary Anna got caught up in the gaiety. She cooked for two days, and when the day came, she spent a long while grooming herself for the party.

"You look like a bride," Daniel told her. Her eyes sparkled. "I haven't seen that joy in your eyes in a long while." He gathered her into his arms and danced her around the small cabin.

"Turn me loose! I've still a hundred things to do," she scolded him with a smile.

She had smoothed the dirt floor with her broom and washed the quilt on their bed. The tablecloth was bright and cheerful, and she had polished the dishes with her dishcloth until she could see herself in them. She had done the best she could to make this a nice place. She was careful Daniel didn't see the frown on her face as she looked around the starkness of their home. For a fragment of a moment, she wondered if it would always be like this and then hurried on with her dream of having a beautiful home some day.

Hearing the rattle of wagon wheels, Mary Anna smoothed her dress and moved to answer the door. Virginia, Caleb, and Albert were the first to arrive, followed closely by Otto with his friend in a borrowed buggy.

"He must be serious about her if he borrowed a buggy," whispered Daniel. Mary Anna grinned. It would be nice to see young love in bloom.

Otto took off his hat. His cheeks were a high color and his grin self-conscious. "This here is Miss Angel Gilbert. Miz Thornton, Mr. Thornton, Mr. and Miz West."

"I'm pleased to meet you," Angel replied to their greetings. She was tall and slender with curly brown-gold hair pulled back modestly into a soft bun. Some of the curls had escaped her comb and fluffed over her oval face in a most becoming way. She seemed perfectly at ease. The only thing that gave her away was her cold hands.

Food was brought in from the outside and added to the spread Mary Anna had prepared.

"Don't stand on ceremony," Daniel instructed them. "Dig in. Dig in."

"Miss Gilbert doesn't eat much, does she?" Daniel whispered to Mary Anna.

"No young girl is going to eat much when her beau is watching, no matter how hungry she is. It isn't ladylike."

"So that's why you picked at your food when I was courting and now I can't fill you up," he teased.

Otto and Angel were sitting close together on a split log bench, doing more talking than eating. She was hanging on to his every word, and Mary Anna could see how important it made him feel. *She'll have him roped and tied in no time,* she thought, and she grinned at Daniel, who was also watching the tableau. Miss Angel was careful to touch Otto's arm often and gaze into his eyes with big saucers of her own. Her laugh was pleasant, and each time it gurgled, Otto's chest got a little larger.

As Mary Anna listened to them talk, she was reminded of that day on the quilt when she and Daniel had exchanged dreams. *She has the same dreams I had when I came here,* she thought with a start. *She's only seventeen, three years younger than I am.* But Mary Anna felt much, much older as she listened to the girl's prattle. She smiled up at her husband. "Do you suppose that's the way I sounded when

I talked to my stepmother before we were married?"

"Were we really ever that young?" Daniel countered.

With the three couples together, everything seemed funnier and the food tasted better. They were good friends gathered together to celebrate.

"Daniel, get out that fiddle of yours. I'm pining to be dancing with my wife," called Caleb.

Out under a checkered picnic cloth of stars, they spun and wheeled as Daniel's fiddle spun melodic magic and made the gingham skirts whirl.

The courtship going on lent a delicious flirtatiousness to the married couples. They forgot the hardships and remembered the beginning of their own romances. For a while each couple seemed wrapped up in their own world of memories, and mouths hardened by life softened with new smiles.

Caleb spelled Daniel with his mouth harp, and Mary Anna found herself in Daniel's arms waltzing to the sweet strains of "Aura Lee." *How tall and handsome Daniel is,* she noted with pride. *Probably the best-looking man here.* She felt his lean body moving to the music, and the cold stone buried deep inside her flaked off one chip. *Concentrate on what you have today and forget about yesterday. Let it go. Keep your eyes on the Master.* She lay her head down on Daniel's broad chest and gave herself up to the rhythm and the movement of the moment.

The September wind had a decided bite to it as Mary Anna struggled back up from the stream with the heavy bucket of fresh water. Short of hiking up her skirts, there was no way to keep them dry, and they dragged around her ankles, making the task harder. Soon the relatively easy task of getting water to the cabin was going to be a miserable chore.

Daniel had been pleased to feel the air. "The cotton bolls will pop open," he promised.

Then all of them would share in the backbreaking job of picking the fluffy white fiber for Mary Anna to make cloth and then new clothing during the cold winter months when they were cabin-bound.

She was fairly certain she carried another child for a June delivery. A smile crept around her mouth as she remembered the red flannel clothes waiting in the trunk.

The men were out planting peach trees for an orchard. The thought of ripe peaches made her mouth water. *One day I'll be putting up preserves and baking peach cobblers.* Patience was one virtue all pioneer women were forced to practice unendingly. Everything they did took a long time to finally enjoy. *From babies to peaches,* she mused.

Soldier, now a leggy adolescent, had monitored her trip to the spring and now lay down in his hole by the cabin door. He had reached his full size, though he would add a few pounds.

Mary Anna gathered a few scraps and tossed them to him. As he gulped the food impolitely, she stroked his black and white coat. His long tail beat the air in pleasure.

Columbus came steadily out the door, plopping down beside the hound. His curly hair hung in ringlets around his chubby face.

"Careful now. Pat him softly," Mary Anna instructed as he tried to grab a handful of hair from Soldier's back. The dog licked her hand, getting the last traces of crumbs from her fingers.

Mary Anna left them and went into the cabin. It was bread day, and she looked forward to getting her hands into the fragrant dough.

She had just put the first batch into the fire to bake when she heard Soldier's low warning growl. She shaded her eyes and saw a band of Indians on the horizon. Soldier was in a guardian stance as they watched the Indians move away from them.

Mary Anna's pounding heart settled a bit, and she took her hand from the gun on the shelf by the door. A good deal of the sorrow she had felt for Indians had died with her baby.

At noon Daniel and Otto came in from the fields hot and dirty. "Got the peach trees in and the cotton hoed," Daniel said. "Shouldn't be long now 'til we can pick it."

"I saw a band of Indians awhile ago." Mary Anna put the hot stew and fresh bread in front of them.

"We did, too. It was a mixed band, not a raiding party," he added reassuringly. He took a bite of stew and chewed it carefully. "Robert Wylie and I are going to take some cattle to Palo Pinto tomorrow."

She wanted to argue with him, to ask him to wait a day or two, as though that would make some difference, but she knew it would be useless. Raising cattle and horses was their primary reason for being here.

"I need some cash money, and this is a fast way to get it," he continued. "You'll have Soldier and Otto to protect you."

They exchanged steady gazes.

"We'll be fine," she said a little too brightly. "It's you I worry about."

"Wylie has been to Palo Pinto before. We should only be gone a few days. We don't have a big herd to move, but we have to do it before the winter sets in." He took a bit of bread. "I'll stop by town and pick up a few things. Can't bring much by horse, though. Make me a desperate list." He tried to get her to grin.

She made the effort and then enumerated the critical list and said no more. Uneasiness made her mute.

When Daniel left the following day, Mary Anna hugged him tightly. "God speed" was all she said. But she prayed for him off and on throughout the day and was more alert than usual to everything around her.

"Lord, I know I've been mad at you about the baby. And my heart has hardened against the Indians, but please take care of Daniel in spite of my sins."

❧

*Being on the trail again feels good,* Daniel thought as he began the drive. It was a welcome break from his steady chores at home. Rocking in the saddle of a good horse, new sights, and a feeling of adventure made him feel keenly alive.

Beyond the dust his small herd kicked up, Daniel could see another sandy cloud, and he pushed his cows toward it. There was always a risk it was Indians, but the cloud stood over the rendezvous spot he had agreed on with Wylie. He loosened his rifle and pulled it across the saddle horn, just in case. Then he saw the familiar roan Wylie rode and Wylie himself waving his hat high in the air.

They had to work hard to mix the two herds of cows. Cows, like some people, don't accept newcomers. So it was a skittish group the men tried to move.

The men alternated the dirty job of riding the dusty drag and the relative pleasant point. Even so, Daniel's white shirt was the color of the red trail dust in no time at all. And in spite of the neckerchief he wore over his mouth, he had eaten a pound of dirt.

They pushed the cattle hard and fast, getting them away from their home range as quickly as possible. "Don't give 'em time to think" was one of the first axioms of herding.

They had only been out about an hour when Daniel saw another cloud of dust on the horizon. The chances of it being another herd were slim, and as he began to make out the riders, his worst fears were realized.

Daniel waved his hat in the air and shouted to Wylie, "The fort!"

The Indian raiding party was bearing down on them at full gallop.

Daniel raised his rifle over the head of the cattle and fired, starting the herd into a mad run. Using his horse to loosely point the leaders toward the fort, he hoped his mount wouldn't stumble and throw him under the pounding hooves.

The fort was close by, and soon part of the band gave up the chase, but Daniel saw three braves riding low and fast toward the remuda. The remuda was made up of Wylie's horses, but Daniel was determined the Comanche wouldn't get them. Fury rose like a gorge in his throat, and he reined his horse to a stop, knelt down, and took careful aim at the marauding men. His first shot was too high.

*Take your time. Easy now.* He squinted down the barrel and squeezed off another shot. The man dropped from his horse. The herd was racing past him, their dust choking his eyesight. He quickly wiped his eyes and pulled the trigger again. He missed, but the other two Indians turned their ponies and made a pass at their downed comrade, swooping him from the ground between them. One man skillfully maneuvered the body in front of him, and the would-be cattle thieves rode away, sitting high once they were out of Daniel's range of fire.

The cattle were milled to a walk outside the fort and then driven inside.

Wylie had a big grin on his face as he came alongside Daniel's horse. "Good shooting there."

Daniel's anger had subsided, but his heart was still racing. "Maybe next time we ought to take a couple more men with us, Wylie. I'd like the odds better," he said wryly.

"Seemed like a good idea at the beginning. Ain't had any raids in a while. But we'll scare us up a couple of good pokes before we set out again."

"Want me to go back to town for them?"

Wylie grinned slowly. "The way you fight Injuns, you're sure to get there. I'll jest wait here. Try the mercantile store. There's usually either someone hanging out there or someone who knows where to look." He stepped down off his horse and knocked some of the dust out of his well-worn hat. "At least we won't have to ride drag no more. Low man on the totem pole gets the drag. And we're the bosses." His smile grew larger at the thought.

When Daniel returned to the fort, he had two men with him.

Wylie stuck out his hand as they introduced themselves.

"MacDougle's the name," said the huge, red-haired, bearded bear of a man. His Scottish burr gave away his homeland.

"Snake." The man looked like a Baptist deacon, dressed in black with a large black hat. His hair was thin and blond and blew in the wind unrepressed as he took off his hat and shook hands. "Kind of a small herd. How far you going?"

"Palo Pinto to join up with another herd," said Wylie.

"They're likely to be hiring on for the drive to the railhead," said MacDougle. "Beautiful country, America. Texas has been my favorite by far, though."

Daniel was curious about why a Scotchman was in Texas, but it was taboo to ask a man about his past. Everyone came to Texas with a clean slate. His actions from then on would make his reputation. At the end of the drive, Daniel would know no more about the man than he did this day, for he never spoke of the past.

Wylie was the talker of the bunch. He told hair-raising stories at the campfire of his growing-up days with eight brothers. And there were the ever-present card games. No cowboy worth his salt would say no to a card game after supper. They bet smooth river stones and played as hard for them as if they were gold pieces.

They took turns with the night watch, but there was no more trouble with the Indians. All four men looked calm, but a sudden noise in the night could cause even the deepest sleeper to rear up with his gun in his hand.

"Don't shoot! It's me, Snake!" called a frightened voice as he returned from a trip to the bushes to find three guns pointed at him from the rim of the firelight.

Mumbled grumblings of relief sounded as the men settled down again.

Daniel squirmed around, trying to make his neck more comfortable on the saddle. Riding in the saddle had been wonderful at first, but as he used it for an uncomfortable pillow, Daniel was sure the saddle would make both ends of his body sore by morning. For a brief moment he wished he was in his soft bed with Mary Anna. *This isn't as much fun as I remembered,* he thought as he drifted to a light sleep.

The days were filled with dirt and tension, and the nights with sore muscles and more tension. The only time Daniel relaxed was when Wylie was telling one of his improbable stories about his family around the campfire after supper.

"Yes, sirree," Wylie said, "we bet my little brother he couldn't git his mouth around that brass doorknob. Mama was plumb sore at us when he did. And then there was the time we told him to put his tongue on the wagon wheel. 'Course it was about twenty below freezin' at the time." He laughed at his memory.

"Never heard a kid yell so loud withoutten him being able to use his tongue. Now this time it was Daddy that took exception to our funnin'. I don't think any of us boys sat down for near to a week after he took us to the woodshed." He took a deep breath. "Spent a lot of time in that there woodshed," he finished. "Miss my brothers, too." He didn't offer to tell what had happened to them, and no one asked. Each man took the time to miss his own family rather than question Wylie about his.

They finally met up with the other herd, and business was concluded. Snake and MacDougle signed on with the herd as they had planned. Wylie and Daniel turned their horses back the way they had come.

As the two men started out for home, the skies rumbled over them and darkened. They brought out their slickers and pulled their hats down lower. The first day's ride was a long, wet one.

That night they made a rude shelter from a tarp and a smokey fire.

"Sure is a glamorous way to make a living, ain't it?" Wylie said as he wrung out his wet socks.

"Says so in all the pulps," Daniel replied. He looked out over the wet range land where an ashen white moon was struggling with the threads of the storm clouds for room. "Not glamorous, maybe, but it's real." He leaned against the tree they had strung the tarp from and said, "I'd rather be out here right now than sittin' in some fine office in fancy clothes."

His blue eyes shone in the firelight. "Out here I can touch and hear what I'm working for. I have a goal, and each day I can measure how close I am to it." He laughed. " 'Course some days it seems to gallop away from me."

Wylie laughed with him. "I know what you're sayin'. Men have said it in fancy ways, but I understand. Out here we take life by the throat and shake out a living, make it give us the dream."

And that night Daniel slept with a big wad of that dream under his saddle. That money would see him through the winter months until he could do it again. And next time it would be a bigger herd.

When at last he held Mary Anna in his arms and tossed a squealing Columbus into the air, he drew his first easy breath.

"How was the drive?" she asked.

"Hard work. But I got my cash money." He reached inside his swinging leather vest. "And I got my best girl some peppermint."

She laid her head on his dirty white shirt and hugged him more tightly.

"Oh, and I found some material that'll better suit your needs for making clothes for the new baby," he grinned.

He shook hands with Otto. "Thanks for being here. It sure took a load off my mind."

❧

As winter closed in on them, Mary Anna was not hard-pressed to find things to do. She spent hours picking the cottonseeds out of the fluff and carding the fiber to make thread. For days the hum of her spinning wheel was the music to which she worked. Then she wove the thread on her loom into soft cloth and replaced their worn summer things and added to their winter wardrobe.

There was still the cooking to do and Columbus to keep up with and the laundry that never seemed to end. But she felt energetic, and her pregnancy didn't slow her down.

She still tended the grave occasionally on a fair day, but with the prospect of another baby, her deep grief eased.

*Lord, I can feel Your healing hands helping me to walk across the water to the boat, and for that I thank You,* she prayed as she walked away from the little grave site.

The weather grew steadily colder, and Daniel recaulked their cabin. There was a good stack of firewood by the back door, and Mary Anna hung her extra quilts over the walls by their beds. They looked cheerful, and they kept the cabin warmer. Warmer was what they would need as the thermometer steadily dropped.

Daniel and Otto were wrapped up in many layers of clothing as they tended the animals. Even so, their faces were red with the cold as they came stomping into the cabin.

"I don't like it, Otto. I think the bottom is going to drop out tonight. It's too blue over in the west." Both men took off their work gloves and hats, shucked off their heavy coats, and hung them on the pegs by the door.

"Yup, sure as shootin' it's gonna freeze hard tonight," he agreed. "But we've done what we could for the animals. They should be all right."

71

"Got a hearty, bone-warming supper for you two," Mary Anna said as she rose from her rocker by the fire.

The men dug into the thick meat pies, and Mary Anna asked innocently, "Is there going to be a wedding anytime soon, Otto?"

Otto's spoon stopped in midair. He looked as guilty as a boy caught with his hand in the cookie jar. "Why, ma'am, I'm not sure."

"You have asked her, haven't you?" Mary Anna grilled him.

Otto dropped his eyes and laid his spoon down carefully by his plate. "Now, ma'am, I have wrote out several things I'd like to say to Angel—I mean Miss Gilbert—but none of them seems to be just the thing I'd really like to say to her."

Mary Anna settled down in her rocker again and took up her sewing. "Just what would you like to say to her?"

Otto turned positively scarlet. He was caught. He couldn't be impolite to Mary Anna, and there was no way in the world he could tell her what he'd like to say to Angel. He took a big bite of food and chewed thoughtfully. Mary Anna waited him out.

He was about to take another huge bite when she said, "Well, Otto?" The shadows hid the amusement on Mary Anna's face.

Otto sputtered a bit and then stammered and added a few hems and haws.

"Mary Anna, have pity on this boy," Daniel pleaded. "You don't need to know what he and Miss Gilbert are planning or are not planning."

Otto sighed in relief, sure he was off the hook.

"But I do! I'm the one who will have to look at his miserably sad face if she says no or put up with the silly grin and half-brained job he'll do if she says yes. I need to get myself ready for either event."

Otto opened his mouth to respond, but nothing came out, and he closed it thoughtfully.

Daniel jumped in. "I would need to know so I could get the shivaree organized. And of course, you'll probably bake the wedding cake as a gift to the bride and groom," he added hesitantly. "And there's the parson to get hold of. Lord only knows where he's at on the circuit right now."

"And it will take months to get a proper wedding dress made. She probably already has a good hope chest started, but they will need a place to live. Do you think you should build a cabin out here close to us, or will you live in town close to her parents?" Mary Anna was having a hard time stifling her laughter as she saw the panic grow on Otto's face.

"Which do you think you'll do, Otto?" asked Daniel innocently.

"I—I—I think I'll check the stock one more time," mumbled a frantic Otto as he rose and grabbed his hat and coat. He exited to gales of smothered laughter.

"He may not show up 'til next spring, Mary Anna. Your foolishness may have cost me a good hand," laughed Daniel.

"And you didn't help, did you?" she retorted.

Almost as soon as the door shut firmly, it opened again. It was Otto, but there was no merriment or embarrassment on his face.

"Mr. Thornton, Indian family here." He wasn't frightened, so Daniel took time to put on his coat and casually reach for his rifle. As he stepped through the door, Mary Anna put on her heavy shawl and stood in the slightly opened door to watch.

It was the same young family that had come to them in the spring. The young, blue-eyed girl was swathed in a buffalo hide blanket against the bitter cold. Mary Anna could just distinguish the lump of her baby inside the robe against her. The young warrior was haughty as he asked for food for his family. They were a pitiful sight. Proud and hungry. A once mighty nation fallen and asking for crumbs from their enemy's table.

Daniel turned to come back into the cabin. Mary Anna wasn't sure if it was to get food or to leave them there in their misery. But his eyes saw the great mercy in hers, and he barked to Otto, "Get them some meat and potatoes." Then he pushed past Mary Anna and entered his own warm home to finish his nurturing supper.

"Thank you," Mary Anna told her tight-lipped husband as he firmly closed the door.

Gruffly he replied, "Better to give them a few things than to have them steal a whole cow from us."

Mary Anna wasn't sure if he was being practical or had shown a kindness to the people he hated, but she was satisfied he had fed them.

His kindness was not rewarded, for that night a cow disappeared. Daniel ranted and raged against the Indians, swearing never to help them again. That night an ice storm blew in and killed a few more cattle and probably many of the baby peach trees they had so carefully planted.

Daniel was unrepentant. "I'm not going to feed even one more family. It does no good. And if that makes the Lord mad at me, so be it."

Mary Anna said, "Daniel, it makes me go cold all over to hear you speak like that!"

"What's made you cold is the weather." And he stomped out to the pens to work out his anger.

"Forgive him, Lord. He doesn't mean to be disrespectful to You," Mary Anna prayed. "Help his heart to soften a little and his tongue a lot."

# Chapter 10

As February doggedly locked her harsh wintery arms around the earth, Mary Anna began dreaming of the warm spring. She hated the long winters and suffered in the frigid temperatures. Her feet were never warm, and her hands were chapped almost to the point of bleeding, no matter how much she tried to protect them.

March followed its normal course and came in angry and growly. They had a small party for Columbus's birthday, and Mary Anna made honey cakes with the precious little sugar they had left. Provisions were growing slim in spite of their careful stockpiling. She knew it wouldn't be long until Daniel would have to leave for more supplies. Or send Otto.

Mary Anna could feel spring coming. She imagined she could smell roses from the garden back home. Little by little, winter began to lose ground to the insistent sun, and the days began to hold the promise of warmth.

Mary Anna's spirits rose with the temperature. She yearned to feel the rich soil of her garden. She began to go outdoors again and revel in the sweetness of the still-cool air.

Daniel made his trip to town for provisions uneventfully, and Mary Anna was able to relax with Otto and Soldier for protection. But she didn't forget to ask the Lord for His guardianship for all of them.

Daniel brought back all the news of the town. Virginia West had borne a girl. His smile was lazy as he added, "But we'll have the first boy born in Erath County."

"How can you be so sure?" she challenged.

"Oh, I just know this time," he said smugly.

April's rain washed away the last of winter, and the whole earth seemed to open its eyes at once. Mary Anna felt dizzy with relief. *We made it through our first winter,* she exalted.

Thomas Peter, to be called Peter, was born at the end of May. He was healthy and his cry hearty as Mary Anna proudly showed him off to Daniel, Columbus, and Otto. Virginia shooed them out the door and finished caring for mother and child.

"It's such a comfort to have you here, Virginia. A good midwife is more valuable than gold."

"I know that, for I had one to help me." She sat on the edge of the bed, smoothing the covers as she talked. "I never considered medical care such a precious thing until I didn't have any out here." She looked sad. "Maybe a doctor could have saved my little girl. Maybe not. But having someone with you in a crisis is—well, no one should ever have to be alone and go through serious illnesses."

She looked Mary Anna in the eyes squarely. "You are a healer. You aren't using your talent fully yet, but you have it. The time will come when you will be valued and loved for your very presence," she said softly. She took Mary Anna's hands in her own. "Yes, you have a talent for doctoring. And you will use it well and wisely."

Mary Anna felt protests begin to rise in her throat, but her heart heard the words, and they touched a resonance of perfect harmony.

Virginia saw her words had been accepted and said, "Well, now I'll get some supper fixed for those young men out there while you care for Peter. He's a fine boy." She beamed with the joy of having helped bring the tiny being into the world.

Mary Anna smiled, too. The spring of 1858 was starting off with great joy and expectations for the young Thornton family.

~⌘~

Mary Anna was working in her herb garden. She knew she would be needing an extensive one. Virginia's words had opened her eyes to a calling she felt deep inside, and she was preparing herself to be helpful whenever she could. She knew a lot about herbs from Louisa, and one of the books she had brought with her at her stepmother's insistence was a book on herbal healing.

She glanced up every now and then to check on the baby sleeping in his basket close by. Four-year-old Columbus was playing with Soldier, throwing a stick for the dog to retrieve. Mary Anna had her new rifle propped against the rude fence that surrounded the spacious garden. They were still having trouble with the Indians, and she was ever mindful of danger. Daniel and Otto were plowing the fields, and she could see the little puffs of dust behind the plow float up into the soft spring sky.

The sun made her long-sleeved dress and poke bonnet warm to work in, and the cotton gloves on her hands were damp with perspiration where she held the hoe. Carefully she worked the rich soil around the tender plants until she heard the steady pound of horses' hooves coming up the rough road. Shading her eyes, she recognized Caleb, and he was riding hard, a sure sign of trouble. He headed straight for the men, and then Daniel came to her with the news.

His face was set hard as granite. "The Lemley girls have been kidnapped by the Comanche," he said without preliminaries.

"Oh, no!" she gasped.

"We're going to try to get them back."

There was no point in exploring the possibilities of what might happen to the two girls if they weren't rescued. Mary Anna was torn between her fear for the children and the terror the parents were going through.

She watched the men ride away from her and silently prayed for all the people involved in this ordeal. Then she spent her energy on the plants and her thoughts of why the Indians did what they did.

"Lord, I can understand the Indians fighting with the settlers to keep their land, but I don't understand the cruelty of their revenges. Why can't someone sit down and work this out? It could all be so simple. We get this land, and they get that land, and everyone should be happy. Why does it have to include the children? I've heard what they do to the children. And to the women they steal. Lord, why can't this be settled between the men? I don't understand. Oh, please, dear Lord, keep those little girls safe and let Daniel and the men find them quickly to bring them home to those who love them. Please." Tears filled her eyes. Her heart tore as if it had been her boys taken away.

Then fear struck. Was she being watched right now? With fear pulling at her, she grabbed the children and ran for the cabin. Columbus was very unhappy at being inside on such a nice day, and she was hard pressed to keep him occupied. She was jumpy, and Columbus's irritability plucked at her tightly strung nerves.

Daniel and Otto didn't come home for dinner, but then she didn't know when to expect them. She sat in the rocker with a small fire in the fireplace to mend by until her eyes were aching with fatigue. There was no question of sleeping until Daniel and Otto returned.

It was close to dawn when they returned, haggard and saddle weary. She peeped out cautiously before she opened the door all the way. Daniel's grin was weary but victorious.

"You got them! Are they all right? Were they hurt? Poor babies, they must have been scared to death. Oh, Daniel, talk to me!"

"I'm just waiting until you take a breath." He smiled and hugged her at the same time. "Yes, they were scared, but they're fine and back home." He sighed. "We followed the Indians to a camp and waited until they were bedded down. We stampeded their horses and cut them down."

"You killed them?"

"I don't think they would have been willing to just hand the girls over to us," he said wryly.

She wanted to say, "You could have tried to trade for them," but bit her tongue. She hadn't been there, so she couldn't know what it had been like. Maybe they had done the only thing they could. She looked carefully at his face and saw nothing. Daniel was numb. His eyes held a haunted look and his color was ashen. She wanted to ask if killing those men would mean more retaliations by the Indians on the settlers. Instead, she said, "Come and I'll feed you."

"Too tired to eat. I just want to go to bed." Daniel knew nothing would stay in his stomach. The sights and sounds and smells of the killing had sickened him. Indian or white man, death like that was ugly, and he hated being a part of it. He tried to tell himself it was like killing a rabid animal to put it out of its misery and keep other people safe, but he wasn't sure he could accept that measurement of human life.

Mary Anna noted a similar look on Otto's face as he headed into his sleeping room.

She lay next to the person she loved most in the world, wondering if she would ever really know him. With this incident had God begun to change Daniel's hatred of Indians? *Please, God, take away the hate and replace it with a desire for peace.*

&#8766;

Daniel knew full well what the Indians might do in retaliation for rescue of the Lemley girls. He and Otto were more vigilant than ever. News had come in the way of a passing stranger. He wouldn't talk in front of Mary Anna, but as he and Daniel and Otto sat outside under the tree, he had warned them.

The stranger's story made Daniel think of the stories he and his brothers had told under the covers at the plantation when they had wanted to scare each other to death. But this was real. And he was here with his family.

The man's story dripped with the blood of innocents murdered and mutilated by the renegade Indians. He spoke in low tones that added to the horror. He said names like Nocona, the Comanche chief, and Geronimo, the Apache warrior. And then he said the most horrible thing of all. "You do realize that you are sittin' smack dab in the middle of one of the Comanche war trails down into Mexico, don't ya?"

Daniel's hair rose in a prickle from his scalp and his heart skipped a beat. "Yes." Yes, he knew, but he hoped it wasn't true.

"Yup." The stranger wiped his dirty face with an equally filthy hand. "The gov'ment ain't gonna be no help either. There's too much land for the few men they have. Gonna have to be some changes made iffen they expect white folks to stay out here on the frontier." He saw the fear in Daniel's eyes and said, "Don't worry. I won't say anything to the little lady." Then he looked at Daniel again. "I'd dare to say she knows she ain't in civilization, but there's no need to scare her to death."

Daniel nodded his thanks and looked at Otto. The younger man was white as the moonlight, and his eyes were as frightened as Daniel's.

"We've had our run-ins with the Indians, Comanche mostly." He told the story of the Lemley girls.

"You know you're a marked man," the stranger said flatly. "They'll never forgive nor forget you." He sighed deeply. "If I was you, I'd pack up right now and move back a ways. At least close to a big fort. There's time enough for you to make your fortune after things are settled with the Indians."

Something inside Daniel recoiled at those words. "I didn't come out here to do things the easy way. I came out here to make something of this land. I can make something productive out of it. More and more whites are moving in. We'll take care of ourselves."

Even in the moonlight, the stranger and Otto could see Daniel's resolve. The strong planes of his face were set hard. The stranger shrugged and tapped out the ashes of his pipe. "I'll be pleased to sleep in your barn tonight. That straw sounds mighty soft. I'll be going at first light."

That night as Daniel lay beside Mary Anna, he had his first serious inspection of his thoughts on God since coming to Erath County. *Does God care what happens to me and mine? Or did He just start the world and now He sits back and watches? People say miracles happen, but I'm not sure if they're miracles by God or extraordinary good luck. Why would God let people like the Indians exist? How can He let them do such terrible things to other human beings and not wipe them out with His power—if He has so much?*

Logic chased reason and knowledge from his childhood around in his head. The things he knew about religion didn't fit out here in the frontier. Long ago he had ceased to depend on God for anything in his life. Now didn't seem to be a fitting time to begin again. Stubbornly he thought, *I'm not going to turn to God in fear. I don't want that kind of God. Mary Anna can do the praying for both of us.* And he turned over and fell into a restless sleep.

≈

Mary Anna was serving Daniel his breakfast when she casually asked, "What did the stranger say about the Indians? Any retaliations because of the Lemley girls?"

Daniel knew better than to lie to her. "Some. We're well warned and armed. Just be a little more careful than usual." His voice was level, but for Mary Anna it held a world of frightening information.

Soldier gave a low growl and ran to the door barking. Daniel was quick to get his gun and hurry to the door. When he opened it, the rattling of a wagon could be clearly heard. Shouts of "Hello!" and "Look at the house!" drifted in. Then came those sweet words: "Mary Anna, it's us! We're here!"

Mary Anna grabbed her shawl and almost got it around her before she hit the cold ground in a dead run. "Papa! Louisa! I can't believe it! It must be a dream!" And then everyone was hugging everyone.

"Jacob, you've grown a foot since I last saw you," Mary Anna exclaimed to her oldest brother. And to each of her four other siblings she made similar remarks, but the one who had changed the most was baby Vera. "How pretty you are, and so grown up! Give me a big hug!" Baby Vera's little curls danced up and down excitedly as she reached for her big sister. "I'm not a baby anymore," she said in a six-year-old voice.

"Of course, you're not. Oh, you and Columbus will have such a good time playing together. And you can help take care of little Peter." Vera's face shone with grown-up joy at the thought.

"Well, come on in and let's get all of you fed." There was a lot of talking and laughter as the food was passed around and gratefully consumed. As she saw that each one was cared for, Mary Anna asked a hundred questions and got a hundred in return.

Peter Garland sat in Daniel's chair and happily ate the venison offered. Louisa sat in Mary Anna's chair thoroughly enjoying a hot cup of coffee laced heavily with cream. Peter wiped his mouth carefully on his sleeve and said, "You haven't lost your touch, girl."

Mary Anna still felt she was in the middle of a dream.

"You look plumb surprised, darlin'." He was delighted he had caused such a stir. "We got tired of the soft life at the hotel and decided to have an adventure, like you."

"Humph! He decided, not me." Louisa took a spoonful of hominy and then added, "I'd have rather stayed in the soft life." But her face gentled as she said to Mary Anna, "You're looking well. Pioneer life hasn't hurt you. You look older but somehow more handsome." She smiled. "And two fine sons!"

She saw the look of pride as well as the knife edge of pain in Mary Anna's eyes. She knew that look, the look of a dead child. Later she would find out about it.

"Tell us your plans, and Otto and me will help you get settled out here," Daniel offered. Otto gave them a shy smile of assent. He looked completely at home among the Garland clan.

"I guess it's simple arithmetic. The more white people there are, the fewer Indians that can stay around. We're here to help settle this part of Texas. The land is beautiful. Soon Stephenville will be needing a good hotel, and we just happen to be in the hotel business." He smiled benevolently.

"From the news I've been hearing, you might not have anybody to rent those rooms to," Louisa said tartly. "Is it true the army is gone? That scares the Irish out of me."

Daniel answered her honestly. "Yes, most of them are gone. And the Indians are riled up because we rescued the Lemley girls. Things are a bit frightening right now."

"We heard about it in town," Peter replied soberly. "I guess our arrival is a timely one. We can help keep watch until this thing has settled down."

"It isn't going to be settled down until all the Indians are on a reservation," Daniel said flatly.

Mary Anna and Louisa exchanged looks of mutual concern.

"But they are on a reservation. Most of them, anyway," Mary Anna said reasonably.

"They aren't staying there," Daniel argued. "If they did, we wouldn't be having all this trouble."

Mary Anna bit her tongue and said carefully, "If they were getting what they needed, they wouldn't come to our door and beg for meat."

Peter and Louisa exchanged covert looks as the marital discord hung in the air. "No matter," said Peter, "we've come to be together as a family again. Now, lass, come outside and see what we've brought you." The tension melted in the warmth of wonderful gifts: spices, pieces of lace, and for Columbus, a metal monkey that clanged cymbals together when he was wound up.

The evening was festive and full of remembrances. When it was time to bed everyone, there was a very short discussion about the two older boys sleeping in the barn. "We can't chance it, boys," Daniel said. "If the Indians raid us, you'd be off by yourselves."

Otto added casually. "Why, I'm even going to sleep here in the cabin. If trouble comes, we all want to be together to help." That settled any discussion. When all were bedded down wall to wall on pallets, Daniel kissed Mary Anna good night quietly in their bed.

"I'm sorry I lost my temper," he whispered.

"I'm sorry, too," she said as she snuggled closer to him in the faded light of the banked fire. She wanted to say more. To tell him there had to be an answer to all the killing and raiding and hating. But there were too many people in the cabin to have a heart-to-heart talk, so she snuggled close to him and held her peace.

*Lord, keep us safe tonight, and thank You for bringing my family together again. Help us to see the Indians as Your children, too. Please, let there be peace among us. And help Daniel to come to love You as I do, for I'm sure then he will see the Indians as human beings, too.*

She gave a tiny grin as she felt another piece of the stone in her heart flake off. Virginia was right. Time was a great healer. It gave her a fairer perspective. Virginia's promise that Mary Anna was a healer flitted through her mind. *Physician, first heal thyself.* And she drifted off to sleep hearing the gentle snoring of her family and feeling a cabinful of love.

⋙

Awful screams and loud cries of horses woke Mary Anna as the sunlight struggled to filter through the tiny chinks of the cabin walls. The shrill battle cries of the Comanche made the hair rise on her arms. Terror cramped her heart, and she couldn't pull any air into her lungs.

Daniel was already springing for his pants and his guns, hopping over sleeping bodies that were beginning to sit up in the din. "Indians!" he shouted, "Get your guns! Everybody stay down! Otto! Peter!"

There was no need to call Peter's name. The old military man was clutching his rifle, heading for the one shuttered window in the cabin. It had gun ports in it, and he peered out into the cold, misty half-light. A cry of dismay slipped through his lips as he saw the raiding band emptying the horses out of the corral and killing the cows randomly. In all his military years he had never seen such a sight as the magnificent horsemen wheeling and charging. Even in his fear he could appreciate the riding skills of the Comanche. He searched for a target and fired. He grunted with satisfaction as a man fell, and then gasped in astonishment as two other riders came in and picked up the wounded man between them.

Daniel was shooting through the gunport in the door. His mouth was dry with fear at the sight of the men. *There's never been so many before,* he thought. And then tears stung his eyes as he saw the first of the flames begin to lick at the corral that had been built with so much hard labor.

But as he saw those flames, fear knotted his stomach. He fired like a wild man trying to keep the raiders from getting close to the cabin. *Dear God, don't let them burn us out! Help us!* The prayer was said without a thought for theology. Instinctively he turned to the only One he knew who had the power to keep them alive—the God of his childhood. He felt they had a good chance of withstanding the firepower and arrows of the Indians, but there was not a chance in a thousand of them surviving without the safety of the cabin.

Mary Anna tried to calm the children and reload Daniel's rifle as quickly as he emptied it. The acrid smell of gunpowder, the ear-splitting noise of the guns, the screams of the terrified children, all made up the cacophony overpowering the small confines of the cabin.

Louisa was white with fear. One of her girls clung to her nightgown, screaming, but she busily reloaded for Peter.

The Indians were riding past the cabin, taunting the gunmen with their riding tricks to stay out of the line of fire. The men could see the horses but not the riders until the arrow or the gunshot came.

When Daniel heard the thud against the back wall of the cabin, he shouted to Otto, who was manning the small gunport, "What's going on back there?"

Otto looked, and his blood ran cold. The raiders in back were shooting flaming arrows at the cabin. His mind raced as he tried to decide what to do. Already smoke was beginning to seep through the tiny chinks.

Daniel ordered the older children to get rags and dip them into the water barrel on the other wall of the cabin where the kitchen things were. "Put them over your faces and lay down on the floor!" he shouted over the pandemonium. *What do we do when it gets too hot to stay in here? Think, Daniel, think.* He tried to remember the landscape behind the cabin. How far was it to the creek? To the woods beyond it? Was there any other place of safety? The five adults, Mary Anna's two half brothers and three half sisters, and his two small ones. Seven children and five adults. He groaned. The smoke was getting thicker, and he was beginning to cough, too.

Sudden silence from the raiders and their retreat gave a surge of hope to Daniel. Were they going? Or was it a trick? Wait until they were forced out and then hit them again? He peered through the gunport hole. "What's going on in front?" he asked Peter.

"They're pulling back. Is it a trick?" He looked at Daniel for information about Indian fighting.

Daniel looked at Otto. "Is it?"

"Yup. They're jest awaiting fer it to git too hot in here." His face was grim.

Daniel ran to the back and felt the heat coming off the logs and the sinister crackling of the roof. "Makes no difference, we're going to have to get out of here."

"We can't go out the front, that's for sure." Peter squinted one eye and peered out again to confirm what Otto had said. "Time to start doing some serious praying."

The wind made the war feathers in the braves' hair dance gracefully. The Comanche were covered in colorful paint, each man with a different design. Even the horses were decorated with paint and fluttering strips of cloth woven in their manes and tails.

"Fearsome looking, they are," said Peter with awe. "Just sittin' there on those ponies, waiting." The silence was nerve-racking.

Daniel hurried to his tool chest and took out a one-man saw. When Peter saw what he intended to do, he took over the window gunport. The logs were hot, putting off enough heat to cook a deer, but the two men hacked at the burning logs until the first one fell to the outside. Quickly water was doused around the small opening, and unspoken prayers were sent up to God with the fervor bred from fear of a gruesome death. *Please don't let them come around to the back of the cabin and find us!*

Under his breath Daniel whispered to Peter. "Save some bullets. Don't let them get the women and girls. If you can, save one for each member of your family. I will for mine. And one for yourself." Peter nodded mutely. Daniel knew there was no need to remind Otto to save a bullet.

"Stay low and run for the creek. Make for the woods as fast and as quietly as you can. We've got to get into the woods." There was an ominous crack overhead as the fire ate through some of the supporting logs. "Go!"

Through the sooty, still-hot logs, the women and children crawled and ran for the creek and the haven of the woods, staying as low as they could.

As Daniel, Otto, and Peter climbed though, the battle shrieks of the Comanche started again, spurring the men into a dead run. Shots were ringing out, but no one was coming around to the back.

Mary Anna's nightgown was soaked up to her waist, and she was covered in greasy soot. Her lungs ached from the smoke, but she had Columbus in one arm and the baby clutched in the other as she sped into the woods. Leaves and small branches tore at her face and clothes. Thorns like living hands ripped at her ankles, tripping her and tearing the flesh. She ran for the hollow where she had seen the young girl giving birth. Louisa was right behind her with her children. They crashed and thrashed their way through the undergrowth until they could run no more.

*Even if I'm about to die, I don't think I can go another step. Lord, help us!* She fell heavily to the ground, turning so as not to fall on the boys. A rock bit deeply into her shoulder, and the fall knocked the wind out of her momentarily. She could see her father, Otto, and Daniel coming in, too.

"Are we all here?" she asked softly. They could still hear gunfire coming from the front of the cabin. The men were stretched out on the ground facing the cabin though the brush.

Louisa was silently crying and rocking her youngest child in her lap. Her hair had come loose from her night braid and flew wildly around her dirty face. The tears made odd tracks through the dirt. "We're all here, I think," she said, gulping in air and letting out tears. "Who is shooting?"

"Praise the Lord!" exclaimed Peter. "It's soldiers! I can see them riding after the Indians! It's soldiers!" he shouted and stood up.

Daniel stepped to the edge of the woods, waiting in their safety as three men rode toward them. The horses' hooves made a clicking noise as they stepped across the rocks in the stream.

"Everyone all right?" called the lieutenant in charge. He rode up close to Daniel and dismounted. "Early morning callers, sir?" he asked grimly.

Mary Anna moved to the edge where she could see her worldly goods being offered up like a morning sacrifice to a pagan god. Her eyes were red and dry as she walked to the lieutenant. "Thank you for coming when you did. The Lord surely sent you to us."

"Yes, ma'am, He did. We don't usually patrol this area this time of the morning, but we had to go into Stephenville, and we saw your smoke and heard the gunfire." Ruefully he looked at the cabin. "Sorry we couldn't have been here a lot sooner."

"Don't be sorry, Lieutenant. You saved our lives. For that we thank you and the Lord."

Falling timbers fell into the shell of the cabin, sending a shower of sparks high in the air. The stench of burned meat and damp logs, of trunks filled with clothes filled the air. Bottles popped from the heat. Pages of a book floated, half burned, over the cabin and landed near the creek. All the small crowd of people could do was watch. They could see the skeleton of the Garland's wagon in front of the cabin. The iron wheels were turned inward and leaning on each other as the wood was consumed from them. Over all of this floated a black cloud of smoke. Smoke that spoke of the ruin of their possessions, and the cloud that had saved their lives.

Mary Anna sank to her knees and folded her hands. One by one the rest followed. "Thank You, heavenly Father, for Your care. Thank You for sending these fine men to rescue us, for they are Your army here on earth for the settlers. Angels in blue uniforms. Amen."

The lieutenant put his hat back on and said gallantly, "Thank you, ma'am." Turning to Daniel he asked, "Is there somewhere we can take you? To town, perhaps?"

Daniel looked around at his bedraggled family. There was no place else to go. Fear sparked his eyes. "The Wests! Lieutenant, you've got to send some men to see about the Wests!"

The lieutenant shouted some orders and half his men mounted up to head for the Wests' cabin. "Let's get you to town and get you settled."

The families huddled in the rattling wagon, sitting on and around the supplies for the army post, as it took them to Stephenville. Daniel and Mary Anna watched their smoldering cabin disappear into the distance. They looked at each other, and Mary Anna saw tears in Daniel's eyes. "It's all gone," he whispered as he held her close. "It's all gone."

"What are we going to do?"

"I don't know. I don't know." He shook his head as they went around a bend that shut off the sight of the pile of ashes that had been their home.

Mary Anna was numb. Her only thought was to get to town quickly and stay there. Maybe for a long time. Maybe forever. Maybe their dream was supposed to come true in the town and not out in the wilderness. A germ of hope seeded itself in her mind.

# Chapter 11

When they arrived in Stephenville, the Thorntons and Garlands found clothes for everyone, and town families took them in. Otto made arrangements to stay with another family close to Miss Gilbert's house. He wasn't unhappy about that. Perhaps he would have time to do some serious wooing.

While they all had places to stay, they knew it wouldn't be for long. Their presence crowded the host families, and even frontier courtesy had its limits.

Neither was the horror of the early morning attack easily forgotten. The children had persistent nightmares, and Mary Anna woke, hearing screams in the night.

Daniel, Otto, and Peter were sitting around the potbellied stove in the general store with some of the other men. They all knew the story of the raid.

"Thinking of staying in town?" asked Bill, the owner.

"I am," answered Peter. "I'm thinkin' of opening a hotel."

His enthusiasm began to grow as the men around the stove nodded their heads in agreement.

"I can see it now. Finer than the one we sold in Tennessee Colony. Mary Anna can do the cooking again. Ah, it'll be grand to have us all together like it used to be."

"And what will I do?" Daniel asked, his voice heavy with bitterness.

"How about setting up a livery stable and raising cattle for our meat and milk at the hotel?" Peter said reasonably.

"We could use a good hotel," Bill said.

One man standing in back of the larger group made an ugly sound with his mouth. "Iffen it was me, I'd be out huntin' me down some red meat, not raising it." He spit an admirable spurt of tobacco into the spittoon from an eyebrow-lifting distance. Some of it dribbled down his dirty beard, and he wiped it away with an equally dirty hand.

"Seems to me if them Injuns are gonna burn us out one at a time, we oughter jest go over to that there reservation and help ourselves to a few scalps ourselves. Mebbe it would make 'em think twice before raiding agin." His eyes were serpentine slits, a cold glitter lighting them. His hat hid most of his face, along with his beard, but those eyes burned with hatred.

"You're talking about a government protected place. A peace treaty promises them safety there," Bill objected.

"Yeah, a place where they can hide after they burn and kill and destroy." He turned his stare toward Daniel. "What do you think would have happened to you and your family if them soldiers hadn't come along?"

A shudder passed through Daniel's body. There was no need to answer. All the men knew.

"But why do they kill and then mutilate the bodies so bad?" asked Bill. "And I can't understand torturing any human being."

The man spat another stream of tobacco, but it missed the mark and slid down on the floor. "They kill to make themselves more powerful in the tribe. They mutilate so the dead person cain't be recognized and git into the next land."

"You seem to know a lot about the Comanche," Bill said softly.

The man nodded. "Make it my bidness to know all I can."

Otto noticed the man never seemed to blink, adding to his snake-like appearance. He measured the man with his eyes and found him a person without a soul. Something in his life had robbed him of the last grain of kindness or compassion. It was probably something about the Indians, but no one was going to ask him.

"I like to pay back the Injuns any time I have the opportunity, gentlemen," the stranger added. He took off his greasy hat, and the men gasped. The entire top of his head was one large scar. His hair was gone. "I like to take me a scalp ever' now and then to replace the one I lost. I ain't gonna show you the rest of my scars. All you need to know is that I survived. And I'm here to help anyone who wants to do any payin' back." He looked directly at Daniel.

Daniel felt the swirl of emotions he had so carefully guarded become a tornado of anger. Anger at the Indians, anger at the total loss of his home and possessions and the back-breaking labor he had used to begin his kingdom.

"First time I was wiped out, they took all my stock. This time they took everything. Only thing I have is my family, and for that I'm grateful, but how am I going to take care of them now that the Indians have burned me out?" All the frustration, hatred, fear, and anger moved up through him like pus to a boil.

"Why don't we pay them a little call?" the stranger suggested. "Kill us a few women and braves. Take their little ones to make white." He tipped his head and spread his hands wide in a gesture of questioning.

"I don't know," Bill said hesitantly. "We're getting into some deep water here. Doing what they do don't make it right."

"You don't have to go iffen you don't want to," the stranger replied in a condescending tone.

Boots scraping the floor was the only sound in the room for a few seconds; then someone offered hesitantly, "If the army isn't going to be able to help us, maybe we do have to help ourselves."

Daniel let out a long breath and unclenched his fists. The memory of the harrowing raid, the noise, the smell, the fear came crashing through his brain with deadly clarity. He began to tremble and sweat. He could taste the hatred in his mouth for the men who had been a constant threat to his family's existence. But in his mind's eye he could see one man, his face painted with black circles around his eyes and yellow stripes across his forehead, pulling on his bow, an arrow aflame with fire, aiming for Daniel's cabin. That man had wanted to burn Daniel and his family to death. He'd wanted to kill them all. Through clenched teeth Daniel asked, "Peter?"

Daniel's overpowering anger spread from one man to another, and Peter's encounter with the Indians had been so recent that he exploded with his anger. "I'll organize it and lead it. No one is going to burn out my daughter and her family!"

News went from one man to another all over town. The sheriff's pleas went unheard in the tide of fury that swept the town. The men, loaded with ammunition and every weapon they could find, pounded out of town like an avenging army to kill the men who had killed so many of them. The dust around them was like a cloud of energy, charging each man to the depths of fury needed to murder.

Peter planned the raid well. They waited until dawn at the edge of the reservation on the Brazos, whipping themselves into a frenzy. But when they swept down on the camp, it wasn't the raiding warriors who were killed. Men who had never killed anything but a deer or a buffalo murdered two young warriors, eight women and two children, one old man, and several horses. Peter led them on their glorious raid, but later no one would tell of the things that happened. No one wanted to remember that he had been part of such a holocaust on the innocent.

The men were gone and back so quickly, each one wondered if he had experienced a nightmare of epic proportions. Only the stranger had howled with joy as he had slaughtered the tribe. But when the men had ridden back into town, the stranger had not been with them. He had disappeared as he had appeared. And after it was over, no one could explain why men of stature and honor had done such a dishonorable deed.

Daniel was riding away from the massacre, running away from the ghastly scene. He saw three braves riding toward him on their way back to camp. He veered from them, heading into some brush. *Where are the other men?* he worried. He was alone, and there were three men coming to kill him for killing their people. Terror became his body, the living thing that covered him and gave him the power to run. He saw a plum thicket up ahead. As his horse passed it, he jumped off and into its thick bracket, hoping the men would follow his horse. It only put them off for a minute. Then they returned, calling to him, "John, come out, John. We won't hurt you."

Daniel was so terrorized every sense was heightened. He had almost stopped breathing in his efforts to stay hidden.

Then the arrows flew into the thicket. The first ones missed, but one arrow found its mark, slicing Daniel's forearm to the bone. Pain screamed through his body. In a way he was almost glad he had been hit. The pain had a cauterizing effect on his conscience. When the men finally went away to help their people, he whistled for his horse and passed out saying, "Mary Anna. Forgive me, Mary Anna."

His horse took him to the house where they were staying.

"Daniel! Where have you and Papa been? What happened? Oh, dear Lord, you look terrible. What happened? Talk to me!" Mary Anna came out and got him into the house.

When he finally regained consciousness, his eyes were hollow with horror and his head rang with the sounds of death. Of babies screaming. He couldn't get the sound of the babies out of his head.

Neither could he look Mary Anna in the eye. He kept his eyes averted, but when his gaze came to rest on his baby son, the pain exploded into tears. "Oh, what have I done, what have I done?" Tears of bitterness scalded his face with shame.

Mary Anna was shocked, but she continued to tend his wounds and comfort him as though it were the most normal thing in the world for her husband to cry with a broken heart.

A soft knock sounded on the door, and Frances came in. Her silvery hair shone in the lamplight and her kind face was filled with pity. "Do you know what happened?"

"No." Mary Anna wanted desperately not to believe what she thought.

Frances sat down carefully in the rocking chair and in a sad voice told the story of the raid. "I saw them riding out of here, tall in the saddle, like knights in shining armor. And I saw them come back in. Slumped and broken-like. They were not proud of what they had done."

Frances was a widow and spent her time in acts of kindness for others. She rose and took Mary Anna in her arms to comfort her. "Don't be hard on him. He'll punish himself much harder than you ever could. He needs your love right now. And your understanding. Even if you don't understand."

There were tears of compassion in her eyes as she patted Mary Anna's hand and left.

The next day Daniel was still in and out of consciousness, but Peter came to call. He was blustery about the raid.

"It had to be done, daughter," he declared confidently, but he couldn't look her in the face, either. His face was flaming with shame. Less certainly he pleaded, "You have to understand how it was there at the store. What the man said was right. If they raid us, then we should raid them. Then they will leave us alone."

Mary Anna's cheeks were red with anger, and she had to hold the knob of the bedstead to stop her trembling. Her voice was low and cold. "When does it stop, Papa, this killing? Where will the circle stop? We are not speaking of animals. We are speaking of people. God's people. No, they're not like us. How could they be? I heard there were women and babies and old people out there. You killed babies? Papa, how could you? How could Daniel? How could anyone?"

She shuddered. "It doesn't matter what they did to us. The circle must be broken. If it isn't, then it means we will all have to die. All of us. And then who will own the land? Who will build your precious hotel or ranch?" She had not yet vented all her fury. It felt like a volcano in her chest, and she was afraid it would literally blow her apart if she let it go.

Peter watched the anger in his daughter's eyes grow. Her blue eyes blazed with an intensity he had never seen. He knew she would never love and respect him as she once had. And he knew he deserved all of her hatred. He hated himself. Louisa hated him. He put out his hand to reach for her, to try to explain, but Mary Anna turned her back.

Tears flowed down his cheeks as he left silently.

Mary Anna knew it was wrong to turn her back on her father, but she couldn't stand the sight of this man she suddenly didn't know. She looked down at Daniel. Would she be able to love him? How could she ever respect him again? How could she ever stand for him to touch her again?

She moved closer to his bed and looked hard at his face. It was twisted with torment as he dreamed the ugliness of his life over again. She thought of the first time they met. When he first held her in his arms. Their happiness in their first cabin with the baby. She held on to the vision of the man she knew and loved, trying not to see this one in front of her. Her eyes filled with tears. It was the first time she had ever given in and cried with grief. And she reached for the only One who could help her.

*Lord Jesus, Who loves us all, help me to love this man. He's my husband and the father of my children. I don't understand what he's done. Maybe You do. I don't want to understand. I just want to be able to forgive him and help him to forgive himself. Give him the love and faith he needs to be able to live with himself again.*

Peace flowed through her. Slowly she picked up Daniel's limp hand, hoping some of the peace she felt would flow through her into his heart.

She remembered telling Virginia how she felt she was sinking in the water like Peter. How long ago that seemed! She closed her eyes and reached out for the Lord as Peter had on that lake so long ago. She could feel His goodness and mercy surrounding her, and trust replaced the doubts she'd had. She belonged out here in the wilderness with Daniel. The Lord would take care of them. He wouldn't shield them from dangerous events, but He would use those trials to build their trust in Him. His hand was there, pulling them both out of the icy water.

Daniel stirred in his sleep, restless in his pain. She took some of the willow tea and spooned a little into his mouth, urging him to swallow it. Then she checked his bandage and washed his face gently. She looked at his face, really looked at it. It was still the face she had fallen in love with in Tennessee Colony. It was the face of her husband. The father of her children. And she loved him. Her heart ached for him, for she had seen the beginning of his pain.

Daniel opened his eyes at her touch. "Mary Anna" was all he could say before the tears began.

"Shh, shh. I know, my darling, I know. It's going to be all right." She softly wiped away his tears. "Some people return to the Lord easily. Some have to do it the hard way. You chose a hard way, my sweet husband, but God has never let go of you. I guess He had to use the big artillery to get your attention. He loves you, Daniel, and forgives you. And so do I."

With his good hand, Daniel lifted her fingers to his mouth and kissed them one at a time with his eyes closed in concentration on the loving task. "I'm sure the Lord does love me. He gave me you."

"We have a lot of things to discuss, my love." She smoothed back a straying lock of hair from his forehead. "And the Lord has given us this time, while you're recuperating." Gently she kissed his forehead where her hand had caressed his hair. "We're going to start over. Everything."

He gave her a weak smile. "Everything?"

"Well, not everything," she conceded. "But our lives. Daniel, let's not rebuild in the same place. There's no reason to live on the Indian's highway. Can't we go somewhere else?"

"Heard the men speaking of the North Bosque. Pretty up there. Not so many Indians." He looked up into her eyes, matching her hope with his pain. "I know them as people now. I saw too much of their humanity. I never saw them as people before. They were a nuisance, like rats or something. Then I saw them as families. Like ours. And their blood."

He closed his eyes in horror. "Dear Lord, their blood, everywhere." He took a steadying breath. "I don't want to fight with them. I just want a place where I can build my ranch and bring up my family. Let's go to the North Bosque. We can start over. I can start over." He smiled tiredly. "You were right about the Lord using the big artillery on me."

"But He didn't sink your boat, Daniel. He pulled both of us back into it with Him. We're back in His boat again. We're together with Him."

With as much vigor as he could muster, Daniel said, "Look out, world. Here comes the Thornton boat with the Lord doing the rowing!"

"Yes, that's the right way to begin. You sleep now, and I'll sit here with you."

"No, come lie beside me," he said softly. His eyes were glazed with pain, but he said, "I still can't believe you're mine."

Deep pain that had nothing to do with his wound came into his eyes. "I'll make it up to you somehow, Mary Anna. I know I did a terrible thing. An unforgivable thing."

She gently laid her finger on his lips. "There is only one thing God can't forgive: not acknowledging him as Lord and Savior. He has already forgiven you." She took a deep breath. "And I have forgiven you, too. It may be a long time until I forget. Maybe I won't ever forget. But I do love you and I see your sorrow, too."

She nestled against him. "I think the one who will be the last to forgive you is yourself. But if you let the Lord work in you, healing will come." She rested her arm across his chest and her head in the crook of his neck. She could feel his warm tears, and she hugged him tightly.

His voice was soft and whispery. "Lord, I do believe You love me and forgive me. I'm more sorry than I can say for what I did. Help me to change my life and my ideas about the Indians. I'm afraid it will be a powerful task, but Mary Anna says You will do it. And God, thank You for Mary Anna."

He had to stop for a moment because the tears were making a huge lump in his throat. "She is more than I could ever deserve." Then he broke down and cried hard, pressing his face into Mary Anna's shoulder.

She couldn't say a thing, but cried silently with him. All her waiting was being rewarded. Daniel was returning to the Lord and asking His forgiveness. Peace flowed through her and around her, and for one wonderful moment, she thought she might die of happiness. Life was going to be too beautiful for words. The Lord had used an awful, bloody event to completely remake Daniel. It had been a high price to pay for serenity. And then she remembered the price Jesus had paid for the sins of the entire world. And she wept in gratitude.

# Chapter 12

The next day Mary Anna and Daniel were still walking in a glow of renewal when she had a terrible thought. She was changing his dressing when she voiced her concern.

"Daniel, do you think there'll be trouble about this? You did raid a reservation. Will the army take any action?"

"I doubt it. They're probably glad to have someone to help them settle the Indians down."

"And what about the sheriff? I heard he tried to stop you."

"Yes, but why would he care?"

"I don't know, I just have a funny feeling about all this. Reservations are government land, and there's laws protecting them. It's already all over the county about the raid."

His pale face blanched. "And what are people saying?"

She turned away from him so he couldn't see her face. "Oh, different things," she hedged.

"Like what?"

"Some are for it, and some are against it. You can't go by what you hear."

"Turn around and look at me," he ordered. The worry on her face told him what he needed to know.

"There's talk of retaliation by the Indians?"

"No. There is a rumor that Judge Battles in Waco has issued warrants for the arrest of Papa and you and all the men who were in the raid."

Daniel's face was somber. He wrestled with his new view of the Indians against what he had felt right after the raid on his cabin. "What we did was wrong, but it is fair in the face of what the Indians have done to all of us. We're supposed to be protected by the army from harm from the Indians, too. I don't see any arrest warrants being issued by any judges for them."

"Daniel, what if they do execute those warrants? You could go to trial for this. And if they find you guilty. . ."

"Call your father in here for me. We need to talk."

In a short while Peter was at Daniel's bedside.

"Well, what do you think?" Daniel asked his father-in-law.

Peter took a deep breath, avoiding Daniel's eyes. "I think we could be in big trouble if this judge carries on with this."

"What can we do?"

"Let's talk around the town, explain our side to the people. Since the massacre of the Jackson family outside town, people might not be so quick to judge us harshly." He walked over to the window and stared out unseeingly.

"There isn't a single family out here that hasn't had some horrible thing done to them by the Indians." He turned back to face Daniel, his eyes flinty blue and cold as he said, "I don't intend to go to jail for doing the same thing the Indians are doing."

"But we're supposed to be the law-abiding ones," Daniel argued. He was propped up on pillows, pale and weak and worried. "If we go to jail, what will happen to our families?"

"If we go to jail for protecting our families, no one out here is safe. We might as well all go back to Tennessee Colony," Peter stated flatly.

Daniel wrinkled his brow. The pain in his arm made his mind work more slowly. "Will the sheriff execute the warrant?"

"No. He's on our side."

"Then who would do it?"

"Mr. Neighbors, the Indian agent, has been writing to Governor Runnels. They're trying to get Captain Ford to do it, but he says it's a civil affair and he doesn't have any authority." A smile gleamed in the cold eyes, warming them briefly. "Divide and conquer."

There was no smile in Daniel's eyes. "I don't want to go to trial for this. What's done has been done by both sides. It should be over."

Peter sat down in Mary Anna's rocking chair. "I think we can make it plain to everyone that we don't intend to be dragged through two counties to stand before Judge Battles in Waco. I'll talk to the others." He rose and placed his right hand on Daniel's good arm. "Now, son, you just rest and let me take care of everything. Rest."

Mary Anna came in right after her father left. "Well?"

"Your father is going to get the other men together and let it be known to all that we won't allow ourselves to be arrested and taken to Waco for trial."

"And what will you do if the army comes in here to arrest you? Shoot them, too?"

Daniel grimaced. "Of course not. All we did was protect what was ours."

"You killed women and children on a protected reservation."

He looked at her with pain in his eyes. "At the time it seemed to be the right thing to do. The Indians were raiding us in our homes, so we raided them in theirs. They've killed our women and children, and we killed theirs."

He shuddered. "It sounded so simple and just. I never dreamed it would turn out like this." He lay back in the pillows and covered his face with the hand of his good arm. A groan escaped through the closed fingers. "We can't take on the army. And if they take us to Waco, where they're not having problems with the Indians, they're liable to find us guilty and then jail us or hang us."

"Oh, Daniel, don't talk like that!" Mary Anna fell on her knees beside his bed and buried her face in the covers. "You'd get a fair trial. People can read the newspapers. They know what's going on out here in the West."

"I hope you're right." He looked in her face with new hope. "The Lord will take care of it. He's the only one who can. Right?"

"Absolutely." She bent to kiss him. "You are learning quickly, my love."

A few days later, Peter was back with more news. There was a bit of a predatory gleam in his eyes. "I think we've created a tempest in the teapot of politics."

"Oh? Is this good news?"

"It seems Captain Ford has refused to come in and arrest us."

"He told the governor this?"

"In a polite and diplomatic way. He said he thought they should try other things first. The sheriff won't do it, Captain Ford won't do it, and now they're trying to get Major Thomas to come help. Only he can't, because he's short of men."

"Let's end this thing, Peter. Let's publish a letter stating our side of it."

"I don't intend to leave Palo Pinto County."

"Let's put that in there. Reach some sort of compromise."

Peter frowned. "It's near to time for the men to be working their farms. No one wants to leave now. Can't. Mary Anna," he called.

"Yes?"

"Get us some paper and a quill and ink. We're going to try to get this thing settled." He looked sternly at Daniel. "I intend to be the one to put my name on this. I feel responsible for the whole thing, in a way. I'm an army man. I was in charge of the raid. Planned it. And I'll be the one to stand up and take the blame if there's blame to be taken."

Daniel closed his eyes and sighed deeply. "All right. But I'll be by your side all the way. I was there that day, too."

They made a rough draft of a letter to be sent to Governor Runnels. It was circulated among the other men involved, and each one had some say about it. New ideas were incorporated and new arguments made until it said all the things they thought were important.

"We need to let the governor know that the army can't always protect us. It takes a civilian group to help," Peter said to the assembled men. "I suggest we call ourselves the Frontier Guards."

"That will give us more dignity than a raggedy band of raiders," agreed one of the men. "I'm fer it."

And so a strong letter defending their actions and agreeing to go to trial, but only in Stephenville, Palo Pinto, or the Jamison Peak, was sent.

It included a protest about Major Neighbors not allowing an Indian on the reservation to be arrested for the murder of Allen Johnson's son and stated firmly that the citizens of Palo Pinto County and the surrounding counties concurred with them fully in their views of their right to defend themselves however they had to. It was signed, "Peter Garland Company, The Frontier Guards."

It took a long time for the letter to get to Governor Runnels, and longer for any type of response.

In the meantime, the men let it be known far and wide that they had no intention of giving up peacefully to the army or any other authority. If they were to go to trial, it would be on their own terms and in their own territory, where they were fairly certain they would be found guiltless.

Mary Anna prayed incessantly for strength to endure and that the men would be found innocent if they went to trial.

*Please, God, I know they did something terrible. I also know that Daniel is sorry for his part in it. Maybe even Father. But now they have their backs to the wall. It's true the Indian agent won't let that Indian be arrested for the murder of a white man. It wouldn't be fair to make them go to trial for killing the Indians.*

*Help us, Lord. Please. I couldn't live without Daniel. Not even one day. I know he'll never do anything like that again. He's sorry, Lord, and You know that. Please, please don't take Daniel from me. Let us live out our lives together until we're old and gray and sitting on the porch in matching rocking chairs.*

She wiped the tears from her eyes and prayed pieces of the same prayer over and over as she worked and took care of the family. She reminded God that they were planning to move as soon as Daniel was able. To get away from the Indian problems. To get away from the killing. She felt time slipping away, for she knew she would have another child soon. She wanted everything settled before the baby was born. Then they could pick up and go on.

Time dragged. The sheriff wasn't any help when it came to information.

"I don't know a thing," he said honestly when Peter asked him about the warrant being served. "It's in the army's hands now."

Daniel turned to leave, but the sheriff continued. "Of course, you've heard about the army, I guess."

"No, what?"

"There's a lot of hoop-de-la in the South about the government trying to abolish slavery. Lots of unrest. So much, in fact, that the government is beginning to pull a few of the troops out of Texas to help with the problems in the South. The South is threatening to secede from the Union if the North doesn't leave them alone."

"Some of the troops are leaving?"

"Kind of good news and bad news, eh? Gets the army off your back but puts all of us in danger of more Indian raids."

Daniel walked slowly out of the sheriff's office with new resolve. *Even if I'm not up to par, we've got to get out of here while we still can. I've got to get my family to the North Bosque. If Peter goes with us, we can get the cabins up quicker, and maybe the army will forget all about us.* He hurried as quickly as he could to tell Mary Anna about his plans.

They held a full family meeting with all the adults. Daniel made his proposal, and there was only a small hesitation in Peter's agreement to it.

"Pulling out of here means leaving all these people less protection. It's safer with more of us out here. We'll be letting them down."

"Maybe some of them will go with us. Maybe they'll see things the way we do."

Peter folded his arms in front of his chest and his spreading, middle-aged belly. "Are you running?"

"Yes, but not from the law. I believe the army would call it a strategic relocation. We've got to get off the Indians' highway to Mexico." Daniel's face held firm resolve and certainty. "I don't want to die out here. I came west to build a ranch, and so far I haven't accomplished anything I've set out to do. Maybe the Lord is trying to tell me something."

"The Lord? And when did you get on such familiar terms with the Lord," Peter asked sarcastically.

"Since He let me live through the raid and see how wrong I was about the Indians."

"Wrong!" Peter's face turned almost purple with anger. "How dare you say we were wrong to avenge our dead!"

"It was wrong for me. Seeing those dead women and babies made me see things in a whole different light, Peter." He looked hard at his father-in-law. "Surely it's changed you, too."

Peter dropped his murderous stare. "No. I still think we did the right thing." His chest heaved with his deep sigh. "Well, maybe it wasn't the right thing to do, but it was a necessary thing to do."

He looked Daniel in the eyes. "I'm sorry it turned out like it did. But I thought at the time it was the right thing to do. I can't take back what I did. But each day I pray that Mary Anna can forgive me. I've let her down terribly. I think she still loves me, but it will be a long time of healing before things are the same between us again. Maybe never," he added sadly.

"But I do see the good reasoning behind leaving this area now that the army is beginning to pull back," Peter added. "Things'll only get worse. I agree with you. I didn't come out here to be an Indian fighter. I wanted to build a fine hotel."

He almost grinned. "And I doubt the Indians have the money to stay in one of my fine rooms." He looked at Daniel hopefully. "You're sure it's all right with Mary Anna if we go with you to the new place?"

"I'm sure. We've already talked about it. She's a loving woman. Just give her a little time. And she does love you. Okay?" He clapped Peter on the back.

Peter nodded his head and said, "You're a fine man, too, Daniel Thornton."

"All right," Daniel replied in a somewhat embarrassed voice, "no sense in wasting time. Let's get to bed and pack things up in the morning."

"Guess if the army wants us, they'll know where to find us," Peter said philosophically. "But I don't think they're going to have time to fool with us now."

Daniel told Mary Anna about Peter and Louisa wanting to go with them.

Mary Anna gave Daniel a weak smile. "Maybe this is God's way of settling things." Her smile strengthened. "We can make a brand-new start. We're smarter now. We've been through 'most everything." She laughed. "The Lord is giving us a chance to build that kingdom you spoke of so long ago on that blanket at the dinner on the ground." And in her heart she thanked God that she and Daniel would be allowed to grow old in those rockers after all.

❧

The next morning at sunrise the adults began packing the few basic things the townspeople had gathered up for them. Daniel had bartered his gold watch for a wagon and two mules to pull it.

"I'll keep the watch for you, Daniel, until you can come back with the cash to get it." Jeb looked steadily at Daniel. "I know how much this watch must mean to you."

Daniel nodded gratefully. "Yes, it was my father's. Thanks for the help, Jeb."

The little boys had no idea what was happening, but the festive air made them happy, too.

About midday, Caleb came by the boardinghouse.

He stepped up on the porch and took off his hat to Mary Anna.

"Morning, Caleb," she smiled.

"Heard you was fixing to move up on the North Bosque. Thought I'd come by to say fare-thee-well." His face revealed the sadness in his heart. "Can't hardly stand for you to leave. Virginia said to tell you good-bye. Her heart is about broke."

"I'm sorry you feel so bad about us leaving," Daniel replied. "It won't be the same without you and your fine family. You know, Mary Anna and I were talking about this just the other night. How it isn't going to be safe out here with so many leaving. We were wondering if maybe you and Virginia might care to come along with us and build close by. We've a mind to put up a sort of little town of our own with her family. We'd be so happy, and so much safer, if you'd come along."

Caleb's face lit up like a boy with a new puppy. "Well, now that you mention it, Virginia and I did talk some about moving away from this place, too. We hadn't made up our minds yet about which direction to go. Might as well go with good friends, I always say. It's way past friendly for you to invite us, and we'd be more than pleased to go with you to the new promised land. I'll just hurry and go tell Virginia. We don't have much. We can be ready to travel whenever you are."

His eyes shone and his smile went clear across his face from one big ear to the other. "Whoooooeeee!" he shouted. "We got us a wagon train!" And he jumped off the porch, hit the ground running, and forgot his horse waiting patiently at the rail.

Mary Anna hugged Daniel. "I think you made him happy. And I know you made me happy." She kissed his mouth softly. "Thank you, Daniel."

Daniel grinned a little self-consciously. "It just makes good sense. And they're good people. But I'll take the kiss anyhow."

"Speaking of kisses, have you talked with Otto lately?"

Daniel looked at the big smile on her face. "Go on, tell me. I know you're dying to."

"He and Angel are getting married. They've already chosen a little house at the edge of town."

"When?"

"Autumn. Can we come back for the wedding?"

"Why, we couldn't miss that wedding. We've watched this romance blossom from the beginning." Daniel sighed deeply. "Too bad. He was the best hand I ever had." But he grinned when Mary Anna glared at him.

❧

By the next week, the little caravan of three wagons and assorted animals was ready to make its way along the Brazos to a new promised land.

Daniel was in the saddle of his favorite horse riding beside Mary Anna as she drove their wagon.

"This is the right thing to do, Daniel. I'm certain of it. I prayed that you and I would be able to grow old together in our rocking chairs on the front porch, and this is God's way of making that come true. I couldn't bear to be separated from you even for a day." A chill passed over her. "When I thought of you having to go to jail, or worse, I couldn't take it. Now I'm sure this is the answer to my prayers."

He grinned broadly at her as he rocked in the saddle. "There's no way you can get rid of me. We promised each other forever, and that's what I'm promising to give you. Besides, I still owe you that star."

"You did promise me a star when we were coming out here," she remembered, smiling. "And I intend to collect it."

"No more than I intend to give it."

# Chapter 13

The three families selected a good spot out in the open but close to water. The foundation for the first cabin was laid in dogtrot style. There were two rooms connected by a large porch. It was called a dogtrot because on a hot day, the dogs could usually be found resting on the cool porch. One room was used for living and cooking, and the other was for sleeping and storage.

"Oh, Daniel!" Mary Anna exclaimed. "I have all the room in the world! It's so big!" She danced around the nearly finished cabin, furnishing and arranging things in her mind.

"And for safety, I used a tin roof. No more fires from arrows," Daniel said soberly. "I've saved a piece of tin to put on the wooden floor under the fancy cooking stove I intend to buy you a little later on. Then we can use the fireplace for warmth, and you can cook like a real lady."

She walked up to him and wrapped her arms around his neck. "Thank you, my darling husband." His blush was seen only by his two boys, and they giggled as they watched their parents embrace.

Caleb assumed Peter's cabin would go up next. There was a stunned silence at Peter's reply.

"Daughter," he looked fondly at Mary Anna, "I think I've brought enough sadness into your life. Louisa is ready to live in the city again. And if I'm to have that hotel, that's where we'll be needing to go. We'll stay here until we get the Wests' cabin up, and then we'll be heading for Young County."

"I know you only came out here to help us get a new start, Papa. I'm grateful for that." Tears gathered in Mary Anna's eyes. "And I also want you to know I'm sorry to see you and Louisa go. I still love you very much, and I have forgiven you. But I know you will be happier in town. We won't be that far apart. We'll see each other now and again."

Through their Herculean labor, the second cabin was ready quickly. It was far enough away for privacy but close enough for safety. The women planted a communal herb and vegetable garden. Mary Anna and Virginia would dry and make medicine from the herbs.

Then it was time to say good-bye to the Garlands. Louisa held Mary Anna close and said, "I'm sorry I won't be here to see that new little one born. Write me and tell me everything." Love shone in her eyes.

"Virginia will be here with me. I'll be fine. I'll let you know right away if you have a grandson or a granddaughter."

"It'll be a daughter this time. I'm sure," Louisa said.

Hugs and more hugs were exchanged, and then the wagon disappeared down the indentations of grass that served as a road.

❧

The cabins were sitting in a low place close to the river, and the night fog drifted up to the house, bringing with it mosquitoes and mysterious fevers.

September came, but it brought with it more rain to add to the heat. And with the rain came even more mosquitoes. The nights were so sultry it was hard to breathe, but if the door was left open, there was little sleeping because of the drone of the humming insects.

During the night Mary Anna heard the baby coughing. Daniel woke as she climbed out of bed.

"What is it?"

"Peter is coughing. Will you get me some of that cherry bark syrup I made?"

She sat down in the rocker with little Peter, and Daniel helped her spoon a little of the cough syrup down the baby's throat. "He doesn't feel hot. Maybe he's just teething." She rocked him until he feel asleep again and crawled back in bed with Daniel.

"Are you all right?" His voice was carefully controlled to hide the anxiety he felt. "You've lost weight. Why, by now I should be able to easily see that baby of ours." He didn't mention the dark circles under her eyes or the mild cough she seemed to be developing.

"I'm worn out from the heat and the mosquitoes," she snapped.

Daniel knew when to be quiet, but he slept lightly in case the baby woke so he could be the one to get up with him.

Everyone was short tempered from lack of sleep and from the constant itching of the large welts the mosquitoes made. Mary Anna concocted a salve from lard and boiled willow root, and it helped some.

She woke one morning, shivering. *The cool weather has finally come,* was her first thought. She got up to check the boys. They were warm enough, but she was thoroughly chilled. When the room began to spin, she realized the temperature of the house had not changed. She had come down with a fever. She crept back to bed and woke Daniel.

"I'll get Virginia," he said as he pulled on his boots.

"Take the boys with you. I don't want them here." It was all she could manage between her chattering teeth.

The world became a hazy place of hot and cold. And then the hot and cold was replaced by hot, ripping pains ravaging her body. There had been no faint

100

cries, so the baby hadn't been born. *Besides, it's not time.*

Daniel kept trying to tell her something about everything being all right. She wanted to tell him she was getting better. The terrible pain had stopped, and now all she felt was the heat.

But she was so tired. Too tired even to push away the spoon of warm liquid Virginia kept trying to push between her tightly clenched teeth. She wanted to drift with the lovely tide that ebbed and flowed through her. She was too tired to feel guilty that she wasn't taking care of anything for Daniel. If only the heat would go away. It kept pulling at her, sucking away her strength. Daniel kept telling her he needed her, but she couldn't figure out what it was he wanted her to do.

She wanted to invite him to come with her to her nothingness land. It would be so lovely with just the two of them. *No, there are the boys. Where are the boys? Virginia must have them. They're fine. Isn't that what Daniel said?*

She drifted on, sorry that Daniel couldn't go with her.

The dream began to fade, and she opened her eyes to find Daniel asleep in a chair beside her bed. Why wasn't he in bed with her? She tried to call him, but the effort was too much. His hand on the coverlet was close to hers. Slowly, she moved her fingers to grasp one of his.

He awoke with a start. "Mary Anna! You're awake!" He buried his head in the covers and wept. She was astonished at his crying. She wanted to tell him she had only slept a long while, but he sat on the edge of the bed and cradled her, all the while chanting, "Thank You, God. Thank You."

With tears running down his cheeks, he kissed her gently on the forehead. "I thought I'd lost you!" He held her tenderly, and she wanted to ask him many things, but she felt so exhausted. How could she have slept so long and yet be so drained?

Reluctantly he rested her head back on the pillow and hurriedly got a bowl of soup from the big pot in the fireplace. "Here, drink a little of this. You had me scared to death."

Shakily she put her hand up to stop the spoon. "What happened?" she asked in a voice that didn't belong to her.

"You've had a fever. You've been sick for a long time."

"How long?"

"Almost five weeks now." Cautiously he added, "You don't remember anything, do you?"

"No." From her reclining position she followed his eyes to the flatness of her middle. "I lost the baby." Her voice was expressionless.

"Yes." His eyes filled with tears again. "It was too soon."

"A girl?"

"Yes."

She could feel the tears inside, but they were too far away to spill over onto her cheeks. "I guess we'll never get our girl, will we?"

"Some day, my darling. Some day," he said softly. "Right now all I can think of is that I have you, and I am so thankful for that."

The days passed between healthful sleep and a cautious returning to the real world. Virginia and Daniel took turns nursing Mary Anna. They brought the boys over for brief visits and then hurried them away.

She spent her waking hours regaining her strength and dealing with the news that her baby was dead. Her grief felt odd. No one spoke of the baby. She had to ask Daniel about the little one's birth and burial. His recital was short. And all she could think of to say at its end was "Another house, another grave." *Lord, your ways are hard. I only get to keep every other child You give me. Take care of her, Lord. Be sure she gets to know her big brother.*

"What month is this?" Mary Anna asked Daniel one morning.

"Beginning of December, why?"

"I went to sleep in the fall and woke up in the winter."

"Guess you know a little of how a bear feels," he grinned.

They were sitting in front of the fire—she still in her nightgown and with a quilt wrapped about her legs and feet.

Daniel watched her carefully, as if to see if she had been damaged by the fever for life. He was gentle with her.

On a December morning when the wind was still and the sun warmed the earth in a promise of a faraway spring, Mary Anna dressed warmly and went out to the place where Daniel had buried their daughter.

The grave was very tiny, but it was properly marked with a piece of rose limestone. It had come from the same place where they had gathered rocks for the foundation of the cabin. Daniel had smoothed one side and scratched "Thornton" on it.

Daniel watched his wife from the window of the cabin. His heart ached for her, but he left her alone.

She stayed only a short time, but when she returned to the cabin, a great weight had been lifted from her heart. She felt whole again and ready to pick up her life and go on.

"It's time for the boys to come home," she announced as she took off her heavy winter things.

They were a family again, and Mary Anna felt joy beginning to slip back into her heart like tiny sun rays that refused to be held out by clouds.

As she served their noontime meal, Daniel said, "You're filling out nicely." When she bent to kiss him, he added, "There are little roses blooming in your cheeks, too." His grin was broad and his happiness complete to have her whole again.

Five-year-old Columbus and two-year-old Peter were thrilled to be home again. Mary Anna and Daniel decided to have a simple Christmas celebration, and the boys reveled in the furtive activities and accompanying giggling.

Peter was trying to talk. His vocabulary was fairly well developed but didn't always come out the way he wanted it to. For no understandable reason, he called his older brother Tump, and no amount of correction could change him. Soon, everyone called Columbus Tump.

Tump adapted quickly to his name change. Mary Anna began teaching him his letters that winter. He learned to spell his new name and then asked to spell Peter's. Mary Anna explained Peter's full name was Thomas Peter but that they had called him Peter.

"So, the first letter of his name is T and the first letter of his next name is P?" And in the fairness of life, Tump renamed Peter T.P.

"I don't know why I bothered to name those boys at all," Mary Anna grumped to Daniel.

"Why don't you just let them name the next one to start with?" he grinned.

Mary Anna didn't answer. She wasn't sure her heart could stand the risk of another loss.

There was talk now and again of an occasional Indian raid, but none occurred on the North Bosque. Yet the men remained careful when they were out. No one went anywhere without at least a sidearm.

The men hunted frequently and kept the smokehouse full of meat and poultry. When Daniel returned from one of those hunts, Caleb met him. Caleb grimly related the story of a raid on a nearby neighbor.

"We're getting together to track those thieves down. They got close to twenty-five horses."

Daniel agreed the raiders should be pursued. The horrors of the retaliation on the reservation were still very much on his mind, and he made it clear that his only goal was to retrieve the horses.

The eight men, Caleb, and Daniel left immediately and tracked for the rest of the day. They made camp and rose at dawn.

At about noon, Daniel said to Caleb, "They seem to be taking the horses to Mexico." There was absolutely no humor in his voice.

"Let's make a noon camp and decide what to do," suggested Henry.

"I had no idea they'd bring them this far," complained O'Brian. "I can't be away from my farm. My family is without any protection."

The other men nodded their heads in agreement.

But when night came, they were still a long way from home and the temperature was dropping, with a steady wind picking up.

"Hey, ain't there a schoolhouse that's being built out here somewhere?" Pee Wee asked. "I'm beginning to freeze to death in this here saddle. We could make us a camp there and get out of this cold."

The partially constructed building was found. Knowing there could still be Indians around, the men hid their mounts and saddles and slipped quietly into the building carrying their saddle blankets.

The windows had not been set in the building, nor had the ceiling been closed. Boards were placed loosely on the rafters. The men decided to sleep on the loose boards rather than the cold floor. They'd barely settled down to sleep when Daniel heard a shuffling noise down below. With his heart in his throat, he nudged the man next to him and motioned below.

A large band of Indians, including women and children, were entering the building. Weary and cold, they began preparing for sleep almost immediately, rolling out buffalo robes and blankets.

Frantically the word was passed in the rafters of the settlers' danger. They were outnumbered. There was nothing to do but wait until the Indians slept and then try to slip out of the building.

Cold perspiration ran down Daniel's back as he hugged the board on which he lay. Silently, he prayed that none of the men would accidentally make a noise that would give them away. It seemed an eternity before the tired band of Indians at last fell asleep.

The moonlight glinted now and again on the cold steel of a rifle barrel sticking out of one of the blankets, so Daniel had to assume that each man below was armed. Even if the men had only bows and arrows, Daniel was not eager to feel the bite of an arrowhead again. He concentrated on staying still and breathing as quietly as he could.

Finally, the only sound was the soft snoring of deep sleep below. Using hand signals, the settlers agreed to go one at a time down the outside ladder. Daniel would be next to last, and Pee Wee would be last. There was very little breathing as the men slipped out one at a time down the ladder.

When Daniel's turn came, he willed himself to keep his boots totally silent as he eased himself down. His head was level with the boards when he saw Pee Wee start to move toward the exit.

Suddenly Pee Wee's foot slipped, and he fell with the board to the middle of the sleeping band. He leaped through the door frame and began giving orders like he was commanding troops, all the while firing his gun outside the building.

The frightened Indians charged through the doors and windows and quickly vacated the building. One of the Indians threw his tomahawk at Pee Wee as he ran out the door. It stuck in the frame just above Pee Wee's head.

As the Indians fled, the settlers stood frozen by the outside wall. When they finally realized the danger was past, each man collapsed to the ground. Nervous laughter broke out.

"That's the craziest thing I ever saw," said O'Brian shakily.

"Pee Wee, you've got the quickest brain I ever saw," Daniel said in awe. "How'd you think of doing that?"

Pee Wee pulled at his scraggly beard. "Ah, I used to be a scout in my younger days. It just come to me."

The men pounded Pee Wee on the back and laughed with relief.

"Craziest thing I ever saw" was repeated frequently on the long, cold ride home that night.

The story made a sensational hit in the settlement and was told from cabin to cabin with great glee. Soon it was being called the Schoolhouse Scramble, and Pee Wee became a local celebrity for his bravery and quick thinking.

# Chapter 14

Daniel was working in his fields when he saw the small cloud of dust coming toward the cabin that indicated a rider was on the way. He stopped and said to Caleb, "Better start moving toward the cabin."

They were there when an old friend rode up wearing a very sober face.

"Hello, Sheriff," said Daniel cordially. "Get down and have something cool to drink. It's been a long time since we've seen you. What are you doing away from Stephenville?"

The sheriff climbed from his roan and led the horse to the trough for a drink before he eased his own thirst.

"This is not a happy call I'm making on you, Daniel," he said as he sat in one of the rawhide-bottomed cane chairs under the tree. He accepted some cold buttermilk from Mary Anna and took a deep drink.

"I didn't think it was."

"I've come to ask you to give yourself up for trial in Stephenville," he said quietly. "I didn't bring a posse. You're a man of honor. Either you'll come with me or you won't. I didn't want a gunfight over it."

"Have you found any of the other men?"

"Some. I told them the same as you. I won't know about all of them until time for the trial. Some had work they had to finish before they could come in."

"You're a brave man to do this by yourself," Daniel said with honesty.

"No point in having another war over it. I'd like to get this cleared up, and I think you would, too." He eyed Daniel for a response.

"No, I can't say that I am eager to get it over with. I thought of it as over with when I moved up here on the North Bosque."

"Unfortunately, the government don't think of it quite that way." He shrugged his shoulders and handed Mary Anna the empty glass. "The trial will be in two weeks. You can get you a lawyer, or you can defend yourself. Up to you." He swung up into the saddle again, tipping his hat to Mary Anna. "Thank you for the buttermilk. I always did love buttermilk." He turned his horse to the west and began another slow ride looking for the next man.

Mary Anna stood frozen in place holding the empty glass.

Caleb looked at Daniel. "Do you know what you're gonna do?"

"No point in pretending they don't care anymore. Guess I'll go in."

"He didn't ask about Father," said Mary Anna. "I wonder if he'll be there."

"I imagine he will if they find him." Daniel walked to the washbowl set in the side of the cabin to splash his face and hands. "Let's have some dinner and then get that field finished," he said to Caleb as though nothing had just ripped his world apart.

～

That night in bed there were decisions to be made. Mary Anna was chilled to the bone with the bleak prospects that faced them.

"Are you going to get a lawyer?" she asked.

"I don't know a lawyer. I can tell them what happened. I'm not a deceitful man."

"But lawyers know tricks they can pull and things to do to get people out of trouble." There was panic in her voice.

"I don't need tricks." He looked in her cornflower blue eyes and said, "You're the one who taught me to depend on the Lord. Well, now will be the most important time we've ever called on Him." He tipped her chin up with his fingertips to kiss her lightly. "I'm depending totally on the Lord. And whatever He decides, that's how it will be."

"Ohhh, Daniel," she wailed. "I know you're right, but this will take most of my time to pray about. I know I can't meet this by myself."

"You'll have to pray and work at the same time," he said reasonably.

"I already do that." She sighed. "This is no teasing matter. They could hang you if they find you guilty." Tears filled her eyes.

He pulled her hard against his broad chest and held her close. "The Lord is in charge of this. Let's ask Him for the strength to face whatever we must. This will be our biggest test of faith ever."

～

As it turned out, Daniel would be tried by himself. The other trials were scheduled for later.

True to his word, he did not hire a lawyer. He prepared himself with prayer and trying to remember exactly what had happened.

A strange quiet permeated Stephenville when Daniel and Mary Anna drove into town with Caleb and Virginia. The children had been left with a neighbor.

People on the wooden sidewalks stopped to look. The Thorntons gave a little wave to familiar faces, and some of the people waved back.

"Town don't seem as friendly as it used to be," remarked Caleb.

"Looks like the whole town is holding its breath," said Virginia.

"I saw some smiling faces," argued Mary Anna.

"Wonder what they were smiling about," Daniel added darkly.

Frances Gerald was waiting for them on her porch as they rode up. There was genuine joy in her face when she and Mary Anna and Virginia hugged.

107

"It's so good to see you again. And don't you worry about that silly trial. Everyone around here knows what kind of people you are. They're not going to find you guilty," she said confidently as she led them to their rooms. "I've been talking to everyone around town. Now don't you worry about a thing." Her blue eyes shone under her snowy white pompadour. "Everything is going to be just fine. It's all in the Lord's hands."

Mary Anna looked at her wistfully. "I'm positive it's in the Lord's hands. I wish I could be so sure Daniel would be found innocent."

❧

It was stuffy in the courtroom. Mary Anna had worn her best dress—the one with the long sleeves and too many petticoats. *Vanity gets me again. I should have worn my simple frock. It would have been so much cooler.*

Daniel didn't look comfortable in his long coat and dress pants. "I think you're the handsomest man in the entire world," Mary Anna had told him. But the clothes did give him a measure of confidence. He didn't look like a county rube.

The prosecuting attorney looked mild mannered but had a reputation for high intelligence. Daniel was frightened of him, for this man could have him hanged or put in jail.

Mary Anna stood beside him waiting for the trial to begin.

"The judge looks so serious," Mary Anna remarked. "I hope he's a fair judge. If he is, then everything will be all right." Hope shone in her bright blue eyes as she looked up into Daniel's face for confirmation.

"Make no mistake about it. This is a serious trial," he said gravely. "I had no choice but to come in and face this thing. It's in the Lord's hands."

"Order in the court!" said the judge loudly and banged his gavel on top of the table that served as his desk.

Twelve men were chosen for the jury, though Daniel's knowledge of this art was limited to sizing a man up by his eyes and his manner. Once again he had to rely on the Lord for help.

The proceedings were informal. Daniel told his side of the story, and the prosecuting attorney challenged him at different points. He was allowed to clarify his answers.

When he got to the part in his story where the men were riding into the reservation and the killing began, he broke down.

"I'm sorry. I can still hear the screams of the women and children. See the blood splattering everywhere. I had hated the Indians for so long, and I didn't think of them as human beings. When I saw where they lived and was in the middle of their family life, shooting and killing, it was like I was in the middle of any family. The one picture that will never go away is of the young mother holding a baby in her arms. I can still see the fear on her face, the way she tried to run, and how she fell when she was shot from behind."

He shuddered and squeezed his eyes shut, trying to make the scene go away. "I could hear the baby screaming after she fell on top of the child." He stopped to gain his composure. "I don't know for sure who I shot or who I killed. I'm grateful to God for that. But I was there when I shouldn't have been. I fired into the village as we rode in. Lots of shots. But after I saw the woman and the baby, I rode out with the braves chasing me.

"I helped plan that raid. I was there. I did a lot of shooting. But I learned something that day. I didn't know my enemy the way I thought I did. I was still hating the men who killed my grandfather, and the men who stole my cattle, and the ones who burned my cabin and tried to kill my family. I should have been fighting them—not the women and children. And not on the reservation. At the time there just didn't seem to be any other way."

The courtroom was quiet. Mary Anna listened intently to her husband confess. She had never been prouder of him.

The attorney asked a few questions, but he could see it would do little good to harangue or harass Daniel. It had been a sincere recital. He simply reminded the jury of their responsibilities and what the law said.

Then the waiting began. It was mercifully short. Mary Anna moved to sit beside Daniel at the table as the jury filed in.

The judge looked questioningly at the jury. "Would the foreman please stand up?" When one man stood, he asked, "Have you reached a verdict?"

The man nodded. Harland Lathman, a man in his midthirties and foreman of the jury, stood with his maimed hat in his hands. It was black and had a bullet hole through its battered crown. He twisted the hat at finding himself the center of attention of the courtroom. His black hair was slicked down to follow the contours of his bumpy skull, and his mustache had run riot across his upper lip. He had worn an almost clean shirt for this special occasion but had forgotten to put on clean pants, and stains covered both pant legs. His boots bore the unmistakable marks of a true cowboy.

He cleared his throat and shifted his weight from one leg to the other.

"Well, Judge, I mean, Your Honor, we've been studying about this and we did some careful thinking. We feel like it's prob'ly true that Daniel Thornton did go on that raid. And we're sure if he went on the raid as mad as he said, then he was sure to have kilt someone. I've been in some wild fights when ya didn't know fer sure who you was shooting at and if you kilt anyone until the whole thing was over.

"We know that he knows that he mighten of kilt some women and children." He paused and looked straight at Daniel, and Daniel felt drops of sweat rise up like raindrops on his brow.

"Now we considered where this happened and when it happened. What went before and after." He took another deep breath but was interrupted by the judge.

"We appreciate that you took so much time in deliberating this case, but all of this should have been done behind closed doors, not now. All you have to do, Mr. Lathman, is give us the verdict." The judge's face was lightly twisted in a smile. Frontier justice was the common fare of his court.

"Thanks fer remindin' me, Judge, I mean, Your Honor. But I think it's important for the people to understand why we called this thing the way we did." The hat went around a little faster in his hands.

The judge sighed. "Very well. Continue."

The hat stopped. "Daniel shouldn't have gone out there 'cause it was protected land. But the Indians should have stayed on that land to start with. They shouldn't have kilt any white people. And they shouldn't have tried to kill the Thorntons or burn down their cabin or steal their stock all the time. But there's one of us on the jury that thinks we shouldn't be out here taking the land from the Indians to begin with." All eyes turned to the only Quaker on the panel, and he blushed deeply but held a firm look in his eyes.

"I don't know what the right and wrong of all this pioneering is about, but I do know the Bible says not to kill."

Daniel felt the sweat begin under his arms, staining his shirt under his coat.

"I guess what the jury wants to know, what most folks want to know, is when is it all going to stop? Feuding like this will not get us anywhere."

The judge was beginning to turn a little sour with all this philosophical rhetoric, but he held still.

Mr. Lathman recognized the impatience of the judge. "So the jist of it is that Daniel is guilty of killing those Indians. And he should be punished for it."

Mary Anna felt the gasp go out of her mouth and the life from her body. Daniel's ramrod-straight back went limp.

"But," Mr. Lathman went on, "unless you also bring in them renegade Indians to trial and find them guilty, then you shouldn't punish Mr. Thornton by hisself. So we, the jury find Mr. Thornton guilty, but we don't want him punished."

The courtroom erupted into whoops of joy. It was a popular verdict and, by frontier standards, a just one.

"Order, order in the court!" shouted the judge as he banged his gavel on the table. "Order, or I'll throw you *all* into jail."

Gradually the people settled down to excited, quiet whispers and then the silence that the judge had ordered.

He sighed deeply, pondered the verdict of the jury, and looked at Daniel's hopeful face. "The jury has spoken, Mr. Thornton, but I have something to add. We are trying to civilize this part of the United States. This brand of justice will not serve to further that cause. Vigilante activities are not helpful, even in the absence of the army. If that type of justice were turned against you, you would more fully understand the dishonor of your deed."

Daniel's head dropped in shame at the truth of the judge's words.

"I am not going to punish you, as the jury asked me. I saw repentance in your testimony. I believe you know what you did was wrong, and I'm fairly sure you have suffered because of it. My only choice if the jury found you guilty was to hang you. However, I don't think that would serve any good cause. You seem to be an upstanding family man and a hardworking citizen. We can't afford to lose men like you on the frontier. I do need to know. Do you intend to kill a man or woman again in anger? Do you understand that taking the law into your own hands will bring nothing but heartache?"

Daniel stood to his full height and straightened his shoulders. "I understand what I did was wrong, Your Honor. I've lived a lifetime since all that happened. I believe that God has forgiven me for what I did. I will still protect what is mine as long as the Indians continue to steal from me. But I will take back only what belongs to me, and I won't do any killing. I think I've already proven that by what we now call the Schoolhouse Scramble." Soft laughter rippled through the courtroom. "I want to thank the men on the jury for listening so carefully to the things I said and maybe some of the things I didn't say, but meant to. My family thanks you, also." He sat down, and the room exploded with happy talk and applause.

Mary Anna turned to Daniel and kissed him fully on the lips. Then she burst into torrents of tears, sopping at them with her lace-hemmed handkerchief. Daniel could hear her soft, "Thank You, God," murmured over and over to herself.

❧

Later that day, as they were riding out of town, Caleb said, "I notice the people seem a little friendlier," and he smiled his slow cowboy grin.

Mary Anna cuddled next to Daniel in the front. "I was so afraid we were going to be parted, one way or the other. My heart is bursting with the joy of knowing we don't ever have to be apart again."

Daniel slipped his arm around her. "We're still together, my love."

❧

Another story joined that of Daniel's exoneration in traveling as fast as a Texas prairie fire. The government was trying to tell a man how to run his life and business by forbidding slavery. The counterpoint was that no one had the right to own another human being.

When Daniel went into town for supplies, he heard the arguments back and forth around the potbellied stove of the general store. It spilled out on the street and around the watering troughs.

He listened as he waited for his supply list to be filled at the general store.

"I'm telling you, there's going to be a war over this," spouted one red-faced citizen to another.

"You tell me that deep down in your heart you think it's okay to buy and sell human flesh just like it was a horse," replied his opponent.

A man with his feet propped up close to the stove spoke. "Slavery's not the problem. It's the Knights of the Golden Circle causing all the trouble."

"Who are they?" asked Daniel as he leaned on the cluttered counter of the store.

"A secret society." The man's bushy beard was streaked with gray, and he stroked it as he puffed a corncob pipe. "They go around recruiting new members and then go 'visit' people that don't think like they do. Hung two men in Fort Worth last week that disagreed with them."

A chill passed through Daniel. "What about the law? Don't they do anything?"

"Some of the law may be members," replied the bewhiskered man quietly. "My name's Johann Wilham." He offered his hand to Daniel.

"Daniel Thornton."

"Exactly what do these men want?" asked the storekeeper, Charlie Billinger.

"Well, Charlie, they want all of us to know that there are some people in Texas that are trying to start a slave uprising. I think they have killed a lot of people who argued with them all over the state."

"But there aren't that many slaves in Texas," Daniel pointed out.

"There are getting to be more all the time," said Johann. "The Knights said they found poison on some of the whites, so they took them to the outskirts of town and hung them, too. They are stirring up trouble."

"Fort Worth ain't that far away from here," said Charlie nervously. "But I ain't heard of no trouble with the slaves."

All the men nodded their heads in agreement.

"All I know is rumors I picked up when I was back that way last week." Johann sucked slowly at his pipe. "I also heard that they're trying to force old Governor Sam to call a special session of the legislature so they can vote on whether to join in with the South. Of course, they want everyone to vote for it. It could be they are making sure the vote goes their way."

"Houston ain't going to be run around by a bunch of hooligans," said Charlie. "He's made it plain he thinks if we leave the Union we'll get into war and," he added ominously, "a war we can't win. I go along with Sam. If we're going to do something, we ought to just go back to being a republic and stay out of all this."

There was silence as each man weighed the words of their beloved leader. Sam Houston had made his position well known all over the state and been quoted in the papers extensively.

"Gentlemen," began Johann, "I am going to take a step out in faith that none of you belong to the Knights and speak from my heart. I left Germany to get out of all the civil wars. You men aren't Southerners any more. We're all Texans. If the South wants to cut its own throat, let it. We have all we can handle here with the Indians and the Mexican bandit, Juan Cortina, running back and forth across the river.

"I am scared to death of this thing. It is going to get us into war for sure. Here it is the first of January, and it looks like Old Sam is going to have to give the Knights that session. When he does, it's going to be a big fight as to who we join. For me, I think we should be a republic again. Too much blood has been spilt to go back on that."

He looked into the eyes of the closest man. "I know because I was there. And I'm not willing to go fight for something that doesn't concern me. I don't got slaves, and I don't plan to have any." He puffed on his pipe and, a practical German to the end, concluded, "I can't afford them."

Daniel saw men nod their heads at different points in his argument. Covertly he watched to see if he could detect anyone who might be a Knight. It didn't seem likely by their expressions.

"I've still got family in the South. Pickens County, Alabama," he offered quietly.

"I guess a lot of us do," sighed Charlie. "But I have a family out here that needs me. Got to take care of them first," he added firmly.

"Well, the South's fight seems pretty clear to me," said Daniel. "The Union doesn't have the right to take away their way of making a living. They need those slaves to do the work."

Johann nodded his head in agreement. "True, but still it is a thorny question. You keep slaves, Mr. Thornton?"

"No," said Daniel. "I'm like you. Can't afford them."

"But you feel the South has the right to own them?" Johann persisted.

Daniel hesitated. "I guess I think the government doesn't have the right to come in and tell a man what he ought or ought not to do with his life."

Most of the men nodded their heads in agreement.

"We're an independent lot, we Texans," noted Johann. He laughed. "That's how we got to be Texans to start with."

On that note of general agreement, Daniel quit the conversation. It was too big a problem to be solved around a potbellied stove in the rough country of Erath County.

"Been very interesting talking to you, Mr. Wilham," he said cordially as he gathered up his needed provisions.

As he drove the oxen home, the conflict he had heard was reflected in his eyes. He thought his way through what he knew about slavery. *It's so natural. Someone has to do the grueling work. Slaves are the ones chosen to do that. In return, Pa takes care of them, gives them food and shelter. He is a temperate man and has never punished a slave unless he really needed to. Besides, all good businessmen know better than to let an expensive slave be damaged any more than he'd let his farm animals be hurt.*

His father seemed to have a genuine affection for some of his favorites that had been with him all their lives. The house servants especially were more like part of the family. *Wasn't I raised by Tildy? Slaves are just like overgrown children. They need constant supervision. Except for those special ones, and they are treated almost like family, never punished bad or ever sold.*

*Did the North know about that? How could they know about this way of life?*

And yet Daniel couldn't forget the times he'd seen a mother wailing as her young were sold off or the treatment he'd seen other planters impose on their slaves. Whippings and worse. He shuddered as some of those scenes filled his mind.

By the time he'd gotten home, he'd decided that nothing could be done about any of the problems from way out here in Texas. It was probably just the politicians stirring up the people in order to get reelected to their places of power. It had no bearing on how he made his living. He kept no slaves. Wanted none.

There was a deep satisfaction in pitting himself against nature and carving out his place in the frontier wilderness. He enjoyed feeling his muscles strain to build his kingdom. He said nothing to Mary Anna about the ugly talk he'd heard.

But Mary Anna was aware of the secession talk. It frightened her to think that something so awful was stalking their horizons while they were snug and warm in their new home.

Even the Indian raids were less frequent. Talk was that the Comanche had been rounded up and moved to another reservation up in the Oklahoma Territory. There were still renegades, but they spent most of their time evading soldiers.

Mary Anna grew larger with their next child, praying this time it would be the girl she longed for and that she would be able to keep the child rather than lay it to rest with the others.

She was beginning to get the soil in her garden ready to plant when her time came. Virginia was with her; Daniel paced outside the door of the bedroom.

It was Virginia's bright smile that told him of his new baby daughter.

"She's all right? Both of them, I mean," Daniel stammered.

"Yes. Both of them are fine. Come in." She held the door ajar and stepped aside.

Daniel knelt beside the bed, his face lit with joy as he took Mary Anna's hand in his big ones.

"She's so pretty, Daniel. And very strong." Mary Anna pulled the blanket away from the tiny face pressed against her breast. "See."

Daniel did see. "We finally have our daughter. I'm so proud I could pop!" His big fingers brushed the baby's cheek, causing her to turn in confusion to seek another source of nourishment and to howl at the deception.

"She has a big voice for such a little thing," he said, embarrassed at his mistake. They sat quietly for a while just admiring the new baby. The two boys came in to greet their little sister and then were quickly shooed out.

March turned into April, and with it came full spring. Mary Anna felt hale and hearty, and her baby flourished with all the love and attention heaped on her. It was easy to love this child they'd named Elizabeth for Daniel's mother.

She was a true child of the Old Country. A cinnamon sprinkling of freckles powdered her pert nose, and her hair was the deep auburn common to the Irish of Mary Anna's family. From her infancy, she, more than the other children, loved the sound of Daniel's fiddle.

"The melodies of Ireland flow through that child's veins," remarked Daniel as he watched her uncertain baby grin. He drew the bow softly over the strings and delighted anew when she turned her head toward the sound.

The days were almost unbearably sweet for a while, but the talk of secession seeped through the cracks of the logs and under the strong door. It was impossible to ignore. Lincoln was elected. In February Texas had formally seceded from the Union over Sam Houston's strong objections. The time had come to make hard choices.

One evening Daniel and Caleb sat before the Thornton cabin. Fireflies winked around them, and the soft gurgle of the river added to nature's song.

"What are you going to do now?" Caleb asked. He was sitting in a chair with a rawhide seat, and it squeaked comfortably beneath his weight now and again.

Daniel shook his head. "I honestly don't know. I feel a strong call to help the men with the fighting. Yet I can't stand to leave everything here that we've struggled so hard for."

"With the soldiers gone to fight, there'll soon be no one to help us fight the Comanche." An undercurrent of fear colored Caleb's next words. "You know what can happen if there's no one to defend our women and children."

He and Daniel locked eyes, understanding the consequences of an unchecked Indian raid. Erath County had set up a brigade of men to fill the place of the departed army, but no one knew how effective the group of men would be.

"The South will beat the Union boys pretty quick if it comes to war," Daniel said confidently. "Question is, where do we stand our ground and what do we defend?"

"I'm planning on staying right here and protecting what I have," Caleb said quietly. "We ain't in it yet. Ain't been no shooting that I know of."

"Then there's no need to make any decisions tonight." Tired, Daniel rose and stretched his long arms. "Got plowing to do tomorrow." He shook hands with Caleb.

"We'll do more talkin' when we know what we're talkin' about."

Daniel nodded in agreement.

Only a few weeks later, Caleb spurred his horse into the yard hurriedly, kicking up puffs of loose dirt.

He accepted Mary Anna's offer to come inside, and she called Daniel in from the fields with the big triangle he'd forged for her. He barely had time to knock the dust off his hat before Caleb spoke.

"It's finally come, Daniel. The South fired on Fort Sumpter."

"That means there's war then," he said grimly.

Caleb nodded.

Mary Anna felt sick in the pit of her stomach. "But that doesn't have anything to do with us," she protested.

Both men smiled at her. "We've been trying to decide that for ourselves," Daniel said.

"Waco is getting up an infantry," offered Caleb.

"Kind of in a hurry to get into it, aren't they?" Daniel said. "I think we ought to bide our time and see how the fighting goes."

"But if all of us stay, who will help the South?" argued Caleb. "They'll be needing every man to keep it quick."

"But we can't go traipsing all over the countryside," Daniel argued back. "We could get there after it's over, only to come back here and find we've lost everything we've built." Frustrated, Daniel sipped the coffee Mary Anna had given them.

"Does seem to be an unsolvable problem," Caleb agreed.

"I'm going into town tomorrow to see what I can find out about the war." Glumly, Daniel added, "I'm afraid that either way, we're going to lose a lot."

❧

Daniel said nothing to Mary Anna as they prepared for bed late that night, but she knew he was wrestling with the news. By ignoring it, she had hoped it would go away. After all, the fight was happening far away from them, and Daniel knew how important it was for him to be with his family. She left him to work the issue out in his own mind. Snuggling down in the deep quilts of their bed, she fell asleep praying, *Lord, help Daniel work his way through the problem and give him some peace. Help him to see we need him here. Don't let his love of the South overcome his love for us. Help the South to win their battles without his help. And let it be a brief battle, Lord, for everyone's sake.*

❧

During the next few weeks, Mary Anna heard Daniel say often, "I'm going into town."

"Again? You've just come back." She was cross at his obsession for war news.

"I want to see the *Waco Tribune*. They get their information directly from the eastern newspapers who are there on the scene every day."

At the store he pored over the battered newspaper.

"Hey," said Charlie, "I read where the generals plan their troop movements on what they read in the newspapers. They find out where the enemy is by reading about it!"

"Yeah," added Ted Westmoreland, "Brady and Sullivan and a bunch of other men are taking pictures of the war. They have a big carriage fixed like a darkroom, and they're publishing pictures in magazines!"

"I've even heard," Charlie continued, "that some of the people drive out from the towns with picnic baskets to watch from a safe distance. Imagine sitting on the top of a hill eating cold fried chicken and seeing the war taking place below you!"

Daniel relayed all this to Mary Anna. "That's disgusting!" was her only comment.

Still they didn't discuss his leaving.

As the weeks turned into months and almost a year passed, Mary Anna knew time was on her side.

Until one day. She was putting the Dutch oven in the coals to bake their bread when Daniel approached her.

"I'm joining up to fight. I want you to go back to Anderson County. You and the children should be safer there."

Mary Anna looked at him as if the words had absolutely no meaning. "What?" she asked stupidly.

"There's no other way to do it," he said. "I'm joining up. I can't leave my family here at the hands of the Indians."

Anger swept through Mary Anna. "*You* decided all this without asking me what I thought?" Her voice whispered the words, but they rammed into the walls of the cabin, careening against one another.

He looked at her dumbly, totally taken off guard. He had been prepared for tears. But not hostility.

"*You* decided what we're going to do!" she repeated.

"Haven't you been thinking about all this?" he asked. "You knew I couldn't let the South fight this thing without helping. Texas has been invaded at Fort Arbuckle. Colonel Young fought off the Yanks."

"But that's on the Red River," she argued.

He stared into her eyes steadily. "I've got to go, and you know you can't stay here." Softly he added, "I'm afraid the Comanche would get you."

"And you don't think the war will?" she challenged.

"There won't be any more fighting in Texas," he said confidently.

"You don't know that." She turned her back on him, moving to the planked table to clean up her baking mess. Silence was a living thing between them.

Finally, Mary Anna spoke. "I don't want to go back. I want to stay here." She looked at him evenly. "And I think you should, too. The South has enough men. It's not our fight. Besides, it'll be over before you can get there."

"What do you mean, it's not our fight?" Now he was angry. It had taken him almost a year to work this thing out, to finally come to the best decision. And his own wife was arguing with him.

"Why? We don't keep any slaves. That should be fought out by the people who do. Our place is here, where we've fought it out with the Indians. Did anyone from the South come to help us?"

"As a matter of fact, they did. Your mother and father being one example. And the Wests." He was afraid to move, afraid the logic he had laid down would be ripped apart by her feelings. He had made the choice, and it was the right one. Why was she balking?

Deliberately she turned to face him. "Daniel, I don't want you to go to war. There's enough danger here every day of our lives." She closed her eyes and added, "I know you could be killed any day, but at least I'd know what happened right away. If you go to war, I'll never know what is happening to you. I might never find out why you didn't come home." Tears formed in her eyes. "We promised each other after the trial that we'd never have to be apart again. We promised!"

He crossed the room, taking her in his arms. "I'm not going to get killed in either place," he said against her soft hair. "I have too much to live for. I haven't given you any of those stars I promised yet." He leaned back to look her fully in the face. "This is important to me, Mary Anna. I feel honor bound to fight for a way of life I've always known. The government has no right to tell anyone what they can do on their own land. They need us. They need *me*."

A tiny cold place had begun to form in the corner of Mary Anna's heart. It was next to the one where the death of her children lay. But when she looked into his azure blue eyes glowing with commitment, she felt the will to stand against him slip a little. "But everything is so good here. I don't think I can bear to go off and leave our hard work. . .our little girl out there under the oak tree."

"The baby sleeps in God's arms and our hearts, not in that earth out there," he said gently. "We carry both our lost ones with us wherever we go." He pulled her hard against his broad chest. "And we will build and keep building. We're going to build us an empire. But right now, I must do this. It will weigh heavily on me all my life if I don't." His eyes bore into hers with increasing intensity. "I have to go."

One level of consciousness reached for him, exalted with his honor, and another enlarged the cold spot of dread in her heart. Her mind's eye reached across the days ahead, and all she could see was loneliness and desolation. "I know if I don't give you leave to do this, it will always be between us. I have no right to keep you from doing something that is this important to you. Even the love between us can't protect me from your need for honor."

She heaved a great sigh. "But I don't understand why men must find honor only in war. I would think there would be great honor in building your empire." She looked to see if this made any difference to him. She could see her answer in his handsome face. "When?"

He kissed her with great tenderness. "As soon as we can get packed up. The sooner I go, the sooner I'll be back."

"That's a lie, and you know it. You'll go, but you won't be back soon. War isn't like that. It's long and ugly, and it doesn't always settle the things it's supposed to. I'll pray for you and your safety." She held on to him tightly. "Promise me you'll come back. Even if you're horribly maimed. Come back."

⁓

Even the weather seemed to disapprove of what they were doing. It was the end of February, but the day that had begun warm turned hot, the sun glaring at the busy activities below his scorching fingers. The heat made the job of sorting and packing their family belongings harder.

Thunderheads were building up in the west, threatening to put out the sun's heat with a pelting rain guaranteed to drown the snakes out of their holes. Daniel kept a worried eye on the towering clouds that made him work faster. The humidity was building steadily, and his shirt was soaked with perspiration.

Mary Anna looked in consternation at all the goods they had accumulated. Not all of them could go. She was back to taking the necessities of life with her, giving the excess to her friends.

Daniel rode into town the next day to pick up some supplies. He came riding back rapidly and handed her a well-worn letter.

"It's from Father," she read. "They're coming here. He wants Louisa and the rest of the family to live with us while he joins up. According to this letter, they'll be here soon!"

"I should have known. Once a captain, always a captain," said Daniel. "That'll work out just fine. You and Louisa can go back and open up a hotel, and we'll ride together to sign up."

Mary Anna bit back the barbed reply on the end of her Irish tongue. Her one consolation was that she wouldn't have to go back alone.

When they revealed their plan to the Wests, Caleb said, "I'm proud you are going, son. I know the South needs men like you. Virginia and I have talked about it, and we both agreed I'm too old to go."

Mary Anna saw the pain in his Southern heart reflected in his eyes, but she also saw the joy in Virginia's eyes at his staying.

"We'll keep an eye on things for you," she said softly. "And the things you've left with me will be waiting for you when you come back."

Mary Anna tried to return the offered smile. She had turned to stone inside.

"Just think," said Virginia, "you're going back to civilization; stores, close neighbors, church. No more Indian raids, and your boys can go to school." In spite of her joy at staying, there was envy at what Mary Anna would have again. "I'm glad Louisa is going with you. It's a long trip."

She put her arms around Mary Anna's stiff body. "The ways of the Lord are mysterious, but He will take care of you now that you know His will."

Mary Anna's voice was low and gruff. "I'm not sure if it's His will or Daniel's will." She sighed tiredly. "I know He will care for us." She gave Virginia a tired smile. "The boys think it's a great adventure. Daniel told Tump he could ride the dun-colored mare."

Tump was close by, and he grinned his toothless six-year-old smile as he fed the mare a handful of soft grass. T.P. was entertaining Elizabeth with a small wooden toy. Everything was the same, and everything was different.

"Virginia, I remember the first time we visited you and Caleb," said Mary Anna.

"I do, too. That was such a happy day for me." She gave her friend a loving smile. "You've given me a lot of happy days."

"It's not going to be the same without you." Something suspiciously like tears were forming in Mary Anna's eyes. "What will I do without you?"

"Oh, I 'spect you'll find a lot of friends in town."

"It'll be so strange living in a town. Sometimes I think of all the good things you mentioned. But I have the strangest feeling of being crowded, living so close to everyone. Odd, isn't it?"

Virginia nodded in agreement. "You going to be all right for money?"

"Daniel said he'd send me his army pay. It's thirteen dollars a month. I'll get a job until Father can get his own hotel. We'll be fine. I'll have my garden, and Louisa is planning to raise a whole flock of chickens."

"It sounds like y'all have thought of everything."

They both knew they were running out of small talk, and they couldn't bear to say the things they wanted to say to each other.

"It's best we go so you can get on with your packin'."

"I'll write," Mary Anna promised.

Virginia laughed. "I'll watch for that letter. It'll be almost as good as a visit."

"Virginia, stay safe." Mary Anna's brow puckered with concern. "If things get too bad out here, come to Tennessee Colony. You'll always have a place to stay. The future is so muddled right now with the war and all. If you need help, come to me."

Virginia couldn't get her voice past the hard knot of sadness locked in her throat. She hugged Mary Anna, blew a kiss to the children, and climbed up beside Caleb in the wagon. "God bless," she whispered as they headed the horses back to their cabin.

Most of the packing was done by the time they turned in for the night. They had a cold supper, and the only conversation came from the children. Neither Daniel nor Mary Anna could find anything to say.

Mary Anna ached to tell Daniel not to go.

Daniel ached to remind Mary Anna of why he had to.

When they climbed into their bed, Daniel finally said, "Your folks should be here tomorrow. If they're not, we'll leave them a note and go on. The weather is very changeable right now, and I don't want to leave in a rainstorm."

Mary Anna prayed for a rainstorm to end all rainstorms, but when she climbed wearily out of her side of the bed, the new day was clear and bright.

She couldn't afford to waste this day. She would squeeze every piece of time like a miser giving out coins. This would be her last day with Daniel. She looked back at their bed. Daniel appeared to be sleeping. On silent feet, she went back and slid under the covers with him.

"I'm glad you came back," he whispered as he gathered her up in his arms.

"It's still cold out there," she whispered as she snuggled closer to his body.

"I'm going to miss you more than I can say, my love."

"And I, you," she breathed.

He stroked her hair with a practiced hand and ran his fingers across her mouth in the way that made her tingle with delight.

Mary Anna knew that if she took advantage of his desire to make love to her, she might have a chance to talk him out of going. He was vulnerable. She could beg him not to break the bonds of love that held them together. Remind him that there was no way to know when they could be together again like this. She could use his desire to make him stay. But she chose to make it the most memorable time of their lives, a celebration of their love that would endure even a wartime separation.

And when they lay in each other's arms spent, she stroked his face with her fingertips to memorize every line. She kissed his mouth a hundred times to make her lips remember his. She molded herself to his body in an effort to be able to recall its feel in the lonely times to come.

All day she watched him with covert eyes, saving every scrap of his voice, his walk, his face, and his hands. She watched him all during the favorite breakfast she prepared for him. She watched while he played with the boys and little Betty.

Daniel felt Mary Anna's eyes on his every move. He was watching her in the same way. He was a man tied on two horses going in opposite directions. Duty called him. His love for Mary Anna and the children ripped at his heart.

He had thought one or the other would finally win out and he would be at peace with his decision, but the war inside him raged as hard as the one to which he was going.

Why did he have this compelling need to help the South? He hated himself for it. But it wouldn't go away. The South had sent out a call for help, and he couldn't ignore it. The shining honor he called his manhood was being challenged. Not to go would dishonor himself and his family. But when he looked at Mary Anna, he felt his will begin to slip. It would be so much easier and happier to stay with her.

With great deliberation he prepared himself to leave. As he was tying on his saddlebags and bedroll, he saw the cloud of dust coming from the distance. "I think your folks are here, Mary Anna," he called to the cabin.

She came outside with a slow step to watch the dust get closer.

There were no excited exchanges of greetings. Louisa was cold and withdrawn. Mary Anna was numb. Only the boys were excited to see their grandparents again.

Daniel took Mary Anna in his arms one last time. She tried desperately not to cry. She summoned strength from deep within to meet the sweet passion of his lips on hers for the last time.

And then he was astride his tall horse.

A strange swelling of pride that she was able to send her man into battle with clear, bright eyes filled Mary Anna's soul. She stood as tall as she could and waved him out of sight, wearing her frontier eyes until she was sure Daniel could no longer see her. Then she cried quietly to herself, fearing the tears would upset the children who had so proudly sent their father and grandfather off to fight the war to save the South.

*Lord, keep both of them safe and bring them home soon. Give us all the courage to face this terrible time of testing. I don't know who is right, the Union or the South, but let it end quickly. Spare our men, please, Lord. Daniel belongs to You now. Bring him back home so he can live out the kind of life You'd be proud of. You can use him to build more of Your kingdom. Lord God of all creation, I beg You to bring back my love to me.*

And she poured out her tears as sacrifices to God for Daniel's safe return.

# Dreams

## of Glory

*For Mary Anna Thornton Smith*
*who started the wheels turning.*

# Chapter 1

No," she whispered, "I won't cry. I won't."

Mary Anna refused to let the tears dammed up behind her blue eyes relieve the pressure growing in her throat. She watched the figure of her husband on horseback grow smaller until it finally became a blurred mirage as he and her father rode away to help save the South.

It was a small, sad band that watched the men ride out of sight. Mary Anna stood holding her ten-month-old baby, with her two other young children huddled around her long skirts. Her stepmother, Louisa, stood surrounded by her own three children.

"Mama," asked Mary Anna's seven-year-old son, Tump, "when will they be back?" One front tooth was still missing, and it gave him a soft lisp.

She tousled his reddish hair with a gentle rub and said, "As soon as they're able." She pulled him close to give them both comfort and asked, "Would you help me get Baby Betty into the wagon? We need to get started, too."

Tump waited for Mary Anna to get settled on the hard wooden seat and handed her the basket that held ten-month-old Elizabeth, known affectionately as Betty. "How far is it to Tennessee Colony?" he asked.

"It's on the other side of the world," his mother answered tiredly.

Tump squinted up to her. "How far?"

Louisa came up on the other side of the wagon. "Your Ma is teasing you, son. It's right close to Fort Parker in the east part of Texas." Her eyes were red from crying. She had made no effort to hide the tears of anger and sadness at her husband's leaving.

She made a swipe at her nose and eyes with her sodden handkerchief. "There's no use in lying to the child, Mary Anna. The Lord knows we've got a long ways to go." She looked reprovingly at her husband's beloved daughter. "Let's not start the trip off that way." Then in an apologetic move, she patted Mary Anna's hand. "We'll all be together soon."

Her words were not a comfort to Mary Anna, nor was her touch. "God alone knows what's in store for us," Mary Anna mumbled to herself. To Tump she called, "Help Peter up into the wagon, too."

Four-year-old Peter was so excited about going that he used his chubby little hands to grab hold of Tump's shirt to haul himself up higher. "Help," he commanded. "I go, too. Get my dog. Here, Soldier, here, boy." He made a valiant effort to whistle, but all he did was purse his lips and blow bubbles, most of which got on Tump's shirt.

"Don't get that slobber all over me!" he complained as he hoisted the heavy little boy up high.

Louisa's nine-year-old son, Thomas, got his two little sisters into the wagon, too. The normal bickering of siblings was missing, so cowed were they by the tension in the air.

Louisa climbed in just as Soldier jumped in the back of the wagon. She sighed deeply as she settled her skirts around her and tried to find a more comfortable place for her bony hips to ride. "Thought I was through with all this traveling across country."

Mary Anna nodded her head in agreement. "Before we go, I want to say a traveling prayer." They all clasped hands in the wagon and bowed their heads.

"Lord, this is a terrible time of testing for all of us. Having our husbands gone gives us a feeling of being alone in the world. Help us to remember that You are always with us and You are there to protect us even when we're apart from one another. It's Your love that binds us and it's Your love that saves us. Keep all of us from harm and danger. You know how much travel there is between us and Tennessee Colony. And put a protective shield around Daniel and Father and bring them back safely to us. And Lord, could it be pretty quickly? Amen."

After a moment of silence, the two families raised their heads. "Okay, Tump, you can get on your mare now. Stay close to the wagon," Mary Anna commanded. "And keep an eye on that milk cow. Be sure she's tied good."

Mary Anna flipped the reins over the backs of the horses and said to Louisa, "I don't like the looks of those thunderheads." They hung ominously on the horizon, a fitting portent to their journey, Mary Anna was afraid. "They remind me of the clouds of war hanging over our heads. Likely to strike at any time and give no warning."

Louisa sniffed. "No need to get fanciful. They're just clouds. If they come, they come, if they don't, they don't."

She wasn't singing that same tune later when they camped for their first night out on the trail. The rain came in slanting fury that permeated the canvas wagon cover.

Mary Anna lay on her back listening to the rain and wondering what she was doing on the trail instead of in her warm, safe cabin. *Men. Why are they so all fired up about saving the South when our life is out here in Texas? Daniel, where are you? Are you safe?*

She knew Daniel and her father were riding to Fort Stockton in West Texas to join up. She wasn't sure how long it would take them to reach the town, so she had no idea where to picture her husband.

*I miss you so much already. How can I stand to be apart from you for a long time?* A tear she had refused to spend in front of Daniel earlier in the day now slipped down the side of her eye and into her hair. She didn't try to wipe its companions away as they hurried after each other.

*I loved living in our cabin. I felt safe there, and we were finally getting things going. You wanted to build a kingdom where you could ride your horse from your bed to the breakfast table. That's what you told me when we spent that lovely day on the quilt at the dinner on the church grounds when we first met.* She couldn't stop the angry thoughts erupting from her heart.

*And where are you now? Riding into worse danger than when we fought off the Indians. It isn't fair. It just isn't fair. We were finally getting somewhere and you had to decide to defend the honor of the South. You don't even believe in slavery. We've never had a slave. Why do you think it's your job to keep the government from telling the South what to do? Where do men get such ideas?*

Mary Anna felt the pressure building in her temples, a sure sign of a headache coming on. But she had no way to express her anger, and she tried praying herself to sleep.

"Lord," she whispered in the darkness, "I'm sorry I'm not a patient Christian, and that I have a bad temper. Forgive me and help me to be strong for Daniel and the children. Keep us safe and bring us together soon. Amen."

The peace was not immediate, nor sleep instant, but she felt a measure of relief just by giving things she couldn't control to the Lord. And sleep did come.

But because of the soaking and the late hour, she woke up cranky and tired. She knew the days ahead would be a test of her fortitude. At twenty-five, Mary Anna had already settled on the Brazos River in Texas, fought the Indians for the land, sat through a trial in which her husband was accused of killing Indians unjustly, and learned to live the life of a pioneer woman. It seemed that this trip to Tennessee Colony was turning back the clock on all her accomplishments. And it made her mad.

Bleak days strung out ahead of them, each one spent in deadening whiteness. The rutted "road" they followed was brutal, and the weather unforgiving.

They were spared actual attack from Indians, but signs of Indian presence were everywhere and made the weary travelers tense. Even Soldier seemed on edge as he walked alongside the wagon, watching alertly for any danger. Occasionally he accepted a ride in the wagon to rest his weary paws.

While Mary Anna could keep her eyes busy looking for trouble on the trail, her thoughts wandered where they willed. Part of the time she was fighting mad at Daniel for putting her in a position in which she had to single-handedly care for herself and her family on the trail. Other times she was so tired she didn't care if they were all killed. *At least I'd get some rest then,* she thought as a wry smile crossed her lips.

As they rocked along, Louisa observed, "There are more cabins than when we came out here. Why, we saw two yesterday, and look, there's another one over there. Texas is getting full of people."

"It was full of people when we got here," Mary Anna said softly.

"Indians," Louisa retorted. "You and your liberal ways." She looked sideways at Mary Anna, pulling away slightly so her older eyes could focus well on her stepdaughter. "Wonder if you could have some Indian blood in you. Why else would you be so caring about them that are always trying to kill you and your kin?"

"They're people, just like us," Mary Anna said for the hundredth time. "They were here first."

"I don't want to hear that song again," snapped Louisa.

Mary Anna's eyes blazed a cold agate blue. "Then don't provoke me."

Since they could not retreat physically from each other, they retreated into silence, sitting side by side. After five years of living on the frontier, the question of how Indians should be treated was still too volatile to be talked of lightly.

Mary Anna saw Indians as people who had been invaded by ruthless men, exploited by the white man's greed for land. But she didn't understand the deliberate cruelty the Indians used to drive the white man away. She had always been taught to fight fairly. There was nothing fair about the way the Indians fought the white man. This muddled her feelings about the right of the Indians to the land. And she stood alone in her feelings.

The threat of those very people was ever on Mary Anna's mind, and she slept lightly, even though there had been no attempts to steal their animals. She kept her rifle by her side day and night and breathed with the land, listening keenly for any change in its life rhythms. She relied on Soldier to listen, too, and thanked God for the vigilant dog.

It took all her patience and ingenuity to keep them going. The constant pounding her body took on the rutted trail made her bones ache at the end of each long day. But when it rained on them, it was even worse, turning the road into a boggy mess. The infant spring blew its cool days and colder nights over their weary bodies, and Mary Anna thought they would never get away from the endless buffalo grass.

The grasslands finally began to give way to low foothills of standing cedar and small pines. Out on the plains it had been easy to see for miles. Now they faced the prospect of being ambushed in the brush. The shelter the trees offered was offset by fear of attack. Mary Anna never felt rested, so strong was her sense of alertness. Thankfully the children stayed well and their main health problems were the common ones of travel.

"Mary Anna, there's a cabin up there a ways," said Louisa as the sun crept down closer to the horizon. "Let's camp there tonight." Hunger for companionship was the most prevalent and consuming need for women on the frontier, and gratefully Mary Anna guided their wagon to the cabin.

As they neared, their host ambled out to meet them, rifle slung across his arm. "Howdy," he said hospitably, but his eyes were cautious. "Traveling alone?"

"We're on our way back to Tennessee Colony in East Texas," Mary Anna replied. She was equally alert to any signs of hostility or danger.

Her voice tinged with anger, Louisa added, "Our husbands have gone to fight for the South."

The man didn't miss the unspoken question of why he was still in Texas. "Some men gotta go, some gotta stay."

His wife appeared at the door of the cabin. She was gaunt and her skirts hung around her like the rags on a scarecrow in the fields. "Who is it, William? Is it Mother? Tell her to get down and bring her friend." As she moved from the door, her husband explained, "My wife isn't well. Y'all excuse her." Great pain covered his face as he added, "She don't live in this world anymore."

The tattered woman fluttered around them as she provided a simple meal, mumbling about family things and asking questions of Louisa, whom she had deemed her mother. Louisa was sadly kind in her answers.

Mary Anna was almost sorry they had stopped, for the atmosphere was as gray as the woman's hair, until William brought out his fiddle.

He played cheerful tunes while the children danced around. They moved outside into the cool night and circled the small fire William built. The trees stood around them like silent guardians, and Mary Anna expected to see even their roots tapping to the happy tunes.

But for Mary Anna the sound of the fiddle brought back sharp memories of the man she loved. When she closed her eyes, Daniel's blue eyes flashing in the firelight and his quick fingers on the fingerboard came back in painful clarity. Still she tried to enjoy the brief respite of company and music. She loved her husband and her children. He would come back to her, and they would go home again. This dream would keep her going for as long as the war made it necessary.

~

When they finally pulled into Tennessee Colony, Mary Anna was amazed at how it had grown.

"My lands," said Louisa, "this place is twice as big as it was when we left." Her gaze skittered across all the new buildings. "Shouldn't be hard to find us cabins."

Mary Anna was quick to note the plural in cabins. She was glad Louisa didn't intend to live with her. It was going to be hard enough to live in a town again without Daniel.

After a few days they were able to secure two cabins and move in. Mary Anna felt closed in immediately, but she knew it was to her advantage to be so close to people. "I hope the time will pass quickly," she sighed as she unpacked their few belongings.

It wasn't hard to settle into a routine. The needs of her family still ran the clock of her life. She made their cabin as comfortable as possible and welcomed each visitor.

Louisa's grief over Peter's absence was quickly assuaged by all the old friends she found. Quickly she adapted to her social ways, more or less dragging Mary Anna along with her.

"I don't know why we have to go see Mrs. Bloomingthal today," Mary Anna would grumble to herself, but she was almost smiling when Louisa came to get her. And by the time they had returned, Mary Anna either was refreshed by the visit, or she had a bad headache.

The two women began a late garden and prepared for the coming winter months. Mary Anna also looked for signs of a coming child. When none appeared, she took comfort in the three happy children around her table. She had hoped to give Daniel another child as a homecoming present.

Tump was not pleased with being at school after learning at his mother's knee. "Mama, Mr. Green is so strict," he pouted. "He yells all the time, and he's not as smart as you are," he added hopefully.

Mary Anna smiled when she remembered the brush arbor in which she had taught at the tender age of sixteen right here in Tennessee Colony. Now there was a real school, and her son a student in it. "I want you to be well educated, Tump. Some day I even want you to go to college. I want people to look at my family and think what good manners you have and how well educated all of you are. I promise you, some day you'll be so glad you had a good school. There's so much out there to learn, son."

Tump saw the dreams in her eyes, and he wanted to make them come true. "All right, Mama. I'll try real hard. For you."

She smiled and gave him a big hug.

Many women in Tennessee Colony had sent their men off to war, and they looked out for each other. Women joined together to do the things their men had done. Plowing wet earth was what Mary Anna hated most. It was backbreaking labor and slow going.

Mary Anna held back her anticipation of Daniel's first letter for several weeks after her arrival. But the weeks turned into months, and her anxiety grew. She knew only that the men had intended to ride to Stockton to enlist. She questioned each passing rider for information, but none knew anything to tell her. She remembered the men in her daily prayers and commended them to God. There was little else she could do.

The labors required to maintain a family even in a settled area kept her plenty busy. She got wool and mixed it with cotton to make homespun clothes. There was food to be put away for the winter and their few animals to care for. And she was a constant worker in the community church.

The circuit rider who came around once every two weeks was a godly man not much older than Daniel, and he took some of his meals with Mary Anna and her family.

He was an enormously tall man, well over six feet, with a full head of curly brown hair. He wore the traditional black suit and hat that marked him as a minister and carried a very worn Bible. She liked his gentle voice and the fact that he didn't quote Scripture to her at every opportunity. When he dined with them, she was pleased with his good manners and scholarly ways. He genuinely enjoyed being with the children and always took pains to spend time with each of them.

"As usual, Mrs. Thornton, an excellent meal." Mr. Amos Strong carefully wiped his mouth with his handkerchief and placed his eating utensils across the china plate. Mary Anna refilled his coffee cup, and they moved to the rockers placed around the cheerful fire. The boys immediately vied for a place close to his feet and waited for the usual Bible story he told each time he came. Even Soldier seemed to listen.

As the pastor's pleasant voice entertained and enlightened her boys, Mary Anna readied the toddling Betty for bed. There was a sense of peace and contentment in her home. All that was missing was the man she loved and missed so achingly. A tear threatened to form in her eye, and she willed it away. She had nothing of which to complain except the absence of her husband.

After the boys were tucked into their beds, she took the other rocker and shared a cup of coffee with Mr. Strong.

"I did as you asked, Mrs. Thornton. I talked with every man and woman I saw on my last trip back, but I wasn't able to find anyone who had spoken with or knew of Daniel and your father."

"I thank you for your vigilant efforts. The war news seems to be first good and then bad. What is the latest you've heard?"

His big hazel eyes didn't hold back the truth. "It's not as good as we would like to hear, I'm afraid. There was a big battle, and our boys took quite a beating. I read the list of killed and wounded in the newspaper, and," he added as he noted her alarm, "their names weren't on the lists."

"I don't understand why he doesn't write. Why hasn't he sent me a single letter? It would mean so much." She sighed tiredly.

Mr. Strong's voice took on a comforting tone. "It's harder not knowing, but the time will come when we'll find out something." He smiled at her. "You've been a good wife and mother and borne your burdens well for one so young. Take heart in the promises God has given each of us. Patience is something we must practice unendingly. Especially now."

They rocked in an easy silence, and then he said, "I spend a lot of time in other people's homes, Mrs. Thornton, and I want to compliment you on the serenity I find here each time I come. You're doing a fine job of raising your family, and I know your husband will be proud of you when he comes home."

Her cheeks colored slightly. "Thank you, Mr. Strong. Your words of praise mean a great deal to me." She was curious about his family but hesitated to pry into his private life. Still, she wished he would share this information with her. But he was content to speak of everyday things and generalities.

He pushed himself from the rocker. "I must be going. Mr. and Mrs. Gottlieb will be waiting for me." He never stayed at her cabin. It would have been highly improper, even if he had slept in the little barn behind the house. When she had first hesitatingly offered it to him, he had declined.

"Thank you, but no." His eyes sparkled with mischief as he added, "Let's not give Satan any tools to work with." She had never offered the barn to him again. He was scrupulous with the reputations of all the women who lived alone, staying only with married couples but eating at each home in turn.

All that winter he observed a fairly stable routine of eating and lodging with the same families, and she found herself looking forward to the friendly evenings of conversation they shared. It filled some of the quiet Daniel had left behind.

The winter was kind to them, staying within the bounds of reason during the cold months. She prayed Daniel was somewhere well fed and warm and safe, for no letter came. Her quest for news of him was a constant anxiety that wore her thin. But she practiced patience as Mr. Strong had urged her to do.

There was a light snow in late February, but Mr. Strong was able to keep his rounds. Mary Anna found herself planning special meals when she knew it was her turn to feed him supper.

He was a capable preacher, and she found consolation in his sermons. She had heard a few wandering evangelists who distressed her. Their sermons rang hollow when measured against their actions. They wore hypocrisy like an invisible mantle.

It reminded Mary Anna of the story her mother had told her as a little girl about a king who thought he was wearing regal clothes when indeed he was only in his underwear. It caused her a few desperate battles against smiling during their sermons as she imagined them in their long johns.

Still she fed them with great courtesy and endured their eternal sanctimonious ramblings around her fireplace. After all, they were men of God. But it made her appreciate Mr. Strong all the more. He was real.

Mary Anna was preparing one of her special meals for him when Louisa came to call on her afternoon off from her new job cooking at the hotel. She was full of town news and more news about the war, but she still hadn't heard from Peter—her husband and Mary Anna's father.

Louisa looked tired and drawn. She was not a young woman, and worry over her husband combined with staying on her feet all day cooking was taking its toll. "You have to be realistic," she said. "What if neither one of them comes back? What will we do?"

"What we are doing now," Mary Anna snapped. "I really do not want to discuss the possibility of never seeing Daniel again. Please don't speak of it again."

Louisa took a breath to say something else, thought better of it, and picked one of the apple pieces out of the cobbler Mary Anna was about to bake. "I see you're getting ready for Mr. Strong's visit." Was there the tiniest bit of ugliness in her question?

"I enjoy cooking, and this gives me an excuse to do some extra baking for the children, too." Mary Anna's forehead wrinkled in a frown. "Although, it is getting more and more difficult to find sugar. The war is cutting into our supplies."

"Strange man, Mr. Strong. Heard he had come out West to be a missionary to the Indians. Brought his family, too. A wife and four kids, I think. They were killed in a raid on the mission while he was away. It was so sad."

Mary Anna felt the hair rise on her arms. "How awful!" she gasped.

"Yes, he took to drink for near a year before he came to his senses." Louisa sighed and took her cup of coffee to the rocker. "After that he just began wandering and preaching. When they asked him to stay here permanent, he decided to make a regular route to ride." She sipped her coffee. "I think he's a good preacher." She looked sideways at Mary Anna who had just slipped the cobbler in the fire. "I like him better than the others who come through here."

Mary Anna chuckled. "Me, too. The others are just too righteous for me."

Louisa joined her chuckle. "My thought exactly. They make me feel like an unsavable sinner."

There was a hearty knock on the cabin door, and Mary Anna smoothed down her hair as she went to answer it.

"Hello." Mr. Strong stepped through the door. "Miss Mary Anna, Miss Louisa," he said with a little bow. Mary Anna hung his hat on the peg by the door.

He smiled broadly. "It smells good in here. Apple cobbler?"

"You have a good sense of smell," Louisa said.

"I need it on the trail," he responded affably.

The word *Indian* was not said aloud, but it caused the hair to rise again on Mary Anna's arms.

"Did you bring us any news of the war?" she asked.

"Only general news, I'm afraid," he said. "There's been a big battle at the Arkansas Post. The 15th Regimental Texas Cavalry was whipped badly enough that it was dismounted. The survivors will be infantry now. I couldn't get a list of the wounded or killed. I'm sorry."

"Arkansas," said Mary Anna. "That's not close, but it's too close for comfort." A shadow of fear crossed her heart.

"We'll be all right," Mr. Strong said easily. "If there's danger, we'll have plenty of warning, I'm sure."

"Certainly," Louisa agreed. "We're safe enough here." Quietly she added, "Of the two choices, I think I'd rather take a chance with the boys in Gray protecting us against the Union soldiers than to fight the Comanche alone."

Mary Anna knew she was right. They couldn't leave. She couldn't take the chance of missing Daniel's letters. Or even his coming home to find her gone. No, there was nothing to do but stay and pray that the Rebs could hold back the Blue tide.

"Will you and your family take dinner with us?" Mary Anna asked Louisa politely.

"No, thank you. Thomas has been out trying to do the spring plowing with that balky old mule. He'll probably be too tired to eat. I need to go home and take care of all of them. Spring," she mused. "It's spring, the time of renewal and hope." But there was such a sadness in her eyes that it contradicted her statement.

Amos saw it. "Yes, spring is always the season of hope," he echoed encouragingly as he opened the door for her.

Mary Anna was setting the table. "It's true about spring being a hopeful time. It's always been my best time of the year."

Amos watched her as she moved gracefully around the rude table. He was painfully reminded of another woman moving just so around his table. She had been very much like Mary Anna. Especially her spirit. She had the same quality of endurance that he saw in Mary Anna. Only Eleanor hadn't been able to endure the hateful arrows of the Comanche.

His loneliness was appeased somewhat by his visits to the Thornton cabin. Here there was a loving wife and mother and three fine children. He could enjoy the homey atmosphere with a little less pain than he usually carried in his heart. It was easy to imagine Eleanor doing these things in heaven as she waited for him to join her.

He was well aware he was using Mary Anna and her family as a substitute for what he missed. It was all right. There was no harm in bathing the wounds he carried in the tranquillity of this home. And he was determined nothing he would do or say could in any way dishonor Mary Anna. And so he drank deeply each time he came to sustain him for the times in between. He doubted very much he would ever love and marry again. He felt too old to begin again.

"Spring has always been a good time for me, too," he agreed. "Something about the very air promises new life."

Mary Anna's eyes sparkled. "Getting geared up for your Easter sermon?"

"As a matter of fact, I am. Easter is my number one celebration of the year. The hope of being reunited with God and the people we've loved and lost is my greatest comfort."

Carefully Mary Anna said, "Sometimes it's not easy to give up what we've lost. I've left two babies. One buried on the North Bosque and one at Dripping Springs."

His eyes were full of compassion. "I'm sorry."

"Not many days go by that I don't think of them, even with the three I do have." The sounds of their laughter drifted from outside the cabin. Tump and Peter were showing Betty how to make Soldier retrieve a stick.

"The Bible says God gives us only what we can bear, but sometimes He gives some of us a might heavy load." Amos's eyes were sad, but he deliberately shook off the melancholy of the moment and offered to call the children for supper.

After they were seated and he had said the prayer, the ambience of the cabin shifted to joyful as the children showered him with attention and affection.

Mary Anna knew this was as close as the pastor would ever come to speaking of his tragedy, and promised herself she would never approach the subject again. It was his alone to bear.

During their quiet time alone in the evening, she did broach another subject that was tugging at her. "I've been thinking if Daniel's letters and the money he promised to send don't come soon, I'm going to have to take up Louisa's offer to work at the hotel. Did you know that my father once owned that hotel? It was years ago," she mused. "Imagine Louisa now working there." She smiled.

"Working at the hotel is honest work." His rocker moved rhythmically.

"Hotel is a fancy word for that building," she laughed.

"It's not overly large, but it does serve to take care of the people we have passing through. And that's beginning to be more and more. We're getting to be a regular city." Amos noted his hostess's eyes were far away. "Miss Mary Anna?"

"Daniel and I met in this town. I saw him at the mercantile. Then he came to dinner at the hotel where I was working as my father's cook. In some ways this town is a comfort to me. In some, a constant heartache. I don't know, it's as if he were dead and I kept rummaging through his things and his memories."

"Choose to remember the times so you can share them with him when he comes home again."

Mary Anna wiped a suspicion of a tear from the corner of her eye. "Thank you, Reverend Strong. The Lord sent the right man to Tennessee Colony when he sent you. We need your comfort and your strength."

"Lean on the strength of the Lord, Miss Mary Anna, not me. I'm a hollow rock compared to him."

"Maybe so, but you're our rock right now. A visible promise that God is with us during this terrible ordeal."

"Thank you for those kind words." He looked at her blue eyes so deeply she had the feeling he could see right through to her soul. "They will comfort me through my long nights."

# Chapter 2

Daniel joined the 15th Regimental Texas Cavalry, D Company, on March 2, 1862, the year after Texas ceded from the Union. It wasn't a splendid outfit. The men had uniforms and supplies. They were well armed and in most cases rode fine horseflesh. There was a spirit about them that warmed Daniel's heart and made up for their lack of spit and polish.

It didn't matter; Lincoln himself had said the war would last only three months at the most. It had been a full year already. It mattered only that the South won, and that he got home quickly.

Camp life wasn't much different from being at home, except that Daniel had to do a lot of the things Mary Anna had done for him. For the most part, each man provided his own food. Shelter was provided by the Confederacy in the form of two-man tents.

They drilled until Daniel was thoroughly bored. But when their marching orders finally came, what a send off they got!

The prettiest girl in town presented their captain with a handmade flag and a blushing kiss. The local band played spirited marches and led the way out of town. The townspeople went along, either riding in carriages or walking. The troops marched about ten miles to a prosperous-looking farm where a big barbeque was held in their honor. The pretty, flirtatious Texas belles laughed and talked with the soldiers, urging them never to carry the flag backward in a retreat. And the men promised never to bring disgrace on so honored a treasure.

At the end of the festive evening, the carriages filled with the townspeople and returned home. The troops camped, happy and full, on the farm.

In the morning the troops began their march in earnest, and the band cheered them on, falling back after they had gone a mile or two.

Daniel smiled as the music began to fade. "What a way to go to war," he said to the man riding beside him.

"Makes a man proud to be part of this glorious cause, doesn't it?" he smiled back.

Daniel nodded, thinking of his faraway wife and family.

"I wonder how long it will be 'til our first fight," the eager young man pondered.

What came first was the rain. It was late May and the spring rains should have been over, but the roads were boggy and the men perpetually soaked for days at a time. Some got sick and dropped out at the nearest farmhouse to recuperate.

Daniel hung on, resolutely grinding out the soggy miles on his strong sorrel, Beau. He was beginning to think the rain would last his entire time in the cavalry. Worse yet, he hadn't even seen a Union soldier.

It was getting darker. He hadn't seen the sun all day, but he knew by the way his muscles felt that it had to be getting close to bedding-down time. When the captain finally reined his horse underneath some dripping trees, Daniel was almost too tired to help put up the tent he shared. He unsaddled Beau and let him graze nearby.

Jimmy Joe, the fresh-faced seventeen-year-old with whom Daniel had become friends, settled down beside him. Daniel felt old when he looked at the faces of the men in his company. They were mostly in their early twenties except for the captain, who was probably in his thirties.

"Cold beans and biscuits again tonight," Jimmy Joe complained. "What I wouldn't give for some of that barbecue right now. Or some of Ma's thick black coffee with molasses for sweetenin'."

They put their saddle blankets and bedrolls side by side to form their beds and shared the unappetizing fare in the tent. The water dripped monotonously off the tent flap.

"I think I know just how old Noah must have felt," Jimmy Joe said dolefully.

"Complaining won't make it better," Daniel replied tiredly. "Better try and get some sleep." He knew it was too wet and he was too tired to write another letter to Mary Anna.

He had left three letters for her along the way. Each of the men to whom he had entrusted the letters had promised faithfully to get it to her. Everyone knew how important letters were. Daniel himself was carrying one for a man who had been wounded. He would mail it in the next town they reached.

He rolled up in the damp blanket he carried and used his saddle for a pillow, not even bothering to take off his boots. He hadn't expected it to be all glory and excitement, but his experiences so far had been a dreadful disappointment.

"I hate sleeping on the ground," he mumbled to himself.

Several days and many miles later, they finally encountered a small company of Union men. It surprised both of them. Each unit charged wildly at the other, shooting at whatever appeared to be the enemy. *All that drilling and I can't remember what to do,* he raged silently at himself.

Daniel was so scared at the suddenness of the foray, he couldn't get his bearings. He just shot and prayed. It was over almost before it began.

There were several dead Union boys lying on the ground. Two of their men had been wounded. One severely shot in the stomach took the entire night to die. The surgeon traveling with them did what he could, but at first light a burial detail was called out to lay the boy to rest not far from where he had fallen. Daniel guessed him to be about fifteen.

"How in the world did he get into the army?" Daniel whispered to Jimmy Joe as they watched.

"Lied about his age, I reckon." Jimmy Joe avoided looking at Daniel's eyes as he spoke.

It dawned on Daniel that Jimmy Joe had done exactly the same thing. "Pretty stupid thing to do, I think," Daniel said pointedly. "This is a man's war."

Jimmy Joe's face reddened, but he didn't reply.

The captain wrote the dead boy's name in a little book he carried tucked inside his gray coat. The coat had gold fringe sewn on the shoulders, and the hat bore a golden colored cord wrapped around the crown that hung down off the brim. He wore his beard long but neatly trimmed.

Daniel himself had let his beard grow. He had little time or energy to keep himself sharply shaved. Nobody shaved, but then many of the boys had few whiskers to take off.

They were ready when the next battle came. The 15th had dug into the side of a bluff overlooking a river. The scouts had done a good job of gathering information about the Union troop movement. The only mistake they made was not seeing the big cannon at the rear of the column.

It pounded the 15th for several hours. Each time Daniel heard an incoming shell, he felt death chasing him. The explosions rocked the ground and left an acrid smell in the air. Sometimes all it threw up were rocks and dirt, but sometimes a body sailed high in the June sky.

He tried to find a target to shoot at, but the heavy foliage along the river hid any possible targets. He watched for puffs of smoke and then fired into that place. Occasionally he heard a cry or a scream. He assumed he was responsible for it.

The battle went on until dark with neither side gaining any advantage. He saw three men carry a white flag out into the middle of the river, cautious and expecting to get shot. They were met by shouts from the other side, and a truce day was arranged.

When dawn came, men from both sides came out of hiding to gather up the dead and bury them. By noon they were sharing the river for bathing purposes, and by afternoon there had been many exchanges of Yankee sugar for Confederate tobacco. Daniel stayed away from the friendly intercourse. He knew he couldn't laugh and joke with a man in the afternoon and kill him in the morning. Either they were the enemy or they weren't.

Perhaps it made it harder on the other Rebs, too, for they were overrun the next morning by the Union boys. Daniel took to his heels, chased down Beau, and rode as if all of Satan's forces were behind him. They regrouped in a hollow. When the captain called the roll, more than half of Company D was missing, presumed dead. They never knew, for they took a roundabout route when they retreated farther to avoid more fighting.

"Daniel! Over here!" called Jimmy Joe softly.

"Glad to see you made it," Daniel grinned.

"I've got a fast horse," Jimmy Joe said wryly.

"Me, too," said Daniel, but there was a tinge of shame in the admission.

Daniel was relieved to see the boy among the living. He had grown fond of him against his better instincts. He needed someone with whom to share a friendship, but he was afraid of what might happen if that friend were killed. He tried to stay friendly but uninvolved with the rest of the men. His age made a natural barrier.

In their next battle, the men fixed their bayonets and rode through the Union lines. Daniel took aim at the chest of a man trying to shoot him but avoided the man's eyes as he rammed the sharp blade deep into his chest. His ears couldn't avoid hearing the man's scream.

Everything about the war sickened Daniel and went against his principles. Over and over he had to keep sorting out the reason he was killing men each day. *Lincoln hasn't given me a choice. Every man has the right to decide his life for himself. Maybe I don't totally understand about the political advantages of secession,* he admitted, *but if Jeff Davis is for it, then it must be a good thing. The South has to be free to run the plantations the way they always have with slave labor. And that's true in Texas, too, if a man wants it,* he thought belligerently.

*There's no way to turn a profit if the owner has to hire someone to plant and pick his cotton. And if the plantations don't ship the cotton to Britain, then the South will be economically ruined. Cotton is the only thing the South has to offer on the market. Tobacco is coming along,* he reasoned, *but it needs slave labor, too.*

His mind rumbled these things around and around in the evening when Jimmy Joe would let him think. Jimmy Joe was losing the boyishness in his face. It was becoming increasingly difficult to guess his age. After only three battles, Jimmy Joe was old. *Guess that makes me a grandpa,* Daniel thought. *Or maybe that makes us the same age. Three battles old.*

They'd lost a lot of horses in the shelling. Many of the men were riding double, and the rest walked. It made a mockery of the word *cavalry.* Little by little they were being whittled down to an infantry company.

Beau wasn't in the best shape. He'd grown thin with the screaming of the battles and the foraging. Daniel tried to care for him as best he could, but there was little he could do. He barely had enough food to feed himself, let alone the horse.

The worry was soon over. Beau was shot out from under him in a skirmish. Daniel used his body for cover. Jimmy Joe was running low to join him when the boy's head snapped back from the impact of a shot. Daniel pushed the boy away from him and felt something akin to iron grow inside his chest. He saw a Union man charging him with a fixed bayonet, and he took careful aim and shot him between the eyes, feeling nothing but satisfaction at his marksmanship.

His mind flashed back to the time when he had been defending his cabin against a Comanche raid and he had so carefully shot at each rider who was trying to kill his family. For a brief moment it seemed as though he had spent his whole life killing someone else to stay alive. He bent over and vomited, wanting his deeds to come out with the bile that spilled from his stomach. Wanting forgiveness and wishing the killing would stop, he lay in the churned up grass and called to God for mercy.

After they had won the skirmish, Daniel and his comrades saw that the wheat field was littered with blue clad bodies. They walked through and took the things they needed. Daniel felt deep remorse as he took a pair of boots from one of the Union men. And he took another blanket to keep him warm at night, trying not to see the grotesque posture of its former owner.

He wasn't surprised when they were renamed an infantry troop. It only formalized the shape of their company. It was the early part of July near Little Rock. The 15th, 17th, and 18th Texas Cavalry regiments were joined by the 10th Texas Infantry under the command of Colonel Allison Nelson. For several months they drilled again, and then were ordered to a garrison of Arkansas Post, near the mouth of the Arkansas River. Daniel was relieved by the respite from killing.

By the fall they went into winter quarters, where they were joined by more men. The entire group was then known as Granbury's Brigade.

On January 11, at the Battle of Arkansas Post, Daniel was ashamed to find himself cornered by a bluebelly younger than himself.

"Hold it, Reb," said the hardened young man. "Just keep your hands where I can see them and drop that gun." His eyes skittered around looking for more Rebels.

"Don't shoot," said Daniel as he carefully laid down his rifle. He felt his stomach recoil in fear. Death felt very near as he watched the sun glinting off the cold steel of the Union soldier's gun that was pointed straight at him.

"Sandy!" came a voice from close by.

"I'm over here. Got one. You okay, Clarence?"

The noise of marching boots through the brush got louder. "Got two. Well, now, seems to me we got us a gaggle of gray geese." There was derision and pride in his voice as they gathered the men together and herded them to a larger group.

Daniel felt the sweat of fear run down his back. He fully expected to be executed on the spot.

The men looked at one another, trying without words to encourage each other, no matter what happened.

Daniel was honestly surprised when they were marched to a holding pen by the railroad and after several days loaded onto trains to be taken to Camp Douglas in Chicago.

"Camp Douglas," spat one man. "Be more merciful to shoot us now."

"What do you know about this place?" whispered Daniel.

"I know most of the men who go there die. Watch for a chance and run for your life. The odds are about the same—it will just be quicker."

The next day as they were being loaded, Daniel heard a shot ring out.

"I got him. Just one more Reb we don't have to feed," said a Union soldier. Daniel's empty stomach was not comforted.

It was as bad as the man had said. Winter was at its full strength, and Daniel spent most of his time trying to stay warm. The building where they were quartered was a long low dormitory set up off the ground a foot or so. The Illinois wind blew its cold breath into every corner.

Thirteen of these buildings were lined up in a neat row and surrounded by a high wall. It had once been a volunteer training camp for the Union soldiers but had been pressed into service for a prison camp.

When the morning came, Daniel woke, wondering if this day would be like all the rest. The smell was the first thing that had hit when he had entered the long building. After a while his nose was permanently immune to the stench of unwashed bodies, the secretions of illness, and offal.

At first the Union soldiers tried to get the men to police the outside areas, but they gave up trying to make anybody do anything in the winter as they searched for warmth themselves.

Besides, they would have to slog through the standing water in the yard to get to the men, and the Rebs were known to simply open the door to empty the slop jars. It was too cold, and they were too sick to do anything else.

When the soldier came to their building to bring the morning's rations, the men who could took food to the men too weak to move. The bread was stale and the gooey gruel cold, and it made a large undigested lump in Daniel's stomach, but he ate it.

He moved to wake the man sleeping next to him and found him dead. Daniel tried to catch the attention of the guard who had moved toward the door. "Sir, there's a dead man here."

The guard, a grizzle-haired veteran, shouted out the door to the next building. "Here's another one. Come help me."

They touched the dead man as little as possible, holding on to what they could grasp and still carry him. Daniel watched the men through the windows and saw the one man lose his grip on his end of the body, dropping it in the cold mud. Daniel turned away, unwilling to see more. He knew better than to make any protest.

James Horner had told him not to make any trouble. "They have a way of punishing troublemakers," he whispered in the cold, stench-filled night. "Morgan's mule, they call it. It's named for a Confederate raider, John Hunt Morgan, who was the terror of the Midwest. It's a sawhorse that's ten feet high. You can imagine what shape a man who has to sit astride that narrow rail with his feet swinging in midair for a long time is in by the time they let him down. Just keep your mouth shut if you don't want to ride the mule."

It was good advice.

Most of the time Daniel spent stretched out on the pile of hay that served as his bed with his feet carefully wrapped in the remnants of a tattered blanket. His boots were only shreds of leather, but they were better than the bare feet that too many of the men endured. He crossed his arms under his head to form a pillow and moved only to scratch his lice bites.

The quiet times were when he dreamed of Mary Anna and his family. Their pictures in his mind were fuzzy, and he was sure the children were much older than he remembered them, but he clung to the thought of them like a drowning man holds on to a piece of flotsam. Mostly he thought about Mary Anna. Sometimes in the night he could swear he smelled the sweetness of her skin and hair and feel her sleeping next to him. He ached to be with her, and the thought of not seeing her again almost drove him mad. His prayers for her and his family were constant and sent with tears to God.

As men always do when faced with hardship and privation, they found ways to entertain themselves and pass the time. One man had a deck of greasy cards with which to play poker, using straws for ante. And once in a while they had lice or cockroach races.

Boredom, illness, and death were their constant companions. Before it was all over, more than thirty percent of the men would die. Most of the men were sick with fevers. The food was poor and medical care primitive. Daniel took care of the ones he could and prayed for the souls of the ones he couldn't. He wasn't surprised when the day came that one minute he was freezing and the next, throwing off his blanket.

His stomach cramped, but he was too weak to move to the slop bucket. Finally, he couldn't keep down the gruel that one of the boys tried to feed him. He couldn't understand why Mary Anna didn't come and take care of him the way he had cared for her when she was sick. And he called for her constantly.

He came to himself one day and realized where he was.

"Good. You're awake." A black-bearded man was leaning over him with some kind of soup. "If there's any way you can sit up, you may have a good chance of being sent for exchange." The man propped Daniel against a wall. "They want the ones sick enough not to be able to fight again but well enough not to die on 'em."

Daniel felt a flicker of hope lick at the iron bar in his chest. "For truth?" he asked weakly of his companion.

"For truth. Think you qualify?"

Daniel nodded.

"Then I'll see if I can get your name on the list."

Daniel grasped the man's dirty shirt numbly. "Does this mean I can go home?" Visions of his wife exploded in his head.

"All I know is that they're sending them out. The Express List had new names on it today." Grimly he added, "It's got to be better than this."

When Daniel found out what month it was, he figured he had been in prison roughly three months. He could make it home from Virginia where he was sure to be exchanged. He was positive of that.

On April 5, 1863, the soldiers were on their way to City Point, Virginia, near Petersburg. As the train crept along the swaying tracks, the air around him warmed a little. Each day he felt more hopeful, but he didn't get any stronger. He knew the Union men didn't want him to be able to fight again. The truth was he didn't want to fight, either.

He was traded and then housed at a farm with the other men.

It was a poor place, and there were no men around to work the fields.

Mrs. Harrison was a tall woman, nearly six feet. But she was so thin she looked even taller. She was strong from doing the farmwork left by her men, and she put up with no nonsense from anyone. She had a job to do and she did it. She fed and nursed the men. Once they were on their feet again, they helped with the lighter chores.

"Put him over there on that clean hay. Here's a blanket for him. I'll bring some good hot soup for you. What's your name?"

"Daniel Thornton, ma'am, and I'm more than grateful for your help."

She gave what passed for a smile. "I'll be back to wash and bandage your wounds," she told the man next to Daniel.

"I've gotten so's I don't even mind that skin-eatin' lye soap, ma'am," he grinned.

"Just think of it as eating away the bad infection," she barked. But her rough words and appearance couldn't hide the basic kindness behind her deeds.

It stayed cool at night, but it was nothing compared to the icy cold of Chicago. And Daniel was on Southern soil. He had been afraid he would die up north and no one would ever know. Now if anything happened, he felt he would at least be listed and Mary Anna would know he was dead.

*Mary Anna, why haven't you written?* he anguished. Other men around him had gotten letters. Some were hand carried to the towns, some went through the undependable mail. But they had gotten letters. *Why haven't I?* He fought the terrible temptation to think she had forsaken him for another. Or that she was dead.

*I would rather think of her as dead than in someone else's arms,* he grimaced in the dark of the barn.

Over and over again he thought of how she looked, how she smelled, her smile, the soft touch of her hands. He remembered the wonderful meals she prepared from the food he brought her, and the laughter of his children. And he wept on the clean straw, quietly and almost in despair.

A voice came softly from the adjoining blanket. "Pray, brother. Pray for strength and faith. Only prayer to God will end all this suffering. Talk to Him and ask Him for His help. And I'll pray for you. Peace, brother. Accept His peace and sleep with His promises in your heart. He can heal everything and anything. Pray."

The voice was like an angel's, and Daniel held on to the promises and did pray until he felt that peace come back and he was able to sleep. He had been through hell, but he rested on the promises of God and he got stronger.

He found himself trying hard to get well just so he could get out of the barn. The doorway to the barn became his goal. Gingerly he tried sitting up. Gradually he was walking weakly to the door of the barn and barely getting back to his pallet of straw. That being accomplished, he offered to help with the small chores around the farm.

Mrs. Harrison looked him over. "Well, you do look some better. Hardly the mean fighting machine the South needs, but you're coming along. Why don't you take this and go feed my poor scrawny chickens? They look near as bad as you do, but they can still make chicken soup when I need it."

Daniel smiled broadly.

"It's nice to see you can smile. You're on your way now," Mrs. Harrison said.

He felt a little silly throwing hen scratch to the carefully stepping chickens. *I came all this way to feed Mrs. Harrison's chickens. Boy, the South is bound to win the war with me taking care of the barnyard,* he thought grumpily. Yet there was something soothing about the familiar sound of the squawking and arguing of the hens. The rooster strutted around, stepping high and proud. Daniel smiled again. *I think that's what we must have looked like when we left Fort Stockton to go join the war.*

He wrote another letter to Mary Anna to let her know where he was and that he was doing fine. He apologized for not being able to send her any money this time. The last time he had sent her money, he had gotten it from one of the dead Union men on the battlefield.

Though he had no family news, there was plenty of war news. As though to stamp the date on the mind of man for all eternity, both the Battles of Gettysburg and Vicksburg had been fought and lost for the South. Grant had managed to cut the South in half.

Daniel felt a moment of relief and a moment of shame that he had come so far to miss the battles that seemed to have tipped the scales for the Union. The battles he had fought were desperate battles; men had been wounded or killed. Yet here he was, sick. "I could have stayed home and helped out this much," he muttered to himself as he sprayed the yard again with feed for the patient hens.

That night as Daniel lay on the straw, Ely Bell strolled over. "Want to play cards?" he asked. When Daniel consented, he sat down and began to deal the tattered deck.

They played a round or two, but it became apparent that Daniel's mind was not on the game.

"Feeling homesick tonight?" Ely asked.

Daniel heaved a sigh. "Yes. I haven't heard from my wife, and I can't be sure she's been getting my letters."

"Thinking about deserting?" A glitter showed in Ely's eyes.

"Now, Ely," Daniel growled, "if I was, I wouldn't be telling you about it, would I?"

"I've been thinking serious about it," said Ely in a soft voice. "Rumor going around is that we're about ready to be sent to the front again. We're to be Hood's replacements."

"Hood's Texas Brigade?" Daniel whistled. "Best outfit in the Rebel army, I hear."

"You being from Texas wouldn't have anything to do with that opinion, I guess," Ely grinned.

"I hear the Waco boys are in there." Daniel folded his cards thoughtfully. "It would be nice to see someone from home. Maybe they even have some news for me."

"The only news they're likely to have will be death notices," Ely growled.

"The Lone Star Guards, they call themselves." Daniel was thoughtful. "Some of the first men to volunteer from Texas. I wonder if Ryan is still in command?"

"What difference does it make?" Ely was getting testy at Daniel's admiration.

"It means I should have joined up with them right away instead of waiting a year. It also means I'll be with men who will go home to the county next to mine. McLennan County is right next to Erath."

"If you get to go home," Ely added.

"Ely, I don't know what you have in mind exactly, but at this point in the war I'd rather take my chances fighting against the bluebellies than be shot for desertion. Or face disgrace," he added. "I couldn't live with that."

Ely scratched at his chin whiskers. "I guess that's something each man has to decide for himself. Another round?" he asked as he shuffled the cards.

"Sure."

The next morning Daniel wasn't surprised when Ely was missing. He had no information to give and said nothing about the conversation he and Ely had had the evening before.

Neither was he surprised when a sergeant came riding into the yard and started rounding up all able-bodied men.

Daniel got his gun and blanket. Mrs. Harrison offered them hardtack and salt pork to take with them, apologizing that there was no coffee to spare. He pulled on his well-worn boots and prepared to leave.

"Hood need some more good men?" he asked casually as he climbed up into the back of the wagon.

"No. Bragg does. You're now in the Army of Tennessee." He ordered one of the men to the seat of the wagon and started off down the road.

Daniel felt the gorge of disappointment rise in the column of his throat. He tried to deal with it by telling himself he was sure to meet up with someone from Texas. Perhaps all was not lost after all.

They caught up with Braxton Bragg at La Fayette, Georgia, about twenty-five miles from Chattanooga. Bragg was dug in there waiting for reinforcement, while Rosecrans was in the city itself, where he felt safe for the moment from the boys in gray.

Daniel threw his blanket down beside a man who looked to be about his age. "Howdy. Name's Daniel Thornton." He stuck out his hand.

"Randolph Young, formerly of Virginia. Of late, whatever state we're in now." Randolph was well groomed and made Daniel feel like a country hick.

"I'm from Texas. I'm looking for anyone else from there." He sat on the blanket and resolved to up his grooming program.

"Can't help you, I'm afraid." Randolph measured Daniel with his eyes.

"Just back from a sick leave, I gather."

"Yes. What's the situation around here?"

"You'll have to ask Bragg himself for a detailed account, but from my end of the spectrum, I see Old Rosy feeling quite secure until all you men moved in. Scouts say he's moving out of the city to about twelve miles below Chattanooga to a river called the Chicamauga." Randolph paused. "Do you speak Cherokee, Daniel?"

"No."

"Chicamauga means 'the river of death.' I sincerely hope neither of us adds our blood to its journey." Randolph sighed and took a deep drink from his wooden canteen. "We'll know soon, I think."

# Chapter 3

It was September 19, 1863—a clear, crisp day with clouds framing the mountains just behind the river, making Daniel wish he were back home working in his own fields.

He could hear the sounds of rattling wagons and horses neighing nervously. "That's too many horses just to be for the wagons," he said to Randolph. "Cavalry somewhere. I hope it's ours."

In fact, both sides had ample cavalry.

Daniel tensed as he heard shots being fired ahead of him. He had been assigned to General James Longstreet's men. And then it was a matter of killing and trying to stay alive. The crisp air turned sour with cannon fire and thousands of arms being fired. It was ripped by the bloody screams of the wounded and dying.

Randolph nudged him and nodded to his left. Daniel's gaze followed Randolph's, and he saw bodies being stacked like cords of wood to allow the supply wagons and men to get down the small roads. He was sick to his stomach but dared not drop his guard long enough to vomit. Almost immediately a long blue line of men charged toward their position, and he fired at will as fast as he was able.

Some of the Union men broke through, and there was hand-to-hand combat with knives and bayonets. Daniel found blood all over the front of his shirt. Frantically he searched for his wound. It was the blood of the men he had killed. There was no time to think or plan. All he could do was keep firing and hope his ammunition held out.

As it grew darker, the fighting died down except for sporadic sniping from both sides. He fell down heavily with a tree at his back. He was too worn out to eat more than some hardtack and water from his canteen.

Pulling his blanket around him, he stretched out, sleeping on his gun. He had no idea where Randolph was.

Cannon fire woke him at dawn. The Army of the Cumberland was trying to find a range on them. Another day of horrendous noise, smell, and the taste of blood in his mouth.

It was man to man, until suddenly Daniel realized the Blues weren't running at him anymore. They were retreating!

The Rebs poured into the Union line unchecked, chasing the enemy back in the direction of Chattanooga.

Above the tempest of the battle, no orders could possibly be heard. Fugitives, wounded, caissons, and ambulances clogged the narrow pathways.

Daniel dropped down in a hollow behind a fallen log and breathed a huge sigh of relief. He had survived another battle. *Thank you, God, and have mercy on the souls of those men who died here today.*

The sound of rustling grass behind him caused him to whirl and aim his gun.

"Whoa! I'm on your side," said a battle-weary Reb. He was a little younger than Daniel and dressed in a tattered Confederate hat and full buckskins, complete with fringe. He dropped down beside Daniel and stuck out his big calloused hand. "Samuel Beardsley."

"Daniel Thornton."

"We did good, Dan," he bragged.

"We have orders to move up to Missionary Ridge and hold it. Old Rosy is heading for Chattanooga. We'll just sit back and starve him out."

A sergeant interrupted them. "I need you men for burial detail. Look alive."

*Look alive for a burial detail?* thought Daniel, and he grimaced at the paradox of war.

He and Samuel joined the other men on the recent battleground. It was a gruesome task he had been assigned. Soldiers were going through the field gathering what things could be useful for them. But as Daniel worked his way through the clothing of the men looking for identification, they ceased to be grotesque corpses. They were men torn away from their families, and the ambrotype pictures they carried of their loved ones was a wretched reminder of his own. Would some sickened soldier go through his pockets some day trying to identify him? He tried to put away the thought and distance himself mentally from the process of going through the dead soldiers.

Other men dug trenches about six or eight feet long, six feet wide and about twenty inches deep. The bodies were laid beside them and articles of clothing and blankets on the bottom. Then the men were laid tenderly side by side and covered with other blankets, and the soil for which they had so gallantly died was spread over them.

Daniel took a pair of boots from a dead Yankee. They were new and polished to a high sheen. Obviously he hadn't been in the field long. Or maybe he had taken them from someone else, too. By and large, the Union men were well outfitted and carefully dressed, in stark contrast to the ragged Confederate soldiers.

The carnage was awesome. Only later would Daniel find out both sides had suffered causalities of thirty percent.

"The only good thing I see about this is that we'll have plenty of artillery and guns and ammunition," said Samuel as he worked beside Daniel. He leaned over and helped himself to a brand-new rifle lying beside a dead Yankee. "Got you some boots, I see. I think it's right nice of the Union boys to see we're well provisioned. The South seems to be having a hard time keeping up with our needs. I haven't gotten a paycheck yet."

Daniel's worry over Mary Anna's financial plight escalated. He had promised to send her cash, but so far he hadn't been paid either. When he found some money in the pockets of the men he was helping bury, he stuffed it in his own pockets. "For my wife," he explained to Samuel.

Quietly Samuel said, "You don't need to justify taking anything from these boys. They won't be needing it anymore."

When the ghastly job was done, they returned to their camp.

Daniel asked several men about Randolph, until finally one man said, "I saw him fall. Cannonball got him. He's dead, friend. It was the most merciful thing that could happen. One minute he was and the next minute he wasn't."

They were allowed to build fires for the evening meal. Daniel found he couldn't swallow, but he shared the small comfort of the fire with his new friend. "You're not from Texas, by any chance?" he asked.

"Practically, Arkansas, neighbor." Noting the disappointment in Daniel's face, he added, "I know some boys from Texas. Hood's Brigade. They're camped on down the way. Like me to introduce you?"

"I'd be obliged. I'm trying to find someone from close to home and see if they're carrying any mail for me."

"Always a chance. Looks like we're going to be here a spell. Be safer to wait until daylight. Wouldn't want you to get shot before you got your letter," grinned Samuel.

Daniel returned his grin. "I think I might be too tired to go hunting up the brigade tonight. First thing tomorrow'll be fine."

They got permission from their captain and began the walk along the ridge. They were careful not to skylight themselves in case there were Union snipers still in the area.

"Reminds me of being in Indian country," Daniel remarked.

"Same principle, only this time we're fighting our kinfolks."

Daniel saw a brief flash of pain across Samuel's face. "You got kin on the other side?"

"My brother. We never did see eye to eye on most things. Still, he's my big brother. I pray to God I never meet him on the battlefield."

The enormity of the situation left Daniel with nothing to say. He knew a lot of families had the same problems. He was thankful such was not his case.

They finally located some men from the Lone Star Guard, but after questioning as many soldiers as they could, Daniel still knew nothing more. He was cheered by seeing men who could at least speak of the place he called home, but it also depressed him. It made him homesick for the quiet of his fields and the sight and sounds of cattle and horses. It made him ache to be with Mary Anna and the children. He wondered if Mary Anna was carrying another child.

*No, I've been gone for almost two years. If she had been in a family way, the child has already been born.* The thought of an unknown child plunged him deeper into the doldrums.

Back in their own camp with little to do but the usual duties, Daniel's mind had plenty of freedom to roam. It was one of the hazards of army life that he was either in the middle of a furious battle or doing his laundry.

He summoned up the picture of the cabin Mary Anna would be living in. *Is she living with Louisa? Doubtful. Probably has her own cabin. I can see it now. Hear the kids outside playing. Kids are a foot taller. Maybe a new one. Mary Anna. Dear Lord, how I miss her.*

Tears dropped on the underwear he was washing in a pan of dirty water. His chest ached so badly, he thought there surely must be an open wound there. Her picture kept floating up out of the water, teasing his senses. He remembered her long silky hair and how he used to brush it for her at night as she sat in her mother's rocker. Her soft skin with its freshly scrubbed smell rose in his nostrils, and her lips seemed to move closer to his.

*She's so tiny. So full of vinegar. God, keep her safe.*

As she moved closer to him, into his arms, he felt the familiar stirrings in his body. He could envision the children sleeping and the darkness of the cabin. The soft bed they shared. And then another tear fell into the water, plopping and breaking the dream. With the daydream over, another tear fell; this one was an angry tear. *What am I doing here? I should be with Mary Anna.* And he understood full well why Ely had left. Deep inside, Daniel hoped Ely had made it back home.

Roughly he scraped at the tears and shook them from his eyes. He walked over and hung the underwear, the only other pair he owned, on the small branches of a bush, hoping it would dry quickly so he could change. Even though the days were only crisp, the evenings were still very cool.

He had been well outfitted when he joined up. Even during the first few campaigns, he had what he needed. Each soldier seemed to be an expert at foraging for himself and his friends. In fact, he'd heard that Lee had called them "the best Moonlight Requisitioned of any war."

Early on the morning of September 22, the army began its march through Rossville and the Chattanooga Valley toward the Tennessee River. They spent the night in a skirt of woods east of Lookout Mountain.

Daniel and Samuel shared in an ample breakfast the next morning. The men of their company cooked Union food in Union pots.

"Best breakfast I've had in a long time," said Daniel.

"We'll be eatin' good for a spell, I suspect. Then it's back to the way it usually is," Samuel responded philosophically. "Maybe we can chase the Blues out of Chattanooga and they'll leave us another banquet."

There was general laughter around the campfire, and a few heads nodded in agreement. They were winning now. The Yanks were on the run.

The sergeant strolled up. "Glad you fellows have had a good meal. You'll be needin' all the strength you got to get those breastworks built before dark."

There was soft grumbling, but the men would rather fight from behind a breastwork than in the open field or trust a tree, so the work was done carefully and completely.

The next day Daniel and Samuel sat by the morning cook fire and enjoyed a real luxury—coffee.

"Why do you suppose we didn't keep running after them bluebellies when we had them going? We could have chased them all the way back to Washington," Samuel said.

Daniel was surprised at the question. He had been so glad the shooting was over, it never occurred to him they should have pursued the enemy.

"If he gets dug in at Chattanooga, he's liable to be mean to dig out."

"Not if he doesn't get any supplies," argued Daniel. "It'll be a long, cold, hungry winter for him."

"And not for us?" challenged Samuel. "Where do you think we'll get our supplies? The South seems to be a might short on the things I crave."

It was a worrisome question. Why were they stopped? "Surely Bragg has a plan," Daniel protested.

Samuel helped himself to some more of the precious coffee. "I sure do hope you're right, friend."

They spent the month of October in leisure. Many of the men liked being on Lookout Mountain, Raccoon Mountain, and Missionary Ridge and took easy hikes along the timbered areas. At the top of Lookout Mountain, Daniel could look down into the Federal camp in Chattanooga and see the men doing their camp chores, drills, and recreation.

"Look through these glasses, Sam. They're playing baseball."

"Maybe we ought to get us up a game."

"I'd rather just sit here and look." Daniel breathed in the fresh, brittle air. The pines were deep here, and he could see the Tennessee River threading its way through the valley. The trees had started to turn, and October had splashed a colorful hand across the timber. It was the closest thing to peace he had felt in a while, and he wasn't eager to leave it.

When they did arrive back in camp, they checked the duty roster. Daniel hated to do picket duty. Some of the outposts were less than a hundred yards from the Blues, and the pickets were back to visiting with the enemy. He hated all the chatting back and forth and the trading of newspapers and food. He knew it was strictly against orders, but that's not why he didn't engage in all the socializing. He still couldn't bring himself to get to know the men he was supposed to kill. Sometimes the men even played cards together. He couldn't understand it. The vision of Chicamauga's grisly battlefield was forever etched in his mind. And he knew it would happen again.

They had constructed small log cabins in which to spend the progressively colder nights. The larges of food had dwindled to the usual Confederate rations.

"I'm sure glad we've got Old Rosy under siege," said Sam sarcastically. "I'm sure he's really hurting for food by now." He looked at the musty corn and blue beef he was supposed to eat for his meal and laid it down in disgust.

Daniel tried to convince himself it was better than the weeks it rained and there was nothing at all brought up for them. "I doubt I'll ever eat corn bread again as long as I live. Not even Mary Anna's."

With the encampment, rain, and cold weather, sickness had visited the soldiers again. Fevers were rampant. Some men said the water made them sick, but it looked clean and clear. All the men knew not to drink befouled water, but still diarrhea was a constant companion for most of the men.

Foraging where there were few farms didn't produce much food, and many days the food that was brought in was not fit to eat, leaving the men open for every type of disease.

With the cold weather and constant rain, men stayed in the little huts. Samuel had several books in his haversack he gladly shared with Daniel. *The Autocrat of the Breakfast Table* was one of his favorites, and they discussed the story frequently. They also shared the small Bible Daniel carried with him. Death was an ever-present companion, and eternity was discussed endlessly.

"Sam, do you believe in God?"

Sam was whittling on a small piece of wood and dropping the shavings into the small fire as they huddled in their hut. "Yup. I was saved when I was twelve. Baptized, too." His eyes hooded a bit. "I haven't been the best churchgoer in the congregation, but now that I'm here, I do more praying than I ever did at home."

"Me, too," admitted Daniel. "Wonder what the men who don't believe in God do?"

Samuel laughed. "A lot of ducking, I imagine."

"He's gotten me out of a lot of bad spots, I know that. But why do you suppose He lets the war keep going on?"

"I suspect it's not God that keeps it going. It's men." Samuel scratched his beard. "I've always thought a man had a right to protect what was his, but when I see all the dead men spread all over the battlefield, I'm sure there has to be a better way to solve all this."

"I wish you'd share this solution with General Lee!"

"You can be sure I would. I just want to get back to my farming."

Daniel nodded, and then added, "But nothing would have been solved. The government would just keep on telling us what to do. We've made a new country. Old Abe's side doesn't think we ought to do this."

Samuel looked Daniel in the eyes. "Do you think slavery is wrong?"

Daniel dropped his chin and nodded his head in confusion. "Is it wrong for one man to own another?"

"But are slaves men?" Samuel challenged.

Daniel shook his head. "I thought I had all this figured out once. Now that I'm here and see what it's led to, I'm not sure about anything. Back in Alabama it never occurred to me to ask questions. They were just there and they did the work. Now when I think about the mammy that raised me, I remember seeing her cry when Papa sold off her babies. She was kind to me. Took care of me when I was sick. Bathed me, fed me, scolded me.

"Once she even lied to Papa and said she broke the big bowl on the wash-stand to keep me out of trouble." He looked steadily at Sam. "And then there was Tom, the houseboy. He was a good friend to me all my growing up days. But there was an invisible line drawn between us where he couldn't go. He knew it and I knew it. It didn't seem fair or unfair, it was just the way things were."

He sighed. "I don't keep slaves in Texas. Can't afford them," he admitted. "But does that mean it's wrong for other men who can?" He turned to Samuel. "Does it? And can the government tell us what we can do with our own lives?"

"I went to an Abolitionist meetin' once. Just to hear what they had to say. I have to admit, it jarred me some." He looked at Daniel again. "Seems to me you've been a bit jarred yourself."

Daniel chuckled. "I thought I was real grown-up when I enlisted, especially with all those fresh-faced kids." His chest heaved in a thoughtful sigh. "Now I'm not sure that the reason I joined up is the one that keeps me in. I'm not sure about anything anymore." He looked up in time to see Samuel's eyes misting.

"You sure about God?"

"That's the only thing I'm sure of. He's going to get me back to Mary Anna. He gave us to each other. He'll take me home to her."

"My wife is dead. Died of a fever three years ago. I have nothing to go home to."

"Yes, you do. You have a new life to build. Sons to sire. Daughters to sit on your knee and twirl your beard," Daniel joked with him. He was frightened by the resignation he saw in Samuel's eyes.

"Dan, we've been in some awful battles, but I think Armageddon is yet to come for us." He shrugged his shoulders. "I may be joining my wife."

"It's not the worst thing that could happen," Daniel said softly.

In the silence that followed, they could hear someone playing a mouth harp. The sad strains of "Aura Lee" wafted across the campgrounds. Questions of right or wrong blurred with the one burning desire of each man: to go home again— wherever that might be.

After the heavy losses at Chicamauga, both Samuel and Daniel were reassigned to Cleburne's Confederates and positioned to defend the north end of Missionary Ridge. In late October the Yanks had grown tired enough of the stringy beef hurriedly driven on the hoof to Chattanooga and had seized Brown's Ferry downstream from the city, opening up a supply line again for them. On November 23, Thomas's troops took Orchard Knob, a spot he thought good enough to take Missionary Ridge. On the following day, Joe Hooker's Easterners took Lookout Mountain.

"We're in big trouble," Daniel said, trying to hide the fear raging through his body like hot lightning.

The ridge was swathed in early morning mist, giving everything a ghostly feeling.

"I don't feel good about this either," Samuel agreed through clenched teeth. The war wagons could be plainly heard echoing in the morning as they positioned the artillery.

"We're high enough up above them to make the pickin' easy," bragged a Reb on Daniel's left.

It was true they were looking down on the enemy lines from the ridge. There were rifle pits at the base of the ridge below them, but both men knew Bragg had sent Longstreet's men to help out in Knoxville, and there had been some heavy reinforcements along the Union line, leaving the Rebs badly outnumbered.

"The only thing we've got going for us is the height," said Daniel.

"Then we'd better make the most of it," replied Samuel. "Here they come!"

"Lord God, help me" was all Daniel had time to pray when the Rebel cannons opened fire.

"No, no! They're firing over their head! Lower those noses, boys!" shouted the bragging young Rebel.

The cannons were fired again, but the shells were still sailing over the advancing men.

"Look!" shouted Daniel. "Their men are lighting the shells and throwing them back!"

Rebel yells split the air as the men spurred each other on in their efforts. The line held until the middle of the afternoon.

Daniel took a long drink from his canteen and offered it to Samuel.

"Thanks. Don't guess you've got anything stronger somewhere, have you?" he joked.

"Even if I did, you wouldn't have time to drink it. Here they come again!"

This time the first line of Rebels fell to the Union effort. The rifle pits were still holding, though, and the men from above laid down a blistering barrage.

Suddenly the bluebellies were swarming all over the rifle pits and firing up onto the ridge itself.

"Getting hot around here," observed Samuel.

"They're not backing down," shouted Daniel over the noise of the incessant firing. Clearly from below them could be heard the word "Chicamauga!" being chanted by the stubborn Union men.

Desperately the Rebels tried to hold off the enemy, but it was soon apparent to all that the men could not hold back the surging Blue tide crawling up the side of the ridge.

The Confederate men began a backward fight, firing as they retreated. And then it was every man for himself.

Daniel broke out in a cold sweat and ran swiftly for cover. He saw Samuel following after him out of the corner of his eye. They slid behind a fallen log and gasped for air.

"Run for that little valley, Sam." He turned to see if his friend was behind him and saw Samuel stumble and fall. Daniel dashed back.

"Get up, Sam! Run!" That's when he saw the blood gushing from the wound in Samuel's chest.

"Best you go on without me," he gasped. "I'll be along directly. I think a mosquito bit me." When he saw Daniel hesitate, he pushed him with a bloodied hand. "Go! Go!"

Too scared to do anything but obey, Daniel ran. He crouched as best he could, but bullets were singing all around him. He headed for the road.

Men were everywhere, and all were running. He jumped over a fallen standard bearer. He ran with the men until the sounds of battle were behind them and then fell into a deep ravine, panting. He wiped his eyes, expecting to find blood on his hand. There was nothing but sweat and the tears that were streaming down his face. He jumped at every noise, relieved to find it was only another Reb hiding as he was.

Gradually the men found one another and got what was left of their company together. They continued to move deeper toward Georgia, stopping only when they hadn't the strength to go one more foot. In the days that followed, Daniel was morose and spent as much time as he could sleeping. The unit of men had lost their captain and argued a good bit about who ought to lead them.

"We don't even know where we're going. How can anyone lead?" asked a belligerent man. It was finally decided to have Daniel lead on the sole basis that, at thirty, he was the oldest one among them.

He decided Atlanta would be their best bet, so he headed the men in a southerly route, always alert for other companies.

They never made it to Atlanta. They met up with other remnants of the Army of Tennessee, now led by Joseph E. Johnson, entrenched on the low mountain ridges northeast of Dalton, Georgia, a few miles from the bloodstained field of Chicamauga. There they dug in for the winter months.

The men built rude shelters and tried to live off the land. The land had little to give them, for it had tried to feed thousands of people for two years.

There was an attempt to celebrate Christmas. Mostly the men sat quietly, many of them crying.

Daniel read the Christmas story from his battered Bible. After he finished he tried to see his family celebrating. The picture wouldn't come. *Here I am, Lord, on Your day. Forgive me if I can't find it in my heart to rejoice today. Thank You for keeping me alive through all this. Bless my family.* He choked on the word "family." *I ask only one thing today. Could I please get a letter from Mary Anna? I've written and written, but I haven't heard from her. Lord, it's been a long time.* Frank tears flowed down his grizzled cheeks. *I love her so much. Please let her still love me, too. A letter, Lord. That's all I ask.*

It didn't come.

The ever-present trio of bad water, bad food, and cold felled the men with disease and illnesses. Daniel survived one bout, only to fall victim to pneumonia. Most of the time he was more dead than alive, and it was finally decided to furlough him home. No one expected him to make it.

Later he wouldn't recall much about the trip. He knew only that sometimes it was by wagon and sometimes by rickety train. He never knew the route. All he knew was that he was being sent home, and he had a raging desire to stay alive long enough to get there.

The only question was, would Mary Anna be there when he got home?

"I never got a letter," he mumbled in his delirium. "I never got a letter."

# Chapter 4

It had been a year and eight months since Mary Anna had tenderly kissed Daniel and sent him off to war with carefully guarded bravado. Twenty months and not one word from him.

She was working full time at the hotel. She toiled over the hot, big black stove and listened to the gossip of the travelers. True, there weren't as many as there used to be, but things would get better. At least, that's what they all told one another on an almost daily basis.

The town of Tennessee Colony had sent everything it could to help the war effort. Consequently, there weren't a lot of things for Mary Anna to cook. Her brothers were long gone to war, even the very youngest at fifteen. The only men left were cripples and the infirm.

Her summer garden had provided them with just enough food to get through the winter. She tried not to eat the chickens, for the eggs were such a treat, but as the feed for them became scarce, the eggs became fewer and fewer. When two of the hens mysteriously disappeared, she decided to feed her family rather than strangers.

Once she had taken the rifle out in hopes of getting some meat or game. She did get one wild turkey. As she carefully smoked it, she silently laughed as she remembered how Daniel and their friend Caleb had tried to catch the wild turkeys and put them in pens to raise them out on the Brazos River so long ago. What a mess that scheme had turned out to be! Texas wild turkeys were not of a mind to sit in a pen.

She made corn bread and had a big pot of red beans on the cast-iron stove in her cabin. Mr. Strong would be coming for dinner tonight, so she made a quick apple pie out of the last of her dried apples from the summer.

She thought of Daniel every day, though his sharp image had grown fuzzy and she mostly remembered his essence. Sometimes she tried to remember if he was as tall as Mr. Strong. They might be the same height. There was so much of Daniel emblazoned on her heart forever, but it felt as if it had all happened in another life. Here in Anderson County, her life with him in the pioneer county of Erath held a dreamlike quality.

*If only he would write, I would know he was alive. I could dream for us and make plans.* She frowned. *If he's dead, that also calls for making plans. No, he's alive. I feel it in my heart. Lord God in heaven, please keep him alive. You're the Almighty. You can do anything. Please don't take him from me. I need him. I love him.*

She walked to the end of her bed and opened her brass-bound traveling chest. Carefully she pried off the lid of a small velvet box. Inside was the only picture she had of Daniel. She made a small gasping sound as she saw the handsome features and ran her fingertips around the edges of Daniel's face. Then she kissed her fingertip and placed it gently on his mouth. He looked so young and vibrant. *He's alive. I know he is. He has to be. Oh, Daniel, I love you. I love you.* Painstakingly, she slipped the ambrotype picture back into its soft box and the tray into the trunk.

Amos came to the cabin for supper that night. They sat at the table together, looking for all the world like a happy family.

There had been quiet talk about Amos not joining the war effort, but he had proven so helpful to the women left behind, his kindness blotted out their doubts about his loyalties.

The cold December wind blew outside, daring hearty souls to brave its iciness. The fireplace offered comfort and security from the stark world.

There was the usual cheerful chatter from the children. Tump was getting close to nine years old. Peter was almost six years old. Betty was a baby no longer. At three she fairly bristled when anyone called her Baby Betty.

While Mary Anna got the children in their beds, Amos pulled a rocker closer to the fire and propped his boots up on the hearth. He was sipping sumac tea when Mary Anna came back to join him.

They sat in companionable silence for a while. They had spent enough time together to not be embarrassed by their lack of conversation.

"So you bring any news of the war?" she finally asked.

"Bad news, I'm afraid." He met her frightened look with a quick explanation. "We lost bad at Missionary Ridge. Chased our fine men all the way back to Georgia. Bragg's been replaced by Johnson."

"That means Grant has the South by the throat." Her eyes were large with worry.

"True. But the invasion of Texas has been aborted."

"I'm grateful to God for that, but. . ." She saw the shadow of grief in his face. "We're beaten," she said in a dead tone.

"Unless a miracle happens, it does look that way. Richmond is sure to fall." He let out a deep breath. "We just can't give the men the supplies they need. The North keeps pouring men and materials in an endless river."

"A man came through here two days ago and gave me a copy of the *New York Herald* newspaper. It said the same thing. I was hoping they were just bragging." She stared at the fire for a few minutes and then said, "Maybe that means Daniel will be coming home soon. There's got to be something good in there somewhere."

Gently he said, "You still think he's alive even after all this time with no letters?"

"He's not been on any of the casualty lists we've seen, and I have to believe he'll come back to me." Her eyes were steady.

Her deep devotion to a man she had not heard from in twenty months touched him deeply.

"They say swans mate for life. You strike me as a swan."

"Amos," she said turning to him and looking him squarely in the eyes, "I have loved only one man in my life. I'm waiting for someone to either send him home to me or tell me where he's buried. Then I'll deal with the problem after I know what it is. Until then, I'll wait for him." Her eyes reflected the dying glitter of the fire.

"I'll wait with you." He reached across the short expanse between them and put his hand on hers, which rested on the arm of the rocker. "If he comes home, I'll rejoice with you. If he doesn't, I will mourn with you." Softly he added, "And when your mourning is over, I'll come to supper again. And for as many times as it takes to win your heart for myself." He looked deeply into her wide blue eyes.

"I won't pretend to be shocked. You're a fine man and have never been anything but a complete gentleman with me. And I know about the pain you carry. We are good friends and comfortable with each other, and the children adore you. But right now all I can say is that I love Daniel." The bright blue of her eyes was shaded to a deeper color by the tears that welled up. "Next to Daniel, you're the finest man I've ever known, and I thank you for all your care and kindnesses to me and the children."

He gave her hand a loving squeeze and took it away, settling back into his chair, content.

She felt no guilt at the conversation that had passed between them. There were no remarks to sully her honor, only an honest statement of Amos's feelings. And she had been candid with him. Something inside said she would never love again if she lost Daniel. And something else even deeper recognized that there were many kinds of love. Being married to Amos would not be a horrible fate.

Later that night as Mary Anna lay in her own bed, she carefully tested her feelings. Amos's image was clear in her mind, even to the different colors of hair in his carefully trimmed beard. But she had to struggle to see Daniel in her mind's eye. Not the picture of him, but what he was like in the flesh. She began with his eyes. Blue ones, like hers, that lit up his young face. His mouth. Mobile and quick to smile. And his hands, eager for her. He had been able to start a lightning-fast fire in her, a fire that consumed both of them and left them breathless with the wonder that passed between them. She wrapped her arms around herself and cried with the ache that memory brought her.

She was twenty-six years old with three children and had spent the long lonely year and eight months bereft of his love. *Are you alive, my darling? Are you warm and well? Oh, Daniel, please come home to me, please.* She prayed and fell asleep with her pillow damp with prayers and tears.

When she awoke in the morning, she felt safe, protected. The Lord had provided her with a husband and now another man who was her good friend. *Lord, I know You'll show me what to do when the time comes. Keep my husband and my friend safe, and bring Daniel home to me. And ease the pain and loneliness in Amos's heart.*

The month of December fluttered by like the limp leaves still clinging to the tree outside her window. Mary Anna felt her resolve not to give up on Daniel begin to slip a fraction. The gray days added nothing to her state of mind. Christmas was on the way, but she dreaded the thought of trying to be cheerful for the children. Their gaiety irritated her.

*Lord, I need some big help. It's time to celebrate the coming of Your Son, and I can't feel anything but sadness in my heart. For my sake and the children's, would You please ease the doubt in my mind and give me hope? Help me to make it a happy time for all of us.*

She carded some of her precious wool and made yarn to knit into mittens for each of the children. The task was pleasant enough, but she enjoyed making the fruitcake, skimping and substituting ingredients to make something really special for Christmas Day.

Amos came to preach and brought her a wild turkey already smoked for Christmas dinner. He had gathered pecans for the children, and she put them away. She felt a small flutter of excitement as she readied things for the holidays.

She decided to knit a neck scarf for Amos. After all, he would be there for Christmas Day and the dinner following church.

She listened to his sermons when he came and tried to take comfort from his words, but something inside her was shriveling. His actions toward her both publicly and privately never reached the intimacy of that one evening. It was as though he had never uttered his thoughts to her.

Mary Anna worked on the scarf while the children decorated the Christmas tree with scraps of material, paper, and brightly colored berries.

Tump came over to her with his eyes lit with the wonder of Christmas. "Mama, can we please borrow your shiny silver broach to put up on the top of the tree? Please?"

She laughed at the intensity of his plea. "Yes, but you please be very careful with it. Your father gave that to me. It's special."

"I know," he said proudly, "that's why we want to use it. It will remind all of us about Papa." He looked hopeful. "Do you think he'll make it home for Christmas? Maybe?"

A stab of pain pierced her heart. "Maybe," she echoed sadly.

On Christmas Eve the church was softly lit with candles, and the sound of the reedy organ whispered familiar carols. The smell of sticky pine boughs bathed the air, now crisp with a light December snow.

Mary Anna tried to sing with the congregation, but the sounds stuck in her heart. *Where are you, my darling? Are you well? Do you have anything to eat? Who will kiss you awake and say, "Merry Christmas!" I have a gift for you. I made it from the best pieces of leather I could find. House slippers for you to wear as you sit by the fire and read. I lined them with bits of rabbit fur. Daniel, my love, why don't you write? Are you dead and in heaven with the Lord?*

In spite of her resolve to have a happy time for the children, a tear escaped and coursed down her cheek. Furtively she swooshed it away with a nonchalant hand as though smoothing her cheek.

But it wasn't so easy to escape the tears when Amos prayed for all the men who were away from their families. And she frankly wept when they sang the closing hymn, "Silent Night."

Mrs. Cocheran was not a skilled organist, but she brought out the best in the wheezy old pump organ this special holiday. There were many damp eyes and hurting hearts in the church that night. Perhaps only the youngest had anticipated and enjoyed the season.

The next morning the squeals of delight from the children and their happy cavorting brought a genuine smile to Mary Anna's face. For a few minutes, Daniel's absence was forgotten and she immersed herself in their joy.

For the big noon meal, Louisa brought food and gifts and her children. There was plenty for all. The cousins exchanged gifts and displayed their favorites. It was a slim Christmas by some standards, but the family celebrating could well relate to the story of the baby born in a stable, and they thanked God for the bounty of His hand in such desperate times.

Amos came after the meal, having eaten with the Gottleib family. He had peppermint for the children and a little saltwater taffy "for the lovely ladies of the house."

Tump came to him bearing a brown paper-wrapped present decorated with a real silk ribbon. "For you, Mr. Strong, because we love you."

For one moment Mary Anna thought he was going to cry.

He took a deep breath and opened the present while the children circled him with glee. "I've never seen a finer scarf in all my born days," he exclaimed, and gave each child a warm hug. For Mary Anna, he said, "Thank you," in a way that made her heart happy, too.

Louisa's quick eyes noted the happy exchange between them. But even Louisa's old rivalry with Mary Anna couldn't begrudge her stepdaughter a moment of happiness. In her heart she knew Mary Anna to be a woman of great character. Mr. Strong was an honorable man.

*If they have feelings for one another, it's none of my business. Lord knows, there's enough sadness in this world. If Daniel doesn't come home, Amos would make a fine husband and father. And if my Peter doesn't come home and I were ten years younger, I'd do my best to win him away. Growing old by yourself is not a happy life.* The smile she felt never reached her lips as she pretended not to see anything.

Amos was quick to sense her melancholy mood. He didn't try to cheer her up, but spent his energies responding to the happiness of the children. She was grateful for his sensitivity to all their needs.

Mary Anna was exhausted by the time everyone went home. She had watched Christmas from inside a glass box that was tightly sealed away from all the joy.

The walls of the glass box began to thin a little as the calendar moved them inexorably toward spring.

Resuming her spring ritual revived her a bit. She got the garden started, and she and her sisters got the small fields plowed. There was still a little cottonseed left from the crop last year. It wasn't much, but it was something. There was no seed for the wheat. She had to use it for their bread, but there was a little corn seed. Carefully she dropped three kernels into each little hill and tapped them down, watering them as she moved down the row.

Late that evening she was mending Tump's worn pants when she heard a wagon rattling up.

She wrapped her shawl more tightly around her and opened the cabin door. In the darkness she could make out a man sitting up on the seat of the wagon but couldn't identify him. Stealthily she reached up to the shelf beside the door for the gun.

"Is this here the Thornton cabin?" the man called to her.

"Yes, it is. Is there something I can do for you?" The man looked harmless, but she still felt uneasy.

"Yes, ma'am, I could use a little help getting your husband outta the back here."

It took a few seconds for the words to register in her brain. "Your husband" ricocheted against her skull. When the message finally got to her feet, they began running toward the wagon.

"Is he alive?" she shouted breathlessly.

"Mostly, ma'am, but he's powerful sick."

For one horrible moment she thought the man in the wagon had played an evil trick on her. The man in the back of the wagon was only a sack of bones with a matted beard and sunken eyes that were closed.

"Daniel?" she said softly as she reached for the tangle of hair. "Daniel?" she repeated as she stroked the hair.

"Mary Anna. Is that you, Mary Anna?" The words were a mere whisper. "Are you real or just another of my dreams?"

"I'm real, my darling." She tried to hold back the tears as she and the man helped Daniel move out of the wagon.

He helped them a little and leaned heavily on the man as the two of them half walked and half carried Daniel into the cabin.

As they laid him on the bed, one sigh, made up of all the sighs he had uttered while he was gone, passed his cracked lips. "I made it" was all he said as he slipped into a deep sleep.

Mary Anna never heard the man quietly leave, never had the opportunity to thank him or even find out his name. All she knew at that moment was that Daniel had come home. And he was very sick. The chilling thought that he might die here at home made her shiver. Tenderly she laid two more quilts over him. Then she got a basin of warm water and began to wash his face.

It was the face of a stranger. His blue-black hair was streaked with gray, and he had grown a full beard, also streaked with gray. It covered the lower part of his face, hiding the jawline she should have been able to recognize. Both were matted and tangled, bearing no resemblance to the carefully groomed man she had sent away. His face was thin and the skin like parchment. Had he not called out her name, she would not have recognized him. She never would have found this man, for he bore no markings she remembered.

She sat on the bed all night watching him. He mumbled unintelligible things in his deep sleep, and she wiped away his many tears with gentle hands.

When dawn came, she made a nourishing soup for him, mashing the vegetables into nothingness to pour down his throat.

She woke him gently. "Daniel? Can you hear me?"

With tremendous effort, he opened his eyes. "Mary Anna? Is that you?" When he saw it was, he began to cry again, silently, the tears mixing with the warm soup she fed him.

Mary Anna's heart was breaking with the sight of him. For an instant she wished him dead rather than trapped in this body. *No*, she assured herself, *I can nurse him back to health. Help me, God. Help Daniel.*

Tump woke first and stumbled over to her sleepily. Seeing the man in bed, he asked, "Is that our grandpa?"

"No, Tump, this is your papa." She beckoned him closer.

"He's home?" He looked more closely and slipped his arms around his mother. "I'm glad he's home. We've all prayed for him a whole bunch." Anxiously he asked, "Is he going to be all right?"

"He needs time, son. He's been through an awful ordeal. He just needs time," she repeated.

Tump turned and ran for the bed he shared with Peter and the trundle where Betty slept. "Shhh," he admonished. "Come and see. Papa is home. Be real quiet. He's awful sick. He's been through an awful order."

Mary Anna smiled at Tump's translation of the word *ordeal*, but in a way Daniel had been through an awful order. An order to fight a war that had almost killed him.

The next time he awoke, she took off the rags he was wearing and was even more shocked by his wasted body. But she carefully sponged him off and covered his bony frame with clean clothes.

The children were obediently quiet and surprisingly thoughtful of her. Chores were done without asking, and there were only carefully whispered arguments.

Early in the morning, Louisa burst through the cabin door. When she saw the sleeping Daniel, she quieted her hurried footsteps to Mary Anna's side. "Has he said anything about Peter?" she whispered urgently.

"No," Mary Anna whispered back. "He hasn't." She saw Louisa's eyes redden.

"If Daniel looks like this, I can't bear to think what Peter could look like," Louisa cried. "He wasn't a young man when he left." A soft sob escaped her.

"Oh, Mary Anna, I'm so scared he's dead. The old fool. Why didn't he stay home with me? I need him. Not the South." She pulled out her ever-present lace handkerchief and blotted her eyes. "Please let me know the minute he says anything to you." Her eyes inventoried Daniel. "I'll be praying for Daniel, too. Mary Anna, I wouldn't have known it was him. He's got a long way to go to get his health back. I'll be back after work to help you."

Mary Anna started to protest, but she knew it would be useless. Louisa would stay until Daniel could tell her something about Peter.

Friends began arriving the first day with small packages of special food for Daniel's recovery and offers to spell her.

She graciously thanked them but knew she could never leave his side until she was sure he was out of danger.

The week passed with her sleeping lightly, instantly awake each time Daniel moved or spoke in his delirium. She laid her head against his chest and cradled his head when he had bad dreams and cried out.

Even with Louisa's help, she was limp with fatigue by the second week and had fallen into a deep sleep in spite of herself, when she felt a hand on her face. "Oh!" she gasped, frightened out of her wits.

"I'm sorry, I didn't mean to scare you. I only wanted to touch you." Daniel was looking at her through his stranger's eyes with all the love in the world shining through.

She grasped the hand and kissed it softly. She looked into the gaunt face of her husband and saw the love in his blue eyes. His mouth was smiling at her weakly.

"Hello." she said.

"Hello. I've been watching you while you slept. You looked like an angel from heaven itself."

"For a little while I thought that's where you were bound," she smiled.

"That's where I am, for sure."

She leaned over and tenderly kissed him. His mouth felt warm under hers, and the kiss familiar. Her Daniel was here. Safe. A silent stream of thanksgiving flowed from her heart straight to the throne of God for His goodness and mercy. Tears of complete joy plummeted down her face.

"Tears? For me? My true love cries when she's happy." Weakly he traced the path of tears to her chin and smiled. "You must have been saving up for a long time."

She sniffed heartily. "I thought you weren't ever coming back." Her eyes narrowed with a glint of anger. "You said you'd write. I never got a single letter!"

Shock registered in Daniel's eyes. "Neither did I!"

"Not even one?"

"Not even one." He sighed. "Guess I'm going to have to write an ugly letter to the post office about this." Then he grinned. "But they probably wouldn't ever get it either." They laughed and cried together, holding on tightly and exchanging words of love.

Daniel said with as much fervor as he could muster, "I intend to make the world's fastest recovery and claim my wife again." His hand fell from her face weakly. "Maybe I could use a little soup and some of that good bread you make. But no corn bread," he added bitterly. "I never want to see or smell corn bread again as long as I live."

Quickly she dashed the tears away and scrambled to get the food. She soaked the bread in the soup and spoon fed him.

"Hmm," he crooned, "this is manna from heaven."

He ate only half the contents of the bowl and then turned his head away from the spoon. "I'm so tired, Mary Anna. I can't seem to keep my eyes open." Instantly he was asleep.

Only then did she remember her promise to Louisa to ask about Peter. Late in the afternoon, Louisa came by and stayed until Daniel awoke again.

"I'm sorry, Louisa," he said sadly, "I can't tell you anything. We were separated right away, and I never saw him again." He saw the lines of worry that had aged her, deepen. "If I made it, though, he probably did, too. Don't give up. He'll come home," he tried to assure her.

On Sunday Mary Anna didn't leave Daniel to go to church as she usually did.

She dressed the children and sent them with an invitation for Amos to come after the service.

The door opened quietly, and the children filed in, bringing Amos with them.

Daniel was asleep. Mary Anna and Amos looked at each other across the room, and his eyes were at once sad and happy for her.

"God has answered your prayers, and I am happy that your waiting is over," he said softly.

She nodded in assent. "Daniel," she said, "wake up. There's someone I want you to meet."

She couldn't help but note the firm tread that brought Amos to Daniel's bedside, nor the strength of his frame.

Daniel opened his eyes.

"Daniel, this is our minister, Amos Strong. Mr. Strong, this is my husband, Daniel," she said formally.

Daniel offered his hand, which Amos took heartily. "Your wife has been an example to us all in her faith and patience. I thank God that He has sent you home safely. I'm sure in no time at all you'll be well and strong again."

"Thank you. It was good of you to come by." He eyed the antics of his children as they vied to stand beside Amos. "And I'm grateful for anything you might have done to help my family while I was away."

"It has been my good fortune to have dinner here occasionally. Each of the families takes turns feeding me. Your wife is a fine cook and an excellent mother. Her name should have been Ruth for her faithfulness to you and the children. You can be proud of the things she has done while you were away fighting for the cause." His eyes were clear and his words straightforward as he spoke to Daniel.

"Thank you for those kind words. I can only thank God I'm here." Daniel asked that a chair be brought so Amos could sit beside his bed.

"I don't want to tire you, Mr. Thornton."

"Please, I'd count it as a favor if you would stay awhile. You're the first person I remember being here as a guest."

Amos noted the gauntness and Daniel's weakness. "You've been through a soul-searing experience, haven't you?" he asked in a gentle voice.

Daniel met his gaze steadily. "Yes. And all for nothing," he added in an empty tone.

"Wars always seem to be for nothing. Some man somewhere dreams a dream and sends men to make it come true. I'm only sorry you had to be one of those men."

"You were smart not to go. It wouldn't have helped us," said Daniel without rancor.

"Mr. Thornton," said Amos sadly, "some men carry their wars with them all their lives. They have no need to fight another man's battle when they can't win their own." The terrible sadness in Amos's eyes spoke more eloquently than words of his tragedy could.

Softly Mary Anna said, "Amos lost his wife and four children to the Comanche."

If Daniel noticed she called Amos by his first name, he didn't show surprise at the familiarity. He recognized only the pain. "I'm sorry."

"It's a common tale told by many men today. May I call you Daniel? I feel I know you so well from all the things Mary Anna has told me about you."

"I'd be pleased."

As the men conversed, Mary Anna prepared supper and watched the two of them. It felt odd to see them together. She loved both of them in different ways. One had been her husband for eleven years and one had been her emotional support for almost a year and a half. Did Daniel feel he had a rival in Amos? It didn't appear so. In her heart she knew he didn't.

When supper was served, Daniel surprised them all by insisting he sit at the table. It was a merry meal, but the children were obviously more comfortable with Amos than with their long-absent father.

Seeking to prove the importance of Amos, Tump told Daniel proudly, "Mr. Strong gave me a pocketknife, Papa. I can make things with it. He said he would show me how to skin a rabbit, but we never found one," he added.

"Maybe when it gets warmer and I'm stronger, we can go hunting for one," Daniel said kindly.

Not to be outdone, Peter said, "Sometimes Mr. Strong lets me ride with him on his horse. And he brought Betty a cornhusk doll." His eyes glowed with the pleasure of these memories.

Gently Amos said to Daniel, "I know you will forgive me for borrowing your family in place of my own. They have been a great comfort to me."

Daniel studied the man sitting at his table. He was a man who had stayed home, a man who knew his family better than he did. "I'm obliged to you for looking out for them." He hoped he meant the words as strongly as he uttered them, for he felt a stab of jealousy at the way the children reacted to Amos. Each time the children told him of the things that had happened while he was gone, it seemed to include Amos. Perhaps they were only trying to catch him up on all the things that had happened, but in each event Amos played a major role. A dark part of his soul shouted, "And what did he do for Mary Anna?"

His love answered, "She loves me. Of that I'm sure."

Soon he was too tired to feel much of anything. "If you'll excuse me, I think I'll lie down for a bit."

Amos helped him back to bed. "I do apologize for staying so long. We'll have plenty of time to get to know one another better. Sleep well, Daniel." He shook the thin hand offered him and took his leave. Daniel fell asleep even as Amos was saying his thanks and good-byes to Mary Anna and the children.

"Thank you, Amos" was all she said to him as he left the warmth of the cabin. When she finally got into their bed, she crept up against her husband and put her arm across his bony chest, grateful he was there.

By June Daniel was up and moving about, though he rested frequently. He had been furloughed and given the job of guarding the provisions for the Southern Army.

"That's really funny," he told her. "I can barely take care of myself. How do they expect me to gather and guard provisions?"

Her laugh was not a joyful one. "There's precious little to guard. We send what we can, but I doubt it will help much."

At the first of July, Mary Anna began to think of their anniversary coming up on the twenty-seventh. *I'm twenty-seven. We've been married for eleven years.* Since the war she rarely spent any more time in front of the mirror than it took to arrange her long hair in its usual large bun. But today she took a good look.

*I've aged,* she thought ruefully. *Isn't that how life goes? In those eleven years, we've done a lot of living. Not much of it easy, either.* She leaned closer to the mirror and stroked the hair at her temples. *Each of these gray hairs represents a day of my life. I've earned them.* But when she looked for wrinkles, she found few. *My face looks thin and drawn, though. "Life is what happens to you while you're making plans,"* she quoted Louisa's favorite saying. She moved away from the mirror, satisfied that she didn't look as old as she felt.

The strain of nursing Daniel, taking care of her family, and working at the hotel showed in her eyes, but her sturdy Irish body was still strong.

Daniel didn't object to her working at the hotel. They had no money but what she made. It made him angry to see her tiredness, but there was no alternative right now.

Mary Anna wondered, *Won't things ever be good again?* She didn't expect things to be easy. Life for her never had been. But she was tired of all the bad war news and seeing her husband only a shadow of what he had once been. She hated the food shortages and having to give up part of their skimpy stores for the cause. There wasn't a good horse or mule in the county. Everything had gone into the war effort.

And she hated the unnatural lack of young men in the town. A few more veterans had managed to come home, broken and ill. Only remnants of the glorious manhood that had been sent out had come back to them. Those were horribly maimed or sick.

One of her brothers had come home, his right pant leg empty and the stump a sickening sore. He had been only fifteen when he left, but he came home an old man with shocked eyes. And still both sides demanded more men and materials.

At night when she slept beside Daniel, Mary Anna dreamed of their cabin in the quiet woods of Erath County. Horses grazed as she milked the cow. Indians ceased to be a menace as she walked in the woods to gather the first sweet berries of the spring. And she remembered the strong body of her husband pressing against her in the glow of their lovemaking.

But when she woke in the morning, she dealt with the reality of the day. She took careful pains to feed Daniel well, always giving him the best food she could find.

"Breakfast, Daniel," she called as she put hot cereal on the table for him. He had been outside since he got up, and the man who walked through the door had a smile as big as Texas on his face.

"You look beautiful!" she breathed.

"A long bath, a good close shave, clean clothes, clean living, a loving wife and family," he grinned. "What more could any man want?"

She studied him carefully. "I do believe you're looking better every day. Hmm, handsome and like my Daniel today."

He came inside and sat at the table with his family. "Kids, do you know what today is?"

To the negative shake of their heads, he said, "Today is the day your mother and I got married eleven years ago. And in keeping with the spirit of that day, I've brought your mother something." With a flourish he produced a small, brightly wrapped package.

"Daniel! However—where—how did you—?" she stuttered.

"Just open it. It isn't the diamond I promised. Not yet," he warned.

Mary Anna smiled broadly and laughed with delight. "Peppermint! How did you manage to find peppermint candy?"

"Amos gets around. He found it for me." He was as pleased as a little boy with his first girlfriend.

Mary Anna shared the candy with her wide-eyed children. It was eaten slowly and licked carefully.

"Mama, have you always known Daddy?" asked Tump.

Mary Anna smiled at Daniel. "Yes, I think so. At least in my heart." She saw Tump had no idea what she was talking about, so she said, "He came to my hometown, right here in Tennessee Colony, when we were both very young." Her eyes were dancing with happy memories. "He was the handsomest man I'd ever seen, with that gray cowboy hat and his smooth manners."

"I knew right off she was the woman for me," Daniel added. "I met her in the store and offered to buy her candy." He tipped his head at Mary Anna and added,

"Peppermint, I think it was."

"You know it was, you rascal."

"I courted her for some time before I was able to convince her to marry me and go west."

Mary Anna's mind skipped over the part where she and Daniel had disagreed for a long time over his early hatred of the Indians. It almost caused them not to marry.

She skipped it because it was painful and he was not the Daniel she knew today. Now he was the Daniel who had renewed his faith in the Lord and faced the consequences of going to trial for being in a group of men who raided an Indian reservation and killed thirteen people. That was the old Daniel. Now she had her beloved Daniel back. Ah, the Lord was indeed good.

Daniel spoke of their trip to Erath County and how they had built their dream cabin on the Brazos.

Mary Anna could plainly see that all those early dreams had not died. She knew they would be going back as soon as Daniel was able. It made her heart beat fast with joy. Pioneering, hard as it was, was the dream they shared.

They told the children more of their adventure stories until the children were wide-eyed. Mary Anna finally broke up the reverie and shooed them off to bed.

That night Daniel had another present for her. For the first time since he had come home, he held her close to him. It was a tender night. Two people who had known each other for so long and had been through so much came together with gentleness and the smoldering passion pent up for so long. When at last Daniel slept, Mary Anna felt a wave of relief wash over her. The war hadn't broken him after all. She knew he would regain his strength and they would go on with their lives as before. More sons and daughters would come out of their love, and they would be able to build their kingdom after all.

Tennessee Colony wouldn't be their home. She began to think of it as a place where they had paused to rest and gather their strength before tackling the wilderness again. But she said nothing of this to Daniel. She offered herself to him each time he approached her, and he grew stronger with the passing of the days in the healing power of her love.

She threw away the rags of his uniform, keeping only the hat with the shiny gold tassels hanging rakishly from the crown. He wore it when he had to take his turn guarding the military provisions.

When the fall came, she thought he might speak about moving back to Erath County, but he resolutely helped pick their small cotton crop. They kept some of it with which Mary Anna might make clothes and sold the rest for a small profit.

The crops they gathered were poor ones, but the food would probably see them through the winter. Daniel hunted as often as he could, and they had smoked meat for the winter. He took the boys fishing and brought home fresh fish to eat and some to salt down. They took along one of Soldier's pups, Shep, to train him. Soldier made sure the pup behaved as he should.

When he was there, Amos was a big help. The men sweated and fought the land together. And their friendship flourished.

One night as Mary Anna and Daniel lay cuddled in bed, Daniel said, "I really do like Amos. He's a fine man." He felt Mary Anna nod her head against his shoulder.

"Yes, he was very good to us while you were gone."

"The way the children act, they sort of thought of him as a father, didn't they?"

Again he felt her nod in agreement. She lifted her head from his shoulder and looked in the dim light into his eyes. "But I never let them forget about you, and that I was sure you were coming home."

Softly he kissed her. "I know."

She lay her head back down on his shoulder.

Daniel sighed deeply with both contentment and acceptance. "I know that Amos loves you. I know you love me. And if I hadn't come back, it would have been all right with me for you to have married him."

With her heart overflowing with love, Mary Anna's words were pure and honest. "I wanted you to come back with all my heart."

"I know. Maybe that's why the Lord let me live. And after seeing you and Amos together, I know you waited for me." He grinned in the darkness. "I sure do feel sorry for Amos. My homecoming must have been very hard on him."

"You're awful!" she whispered.

"I know. And I'm home." And he reached for her.

## Chapter 5

The soft budding of the leaves on the trees brought tears to Daniel's eyes, and the sight of a butterfly riding the soft spring breezes on a flower caused an ache of happiness in his chest. Life was so sweet. His ears were tuned to every nuance of the changing season.

He was proud of his children. Tump had grown so tall. He was intelligent and ever thoughtful of his mother. Peter had lost all signs of babyhood and was helpful when it came time to till their fields.

But it was Betty who remained a constant delight to him. She was round faced and had long, dark red curls that Mary Anna kept in ringlets by wrapping them in rags at night.

Betty would crawl up into his lap and look up at him with her blue eyes, his own he realized in surprise, and smile her sweet smile, and Daniel would melt like butter in a hot sun. He wanted to pull her to him and squeeze her hard, somehow hoping that with that act he could keep anything from ever hurting or frightening her.

He watched his wife and children through the eyes of a man who couldn't see enough of them if he lived to be a hundred years old. He had come home almost dead, and now he was filled with the new life of spring. He could feel renewed strength moving from the warming earth through the soles of his feet and spreading up into the rest of his body.

His love for Mary Anna became a fevered desire. He could barely wait sometimes until the children were safely in bed and he could kiss and pull her against him. He wanted to feel her soft skin against his. He wanted to blot out all the ugliness of the war with the beauty of his passion, and she responded with an openness that astounded him. The heat of their passion seared the wounds of war for him, and there was only peace in his dreams now.

He had a burning need to see new life after the stench of death had finally left his nostrils. The earth burst forth with verdant life, and it soon became clear that Mary Anna would bear a child in September.

She was still helping out at the hotel part time with the cooking. Sometimes her family came there for their supper.

She was serving Daniel and the children one night when a traveler joined their table. He was dressed in expensive clothes and was well groomed.

"I'm Bartholomew Brown." He had good manners and waited to be asked to sit down. The usual pleasantries were covered, and he told them he was from Washington.

Daniel felt uncomfortable with this stranger. He covertly watched the man as they dined together. Brown's face was thin, and his eyes shifty-looking. The big diamond ring on his finger glittered each time he moved his big hand to eat. He had all the latest war news, but his voice was nasal and irritated the ears of those around him.

In spite of that, Daniel listened carefully to his conversation. He also guarded his temper, for the man was obviously a Union sympathizer.

"No doubt you have heard of Sherman's march through the South to the sea. Burned his way into history." Brown took a large spoonful of Mary Anna's hearty soup, careful not to get any spots on his costly cravat.

"Yes, we have. And of the gallant Wilderness Battle in Virginia."

Brown lifted a sparse eyebrow. He knew he was in the presence of Southern supporters, but he was so arrogant, he continued. "Yes, it's only a matter of time. The South is bloody and bowed. The death toll is staggering and the devastation complete. I can't imagine why they don't throw down their arms and surrender. This winter will surely break them."

Mary Anna warned Daniel's more stormy eyes with her own. Then she said softly to the crude man, "We are Southerners, Mr. Brown. If you are to sit at our table and eat our food, please remember that."

Mr. Brown had enough good manners and good sense to color slightly. "Yes, of course. I thought it was a foregone conclusion that you people knew the end is in sight."

"If we do, it is not your place to remind us of it," Mary Anna said coolly. "I'll send your dessert to your room." She dismissed him as she would a rude child.

Hastily he rose, looking nervously at Daniel, and in the process, he bumped the table, sloshing a bit of soup on his resplendent trousers. He didn't take the time to blot them, but made his way quickly up the staircase to his room.

Daniel leaned back in his chair, playing angrily with his dinner knife. "Why didn't you just let me pop him one?"

"Because I don't want anything broken in here," she said tiredly.

Daniel leaned forward with his elbows on the table. "He's right about the South. Winter will break them. I can't even imagine the hunger and privation of those men."

Mary Anna wanted to ask him why the South kept fighting, but it would stir up old wounds better left alone. Silently she served the baked apples.

The children had been quiet at the table, but there were a lot of questions in Tump's young eyes. He timidly asked, "Why doesn't Mr. Lincoln tell them to stop?"

Daniel ran a hand through Tump's hair. "I don't think he can. I don't think there is any one man who can stop this thing now."

But when they heard that the final battle had been fought in April and General Lee, carefully dressed, had met with General Grant at Appomattox in the McLean home to formally surrender, Daniel wept with the rest of the South. In his heart he was glad the awful slaughter was finally over, but the waste was too awesome to comprehend.

And then the day came when news of Lincoln's assassination ran like wildfire through the town. Some cheered openly. Others wept.

Lincoln had been killed five days after the war ended.

Daniel received his parole, along with the other men who had fought in battles against the Union, and he prepared to work as did the others, to rebuild the broken country.

He rejoiced with the birth of their son Henry Clay on September 9, 1865.

The town gradually gathered its men back home. The trickle of broken humanity that made it back were worse than pitiful.

Mary Anna's father showed up, older and angry. He had almost recovered from a wound to his arm. It was only God's grace that had kept the arm from being amputated, and though it pained him greatly, he was thankful to still have it when other men had lost so many limbs.

None of the returning men were healthy or whole. Even if a man got home with all his limbs intact, his body and spirit were sick with the gruesomeness of battle. Daniel felt the world would never be the same again. There was no way to escape the vacant eyes and the dirty bandaged stumps of the men. Everywhere he looked he saw death again, and it made him sick. The elation of Henry's birth was almost erased.

The gloomy days of the winter closed in on them, but the town had several activities to keep the doldrums away. There were taffy pulls and quilting bees, and every holiday was celebrated. One of the advantages of living in a populated area was that the Thorntons could attend most of the socials, enjoying the company of their friends.

By May, Mary Anna was certain she carried another child. At first she was a little distressed. If she was right, the babies would be fifteen months apart. But Daniel had been so enlivened by Henry's birth, she couldn't help but be pleased.

She waited until she had nursed Henry and put the other children in their beds. She took down her hair and sat in the rocker. "Come brush my hair for me," she asked Daniel, and the love she felt for him was burning in the look she offered him.

He sat on a low stool behind her and pulled the silver-backed brush that had been her mother's carefully through the long, clean strands, feeling the sensuousness and smelling her scent. When he could bear it no longer, he took her in his arms and carried her to bed.

"Daniel," she whispered, "I'm going to have another son."

"So soon!" he breathed against her mouth.

"We need a reminder that life can be sweet and that it goes on, even in the midst of horror. A child is a promise for tomorrow."

He moved back from her to look into her eyes. "You aren't upset at another one so quickly?"

"A little surprised but not upset. It's your child, Daniel. Our future. Part of us conceived in our love for each other. How could I be upset?"

He chuckled softly. "Not all women have your view on that subject, I think."

"Not all women have a man like you for a husband. I want to have your babies." She ran her fingers gently through his soft beard. "When I'm pregnant, I feel like Mother Earth." He smiled, remembering the spring. "When I finally hold that child, I feel hopefulness and wonder what this child will do for the family. Each new baby brings with it so many possibilities."

"I don't think it will be a boy," he said. "I think it's time for another girl." He kissed her slowly.

"It doesn't matter." She returned his kiss. "But I still think it will be a boy."

William Luther was born December 11. It took Mary Anna longer to recover from this birth. Willie was a good baby, but Daniel was careful of Mary Anna, remembering when she had been so sick that he had nearly lost her that one winter. He was the one who took care of the children's various illnesses.

It was he who stayed awake all night after Peter had been bitten by the rattlesnake and had been delirious. Mary Anna had made the poultice and then fallen asleep in her chair beside the boy's bed. Daniel carried Mary Anna to their bed and stayed with the boy himself, praying that the chewing tobacco poultice would work. He didn't intend to build any fences around any cemeteries if he could help it, and he fought off death the way he had in the battles of the war, with prayer. He knew he had won by the morning when the boy was sleeping quietly and the swelling around the fang marks had stopped getting larger. Together Daniel and Mary Anna nursed Peter back to health and watched the others more carefully lest they get hurt, too.

As 1867 began, Mary Anna sensed a restlessness beginning in Daniel. He was strong again and working the land, but she recognized the signs. Daniel was ready to go pioneering again.

There was no real government in Texas, only the chaos of the Union trying to reorganize. General Sheridan was the commander of the Military Division of the Southwest, quartered in New Orleans. The Freedmen Bureau had been organized by the War Department to help the Negro adjust to his new lifestyle, and its policies were being dreadfully abused. Daniel had tried to hire someone to help him with the farming, but he had no cash to pay. Too many of the newly freed Negroes expected a life of plenty. They were angered by the promises that hadn't come true.

Carpetbaggers had taken over everywhere, and the economy was in terrible shape. President Andrew Johnson's stringent policies did nothing to aid the healing of the North or the South, and discontent was the tenor of the day. The crime rate in Tennessee Colony was rising with the confusion, and Mary Anna was afraid to shop by herself in the town where she had spent so many happy times.

She wasn't surprised when Daniel came in red faced with anger after a visit to the general store.

"Things are going from bad to worse." His jaw was clenched, and a white line played along his mouth.

Mary Anna got him a cup of sumac tea as he threw himself into a chair at the table. "What happened?" She got a cup for herself and joined him.

"How am I supposed to pay cash when I don't have any? The Confederate money I have is no good. I can't trade for the things I need, and I don't have any gold. The town's crawling with freedmen who won't work, and I need help. The carpetbaggers are strutting around fat and sassy and looking down their noses at those of us who fought with the South."

His face was red with anger. "Saw that charming Mr. Brown. He's now the owner of a store and has already announced he is running for public office." Daniel practically shuddered. "I can't stand the thought of that kind of person holding public office in our town."

"It's time, Daniel," she said quietly.

He looked at her long and hard, but with rising hope. "You know what it means if we move back to Erath County?"

"I know. We'll be back to the problems with the Indians," she said.

"It will be worse this time around. The military can't patrol the whole frontier. Lots of men are gone from the area. We'll be on our own."

She took his hand. "If we stay here, maybe in a few years we'll be able to make it. But I'm beginning to feel hemmed in again. You need a place where you can have a chance at making a good living. We'll have nothing to leave to the children if we stay here."

He kissed her hand. "You truly are the other half of my heart." He looked deeply into her eyes. "I won't lie to you. It will be hard. But there are cattle roaming all over that place." His face and hands became animated. "We could get rich in a short time if we're willing to work hard and contend with the Indians. It's really what I want to do."

There again was the face of the young man she had married. The years and sorrows slipped from his frame as he dreamed his dream. The two of them were not the fresh-faced innocents of so long ago. They were world wise and knew what lie ahead of them.

"I want us to pray about this, Daniel. The Lord will let us know if we're to go back or stay here. He has always led us in the past," Mary Anna said solemnly.

Daniel gathered her into his arms. "I know. I didn't always know that, but I do know it now." He closed his eyes, and still holding Mary Anna close, he prayed. "Lord, we need to know what You want us to do. We think the best thing is to go back to the Brazos River and start over. Would you please let us somehow know if that's the right thing? We'll start working toward that goal. If You approve, make the way smooth. If You don't approve and want us to stay here, make it very clear to us that we are to stay. Amen."

Mary Anna sighed. "That's plain enough. Now we'll start getting ready and see what happens." She looked up into Daniel's blue eyes. "I never thought I'd live to see the day when you would be asking God what to do next. You've always been such an independent man. And now these past years I've watched you change from a skeptic to a man of God. And I praise God for your change."

"I know you spent a lot of prayer time on me," he smiled. "I seem to need to find out things the hard way. Living on the Brazos the first time, going through the war, those can be powerful teachers of who is in control of life and death. I know in my heart that things don't just happen. There is a plan and sense behind everything. Even though I don't always know what it is, I know God is doing something. I have learned to be a patient man and listen to what He's saying."

Mary Anna strengthened her hug around Daniel's neck and cried softly in his shirt collar. "I love you, and I thank God for the day He gave us to each other."

"I feel the same way about you," he said softly. Daniel heard a little giggle coming from behind him. He grinned at Mary Anna. "I think I hear a mouse over there in the corner," he said in a stage whisper. "Maybe you'd better get the cheese and I'll get the broom." He turned and moved toward the sound.

"No, no," Betty shrieked. "It's me!" She laughed hard when Daniel caught her up in his arms and whirled her around the room.

"Why, it is a little mouse with red hair. What were you doing over there?"

"Watching you and Mama hug," she grinned. "It was nice."

"Well, I certainly enjoyed it," Daniel laughed. "Now why don't you go help your mama get our food on the table?"

As they had their supper that night, Mary Anna said, "Do you think Louisa and Papa would want to go with us?"

Daniel shook his head and took a deep drink of buttermilk. "I doubt it. Your father is still pretty weak from the war. And I think Louisa might tie him up if he tried. She loves living here with all the social events." He looked at Mary Anna soberly. "You still want to go?"

"We're going unless the Lord tells us differently," she said confidently.

As they gathered the things together that they would need for their trip, everything went relatively smoothly. Even Louisa and Peter agreed it would be a good move. Peter seemed a bit mournful about their leaving, but he was not in good health and told them, "Even the thought of traveling that far makes me tired. I wish you God's blessings and good hunting."

Each night Mary Anna and Daniel measured the day's activities.

"I do think He wants us to go," Daniel said positively.

"It looks that way to me, too. It will be a completely different trip this time, won't it?"

"How?" Daniel asked.

"I feel we're on a mission this time with God's blessing. Before I was going with you because I loved you and your dream of pioneering. But now I feel the Lord has something He wants us to do. I don't know what," she admitted, "but He hasn't told us not to go."

"How will we know what we're supposed to do?"

"We'll wait and see what happens. It's all I know to do, unless He sends an angel messenger with a letter," Mary Anna laughed. "We live our life and pray for His guidance—we pray every day."

"I have been. Especially about the Indians."

Mary Anna thought back to Daniel's earlier hatred of everything about the Indians because of his grandfather's murder and their experiences at the hands of the Comanche the first time they lived in Erath County. There was too much to remember, but the feelings were still there. "Do you think you can live in peace with them?"

He hesitated and cleared his throat. "All I can tell you is that I'll try. I have changed my feelings about them. I see them as real people. What I'm worried about is how they will treat us." He looked steadily at her. "You know I'll have to defend us if we're attacked."

"But the intent would be different this time, wouldn't it?"

"Yes. I have no vendetta with them now. I want to be through with all the killing. I've had enough killing to last many men many lifetimes."

His eyes got that tired, old-man look in them. The one that always came when he spoke of the war.

She walked into his arms and hugged him fiercely. "I love you. I've loved you from the first time I ever saw you. But I love you more now. All the things I've prayed for, all the things we've been through, all the time we've spent together have changed both of us. For the better, I think. This time on the frontier will be different." She grinned up at him. "If nothing else, we're both older and wiser." He returned her grin.

"Yep. Those Comanche had better watch out. They're up against some mighty smart people now."

Reluctantly she turned loose of him and turned to finish packing. "It won't take me too long to get things ready."

Daniel half dragged and half carried the brass-bound trunk out to the wagon.

"Here, neighbor, let me help you with that," offered Mr. Gibson from the house next door. "We're going to miss you and your family." He offered his hand. "We wish you God's blessings on your new life out there."

"Thank you, Mr. Gibson."

While they talked outside by the wagon, Mary Anna was standing in the bedroom holding a quilt. She smoothed the soft pattern with gentle fingers and thought of the meaning of each of the pieces of material. She was literally holding the fabric of her life. Pieces of material from her dresses and the boys' clothes formed into lovely patterns. The new trousers she had made for Daniel after he came back home. A warm coat sewn during the spring for Betty from a soft blue. The quilt was a picture book of the past few years. And now it was to be taken to the frontier.

*I wonder how it will be this time. Starting over again. When does one get too old to start over again? My enthusiasm is more for Daniel than for me. It is the right thing to do, but my heart is not in it the way it was when we were first married. Gotten soft in your old age, eh? I can't tell Daniel about my reservations. He will shrivel up and die here in town. He needs his dream and I need him. The Lord must want us to go, because He hasn't done anything to keep us from it. Lord, give me the strength I need to help Daniel with his dream. Make it mine, too.* She smiled after praying and placed the quilt on the kitchen table. Then she used it to wrap another precious item. Her medicine cabinet.

Daniel had found some cherrywood and made her a beautiful little cabinet filled with drawers in which to keep her dried herbs. There were tiny brass pulls on each drawer. She had filled it up with all the herbs she thought they would need to stay well on the frontier. It would be her duty to keep the family well and to nurse them when they became ill. After the cabinet had been wrapped carefully, she laid it in the cradle Daniel had made. Sighing, she carried the wooden cradle out to the quickly filling wagon.

Friends and relatives had given what they could spare in the way of staples, and Daniel had worked out some things in trade. Once again all their worldly possessions were packed into one wagon. This time, though, there would be no cattle to drive before them. Only the milk cow was tied on to the back. The cattle and horses would come later. That was the dream: to get the ranch going and productive with horses and cattle. There was a desperate need for beef in the North, and there were cattle ranging wide over the Texas plains. All a man had to do was gather them together. And keep them from the Indians.

The children were excited at the prospect of traveling. Tump in particular remembered the adventures from a child's perspective, forgetting the real dangers he'd witnessed. His grandfather had proudly marked one of the horses he gave as Tump's. But it was Daniel who gave him the one thing his heart desired above all things: his very own rifle.

Daniel worked with him, teaching him how to shoot and care for it. "You're my righthand man, now," he had told his son. Tump straightened his shoulders and held his head a little higher with Daniel's fatherly trust in him.

Mary Anna gathered the children together, along with her parents, and Daniel led them in prayer as they left for the hostile frontier. "Father, once again we need Your help as we head out to try and make our dream of a ranch come true. We pray that it is Your will for us to do this, and that You would bless our efforts and keep us safe from all harm and danger. All these things we ask in Your Son's name. Amen."

He put his hat on and started lifting kids into the wagon. Peter, now nine, was a little jealous of Tump's getting to ride with his father on his own horse, but Mary Anna let him drive the wagon to salvage some of his manly pride. Betty was six, and she helped keep up after little Henry, almost two, and baby Willie.

Daniel moved his horse up beside the wagon seat and said to Mary Anna, "We'll do it just like before. I'll ride ahead and scout the area. I'll fire the rifle three times if there's any danger. You're well armed. Don't be afraid to use the weapons," he added grimly. Their eyes met, and many silent messages passed between them. She nodded her head in agreement and leaned toward him for a last kiss.

Daniel leaned back into his saddle, the squeak of the leather a pleasant sound to his ears, and said, "We're off to the Promised Land. God be with us!"

Peter whistled to the horses and slapped the reins across their backs. The two dogs began barking joyously in all the excitement. Mary Anna turned and gave a last wave to her father and Louisa. Her eyes swept quickly across the town, memorizing the buildings and saying good-bye to its comforts. Something deep inside her wanted to say, "No, let's don't do this again." And something else said, "Follow your husband to his dream."

She thought of Virginia and Caleb West. Would they still be there? Virginia hadn't wanted to come to the wilderness, but she had followed her husband. And she, like Mary Anna, had left tiny graves and shed many tears in her loneliness. Mary Anna and Virginia's friendship had flourished, each fed by similar trials and happiness. What had happened to her since the war?

Daniel rode ahead, sometimes out of sight of the wagon. One day as he topped a bluff, he saw what he had hoped he never would again. A wagon lay on its side at the bottom of a dry ravine. A man lay sprawled as he had in his last agony. He had an arrow in his chest and had been scalped. His wife lay half under the wrecked vehicle. She, too, had been killed and scalped.

There was no sign of any children. Daniel knew if there had been any, they had been taken. He dug a large grave and said a few words over the tragic couple.

He stayed close to Mary Anna and their wagon for the next few days and tried to hide his edginess from her, but he saw no more signs of the raiders.

"You're not straying very far from the wagon. Do you miss me, Daniel?" Mary Anna asked lightly. Then more quietly she asked, "Did you see Indian signs?" Her sharp eyes sought his under the shaded brim of his hat.

"Yes." He tried hard not to remember what he had seen.

"What did you see?"

"A husband and wife who will sleep together forever now." He dipped his head slightly, and the shade completely covered his eyes.

"Oh. I'll be extra careful." She glanced to her side where the rifle lay within easy reach. They had packed what she thought was more than enough ammunition, and it was within easy reach, too.

Often Mary Anna turned to her sustaining solace—prayer. There was always comfort in talking with her Lord, but it did not replace vigilance.

"Thank the Lord," she breathed when they spotted a lonely cabin. "A safe place to camp for the night." There was no need to confer with Daniel. She headed straight for the log cabin.

A one-legged man came out of the front door carrying a rifle loosely in the hand that he wasn't using to support himself on his crutch. He waited until they got close enough to hear him and then called out, "Howdy." His eagle eyes saw a family and he relaxed slightly. There was less danger than in a single male. He watched the dogs who were in an alert stance.

"Howdy, yourself," Daniel said. He sat loosely in the saddle with his hand close to his pistol. "Mind if we spend the night here on your property?"

"Nope. Hep yourself to the water in the well. Iffen you're a mind to, you can sleep on the straw in the barn in back. Sorry I ain't got no beds fer ya. Came back from the war and found my cabin had been stripped bare as a baby's bottom. Ain't been able to get around to making anything yet."

Daniel nodded his understanding. "We thank you for you hospitality." There was instant rapport between these two veterans. They spoke volumes with their eyes.

The man shifted uncomfortably on the crutch. "Gettysburg," he said.

Daniel nodded again, but he didn't ask which side the man was on. It didn't matter anymore. They were brothers by the simple act of staying alive in such an awful time. "I'm Daniel Thornton, and this is my family. We're going back to around Stephenville."

"Willard Abbacrombie."

Daniel tipped his hat, and Mary Anna smiled at the ragged man.

When she began cooking over the campfire behind the cabin, she wasn't surprised to see the man come out. He limped over to the fire and tried not to look hungry.

"Them beans smell mighty good, ma'am."

Mary Anna's heart went out to the starved-looking man. "You're welcome to have some supper with us. And your wife, too, of course," she added.

"I live alone" was all he said as he eased his stringy frame to a log Daniel had rolled up for them to sit on.

"You live so far from everyone. Is that the way you want it?" Daniel asked as he sat down across from the man.

"I did at first. I'd had all the company I'd ever wanted after the war. It seemed so peaceful out here." He glanced carefully at the children playing around the wagon, and he lowered his voice. "Now I know why it is so quiet. Them Injuns is running wild. No soldiers to corral them." His eyebrows crunched up in concern. "You got to be real careful out here. In some ways it's more cruel now than ever." He accepted a plate of beans and campfire bread from Mary Anna. "Truth be told, I've been waiting for someone to come along so's I could hook up with them." The look in his eyes was shy as he asked softly, "Would you mind me tagging along? I have what's left of a horse. I can help keep watch and do odd jobs to make the trip easier."

"It'd be good to have another man along," Daniel said kindly.

That night as they slept in the barn, Daniel said to Mary Anna, "Things have really changed since the first time we came out here. There wasn't a cabin from the time we left Tennessee Colony until we got to Dripping Springs."

She laughed softly. "And we built that one." She rolled over closer to him. "Those were good days, weren't they?"

Daniel's fingers played with a lock of her hair. "Yes, they were. Innocent days. A hundred lifetimes ago."

"Do you still want to go to Stephenville?"

He was silent for a while. "Yes. Things will always be different. Life is that way. But we're going into this thing with a lot more living behind us. I still think this part of Texas is where we can make our living." He smiled in the darkness. "Why, who knows? We might even get rich."

"We are rich."

"I knew you would say that." He sighed softly and nestled more deeply into the straw.

# Chapter 6

The weather stayed good for most of the trip, but when it did rain, it nearly washed them away. The children were huddled in the damp wagon, and Mary Anna was driving the team from under a heavy tarp set up like a small tent over her. Daniel and Willard had on their slickers, and the rain ran from their hat brims in rivulets.

"I'm worried about fording the Trinity," he shouted to Willard over the thunder.

Willard nodded and shouted back, "Let's head for that stand of trees and make camp." It was futile to try to hold a conversation at this point.

They unfolded the tent Mary Anna used and attached it to the wagon bed. Everyone huddled under the makeshift shelter.

Tump said miserably, "Cold supper tonight."

"I'm afraid so, son," Daniel said sympathetically.

Then he and Willard made plans for crossing the Trinity.

When they did get to the river, Willard whooped. "I'll be double dipped in chocolate sauce! Look at that purty sight. It's running smooth and low!"

"Praise God!" added Mary Anna.

Their work was far from over, but with the river calm, the crossing was accomplished with minimum trouble.

Then they hit the Brazos.

Willard and Daniel stopped their horses well away from the fast-running current. "I was afraid of this," Daniel said.

"I guess our luck was too good to hold," said Willard.

Mary Anna climbed down from the wagon and walked over to the men, still sitting on their horses. "Want to camp first and make a run at it first thing in the morning?"

Daniel squinted at the sky. "Don't think we'd better take the chance. It might rain some more tonight, and we'd be stuck here for weeks."

It was around four in the afternoon, and there wasn't much light left in the day. Everyone hurriedly helped lighten the wagon and made small rafts to float some of their things across.

They discussed the safest way to get the children across. "I'm afraid the horses will founder in the water with the extra weight. Better to keep them in the wagon,

I think," said Daniel.

"It'll be hard enough for the horses to get us across without the kids. I agree," said Willard.

Daniel looked hard at Mary Anna. "Can you drive the wagon across?"

Mary Anna was clearly frightened. "Yes. But can we secure it somehow with ropes on the other side and sort of ferry it across?"

"You've got a good head on your shoulders, woman. We'll give it a try. And everyone pray hard. This is going to be a humdinger of a project," Daniel said.

The plan was played out a piece at a time. The men tied ropes on the little rafts and swam their horses across, where they secured the ropes from the wagon to the trees pulley-fashion. Then Mary Anna and the children rode the wagon across, helped along with the ropes to keep them from being pushed downstream.

By the time they reached the other side, Mary Anna's arms ached with the strain of urging the horses into the swift water. Daniel helped her down from the wagon seat, and she fell against him. "I hope I never have to do that again!"

"Me, too," Daniel said grimly. Everyone pitched in to help prepare a good hot meal. Then Willard volunteered to keep first watch while the others fell asleep almost before they had finished their meal.

Willard was uneasy about the night. It didn't feel friendly. He felt it was watching the little camp with hateful eyes, and he was extra careful of every little sound and movement. Soldier and Shep prowled around, adding to his edginess. By the time Daniel came to take his turn, Willard was shaking with fatigue.

Willard's whispered warnings sharpened Daniel's watch, too.

He was sure there was someone out there watching them, but he couldn't pinpoint any one specific place. He felt surrounded, and he silently prayed for protection.

In the morning when he and Willard were hitching up the horses, they found moccasin prints not far from where the team had been hobbled. They exchanged knowing looks.

"I'd say we're in for some excitement if we're not real careful," said Daniel. "I wonder why the dogs didn't bark?"

"Kind of a lucky thing they didn't find them. They'd have their throats cut before they could git out a single bark. Tonight we'll tether the horses to the wagon. Better do some sleeping in the saddle today if you kin." Willard looked haggard and worried.

"Willard, do you believe in God? Trust in Him to keep you safe?"

Willard didn't answer right away. "I guess I do. I made it through the war, though I lost my leg. Why?"

"You'd rest a lot better if you could put your trust in Him. The load of fear we're carrying with us right now is too heavy for either or both of us. Give some of it to the Lord." He added, "Oh, you'll still have to stand night guard, but you won't be so scared and tied up in knots if you let the Lord do some of the watching with you."

"You a preacher?" It wasn't an angry question.

"No. I learned what I know about the Lord the hard way." Daniel grinned. "And I think being out here right now might be the hard way for you, too."

Willard pulled his hat down harder on his head. "I'll try to do it the way you said, but it ain't easy. Doesn't sound like it would work, really."

"You saw the moccasin prints this morning, didn't you?"

"Well, yeah."

"And we are still just fine this morning, aren't we?"

"Maybe it was just dumb luck."

"Nope. We had the Lord keeping us safe last night. He'll do it all the way if we ask Him."

"I'm going to do a lot of asking, Daniel. And I'll think on the things you've said." Willard scratched on his scraggly beard. "I didn't plan on getting religion this late in my life. Especially not after the war." He looked again at Daniel. "Still, there is somethin' to what you said about us still being here this morning."

They made a cold stop at lunch, as was their habit, and hurried on to use up all the daylight they could.

When they camped that night, they put their backs against a low bluff. There was a small stream flowing by. Farther down were some cattails waving gently in the cool air. Daniel walked down there very carefully. It was spring, and all manner of creatures were coming awake after the coldness of winter. He put his foot down and froze. A water moccasin sleepily moved away from the intrusion of his boot. Daniel broke out into a sweat and stood perfectly still until he was sure the snake was out of striking range and that there were no more close by. He came back to the friendly fire and a warm supper.

"Stay out of the cattails," he warned everyone. "Use only clear water where you can see. The moccasins are waking up."

"Pa," asked Tump excitedly, "can I go down there in the morning and see if I can shoot a snake?"

"Absolutely not," his mother said firmly.

"Better mind your ma, son," Willard said. "Once I saw a whole passel of moccasins come together in a circle and then raise up on their tails and sway to the sound of the wind. Nearly scairt me half to death." Willard's eyes were wild and frightened.

"Ah, you're just making that up, Mr. Willard," Tump said with a heavy touch of wishing. "Aren't you?"

Willard set down the plate of rabbit stew he was eating. "Son, I've seen things out here I never hope to see agin in my lifetime," he said honestly.

"You stay away from the cattails," his mother repeated. "You, too, Peter. And Betty, you watch extra close with the little ones."

Betty shivered. "Yes, ma'am."

Willard's story still hung in the air when it was time to bed down, and the children insisted on sleeping up in the wagon. Mary Anna was still considering what she would do.

Daniel walked over to Willard's sentry post. "Did you really see those snakes do that?" he asked casually.

Willard looked solemn as a preacher finding a boy out smoking behind the barn. "Yes, sir. But then, that was during my drinking days," he winked.

The next day as they pushed westward, Mary Anna talked to Daniel as he rode on his horse beside the wagon. "You know, when we went back to Tennessee Colony, there were cabins everywhere. All up and down this area. But I don't see many now."

"Some have been deserted and I suspect some have been burned down," Daniel replied.

"I feel the danger all the time. I'm not used to being so alert for every sight and sound."

"It is nerve-racking, but we've got Willard to help us. We'll be all right."

"How much longer do you think we'll be on the trail?"

"Should be getting to Dripping Springs in another couple of days."

"Daniel, I know the Lord is with us, but I can't help being frightened. And I know that it isn't going to go away when we get there. I remember what it's like to live in Indian country."

Daniel frowned. "I know you really didn't want to come out here. We've been married too long for me not to figure that out. But I honestly feel we can make a go of a ranch. The Indian problem is going to be settled eventually. If we get here first, we get a chance to pick out the best land. Dripping Springs was ideal. If the cabin is still standing and any of the outbuildings, we've saved ourselves a lot of work already. Willard and I can get started right away collecting the cattle. I want to make the first drive next fall." His face was glowing, and excitement made his blue eyes electric.

Mary Anna couldn't bear to think of doing anything to put a damper on her husband's dream. She tried to see down the future, too. She tried to imagine a town like they had left. A nice home, a church and good school, neighbors, parties, stores. She trembled with the thought of what they might accomplish. "With the Lord's help, we'll try to make that dream come true." Her eyes danced with mischief. "But I think if I have to endure all that must come before, you should promise to build me the nicest house in town."

Daniel was feeling expansive in his dreams, and in the largess of that, he said, "I'll build you the most beautiful house I possibly can."

"Better watch out what you promise me," she warned. "I intend to collect on it."

"Done," he laughed and spurred his horse as though to hurry along the day.

"What are you and Papa talking about?" asked Betty.

"About building a lovely place for you and your brothers and sisters to grow up in. It'll take a lot of hard work, but some day, Betty, you will live like a real lady. Educated and beautiful." Her heart ached in a sudden realization that she couldn't always keep Betty innocent and protected. That day would arrive when she would watch her daughter marry a stranger and make her own home. She could only pray it would be close by.

Willard had been riding point, and in the distance they could see him coming at a swift gallop that meant business.

Daniel rode out to meet him. "Trouble?"

Willard rubbed the stump of his leg. " 'Fraid so. I saw a small band of warriors, or maybe a hunting party, out northeast of here about two hours ago."

"Could you tell which way they were riding?"

"Iffen we keep going this way, we'll hit 'em. Let's turn more westerly. They wasn't wearing no paint or anything, but it don't take much to get 'em riled up."

Daniel relayed the information to Mary Anna. Prickles ran down her spine. So far they had managed to avoid seeing any Indians, and that was the way she wanted it to stay.

But when they camped for the evening, their last evening on the trail before they arrived at Dripping Springs, the entire camp was tense. The horses nickered nervously, and they pawed the ground restlessly. Soldier and Shep's senses were working overtime.

Mary Anna tried to make the supper a pleasant affair, but the food went largely uneaten, even by the children. The children were quarrelsome and the baby fussy. Mary Anna looked across the campfire at Daniel.

"Better sleep inside the wagon tonight," he ordered.

Willard kept rubbing his stubby leg as the coolness of the air settled around them. "That's a sure sign of something," he said softly. He cast a glance to the starlit sky. "And I don't think it's rain."

Both Daniel and Willard sat around the low fire and drank endless cups of coffee as the night deepened.

"Notice I don't hear no birds calling," Willard observed.

"If you do, we're in for it."

Willard nodded his head in agreement.

Mary Anna, inside the wagon, could hear them talking softly but couldn't make out what they were saying. It was not chatty talk. It was not cheerful. It was careful, and there were long pauses.

During the pauses, her mind thought the worst, and she was relieved to finally hear one of them make a comment. *Oh, Lord, we need you tonight. Send Your angels to protect us and let us get safely to Dripping Springs. We're so close now, Lord, and this is what we think You want us to do. Help us, Lord. Help us.*

She drifted in and out of slumber and was annoyed with herself that the prayers she prayed did not ease her fears. Every time she woke up, she prayed some more.

She watched over the sleeping figures of her children, in their innocent dreams oblivious to the dangers around them. She positioned herself by the tailgate to protect the children.

Mary Anna felt a faint shadow cross her face. She looked up to see if it was Daniel coming into the open end of the wagon. Her mouth was open slightly to whisper to him to be careful of the children. Instead of Daniel's loving face, she looked into the war-painted face of a Comanche warrior. His knife was in a striking position over her. There wasn't time to pray or scream. A single shot rang out, and the warrior's face lost it's grim expression and slid out of sight under the wagon bed.

A bedlam of shouting, screaming, and shooting echoed in the camp. Horses squealed in their fright, and their eyes were wild with the sound of gunfire so close to them.

Mary Anna had no idea what was happening outside the wagon, and she was afraid to look. She held the rifle, ready to shoot at any other Indian who might put his face into the wagon. But she was unprepared for the ugly slashing sound of the cloth of the wagon being ripped open by a large bladed knife. She turned and aimed at the dark hand holding the knife. Without hesitation she fired and heard the awful scream that joined the sound of the rifle going off in so small a space. Where was Daniel? Willard? Were they still alive? She couldn't hear their voices, just a jumble of fighting.

And then someone reached through the huge hole in the torn fabric of the wagon and grabbed her by the hair from behind. She could feel herself sliding backwards, but she wasn't able to get the gun pointed to stop the terrible pain of being dragged against the side of the wagon. For one brief instant she envisioned her beautiful hair hanging from a Comanche lodge pole. She twisted around in time to see the face of the man trying to jerk her from the wagon. He was wearing an eerie half smile that changed before her to a grimace of anger. A dark liquid began seeping out of the front of his buckskin shirt, and his hold on her hair loosened. Just beyond the man, Mary Anna could see Willard's hand pulling back the huge knife with which he had just stabbed the man in the back.

The Indian took one step backward and turned toward Willard.

"No!" screamed Mary Anna. Willard was leaning on his crutch with one hand and holding the knife with the other. She fumbled for the rifle that was supposed to be beside her. In the dark, with fingers like stone, she found it and quickly swung around to help Willard. She was just in time to see the Indian swing his knife and fall heavily on top of her rescuer. "Willard! Daniel! Help!" Suddenly the only sound was baby Willie screaming at the top of his lungs in fear and anger. The other three children were huddled together in the bottom of the wagon in terrified silence.

"Mary Anna! Are you all right?" called Daniel as he ran to the open end of the wagon.

"Yes, but Daniel, help Willard." She pointed to the two fallen men, and Daniel cautiously went over to pull the Indian off Willard.

"Thank ya," Willard said in a raspy voice. "He was gettin' a mite heavy. Help me sit up, will ya?"

Mary Anna moved quickly out of the wagon to his side. Daniel was supporting Willard in his arms. "Willard, you saved my life," Mary Anna said softly.

"You know, Mrs. Thornton, I'm glad I was able to die doing something worthwhile. I've always worried that I didn't do my part in the war. Else we would have won, wouldn't we?" His face was streaked with blood, and his scraggly beard almost hid the small smile that came before the pain of the knife wound in his belly caused him to grimace. He coughed with a great shudder.

"Willard, tonight I prayed that the Lord would send His angels to watch and protect us. I had no idea that you were that angel." She stroked his face with her fingertips. "Thank you for saving my life."

"Will you pray me out of this life into the next? Daniel and I had a serious talk the other day, and he set me to thinkin'. I'm grateful for that, Daniel. I think I hear Jesus calling to me. Thank you for that." He closed his eyes as Mary Anna began a prayer of intercession for Willard. Daniel held him in his arms until the last breath had left Willard's thin body.

By the first light of dawn, they buried Willard, and Mary Anna and the boys wept at the loss of their new friend. "He truly was an angel of mercy sent to us to get us to Dripping Springs," she whispered as she placed a tiny bunch of early spring flowers on his grave.

"He certainly was a good and brave man," Daniel agreed. Sighing deeply, he stood a board with Willard's name carved out on it at the head of the grave. He wondered if this was the beginning of another long line of people he would have to see die and be buried before it all finally stopped. And for a moment he doubted the wisdom of coming back to Dripping Springs until it was safer. He certainly knew it wasn't safe to stay put. The Comanche would be back for their dead.

"We've got to get out of here quick."

Mary Anna hurried the children into the wagon, talking constantly to keep their minds off the bodies of the warriors.

"Mama, where are the dogs?" asked Tump. There was fear in his eyes.

"Let your father look for them. You stay with us."

Daniel found the dogs not far from camp. They had serious knife wounds, but he placed them carefully in the back of the wagon, and Mary Anna did what she could to doctor them.

"Are they going to live?" asked Peter. His small face was marked with fatigue and sadness.

"Pray about it, son. Dogs have an amazing ability to heal," Mary Anna assured him. She kissed her grieving son as he sat down between the two dogs and gently patted and talked to them.

Later, as they rode in the wagon together, Daniel looked at his beloved wife and asked earnestly, "Should we turn around and go back?"

"No," she said firmly. "The Lord has taken care of us through all of this. He'll not let us down now. This is what He wants for us. I think I can see that." Her eyes misted over, softening the bright blue to a soft baby blue. "Willard would have wanted to see that dream come true, too. He's part of it even now."

Daniel looked deeply into the eyes of the only woman he had ever loved and said, "How God blessed me the day He brought us together. I'll cherish you all the days of my life."

They pushed hard that day to reach Dripping Springs, where they hoped their cabin still stood. Daniel was exhausted with Willard and the dogs not around to help him keep watch. He stayed right with the wagon, dozing off and on in his saddle.

"Daniel, I think I see a rider coming this way. Just one man."

Daniel tried to focus his tired eyes in the direction Mary Anna was pointing. The distance played tricks, and he wasn't sure what he saw. But as the figure came closer, it was indeed a single man. A young man. Daniel eased his finger closer to the trigger of the rifle laying casually across his lap.

The stranger didn't alter the gait of his horse, nor did he seem to make any threatening moves. His hand, too, was on his rifle. Soon Daniel could see that the young man was dressed in what was left of a Confederate uniform. His horse was old and plodding.

"Howdy," the stranger called out.

"Howdy," Daniel responded as the man continued closer.

The man stopped a short distance away. "Name's Kirk. You heading to Stephenville?"

"Just beyond," Daniel answered vaguely. "You?"

"Going home." He took off his slouch hat and wiped the inside of the hat-band with his neckerchief. "I've been out hunting." His grin was engaging. "As you can see, I didn't bag anything."

"Is the hunting bad out here?" Daniel didn't have a good feeling about this young man. He was just a little too slick and smiley.

"It is if you run out of ammunition." He smiled and looked embarrassed. "I'm not a very good shot, and the few chances I did have, I missed."

"You are out here in Indian country hunting by yourself," Daniel persisted, "and with no ammunition?"

"Oh, they won't bother me. All they want are the horses. One, I know they don't want this old oat-burner, and I'm not rounding up any good ones. Two, I'm not gathering up cattle. That'd be a little like walking into the middle of a pack of wolves carrying a dead deer." He smiled that charming smile again. "I just wanted a rabbit for my supper."

Daniel considered the information. It contained some things in it that fright-ened him, but he wasn't sure he could trust the source of these facts. Daniel was out here to collect horses and cattle. That wasn't going to make him popular with the Comanche. He had figured that out for himself. The young man seemed benign and affable. All the same, he made Daniel wary.

Mary Anna was pleased with Mr. Kirk. She looked at the recovering dogs watching the young man. They seemed to be trying to make up their minds. They weren't barking, neither were they wagging their tails. That perplexed her, but she had such good feelings about him. "Since you failed to get your rabbit, perhaps you'll ride along with us and share our supper when we stop for camp. We're on our way to Dripping Springs. Our cabin is there. Well, I mean, maybe it is. We're going to see."

Daniel looked at his wife as though seeing a teenage girl gone crazy. She was talking fast and giving the man all sorts of information about them that Daniel didn't care to share at this time.

Kirk gave her a blinding smile. "I'd surely appreciate that, ma'am," he answered as he took off his hat and gave her a slight bow from the saddle.

One thing that Mary Anna always judged a man by was his manners. And this one got an A in decorum and charm in her grade book. She saw Daniel's frown and realized she had been gushing like a schoolgirl, so she smoothed her skirts and added, "We have rabbit for supper. Isn't that a coincidence?"

Kirk moved closer to the wagon. He spoke to Tump. "Did you get the rabbit? You look like you'd be a good hunter."

Tump grinned from ear to ear. "Yes, sir, I did. Thunder and I rode it down, and I shot it." He wanted to be sure the stranger knew he had his own horse.

Now Daniel got grumpy. The man had charmed his wife and his oldest son.

"After putting in all that work and driving the wagon for your mother, you've had quite a day. Maybe you'd do me the honor of driving for you for a while. Who knows? You might find another rabbit, and we'd have a real feast."

Tump wasn't reluctant to turn over the reins at all. But it was supposed to be Peter's turn, and Peter immediately decided he didn't like this intruder at all.

Kirk saw the flush on Peter's face. "Oh, oh. I think I've butted in where I don't belong. It was going to be your turn, wasn't it?" Kirk stuck out his hand to each boy and introduced himself. "Tump and Peter. What fine young men you are. I can plainly see you wanted your turn, Peter. How would you like to ride my horse for a while? I'd sure appreciate sitting on a soft wagon seat for a change."

It wasn't much of a horse, but Peter jumped at the chance to ride like his big brother. "Yes, sir."

"You boys stay by the wagon," Daniel said with great authority. "We're going to be getting close before long. I want to be able to see you all the time."

"Yes, sir, Pa," they chorused and moved the horses up to a modest gallop, which was a good thing, because it looked as if that would be Kirk's horse's top speed.

Daniel looked at his attractive wife sitting on the wagon seat with this slick-talker and felt his hackles rise. They were chatting like old friends. He could hear much of what was being said, and he didn't like any of it. The man was too familiar, too quick to make himself part of the family.

"And you stayed out there until the war was over? You're a brave woman to keep your family together until your husband came home," he heard young Kirk say.

It went like that all afternoon. Mary Anna seemed to be telling him their life's history, and Kirk was eating it up with a spoon. Or so it appeared. Daniel wanted to tell Mary Anna to shut up, but he couldn't for the life of him figure out how. He was too far away to be included in the conversation.

Daniel was soothed only by the fact that he was beginning to recognize familiar landmarks. They were getting close to where they had built their first cabin at Dripping Springs.

Topping the rise, Daniel reined in his horse. Below him lay his valley. Through a haze of tears he surveyed it. There was the stand of majestic trees from which he and Mary Anna had cut the logs for their first cabin. The stream ran clear and sweet through the rich grass. And he could see the remains of their cabin. The land had begun reclaiming it, spreading green lacy fingers over the half-burned timbers. A startled fawn dashed for the safety of the trees. Here and there crocuses had begun to poke up cautious heads, dotting the landscape with spots of yellow. The land spread before him as if waiting for his return. He turned his horse around and rode hard for the wagon not too far behind him. He took off his hat and waved it in the air, whooping and shouting, "Yahoo! We're home!"

Mary Anna hurried the horses as fast as she could, but when she topped the rise, she had to stop and survey the scene as Daniel had done. He rode up beside her, pulling his horse up short.

"It's the same land, Mary Anna. It's still paradise."

"It looks as though it's been waiting for us to come back, doesn't it?" She looked at him with bride's eyes of love.

Kirk sat stone still. He realized he was in the midst of a tender moment, and he held his tongue for the man and his wife to claim their dream again.

"Well, what are we waiting for? Let's get down there," Mary Anna said, and slapped the reins over the backs of the horses. Daniel whistled to the boys and pointed to the cabin ahead. They spurred their horses in a race as all brothers do.

Mary Anna laughed out loud to see her two young sons urge their mounts toward the cabin. Then a warning sounded in her head. A pioneer woman's warning. The boys had no idea what they were racing into, what dangers could lie in wait for them. But there was no way to stop their headlong flight.

"Lord, let those boys be safe," she whispered as she pressed her team harder to catch up with them.

## Chapter 7

Mary Anna pulled the wagon up close to the ruins underneath the huge old hackberry tree that had once shaded their front door. A quick glance revealed no overt dangers. It was a good thing, because Tump and Peter were already on foot exploring, with Betty crying after them to wait for her. Mary Anna held Willie and Daniel took Henry as they began their walk around. They surveyed the falling down walls, remembering the beginning of their married life.

"Foundation's in pretty good shape. Shouldn't take much work to get it solid again," remarked Kirk as he poked at it with the tip of his boot.

Daniel thought of the long hours it had taken him to collect the big flat limestones to lay the foundation and the days it had taken him to cut the trees for the logs. He looked disdainfully at Kirk's back, doubting the young man had ever done a full day's work in his life.

"Watch out for snakes and fiddlebacks," Mary Anna admonished the boys. She looked up at her tall, handsome husband. "Welcome home, my love."

In a show of ownership, Daniel leaned down and kissed her fully on her upturned mouth as he hoped Kirk watched. "Welcome home to you."

Kirk was quick to know when he wasn't needed—or wanted. "I'll unload whatever you need for night camp," he offered.

Now that he felt master of the house again, Daniel said confidently, "Why don't you plan to stay here and help me with the rebuilding? I can't pay you much, but I can give you food, shelter, and some cash."

A big smile broke out on Kirk's face. "I'd surely like that."

In short order the night camp was made and supper was ready. After the hot meal, Kirk pulled out his harmonica and played a soft tune. The two little ones were already tucked into the wagon for the night, but Mary Anna had allowed the two older boys to sit around the fire for a little while longer.

Mary Anna turned to Daniel. "This is the way it should be. This is what I've missed without even knowing it."

"I thought you were sad about leaving the city," Daniel said softly.

"I was," she admitted. "But when I saw our cabin again, I knew this is where we belong. What's wrong, Daniel? You're the one who looks sad."

"Oh, it's just that hearing that harmonica brings back the war. Too many bad memories attached to that sound."

Kirk quickly apologized and shoved the instrument into his shirt pocket. "Sorry."

"Don't apologize for having the gift of music," Daniel rebuked him. "I play the fiddle some myself." He looked warningly at Mary Anna. "And before you get any ideas, not tonight. I'm just too tired to hold up my head, much less my fiddle."

By tacit agreement the fire was banked, Kirk took the first watch, and everyone else went to bed.

Daniel found it hard to sleep. His faith in Kirk was shaky, and the dogs were still recovering from their wounds. Daniel's ears heard the tiniest rustle of the leaves as the wind fingered the trees. He was decidedly unrested when he took his turn to watch.

Kirk rolled up in his blankets close to the fire, using his saddle as a pillow. He put his hat over his face and seemed to go to sleep instantly. Daniel saw that Kirk had his hand on his pistol, which still rested in its holster.

While Daniel guarded his family, part of his mind tried to work out the knots of doubt he felt about Kirk. What was it that just didn't ring true about the young man? It worried him to feel he couldn't trust this man with his family's life if push came to shove. One characteristic that brought a sour taste to his mouth was a man who was just too polished and polite. Envy? He shook his head.

*I like a man with good manners. He hasn't made a move on Mary Anna that I'm aware of, and I'm sure she'd tell me. What makes you tick, Kirk? What is it about you that makes me never want to turn my back on you?* The sleeping figure gave him no answers.

The sun hadn't quite made the top of its head poke through the atmosphere when Mary Anna woke and dressed for a hard day's work. She put her hair up in braids and secured them about her head as the coffee gave off its first tantalizing scent.

Daniel came strolling over to the fire. "Good morning, glory." He put his arms around her and pulled a welcoming kiss from her upturned mouth.

She smiled at him and ran her hands over his stubbled chin with her thumb. "You look so tired, my love. Why don't you sleep until I have your breakfast ready?"

"I could use a little more sleep," Daniel acknowledged. Wearily he walked over to the wagon and climbed around his sleeping children. He never slept on the ground if he could possibly avoid it. He'd hated it before the war and he hated it even more now.

Kirk kicked off his blanket and sat up wide awake and rested. "Howdy, Mrs. Thornton. That coffee surely does smell good to this old country boy."

Mary Anna poured him a cup and gave him a brief good morning smile. She knew Daniel didn't like Kirk for some reason, so she was circumspect with him, especially when they were alone. She liked the honest young face she saw. And his good sense of humor. He had made their camp and their time on the trail more pleasant. *Why doesn't Daniel like him? Or is it that he doesn't trust him?* She decided to make up her own mind but to be watchful of Kirk.

She finished making a good breakfast of fried bacon and biscuits with gravy, even putting out a jar of her summer mustang jelly she had made back in Tennessee Colony. The grapes were tart and left a deep stain on the careless eater's hands, but they were a taste of summertime.

Tump came out of the wagon as she was stirring the gravy.

"Go check the dogs and take them a little food. Don't forget the water. And don't move the bandages I have on them. If the bandages smell bad, come and tell me right away."

He grinned at the list of commands. "Then can I go to the bathroom and have some breakfast?"

"I'm sorry, Tump. There are just so many things going through my mind right now. You take care of your dogs, and I'll feed you a cattleman's breakfast. Okay?" she smiled.

"Bathroom first." Tump grinned wickedly at her.

"Tump," she added quietly. "Use the new one, but be careful. Everything out here is attached to a price."

His young face was somber. "Yes, Ma, I know."

Maybe he did. Maybe he didn't. But it was Mary Anna's job to remind him constantly.

Daniel was in a hard, deep sleep when she went to the wagon to wake him. She looked at his sleeping face, so far away from her in his dreams, and hated to wake him. But she knew he'd be angry if she didn't get him up. She climbed in the wagon and kissed his mouth gently. Then she slid her mouth across his cheeks up to his eyes and kissed each one. "Is there anybody in there?" she asked softly.

He groaned. She ran her hand across his chest, rubbing it back to life. He groaned a more pleasant groan. "Now rub my arm—my hand's asleep." She obediently rubbed his hands and arms, and then he said with a straight face, "Now my eyes and mouth have gone back to sleep. Guess they need some more attention, too." She chuckled and then repeated her first attempt to wake him.

Daniel smiled broadly with his eyes still shut. "What a wonderful way to wake up in the morning. Can we do this every day?"

"Not when you're usually the first one up."

"I can guarantee you I won't be from now on."

"Oh, yes, you will. But maybe we can save this for special days like Sunday mornings," she promised in a sultry voice.

"Lady, you got yourself a deal." He wrapped his arms around her and gave her a bear hug. "Now feed me some of that fantastic-smelling breakfast."

While Daniel sat on the knocked-over logs on the south side of the cabin and had breakfast he said to Mary Anna, "I sure would like to know where Caleb and Virginia West are. Do you think they'd still be in Stephenville?"

Mary Anna shook her head. "I'm afraid to guess they could still be that close by."

"After I get the cabin rebuilt, I'll go over to Stephenville and find out what I can."

"If you want, I could do that for you," Kirk offered. " 'Course I know you really need me here to help with the cabin. But I could do it." He looked at Daniel expectantly.

Mary Anna held her tongue and her breath. To find the Wests would be a wonderful thing. It would seem they were really back home again.

Daniel saw the hope in Mary Anna's face and said, "I think we could spare you for a day or two. They had a cabin about twelve miles northeast of Stephenville, but they might have moved into town during the war."

"I can check with the post office and the local stores. They always know where people are." Kirk's face was lit with joy at his mission. "I'll leave right after breakfast, unless you have something you want me to do first, Mr. Thornton."

"No, I don't have anything." Daniel frowned when he thought of all the work he had done on the first cabin without a young whippersnapper to help him. *Course I was a little younger then,* he admitted to himself.

"As long as you're going into town, you better bring us a few things," Daniel ordered. "Mary Anna, you give him your list." He walked to the back of the wagon, rifled through until he got to the big brass-bound trunk. There was precious little money, but he took it out, guessed at what the cost of the supplies might be, and gave part of the money to Kirk.

"This ought to cover it. We'll be looking for you about tomorrow sundown."

Kirk heard the doubt in Daniel's voice. "I'll be back with your supplies, Mr. Thornton. And I hope your friends. All I want to do is help you and make a little money for myself. But I'm no thief." He stood a little taller.

Daniel didn't drop his eyes from the ones staring at him. "We're counting on you, Kirk." Then he added in a conciliatory tone, "Be careful out there."

Kirk mounted his swayback nag and nudged him toward Stephenville. "I'll bring you kids a surprise," he shouted back over his shoulder.

"Oh, Daniel, I'm going to pray real hard that he finds the Wests." Mary Anna stood at his side as they watched Kirk disappear in the grass and trees.

"I'll pray about that, too, but I think I'll concentrate on getting our supplies with that money I just gave him." He sighed. "I hope that wasn't a fool thing to do, give my money to a stranger."

Quietly she said, "Think of it as casting your bread upon the waters. It'll come back. So will Kirk. He wants you to like him."

"Everybody wants to be liked."

"But why don't you like him?" she pressed.

"I've been thinking about it. Can't quite put my finger on it. Maybe he's just a little too nice. A little too slick." He shook his head.

"Maybe he's just young," Mary Anna said hopefully. "I like him," she added.

"I know," Daniel grinned. "Maybe that's why I don't like him."

"You know you have no rival in my life." She stood up on her tiptoes and gave him a gentle kiss.

Daniel's arms went around her, and he deepened the kiss. "Got you all to myself again," he said in a softly seductive tone.

"Yeah, except for the five kids," she said with a sparkle in her eye.

He laughed out loud. "Let's get those five little urchins to work. We can have our cabin rebuilt in no time with all that help."

The work did go well that day. Most of the logs they needed were still there, piled about haphazardly. Daniel wore leather gloves to avoid getting bitten by something he couldn't see. The boys played and romped while making the caulking and smearing it in the cracks as Daniel set the logs in place with the help of Mary Anna and the horses.

The sound of crashing logs and family laughter rang down the slope of the land to the little river where they got their water. It traveled on, trapped in the tiny bubbles, to the land beyond, swirling and pirouetting over rocks and rubble, traveling many miles until it finally passed in front of the Indian reservation of the Brazos where the women were gathered to do their laundry and bathe. There it mixed with similar sounds of laughter and family business.

This time as it left, the two were one, and as the bubbles passed another camp, more bubbles were added until at last they reached the ocean. There, all the laughter and tears and work sounds were released to become the sound of the surf of the Gulf of Mexico.

The Thorntons worked, as people say in the South, "From cain to cain't." Everyone was ready for a quick supper and a fast sleep. The children were put inside the partially finished cabin.

Tump looked up at his mother as she arranged his covers. "It's good to be in a house again," he said as he yawned.

"Yes, my sweet, it's good to be home again." She checked each child, helped them say their prayers, and then went out into the starlit night with Daniel.

Daniel reached for the blue-enameled coffeepot standing on the grill over the fire. He sighed a tired sigh and drank carefully from the tin cup.

"It's going to be a long night for you, isn't it?" Mary Anna asked.

"Looks like it."

"Would you let me stand a watch for you?"

Daniel took another sip of the hot coffee. "Hadn't thought about it."

She let him think a minute and asked him again. "Well?"

"You really want to?"

"Yes." She added with confidence, "I can listen as well as you. And the dogs are getting better each day. I'll move them here with me by the fire. If anything happens, you'll be the first to know."

She tried to make her voice light, but they both knew the night would be dangerous with two injured dogs and without the protection of a full cabin. If there were Indians in the area, they were sure to know about the Thorntons' return. News had reached them that Swift-as-an-Antelope was dead, but there would always be new men to take his place.

Daniel measured his tiny wife against the evils of the night. She looked so small to be the protector of their family. He knew he couldn't go without sleep and keep working and guarding. "You and the Lord will have to take care of it tonight. I'm too tired to worry about it."

Mary Anna smiled because she knew that was a lie. Daniel had never been too tired to worry about anything. She loved him the more for making it easy for her to help him.

The idea of the Lord helping her keep watch was not a lie. Mary Anna spent most of her time divided between listening and praying. At first every little sound made her heart pound a little harder, but then she began to feel the rhythm of the night and relaxed a little.

*Lord, thank You for this day and its blessings. Out here where there are so many things that can go wrong and snatch life right out of our hand, I thank You that my family and I are safe. Send Your guardian angels to protect us. And, Lord, would You help the white man find a way to talk to the Indians and live in peace with them? You died for them, too, though I know this is not a popular idea around here. I'm scared of them now. They seem like wild animals trapped with their backs against the wall and the hunter bearing down on them. I didn't mean to take anything away from them when we moved out here. We only wanted to follow Daniel's dream of having a ranch of his own. This is the only place where we felt we could do this. Everything is tangled like a ball of yarn the cat has been playing with. Help us get it straightened out so everyone can be safe and happy.*

It had long been Mary Anna's habit to talk to the Lord at any given moment, during any time or problem she had. Once she told another woman that she prayed even for things like lost socks, and the woman had been very indignant. "I can't imagine bothering the Lord with something like a pair of socks!" she had huffed.

Mary Anna couldn't imagine not bothering the Lord with everything in her life, no matter how small. And now as she sat under His starry canopy, smelling the cleanness of His creation and listening to the gentle pops of the fire and the sounds of the night, she had plenty of time to talk with Him.

*Lord, please let us find the Wests. Good friends like that should be a lifetime gift. Let them be in good health and happy. And Lord, thank You for the changes in Daniel. He has come to know You and love You. I understand that really getting to know You takes an entire lifetime, but I thank You for his beginning.* She smiled. *Sometimes he's like a little kid, but You've placed some heavy burdens on him. Help him to attain his dream. It isn't a selfish dream. It's for all of us.*

She stopped for a moment to listen more carefully to a sound of movement out over by the wagon. She looked at the dogs. Their ears were up, but they quickly settled down, so she relaxed. Moving over to them, Mary Anna gave a cursory check to their necks where the wounds were and then patted them both, talking softly to each as she ran her fingers through their silky fur, assuring them they'd be fine soon.

The black trees partially obscured her view of the milky moon. It was only a half-moon, so its light was miserly. It made the landscape she could see more frightening. Instinctively, she held the gun a little more tightly. It was heavy and made her already tired arm ache as the muscle cramped.

She was close enough to the fire that the heat began to make her face too hot, so she turned her body slightly away. She also tried not to look into the fire so she could see better into the dark around the cabin.

As time dragged by, she longed to be inside with the rest of her family, sleeping soundly, and she hoped safely. Gently she let the happy news she carried into her mind to nurture it. She was with child once more. It was so soon after Willie, she hadn't been sure Daniel would be pleased about it. When she had told him, he was delighted, then alarmed. The baby was due in December. Willie would be only twelve months old when the new one came, if she had figured it right. It was not good timing.

At first she had been happy, then sad, then hopeful it wasn't true. It was too soon to have another child and make a new home in the hostile land Daniel had chosen. When she was sure a baby was coming, she made peace with the idea and made practical plans to take care of the baby and herself without delaying Daniel's dream.

She hoped for another girl. That would be perfect. Tump, Peter, Betty, Henry, Willy, and another little girl. She tended to think of the baby as a girl and spoke to her that way. She had already chosen a name. Annah. She wanted a middle name that began with an *n*. Then the initials would be A.N.T., and she could imagine her busy little girl hurrying around like a little ant to help the Thornton family. But she hadn't decided on one. She felt that since she had chosen the first name, Daniel might want to choose the middle one. She knew it wouldn't be long until he figured it out. Up to now he had been too busy with all the work involved in the trip to think of it. She smiled when she remembered his surprise. *'Course he probably wants another strapping son to help him on the place.* But she knew he would love whoever came to live with them.

She had just reached the part of the night when she thought she couldn't stay awake for another instant, when she saw Daniel silhouetted in the doorway of the cabin. She was too tired to rise to meet him, but he hurried out.

"You look a little tired," he said kindly. He reached down and picked his small wife up in his arms and carried her back inside the cabin walls. She wrapped her arms around his neck and laid her head on his broad chest. Gently he laid her in the sleeping blanket he had just left.

"It still has your warmth and smell," she said softly and was immediately asleep even as he put the blankets around her.

"Sleep mighty woman," he whispered. "You've earned a good rest." Then he smiled broadly. "You and that little one you carry so quietly."

He looked around the cabin that would soon be whole and surveyed his family. *Lord, thank You for my family. Keep us all safe and help us to tame this land and make it a good place for us to bring up our family. Bless the labor of our hands and help us to live in peace with the Indians.* His face turned grim. *Please don't put me to the test of having to choose between the Indians and my family.* Even as he prayed, he knew the situation was inevitable.

He walked out into the night. The dogs both wagged their tails in greeting. "Get well fast, boys. I need the extra help," he said as he squatted down to pat them. He grinned at Soldier. "I bet an Indian won't be able to get within a mile of you from now on. He had his chance to get rid of you two, and you'll have your ears to hear him long before I do. Many times, I'm afraid." He sighed deeply.

"Many times, I'm afraid," he repeated and wiped his face with his handkerchief. Then he used the handkerchief to wrap around the handle of the hot coffeepot and pour himself a cup. It was still a long time until dawn. *I wonder if Kirk will come back. And if he does, will he have found Caleb? I doubt he'll be back. Something about that boy I can't quite lay my finger on. If he doesn't bring Caleb back with him, I'll make a trip into town myself after the cabin is secure.*

His internal conversation ended when he saw Soldier's ears pop up and his head rise. Daniel stood up and moved back away from the firelight, listening, gun ready.

His heart was pounding as he strained to hear what Soldier had heard. Soldier's face was pointed toward the stand of trees about a hundred yards east of the cabin. Daniel tried to focus every sense in that direction, too. He heard a night bird call, but that didn't mean there was a bird out there. He held his breath and waited for an answering call. None came. "What did you hear out there, boy?" he whispered to Soldier.

Soldier looked at him as if to answer. Then he plopped his head down on his paws as if to say, "Whatever it was, it's safe now."

Daniel relaxed a little and continued to alternately watch the dogs and listen for night sounds that shouldn't be there. It was a lonely vigil.

He sat back from the firelight with his back against the tree that spread majestically across the front of the cabin. While he listened, his mind was busy building his ranch, placing the different buildings around the cabin and catching wild cows to build his herd. In his mind he could see all the improvements he would make.

In the back of his mind was a vague recollection of the preacher reading from Genesis when God spoke to Adam about the Garden of Eden. Something about subduing the earth. *That's what I'm out here to do, Lord. Subdue it and make it a productive place. I'm not fool enough to think I'm doing this for You. I know I'm doing it for myself. But I think this is what You meant for the land to be. Settled and productive.*

And thus he passed the night. The night can go quickly when one is building a lifetime of dreams.

# Chapter 8

When the sun was well up, Daniel went inside to wake his family. "You bunch of no good lazy bums. The sun is almost at high noon, and here you are still warming your blankets. Get up and eat the breakfast I've prepared for you. You're going to need it, 'cause we're getting this cabin finished today." He tickled the boys and Betty for a minute and then went over to sit on the ground beside Mary Anna.

"The sun is not at high noon." She stretched and yawned. "Oh, my arms are sore."

"I'm not surprised. You put in quite a day yesterday."

"I know I should jump up and act guilty that I didn't wake up to fix your breakfast, but I'm just flat too tired. I would have slept until noon if you hadn't wakened me," she admitted.

"You need the extra sleep, I'm sure," he said softly as he touched her middle. She broke into a big smile. "You really don't mind?"

"Honey, we've been married a long time," he laughed. "Surely you know me better than that."

"I thought you were too busy with this big dream of yours to be that interested."

"I had to take everything into account. And I knew I'd need another big boy to help with the ranch," he teased. "I always plan ahead," he laughed.

"Planned ahead. Humph!" she sniffed.

"Ah, now don't go getting your hackles up. We're having another little Thornton. A boy, I hope, but I'd love another girl, too. Someone to bake as well as you do." He nuzzled her sleep-warmed neck and kissed her soft lips.

"You'd better stop that. The children are awake. Besides, that's how I got in this condition in the first place."

"And the second and the third and—"

"All right, you made your point. Help me up. I'll at least help you serve breakfast so I don't have to listen to you brag about how wonderful you are all day long."

He laughed at her mock anger and pulled her to her feet. He walked outside to help himself to another cup of coffee when he heard Soldier bark. He looked in the direction their wagon had come, but he couldn't see anything. "You have good ears, Soldier." Shep began barking to prove he was as good a watchdog as his companion. "You're a little late there, Shep." The dog barked a little louder.

"Okay, I'm convinced you're a good watchdog, too." Daniel patted both the dogs and kept watching in the direction they were looking.

Soon he was able to make out a rider and a wagon. "I hope that's Kirk and the Wests," he muttered. "Mary Anna," he shouted, "company's coming."

She came running out of the cabin. "Is it the Wests?"

He was secretly pleased she hadn't asked if it were Kirk. "Looks like it could be." They both squinted hard, trying to focus on the individuals approaching.

"It is!" Mary Anna exclaimed. "It's Virginia and Caleb." She began to wave her hand in big circles of welcome. It seemed to take forever for the wagon to cover the last distance. The mules had barely planted their tired feet when Virginia began climbing down into the waiting arms of Mary Anna.

"Oh, I've missed you," Virginia said as she hugged her friend as hard as Mary Anna hugged her.

"I was so afraid we wouldn't be able to find you," Mary Anna said. Virginia couldn't see the frown of concern on her friend's face. Mary Anna felt the fragile boniness of Virginia, a woman who had been round and healthy the last time she had seen her.

Daniel and Caleb were warmly shaking hands. There were tears in Caleb's eyes. They threatened to follow the new, deep lines of worry down to his ragged clothes. "Couldn't stay away from Paradise, eh?"

"You know how I love my apples," countered Daniel. He tried to hide his shock at Caleb's apparent poverty.

"It's not the apples that'll get ya; it's the snakes ya have to watch out fer," said Caleb. In a softer voice, he added, "It's not safe out here, Daniel. Keep a sharp eye out. It's not like it used to be when we'd have a few renegades. These snakes have banded together, and they're out for blood," he warned. "When the army pulled out in '61, they turned loose all the mad hornets." He squinted at Daniel and said in earnest, "Remember, we're sitting about a mile off their main path into Mexico."

"I don't want any trouble."

"Us being here is the trouble." His leathery face wrinkled into a warm grin. "Sure are glad you've come back."

An equally thin young boy climbed from the back of the wagon. "You remember my boy, Jim?"

The boy put out his hand politely to Daniel. "Hello, sir."

"Boys," said Daniel. "Company for you." As the oldest Thornton boys stepped forward, Daniel said, "This is Tump and this one is Peter. Why don't you boys go check on the horses for us?" His brow wrinkled. "And be careful out there."

Kirk saw the closeness of the two families and was uncomfortable with the intimacy he saw. He was a stranger, so he said loudly, "I'll go with the boys and take care of the horses, too."

Daniel shook hands with him. "Thank you, Kirk, for finding these dear friends of ours and bringing us safely together again."

Kirk touched the brim of his hat in a jaunty salute. "My pleasure," and he led his horse off behind the boys.

The women were moving toward the unfinished cabin. "Come on, Caleb, breakfast is still hot."

Caleb saw Daniel looking at his pronounced limp. "Shiloh," he said. "Bluebelly got me. Don't slow me down much, just give me a dignified gait."

Daniel smiled sadly. "I was lucky."

"Or faster," Caleb added.

Daniel's face turned grim. "My wounds don't show on the outside."

As Caleb looked at the pain in Daniel's eyes, he said, "Maybe those are the hardest to heal."

# Chapter 9

There was no need to apologize for the lack of furniture or other amenities. Hospitality was solely dependent on the grace of the hostess and the joy with which whatever food was available was shared.

By those standards, breakfast was a social extravaganza.

The women talked and talked. Virginia reintroduced her little girl, Edna, and Mary Anna her Betty. The two girls came together shyly but were soon off to the corner of the cabin's floor, sharing a big hot biscuit.

Mary Anna couldn't get over how Virginia's plumpness had been pared down to a hard thinness. Her heart hurt for the condition of her friends.

"This coffee is heavenly," sighed Virginia. "We used burnt okra during the war, but I got to where I couldn't stand the smell, let alone the taste of it."

"It was hard for you. For all of us. Where did you go when Caleb joined up?"

"I had hoped to keep the old buzzard home, but when the other men started leaving, he felt it was his duty, too, and he didn't want to feel shamed." She licked off some of the butter running down her finger with obvious pleasure. "I took the children and moved over to Waco."

Without asking for pity, she added, "No need to tell you how hard it was. It was the same for everybody." She looked carefully at Mary Anna. "But you seem to be in good health." Suspiciously she looked into Mary Anna's eyes. "Ah, I see the reason for the happy gleam in your eyes," she smiled. "When?"

"December, January, maybe."

"Well, we'll be needing to get this cabin finished up in a hurry."

When they saw the men coming their way, the women prepared to help with the cabin. Even the children helped out.

During one of the breaks, Caleb asked Daniel about Kirk. "Where did you meet up with him?"

Daniel told him the story, and he added, "I don't trust him for some reason. He's been a perfect gentleman and a hard worker, but there's something I can't quite put my finger on." He gave a short laugh. "Maybe I'm jealous of the way Mary Anna enjoys her time with him."

Caleb was covertly watching the young man. "He does seem a bit slippery to me, too. I see what you mean. Why, look at Virginia. She's got a look on her face that makes her look young again!" He turned to Daniel. "That man is dangerous, even if he is honest!" They laughed together, but it wasn't jovial laughter.

"I don't want him in my house. I'm going to build a little lean-to on the side. If he doesn't like it, he can move on."

"You can always use the excuse he needs his privacy as much as you do. You can't build a bunkhouse yet."

"All that's very true," said Daniel. "He's not a part of the family."

With everyone working hard, the cabin was finished except for some work inside. It was ready to live in, and Mary Anna was ecstatic.

"It's better than our last one. Oh, Daniel, I love it. It looks so strong and safe. And pretty. It smells good, too." Tired as they were, Mary Anna and Virginia prepared a good supper. With the Wests staying the night, there was no problem moving Kirk into the little lean-to. He had a grateful look on his face to have a little home of his own. Daniel watched for signs of malcontent but saw none.

After they ate, the children were tucked into the loft and baby Willie into his cradle.

Virginia sat in the rocking chair, drinking one last cup of coffee. The men sat in rawhide leather–laced chairs tipped against a wall. Mary Anna sat in the rocking chair her mother had given her, her hands in her lap and her head laid against its polished cherrywood back. She could feel little butterfly movements inside her tired body as the baby floated about. Her smile was one of complete contentment.

"It's good to feel so safe. I haven't felt this good in a long time. Tired from doing something worthwhile and with good friends," said Caleb.

"It's safe for now, but watch your kids real careful," warned Virginia.

Mary Anna saw the fear in her eyes. "Is it worse than before?"

Virginia nodded. "Before they only wanted the horses and cattle. Now they seem to want to kill off every white person in the country."

Caleb added, "It's the gov'ment's fault. They promised the Indians they'd be taken care of if they stayed on the reservations. They've been lied to and cheated, time after time."

"Looks like you've changed your tune about the Indians."

"I've changed a lot of things since the war," Caleb said softly.

"So have I," admitted Daniel. He straightened his shoulders. "But I still want to live here on this land. I have a right to it. I've built a life here. I haven't hurt anyone or pushed anyone off their land. Why, the Indians are welcome to hunt right there in those woods if they want to," he said as he pointed in the direction of the stand of trees.

"Ain't no buffalo in them woods, Daniel," smiled Caleb. "No deer, either, I'd bet. Even if there was, they don't want you around. They want the land back the way it was. Their lives just like they was."

"No one can turn back the clock," Daniel argued.

"They're gonna try." Caleb looked at the floor. "Guess that's why we're still in town right now. I've been trying to work up the gumption to build our own cabin out here."

"Is town where you really want to be?" asked Daniel.

"I'm not sure." He looked at Virginia as though eliciting a reply from her eyes.

"It wouldn't take us long to build you a cabin here on this land close by. Then you'd be handy when we plan the drives in the fall and make all the other decisions a rich cattle baron has to make." The light in Daniel's eyes danced with promise.

Caleb pushed back in his chair. "You do make it hard on a man to leave now, don't you?" he drawled. "How about it, Virginnie?"

"Live out here close to the Thorntons? Be rich? Are you crazy, old man? Say yes to him before he changes his mind!"

And so they started again, everyone working to raise a second cabin across what they planned to be a big communal garden.

"Why, we're practically making our own little town," Virginia said happily as she slapped some caulking between the logs of her soon-to-be home.

After the cabin was finished, a sturdy corral was built close to the houses.

"I'd put all the cattle and horses inside my cabin if I thought I could. I'm determined not to lose any to the Indians. We'll need those horses for a remuda when we drive the stock," Daniel said firmly.

The next morning, Tump came charging in before breakfast shouting, "Papa, Papa, Thunder is gone!"

Daniel grabbed his gun and started running for the corral. Quickly he scanned the horses. No other ones seemed to be missing.

"That's odd." He knelt down in front of the opening where the logs slid back and forth to make a gate. "Moccasin tracks going in, shod horse tracks coming out."

Tump grabbed his father. "Oh, Papa, what are we going to do! I can't stand for the Indians to have him. Can we go get him?" Tears ran unashamedly down his young face. There were streaks of grime where his dirty hands had tried to wipe some of them away.

"I'm sure they're long gone by now, son." Daniel wrapped the boy in his arms, hugging him hard against his body. "I think I know how much this hurts, son. Your first horse is like your first love. It's something that stays with you all the days of your life. I can still remember the first horse my dad ever gave me. And I still love her best of all my horses."

He tipped Tump's chin up so he could look in his son's eyes. "But we can't leave all these horses to go get Thunder." With sudden insight, he said, "That's it! That's what they want us to do! They baited the hook with Thunder. Well, we're not going to fall for that. Son, you can have any horse in the corral, and I'll help you train him. Let's go back to your mother and tell her what's happened."

"But that's crazy," Mary Anna said. "How would they know to pick Thunder?"

"Somebody told them Thunder was almost a pet." Daniel's face was ashen.

Suddenly Mary Anna knew what he was saying. "Kirk has betrayed us," she breathed softly.

Daniel nodded his head. "Is he out in the lean-to?"

"I don't know. I haven't seen him yet this morning." She pulled Tump against her and hugged him as she watched Daniel walk out the door with his rifle held in his hand.

"I'll check, and then I'm going over to the Wests. They need to know."

The lean-to was empty as he had thought it would be. He sprinted around the big garden plot and banged on the door. "Caleb, Virginia, it's me, Daniel. Open up!"

Caleb was in his trousers and undershirt having some breakfast when Virginia threw open the door and invited Daniel in. Quickly Daniel told them what had happened.

"You're probably right, Daniel. He'd be the only one that could tell them about how much Tump loved Thunder." Caleb let out a colorful string of words Virginia normally would never let him use in front of her or the children. "What are we going to do? We don't have any proof of this?"

"No, only my gut feeling." Daniel scratched his day-old beard. "I think the best thing to do would be to watch him. He's bound to be in trouble that it didn't work, 'cause we're not going to leave to get Thunder. I doubt he'll be back in either case. His cover is blown. I knew there was something wrong with that man! Right in my own home! A white man!" He stood very still and said softly, "The day will come when I find him again. And when it does, he'll have to pay for what he's done."

"Revenge is a tricky thing, Daniel," warned Caleb. "It may be the Lord will take care of it before you have to. Comanche don't like no one talking out of both sides of their mouth. He's in as much danger as we are, I'm thinking."

"Thank God, we found out in time," added Virginia.

"True, but be on the alert, old friend. This is God's way of giving us a warning so we can get ready. Caleb, I want to protect those horses, but I don't want either one of us to be killed. We'll do the best we can to secure the horses, but we'll all stay in the cabin today. One man isn't going to make any difference to a Comanche raiding party."

"God be with us all," Caleb said.

Daniel came back into their kitchen and sat down at the table. He told Mary Anna and Tump what he suspected. "So be careful around Kirk if he comes back. Don't trust him for a second."

Mary Anna's face flamed in anger, her cheeks glowing cherry red and her eyes a deeper blue. "You were right about him. I was so taken with his manners, I didn't see the rattles at the end of his tail."

"Well, it's not anybody's fault. It's just the way things are. So let's get cracking and get ready for anything. If the Indians think we've figured this out, they may come on in for the rest of the horses. Or they may leave us alone, thinking we're waiting for them. And I sure do want to be waiting for them!"

Tump and Daniel moved the outside barrel of water to the inside of the cabin. All guns and ammunition were checked and readied. Fear permeated the cabin. Willie was quick to pick it up, so he was fussy, demanding much of Mary Anna's time.

Daniel, Caleb, and Tump did what they could to secure the horses. Grimly Daniel said again, "Sure do wish I could get them in the cabin."

Caleb's laugh was short. "It may be the only way to keep them safe."

Virginia and her children moved into the Thornton cabin. Daniel and Caleb shoveled out a hollow place in the middle of the floor big and deep enough to accommodate the children. The kitchen table could be placed upside down over it to act as a shield.

Then they formed a line coming up from the stream. Even the older children were included. They passed buckets of water to Daniel on the roof of the cabin as he wet it down. "They burned us out last time. Maybe this will give us an edge," he said.

Mary Anna thought her arms couldn't lift another bucket when Daniel was finally satisfied that the entire cabin had been thoroughly doused.

Caleb brought in a load of meat from the smokehouse. "I can't think of another thing to do," he said as he glanced around the cabin.

"Nothing left to do but wait." Daniel's blue eyes were a steely gray with the intensity of his fear. Shadows of the last time they were burned out by the Comanche darted in and out of his mind. Images of what could happen if the Comanche breached the cabin haunted him.

He handed Mary Anna a pistol. "You know what to do with this if worse comes to worst." Their eyes locked in the single-minded thought of what he was telling her. "They can't take us alive. Especially you and Virginia and the children."

She nodded her head in agreement. "The Lord won't let it come to that," she whispered. Her face was chalk white, making her blue eyes glow starkly. "Last time He provided us with a miracle. The patrol of soldiers came out of nowhere." She knew the Lord could do it, but maybe this time, in His unfathomable wisdom, He wouldn't.

"Well, we're gonna pray to Him about it right now."

They held hands, comforting each other with the touching of their flesh, while Daniel pleaded with the Lord for mercy and deliverance.

# Chapter 10

As the sun began to turn a misty copper and slide down out of sight, the tension in the cabin escalated. There would be a full moon. In Texas a moon like that was called a Comanche moon, for this was the time when the Comanche were notorious for conducting their cruelest and largest raids.

"Who do you think will lead the raid?" asked Caleb as he played with the food on his plate.

"Swift-as-an-Antelope, probably. Can't think of anyone else around here with more power or hatred. Could be a young buck trying to make a name for himself. Doesn't really matter," Daniel shrugged.

"Yes, it does. The more experience he has, the more trouble we're in," argued Mary Anna.

"Mary Anna," Daniel said in a tired voice, "they're all experienced. That's the young man's greatest dream—to go on a raid. And they start early."

"Like Daniel said, it doesn't really matter," Virginia said in a small voice. "They're all alike. Murder and cruelty are all they understand."

Every adult in the room could recite hundreds of stories of the atrocities committed by Indians of many names and tribes. They echoed silently around the room like visible ghosts.

The top sliver of the blanched moon began to appear between the trees. Mary Anna put little Willie in his cradle down in the depression Daniel and Caleb had dug. She made beds for the older children from quilts and helped them say their usual nightly prayers. She calmed the terrified look in Tump's eyes. "God will take care of us as He always has," she assured him.

They kept the cabin dark, banking the fire in the fireplace. Caleb sat at the east window, and Daniel sat at the west one. Virginia offered to take the north window first. Mary Anna sat with Daniel, and they talked softly.

"I've tried so hard not to hate these people," Daniel said. "But I just can't understand why they do the things they do."

"Don't you think the main reason is they don't know our loving God?" Mary Anna answered. "For them life has been completely different. They don't depend on the Father the way we do. They have to do everything for themselves. They have to appease the spirits of everything around them. They love their families just as we do, but they must use different methods to protect them."

"But why choose us to punish? We're not doing anything to them. And the things they do to the prisoners they take—" Daniel shuddered. "I haven't done anything to them."

Mary Anna ran her finger lightly across his tense mouth. "Yes, my love, you did. You took their way of life from them." Before he could protest, she added, "You are the representative of all the people who have harmed them and locked them down to a small space. They've lost everything. Most of all, they've lost their pride and their identity. Maybe you would fight like they do if you had lost that much."

Daniel thought back to the war and how hard he had fought to stay alive. It wasn't always the cause for which he fought. It was merely to stay alive and get home. He measured his feelings against what Mary Anna had said about the Indians, and tears formed a mist in his eyes. He remembered the things he had seen in the Indian village he had helped to destroy, and it melded with the scenes of battle from the war.

For a moment he wanted to pack up all their belongings and go where there couldn't be any more fighting. But the urge quickly passed. They couldn't leave yet. And if they did, where would they go that they didn't bump into someone else's way of life? Despair began to creep over him like the cold coming up from the river on a windy night.

He held Mary Anna tighter. "There is only one way out of this. The Lord must help us fight off the Indians tonight, and then I'll find a way to help get justice for them when we're safe."

Mary Anna smiled in the darkness. "Yes, my love," she responded as she snuggled closer to his warm body against the rough log wall. She knew as soon as they were safe again, he would do the little he could for the Indians and then pursue his dream of his ranch. The dream was an all-consuming thing in his life. What powered this need to own the land and tame it she wasn't sure. But he wanted it enough to take this chance with all their lives.

"Do you think you could talk to Swift-as-an-Antelope and arrange some sort of bargain?"

"I would love to do that, but I think they're way past trusting anything a white man would have to say."

"Could we just let them have the horses?" she asked.

"Never. Those horses are ours, and they're too important to the cattle drive."

"So we're waiting here in the dark, perhaps getting ready to die, for some horses," she said gently.

"No, ma'am," he said firmly. "We're fighting for the right to live our lives where we want to and make a better life for our children."

Mary Anna's head began to throb with tiny pinpricks of pain. She sighed deeply and looked up at Daniel. "I hear what you're saying, but somehow I can't reconcile the two."

Daniel swept away her thoughts as easily as a broom destroys a spider web. "Just love me and help me with the dream. I want it to be your dream, too," he added pointedly.

Mary Anna's mind was too tired and frightened to argue with him. Right now there was only one thing to concentrate on. They must stay alive or there wouldn't be a dream for either one of them.

The moon slipped higher and higher in the ebony sky, painting the landscape an odd silvery color. Nothing looked right in the reflected light of the moon. Every tree took on a personality and posture of its own. Daniel strained to see what was real and what was fantasy. He felt the Indians would come through the woods. It would give them cover for a longer period of time.

The sight of the heavy moon should have been beautiful. Somewhere farther away, it was probably a courting moon for some young couple. Out here it could well be a killing moon.

Daniel rubbed his weary eyes and reached for the ladle of water Mary Anna offered him. In that second his eyes were not on watch, something moved ever so slightly in the woods. The shadow of a shadow slipped from the front of the stand of trees to the back of it.

Quietly Mary Anna said, "It's like a fairyland out there." She felt a desire to run out into the heavenly light and dance and sing.

"And so deadly. You can see everything and you can see nothing," Daniel said. He was angered that he was so frightened. Memories of war battles kept slipping into his mind. Scenes too horrible to see at the time were stored there, and pieces of them kept popping out like a sick jack-in-the-box toy. The pictures were too grotesque. He almost continuously prayed for strength and courage and wisdom. At times he felt he was going mad waiting for the Comanche, remembering all the gruesome things he had heard about them, and fighting back the bad memories.

Daniel looked at Mary Anna in the partial light spilling through the windows of the cabin. His angel of love. Tonight he loved her so much he wanted to squeeze her almost to death and protect her against all the evil waiting out there in the world. And his children, sleeping restlessly in the ground. He wanted to keep all the bad things away from them, wanting them only to be happy and successful. He had placed all the ones he loved the most in terrible danger. Maybe this was all there would ever be of his dream. And suddenly he hated the dream because it had become his worst nightmare.

Daniel's eyes detected a tiny movement in the woods. His heart jumped sickeningly. "I think they're in the woods. Everyone be alert." His voice was raspy with fear.

Mary Anna and Virginia put the upside-down table over the hole where the children were. More ammunition was passed. Mary Anna moved to the window with Virginia. "I don't see anything back here," Virginia reported.

"Nothing on this side, either, Dan. Must be coming your way."

"We'll still need to cover all the windows to make sure they don't surround us." *Please God, don't let this be a large group. Make them a small band that will quit and go home easily. Help, Lord. Keep us safe.*

And then they were riding out of the woods, painted with the glow of the moon. The horses' tails waved behind, plaited with ribbons so they looked like banners. Terrible screams flowed from the mouths of the Comanche, shrill screams and shrieks that strengthened the warriors and scared their enemies.

Mary Anna moved to Caleb's window. "You go help Daniel. I'll watch here."

Daniel and Caleb started firing right away, for the painted men were close. Everything seemed to slow down. The screams of the men Daniel hit and the snorting of their horses seemed to go on forever. He took careful aim and pulled the trigger fast. They kept pouring out of the woods. Their horsemanship was awesome. Some were clinging to the sides of their horses and firing weapons or arrows from beneath the necks of their mounts. Many times Daniel tried to take aim on a man and he disappeared behind the body of his horse. Daniel started aiming not at where the rider was supposed to be but where he would probably show up at the neck of the horse. It was a very small target at which to shoot.

"Dear Lord, there's so many of them," shouted Caleb as he fired continuously.

Mary Anna divided her time between trying to watch her window and reloading for the men. Her throat was constricted with fear, and she couldn't speak for the first few minutes of the powerful sounds of guns inside the small cabin. When Virginia saw what Mary Anna was doing, she tried to do the same. She was pale, but her hands worked quickly to reload weapons for the men.

Daniel shouted, "I see Swift-as-an-Antelope! Shoot him, Caleb, shoot him!" As though he had heard his name called, Swift-as-an-Antelope whirled his horse and changed directions, firing low as he came in closer to the cabin.

Bullets pinged and whined all around the cabin, and the dull thud of arrows and bullets impaling themselves into the heavy logs filtered into the cabin and added to the sound of screaming children and the acrid smell of gunpowder.

At the first shots, Mary Anna's insides melted into jelly, and she thought for a moment she might faint. But as the battle unfolded, she found herself calmly following Daniel's instructions. In her mind was a running prayer to the Lord for help. But her body was busy fighting the Indians.

"Some of them are trying to get behind the cabin," shouted Caleb. "Virginia, watch out!"

Virginia took careful aim and fired her rifle. The sound of a scream brought a brief smile to her face. "You'll not get by here," she promised beneath her breath.

Mary Anna felt the baby lurch inside her. "Be calm, little one. God is on watch." She and Daniel settled into a well-timed team. Smoke stung her eyes and she coughed.

A gentle wind stirred and blew through the windows, pushing the smoke from the gunpowder up the chimney of the fireplace.

Daniel's skin crawled with the sight of a flaming arrow suspended in the bow of one of the men. Quickly he sighted and shot the man. "Not this time," he promised.

The battle seemed to go on for hours, though it had in truth been only half an hour or so. The Indians made a retreat to the safety of the woods, and Daniel slumped down against the coarse wall. Everyone breathed a sigh of relief, but they knew the Indians were not through with them yet.

Mary Anna and Virginia tried to calm the children's crying.

Caleb's craggy face broke into a wrinkled grin. "We laid down a good barrage for them. Onliest thing we needed was a cannon."

"The memories came back for you, too," said Daniel.

"Them memories won't never go away, Daniel. But the experience sure was helpful."

Daniel grinned back at him. "You're right. We're not tenderfeet out here." Warding off the first attack had been heady for them all. They now had hopes that they would be able to drive away the persistent men trying to kill them.

Daniel looked back over the land. During the war there had been bodies everywhere, some dead and some screaming for help. Now there was nothing to indicate there had been a battle. The Comanche worked in pairs and swept up any fallen comrades. The quiet was unsettling.

"Maybe they aren't coming back," Virginia voiced the hope of everyone in the cabin.

"I think we'd better be ready for another assault. And I think we'd better be sure we get every man who's carrying a flaming arrow. That's our weakest point. It didn't get very hot today. Maybe the moisture is still in the logs and roof."

"There's mist beginning to drift up from the streambed, too," added Caleb hopefully. "All we have to do is keep them away. I can feel the hand of the Lord in this battle." Faith shone in his eyes and quickly sparked from one adult to the other.

"Yes, the Lord is on our side," agreed Daniel. Then he added, "Better get ready, there's something going on in the woods."

Everyone went on alert. The raiders were determined to get to the cabin this time. They came almost straight at it, wheeling and dodging and displaying their horsemanship and their disregard for the white man's bullets.

Arrows and bullets again assaulted the small cabin. More than once an arrow flew through the window with a deadly whistle and buried its head into the logs around them.

"Flaming arrow!" shouted Daniel. The Indian fell silently, and the light from his arrow extinguished itself as both Daniel and Caleb shot at him. But they missed seeing Swift-as-an-Antelope as he galloped toward them and shot his fiery missile at the cabin's roof.

Mary Anna waited for the smoke to come pouring down on them as it had before. She got a bucket of water ready to put out the flames that were sure to come through the split shingles, but nothing happened.

"It's a miracle!" she shouted to Daniel.

"Don't be too quick to name it," Daniel said. "Here come more."

But the arrows that made it to the cabin didn't set it on fire.

Daniel saw the puzzled look on Swift-as-an-Antelope's face as he spun his horse away from the cabin. He had come in close, very close. Daniel knew it would be counted as a coup for Swift-as-an-Antelope. But the disbelief on his face gladdened Daniel's heart. Maybe wetting down the cabin had worked. Maybe God had made it work.

More hopes rose as the little fortress held out against another battle.

Neither Daniel nor Caleb could estimate the casualties on the other side. "I think I've shot at least a hundred men," Caleb exaggerated. "Iffen I was them, I'd give up!"

Daniel, Mary Anna, and Virginia laughed out loud at his bragging and confidence. It felt good to laugh after the extreme tension. Mary Anna laughed until tears started down her face as her body gave up the coil of fear in her heart.

The moon was beginning to lose its battle to the sun. It moved toward the other horizon and, in one last attempt to defeat the sun, shone more brightly than it had all night. But the sun slowly erased the moon, and the Comanche evaporated with the morning mist. The only sign of the battle was bloody, torn-up grass between the cabin and the woods, and the arrows that had not fulfilled their hideous duty.

The Thorntons and Wests joined hands once again and gave thanks to God for saving their lives. As they stood in the circle of prayer, Mary Anna heard Tump say confidently, "I heard Mama say it was a miracle. I want to see it. Where is it, Mama?"

She put her arms around him and the other children. "Right here, my sweet boy. Right here."

# Chapter 11

Three days after the raid, life was getting back to normal. The Wests had stayed with the Thorntons in case the Indians decided to try again, but all seemed to be peaceful.

"We'll be goin' over to our own cabin," Caleb announced at breakfast that morning. "I think everythin' is all right." He chewed a big bite of Mary Anna's soft biscuit and added, "Boy, that was a night to remember."

Everyone around the table nodded their heads in agreement. "I don't want to go through that ever again," said Virginia firmly. Her hand still shook a little when she raised her coffee cup to her mouth.

The children were just beginning to sleep through the nights without bad dreams. Loud noises could still make them jump.

"We need to report this to the sheriff in Stephenville so he can relay it to the army," said Daniel.

"We don't want to leave to go to town right now, Dan," said Caleb. "You don't know for sure where them Indians is. We'll do it later."

"But what about the other settlers around here?" Daniel argued.

"They knew before they come out here how bad the Indian situation is. I'm sure they're ready like we were. And the army ain't gonna catch Swift-as-an-Antelope. Let's jest git on with our business. You promised to make me a rich man. Remember?"

Daniel considered what Caleb had said and accepted the advice. "We need to round up some more cattle. There's a place just north of here that looked promising. We could try there." He looked at Mary Anna. "Will you be all right if we leave you women here so we can round up some cows?"

A lightning flash of fear shot through Mary Anna. She pulled herself together and, with eyes that were a little too bright, said, "Virginia and I can take care of each other." She put the hot blue-enameled coffeepot on the table carefully. "I know what to do if the Indians come back, but what should we do if Kirk comes back?"

"He won't." Daniel cut a big bite of smoked ham. "If he does, put a gun on him and tie him up in the lean-to. We'll take care of him when we come back."

Mary Anna looked to see if he was joking. He wasn't.

"Daniel," Mary Anna said hesitantly. "I don't think it's a good idea to go out

218

after the cows so soon. You don't know where the Indians are or even if they'll come back. Please don't go yet."

Daniel was still afraid of a raid, but he felt the chances of the men coming back were slim. Yet in front of him stood his pregnant wife who was still frightened to death. It was a wonder she hadn't lost the baby.

He put his arms around her and said, "I didn't mean right away." His eyes went to Caleb as he spoke to Mary Anna. "We'll wait a while, and then we'll have to get those cows added to our herd, else we'll lose a whole year."

They heard the sound of an approaching horse, and Daniel immediately grabbed the rifle and headed for the door. "Well, I'll be jiggered," he breathed. "Tump, come here!"

## Chapter 12

Daniel threw the door open a little wider, and Tump peered out. "Thunder! It's Thunder! He's come back! Mama! He's back!" Tump ran from the house to check his horse. "He's got a buckskin rope around his neck, but he looks fine to me." He looked at his father. "Is he all right?"

Daniel looked the horse over, too. "I can't see a thing wrong with him." He took the end of the frayed buckskin rope. "Looks like he wore the rope in two." He grinned. "I think what we have here is a runaway horse."

"Yeah, he ran away back to his home," said Tump with a huge smile. He stroked Thunder's nose. "You know where you belong, don't you, boy?"

"Take him around to the corral and give him some feed," ordered Mary Anna. "I hope he's had a long trip. The longer it was, the farther the Indians are away from us."

"I'll go feed him, but Mama, can he *please* stay in the lean-to tonight?"

Mary Anna looked at her son's happy, pleading face and, remembering it was Thunder that was used to start the Indian raid, agreed. "All right, but *you* still have to sleep inside the house."

Tump's face radiated joy. "Thanks, Mama."

"Thunder is just like a trained dog," laughed Virginia. "That horse is a pet."

"Ah, horses come back home all the time," Caleb said. He spit in the dirt and tried to appear unaffected by the horse's return.

"We're sure glad this one came back," Daniel replied. "I was going to have to train a new one for Tump. Now we can use that time to get our herd ready."

Mary Anna was relieved Daniel and Caleb wouldn't be leaving anytime soon. As she lay in bed that night with Daniel, she said, "Thank you for staying. I'm not sure I could cope with another attack—and especially without you."

He held her closer, running his fingertips over her soft face. Love for her caused a happy ache. "I won't leave you alone. You were so brave, my frontier woman. You've been through so much, yet you've never left me or let me down." Gently, he added, "You do know we have to go after those cows, don't you?"

When he felt her nod her head against him, he said, "Believe me, those Indians won't be back around here anytime soon. They'll pick on someone who doesn't live in a fort."

"And whose fort is not surrounded by angels," she added, smiling in the darkness. "That's the way I want to remember it. We were surrounded by angels, and the Indians couldn't get through."

"I wish I had known that at the time. I would have saved some of that ammunition," Daniel observed dryly.

"If you had run out of ammunition that night, you would have thrown sticks at those Indians to defend your home, and you know it," she said.

Mary Anna nestled deeper in his embrace. "I wish I could really understand your dream. I know what it is, but I've never had a dream that I was ready to die for. It's hard for me sometimes because I don't understand it." She could feel the slow beating of Daniel's heart under her head.

"I'm sorry I can't make you see the visions I see in my mind, my love. Maybe what I see is my home back in the South transplanted to here on the Brazos. Big white columns supporting a second floor and making a porch all around the house on the first floor. I don't want slaves, but I see us being rich enough to hire a lot of people to take care of the place. And a cook for you. And a laundress."

"I like to cook," she protested.

"You can cook when you want to, but you won't have to." He sighed. "Big green meadows filled with fancy horses and thoroughbred cattle. Down the road, miles away 'cause we own so much land, is a town. Stephenville. It'll have stores of every kind, and schools and churches. People will live in proper houses with white picket fences around them and flowers in the flowerbeds. We'll be respected cattle people.

"Our sons will be well educated and have wonderful manners, and our daughters will have the same chance to go to college and make fine marriages. I look down the years and see the Thornton name being one that people know and trust. And when our sons and daughters are married, you and I will still be together on the home place. They'll come for holidays and Sunday dinners. Maybe they'll decide to be governors and senators. Maybe even president someday. I want to build for tomorrow. And I want to be an important part of that tomorrow."

Mary Anna was silent as she saw the dream her husband carried, awed by the hugeness of it. "I see why you fight so hard for your dream," she whispered. A new and deeper respect crept over her for this man she thought she knew so well. "Now that I know the dream, I can fight just as hard for it as you can. Side by side."

She leaned up and gave him a soft kiss to seal her promise. "I'm glad we don't have to do this by ourselves. If God blesses this dream of yours, it will come true. Not without hardship, but not without the Lord."

"I've talked to the Lord a lot about this dream." Daniel smiled in the night. "He isn't going to make it easy for us, but I don't think He's said no to it. I still feel He thinks it's all right."

Daniel turned over a little so he could see her face in the firelight. "I'm sorry

I wasn't able to put the dream into words for you before. Sometimes I'd try, but it seemed like, well, like I was just full of myself. And if I failed, I didn't want you to know how grand the dream was. Then I wouldn't be a failure in your eyes, too."

"Sometimes you've let me down, Daniel, but you've never been a failure at anything." She used his new closeness to kiss his mouth again.

"You keep that up and you won't get to hear more about the dream."

"Hmm, tell me more."

"I'd like to travel some day. To some of those countries I've heard about. My family roots go back to Ireland and Scotland. Why, maybe there's a Thornton castle over there just waiting to be claimed."

"Pioneering in Ireland. Now that makes an interesting picture in my head." With a straight face she said, "Getting the wagon across that ocean is going to be a lot bigger job than getting across those rivers was."

The chagrin on his face quickly painted a light blush on his cheeks. "Ah, you know what I mean. That's the very end of the dream. I don't expect that to come true. But the first part is so real to me, Mary Anna. Sometimes in my sleep I think I'm living in our house."

Softly she added, "You said you wanted to ride your horse from your bed to the kitchen table for breakfast. I thought you were teasing."

"Nope. That's just what I want to do. And I want that table filled up with sons and daughters, smiling and neat and clean." He patted her rounding middle. "We're well into the plan on that score."

Mary Anna tried not to think of the small graves she had left behind, nor of the pain and joy that were to come with childbirth. Instead, she said, "Thank you, my love, for sharing your dream with me."

"You're the biggest part of that dream. I had to find you before I could even think of starting it. God gave you to me, Mary Anna, just as surely as He gave me the dream. And He will urge us on when we get discouraged and save us when disaster is near. He made us one." Daniel's kisses became deeper and more possessive. "He made us one flesh."

Mary Anna gave herself up to Daniel and the dream.

## Chapter 13

Weeks later Daniel told Caleb he was going into town for supplies.
"I'll keep watch while you're gone," he said.

The days it took Daniel to drive the wagon and the oxen to Stephenville were tranquil days of gardening for Mary Anna. She could feel her baby growing and felt confident the Lord would protect Daniel as well as the rest of them left at home.

When Daniel returned he brought a lot of supplies and news.

"First things first. Peppermint for you, Mary Anna."

She broke into a huge smile for him. It was now a joke between them. Peppermints had been his first gift to her and probably always would be when he returned from any trip.

"What about us, Papa?" little Peter asked.

"Horehound candy sticks for everyone," he laughed.

Finally, after everything was unloaded and put away, there was time around the table to share the news.

"Everyone is talking about the new state police. I'm not sure how well that's going to work out. Most of them are Negroes, but if they can cut down on crime and catch the Indians, it'll be a blessing. Also, there's a treaty in the works. Government is trying to get the Comanche and Kiowas to stay on the reservation. The peaceful ones are still on the Clear Fork of the Brazos, and the others are guarded by the army on the Lower Brazos." His brow wrinkled. "It didn't work in '58, and I don't think it will work this time either," he said flatly. "There's just too much land and not enough men to guard it."

"So we're still our best protection," said Mary Anna.

"Us and the Lord," Virginia reminded her.

"Of course." Daniel took a deep drink of buttermilk from a cold glass. He had been so busy he had not noticed that Mary Anna had handed him buttermilk instead of his usual coffee. Then it dawned on him. "Where in the world did you get cold buttermilk?"

Caleb smiled and ducked his head a little. "Oh, it was just a little project Virginnie has been trying to get me to do. I built a springhouse down by the stream. The water runs through it and cools the milk and butter and things. It needs a little refinement, but it's working pretty good right now. I hurried so's I'd be through by the time you got home again."

"Caleb, you're a wonder! Cold buttermilk." He savored a big mouthful.

"What else did you hear? Are our friends all right?"

"Going and blowing. Saw Frances Gerald. She's running a full boardinghouse now. Best food in town. Softest beds. She sent a cake for all of us."

"There's something else you haven't told us. Something good. Come on, Daniel, don't hold out on us," said Mary Anna. "I can see it in your eyes."

"I hired us some cowboys to help out with the roundup and the fall drive. They'll be along tomorrow."

"Yahoo!" shouted Caleb and made little Willie cry with the suddenness of his yell.

Mary Anna picked up Willie and said, "It's really beginning now, isn't it?"

"We're on our way to being rich cattle barons, jest like you promised," grinned Caleb.

"We're on our way," repeated Daniel.

He was up before dawn in anticipation of the men coming. Mary Anna heard his unsuccessful attempts to make coffee quietly and finally gave up her sleep to help him get his breakfast. It irked her to be awakened.

"I don't know why everything has to start at dawn," she complained.

"Ah, that's the best time of the day," said Daniel as he poured his coffee.

"It is not. The best time of the day is when all the children go down for a nap at the same time and I get to rest, too."

Daniel noted her larger middle. "It isn't easy to be pregnant," he sympathized.

That really ticked Mary Anna off. What did he know about what it was like? "I get bigger and bigger every day, and I can't bend over and get things I need. And someone inside me is kicking every time I want to rest. And my hands and feet swell, but it doesn't matter, because soon I won't be able to see my feet. And I know how much it's going to hurt when that lump in front finally does decide to come out. And then it keeps me up all hours of the night. And then there's the other children to care for and—"

"Whoa, whoa." Daniel quickly crossed the room and took Mary Anna into his arms. "I'm sorry. You seem to do it so easily every time." He wondered if she was worrying about whether the baby would live. *Maybe she's worrying about dying herself.*

"I'm not as young as I used to be." She laid her head on his broad chest and began to cry big gulps of tears.

"What's this? You never cry tears unless you're happy. Are these sad tears?" Daniel was alarmed at her sudden outburst. This was not the Mary Anna he knew and loved.

"No, they're pregnant tears. I just feel like crying, all right?"

He stood there holding her, wondering what to do or say next. He was afraid he'd make things worse if he said anything. He was honestly confused about her feelings. He remembered her bad temper when they first married. But this was something new.

Betty woke up, rubbing the sleep from her eyes, and hung her head over the loft edge. "Why is Mama crying?"

Tump, Peter, and Henry joined her. They looked like four solemn owls peering down at their weeping mother.

"Why is she crying, Papa?" repeated Tump.

Daniel was rattled by the four children suddenly intruding in their intimate husband-and-wife scene. "She's not really crying," he stumbled. "She's just tired."

"Why doesn't she go back to bed?" Tump asked reasonably.

Mary Anna cried a little harder, knowing that now that the four oldest ones were awake, she didn't have a chance in the world of sleeping. She pushed Daniel away and sat down in her rocking chair, tears streaming from her eyes.

Daniel reacted to the rebuff of his comfort by trying to do something practical. He went ahead with breakfast by getting out the big iron skillet.

He dropped the skillet just short of the fireplace, and all five of the other Thorntons jumped at the sound. Of course, its loudness woke baby Willie, who began to bawl at the top of his lungs. Helplessly Daniel looked from Mary Anna to the baby to the children in the loft.

"Just go away," Mary Anna sobbed. "You've helped me enough for one day. Go away. And don't come back until dinner."

Her angry words stung Daniel. He stomped out of the cabin without his breakfast and fed the cows with angry energy. "Women!" he told the horses in the corral. "If I live to be a hundred, I'll never understand them!"

It was at that inopportune moment that the two new cowboys came riding in. Normally someone would have heard them and come out to greet them, so the older of the two men took the initiative.

"Hello, house," called Coleman.

Mary Anna heard the cry and pulled herself together. She put a shawl over her nightgown and got the rifle as she opened the door slightly.

There on a horse was a man with the most ferocious-looking facial hair Mary Anna had ever seen. And he had another, younger man with him.

Coleman, on the other hand, saw a young woman, obviously with child, red-eyed, auburn hair cascading in a riot around her face, holding a rifle on him.

"Just take it easy, ma'am," he said gently. "We're looking for Daniel Thornton. We hired on for him to cowboy."

Mary Anna lowered the gun. "Oh, yes, he's looking for you. I think he's out at the corral. If he hasn't gone back to East Texas," she added under her breath.

"Are you all right, ma'am?" The other cowboy was a polite young man named Toad. He took off his hat as he spoke to her, turning almost as red as his tufted haystack of hair.

Mary Anna sniffed loudly at his kindness. "Yes, I'm fine. I'm just having a bad morning. You go on around to the corral, and after a while I'll have some breakfast for you." She shut the door without any further ado, a high sin of frontier courtesy.

"Do you think she's crazy?" asked Toad.

"Well, I don't think we'll bother her too much with breakfast. She looks like she's got her hands full this morning," said Coleman through his thick, black mustache. "Let's go around back like she said. I'd hate to think of our dead bodies adding to her bad morning," he drawled.

"Why, I think I'd rather face a stampede than go in that house for a meal," added Toad. "Poor Mr. Thornton. He does need help out here."

Daniel heard them coming and met them halfway. "Morning, gentlemen." He had worked off some of his anger and was recovering some of his good humor now that his working crew had arrived to get on with his business. He hoped Mary Anna was feeling better, too, for he said to the men, "Glad to see you so early. Climb on down and we'll go in and meet the missus. She'll probably have breakfast done in a little while."

"Oh, no," Toad said quickly. "We don't want to put her to no trouble."

Daniel was puzzled at the rebuff. "I'm sure she won't mind." The two men sat still on their horses.

Daniel pushed his hat up a little sideways and scratched his head. "Well, if you really don't want to come in the cabin and meet my wife now, we can do it later."

"I think later would be a really good idea," Coleman agreed.

"Why don't we go over to Caleb West's house?"

"Does he have a wife?" Toad asked carefully.

"As a matter of fact he does. Nice woman. Good cook. Maybe we could have breakfast over there."

"Why don't we wait and see, Mr. Thornton. Sometimes we like to cook for ourselves," Coleman replied.

Daniel decided he had two men who had been by themselves too long and were not comfortable with other people. He led them to Caleb's.

All was in order at the Wests' cabin.

"Y'all come on in and have some breakfast," said the neatly dressed, smiling Virginia. Toad and Coleman relaxed considerably and climbed down off their horses.

It took some talking on Daniel's part, but he finally convinced the men to help him in building the bunkhouse. Cowboys rarely did anything that required them to be off their horses. But they saw the wisdom of getting it done quickly.

They were moving the already cut logs to the site of the bunkhouse when the dinner bell finally sounded at high noon. Daniel started for the house and looked back at his reluctant workers. "Dinner's ready," he announced as though they didn't understand what the bell was for.

Toad and Coleman couldn't see a way to get around going up to the Thornton cabin, so they slowly followed their new boss and prepared for the worst.

Daniel opened the door, and the two new men shuffled their feet a little as though to take the dust off their boots so they could enter the dirt-floored cabin. Hats slipped from their heads. As they cleared the door, their mouths opened slightly in complete surprise.

Mary Anna turned from the fireplace. She was beautiful, and her hair was carefully put up. She had a big smile on her face and genuine welcome in her eyes. The children were clean and playing quietly on the floor. Mary Anna was dressed modestly in a smock that didn't hide her condition but somehow made her look winsome.

"Hello, gentlemen," she said as she put the heavy kettle on the table. "I'm glad to see you. Won't you sit down and have some dinner with us?" Her smile was bright as the sun.

Toad and Coleman closed their mouths, twirled their hats until Daniel showed them the pegs where his hat hung, and sat down dumbfounded.

In both their minds ran the question of whether this could possibly be the same woman they had met early that morning. Was it some sort of trick? Neither one of them said a word.

Toad stiffened a little when Mary Anna approached him carrying a hot pot of coffee. "Coffee?" she asked sweetly.

"Please, ma'am," and he prayed it wasn't going to be poured in his lap. Neatly Mary Anna served the men and then sat down herself.

"I'm sorry you found me in such disarray this morning," she said softly. "I had a bad morning." Then she smiled her radiant smile again. "But everything is all right now. The storm has passed."

Coleman smoothed down his bristled and unruly mustache and said quite seriously, "Ma'am, about how often do these storms come?"

Mary Anna exploded into laughter, clasping her hands together and rocking in her chair in an effort to allow room for all the laughter to escape. "I'm sorry," she gasped. "I don't know what happened to me this morning." She looked at Daniel. "I'm sure my husband is as confused as you are about my behavior." Daniel nodded his head in agreement.

She quickly told him about what had happened when the men came to the cabin.

"Now I understand your reluctance to come to the cabin for breakfast," Daniel laughed. "Her storms are well spaced, I promise. But to tell you the truth, I didn't know what to do, so I made a strategic retreat." The three men began to chuckle a little, and that touch of humor swelled into a good hard belly laugh. Mary Anna joined them, though less heartily since the joke was at her expense.

"Just remember what you saw and don't make me mad," she warned the men half seriously.

"Ma'am," Coleman said gallantly, "I'd want you fighting on my side anytime."

"Spoken like a real Southern gentleman." She nodded her head toward him in a small bow.

"Now that you're not afraid of my wife anymore," Daniel inserted, "let's get that bunkhouse finished."

That night Mary Anna and Virginia fed everyone a hearty supper outside under the softly whistling tree at the front of the cabin. But even in the serenity of the moment, Mary Anna had the feeling unfriendly eyes were watching from the woods, waiting for these white interlopers to get careless. She mentioned it to Daniel.

"I suspect you're right. Swift-as-an-Antelope has his own plans." The meal turned somber as Daniel warned Coleman and Toad about Mary Anna's feelings of being watched.

"Don't you worry none. We sleep with one eye open and our hands on our rifles," Coleman assured them. "We know about the Indian problems around here. Matter of fact, we found some poor white man about ten miles from here. I don't want to tell you what the Indians had done to him, but he must've died several times."

Mary Anna and Daniel exchanged looks. "Could you give us a description of the man. Hair color? Old or young?"

"All them questions are a little hard to answer, but it seems to me he was young and blond. Might have been a nice kid. Handsome, too. Hard to tell by the time we found him."

"Kirk," Mary Anna breathed softly.

"Prob'ly," Caleb answered. "Well, we don't have to worry about him anymore."

"Just Swift-as-an-Antelope," Virginia said grimly.

Daniel filled the men in on Kirk's betrayal.

"Man should never try to play both ends against the middle," Coleman said. "Especially if one of those ends is the Indians. Well," he added sadly, "he got his just deserts. Many times."

"And we'll be watching out for the Antelope fellow," added Toad. "He won't be the first Indian I've had to kill. And he will get killed iffen he tries to raid us or steal the horses." His face reflected the determination and courage of his youth.

Just having two more men on the place made everything seem so much less threatening. Mary Anna made sure they were full before they left the table for their bedrolls down by the half-finished bunkhouse.

When Mary Anna and Daniel were in bed, she sighed deeply as the baby began its usual night kicking. "It's beginning to feel real. The dream, I mean," she said. "Cowboys, bunkhouses." She grinned largely in the dark. "We now own a ranch."

Daniel was lying on his back beside her and added his deep sigh to hers. "Yes, I guess we do." In a soft voice, he began to speak of their kingdom.

"Before the war, I dreamed of helping to save the South. Those dreams of glory faded real fast in the face of the awful battles." His face was sad for a moment, then hopeful. "Now I have new dreams of glory.

"I know the Good Book says the kingdom of God is what we are to strive for. But I also think He could let part of it be a place. I think we live there. And inside His kingdom, I want to put our ranch. We can do so much for this part of Texas."

Daniel turned over to face Mary Anna. "I get this tingling all over me when I think of owning a big ranch and hiring a lot of men and moving all that beef to the railheads for the East." He returned her smile in the half darkness.

"Texas is the only place where all those dreams could come true for me. And God gave me you to help. I feel all of this so strongly. We can make a go of it. The Indians can't burn us out this time. We'll make us the finest spread in this half of Texas. People will come for miles to sit at our table. And we'll feed good beef to the people in the East. We'll build the big house and entertain everyone from beggars to presidents if they happen to come by. And our sons and daughters will be educated way past us and take over the ranch when we're resting in that special part of the kingdom.

"Sam Houston, Stephen F. Austin, and all the other men and women who came to Texas to settle it have left us a legacy. Texas is on the brink of greatness. I want to ride in on that tide of our history." His voice in the darkness was charged with the electricity of a huge summer storm.

Mary Anna felt its power, and huge goose bumps rose on her arms. "When you speak of your dream like that, there is nothing I can do but hold on to you and ride with you." Hope flashed through her and filled her with the confidence that they could survive the Indians and everything else that would be thrown at them to keep them from achieving their dream.

"The Lord says He watches over us. He also says to ask and it will be given."

"I've asked him a million times. He's blessed the labor of our hands so far.

We'll just keep on making plans and living in His promises. If we're on the wrong track, He'll let us know."

"Don't forget the devil has a few tricks up his sleeve, too, you can bet," Mary Anna warned.

"The Lord is more powerful than the devil. God has given us two more fine men. Why, we have our own little army right here on the ranch." Daniel said the word *ranch* a little self-consciously but with pride.

Mary Anna was charged up with Daniel's exciting talk. "Let's go outside and look at this land in the moonlight," she said.

Daniel looked at her with surprise. "I should know you well enough by now not to be caught off guard by anything you say, but sometimes you amaze me." He helped her sit up. "Come on, little mother, get your shawl. It's a little cool out there. And put on some shoes."

"You sound like the little mother," she teased as she slipped her feet into her soft moccasins. "Remember when you got so mad when I made these shoes when I was pregnant the first time?"

Daniel smiled ruefully. "That was another Daniel in another time." He laughed a short laugh. "I guess I could call you Princess Big Feet right now."

"You could, but it would be a bad idea. Remember this morning?"

He guided her quietly out of the cabin into the waning moon. The wind played the leaves like a fairy wind chime, calming and soothing and promising all was well in the kingdom.

"I like to see the moon carved out like that. I won't be able to enjoy a full moon again for a long, long time," she said. She pushed the bad memories of the full-moon raid of the Comanche away and reached for the happy ones the night offered her. Daniel stood behind her with his arms wrapped around her for warmth and love. He kissed the back of her neck, an intimate place, accessible only to him. She shuddered with the heat of the kiss. "I'll have another son for you this time. I'll have many sons for you. For us."

"And some daughters for the two of us. No family is complete without daughters.

"Lord, thank You for the blessings You've already heaped upon us and the safety we require now," Daniel spoke the words with great thankfulness. "I know we're asking a lot of You when we talk about the ranch, but if it's Your will, help us with the dream. We want it not only for us, but for Your glory. I don't know how—yet—but I'm sure You will show us a way. Keep us safe from Satan's claws and lead us in the way You would have us to go."

Mary Anna felt tears of happiness slide down her cheeks. There was no need for alarm. The Lord had granted her the most important thing she had ever asked of Him. She had asked that Daniel return to his Lord. It was very clear that he had. After seeing such a change in her husband, Mary Anna knew the Lord could answer any request they might ask of Him. Her trust swelled and grew like the child inside her. "I'm sure the Lord will bless our new dreams of glory, my love." She turned in his arms, reaching up and putting her lips fully against his. "I love you, Daniel Thornton."

He held on to Mary Anna tightly, filled with power and hope. With God's help, nothing would stop them this time.

From the darkened woods, a shadow stood watching the tender scene. He was not moved by the love he saw. His love was lying wrapped in death clothes with his tiny son. In his heart he felt only hatred. He felt only the desire to recapture his life and his land. He dreamed of the glory of the old days.

*Dreams*
*Fulfilled*

*For Mary Anna Thornton Smith,*
*who turned back the pages of time and showed me my history.*

# Chapter 1

*Barton Springs, Texas—1868*

The prairie sky was marbled with blues and oranges. Wisps of white, feathery cirrus clouds curled around the deep purples of the sunset. Raucous mockingbirds strove to outdo each other in announcing the setting of the sun.

Daniel could hear the soft singing of the small stream behind the cabin, and the smell of Mary Anna's supper teased his taste buds. The babble of their five children blended with their mother's firm commands.

He tipped his rawhide-bottomed chair back against the rude logs of the cabin he and Mary Anna had built the year before with help from their friends, the Wests. Turning his head to the east, he could see the Wests' cabin on the other side of the communal garden Mary Anna and Virginia had planted.

The sudden nickering of horses in the corral made Daniel sit up, alerting all his senses. Any sound of disruption with the horses was cause for concern. They were the prime target of the renegade Comanche, better than gold or silver.

Many of the Comanche and other tribes were off the reservations since the end of the war. Few troops were available to contain them, and the Indians were taking their revenge on the settlers who had torn the land from them.

The startled sound of the horses quieted, and Daniel listened for a minute more. All sounded well, so he slowly eased himself back into his chair. Fear for his horses was replaced by thoughts of the upcoming cattle roundup and the fall drive to market.

*When I first came to Texas, people told me it was a land flowing with milk and honey, and so it has been. But they didn't mention how hard it would be to collect on that promise,* he thought wryly. *Still, the Lord has provided for us up to this point. He won't let us down now.*

Two cowboys Daniel had hired came strolling up from the bunkhouse for supper. Mary Anna had invited them to eat with the family. Daniel hoped it wouldn't be too long before there were too many cowboys to feed and he'd have to hire a cook just for the men.

"Howdy, Mr. Thornton," said Coleman. His ferocious black mustache barely moved when he spoke, giving him a solemn look even when he was smiling. His sidekick, Toad, stuck his thumbs inside the pockets of his heavy denim pants and added his greeting. Daniel stood up, and the three men entered the house, where Mary Anna was waiting to serve the meal.

Mary Anna always had to hide a smile when Toad took off his hat to her. His hair resembled a red haystack, no matter how much water he put on it when he combed through it. And freckles dotted the fair skin that came with the red hair. He looked to be about seventeen. Coleman was in his midtwenties. They looked very young to thirty-one-year-old Mary Anna, but they didn't look untried.

The noise and confusion of four adults and five children finding their places around the supper table quieted when Daniel paused to say grace. As the baked beans, roast, biscuits, gravy, and canned corn from the last year's harvest circled the table, all conversation focused on the upcoming roundup.

During a break in the talk, fourteen-year-old Tump cleared his throat. "Papa?" he asked hesitantly. "I work with the horses and cattle every day. Can't I go on the roundup with you this year? I know I could help. Please?"

Daniel looked at his oldest son in surprise, then glanced across the table at Mary Anna. "Son," he said gently, "I do appreciate how you've taken on responsibilities this past year and been a real help to both me and your mama. That's why I have to say no. While I'm gone, your mama's going to rely on you to take care of the animals that we leave behind and to set an example for your brothers and sister. I'm depending on you to be the man of the family while I'm gone. Do you understand?"

The light of anticipation died from Tump's eyes, and they looked suspiciously wet as he quickly looked down at his plate. "Yes, sir," he whispered.

"Tump," Mary Anna added, "I know that this is a big disappointment for you, that waiting to take part in big adventures can seem to take forever, but I can't tell you what a comfort it will be to me to know you are here during all those months your papa will be gone."

Her oldest son gave her a tremulous smile, but Mary Anna knew it would take some weeks before Tump had adjusted to this latest disappointment.

Supper over, the men went outdoors to continue settling the details of the roundup. Mary Anna was cleaning up the supper things and getting the children tucked into bed when she heard a soft knock on the open door.

"Evening, Mary Anna." Virginia West was skinny as a shadow, as though honed down to her limit, yet she was getting a healthy glow about her with good food and Mary Anna's companionship. "Got my young'uns tucked in. Thought we could talk a little." She helped herself to a cup of coffee from the pot on the back of the stove and settled herself in a chair by the kitchen table. "Caleb wanted to talk with the men, too, about the roundup."

Mary Anna's eyes gleamed with mischief. "Wouldn't it be fun to go with them?"

Virginia was visibly shocked. "It would not! I would never, ever even think of going on that trip with a bunch of men and horses and cattle. I'll stay here in my cozy cabin, thank you."

"But it would be such an adventure," Mary Anna sighed. "Tump was asking if he could go this year, and while of course he can't, I must say I sympathize with his desire. I've never been that far north before. I think they've decided on the Kansas railhead. I've heard it's a big city. Bigger than any I've seen. Think of the shopping and the restaurants and hotels."

"And they'll all be filled with filthy cowboys who haven't had a decent bath or change of clothes since they left home, and they'll probably all be looking for a good time. The only women in that town are most likely the kind we don't talk about." Virginia looked at her friend suspiciously. "You're reading those romantic books again, aren't you?" she teased.

Mary Anna colored slightly. "Daniel found an old *Godey's Magazine* for me in town last week."

"And you didn't tell me?" Virginia jumped up from the table. "Where is it? I want to see the latest fashions." She tried to look stern. "And there was a romance story in it, too, wasn't there?"

Mary Anna clasped her hands. "Oh, it is so romantic and sad. I cried and cried after I finished it. I was going to give it to you as soon as I was done with it," she added contritely.

"You didn't cry," Virginia said flatly. "You never cry unless you're happy."

"But I was happy. The ending of the story was so beautiful." She opened one of her brass-bound trunks and took out the magazine, smoothing its cover with her hand. Then she gave it to her friend.

Virginia's grin was broad. "I'll give it back to you when I'm finished," she promised.

Mary Anna joined her at the table with her own cup of coffee. She sighed as she lifted the cup to her lips.

"Why the sigh?"

"I was thinking of all the work that has to be done between now and the time the men come back from the drive. The land of milk and honey is there for the taking, but my, what a price must be paid."

"Caleb saw Comanche signs out on the north pasture yesterday," Virginia said softly. "It's just a matter of time, you know."

"I know. I have everything ready here in the cabin if they decide to hit the house."

"No one knows what the Comanche think. If we're real lucky, they'll take only the stock." Virginia sipped carefully from the blue-bordered china cup.

"It won't be luck, Virginia. It will be God's mercy. I don't believe in luck. I think the Almighty has a plan for all of us. We may not understand it or even like it, but it isn't luck. And it isn't written in stone. Different people make all kinds of decisions that somehow affect us. Then the Lord brings good out of it to accomplish His ultimate goal for us."

Virginia's face turned a delicate shade of gray, and her jaw tensed. "It's His will about all this killing and my babies dying?" she asked in a rough voice.

"No, but He was there when all that was happening, and He's used it to make you the woman you are today. A fine woman, strong and wise. You are able to sympathize and care for other women who have suffered as you have, because you've been there." Mary Anna patted her friend's rough hand. "God's love and strength have brought us through all our trials to make us what we are today. Think of all the women who are not nearly as smart as we are," she added with a rueful chuckle.

"I'm glad I know the things I know, but that doesn't mean I want to go through them again," Virginia said, a tiny mist of tears forming in her eyes.

"I know. But we will if we have to. And we will survive it." Mary Anna held Virginia's hand briefly and gave it a loving squeeze. "We're in better shape here than we have been the entire time we've been living in Texas."

Virginia dried her eyes on the hem of her apron. "That's true. We have more men to defend us with Toad and Coleman. And our cabins are close together. The new bunkhouse is right there." She laughed out loud. "You should have seen the looks on Toad and Coleman's faces when Daniel asked them to help finish building the bunkhouse. You know, it's against the code of the cowboy to do anything that can't be done from the back of a horse. Building isn't one of those things. Until Daniel agreed to pay them extra and reminded them the Comanche are going to want those horses, they wouldn't agree to help. I think it was Coleman who said he didn't want to be fighting the Indians out in the open, so they worked like slaves to get it done."

After their laughter died down, Mary Anna added, "I'm sure glad I'm not married to a cowboy."

"But you are," Virginia argued.

"Nope, Daniel will have to work as a cowboy for a while, but he says he'll be a cattleman one day."

"Ah. The cattleman owns the ranch and the cowboys work it. Right?"

"Right."

"Then I guess I'm married to a cattleman, too!" Virginia laughed.

While the women talked in the warm kitchen, the "cattlemen" talked with their cowboys outside under the trees in the swept front yard. Big branches swayed in the night air. April weather was notoriously fickle. Today had been a pleasantly warm day, and the breeze felt good.

Daniel and his neighbor, Caleb West, were determined to gather some of the stray cattle that roamed the Texas prairie. The animals had been abandoned by their owners for as many reasons as there were cows, and anyone willing to risk life and limb rounding them up and branding them could claim them. Then the animals would be taken to the railhead, where they would be sold.

"How many horses we got broke?" Caleb asked.

"Oh, maybe two dozen," Daniel answered.

"I'm breaking 'em as fast as I can," Toad said.

"You keep doing what you're doing. Breaking 'em faster isn't what I have in mind. I want them handled gentle. No rough stuff," Daniel said firmly. "Coleman, are you and Caleb going out tomorrow to drive those cows in from the south?"

"Yes, sir. I reckon I spotted about thirty head down there. We could use another hand."

"That'll leave the women only one man on the place. No offense, Toad, but there's a Comanche moon coming up soon. I can feel it in my bones that we're probably going to get hit. Cattle or horses, I don't know. You get those cows up here to the ranch into that cattle pen as fast as a greased pig. Two men out there isn't any more safe than one man on the place."

"You'll be adding more cowboys soon?" Coleman asked.

"I will. Like to find some honest men who'll work for their wage."

"Don't everyone?" interjected Caleb with a laugh.

"Mr. West and me'll swing by Stephenville and leave word at the mercantile store. That'll spread the news," Coleman offered. Stephenville was about twelve miles southwest.

"That'll lose you two days of getting to those cows," Daniel worried. "But we need the help. Do it—but don't tell Mrs. Thornton, or you'll have a list of things as long as your arm that she needs from the mercantile store." Chuckling, he rose and stretched in the glow of the moon.

"I used to love to see that old moon get big and fat like it was so heavy it would fall from the sky," said Caleb. "Now I get butterflies in my stomach every time it gets full."

"I guess we all do. They may not wait that long, so keep your eyes and ears peeled for any signs." Daniel yawned.

"I've already spotted some today on the north pasture. Horse tracks. Unshod ponies. Better sleep with your rifle for a while."

Toad and Coleman headed for the bunkhouse, while Daniel and Caleb headed for the cabin. "You best tell the women," Daniel said.

"Virginia knows. She's prob'ly already told Mary Anna."

Later that night, Daniel took his own advice and kept the rifle handy as he slept. He knew Mary Anna was sleeping as lightly as he was. *I'll look for the day when I can sleep the sleep of the righteous the whole night through. It's coming,* he promised himself, *it's coming. Patience. The Lord is on guard, too.*

⟡

The next few days were a flurry of activity as cows were brought in and put protestingly into the cattle pens. Four more men drifted in to help with the roundup and brand the cattle with the Thornton brand: the Diamond T. It honored Daniel's promise—made way back when he and Mary Anna first came west—to buy Mary Anna a huge diamond as big as the stars.

"I wouldn't know what to do with a big diamond," she'd argued with him. "I'd rather have another woman to come in and help with the chores."

"You know I can't afford that," he'd countered. "I need men for the drive."

A little sourly she'd conceded, "I'm sorry—I got my lists mixed up." But she knew he was right.

Most of the men wouldn't see their money until the end of the drive when the cattle were sold at market value. Until then, food had to be provided for them, and Mary Anna used her experience from cooking in her father's hotel as a young lady to provide large quantities of delicious food for all of the hard-working men.

Toad and Coleman shared their small bunkhouse until it was crowded, and the rest of the men slept in the barn.

"This place is beginning to look like a real ranch," Mary Anna told Daniel. "Cowboys everywhere I look."

"I hope the Comanche are looking, too. Maybe they won't want to take on so big a band of white men."

But instead of the Indians, the army came riding in.

"Lieutenant Mooreland," barked the cocky young man who sat on a prancing red roan. "I'm here to buy horses."

His arrogance was irritating to Daniel, but the possibility of getting cash from the government kept Daniel from making the tart reply perched on the tip of his tongue. Instead, he deliberately withheld the customary invitation for his visitor to get down off his horse and simply asked, "How many horses did you have in mind?"

Ignoring Daniel's rudeness, the lieutenant got off his horse and dusted his clothes. "That depends entirely on the quality of the animals," he responded.

The blue of the lieutenant's uniform did nothing to smooth Daniel's ruffled feathers. *A bluebelly is a bluebelly,* said his Southern heart.

The Union's hand had been hard on the beaten South. Taxes were unjustly high, and the few government men Daniel had had the misfortune of dealing with had been complete scoundrels. Talk in town was rough tongued against Reconstruction policies.

"Been here long, Lieutenant Mooreland?" Daniel asked casually.

The man blushed slightly. "A month," he replied.

"Then you should know that the horses I sell are good. That's the only kind I sell. Kind of a point of honor with me," he drawled.

"Honor for a Reb," one of the men in the patrol snickered. "That's a good one."

Daniel felt his blood rise. Silently he led the men to the corral, where Coleman and some of the hands were working with the horses.

The lieutenant was clearly pleased with what he saw. "I can use ten. I'll give you ten dollars a piece."

Daniel was tempted to ask for fifteen dollars just because of how he was feeling toward the government, but the lieutenant had offered a fair price. Daniel signed the requisition, wondering if the money would ever actually be paid.

"We'll be back in a week or so. I'll bring you the money," Lieutenant Mooreland promised.

Daniel nodded, biting back sarcastic words about the worth of government promises.

"Any trouble with the Indians?" the lieutenant asked as he remounted.

"Just signs lately." He chose not to elaborate.

"You're lucky if you didn't lose any horses or get anyone killed. The farm a few miles from here lost all their stock and had one man killed. Probably Santana's work." He sighed. "We do what we can." He adjusted the ornate saber at his side. "We'll get them eventually. We got Nocona, and we'll get that squirt Quannah Parker, too."

"I believe that was J. H. Cureton and Captain Rip Ford who got Nocona," Daniel said quietly.

"Spangler had twenty men in there, too" was the brief reply.

"Took almost a hundred men to kill him. Parker isn't going to be any easier." He eyed the small patrol. "Hope you don't meet up with him on this trip. He learned everything from his father."

Angrily Lieutenant Mooreland replied, "He'd have one big fight on his hands if we did meet." Without another word, the man and his patrol began herding the horses away from the corral.

"You're a prime target with all those horses," Daniel warned the retreating men's backs. In spite of his anger, he didn't wish the men dead. Frightened out of their haughtiness, yes, but not dead.

As the lieutenant and his men headed out, Coleman walked over to his boss. "The Indians will take the uppity notions out of them the first go-round," he told

Daniel solemnly. "Nothing like a war whoop to take the starch out of a man's underwear."

Daniel laughed in spite of the painful truth of the statement. "Well, men, we're richer now if we get paid. Guess I'll be able to pay your wages this month."

That brought a big smile from the hands.

"Course the downside is that we need more horses broken." He threw a small salute toward Toad. "Go to it, boy, and take one of the new men with you. You can show him what to do."

Toad's chest swelled a little with pride at being made the headman of the team by his boss.

≈

Daniel came in to supper that night exhausted. His greeting wasn't as warm as usual. When he sat down at the table, he simply prayed out of habit, "For what we are about to receive, O Lord, make us truly grateful," and fell to eating.

When Daniel had eaten enough to ease his hunger and tiredness, he looked at Mary Anna. She had been silent through the meal. "You must be as tired as I am," he said carefully. Mary Anna's temper had moderated through the years, but Daniel would never forget those tempestuous early days of their marriage.

"I am."

"I'll get you some help as soon as I can," he promised, eager to lift her spirits.

"I know." She sat down beside him at the table. "It's just that everything is for the ranch right now, and I still have a dirt floor." She burst into a flood of tears that totally unnerved Daniel. Mary Anna never cried unless she was happy.

Clumsily he stood and took her in his arms. "I'll put in floors for you, if that's what you want. You only have to ask me."

"And a cellar," she sniffed.

"All right." He smoothed her hair back from her face. "Anything else?"

"Windows. I need windows so I can see the lovely spring," she sniffed. "I'll need the fresh air for the baby," she added softly.

It took a moment for the message to sink in. "The baby. *A* baby. That's what all this is about. You're going to have another baby! Oh, Mary Anna, I'm thrilled! When?" He held her closer.

"Early January, I think."

"I'll get everything done for you and the new baby before I go on the drive in the fall. You'll be as snug as a big old black bear sleeping off the winter. All of us will be." The laughter in his eyes drifted to his mouth in the form of a big smile. "I love you, Mary Anna Garland Thornton. More and more every year."

"And I love you, too, Daniel Robert Thornton. Thank you for fixing up the cabin into a real house."

"Anything for my love," he promised, knowing that it would be a struggle to find the time to get the project finished. He knew better than to ask the cowboys to help, and he needed them doing cowboys' work anyway.

The next day, Daniel confided in Caleb about his problem.

Caleb looked at Daniel with great sympathy. "She's going to have a baby, isn't she?" he guessed wisely with a shake of his head.

"Yes, and I'm happy about that." In spite of his words, Daniel looked miserable.

"I know. But that's when they start wanting the durndest things. Well, the onliest thing I know to do is fer you and me to get busy so we can git on with the cattle business. We've got to keep our wives happy, else we're doing all this ranching business for nothing."

With the two of them working and their older boys helping, it didn't take too long to dig a cellar with a hinged door over it, set in new puncheon floors. They put in small windows with shutters on either side. The windows could be raised for airing the cabin, and the shutters could either be partially closed for firing a rifle during a raid or shut up tight for the coming winter winds.

When the work was finally done, Mary Anna was ecstatic over the improvements to her home. She pranced around the room and positively glowed with pride.

"This is a real home. Something to be proud of. Oh, thank you two for all this." Much to Caleb's surprise, she grabbed both of the men around the neck and bumped them together with her big hug.

As the men walked outside Mary Anna's hearing, Caleb said glumly, "Well, you know what else this means."

Daniel sighed and nodded his head. "Yup. Your cabin next, right?"

"You're a man wise beyond your years in the ways of women," said Caleb as he reached for his tools and headed toward his cabin.

The raw smell of the beautiful wood on her floor and windows was like the fragrance of the forest after a cooling rain, and Mary Anna sat in her rocker for a little while and let it flow around her. Then she smiled as she heard the familiar sound of hammering and sawing coming from Virginia's home. "We have the best husbands in the world," she reflected as she laid her head back against the rocker and smiled and smiled.

That evening Coleman and Toad were invited for supper so that plans for the drive could be finalized. After the meal, Caleb joined them, and the serious planning began. Coleman used a piece of brown wrapping paper to draw a rough map, indicating the general trails known to him.

"I've rode with Goodnight and Loving." Lest they think him a braggart, he added, "I wasn't their trail boss, but I kept my eyes and ears open. I know that way. We was on the trail about two months. Guess we went close to seven hundred miles. Long miles, too. The trick is to get there first. But," he added, "you have some flooding in the rivers.

"You know we're going to have trouble with the Indians and rustlers. After that, all you have to worry about is having water on them long stretches. There's been some talk that the Kansas farmers don't want us bringing our cattle in because they claim that they cause some kind of fever. Personally, I doubt that. Probably getting it from the Indians. We'll need more men, depending on however many cows we push."

"Before the war I ran a small herd with Wylie, a friend of mine, to Palo Pinto," said Daniel. "We did it with just four of us, but it was a small herd. We drove them to Palo Pinto to put them in with another herd. Now I want a big herd, and I plan to take it all the way." A ripple of excitement passed from one man to the other.

*What is it,* Mary Anna wondered as she listened to the men talk, *that pulls men to take on such a job?* It meant possible wealth for her and Daniel, but the wages for the cowboys could easily be lost in the many temptations of the trail towns. Still, there sat Toad and Coleman with vibrations of excitement running through them. She tried to recapture the feelings of adventure she had expressed earlier to Virginia, but in the reality of talking about the drive, she, too, was grateful she could stay in her home. *Two months,* she thought with dismay.

"How many horses do you think we'll need for the remuda?" Daniel asked Coleman.

"It's best to take about eight or ten for each man. Lots of things can happen to a mount. Seven hundred miles can wear out a lot of horseflesh."

"We can get the horses, no problem there. Finding the men may be another thing. The war seems to have used up a lot of them," Daniel added a little bitterly.

"You've started the word out. The men will find you. Choosing the good ones will be the tricky part," Coleman assured him. "You do understand they will call you captain because you're the one with the money invested."

Daniel's eyebrows rose. "Captain? I never thought to be called a captain at this late date."

"Cattle drive is a lot like an army maneuver. Takes teamwork and good strong leadership," Coleman assured him.

Coleman was just beginning to discuss the dangers of a stampede when Mary Anna decided she had heard enough. When she rose and began tidying up, the three guests hastily excused themselves. Caleb walked back over to his cabin, and Coleman and Toad headed toward the bunkhouse.

Quiet descended on their home. Daniel went to Mary Anna and wrapped his arms around her tiny figure. "Too much man talk tonight?" He kissed her softly. "You won't mind so much when I buy that diamond and build that mansion for you."

"I think I already have that mansion," she sighed. "I'm just worrying about who will defend it from the Indians while you're off playing cowboy."

"Remember? I'm the cattleman. They're the cowboys." He helped himself to a kiss.

In spite of herself, she felt the familiar stirrings beginning. "You're terrible," she breathed, even as she returned his kiss.

"I know. All us cattle barons are like that."

Later as she lay in their bed, she thought about the baby. Her smile was broad as she decided it would be a girl this time. Another girl for her. She loved her four sons and was proud of them. They would help make the ranch dream continue. But the girls were hers. Companions. Dear friends when they grew up. A little sister for Betty. She would name her Annah. And then there would be grandchildren. . . . She fell asleep before she could plan the rest of her life.

## Chapter 2

As the cattle and horse herds began to grow, so did Daniel's fear of attacks from Indians and rustlers. The men riding night guard had scared off a couple would-be cattle thieves. But the Indians had been strangely quiet. That made Daniel nervous. He was anxious to get on the trail, yet he knew he would be more exposed than ever to attack.

Mary Anna knew he was deeply worried. One night after the children were in bed and she and Daniel were sitting at the kitchen table discussing the day, she said, "Daniel, I sense you aren't easy about something."

Daniel stared into his coffee cup, watching the lantern light reflected in the black liquid. After a pause, he admitted, "You're right. No matter what I do, I know our herd is vulnerable to attack, and there's nothing much more I can do to protect it."

Quietly she said, "I think you need to spend a lot more time in prayer. No one on earth can keep your herd together all the way to Kansas. Give your worries to the Lord and let Him take care of things."

Daniel rubbed his index finger around the rim of his cup. Finally, he put his cup down on the table and stood up. "Mary Anna, love, I need to go out and do me some talking with the Lord. Why don't you go ahead and get some sleep? I'll be joining you in a bit."

As he headed toward the door, Mary Anna rushed over and gave him a reassuring hug. Her gentle smile was the last thing he saw as he closed the door behind him. Daniel prayed long and hard that night under the starry sky before he went to bed. Looking at the stars thrown across the black heavens like tiny pieces of mirror put his life in perspective. "Lord," he prayed as he looked out over the land, "I'm not a man of many words, and You know I have trouble relying on anyone other than myself. I've depended on my wits and rifle to get me out of hard places most of my life. But I'm in a situation I can't handle on my own. Please give me peace of mind during the days and weeks ahead, and place Your protecting hand on our venture. Teach me how to follow Your leading and trust You. And more than anything, watch over Mary Anna and our children while I'm gone."

The next morning Daniel woke refreshed and eager for the day. Several more men drifted in asking about the drive. Daniel asked Coleman to screen the men and hire the ones he thought honest. "You'll be the trail boss," Daniel announced. "By the way," he grinned, "are you a praying man?"

"Yes, sir. I was saved during a run-in with the Apaches a few years ago. Found me a town and a preacher and had myself baptized in the river. I'm pretty sure that's how I found this job. Praying for work."

Daniel noticed for the first time how Coleman's dark brown eyes gleamed from his face. Even the bushy eyebrows and mustache couldn't hide the glow.

"It's old Toad you need to work on, sir. He sure does need saving before we get to Kansas." Coleman laughed. "Even a saved man has to be careful up there."

"I know not all the men will be Christians, but choose the honest ones. I want to build a rock-hard reputation as an honest man. I plan to drive cattle to Kansas and anywhere else that we can sell them. I want my reputation to precede me."

"I'll do the best I can, sir, but I can't guarantee you a bunch of knights in shining armor."

"I know," Daniel sighed.

The herd was fast swelling to fifteen-hundred head, and Daniel was even more certain that a raid was inevitable. So when a few nights later, he and Mary Anna were awakened by gunshots, he wasn't surprised. He and Mary Anna crawled out of bed, and Mary Anna heated some coffee on the stove. Guns at the ready, they anxiously hoped for news from the men who had been on guard—but they realized they could soon be facing an attack on their home.

About ten minutes later, they heard a horse galloping toward the cabin. "That's only one rider," Mary Anna whispered as she dimmed the lantern light. "Maybe we'll escape attack, at least for tonight."

Daniel peered cautiously through a crack in the shutters and breathed a sigh of relief when the rider came into view under the moonlight. Peterson was riding in with his report.

Daniel opened the door to the man, and Mary Anna passed him a cup of hot coffee.

"Got about ten head, Captain. No horses. I guess there was about fifteen of 'em. Not Comanche this time—Apaches. Things must not be goin' too well fer them either."

Daniel nodded with satisfaction. Maybe news that the Thornton Ranch was well guarded by watchful men would spread to other bands in the area, and the Indians would decide the ranch wasn't worth the trouble it brought. "Thanks, Peterson. Tell the men, 'Well done.'"

After Peterson left to return to his duties, Daniel pulled Mary Anna into a fierce hug. "The Lord is answering my prayers already," he whispered. "His hand protected us and our children. Let's thank Him—and then get what little sleep we still can."

❦

Daniel had hired on several freedmen: blacks who had been freed by the war. They were good workers, glad to be able to choose their own boss and to roam where they pleased.

Caleb showed up with another freedman at breakfast the next morning.

"Daniel Thornton, I want you to meet one of the best cooks in Texas. This here is Rabbit Washington Lincoln."

What Daniel saw first was a big wagon with pots and pans hanging off every side, clanging with a music all its own. Then he looked at the smiling man driving the covered wagon. The man jumped down and walked over to Daniel, taking off his slouch hat and extending his hand.

Daniel shook the man's hand and surveyed him. Lincoln was close to six feet, four inches tall and was as thin as a Lincoln rail. His hair was a mass of tightly kinked balls, and he looked to be around twenty. His clothes were old, but they were clean and neat.

"Howdy, Mr. Thornton." He held his hat in his hand respectfully. "I'm the best trail cook in Texas. My mammy was the number one cook on the plantation, and she taught me. I've been on two drives, and I can keep the men happy about the grub." Without taking a breath, he added, "They call me Rabbit 'cause I can catch any one of 'em I can see, and I make the best rabbit stew you ever wrapped your lips around."

"I kin testify to that myself," Caleb said. "I met Rabbit back during the war. He's a good man."

"Sounds like you're hired," Daniel grinned. "And this is your supply wagon?"

"Yes, sir. This here is a chuck wagon. Made it with the tailgate to drop down and make a table. Filled it with little drawers and cubbies for all my cooking things."

Daniel looked at the mules pulling the wagon. "You think those two mules can make it all the way to Kansas?"

"Yes, sir. Savannah an' Alabama an' I have been together a long time. They kin pull a wagon all day long and not even be weary at the end of the day. They better than horses er oxes. They the best. I trained 'em myself."

As Rabbit rode off slowly to the barn, Daniel said, "Looks like it's all falling into place. I want to hurry up and get going. We should leave in two more days. Tell the men." Daniel grinned. "That'll be the easy part. Then we'll only have to tell our wives."

❦

Mary Anna took one look at Daniel's face and said, "I know. I can see it in your eyes. When?"

"Two days." He pulled her away from the sink and put his arms around her. Pain clouded his loving blue eyes. "Try not to be mad at me for leaving. The boys will still be here."

"An almost fourteen-year-old who's mad he can't go, a ten-and-a-half-year-old, two more rowdy boys to keep up with, and a babe in arms. The sight of those boys along with Betty and me ought to make old Ten Bears think twice before he comes to call." She paused, her eyes filling with tears. "I know you have to go. I just can't stand to think of something happening to you."

"I made it through the war." He grinned wickedly. "Who told me to pray about everything and that the Lord was in charge?"

She lightly hit him with the damp tea towel she was using to dry the dishes, then ducked her head. "I did. And I meant it." Suddenly she straightened up and looked him squarely in the eyes. "I made it through the war without you. This is only two months, more or less. You'll be back in time for the baby. Things are not that bad." She laid her head on his broad chest. "I miss you already." Then she reached up on tiptoe and kissed his mouth carefully. "I love you."

"I'll bring you some peppermint from Kansas," he smiled.

"That'll be wonderful. But don't forget the money, too," she teased back.

He looked at his petite wife carrying their child, thought of the five other children, and made a decision. "I'll hire a man to stay on the place until we can make it back. He can be your handyman-guard and give Tump some help."

Her face brightened. "Yes, that would be wonderful! Make him big and burly. And smart."

Daniel flashed her a huge smile. "Just like me, huh?"

She pretended to throw the towel at him.

The next morning he rode toward Stephenville, colloquially called "Steamville," and took the two older boys with him. This was partially to assuage Tump for not getting to go on the drive and also to get his and Peter's views on anyone who might be staying with the family. They camped at Daniel's favorite place for the night. It was well sheltered, and they made a cold camp. Daniel felt they were relatively safe from unfriendly guests.

As he lay down on the ground in his bedroll, he remembered how much he hated to sleep on the ground. *And I have two months of this coming,* he complained to himself as he drifted off to sleep.

The next day he asked Charlie, the storekeeper in Stephenville, about a good man for staying at the ranch while he was gone.

Charlie scratched his round head, which amused Daniel, for the storekeeper had very few wisps of hair to bother him. "There's a young fellow kind of like you need around here. His ma owns the boardinghouse. But he don't strike me as the cowboy type. I can't think of anyone else."

Daniel thanked him and headed for the boardinghouse. It was a rude affair made of rough logs, and it served more as a hotel than a boardinghouse, for the people who stayed there rarely lingered more than a few days. He knocked politely on the slab of a door, which was answered by a careworn woman in her forties.

"Yes?"

"I'm looking for a young fellow who lives here."

"Ain't many of them around since the war," she said bitterly. "You work for the gov'nment?" Her eyes were suspicious.

"No. I might have a job for him."

She moved back from the door and invited him in to the common room that served as an eating area. "Someone here to see you, Thaddeus."

A mountain of a man stood up and turned around.

Daniel walked over to him quickly, for he also saw the empty pants leg and the crutch, and stuck out his hand as he introduced himself.

Thaddeus's eyes followed Daniel's to his stump. "Gettysburg," he said quietly. His voice was surprisingly soft for a man so large. He offered Daniel a chair and motioned Tump and Peter to a bench.

"Are you from around here?" Daniel asked politely. He was already doubtful about hiring a one-legged man. No matter how big or how nice Thaddeus might be, how could he possibly be able to protect Daniel's family or do any of the farm chores?

"This is my ma's boardinghouse," Thaddeus replied. "Lived here since the war."

Daniel liked the way Thaddeus looked him in the eye when they talked. There was nothing sly or evasive in his manner.

"I can see you know about fighting. Know anything about farming and ranching?"

"You offering me a job, Mr. Thornton?" Thaddeus asked.

"Possibly." He indicated the missing limb. "That slow you down much?"

"Not when I'm on a horse. And I'm quick with my crutch, too. It's a skill one must acquire as soon as possible."

"You talk like a schoolmaster."

"I did some of that before the war. Not much call for it now. Besides, most people don't like a one-legged man around to remind them about the war—especially now that the Union men are running things and they realize that I fought on the other side." His eyes shone like a blackbird's wing, and he was clean shaven and well groomed, even though his clothes were shabby.

Daniel was liking what he saw more and more. "You appear to be in good health."

"I'm strong—especially my arms, what with carrying all this long body of mine around."

Daniel briefly described the circumstances he faced.

"I'm alone except for Ma. Reckon you could do without me for a few months, Ma?" he asked the woman hovering in the background.

"You going to pay him with real money?" she asked.

"Yes, ma'am. When I get back from the drive."

"You really going to try to take them longhorns through all them attacking thieves?" Skepticism was clearly marked on her face.

"Been done before," Daniel said easily. He turned back to Thaddeus. "Well? You want a job?"

"First good offer I've had since I got back. You just say when." His smile was pleasant, and the arrangements were quickly completed.

After a quick stop at the store for supplies, Daniel and the boys headed back toward home, talking about their experiences in town.

Tump said thoughtfully, "Papa, he seems so sad, even though he did smile."

"He's been through a lot, son. Time will ease the sadness."

Mary Anna was pleased someone had been found, but withheld her complete approval until she met the man. Tump put in a good word for him, as did Peter, and that made her feel somewhat better.

The grueling work of collecting the herd of longhorns and mustangs continued until the last minute, and still they were two men short. That was when old friends from Daniel's first drive to Palo Pinto showed up.

"Heard you was makin' a drive," Mac grinned widely. He took off his hat to wipe his head and face dry. Mac's red hair was mostly gone now, but Snake was as wiry as ever.

"Well, where did you two come from?" Daniel gave each man a hearty handshake.

"Oh, we was in this little scrape the North and South had, and now we're looking to take a vacation up towards Kansas and visit with the Indians a bit." He put his hat back on his head, adding, "No danger of me gettin' scalped, I reckon."

"You still hirin'?" Snake asked. "Sure could use me a job." Snake got his name because of his affinity for eating them. This made him an outsider to most, but his heart was good and loyal, and he had a charming way of playing tricks on everyone to add fun to most everything he did.

"I'm still hiring," Daniel assured him. "Couldn't have saved those last two jobs for two better men. I guess I'd be pushing my luck to find that you've been up to Abilene."

"Yes, sir, you would. But we rode a herd up to Ellsworth. It ain't as big and sin-some as Abilene yet, but they pay good money same as them."

"You men can bunk in the barn or wherever you can find a spot. After you take care of your horses, come and meet with Caleb, Coleman, and me. We need all the information we can get."

"We'll do her, Dan."

Daniel could feel his excitement growing by the hour. Also increasing was the obsession to find out everything about what might lay ahead. Since these men had been to Ellsworth, the trip could be made infinitely easier and safer. Especially if the money was the same. His head swam with possibilities and ideas. "Thank you, Lord," he breathed as he walked toward the house. "You seem to be smiling on this venture at every turn."

That night over coffee and apple pie, Daniel and Caleb made the final decision to go to Ellsworth, based on the experiences of Mac and Snake. Coleman agreed and seemed glad to have two more men who had been on a drive.

"There'd be no point in using the Goodnight Trail. It'd take us way out of our way."

Mac pointed to the map he had brought with him. "See this? We could angle up north this way, sliding east, and hit this trail. Some are beginning to call it the Western trail. Then mosey on over to the east and hit the western fork of the Chisolm. That'll take us straight into Ellsworth. 'Course it's gonna be bad riding through Indian territory, but there ain't no other way to get there. We leaving soon, Captain?"

"Yes," said Daniel. "Are we all in agreement that this way is the trail we want to take? Coleman? Any problem?"

"No," he said carefully in front of Mary Anna, "it will be a big job no matter which way we go. Same problems. Might get us home quicker."

Mary Anna took a deep breath to steady herself. *This is what we came out here for,* she reminded herself. It was impossible not to feel their excitement, or catch some of it. They were just like little boys—only this was serious man's business.

Thaddeus came the next day. She was prepared to like the man, and she did so immediately. He was polite and seemed to fit all the requirements for which she had asked. She pointedly ignored the crutch, and he did nothing to call attention to it.

He was an enormously large bear of a man, but he was gentle spoken and took an immediate liking to the children.

"What happened to your leg, Mr. Thaddeus?" asked Betty with a seven-year-old child's candor.

Thaddeus pulled her onto his lap and smoothed her unruly pigtails. "I lost it in the war, honey," he said calmly.

"Did it hurt?" she worried.

"For a while. Now I can use it to predict the weather. When it gets a little achy, I know it's going to rain."

"Oh, that's good. Papa'll know when to go out and plow now," she said happily. She frowned at the general laughter around her. "Well, that's important," she said, determined that the adults wouldn't get the better of her. She looked up into Thaddeus's black eyes. "If you need anything, I'll get it for you."

"Thank you very much, Betty. You're a very loving child." Thaddeus was clearly touched by her kindness.

Daniel cleared his throat. Betty took the hint, quit talking, and snuggled more deeply into Thaddeus's arms.

The last of the plans were cemented into place, and Caleb and the men began saying their good evenings as they left the cabin. Daniel motioned for Thaddeus to stay behind.

"Betty, it's your bedtime." He kissed her good night and gave her a quick hug as she left. She blew a kiss to Thaddeus.

"She's a fine girl, Mr. Thornton. All your children are very well brought up."

"Thank you. The reason I asked you to stay is to tell you how relieved I am that you're going to take care of them. I'll worry only half as much on the trail," he chuckled. His face turned serious. "Once the Indians know all the men except you are gone, you're likely to be a good target for their raids."

"I know."

Daniel's serious blue eyes met Thaddeus's dependable black ones. "And you know what to do?"

"Yes, sir, I do." Thaddeus put his hand on Daniel's shoulder. "I'll take good care of your family, Daniel." He rose and left the house, his crutch making a soft clunking sound against the new wooden floor.

The next morning they were all still standing together as if posed for a portrait when Daniel nudged his horse away from them. Mary Anna was holding baby Willie, Tump had Henry on his hip, Betty was holding Thaddeus's hand, and Peter was leaning against his mother's side. Daniel could see that Mary Anna was standing her full five feet two inches. She looked like one of the children with Thaddeus in the group. Torn between the exhilaration of finally leaving on the trip and the fear of leaving his family so vulnerable, Daniel prayed silently, *God protect us all.*

Virginia and her two children stood off on the side crying. "Take good care of yourself." Caleb looked near to tears himself. He sniffed heartily into his red handkerchief. "I'll bring you and the kids a present."

Seeing Daniel leave, Caleb hurried his good-byes.

Mac was on the point, leading the herd. He and Snake would share that spot. The rest of the cowboys were strung out in pairs across the herd and riding drag. Rabbit's chuck wagon was ahead and to the left of the herd. They were already kicking up a lot of dust. Daniel's habit of wearing a clean white shirt each day would suffer on this trip. He pulled his gray Stetson down a little tighter over his forehead and rode up to the front of the herd.

The first day out would be bone tiring. The herd had to be pushed hard away from familiar range. The longhorns were cantankerous about being shoved along. They didn't seem to have a leader yet, but challenges were being made for the spot.

Daniel kept his horse well away from the six-foot spread of crooked death the longhorns carried on their heads, always mindful that one swipe at his horse could spell disaster before they even got one day out.

The two freedmen, Oliver and Maxwell, weren't thrilled at riding drag, but everyone had to take their turn at the back of the herd. The dust of a herd of any size and the constant smell of warm droppings were almost more than any man could endure for long. The next day, the two men would be rotated to another spot, much to their relief.

Daniel caught up with Mac.

"We'll stay well to the east of Twin Mountains and then trail on up the Brazos," Mac said pointing to the ragged peaks of the pale blue rock formation in the distance. "I'll scout us a campground for the evening." He shook his head. "If we could really push the herd, we could get to the Brazos in a few days. I'll feel better when we get through Indian territory. It's going to be too tempting for the Indians to see all these horses and cows."

"I doubt we'll be able to sneak through there, if that's what you had in mind," Daniel said wryly as he noted the huge cloud of dust the cattle made.

Mac's laugh was short.

Daniel thought of the three major rivers they had to cross before they got to Ellsworth. First the Brazos, then the Red, and finally the Canadian. *One day at a time*, he reminded himself.

A sudden rifle report threw the cattle into a wild stampede. Daniel quickly moved to the side of the herd. Looking over his shoulder, he could see a large band of Indians bearing down on them. His men began firing into the galloping raiders, and Snake rode up quickly to him.

"All we can do is try to ride the cattle down!" he shouted.

Daniel was trying to see through the dust and fire over the backs of the herd at the attacking braves. There had to be twenty men at least. *We're outnumbered*, he realized with a sinking heart. Some of the Indians had rifles, but most of them were riding low on their ponies and firing arrows from beneath their necks. Daniel dropped one young rider and eased back to help fend off the would-be rustlers. With the screams, dust, and gunshots, for one awful moment he was back in the cavalry fighting the war all over again. The fear in the pit of his stomach knotted his muscles, and he fired frantically at any target that presented itself.

The cowboys were good shots and better armed than their attackers. They staved off the determined efforts of the Indians. A few at a time, the raiders dropped away.

Daniel raced alongside the thundering herd, heading for the lead cows. Praying his horse wouldn't stumble and throw him under the deadly pounding hooves of the cattle, he tried to reach Mac.

Miles streamed by before they were able to turn the herd, crowding them together in a milling circle. It was hours more before Daniel was reasonably certain they had gathered up the cattle that had broken off from the main herd.

Mac rode up. "We did all right," he grinned. He took off his hat and wiped his balding head and the inside of his hatband. "We're closer to the Brazos River. I guess that's one way to move a herd. Not my first choice, though," he added.

"Anyone hurt?" Daniel still had a knot in his stomach.

"Nope. Rabbit's a bit shook up, 'cause his mules couldn't keep up with us and he was sure the Comanche was goin' to get him. That wagon took a beating, but he wasn't hurt."

"He's not the only one that's shook up," Daniel said ruefully. "For a minute I thought I was back in the war."

"You are, son. You are," Mac said grimly.

"Find us a place to bed down. The men can scout for any more strays," Daniel ordered. "We've come as far as any man could hope to come the first day out."

"Yes, sir, Captain," Mac smiled slowly and rode off.

Mac's use of Daniel's title put the new war he was fighting into perspective. He was the man in charge of a group of men fighting their way to Ellsworth.

Rabbit had his promised good meal for the men that night as they camped along the edge of a small stream. Daniel had expected excited talk about their first encounter with the Indians, but the men were too tired to do much more than eat and roll up in their blankets. He sent out the night riders for guard duty and made a point to tell each man how well he had done. Then he checked to see that Rabbit had pointed the tongue of the chuck wagon to the North Star for the night. Satisfied all was well, Daniel headed for his hard bed.

Even Caleb was asleep before Daniel laid out his bedroll close to the banked fire. It had been a rough beginning, and the men had fought the raiders and the cows better than Daniel had hoped at so early a date. Now they were veterans. Surely they could handle anything.

∽

All day Mary Anna fought loneliness. She kept waiting for Daniel to come home for supper, and then she remembered he was gone. She had been feeding so many men that the supper she prepared seemed too large, until she looked at Thaddeus. He could probably eat enough for three men.

"You're a wonderful cook, Mrs. Thornton," he complimented her as he helped himself to thirds of everything. "If you were cooking at the boarding-house, we'd have a lot more business."

She smiled her thanks, remembering the times she had already spent at that job back in East Texas where her father had owned a hotel. Her face took on a dreamy look as she remembered Daniel staying there and how she had fed him supper in the dining room, and how they had fallen in love and married. East Texas seemed years away. The last time she had been there was during the war when Daniel had been away fighting.

The only pleasant memory from those difficult war years was the face of the Reverend Amos Strong. Amos, the man whose friendship had sustained her through those bad years. *I wonder where he is and how he is? And if he ever married. He was so kind to me and my children.*

"Happy memories?" Thaddeus asked.

Mary Anna laughed. "Some. I used to cook in my father's hotel a long time ago. You triggered some memories."

She shook off yesterday and lived through the chores of today. The small herd of choice cattle Daniel had left for breeding as well as the horses Mary Anna would need were all penned in the small corral closest to the house. It would be easy to hear anyone who might come in the night to steal. She also had the two dogs. Surely they were ready.

"I'll check with Mrs. West to see if she needs anything," Thaddeus said.

Mary Anna's final precaution was to retrieve the lovely new rifle Daniel had left for her and prop it right beside her as she crawled into the empty bed, praying that nothing would disturb their sleep.

Much to Mary Anna's surprise, the night passed uneventfully. The day was so beautiful she decided to make soap. She looked around for her two older boys, but apparently they had anticipated the giant job she had in mind and had disappeared. One thing Mary Anna insisted on was that everyone learn to do everything. The excuse, "That's girls' work," only made her more determined that her children would be totally independent when they went out on their own.

She had Betty watch the baby and Thaddeus carry out the huge black kettle and lay the fire. She shouted for Virginia to come out and help her.

"You make the soap, and I'll do the wash," Virginia said. Either job was a backbreaking one, but with the two of them to talk and laugh, both tasks went faster.

Jim and Edna went in the cabin to see Betty and the baby.

Mary Anna and Virginia spread out the clean wash on the rope Daniel had strung out between two poles. But with so many articles of clothing, they used the bushes and anything else they could to let the hot sun dry them.

Almost, Mary Anna forgot to be alert for signs of raiders. But in the lull of the midafternoon, a raiding party of about ten men came swooping in, firing bullets and arrows.

"Run for the house!" Mary Anna yelled at the older children. While she grabbed the baby, Virginia and Thaddeus grabbed the younger children and everyone dashed for cover. As soon as they had the door shut and bolted, Mary Anna grabbed her new rifle and fired through the shutters that the older boys had partially closed. Virginia and Thaddeus covered the other two walls. Tump was manfully watching through the back window and firing at every brave he saw. Jim manned the rifle his father left for him. His face was white with fear.

But it was impossible to see what was happening to the stock behind the corral. Mary Anna had the sinking feeling they were about to be left without a single animal.

The four fired relentlessly until they drove the men away. It was only then that they could check the stock.

Thunder, Tump's beloved horse, was missing.

"They got him again!" wailed Tump.

Mary Anna tried to comfort him. "Maybe he'll get loose again like he did last time. He knows his way home."

Angry as she was at the theft, she almost sat down and cried when she saw what had happened to all the washing she and Virginia had so carefully done. Some of it had been knocked off the bushes and stomped by careless hooves, and the rest was covered with dust. When she started picking up the scattered laundry, she discovered it had been shot through with bullets. She stood there, the bright sun glinting off the red in her auburn hair, and literally bit her tongue to keep from saying the things she was thinking.

The sorrow that for years she had felt for the Indians was rapidly evaporating under the constant attacks on her home and possessions. She sighed. There was nothing to do but wash everything again and try to mend the holes.

As she and Virginia redid the wash together, reality set in. "What are we going to do now?" Virginia asked.

"I don't know. We have Thaddeus and plenty of fire power, but we don't have any horses or any other way of getting word out about our situation. I guess we hold out until someone comes to us." She looked at Virginia's pale face. "You might as well move in with us. I'll feel safer," she said to keep her friend from having to ask. "We can hold out a long time. Don't worry, the Lord will take care of this, too. Lieutenant Mooreland is supposed to bring us the money for the horses. He'll be back soon," she said confidently.

Mary Anna's body ached from bending over the wash kettles, and she leaned back with her hand on her side to stretch. The rapidly growing child inside of her gave a protesting kick. "I'm tired, too," she said to the unborn child. She looked at all the newly washed laundry and got mad all over again.

That night she angrily poked the needle into every stitch she made as she repaired the garments by lamplight.

# Chapter 3

Mac moved the herd away from the Brazos and headed toward the Red River. There had been no more attempts to steal the cattle, but Daniel knew there were too many miles left to hope it wouldn't happen again.

At the noon break, Daniel and Coleman were leaning against the wheels of the chuck wagon. It was hot and muggy, but the sky was a peaceful blue.

"It hasn't been too bad yet," Daniel said between bites of Rabbit's wonderful food.

"Only one stampede and raid," Coleman grinned. His voice sobered. "You know it ain't over yet."

"I know. I can understand the Indian men not wanting to stay on the reservation. It really hems them in. That's one of the reasons I came out here, feeling hemmed in."

"But them stealing from you does nothing to endear them to your heart," Coleman smiled. "You know, we took everything from them. How's a young buck supposed to prove he can provide for a family? Or be brave in battle? That's their way of life, and they can't do that on the reservation."

"With the buffalo gone, they have to use our herd, huh?" Daniel sopped his biscuit in his bean juice. "But the government gives them meat. They have an agent for that."

Coleman's eyes glinted in anger. "Most of those agents are thieves. And the meat the Indians do get—if they get it—is spoiled."

"It's too big a problem for me to solve," said Daniel shaking his head helplessly. "I came out here to make a living for me and my family. I had no intentions of ruining anyone's life." He stood up and threw the remains of his coffee on the ground. "Let's move 'em out."

But the pleasure of seeing his and Caleb's cattle moving to market had been tainted. He wanted a glorious adventure, but not at the cost of people's lives. His motives were pure and simple. He wanted to have a ranch. He needed to move his cattle. That should be all there was to it. He tried to put the rest of the problem out of his mind. He focused his thoughts on Mary Anna waiting at home.

Her absence was like a living thing within him. Half of him was at the ranch and half of him was here. It still amazed him that his love for one woman could have remained so strong through all these years. It had grown from the first desires of the young to the deep need of being together, touching—of knowing someone so well that words weren't needed between them. He loved his children, but they were an extension of his and Mary Anna's love for each other. He loved Mary Anna, and he smiled broadly as he remembered that he was the only man she loved.

The heavy, still air around him made Daniel perspire heavily, and the dust from the cattle stuck to him from top to bottom. The heavy leather chaps he wore to protect his legs from the tearing fingers of the brush they were moving through caught the sun and made his denim pants damp. Worse yet, he knew this was exactly the kind of weather that could change in moments to a bad storm.

He scanned the horizon but saw only a few cumulus clouds floating like fully bloomed cotton bolls. Though they were fair-weather clouds and nothing to be alarmed at, he didn't drop his guard. Things in Texas could move very quickly and be deadly for the man who failed to stay alert.

His sorrel gelding stepped lightly over the rocky terrain. He was surefooted and a comfort to Daniel, who knew he wouldn't have to guide the horse around obstacles like some horses he had ridden. He and Rusty had been together for two years. They knew each other well, moving as one over country that was sometimes the same color as the horse. Daniel paid attention to Rusty's moods. He knew the horse possessed keener senses than he did. If Rusty was restless, Daniel became alert to everything around him, anticipating a problem of some kind. He disliked the days he had to let Rusty rest in the remuda and ride another horse. Those days never seemed to go as well.

That night they bedded the cattle down beside a large spring that fed a small lake. It was still hot at sundown.

"I waited for the sun to go down and those good old Texas breezes to spring up and blow this wet away," complained Mac as he spread his blankets close to Daniel's. He let go of the saddle he was carrying, arranged it at the top of his blankets for his pillow, and dropped down on the lumpy earthen bed.

Daniel sighed audibly. "You aren't going to get much sleep tonight, Mac. The mosquitoes are eating me alive over here."

Mac smiled angelically. "I've never had me a mosquito bite in my life," he bragged. "They don't seem to cotton to me."

"Maybe it's your smell," Coleman shot back from his place nearby.

"Maybe," Mac grinned good-naturedly. "I plan to take me a bath tomorrow if I have time. That little lake looks mighty invitin'."

"Be careful of the reeds," Coleman said casually. "That's usually where the water moccasins are hiding."

Had the moon been brighter, both men would have seen Mac pale in its glow. But he said in a strong voice. "I'll wear my hat and keep my gun in it." Then with a gleam in his eye, he added, "I noticed you hang your boots up on a tree limb. What's that for?" he asked Coleman.

"Keeps the scorpions and snakes out of them, airs them out, and keeps away rheumatism," he said confidently.

Daniel listened to the bantering and joined in. "Did you notice that Maxwell always puts his rope in a circle around his bed?" He paused dramatically. "Says a rattlesnake won't cross over a rope. His mammy down on the plantation told him that."

"Does that work?" asked Coleman doubtfully.

"He hasn't been bitten yet," Daniel said with a poker face.

"Hmm," said Coleman, "it's something to consider."

"I doubt I'll get half a night's sleep worrying about if a snake is going to crawl in my bed tonight without my rope," said Mac in a half-serious tone. Then he grinned widely in the night. He knew Coleman would get less than a full night's sleep, worrying about whether snakes were going to slither into his unprotected bed.

The soothing sounds of the night riders' song to the cattle calmed Daniel, and after a full day in the saddle, he slept soundly despite his dislike of sleeping on the ground.

At dawn he was awakened by the aroma of strong coffee boiling over a clean, hot fire and the smell of biscuits baking in the big covered pan Rabbit had resting in the coals around the edge of the fire.

He rolled out, stretched to get the kinks out, and pulled on his boots. Mac's bedroll was put away, and when Daniel squinted into the eastern sun at the small lake, he could see Mac's hat bobbing up and down as he enjoyed the water.

"Rise and shine, Coleman. It's time for our baths and rinsing out a few things." He nudged Coleman's foot with the toe of his boot.

Coleman slid his hat off his face and took a deep breath. "Not without my coffee first." The two men took their tin cups with them to the lake.

They stripped down to their long johns, and Coleman stretched out at the edge of the water, drinking his coffee. "Now this is what I call heavenly."

Daniel finished off his coffee and waded out to Mac.

"Here, hold my hat while I get under the water for a few minutes. I've got mud in my hair from the trail."

The water felt deliciously cool in the early morning, for the high humidity had not gone away in the night. Their baths wouldn't last longer than their first few minutes on the trail, but they felt wonderful for the moment.

Daniel saw Caleb squatted down at the edge of the water talking to Coleman. "Come on in, Caleb," he shouted. "It feels grand!"

Caleb shouted back. "No, thanks, I don't want to catch my death on the first part of the trip. I'll wait until we have to ride across a river. Too much bathing is bad for the body."

Rabbit rang the big triangle with his cooking spoon to call in the outlying cowboys. The smell alone was enough to have most of the men up and moving around, waiting to be called.

While they ate their breakfast, Daniel and Caleb talked.

"I don't like this weather, Dan," Caleb said. "I 'spect we're in for some big thunder-boomers before long."

"Yeah, I think you're right. All we can do is watch and hope we can find some kind of shelter when it hits."

After the weeks they had been on the trail, the drive was taking on a certain monotony. "Herding is a lot like the war," Caleb remarked. "Either it's boring or gut tearing."

"I like the boring part," Daniel smiled.

They were nearing the Red River. The small settlement of Doans was nearby, and Daniel thought he might ride over and pick up a few supplies, but a cloud was building in the west, and he didn't like the looks of it. A towering thunderhead was rapidly getting larger and taller. Its top was flattening out, a sure sign of a storm cloud. The slight green cast to it suggested hail, and the day was even more oppressively humid. They were miles from any shelter, and Daniel knew they could be in for a bad time. He spoke to Mac. "Do you know a place we could hole up?"

Mac surveyed the sky. "Nothing but a small ravine over towards the west a few miles."

"Better head the herd over that way. We could be in for some real bad weather."

By noontime camp, the wind had picked up and was blowing things around. Rabbit secured the canvas tarp more tightly over the supplies. The men broke out their ponchos and prepared for a dunking. The cattle were edgy and kept breaking away from the main herd. The darkening sky looked uglier as the afternoon moved on.

A single rumble of thunder like a low growl crawled across the herd, causing some of the cows to bolt. The men were hard pressed to keep the herd together. They moved them down into the ravine and circled them continuously, trying to calm them.

Daniel saw small balls of lightning jump from horn to horn on the cows near him. He knew about ball lightning, or St. Elmo's fire, as the cowboys called it, but it was unnerving to see the brightly glowing balls jump between the horns of the cattle or roll along the ground. It made the cows dodge about, and the sound of their long, crooked horns clicked loudly like a hundred demented swordsmen dueling on the endless prairie.

When the hail started, it was pea sized, but it rapidly grew to the size of small plums.

Daniel heard the rumbling of the cattle as they began trying to move away from the pelting balls of ice. The noise was unusually loud. The rumbling was growing out of proportion to the number of cattle. It was then he saw that part of the cloud had dropped down in an evil-looking black tail. It was sucking up dirt and grass as it traveled. It looked to be about a quarter of a mile away, and it was coming right at them.

"Cyclone!" screamed Mac as he raced toward Daniel. "Get off your horse and lay flat!"

"But the cattle!" Daniel shouted back.

"Never mind them. Take care of yourself!"

It was black as night, and the horrible rumbling was growing into a grinding scream as it came closer. Daniel tried to get his horse to lie down, but the animal's eyes were wild with fright, and he fought to get free. A bolt of lightning struck nearby, sending Rusty rearing into the air, pawing and screaming. Daniel felt the reins being ripped from his hands, so he jammed his Stetson tighter on his head and pressed his face closer to the earth. Water from the deluge splashed up into his face as he flattened himself as close to the earth as he could get. The roar was deafening. He thought he'd already seen the worst nature could hurl at him, but past tussles paled in comparison to this cyclone.

The roaring seemed to last forever, but even as the banshee din moved away from them, the rain continued. Great slashing curtains threatened to wash them all away. Daniel struggled to his feet. He was disoriented. In the waves of rain, he couldn't distinguish the herd or hear any of the other cowboys. He stood still, trying to get his bearings, when someone rode up behind him.

"You all right, Captain?" shouted Snake over the rain.

"Lost my horse," he shouted back. Snake offered him a hand up, and he climbed on behind the drenched man. The mare didn't like the noise, and she didn't like the two riders, so she promptly tried to throw them both off her back. They held their seats and steadied her.

A little farther along, they found the chuck wagon. The tornado-force winds had toppled it, and Rabbit was crouched beneath.

"Are you hurt, Rabbit?" Daniel called.

"Naw, sir, jest scairt to death." His eyes were big under his rain-soaked hat.

"Stay here until we find the herd. We'll come back and help right the wagon for you."

"This mother's child ain't goin' nowheres. You can bet your hat on that!" shouted Rabbit.

The rain began to let up a little, and they spotted the herd. The other men had already begun rounding up the scattered cows. To Daniel's great delight, Oliver, one of the freedman, came up leading Rusty.

They made a very wet camp that night. There wasn't a piece of dry wood to be had, so the men wrapped up as well as they could against the drizzle and chose high ground to set up the small tents they carried.

Mac was heard to grumble as he worked on the tent, "And I wasted a perfectly good bath just to get rained on."

Caleb chuckled. "I told you to wait." He climbed into the tent with Daniel. "I'd almost rather fight Indians as to sit out in the night in the rain. Even if it is in a tent." Water was running off his hat from the small hole in the canvas.

"Just try to think of all that money," replied Daniel as he ran an ineffective hand across his face to wipe away the water. His fingers rubbed the new growth of beard he'd acquired since he'd left home. Rarely did any of the men spend time shaving on a drive. Of course, some of them were so young, it didn't matter.

"That beard makes you look nearly as old as me," Caleb remarked.

"It stays until just before we get back home," Daniel said firmly.

Caleb grinned. "Mary Anna wouldn't recognize her slicked-up husband now. No clean white shirt, no shaving, sleeping on the ground."

Daniel took his kidding well. "The only reason I got all slicked up was so I could catch a woman like Mary Anna. Now I got her, but she can't see me. And I'll bet she'll love a slicked-up, rich cattle baron even better."

The morning brought the soggy sun. A clear path showed where the raging funnel had ripped its way across the landscape. Grass, bushes, and a few cows lay sprawled like broken toys. Awe, fear, and relief passed in stages across each man's face as they looked at the evidence of the powerful storm.

"Thank You, Lord, that we lived to finish this drive," breathed Daniel.

"Amen," added Rabbit.

A sobered group of men rounded up the scattered herd. Soon the whistles and shouts of the cowboys urging the cattle along was heard again. This time they weren't battling the dust. It was the mud and other obstacles left by the storm that could have killed them all.

When they reached the Red River, the men were in no mood to get wet again so soon. The last miles to the river had been hard ones, so Daniel ordered a camp on its banks. They would ford it in the morning. He was not surprised to find the river flooded after the recent rain. The sand around the river was treacherous, and the Red had a reputation for dangerous quicksand and slow death.

"Where did you cross before?" Daniel asked Mac.

"Don't matter where we went before, the quicksand changes every day. There's a trading post on down the river. Man that owns it has a squaw that knows the ways of the river. 'Course he'll charge us, but she'll find a safe way over."

The next morning when Mac came back, a squaw rode a pinto behind him. Serenely Kititke, or Precious One, used a long pole and poked out the safe passage for the men and cattle, her money already tucked inside her bright red blouse.

The place she chose was free of quicksand, but the mud and current were hard on horses and cattle alike. It got worse with each churning hoof that stirred it. Daniel went back and forth, pushing the reluctant cows into the swirling water. The current was swift, and he had to post men downstream to block the drifting cattle. Before he had ridden to the other side of the herd, Daniel's saddle blanket was soaked and Rusty was visibly tiring.

On the far side, Daniel got off Rusty and helped the men pulling Rabbit and his chuck wagon across with ropes. Rabbit's hands clenched the reins, looking like claws. But Savannah was surefooted and gave confidence to her partner, Alabama, so they made it across the Red River in good shape.

Rabbit got down and rubbed the mules' noses. "You sure done good, honey. You sure done good."

"The next one won't be so hard, Rabbit," promised Snake.

"Oh, no! The next one! I needs to get over this one before we talk about another one."

Maxwell rode up. "Stop actin' like a sissy schoolgirl. You're a real cowboy. This here is your third drive. You been through most everythin' already. Now, stand up and get them mules moving. Don't make me ashamed of you." He sat proudly in the saddle, and though he was the same age as Rabbit, he looked years older and years more confident. "Move," he ordered again and rode off to help with the herd.

Rabbit was mumbling to himself as he checked over his chuck wagon for damage. But he stood up taller as Maxwell had told him.

≈

Mary Anna and Virginia were feeding corn bread and cold buttermilk for lunch to their combined families when Tump held his piece of corn bread in midair, his mouth open slightly, and stared through the open door.

"What's wrong, Tump?" asked Mary Anna in alarm.

He didn't answer—instead knocking his chair over as he bolted from the house. When Mary Anna stood in the door, she could see the reason for Tump's strange behavior.

"Well, I'll be double dipped in chocolate," she said. Thaddeus looked over her shoulder. There was pandemonium as they all tumbled out of the cabin for a look.

"Thunder!" said Mary Anna. "Thank You, Jesus," she breathed as she ran out to watch Tump throw his arms around the horse's neck and run unbelieving hands across his nose.

"Look at that. Another broken buckskin rope. Thunder, you're getting a reputation among those Indians," breathed Mary Anna. "Well, quit petting him, Tump, and take him to the barn and feed and water him. He looks all right to me." She turned questioningly to Thaddeus.

"Looks good to me, too. He hasn't been mistreated. That's got to be the smartest horse I've ever seen to get away from the Indians twice."

"Well, they won't get him again, I can promise you that," Tump said flatly. "I'm going to sleep with him all the time now." The excited voices of the children almost drowned out his statement.

But mothers have good ears, and Mary Anna said, "No, you're not, but we'll think of something."

While Tump led the procession to the barn, Thaddeus said, "I'll sleep out here, if you like."

Her reply was immediate. "No, I want you at the house with us." She smiled grimly. "Who knows? They may decide no horse is going to escape from them again and come for him just to make a point."

"But he is our only horse," argued Virginia.

Mary Anna thought for a moment. "We'll move Thaddeus into the house and put Thunder in the shed by the house. Sorry, Thaddeus, but you'll have to take out that floor."

"I can do it in the wink of an eye," he promised. "Everything is going to be just fine."

But Thaddeus didn't see the shadow that blended itself into the trees at the edge of the woods. The eyes were mocking. Taking back the horse he had chosen for himself was child's play. This time he had an uglier plan. It was time for these interlopers to be swept from his land. The dappled sunlight barely revealed the copper-colored face and the distinctive triple-braided hair tied with fur, two feathers rakishly stuck in the braids framing his face.

As he strode toward his horse, the face of Santana was grim. His heart still felt like a burning hot stone in his chest. These settlers had taken his wife and child from him. His dry eyes could not let go of the picture of his family as he had found them—dead. The white settlers must pay for taking away everything that was dear to him. His family, his way of life. He slid onto his horse and glided away, still a shadow on the hill.

There was a bit of shuffling to do to accommodate all the people in the cabin that night, but Mary Anna knew it was prudent for them to be together. Even Thaddeus's snoring from in front of the fireplace was comforting.

The scorching Texas days were giving way to cooler nights now that it was fall. Mary Anna thought of Daniel on the trail and wondered if he had reached Ellsworth yet. She prayed for him and his men, and then she prayed for her "family" in the cabin.

≈

The next week she was startled to see two Indians riding calmly up the road toward the cabin. They carried no drawn weapons, and she stood at the front of the door with her hand on the rifle as Thaddeus met them. He had his rifle in his free hand as he hobbled out.

After a few minutes of conversation, he came back to Mary Anna. The men sat impassively on their horses watching him.

"They want tobacco and meat. They said they know only a one-legged man guards the cabin."

"So, we're back to blackmail again," she said angrily.

"I told them because I have only one leg, I have two hearts for courage. And a woman who has the heart of a panther."

She smiled. "And. . . ," she coached.

"And they said since we were so brave, they were sure we could spare some extra meat." Thaddeus's forehead shone with perspiration. "What do you want to do?"

Mary Anna honestly didn't know. The Indians were not starved or poorly clad. One of the men had his hair parted down the middle, then each side had been braided into three braids, ending in a single point tied with fur. Two feathers had been stuck in at a rakish angle and framed his face. The other man was wearing a tall stovepipe hat, much like the one she had seen the minister in Tennessee Colony wear. It made a shudder ripple through her small frame to think of where he might have gotten it.

From the corner of her eye, Mary Anna saw a horse move by the corral. One of the Indians pulled a gun. Thaddeus shoved her roughly into the cabin, slamming the heavy door behind them. Immediately a deep thud was heard against it.

"Close the shutters!" she screamed at Tump. He sprinted for them and got his rifle. They worked together as before. Jim, Virginia's oldest boy, lifted the hinged door on the cellar and led the terrified children down to safety.

"Mama!" screamed Tump. "They're trying to get Thunder out of the shed!" The big horse was shying away from the brave, fighting frantically at the rope that been thrown around his neck.

"Not this time," Tump said as he shot at the brave, who fell gracefully from his horse. But Tump uttered a single moan of anguish as another Indian took deliberate aim and shot an arrow deep into the horse's neck. "No, no, no," Tump kept saying as he shot at the Indians.

Mary Anna expected the raiders to leave once they had shot Thunder, but they continued with a ferocity that deeply frightened her. *It isn't just the horse they want. They want to drive us out. They want to kill us.*

Arrows and bullets were thundering into the heavy sides of the cabin. With the shutters closed, the Indians had few targets at which to shoot. They surrounded the cabin and pelted all four walls with continuous fire until they finally made a retreat, taking their dead and wounded with them.

Tump sprinted for the door, straining as he lifted the heavy log that barred it.

"No, Tump!" shouted Mary Anna, and she pushed him away from the door.

"But Thunder may still be alive!" he sobbed.

"We can't go out there yet." Thaddeus's voice was firm. He went to all the windows, peeking through the gun slits. It looked safe enough, but he knew it could be a ruse to get them outside.

They waited a full thirty minutes before venturing out. Thaddeus and Tump walked cautiously and fully armed to the fallen animal.

Tump flung himself down on Thunder. The horse whinnied pitifully. An arrow buried deeply in his neck, and blood ran into his beautiful mane. Tump didn't try to stem the tears washing down his face. "Can't we take it out?" he cried to Thaddeus. "Mama's a good doctor. She can save him."

Thaddeus saw no blood coming from the horse's mouth. That was a good sign, even though the animal had lost a lot of blood from the wound. He stood up and motioned for Mary Anna to come.

"Oh, Tump" was all she said when she saw Thunder.

"You can make him well, Mama. You saved Pap when he got shot with an arrow at the plum thicket."

Mary Anna and Thaddeus exchanged glances. "He's lost a lot of blood, son." But when she saw the pitiful sadness of her child, she had no choice but to try.

"See if you can get him on his feet. We need to get him to the shed before I try to take out the arrow."

Thunder struggled to his knees and finally to his feet. Mary Anna was amazed at his strength. Gently they walked him to the shed, and he lay down on the straw with a deep sigh.

"Fetch me the skinning knife," she ordered. She tried to do all the things she had done for Daniel. Fortunately, the arrow had passed through the animal's slender neck. She cut off the arrowhead and carefully retracted the shaft. Thunder sensed she was trying to help him and lay quietly under her hands.

She cleaned the wound with witch hazel and made a poultice of healing herbs, holding it in place with long pieces of torn cloth that she wrapped around Thunder's neck. "That's all I can do. It's up to Thunder and the Lord now."

She let Tump sleep in the little shed, with Thaddeus on guard. But it wasn't Thunder she was remembering that night as she lay in bed. It was the black eyes of the two warriors who had demanded the meat. They were not afraid of being at the cabin. There had been neither animosity nor friendship in their faces. Their expressions had been unreadable. Mary Anna cringed in the dark at the memory and prayed earnestly for protection.

When morning came, she fully expected to find a weeping Tump. Once inside the shed she was surprised to find the horse in bad shape but still alive. She changed the poultice and was relieved to see that the bleeding had pretty much stopped and that there were no signs of festering.

"You are a good doctor," Thaddeus saluted her.

She tried not to smile at the compliment. "Let's not get too happy yet. It will be a while before we know for sure if Thunder will live." Even if he did, they were still without a horse for the moment.

Thaddeus read her thoughts. "Someone will come," he said quietly. "We'll be fine until they do."

Mary Anna continued to pray for deliverance, and when it came, she was surprised by the source. Lieutenant Mooreland and a small company of men rode up to the cabin to deliver payment for the ten horses.

"I'm so glad to see you," Mary Anna greeted the young man. "We've been raided, and all we have is one injured horse. Could you ride back into Stephenville and have Charlie send us a horse or two? I can pay him."

"No one was hurt in the raid?" he asked gallantly. Mary Anna was very pleasing to the eye, and her manner was polished.

"My husband has built us a strong fortress. We can defend ourselves, I believe. But we must have a horse." She noted the dusty uniforms of the men. "Have your men feed and water their horses, and I'll feed you all some lunch." She shaded her face with her hand as she looked up into Lieutenant Mooreland's face. He gave a friendly smile and dismounted.

Sitting at the table with the rest of the "family" while his men lounged in the shade enjoying a hearty meal, the lieutenant said, "You can be sure we'll get by here as often as we can. We're spread very thin, but knowing you're here with only one man on the place makes you a priority. How long will your husbands be gone?"

"We hope they'll be back before December," Virginia answered.

Thaddeus was silently watching the lieutenant. He had his doubts about anyone representing Union forces, but it would make things safer if the lieutenant and his men came around more often. Maybe the Indians would stay away when they noticed the military presence.

# Chapter 4

Daniel felt as if he had been away from home for a lifetime. They had successfully forded the Red River and were headed for the Canadian. He used the rivers to mentally count off the stages of the trip.

They had made better time than he had hoped so far. At the rate they were going, he might be home by December—provided there weren't any major problems.

Caleb rode up beside him as they scouted ahead of the herd. "You know, Dan, we've been mighty lucky on this drive."

"Not lucky, Caleb," he corrected, "blessed."

"Yeah, you're right. Anyhow, there haven't been more raids. We've lost a few cows in the night, but we're in the middle of Indian country, so what can you expect? I don't mind feeding a few families."

"Did you double the night guard? I do mind feeding more than we have to."

"Yup. I saw Maxwell sleeping in the saddle on the way up here to you." He took off his neckerchief and wiped his perspiring face. "The nights are getting colder, but it sure do get hot during the day, don't it?"

Daniel nodded. His eyes scanned the horizon constantly, looking for trouble.

"Aren't we cutting back a little to the west?" Caleb asked.

"Yes. Mac heard about a farmer that doesn't cotton to trail drives, so we're skirting his land to avoid any trouble."

"I'm not sure it worked. Here come three riders, and they ain't riding like cowboys."

Daniel and Caleb kept riding, and as the three men drew nearer, they could see them more clearly. "Looks like a man and his two boys," Caleb said.

"They don't look like boys to me," Daniel said through gritted teeth. "Look at all the artillery they're carrying. They're better armed than we were at the end of the war." He slid his rifle out of its holster beside his leg on the saddle and positioned it across his lap. Caleb did the same, only he took out a shotgun, which would do much more damage at close range.

The riders stopped a talking distance away. Without preamble the man said in a nasty voice, "This here is my land. Don't want no cattle spoiling it. Name's Hippleworth and these here are my boys."

"We don't want any trouble," said Daniel in a friendly manner. "Where are the boundaries of your land? We'd be glad to go 'round it."

"Cain't lessen you aim to go into the next territory."

"You own and work that much land?" Daniel asked carefully.

The old man's eyes were crafty. "Between you herders churning up the land and the Indians, I can hardly make a living. Might make a bargain, though," he added as though he had just thought of a plan.

"We're listening and reasonable."

"You could pay me for crossing over my land. Say about a dollar a head. That seems reasonable to me and my boys." The two ugly men with him grinned evilly and shook their heads in agreement.

Caleb and Daniel exchanged surprised looks. It was clearly highway robbery, and everyone sitting there knew it.

"Would you settle for fifty cents?" Daniel countered.

The old man's eyes glittered as he surveyed the herd stretched out for miles behind the men. "Seventy-five," he said.

"Sixty and not a cent more," Daniel pressed.

"Only if you let me and the boys count the cows." The old man had them, and he knew it. Daniel couldn't go around what the old man claimed was his, and he didn't want to risk a gunfight.

"My foreman will be glad to help you with the counting," Daniel added. He was getting perilously low on hard cash. He wondered if there were any other "farmers" waiting between him and Ellsworth.

While the men counted the cattle, he also wondered if he'd ever get home again. If he wasn't helping Mac find water, they were fording unfriendly rivers that tried to suck his cows under. There was always the threat of Indians, rustlers, and rattlesnakes. Storms lurked in every heavy cloud. About the only thing they hadn't encountered was a prairie fire. He figured that was simply waiting for them around the corner.

That night, they camped for the evening well past the "farm" of Mr. Hippleworth and his boys. Of course, the man's count had been higher than Mac's, so they agreed to split the difference. "To keep peace in the family," Mac had grinned falsely.

Even though it had been weeks since the storm, the men talked endlessly about it as they sat around the campfire after supper. Most of them had never seen a storm of that magnitude. Snake said he had seen plenty.

"I've seen 'em pick up a whole barn and put it down a mile away. Or just blow it to smithereens, like four cannons had fired on it at once."

One of the men eased out a low, long whistle.

"I seen a chicken that had been picked up, and then set back down," Snake continued. "The chicken was fine, but every feather on her was plumb gone offen that hen."

"Ah, go on, Snake. That sounds like some of them tall Texas tales," Toad said.

"Naw, it's truth. I've even seen people picked up. Some was fine, and some had ever bone in their body broke."

Silence greeted that last statement, for most of them had thought that could certainly have happened to them, given the strength of the storm they had endured.

"Worse part is, that this is the time of year that they happen most. It could happen again," Snake added with a sad-looking face.

Before Snake could completely spook the men, Mac called for the night riders, and Maxwell pulled out his harmonica and began a cheerful tune, easing the tension of the camp.

Caleb came up to Daniel. "Sure am glad we have that happy soul to cheer us up when things go bad."

"I'm afraid some of what he says is too true to be ignored, but I'll be dipped in lye water if I know what to do about it." Daniel turned his back to the men for more privacy. "Tell you what, Caleb, the Lord is testing my faith on a daily basis."

"You ought ter be getting big spiritual muscles," Caleb smiled. "We're getting close now. Another two weeks. You and the Lord can surely work out something for that time, cain't ya?"

"Caleb, I'll swan if you aren't starting to sound just like Mary Anna. That's all I need," Daniel grumbled, "a trail wife." But he knew Caleb was right, and he prayed longer that night before he fell asleep.

The next morning Caleb noted his friend looked more rested. "We've made good time," he said affably.

Daniel laughed. "Between the Indians stampeding us and the cyclone blowing the entire herd thirty miles up the trail, we've done well. By the time we get home, that storm story will have us flying the last leg of the trip."

Caleb joined his laughter. "Wished it was that easy, Dan."

⁂

Things had eased up some for Mary Anna. True to his word, Lieutenant Mooreland had gone into town, and Charlie, the storekeeper, had sent a man out with a horse for them.

Thunder was walking on wobbly legs, but he had gained his feet again. Mary Anna insisted Tump and Thaddeus sleep in the house again. She was still worried the Indians would come again on the Comanche moon that would soon be rising. Thaddeus, Tump, and Jim enlarged the shed so that both horses could be stabled next to the cabin.

"The Comanche moon will rise in the next few days," Virginia said softly as they cooked supper.

"We'll be ready, Virginia. I've felt such peace today. I feel that Daniel is safe, even though I haven't heard from him."

"It reminds you of the war, doesn't it?"

"Yes." Mary Anna wandered back to that time in her mind and whispered, "I never got a letter from him the whole time he was gone. Two years." She came back to the business of preparing the meal. "But I never gave up hope that he was alive. Amos Strong helped me through that time. You remember me telling you about Reverend Strong, don't you?"

"Yes." Virginia's eyes danced with mischief. "Did you ever tell Daniel that Reverend Strong was in love with you?"

Mary Anna's face softened. "Yes, after he was well healed. I didn't tell him that Reverend Strong had said he would marry me if Daniel didn't come home after the war. He was wonderful about it, Virginia. He never thought the worst. Never accused me of being unfaithful to him. In fact, he became good friends with Amos himself."

"Daniel is one in a million, I got to admit." She couldn't help asking, "Do you ever think of him? Amos, I mean."

"Sometimes when I bake an apple cobbler. He loved apple cobbler." She shook her head in dismay. "We were talking about Daniel. I don't want to go back to the past. Not even one day. Daniel is well and happy and safe. I'm sure of that. And he could be home in a month or less." Her eyes sparkled like deep blue sapphires with anticipation.

Mary Anna, Thaddeus, and Virginia slept very lightly during the Comanche moon, but there wasn't a raid. A few days later, they learned that the Indians had attacked another homestead.

That night Mary Anna was awakened by Henry and Willie coughing. Terror gripped her heart. She had heard that sound too often before. As she feared, when she checked on the younger boys, both of them had scarlet circles on their little dry cheeks. Instantly she woke up the other adults.

"Thaddeus, take the other children over to the Wests' cabin and keep them there," Mary Anna ordered. "I don't want them sick too."

Virginia made a soothing willow tea for the fever, and Mary Anna bathed the boys' foreheads with cool water. They coughed until their tiny bodies were almost too weak to cough again.

She tried every remedy that she and Virginia could think of and spooned hearty soup down their little throats. Sometimes they couldn't get the liquid down because they were coughing so hard. Days passed with no change. The nights were the worst. The little boys would cough until they lost their breath. Mary Anna and Virginia took turns pressing on the children's chests to make them breathe in, and they propped the boys high on pillows to ease their labored breaths. Their eyes were bright with fever, but they didn't have enough energy to cry. Mary Anna constantly prayed that the boys would be healed as she tried all her powders and potions on them.

In the Wests' cabin, Betty clung close to Thaddeus, who was feeling the fear that a helpless man feels when children are dangerously ill. She climbed into his lap, wrapped her arms around his thick neck, and asked, "Will they die?"

"We're all praying that they won't, but they're awful sick."

"I've never seen anyone dead," she said thoughtfully.

"I thank God for that," he said as he remembered the carnage of the war. "Dying is not bad for the people that go. They get to live in heaven, and nothing goes wrong up there."

Sagely she asked, "Then why is Mama so worried about them going to such a wonderful place?"

"She needs them down here with her. She loves them and would miss them if they went away forever." Thaddeus stroked her long pigtails with gentle fingers.

"Like she's missing Papa, I guess." Thaddeus smiled and nodded. "But Papa's coming back, isn't he? Mama said soon."

"Yes, he'll be back." Thaddeus hoped to heaven he wasn't lying.

"Peter says I have another brother and a sister, but they died and went to heaven."

Wistfully Betty added, "I would like to have a sister. I like to play dolls, and the boys won't play with me very much." She whispered to him, "I think that last baby Papa buried a long time ago was a girl. Sometimes I go there and talk to her. I heard Mama call her Snow once when I went down there with her to put flowers on the grave. So I call her Snow, too. It's a pretty name. Mama said that's how long the baby lived. Like the spring snow. I don't remember it." She sighed. "Snow is a pretty name, not like Betty." Her freckled face was solemn.

"I love your name. *Elizabeth* means 'consecrated to God.'"

"But my name is *Betty*," she argued.

"That's your love name. Elizabeth is your real name. Betty means the same thing," he assured her. "It means you're special to Him."

She took in a long breath. "I'm special to God." She turned her light gray eyes up to him. "Mama says God loves all of us and watches over us. He'll take care of Henry and Willie, too. They'll be all right. Even if they die," she added confidently.

Thaddeus choked back the flood of tears forming in his eyes. "Yes, little Elizabeth, they'll be all right."

After days of numbing fatigue for all the adults, the boys' fever broke and the coughing eased. Mary Anna came to get the other children after she was sure the boys were on the road to recovery. Thaddeus told her of his conversation with Betty.

"Would you rather I call you Elizabeth now that you've become such a grown-up girl?" Mary Anna asked her daughter.

Betty thought for a moment. "Yes, I think so. Elizabeth is a much prettier name. And more grown-up."

"When a girl is going on eight years old, she's well on her way to adulthood," Mary Anna smiled. "And you do carry a lot of responsibilities," she added honestly. "Elizabeth it is."

The younger boys began the long journey back to health. Soon they were fussing and crying. "That's the loveliest sound, isn't it?" Mary Anna asked Virginia. There would be no new graves for Daniel to come home to, and Mary Anna gave daily thanks to God for that.

She thought of Daniel all the time, calling him close with her thoughts. She imagined him coming up the road, safe and with the money they needed. His beautiful blue eyes underneath his gray Stetson warmed her. His suntanned face with its hungry mouth moved against her in her thoughts. He would be tall and healthy this time, not sick, like when he had come home from the war. She tingled with the remembrance of him. She ached to hold him and kiss his searching lips.

❧

Daniel estimated they were about four days out of Ellsworth. The men were weary of life on the trail and began talking of being in a real town again; especially when they heard some of the tales Snake and Mac told them about the wide-open manner in which cowboys were not only allowed to live, but encouraged.

All Daniel wanted was a bath, a good meal, and a real bed. He made no plans to spend any more time in Ellsworth than he had to. He and Caleb were planning to turn right around and go home. He suspected Coleman, Mac, and Toad would make the trip with them.

When they could finally see the tiny dots that were the buildings of Ellsworth, Daniel felt as though he were holding the entire herd and all of the men back with his bare hands.

Leaving Coleman in charge, Mac, Caleb, and Daniel left the herd a few miles outside town and went in to strike a bargain with the buyer.

They hadn't ridden far when they were met by a man coming from the direction of Ellsworth.

"Hello, there, and welcome to Ellsworth, center of the cattle industry." He was well dressed and riding a beautiful stallion. "I saw your herd and thought I'd be the first to welcome you."

He rode up even with Daniel. "My name's James P. Quincy. No relation to the president, unfortunately. I'm a cattle buyer." He scanned the distant horizon. "Looks like you have a sizable herd behind you."

When he finally stopped talking, Daniel offered his hand. "I'm Daniel Thornton. This is Caleb West and Mr. MacDonald."

Time must have been money to Mr. Quincy, for he raced on. "I'm here to offer you forty dollars a head." When the men looked at one another, he added, "You won't find a better deal in Ellsworth. I have the cash money in the bank in town. I'll be glad to show it to you."

The price fulfilled Daniel's wildest dreams. He had made a silent agreement with himself that if he could get twenty dollars a head this trip, he'd be overjoyed. Now this man had doubled that! Cattle business was truly a rich man's game. All the long days of danger and boredom had been worth it. He looked over at Caleb, then Mac.

Mac cleared his throat, pointed with his head, and rode off a little way with Daniel following. "He may be all right, but he's the only man we've seen," he whispered. "Cattle could be going for fifty dollars a head. We don't know."

Daniel rode back to the knot of men. "We'll go into town. I'd like to talk to a few more people."

Mr. Quincy was rubbing his hands together happily. "Let's go. You won't find a better deal. Of that I'm sure." He headed his horse to town. "Supper is on me," he added with a flourish.

They rode in with Mr. Quincy chatting like he was sitting in a front parlor on Sunday. He asked so many questions Daniel was glad when they finally reached the town, for his head hurt from all the talking.

Everything checked out as Mr. Quincy had said it would. The deal was agreed to in principle, leaving only the number of head and the total price to be filled in. Mr. Quincy gave Daniel a large advance, promising to see him after the cattle had been counted and loaded the next day.

"You're a fortunate man, Mr. Thornton. Only a few herds have come in ahead of you. You'll get top dollar. Yes, sir, it truly is the early bird that gets the worm."

That did it for Daniel. He politely thanked Mr. Quincy for the advance, turned down dinner, and headed for the nearest hotel with his two friends, trying to keep his money out of sight as they walked along the muddy boards that served to keep their boots out of the mud.

Suddenly every stranger Daniel saw looked like a robber. They took a room, hurried upstairs, and locked the door. He spread the money out on the bed, and the three men stood there staring at it. "I've never seen that much money in my whole life," Daniel breathed.

"Me neither," intoned Caleb.

Mac just shook his head. "And that's only part of it. There's more to come after the cattle are counted and loaded."

"Here, Mac, you take this and go have some fun," Daniel said as he handed him some money.

"Yes, sir!" He disappeared like smoke in a high wind.

"You staying in town tonight, Caleb?"

"Virginia'd kill me if I spent more than an hour in this sinful place," he grinned. "I'll go back with you. Maybe tomorrow we can partake of the pleasures of the bathtub and barbers."

"And what a pleasure that'll be," Daniel grinned. "Let's go let the men loose. Those young fellows probably think they're gonna die before they can make it to the city."

Daniel and Caleb stuffed the bills into their saddlebags as covertly as possible.

They were one of the first herds to make it to the railhead. The town had only a few rowdy cowboys making a racket in the saloon near the hotel. Daniel could hear someone beating a tinny piano to death. "Isn't much of a town to brag about, as far as I can see." They mounted up.

"Beats the choices in Stephenville. I count about six saloons. 'Course, they're mostly tents."

"I'd call this town an egg waiting to hatch," Daniel observed. He tipped his hat to an elderly lady walking primly down the planks that served as the sidewalk. Her skirts were dragging in the dust and mud, and she carried a small parasol to guard against the hot evening sun. Her returned smile was slight.

"Don't guess she cottons to cattle barons," Caleb smiled.

"Don't guess we look like cattle barons," argued Daniel.

They eased their mounts down the street. Ellsworth was a roughly built settlement getting ready for prosperity. Daniel noted the location of the general store. He would buy presents for his family there the next day.

He guided his horse around a very young cowboy, staggering down the street glassy-eyed. "I'll bet he doesn't think this was so much fun tomorrow."

Caleb laughed. "The young are so dumb, but I suppose I did the same foolish things."

"Are you confessing?" asked Daniel.

"Nope. Just remembering."

Daniel grinned. "Me, too." He shifted slightly in the saddle. "I'm glad all that nonsense is behind me. I made some bad choices in the past. I don't need the things I thought I did to make me happy. Right at this moment, the only thing that would make me happier is to be at home with Mary Anna and the kids."

Caleb got a little misty eyed. "Me, too."

Daniel kept a wary eye out as they made their way to the herd and searched in his mind for a place to hide the money.

The men were raring to go. Daniel gave them part of their wages.

Maxwell, Oliver, and Rabbit formed a unit. Two-thirds of the cowboys on the trail were black, freed from the plantations, but they knew there could still be trouble. Even if they stayed at the designated spot for freedmen, there was a high probability of getting into some kind of scrape with some of the white cowboys in town.

Toad and Snake rode up and joined them. One by one the other men did, too. They were going in together, and they would take care of each other like family on this night of celebration. They had been forged into a family by the drive, and they rode out as one.

Coleman hung back. "I don't have a hankering to go spend my wages on foolishness. Reckon you could use some help holding the herd."

"Be back by sunup," Daniel shouted to the men as they rode off. "We've got a herd to move into town tomorrow." He hoped at least one of the men had heard him.

It was right at sunup when the partygoers dragged up. Oliver and Mac were the only ones smiling. Mac was riding beside Toad, holding him onto his horse. Toad's face was the color of the amphibian for which he was named. Snake's eyes held a glazed look, but he was sitting straight in the saddle.

"I had a grand time," bubbled Maxwell. "We found this man that played the piano in this place. Stayed there all night long, singin' and laughin'. I never had so much fun!" He laughed. "You should have seen old Toad doing that Irish jig."

" 'Course, he ain't dancing much right now," commented Snake.

"You look like you could use some of the hair of the snake that bit you," Toad said in a slurred voice.

The chuck wagon was already packed, and the men had to do without coffee or restorative food. "It's a good thing we're only a mile or so out of town," Daniel told Coleman as he watched the men cling to their saddles. He strongly disapproved of their behavior, but he knew only time and experience would cure intemperance. He was mad at them for not being in top shape for the last of the drive but grinned at the knowledge that their bodies would punish them far more severely than he ever could.

There was some evidence to support the claim that they had all had a bath, and they were freshly shorn, but they were a motley-looking bunch right now.

Daniel rode to the point to talk with Mac. "Drive 'em up to the pens by the railhead. When it comes time to count the herd, I want you right there for our tally. You'd better have Maxwell do the white marking. We're definitely shorthanded this morning. Toad or Snake would probably fall off the fence." Daniel was to find that tallying the cattle was considered one step below riding drag. Two men sat at the mouth of the cattle car. One counted and one marked the cattle on the rump with white. It would be a hot day, and the cattle were packed tightly on top of one another, their nervous droppings stamped by their hooves to release the pungent smell. The dust was almost unbearable. It would take many hours to send the herd through the chute one at a time. But it was too important a job to leave to a careless hand. Every cow counted was money in their pockets.

Daniel stood on the side of the pens and looked with pride at the herd they had brought in all the way from Erath County, Texas. It had been an enormous risk, but they had made it. The full extent of the new wealth he had just earned had not yet penetrated, but he was excited by the entire venture.

By noon the heat at the pens had become so oppressive that Daniel sent for Coleman to spell Mac and had Oliver come to do the marking. When Mac climbed down from the top rail, he strolled over to Daniel.

"You did a good job, Mac," Daniel noted. Now that he understood how dirty a job counting was, he added, "There's a big bonus in it for you."

Mac smiled. He took off his bandana and leaned on the rail with Daniel. "Gives a man a good feeling to see all these cows, don't it? Sort of righteous or something." He fumbled with his feelings, but Daniel knew what he meant.

"Yeah." They exchanged broad smiles.

Caleb, who had been on the other side of the huge pens, came up to join them. "Don't seem real," he said as he shook his head in disbelief. Then he slapped Daniel on the back. "We made it, Dan, we made it!"

And then they were standing in the bank once more with the tally from both sides, splitting the difference in the number counted. Daniel finished the paperwork. Mr. Quincy withdrew the rest of the money and handed the large stack to Daniel. Shaking Daniel's hand, he repeated his desire to work with them next year and left with all parties satisfied.

Daniel divided the money roughly in half and stuck it in Caleb's hands. "Here we go again." He eyed the other people in the bank and didn't see anyone paying attention to them.

"I hadn't thought about this part of it. Protecting the cash, I mean," said Caleb.

"We'll think of something, Caleb."

"Onliest place I know that's big enough to take care of this bundle is in here," he said as he removed his hat and stuffed the money into the crown. He settled the hat back on his head firmly and looked at Daniel. "Okay?"

"Okay. Until you meet a lady," he laughed.

"Don't think there's much danger of that in this town." He offered his arm to Daniel. "Shall we repair to the baths, Sir Daniel?"

Daniel struck his arm through Caleb's. "Let's, Sir Caleb. I told the butler of the baths to have them ready for us."

But no matter how relaxed Daniel became, he never took his eyes off the two hats sitting carelessly on the wooden crates beside the tubs.

"Caleb, I'm going to buy my land up on the North Bosque and build that mansion for Mary Anna."

Caleb considered this. "Okay. I'll buy the land next to it. Guess I should build a mansion, too, for Virginia." He sighed deeply, inhaling the warm smell of fresh soap. "We've come a long way, Dan. A long way since the war."

Daniel rose and stood on the wooden slats. He poured fresh hot water over himself to rinse off and began toweling off his slender frame.

Caleb noted the stark contrast between Daniel's sun-browned hands and face and his white body. He laughed. "You look like a lily with brown leaves."

"Look who's talking. Come on, you lazy hound dog, let's go get us the best food this town has to offer."

It wasn't hard to find that. There was only one café in Ellsworth, and the food gave both men indigestion. It was heavy and greasy and sat like a stone in Daniel's stomach. "I'll die soon if I don't get some of Mary Anna's cooking," he moaned.

They left the café, noted Rabbit was getting the supply wagon reloaded, and entered the store to buy gifts for their loved ones. Daniel got a pretty gold necklace with a small ruby in it for Mary Anna, a finely worked gold ring for Betty, and pocketknives for the boys. "One last thing," he said to the storekeeper. "Do you have any peppermint?" He felt a little dizzy at spending so much money so quickly, but he reminded himself there was plenty left.

Caleb and Daniel went back to the hotel and got another room. Daniel sat down with contentment on the lumpy bed. "This will sure feel good tonight."

Caleb had a frown on his forehead. "The money. Where will we hide it?"

"We'll put it all over everywhere, so if they find one stash they may think that's all there is," said Daniel.

When they dressed the next day, they stuffed cash in their pockets, the tops of their socks, inside their hats, and in the supply wagon for the long trip home.

It was getting colder by the day, and Daniel wanted nothing to stop his trip home. He was taking a huge present to the woman he loved.

# Chapter 5

Mary Anna looked off in the distance. Riders were approaching. Squinting her eyes for a clearer view, she identified a chuck wagon and two riders. Daniel! Minutes later, the small party rode up, and Daniel sprang from his horse to fold Mary Anna in his arms. Her heart sang with joy that Daniel was safe at home in her arms, hugging her tightly. Tears of happiness slid down her face, but she made no attempt to wipe them away.

Daniel tipped her head back to look at the face he had conjured up in his dreams so many times on the drive and kissed the mouth for which he had hungered. "You're even more beautiful than I remembered," he whispered. Then someone kicked him in the stomach. He grinned at Mary Anna. "Guess that baby doesn't want to share you with me."

"She's just letting you know she's glad you're home," smiled Mary Anna.

The warmth of the cabin and the greeting Daniel received made his face shine. He gave out the presents, saving Mary Anna's for last.

"Oh, it's lovely," she breathed. "I'll wear it always as a reminder of this day."

"They didn't have any diamonds up there," he apologized, "but I am going to give you the other present. I'm buying the land, and we'll build a mansion on it." He stood prouder than any peacock that ever spread its massive fan of fancy feathers.

"You're a cattleman," she grinned. "Landowner and all."

"The Lord has delivered us to the land of milk and honey at last."

Mary Anna's face was still glowing. "Oh, Daniel, the Lord has been so good to us. I know all of it could be gone in a minute, but I'm just beside myself with happiness. I never thought it would be this easy!"

"Easy!" exclaimed Daniel, "You should have been there." He thought of the cyclone. "You're right about how fast it could all be gone. But I want to bask in the glory of the blessings He's given us." His eyes were full of love for her, and his voice begged her to rejoice with him.

"How can I say no to you when you look at me like that?" she said. "Tonight will be unbridled joy, and tomorrow we'll be sober about all our new responsibilities."

The next day Daniel groomed himself carefully and went to buy the land. He returned that evening with the deed for 1,250 acres of prime land, and Mary Anna thought she would have to buy him a new hat to fit his head, now swollen with pride.

"We have the dream in our hands," she said softly as he handed her the deed.

She rose from her chair, holding the paper. "Yes. But now what will we do with it?"

"Use it for us and our children, and anyone else we choose." He came to her and put his arms around her while she rested her head on his chest.

"Are we different now?" she asked.

Daniel was quiet for a long while. "Yes and no. I don't want the love between us to change or anything bad to happen to our children. I want us all to stay as happy as we are now. And yet it feels wonderful not to have to worry if I'll be able to take care of you all. I know I could lose all this wealth today. I don't want it to control our lives. But I want to use it. I believe the Lord has blessed us so we can be a blessing to others. I want to use it to build a place where all our children can grow up and marry and bring their children back to visit. A center for our world. We have the money to let our children be anything they want to be. We're free to choose."

He held her closer. "But if I have to choose between our love and the money, I'd give the money away in a second." He held her away from him slightly. "Never doubt that," he said. And gently he took her face in his hands and kissed her mouth as he had when they were first married.

"I never dreamed my life could be so happy," Mary Anna sighed. "I didn't think a love like this could exist. I never saw it before. And sometimes I'm so happy, it frightens me. Like now. Hold me a little tighter so I won't be scared."

"I believe everything you said, right up to the 'hold me a little tighter so I won't be scared.' I don't think you're afraid of anything," laughed Daniel.

She gazed unseeingly off into the distance. "Yes, I am. But tonight is not the time to speak of those things."

Mary Anna knew there would be pain and heartache in their lives. There had to be, for that was life. She only hoped she would be strong enough to meet the tests she felt sure were to come with living out the dream. When she went to bed that night, she spent extra time in prayer. And Annah kicked within her, full of life and mischief.

❧

Annah chose to arrive on January 7, a cold and snowy day.

From the moment the baby was laid in her arms, Mary Anna was enchanted. Annah was somehow the embodiment of her parents' dream, a promise for the future of which they had spoken. While Mary Anna loved all her children, somehow Annah seemed to be the child of her heart. In those secret moments when no one was around, she let the full measure of her love fall on Annah without reservation.

Elizabeth was delighted with her sister. "She finally got here. When will she be able to play dolls with me?"

"Not for a while," her mother answered with a kiss to Elizabeth's forehead.

Elizabeth solved the problem herself. She made Annah the doll, dressing her, playing with her, and taking care of her endlessly. "She's a real doll, isn't she, Mama?" And Mary Anna laughed.

During the winter the men rounded up more cattle and mustangs as they ran across them on the winter pastures. The herd was beginning to grow again.

One morning the day dawned brightly, making the sky a cerulean bowl.

It was so clear that they could see the Palo Pinto Mountains dotting the western horizon. Even the air seemed warmer as Daniel brought up water for the cabin from the stream. It was a perfect day. But toward noon the wind picked up from the north and developed a decided bite.

The men complained of the dropping temperature when they came in for lunch. When Thaddeus came thumping in, he said, "My bad leg tells me we're in for one big blow." By one o'clock, the north sky was deep blue.

"We're in for it now," Daniel said, casting a look over his shoulders. "Better get the horses up toward the barn," he instructed the men, "there's a Blue Northern blowing in. We're likely to have snow by supper time."

Everything was battened down and extra firewood added to the pile by the door. By four o'clock the temperature had fallen drastically.

Mary Anna prepared supper for the men, and they came in out of the weather gratefully.

"Can we go sledding?" asked Peter with shining eyes.

"Me, too," chimed in Elizabeth.

The boys ignored her. "Can we, Mama?" they asked again.

"Let's wait and see if it comes before I make any promises," she hedged.

"Snow may be good for the kids, but it's murder on the stock," grumbled Toad.

When Coleman and Toad left for their bunkhouse, huge, fluffy flakes had already begun drifting down. The children were dancing in their excitement. They put on their coats and ran outside, lifting their arms trying to catch the flakes.

By the next morning, the snow was over Daniel's boots that he wore when he went out to check the barn. Coleman, Toad, and Thaddeus were throwing hay out into the snow for the other animals.

The children were content to run out and play for a few minutes and then come in to the warmth of the fire. To keep them occupied, Mary Anna read to them. Daniel enjoyed listening to Mary Anna read in the long evenings. He was a pretty good reader himself, but Mary Anna had never given up her love of reading, no matter how busy she was. Under her tutelage, the children were doing well with their own reading skills.

"I don't want them to grow up ignorant." It was a point of pride for her that everyone in their family could read. Even the little boys were getting their first lessons. Thaddeus was good about helping them.

"Someday we'll have a proper school again," Mary Anna dreamed.

The wind grew fiercer during the night, and the storm continued without letup for days. When the storm finally blew itself out, several feet of snow covered the ground. No one went outside except to feed the animals.

When the temperature finally allowed some of the snow to begin melting, Daniel took the two older boys hunting. They felled a deer.

"Good shot, Tump. That's a nice fat buck." They were just inside the first good stand of trees beyond the river.

"Papa," Peter said in a frightened voice.

Daniel looked up just as low growls began in the throat of the leader of a pack of timber wolves.

"They must be starved," Daniel said quietly. "Tump, get ready. If they charge us, I'll shoot the leader. You get the one right behind him and don't stop firing." He could see the boys were terrified. "They'll turn tail and run if we kill the leader," he assured them.

The wolves were still growling, poised in attack posture. Daniel waited, sighting the leader's head carefully. The wolf was large and heavily muscled. Long fangs showed through his open mouth. Daniel hoped the pack could be bluffed into leaving, but he saw the muscles of the lead animal tensing. The leader's eyes glinted yellow and cold. Daniel waited only a fraction of a second before he squeezed the trigger. The wolf sprung just as he fired, and it fell instantly dead into the snow, its blood staining the white blanket. Tump fired before the report of Daniel's rifle had stopped. He wounded the second animal and Peter finished him off with his shot. Daniel dropped the third one, and as Peter shot at the fourth animal, the rest of the pack made a quick retreat.

"Let's get this buck out of here," Daniel instructed. "They'll be back. They're too hungry not to give it another try." They draped the buck over Peter's horse, and he rode double with his brother.

"Will they follow us?" Peter shouted.

"Maybe." That thought hurried everyone along.

That night as the Thorntons ate roasted venison, they could hear mournful cries echoing across the moonlit land.

Peter shivered. "I'm glad we live in a strong house."

"Me, too, son," his father said. But until the deep winter eased, hunting would be an even more dangerous venture.

Slowly the winter loosened its unkind grip and the spring activities began again.

Daniel was especially pleased with Tump's uncanny ability with horses. He was good at making friends with them and coaxing them to let him on their backs.

One day Tump was trying to work with a horse the men had brought in. The horse had a glazed look in his eyes and his ears were always pointed. This was not a good sign. Tump managed to get the bit in the horse's mouth, but when the time came for the saddle, it was a different thing all together.

As soon as Tump put the saddle on the horse's back, the horse fell over onto his back and lay there.

"What in the world!" said Tump. By now Toad had come in to witness this strange spectacle. Tump took off the saddle, and the horse stood up.

"Never saw a horse do that before," puzzled Toad.

"Whoa, boy," said Tump silkily. He stroked the horse's head. "It's only a saddle. It won't hurt you." He eased the saddle back onto the horse, and the animal promptly threw himself on his back again, lying there calmly.

He called his father to the barn to witness this new horse's antics.

Once again when the saddle was placed on his back, the horse fell down and lay on his back.

Daniel burst out laughing. "A falling-down horse?" he said. "Never have I ever seen that."

Coleman and Mac were consulted.

"That creature is purely stupid" was Mac's assessment.

"Or purely smart," quipped Tump.

"Better let that one alone. We've got too many good animals for you to waste time with that one," Daniel told Tump.

Reluctantly Tump turned the horse back into the pasture and began working with another one. But the odd behavior of the first horse poked at him. He'd never had a horse he couldn't do something with, and this was a real challenge.

At different times he'd try unsuccessfully to get the horse to accept the saddle.

"Looks like you're going to have a long day," Toad laughed from the top rail of the corral.

"Don't you have anything to do but sit there and watch me?" complained Tump irritably.

"I'm giving you moral support," replied Toad. "Some advice, too. I talked to some of the other men, and they gave me some ideas. I'm here to give you some of their horse wisdom."

They hobbled the horse so he couldn't buck without falling down, and snubbed his head to a post so he endured the blanket Tump put on him. But when Tump untied his head, he could swear he saw a gleam in the animal's eyes as he threw his head around and pulled the blanket off with his teeth.

"Hey, Tump, I think you've finally got a horse that's smarter than you." Toad was having a fine time watching the boy struggle with the stubborn animal.

Doggedly Tump snubbed the horse's head close to the post again, but not before the animal managed to nip the back of his pants. The trick caused Toad to fall off the rail with laughter.

Tump rubbed the painful nip and looked into the horse's big brown eyes. "You've had the last laugh this time, but I will get a blanket on you yet."

Mary Anna put ointment on the painful bite, and Tump sat crooked in his chair at supper that night.

The next day Daniel told him, "I'm sure that with enough time you'll be able to break the falling-down horse. But your time is better spent working with the other horses. I'm afraid by the time you do break him, you'll find out he's too dumb to do anything. Just let the horse be. One of the sad facts of life is that a man can't always be successful, even at what he's good at. Just let him be. It'll make a good story to tell your grandchildren," he grinned.

At the end of April, Mary Anna was greatly embarrassed to find herself pregnant again. "I can't be again so soon," she wailed to Daniel. "I'm not ready for another baby."

Daniel was completely confused by Mary Anna's lack of joy.

Virginia comforted her. But by May, Mary Anna was huge.

"Virginia," she said as they spun the cotton into thread and wrapped it in big balls, "I shouldn't be this large so soon. Do you think it's because I'm not recovered from Annah's birth?"

Virginia wrinkled her eyebrows and measured Mary Anna with her eyes. "Hmm. You are big," she agreed. "There's only one thing that could cause that, Mary Anna, and you know it." She grinned widely.

"Don't even think it!" groaned Mary Anna. "You were supposed to say what I wanted you to." She put her face over her hands and moaned. "Not twins! I couldn't survive carrying them, much less taking care of them!"

Virginia knelt down beside Mary Anna. "My dear, twins are special. I know that it's not often they both survive, but you're strong and healthy, and you have a lot of people to help you. Let's rejoice that the Lord has chosen you to be these babies' mother. And let's pray that they both live to celebrate your one hundredth birthday."

Quietly Mary Anna said, "You're a good friend, Virginia. If I have a girl, I'll name her for you."

News of the coming twins spread rapidly among the cowboys and then to Stephenville. Mary Anna had never received so much pampering. She knew that the longer she carried the babies, the better chance they had to live, so she took all the advice and all the pampering given her.

Daniel wanted to begin building the new house right away. He was full of plans and excitement. Mary Anna refused to talk about it.

"But you said as soon as Annah was here, we'd get started," he protested.

"And now I'm carrying two babies, and I really don't want to discuss it. I don't have the energy for it." She tried to rearrange her body in the rocking chair to a more comfortable position.

"But you don't have to do the building!" Daniel insisted.

"If you're going to build me a grand house, I want to supervise every nail that's put in it. Men know nothing about kitchens and the little things that make a house so convenient. We're fine here. And safe." Her voice left no room for argument.

"Daniel," she added softly, "while I was sitting by the window looking at the woods two days ago, I saw the silhouette of a man. I'm sure I did. It was an Indian. I could tell because of the shadow of his hair. He was watching us. Before I could call for anyone he disappeared."

Daniel tried to calm her fears. "He was probably looking for game."

"No, you know he wasn't. He was watching us." She shivered. "And even from that long way away, I could feel death radiating from him. Anger and death. I don't want to leave this safe little fort we have here with the Wests until Santana, Tall Tree, and Ten Bears are no longer a threat to us. If we build the house now, they'll burn us out more easily. Kill us if they can. They're desperate, cornered people, and they are fighting to survive just as we are."

Daniel looked at her earnest face and heard the wisdom in her words. "I wish you had told me earlier about the man in the woods. I would have posted a guard." His words were gentle. "It's a test of having the dream, isn't it, to have the money to do it and yet have to wait?"

"I think maybe it is."

"Well, the money isn't going anywhere unless there's a bank robbery." He thought of the big bank in Fort Worth where he had deposited his money. "It's in as safe a place as it can be." He sighed deeply. "All right. We'll wait. I hope I don't have to get a badge and go out and catch those renegades myself."

"I doubt you will, my love. You'll be too busy building up some other part of your kingdom."

Daniel took to heart what she said and began planting orchards of peach trees and larger fields of wheat and cotton. Then he hired more men to help him with those crops.

In spite of all their night guards, horses and a few cattle continued to disappear in lieu of all-out raids.

Coleman came in one morning with a large, silly grin on his face.

Daniel raised his eyebrows quizzically. "Yes?"

"Remember the falling-down horse? One of the braves tried to steal him last night. I heard the dogs and went out to check, and I saw him slide on the horse's back. That stupid horse rolled over just like a dog wanting his stomach scratched. Near smashed that Indian. I was laughing so hard I couldn't hardly get a bead on him. Guess it was just one man, and he didn't get anything but embarrassment. Bet he's a mite more careful about which horse he tries to take out of here next time."

Daniel laughed heartily as he imagined the sight, but the incident reminded him again that they were still in danger. Mary Anna's advice sounded wiser every day.

He did pick up two hopeful pieces of information when he went into Stephenville. In March Texas had been readmitted to the Union by President Grant, and twenty companies of Rangers were to be sent to protect the frontier.

Daniel's hope rose for building the house soon. "With all those men, we'll be rid of the Indian problem in no time," he told Charlie.

He told Mary Anna the good news as soon as he got home, expecting her to relent about building the house.

"No. Let's see the Indians gone first." She was steadfast in her feelings.

Caleb and Virginia came over after supper, and the men sat outside in the lovely spring night, talking about Daniel's news.

"It's all paid off, hasn't it, Dan?" Caleb gloated. Then he turned sober. "When you and Mary Anna do decide to build the new house, I am thinking seriously about moving Virginia and me into town. I don't think I want to be a cattle baron now. I want to be a town baron and maybe build a house bigger than anyone else's."

"And not have to fight the Indians," Daniel added.

"And not have to fight the Indians," Caleb agreed. "I'm getting too old for all of that. Time for me to sit back and watch my kids grow." He took a deep breath. "Just smell that air." He smiled broadly. "It belongs to you while it's blowing over this land."

"I doubt that," Daniel laughed. "But I sure do enjoy it all the same." He turned serious. "You've heard about the political stuff that's going on?"

"Only about Texas being readmitted and the Rangers coming," Caleb said.

"The radical Republicans have won, and the new constitution has been ratified. But they filled all the offices with extremists." Daniel shook his head. "Texas is wide open for everything. Even Governor Davis has been accused of fraud, and the state police are making a mess of their job. Charlie had a copy of the *Tri Weekly Gazette* from Waco. Headlines said there was a riot and the sheriff called in the U.S. troops to put it down. I don't know if living in town is going to be so peaceful."

"It will be in Stephenville," Caleb said confidently.

Inside Virginia and Mary Anna were discussing things from the feminine point of view.

"You'll be happy in town, Virginia." Mary Anna was lying in bed, sewing tiny stitches in baby clothes, while Virginia readied the smaller children for bed and shooed the older ones up into the sleeping loft.

"Yes. I'm looking forward to it." She finally came over and sat in the chair beside Mary Anna's bed. "You feeling all right?"

Mary Anna sighed happily. "I have never enjoyed a pregnancy so much. All I do all day long is take care of Annah and then give her to Elizabeth to play with. I've made so many baby clothes. The way everyone treats me, you'd think I'd never had a child before."

"Well, not twins," Virginia added. "What do you think they'll be?"

"One of each would be nice."

"Take off your wedding ring," Virginia commanded. She got a sewing thread, put it through the gold circle, and hung it over Mary Anna's ample middle. "If it swings to and fro it will be boys. If it goes in a circle, it will be girls."

Breathlessly they wait for the ring to move. Subtly it began making the motion of a pendulum.

"Boys!" they said together.

"Do you really think that works?" Mary Anna asked.

"It works half the time," Virginia grinned. "Time will tell."

"Well, I certainly have a lot of that," Mary Anna said in a half-cheerful voice.

And they were long days. Soon even sitting in her rocker brought on contractions, and she was confined to bed. This only gave her more time to think about the absence of Indian attacks and fret about when the next one might come.

When she mentioned her fears to Daniel, he said, "They've been very busy in other parts of the county. Santana, Lone Wolf, and Kicking Bird haven't given up, they've just relocated."

"Kicking Bird? Who in the world is that?"

"Kiowa. He and Lone Wolf have joined forces now." He smoothed her hair against her damp forehead. "Don't worry about them. Just be glad they are causing their trouble in other places. Why, they probably took one look at our fortress and decided to try for easier game."

She thought he was probably right.

By late September, the men were through with the roundup and branding. They were running late this year, and that worried Daniel. Being first was important.

Mac would head up the drive. The men were constantly on guard, even though they suspected that trouble had moved out of the area for a while.

There was no thought of Caleb going on this cattle drive; he had made that clear. But Daniel was like an old hunting dog that saw his master take out the gun and then told the old dog to stay home. There was so much to hate about the drive and so much to love. Daniel had two babies that would come when Mary Anna could carry them no longer. That could be any day. He knew where he belonged, but he couldn't quell his desires to be out on the trail.

Tump approached him. "I want to go with the men. Before you say no, remember that some day I'll be a cattleman just like you, and I'll need to know all the things you know. I'll be careful, and I'll be with men you trust." He left nothing for Daniel to say, so Daniel just nodded his head.

The day finally arrived. Daniel hugged his son good-bye and then spoke to Coleman and Mac.

"The Lord be with you, men," Daniel said as he shook their hands.

"He will be," said Coleman. "Tump will be fine, Captain."

"Take care of Miss Mary Anna," said Mac. "And tell her we're real proud of her." They tipped their hats to Caleb as he rode by them to Daniel.

With a huge mixture of feelings careening through his chest, Daniel watched the herd move out.

Caleb spoke the words for him. "I feel like the girl that got left home from the party." He frowned. "I didn't want to feel that way."

"I know. Come on, Caleb. I'll buy you a cup of coffee." They headed for the cabin, and as they walked into the kitchen area, Virginia yelled at them, "It's time! The babies are on the way! Put the water on to boil! And stay out of my way!"

It was the end of September, and Mary Anna had successfully carried the babies eight months. When Virginia finally stuck her head out of the cabin, her smile told the whole story. "Two fine boys, Daniel. Good and healthy boys." She stepped back to let Daniel to the bedside.

"I want to call them Arthur and Oscar," said Mary Anna. "The one with the red thread is Arthur. He was born first." She smiled tiredly at Daniel. "I just couldn't name them Jacob and Esau."

"Arthur and Oscar are good strong names, family names." Gently he kissed her on the forehead and then touched the hand of each little boy. "Thank You, Lord, that You've given us two more fine sons. And that my Mary Anna is safe." He didn't try to hide the tears in his eyes.

He heard Virginia say to Caleb, "I'd better get my sewing thread ready. He's likely not to have a button left on that coat by the time he tells everyone about his little boys." There was no mistaking the joy behind Virginia's gruff voice.

All the next day the family took turns peeking at the tiny bundles sleeping in their mother's bed. Their cradles were ready, and they would go in them, but not yet.

Every time she looked at the scrunched up faces, Mary Anna thanked God. And she learned to tell their personalities almost at once. She didn't need the colored thread after a few days. But everyone else did.

# Chapter 6

Daniel, Caleb, and Thaddeus worked the crops while the men were on the trail drive. It was a fairly successful crop. Daniel was feeling good about all the money that would be coming in this year. He would be set solid for a long time. His lips parted in a grimy smile as the last of the hay was stored in the barn.

Lieutenant Mooreland came by to pick up a few more horses. "You do have the best horses in the county," he complimented Daniel.

"Careful breeding and tending," Daniel answered with a smile. He had come to like this brusk young man trying to do an impossible job with too few men and too much territory.

Lieutenant Mooreland and his men stayed for dinner. After the good meal, he said, "I dislike telling you this more than I can say, but you need to know so you'll be prepared. Santana, Big Tree, Satank, and 150 of their men raided a ten-wagon train. I can't tell you how bad it was. They just missed ambushing General Sheridan. Also the Lee family of six was wiped out, and Mr. Dobs, the Justice of the Peace of Palo Pinto County was murdered. Scalped and his ears and nose cut off."

Mary Anna felt faint.

"We've reached the point where everyone has agreed the peace treaties are not working. We're actively looking for the men to arrest them."

"I didn't think you could arrest reservation Indians," Daniel said.

"Normally we can't. But this is too big to be ignored. The men will be arrested and stand trial. If we can find them," he added. "So be on your guard. The wagon trail was between Fort Richardson and Fort Belnap."

Daniel and Mary Anna exchanged looks of fear. Fort Belnap was about fifteen miles north.

Lieutenant Mooreland was back a few days later with more news. This time there was a big grin on his face. "They got 'em. The trial will be at Jacksboro. It'll be the first time a reservation Indian has ever been tried." Something akin to hope glimmered from his eyes. "The public outrage has demanded the government do something about the depredations of the Indians." He saluted smartly and wheeled his horse, off on more patrols.

Mary Anna sat down at the table and smoothed the calico tablecloth. "I thought I had come to terms with the Indians and the whites. I've always felt sorry for them, that we pushed them off their land. They're a noble people, and yet I simply can't understand the way they wantonly kill."

Daniel sat down with her. Anger smoldered in his blue eyes. "I'm the one who thought the only good Indian was a dead Indian. Then I saw them as a people, living pretty much the same way we do. I fight for my land, and I can understand their fight for their land. But why do they kill everything that gets in their way? Even in the war we didn't kill anybody but the men in uniform. At least we didn't try to." He shook his head. "I want to hate them again. It was easier that way. But now I can't." He looked sad. "I'm angry with them, hate what they do, but I can't know how they must feel inside to make them do these things."

When he knew the trial should be over, Daniel was so anxious to know the outcome that he went in to Stephenville to the general store.

"You ain't gonna like what I have to say," Charlie warned him.

"They're going to hang them, aren't they?"

"Nope. Thomas Ball and J. A. Woolfork of Weatherford did their best to get them off, but the court gave 'em the death sentence anyway."

"But that's what we wanted," said a confused Daniel.

"Yeah, but Santana and Big Tree's sentence was commuted to life imprisonment. Court said as long as the Kiowas behaved and stayed on the reservations, they would just keep them in jail."

"That makes no sense at all!" exploded Daniel. "That's not going to slow down those Indians!"

Charlie nodded in agreement. "Onliest thing I can figure out is that they're trying to avoid an all-out war. Maybe they think if they kill the chiefs, their braves would just rally and raid worse."

"Cutting off the head of a rattler is usually a good way to slow down his tail," Daniel commented bitterly.

"Guess they're afraid this snake has more than one head."

"Quannah Parker?"

Charlie nodded again. "Could be since he's half-breed he has more to prove?"

"No, it's because his father was Nocona." Anger glinted in Daniel's eyes. "This is one big mistake, and we're going to pay the consequences for it."

"You too mad to buy anything?" Charlie asked pragmatically.

"Don't think my mad spell would be a good enough excuse to Mary Anna for not buying what she needs." Daniel took out the list he was carrying in his vest and handed it to Charlie. He stewed the entire time it was being filled and went home angry.

Back at the ranch there was agreement that the trial had turned out all wrong. And they were frightened by feared retaliations.

"In a way, it's the worst thing they could have done to those chiefs." Mary Anna thought of the vast stretches of prairie they had roamed. "Being cooped up in a jail, like that. I don't think they're afraid of death. They'd be heroes then, but it's a disgrace for them to be kept in a cage."

"I think you're right," Caleb said, "but the bottom line is that we ain't ever gonna be safe until them Indians are put somewhere else."

Daniel's anger grew in proportion to the support he found for his views. All he had ever wanted was to make a living. The Indians' sole purpose in life was to make this impossible for him. Now the government had betrayed him. A government he didn't want, one which he had fought against. And now his own wife was taking up for their enemy.

He jerked his hat off the peg by the door and stomped out. The embarrassed silence that he left behind was not broken. People slid out of sight. The discussion of the trial and its outcome was over.

Word had gotten around about Mary Anna's healing of Thunder. Out where there were no doctors at all, people saw this as a gift. To her surprise, a frantic young husband showed up at her door asking for help with delivering his wife's child. It was the beginning of her career as a midwife.

It also became commonplace for the men to come to Mary Anna for stitching up a bad cut or for her to prescribe something from her medicine cabinet for their various ailments. She had a natural instinct for diagnosing and even helped with the stock once in a while.

She was also looking for her son to come home from the drive any day now. When the cloud of dust surrounding a group of riders finally was sighted, she waited anxiously until she could make out Tump's figure on Thunder.

Daniel pounded him on the back, but Tump had to tell him, "We didn't get there first. We didn't do as good as you and Mr. West did." There was sorrow in his face.

"Whatever it is, it was worth the drive, and I'm proud of you, son." He pounded Tump on the back and then gave him a big bear hug. "I'm so proud of you," he echoed.

Peter was glad to see his brother again but tried hard not to be jealous of all the attention Tump was getting from their father. He had worked hard this summer, and he knew his father appreciated that, but he had never pounded him on the back or given him a bear hug. He made up his mind right then and there that he would be on the next drive, even if he had to sneak off to go.

Daniel further honored his son by asking him to go to Fort Worth to deposit the money. Then he asked Peter to accompany him. "You boys will be running this ranch some day. I'll be sitting on the porch swing, and I don't want you asking me what to do with the million dollars you made on the drive," he grinned.

Peter was mollified, and Tump regaled him with stories of the drive all the way to the bank and back. "You'll be on the next one, Peter. I'll need you." And he gave his brother his best brotherly smile.

Seven-year-old Henry looked up to his big brothers. He copied everything they did. He wanted to be a cowboy and go on the drive with them. He knew they wouldn't let him go for a long time, so he played cowboy every day, practicing for the time when he could go.

He watched the men, too, and the one that caught his eye was Snake. Snake had come back from this drive with a new collection of snakeskins. He wore a hat with a rattlesnake skin wrapped around the crown, the rattles hanging down along the brim. His belt was of rattlesnake skin, and even the sheath in which he carried his skinning knife was made of snakeskin.

The women wouldn't go near Snake, but Henry admired his bravery, which he attributed to killing all those snakes.

A few days later, Mary Anna was feeding the family when she noticed a very unpleasant smell. She was relatively sure something had crawled up under the cabin again and died. She reminded herself to say something to Daniel about it. Each day she would smell the offensive odor, but Daniel couldn't find a cause for it. It seemed to come and go. But when it was around, it was awful.

On Saturday it was terrible, and it got noticeably stronger when Willie and Henry came in for their scrubbing.

"Can't we go down to the river and scrub, Mama?" complained Henry.

"Absolutely not. I want you clean enough for church. Here, let me help you with your shirt, Henry." As she leaned close to him, the smell almost knocked her over. "What in the world!" she said as she lifted his long-tailed shirt.

"Isn't it beautiful?" bragged Henry of his belt. "I caught a snake and killed him and skinned him just like Mr. Snake did."

"Henry!"

"It wasn't poisonous, Mama," he protested as she took the belt from him with two fingers.

"Neither has the skin been cured and tanned properly. It's absolutely rotten!" She opened the door and threw the belt as far away as she could, almost vomiting at the smell. "Next time you want a snakeskin belt, young man," she ordered as she scrubbed him bright red, "you ask your father the right way to do it!"

Daniel roared with laughter when she told him the tale.

"You wouldn't have thought it so funny if you'd been the one to dispose of that rotten mess," she complained. "Those boys will be the death of me yet," she sighed. But privately she smiled at Henry's ingenuity at acquiring something he really wanted.

Daniel wanted something, too. Since he wasn't actively going on the drives, he thought seriously about running for county commissioner. His lodge brothers were encouraging. Stephenville was becoming quite a little town, though it would never fit the description of a boomtown, but it had a good-sized Masonic Lodge, to which Daniel belonged.

A clapboard church had been built, and more stores were going into business. More houses appeared around the square of the courthouse.

When Daniel rode into town, he was greeted by many friends. He made a point of meeting the new people in town, too. In spite of that, he came back to the ranch on election day with a long face.

"Oh, darling, I'm so sorry. You'll get it next time," Mary Anna said confidently.

"I'm not so sure there will be a next time," Daniel said in a gruff voice.

"Of course there will be."

Daniel had a hard time settling down to ranch work for a while, then soothed his dented pride with the purchase of land that brought his holdings up to 3,300 acres. He mentioned the house again to Mary Anna.

"Not until the Indians are gone," she said firmly. She looked into his eyes. "You heard the same rumor I did. The Indians are amassing for an all-out attack. We're in more danger than ever."

"If the meeting President Grant called with all the chiefs in St. Louis doesn't work, I don't know what will happen." He sighed. "I'm not getting my hopes up, but maybe it's a start." For their protection, he hired on more men. He would be ready when the time came.

As though to prove her point, a few nights later they were raided. The children's favorite pet colt refused to leave, and the Indians shot it through the heart with an arrow.

Amid the sobbing children, Mary Anna took one look at the dead colt and knew the story of Thunder's recovery was not to be repeated.

Rarely did a week pass without some losses to the Indians by someone in the area. Daniel wrestled with the question of whether or not he should make a drive that fall.

He and Caleb discussed it over apple pie and hot coffee.

"I'm agin it, Dan. Competition is getting rougher."

"I thought of driving them up there and wintering them, but that blizzard last year wiped out a lot of men. On the other hand, that should pump up the market price."

"We can still run our cattle together up there. 'Course we'll need a traveling brand now. Rustling is getting to be as big a problem as the Indians."

"Comanche and Kiowas are still raiding off the Fort Sill Reservation." Daniel punched his fork hard into the piece of pie. "Isn't it ever going to end?"

"Eventually. We're crowding them out with more settlers every day. We can't kill them all, so we'll muscle them off the land, I reckon."

Daniel still had men out on night guard for the cattle and horses. Sometimes they lost a few head in the night, but they never knew for sure when there would be an all-out attack.

Toad was out with the men one night. The cattle were acting nervous, and Toad pulled out a harmonica and played "Aura Lee" for them. It made him edgy for the cattle to be spooky. His horse shied at the slightest thing, and Toad felt himself straining to hear and identify each sound.

He put his hand on his revolver, reassuring himself it was there and fully loaded. Then he checked to see if his rifle was in its leather holster, hanging down beside the pommel of the saddle. He kept constant check on where the other men were.

It was a clear night, the stars blazing down in all their glory, and the wind barely stirring the rich blades of grass, but it was not peaceful.

Toad was ready. He had felt this all before. He knew it was only a question of where the renegades would hit. He tried to predict their weakest spot, but he felt they had everything covered. "Easy, Beau, easy," he told his horse.

Riding out of the darkness, like spirits on the wind, the attackers came.

The night riders began firing their Springfields and prepared for the cattle to run. There were fences around the pasture, but Toad knew they couldn't hold against the weight of scared longhorns. Right now it was more important to drive away the invaders than to stem the flow of the cattle.

He had one Indian in the sight of his rifle when the man suddenly turned and looked squarely at him. Everything began to happen in slow motion.

Toad could plainly see the man had his hair divided into three braids on each side of his head. He saw the feathers. But when he saw the man's face in the starlight, a shiver ran down his body at the hate reflected there.

This was not some unknown person trying to steal the cattle and horses. This man wanted to kill him. And the smoldering hatred made Toad hesitate for a split second. It was long enough for the Indian to fire his rifle first and for Toad to feel the burning in his chest as the bullet sped across the way and through his flesh. The last thing Toad saw was a tiny gleam of satisfaction when the Indian realized Toad was hit and falling from his horse.

It was only then that the full magnitude of the conflict between the settlers and the Indians became plain to Toad. As plain as the face of death. And the last thing Toad said was "Help me, Lord," as he fell on the hot hide of the longhorn and then bounced underneath the hooves of the moving herd.

After the running battle was over, the men draped Toad's body across his horse, and Snake took him back to the ranch house. Daniel came out of the house with his rifle in his hand. "Who is it?" he asked in a tired voice when he saw the body.

"Toad, Captain." Snake saw the sadness on Daniel's face.

"Have the men build a coffin."

At midmorning Daniel, Mary Anna, Tump, Caleb, Mac, Coleman, and Snake gathered at the little cemetery. Mary Anna put a few wildflowers on the tiny grave of her infant, and then they had the service for Toad.

Daniel read the Twenty-third Psalm and commended the young man to God's keeping. The men covered the coffin with the warm Texas soil, and then Mac placed Toad's saddle over the grave to show anyone who passed by that a good cowboy was buried there. It was the best marker any cowboy could have.

Mary Anna cast one last glance back at the grave. So often she had fought off death for one of her loved ones. The Lord had been merciful to her. She had lost two infants before she had time to get to know them, but so many of the frontier families had lost much, much more.

A chill passed over her as she saw again the tiny grave. "Sleep well, my baby." She was afraid to say more and left the place of the dead for the place of the living.

⟶⟨⟩⟵

One by one the three youngest children came down with a high fever that rapidly advanced to vomiting and runny bowels.

"Daniel," Mary Anna started to say, but he interrupted her.

"I know, take the other children to the Wests' cabin."

Virginia came at once. "The men and older children can take care of things over there. You have your hands full."

Mary Anna used all her tricks to break the fever that sapped life from the children. She tried to get hearty broths down them, but they threw up everything she gave them. She and Virginia literally forced liquids of all kinds down them and even gave them sugar rags to suck.

The nights were the worst. There was little thought of sleep, for while the racking vomiting tore at the women's hearts, they lived in dread of a sudden silence. The specter of three tiny graves doubling the count in the cemetery spurred Mary Anna on, as did her running plea to God to help her and not ask her to give up Oscar, Arthur, and Annah.

"Please, dear Lord," she whispered, "don't take these little ones from me. I can't heal them, but I know Your power can. I knew when I looked down the years with Daniel and we spoke of living out the dream, that this was the sort of test we would face. Help us to pass the test and grow stronger from it. But please, dear God, don't take my little ones."

Most of the time she just prayed, "Please, God, please."

One morning Mary Anna woke with terror. She had slept the entire night through without once getting up to check on her children or nurse them. She ran trembling to their little beds.

They were all sleeping peacefully, and she satisfied her fear by lightly running her hand over each cooling forehead. She watched their dear faces as they slept. Annah was only two. Her illness had sapped the baby fat from her little rounded face. It had a pinched look now. The twins, at one, had the same look about them. Where she had seen a fat little cherub in their faces, now she saw thinness. But they were alive, and she could build them up again. If only there wasn't some permanent damage done to them that wasn't apparent now. She would have to worry about that later. For now she had them back. She kissed each small forehead and crept over to Virginia's bed.

Virginia awoke with alarm when Mary Anna touched her arm. "No, no, it's all right. Virginia, the fever has broken. They're sleeping!"

"Praise the Lord!" Virginia said, and she immediately got out of bed to look at the children for herself. They hugged each other over the little beds and both began to cry with fatigue and relief.

"We'll have to fatten them up," Virginia said as she wiped her nose with a handkerchief.

Mary Anna put her arm around Virginia. "We make a good team." Deep gratitude colored her eyes even bluer. "Thank you for being here to help me."

"Oh, pshaw," Virginia said, now wiping her eyes. "You'd do it for me."

"There are very few women on the frontier, and I'm so grateful I'm with someone I love and can share with," said Mary Anna. "You've heard the same stories I have about women going crazy in the loneliness of their cabins with no one to talk with."

Virginia nodded. "I went through a spell of it myself after my little girl died. There was no one there but Caleb, and he nursed his grief in solitude." The sadness went out of her voice. "All the more reason to rejoice right now."

"It seems to me I spend as much time fighting death as I do living. Between the sicknesses and the Indians, it's a full-time job." She sighed. "I tried to explain this to Daniel when we were talking about how good things are for us now that we have the ranch. We aren't going to be protected from life, no matter what. Life itself is a test. And for the Christian it's a test to see if Satan can separate us from God, even in the little things."

"I don't see how any mother cannot believe in God," Virginia mused. "Who can look after her children every minute of the day? Who can protect them from the unseen and unknown? Prayer is my peace of mind. I know God'll take care of them, even if I can't."

"But that doesn't mean they won't die," Mary Anna said carefully. "I think that's the thing I'm the most afraid of. I love them when they're born, but now that I know them, I'm not sure I could be as strong as you were, Virginia. I think it would kill me to lose any of my children." She turned away. "It would be the ultimate test. Even harder than losing Daniel. We've had a wonderful life together. I'd miss him more than I can say. But a child hasn't had a chance to find out much of anything. They have so much to live for." She shuddered. "I pray daily that I will never have to go through what you have."

"Let go of the fear, and live life to the fullest. You can't trust God and be afraid every day. That doesn't make sense, does it?"

"You're right," she said with a slight parting of the lips. "It doesn't make sense."

Oscar began to cry. "Isn't that the loveliest sound?" Virginia hustled over to him. "Come on, little cowboy. Let's try to get some soup into you.

"He's not a cowboy," Mary Anna corrected her. "He's a cattleman." And she smiled, knowing this was the plan, and if God had mercy on them all, Oscar would grow up to be a cattleman like his father.

# Chapter 7

The spring of 1873 brought the continued recuperations of the three little ones, and the yearly roundup. It seemed to Mary Ann she could set the calendar by the restlessness she felt in Daniel when it was time to get the herd gathered up, counted, and branded. She was reasonably sure he was smart enough not to go on a drive this year and instead send his cattle with the men, as he had done last year. He was hardly old, but the trail was an unforgiving master and made everyone as uncomfortable as possible. There was no such thing as an easy drive.

Daniel and Caleb had their heads together a lot as the summer drew to a close. Mary Anna said nothing, waiting for her level-headed husband to tell her of his plans not to go.

"You're what!" she hissed in the loudest voice she could manage.

Daniel's face wore the look of a man struck by a rattlesnake in his own home. "I'm going on the drive with Tump and Peter."

Mary Anna took a deep breath and squared her shoulders. One eyebrow was raised. She pinched her lips together and gritted her teeth. Her face was a mask of anger he hadn't seen since early in their marriage. "You can't be serious," she said in a carefully controlled voice and crossed her arms in front of her.

Defensive now, Daniel stood a little taller. "I am." Then he took a verbal step too near the edge of the abyss. "I'm the boss of this house and this ranch, and if I say I'm going, then by glory, I'm going." His voice thundered through the cabin. He watched Mary Anna's face turn from anger to surprise.

"You've never spoken to me like that before."

"You've never acted like this before. You can't order me around like you do the children. I'm your husband. Head of the house."

She turned her back on him with that remark.

"The drives aren't going to last for very much longer, Mary Anna," he explained reasonably. "A part of history is passing away. There are more fences and people. Soon we'll be hemmed in." He gave a short laugh. "Just like the Indians. I want to make just one more drive myself." Quietly he added, "Maybe I have to prove to myself that at forty I'm not too old to do it."

When she didn't answer, he walked over to her stiff, silent frame and stood behind her. "I won't say any more. If you want to do some more talking about it, I think we'd better do it later. After you've had a chance to think about what I said." He touched her shoulder, but she shrugged him off. Quietly he left the cabin and went out to work with his men.

Mary Anna threw herself on the bed and cried. Then she beat her fist in the covers. After her temper tantrum was over, she sat up and tried to think. *Why did you get so mad?* she asked herself. *He's a cattleman, and this is what cattlemen do. But he doesn't have to. He has more than enough good men to make that drive without him. You're afraid. Of what? That he won't come back. He's always gone so long, and you hate the loneliness. He's choosing to spend time away from you when he doesn't have to. A little boy, still playing cowboy. He should have been over that long ago. What would he do if he stayed here? What he has been doing. Maybe if we start the new house. . .* That thought frightened her, for the Indians were still raiding at will. Word had come that things were worse in Montana and Wyoming. Sitting Bull and Rain-in-the-Face were leading the Plains Indians, and the government was sending more troops to contain the Sioux. That also meant no new troops for Texas.

Mary Anna got up and poured water in the china bowl from the matching pitcher her mother had given her. As she washed her face, she felt herself cooling down but still angry.

The noise of the children at the supper table covered the silence between husband and wife, but there was no avoiding going to bed together. They were very formal with one another, strangers sharing a bed.

Mary Anna tried hard to get over her anger, but she couldn't let go of it. Daniel left her alone, waiting for his sweet, sensible wife to come back to him.

She was still mad as he prepared to go. "It isn't safe, Daniel. I need you here." The words came out of tight lips.

Quietly he turned from his horse and said, "I'm sorry. But I have to do this. And I'm sorry you don't understand." He leaned down and kissed her still mouth.

She wanted to cry out, "Stay, I love you, I can't bear to see you go, please!" But her lips wouldn't move. She watched him mount up and leave with his men.

She felt as she had when he had gone off to the war. Bereft.

❦

Once on the trail, Daniel began to regret leaving. It was as though Mary Anna had the power to curse the drive. They got off to a late start, and everything that could go wrong, did. When at last they got to Dodge, they couldn't find the buyer they had been guaranteed before they started. Jaye Cook and Company Bank in New York closed and caused huge losses of money among the cattlemen.

Daniel sold his cattle for almost what it cost him to take them up there and counted himself lucky that he didn't have to drive them back home. There was no way he could afford to winter them there. It was too costly for the feed and payroll for the men who would agree to do it. He tried to start home early enough for Christmas, but they missed that by weeks.

He thought of Mary Anna every day on the trail. How would things be between them when he got home? She had been right. He shouldn't have gone. It was bitter to have to face her and admit that after all his bellowing about being the man of the house.

"Papa?" Tump came over to the campfire where they had their bedrolls laid out for the night. Daniel was propped against his saddle, drinking coffee.

"Yes?"

Tump was obviously very uncomfortable about something.

"Sit down, son. Want some coffee?"

"No, thanks."

"Whatever is bothering you can't be that bad. Tell your old papa what's on your mind." Daniel guessed at Tump's age it could be any number of things.

"Do you still love Mama?" Tump looked at Daniel's face to see if he could read the real answer.

Daniel took a deep breath. "Yes, son, I do."

Tump looked down at the fire. "I heard the fight you and Mama had before you left."

Daniel chuckled. "I'm sure half the country heard that fight."

"But you still love her and you're going back to her?"

"With my foot in my mouth and my hat in my hand," Daniel answered. He sighed. "Question is, will she still want me?"

"Of course she will," Tump said quickly. "I mean, what else would she do?"

"Oh, your mama can do pretty well anything she wants to. She's a strong woman. That's why we're still out here. If she wasn't strong, we'd of gone back to Anderson County a long time ago. Or not come at all," he added thoughtfully.

"I know she wants you back," Tump said confidently. "She loves you."

"Maybe. But I sure did a lot to make her not respect me. I said some hard things to her." Daniel took a big swallow of the hot, thick coffee. "She was right, and I was wrong. I shouldn't have come on this drive. Only I was so bound and determined to prove something, I put that first instead of your mama." He looked at his son. "It was a mistake. All I can do is hope she will forgive me and take me back. I've done a lot of damage to the way things are between us. Harsh words are a rocky soil for love to grow in."

"She'll be there, and she'll still love you. I know Mama," Tump said with fervor.

"You can learn a lot from what you heard and saw, boy. Remember not to do it when you're married." Daniel's smile was halfhearted at best.

When they finally rode into the ranch in early January, Mary Anna was not waiting for them on the porch. It was a cold, snowy day. The rain clouds looked like a woman dragging her wet gray skirts across the sky, heavy and sodden.

Daniel had bought everyone presents again. He had been especially careful to pick out a fine silver mirror with a matching comb and brush for Mary Anna. He wondered if he'd ever get the chance again to sit behind her rocker on a low stool and brush out her beautiful auburn hair.

❦

When Mary Anna heard the horses come to a stop in front of the cabin, her heart jumped in fear. Daniel must be home. And with him came the next part of their awful fight. She was afraid he didn't love her anymore. Maybe he had only come back to get his things to move into town. She didn't know what to expect. She smoothed her hair, put on a shawl, and opened the door.

Daniel was climbing down off his horse in a slow, old-man fashion. He looked beaten and tired when he turned to face her. His shoulders were slumped, and there was shame on his face.

All her anger melted away, and she hurried over to him. He looked very much as he had when he came home from the war.

"You're home," she said carefully, watching his eyes for some sign of affection.

"Yes." He waited to see if he would be accepted or rejected.

"Come inside. I have something warm you can eat."

It was a tiny step forward.

She hugged the boys and gave them plates of food, but they were quiet, waiting to see what would happen. All the other children were asleep. Tump pushed Peter into the other side of the cabin. "Be quiet and eat," he whispered to the questioning look Peter gave him.

Slowly Daniel washed his hands and face, drying them on the towel on the peg by the bowl. Mary Anna turned around to face him as she brought the food.

"Mary Anna! Why didn't you tell me you were going to have a child?" he asked as he saw her enlarged figure.

"I thought you might think I was using it as a weapon to keep you home."

"When?" he asked

"The end of March." She put the food on the table and sat across from him.

He didn't touch the food. "You were right. I shouldn't have gone. It was awful from the first day. You were right." He fought the tears that wanted to spill from his eyes. "And now I'm afraid I've lost you, too."

She reached out her hand toward him. "No, I don't think so." She ducked her head for a moment and then said, "I wasn't sure you would come home to me."

He took her hand and stroked it lightly, carefully. "I did what I had to do, but I shouldn't have done it the way I did. I said some things I'm sorry for. Things that, if you let me stay, you'll never hear again. I promise."

"Then you do want to stay with me?" Her face looked hopeful.

"More than anything in the world. Do you forgive me?"

"Yes, I do. And do you forgive me?"

"Yes, with all my heart." He stood up and walked around to her. She sat still while he caressed her face carefully, then she looked up at him and they kissed softly, tenderly, tentatively. At the far end of the cabin, Tump and Peter quietly slipped up to their beds in the loft.

"I think we'll have to get to know each other all over again," she said.

He grinned. "That will be a pleasure for me. And you will find me a changed man, in many ways."

He helped her up out of the chair. "I'm tired now. I want to go to bed," she said.

As they slipped between the covers, Daniel stayed carefully on his side of the bed.

She slipped her hand into his. He gave it a gentle squeeze. Then he lifted it to his lips and kissed the palm of her hand. Everything was going to be all right now. *Thank You, God. Thank You that I didn't lose her in my stupidity. It was a hard learned lesson. But I won't forget.* Mary Anna still loved him. He was her husband. They would carefully find their way back to one another, but they would try to glue the pieces back together in day-to-day living. Their love wouldn't be the same, but it would be a deeper one, one they had chosen to nurture.

❧

As Daniel settled back into home life, he caught up with the local news. Discovering that Santana and Big Tree had been pardoned and released in October while he was on the trail did nothing to lessen his regret over having gone on the trail. "If they had attacked and I hadn't been here, how would I ever have lived with myself?" he asked.

"They didn't, so no harm was done," Mary Anna reassured him. "Remember what the Bible says: 'Sufficient today is the evil thereof.' We've enough struggles to handle without you borrowing trouble from things that never happened."

When, at the end of January, their baby boy was born dead, Daniel voiced his regrets all over again.

He wept as he held the dead infant in his arms. "It's my fault," he said to Mary Anna. "If I hadn't gone on the drive. . ."

"No, Daniel. It wasn't anyone's fault. It's just life." She gathered Daniel and their little son into the bed with her, and they wept together over their loss.

But the seasons of the year can't be stopped, and spring was making a gallant effort to push aside winter. Mary Anna responded to the coming of spring as she always did. She was so finely tuned to its promise, she found healing with the first small green buds. She lavished the love she should have been giving her child on the garden, coaxing each small plant up into the sunlight. And she was able to thank God for the children she did have. She studied them with a new and discerning eye and found new delights.

That summer both Mary Anna and Daniel were glad to welcome Captain Mooreland and his men for a brief visit in the middle of July.

"Congratulations on your promotion, Captain," Daniel said.

"Thank you, but here's what I came out to show you." He was bursting with news. Dramatically, he handed Daniel a paper dated earlier that month.

In it an article described the massacre of Custer at the Little Big Horn by the amassed Sioux. The Indians had been led by Dull Knife, Crazy Horse, Red Cloud, and White Bull. They had wiped out Custer and his men and any chance they had of making peace with the government. They would be hunted down now and eliminated as the enemy. No more peace treaties would be offered.

"They're dead men now," Captain Mooreland said. "And Mackenzie's going after the Comanche up on the Llano Estacado. He'll find them. Every winter they just disappear off the face of the earth. But he'll find them this time." His face was beaming. "We're just about to eliminate our Indian problems."

"And what will happen to the ones who survive?" Mary Anna asked.

"Reservation. But there won't be that many left, believe me. All the leaders will be caught or killed. Indian territory is where they belong."

His prophecy came true as the year advanced. Mackenzie found the Comanche in Palo Duro Canyon and slaughtered them without mercy. Quannah Parker lasted only until the spring. Starving and ragged, he willingly led the last small band to the reservation. Here and there occasional raids were made, but on a practical level, the Indian nations had been totally defeated.

Erath County, along with the other parts of the country, rejoiced that one of their largest barriers to success had been eliminated. Now they had only the weather, the market, thieves and cutthroats, Texas fever, Kansas farmers, and sod-busters with which to contend.

"Well, Dan," said Caleb. "Now that the danger is over, I think we should both get on with the next part of the plan. I'll be moving Virginia into town as soon as I can build us a house there."

"We're going to miss you something awful." Daniel smiled. "We're getting ready to build that mansion I want for Mary Anna."

Caleb shook his head. "I don't know how we did it, but we did. I have everything I've ever wanted."

"You do, too, know how we did it. God has blessed us at every turn. Even the bad ones," Daniel added with chagrin.

Daniel and Mary Anna turned their attention to building their new home. They had chosen a design from an architectural plan book, and Daniel quickly ordered the materials out of Waco.

The Victorian-style house had two stories with a huge porch wrapped around it like loving arms. Its gingerbread trim would be painted dark brown, but the house itself would be dark green. Spacious closets and two bathrooms, an almost unheard-of luxury, were among its finest features.

The men at the Berlin Lodge in Stephenville razzed Daniel endlessly about the bathrooms, but it was in good humor. Before the house was finished, almost every man in the lodge had an opportunity to use his special skills to make the house one of beauty and everyone's pride.

"There is one thing I want," Daniel told the men. "I need running water for the house. I need someone to find it. Know of anyone who can find water?"

"I can take care of that," said Joe, one of his lodge brothers.

The new house was in its last building stages when an old woman as thin and willowy as the forked branch she carried came to the ranch with her husband. Her smile was big as she told him, "There's a lot of shallow pools of water around here. Secret rivers run just beneath the ground and meet up with other rivers." She took one fork of the peach branch in each hand and held the branch level as she began walking. She walked around the front of the house, concentrating on the end of the limb. "No," she shook her head. "Nothing here." She walked to the side of the house.

Daniel was watching the end of the limb carefully, too. He thought he saw it twitch. The woman's skirts swished as she walked through the tall grass. The stick seemed to be pulling her along, and as she got several yards from the house, the end of the stick suddenly dipped toward the ground. The woman stopped still. "Here. Here is where the water is. It's down about fifty feet, but it's here."

Daniel was astonished at the procedure, but he marked the place she indicated. She held out her hand for the money she was to be paid. "When it comes in, I'll come back for the other half of my money." She smiled a toothy grin and climbed up in the wagon with the help of her husband.

"I admit I have some reservations about all this, but you're a mighty impressive woman," Daniel told her.

"It's a gift, Mr. Thornton. I claim no praise and want no shame from it. I use it as best I can."

Several days later the driller came out to dig the well. Mary Anna heard the heavy rattling of his wagons.

He stopped in front of the cabin. "Hello, the house!" he shouted.

When Daniel appeared, the wizened black man scrambled nimbly down from the tall seat. He had an equally thin, dark-skinned boy with him. The old man stuck out his dirty hand.

"Manilla's my name and water's my game. This here is Mandan. Indian kid. Onliest word he would say when I first found him. Name of his tribe, I think. So you want water, do you?"

"Yes, for the new house over there."

They walked over to the work in progress. "Gonna be a big, beautiful house, Mr. Thornton. Mandan is the onliest person alive who can really find water. Never fails. He's the son of a real Indian medicine man."

Daniel looked at the teenage boy who was dressed in ragged castoffs. His hair was matted, and he looked anything but the son of a shaman.

"Cost you a dollar fer him to find it."

Daniel didn't tell the man about the water woman. "That'll be just fine."

"Earn yer keep, boy. Find us some water," the man ordered. The boy moved with grace and ease, striding the front ground of the house. He frowned and retraced his steps to the far side of the house and then moved to the back. He made his way around the house to the side in the general area the water woman had chosen, walking slowly in a careful pattern designed to cover the whole ground. He paused, cocked his ear toward the earth. Then he walked to the exact spot where the water woman had pointed. "Here" is all he said.

"Git the wagon lined up, Mandan. How far down?"

Mandan extended all five fingers of one hand.

"Right at fifty feet," Manilla nodded confidently.

Mandan removed the back wheels, which placed the heavy machinery on the ground. The derrick was raised and the cable spool set. Like a carefully choreographed ballet, Manilla and Mandan pulled the heavy rope off the cable spoon, through the crown and spudding.

Mandan unhitched the mules and secured the pale yellow rope. As they patiently walked their endless circle, they would provide power to turn the machine that would raise and lower the ponderous stem. That in turn pounded the heavy fourteen-inch bit into the ground.

The bit yo-yoed in the ever-deepening hole as the earth it dug was moved to the top. Drilling was hard, dirty work, and it took skillful knowledge to keep the bit chewing at the earth.

"There it is! Fifty-one feet exactly. Tolt ya so!" The water licked at the mud-encrusted bottoms of Manilla's pants, then slowly ebbed out of sight.

Manilla and Mandan had captured the attention of everyone on the ranch, and when the water was found, a shout went up from the crowd. Mandan stooped down, cautiously opened a small leather pouch, and dropped in a pinch of damp earth from the new well.

"All right men, get the pieces of that big Standard windmill and get it set up," said Daniel. They erected the elevated redwood tank and ran the pipes into the house. A simple opening of a valve brought water from the tank. It was a proud moment when Mary Anna opened it and water flowed from the spout. "It's a miracle, Daniel. It's a miracle," she breathed as the water cascaded over her hand.

Daniel went back outside to tell Manilla the job was complete and to pay him. "Best sixty-six dollars I ever spent!" he said as he paid the man.

Manilla handed one of the dollars to Mandan, who climbed up on the wagon seat and sat impassively. Then Manilla joined him and urged his mules on to the next job.

Daniel went into the house. In the kitchen he could hear the groanings of the big blades as they turned in the hot prairie wind. The sound would become a constant companion to the house.

Now that there was water, the work on the house progressed at a rapid rate. The furniture Daniel ordered from Waco came, and soon he and Mary Anna were standing in their dream home.

Daniel was especially proud of the huge claw-footed tubs. It was almost the first thing he showed everyone who came to see their new home. At night carbide lights gave the house a warm glow. The house was built up on a high rock foundation that helped keep it cool in the summer. Thick rugs on the floor would keep it warm in the winter. The house seemed to have everything.

"I've never seen anything like it," said Mac in a voice of awe as he entered the new dwelling. His hat was in his hand, and he was followed by the other cowboys as Daniel gave them the grand tour.

When Virginia and Caleb came for a call, Mary Anna was proud to show them her new home. Caleb and Daniel were a little embarrassed at the girlish joy with which Mary Anna and Virginia met one another. It reminded Daniel of two little schoolgirls who hadn't seen each other in a while. He motioned for Caleb to come into the big parlor on the right side of the house.

"Ah, Daniel, don't be so hard on 'em. They haven't seen each other since we moved to town," Caleb grinned. He looked around the room. "Son, I think you're living in a castle." He sat down in one of the deep leather chairs and crossed his legs.

"Yes, I think I am." He offered Caleb something to drink and said, "You know, you're one of the few people who can truly understand what the culmination of this house means to me."

"It's true. Now our house may not be quite this grand, but it's everything I ever wanted—'cepting I only have one bathroom," he smiled and raised one eyebrow. "And unless I'm mistaken, it looks like you're getting ready to add another child to your family pretty soon. Son, you're doing all right. I don't know if you kin stand another good piece of news."

Daniel was sitting in the matching chair next to him. "News?"

"Yes. The men in the lodge think it's time for you to run again for county commissioner. We think you're a shoo-in."

Daniel flushed and then sputtered, "I'd love to run again. I know this time how to run a campaign a little better than that first time."

"And we plan to hep you."

They raised their glasses, and Caleb said, "To the new county commissioner."

Virginia and Mary Anna were in the master bedroom, sitting on a beautiful sofa in the sitting area, having their refreshments.

Virginia's merry eyes twinkled. "And so when is the new baby due?"

"September. I'm somewhat embarrassed to be having babies still at my age."

"Well, it gets more dangerous, but you can't ignore what the Lord sends. I'll help you when you're time comes."

"And you. How is living in town?"

"Glorious. I love every minute of it." Her glance took in the beautiful room. "You could talk me into living out here with you anytime, though," she grinned. "You have it all, Mary Anna. A husband who loves you, a good family, a beautiful home. What more could there be?"

Mary Anna's big smile faded a bit. "I do have it all. And I'm grateful to God for everything you mentioned. But sometimes I get scared, wondering if I'm supposed to have it all." She looked at her teacup. "Or what price I have to pay for it."

"Don't be silly. God blesses the people He wants without them having to pay a price for it. A blessing is that. A blessing."

"I guess I don't feel like I deserve all this," Mary Anna said truthfully.

"No one does. But we enjoy it all the same without looking over our shoulder for something bad to happen."

"You're still a comfort to me, Virginia. Let's see each other often."

"Let's."

It wasn't long until Virginia made a very hurried trip out to the house again.

Mary Anna was lying at the foot of the big bed in a little labor bed. In between contractions she tried to rest. "I'm getting too old for this, Virginia," she repeated.

"Well, you know what to do about it. Here, push. Push!"

Mary Anna was remembering the three babies who had not cried when she had delivered them or whose cry had been silenced too soon. *Please, God, let this one be all right.*

The sound Mary Anna waited for came quickly. The red-faced infant squalled indignantly at his new world, and Mary Anna laughed out loud at the healthy sound of it. Virginia could barely wait to call Daniel in.

He knelt at the edge of the small bed beside Mary Anna, who was holding the baby. "I want you two to meet properly. Daniel, this is Little Dan. Little Dan, meet your wonderful father."

"Little Dan?"

"I don't want anyone calling him Junior, though his name will be Daniel

Robert Thornton, the Second."

And more blessings were added. Daniel was elected county commissioner in the 1876 elections. At the lodge meeting, he said, "I'm donating two and a half acres of land for the Barton Springs school." Grinning, he added, "I'm not doing this because I'm so noble. I'm doing it because my wife has hounded me to death for a real school building."

The men laughed heartily, and Mr. Trent said, "You know that means a new building for us, too. First floor is the school. Second floor is the meeting place for the lodge." All the men cheered and clapped.

Daniel was feeling very good when he entered his warm, new home. But Mary Anna was crying up in their bedroom.

"What in the world?" he said in alarm and ran to where she was lying in the bed, awash in tears.

"I'm pregnant again!" And she dissolved in more tears. "I'll never get to go anywhere for the rest of my life or entertain in our big lovely house. I'll be in seclusion forever."

Daniel was no fool. He was tickled to death, but he knew better than to say that to his wife. She needed comforting. "I think this thing about seclusion is silly. Everybody knows where babies come from. Why shouldn't you be allowed to go where you please? At least for a long while."

She sat up and looked at him in disbelief. "Do you really think so?"

"Yes, I do. I'm proud you're going to have our child. There's no need to hide the fact that a married woman is going to give birth." He hoped he sounded convincing.

"You know, you're right. I haven't done anything wrong. I'm married. I'm not going to hide away. At least not at the beginning. Let's have a party and invite everyone!"

The town responded pretty well as a whole. The older women seem to be the most sympathetic. They had been through it. The younger women were thankful that someone was breaking a rule they thought was silly.

So when Minnie Kathleen, whom they nicknamed Kate, was born, the town accepted her as a move toward a more modern society.

Daniel and Mary Anna celebrated their twenty-fifth wedding anniversary that summer, and Daniel gave her the last part of his promise: perfectly matched diamond earrings. She cried and cried and protested she didn't need anything else, but she wore them from that day until the day she died.

Life was so sweet, sometimes Mary Anna thought she was living in a dream. She knew that somewhere down the line bad things could still happen. They were not immune to hardship and sorrow. But now were days filled with love and joy.

The joy dimmed when she delivered a stillborn girl, but she knew in her heart there would never be another child. She gloried in the ones she had and loved them with all her heart.

# Chapter 8

## 1886

Daniel looked at the sky again. The early morning promised no clouds on the horizon. He and his neighbors needed the rain badly. He had a big store of grain, but the crops in his fields were burning up just like everyone else's.

He wiped his brow and the inside of his hat with his big handkerchief and said to Mary Anna who was sitting on the porch snapping beans, "We'll still make a profit this year—no need to worry."

"I wasn't worrying. You have those new horses you had sent from England. The mares are about ready to foal. The sale of those horses alone would see us through."

He came up to the porch and sat down on the bottom step. He could smell the greenness of the beans as she snapped them open and pulled down the string to discard.

"Talked to Charlie. Have you seen the paper?"

"No. Something I need to know?"

"Oh, I was feeling a little blue when I read about Santana."

"What about Santana?"

"He threw himself out of the window at the Texas State Prison. He's dead."

"Let me see the article."

Daniel got the paper from inside and she scanned the news about their old enemy. It called him "The Orator of the Plains." It quoted much of his 1867 Medicine Lodge speech about how much he loved to roam over the prairies and he didn't want to settle on the reservation. The speech ended with the words, "I see the white man cut down my timber, kill my buffalo, and when I see that my heart feels like bursting."

Once again terrible guilt filled Mary Anna's heart. They had taken the land, spoiled it for the Indians, and driven an entire nation of people out of their homes into a confined area. Tears formed in her eyes as she thought of the many desperate battles she had fought against this man and others to make her home in Erath County. They were both right and wrong for what they had done to the Indians. Surely it could have been handled in a different way. How did it come to this?

313

"This made you sad?" she asked Daniel.

"Yes. I guess somewhere it will be written that the white man was the good guy and the Indian was the bad guy. If the truth is ever told, it will say there was good and bad on both sides. I needed land to make a living after the war. This was my best chance. It was a lot of people's best chance. When we came out here, we thought the Indian tribes would share with us. We had no idea what chain of events we were setting off." He sighed deeply. "I'm sorry it ended the way it did. But I'm not sorry I came out here and defended my right to own the land and improve it. Just look at what we provide for ourselves and others. Horses, cattle, wheat, cotton, peaches. We have done good things for the community, too. Gave that land for the school." He paused and looked up at Mary Anna.

"Who are you trying to convince?" she smiled.

"Me, of course." His grin was a little crooked. "I wonder what our children will have to conquer to have their dreams come true."

"I'm sure something will turn up."

"I want it to, so they'll be strong and noble and honorable."

"I'm afraid I don't believe some of the things that were done were so honorable," she said carefully.

Daniel's face darkened. "Years ago when your father and I led that raid on the reservation, we thought we were doing the right thing. The jury must have thought so, too."

"No, they didn't think you were right. They said you were wrong, but they didn't want you punished because of all the Indian raids and killing. They hoped the raid you all made on the reservation would stop the Indians, though."

"They were wrong. But I can't see there was any other way to stay alive out here but the way we did it."

"No point in trying to relive and change the past. It's over." She took her pan from her lap and headed for the door. "Do you want me to bring you some lemonade?"

"Please." He wiped his face again. His white shirt was sticking to his body like a wet sheet. He listened to the sound of the windmill turning slowly in the light breeze and smiled at the predictable noise it made. It was as comforting as a mother's lullaby. In the house he could hear Mary Anna talking to Elizabeth through the open windows. The lace curtains fluttered in and out as the wind ebbed and flowed through the house. He was a content man. Well, almost content. He still worried about the rain. He would be all right, but many of his neighbors wouldn't be if they didn't get the rain in the next few days. *Lord, we sure could use some of Your cooling waters on our thirsty crops,* he prayed.

Two riders came toward the house, and Daniel soon recognized them as his sons Willie and Henry. They tethered their horses in the shade of the trees.

"Is Mama around?" Willie asked.

"No, she's in the house."

"Good," said Henry. They sat down on either side of their father.

"What am I getting hit up for this time? Some more money?" he asked suspiciously.

"No, something more important." Henry got closer to his father and dropped his voice down low. "Willie and I want to go back to Anderson County instead of going back to the Huckabee Academy this fall." His twenty-year-old eyes were dark blue and filled with a longing for adventure.

"Anderson!" Daniel exclaimed quietly. "What in the world for?"

"The same reason you came out here. Adventure. We want to seek our fortunes," Willie said dramatically.

"Your fortune is right here on this ranch, and you know it. You may want some adventure, but don't try to sell me a wind-broke horse," Daniel said huffily.

Henry tried a different tack. "You found your true love back there in Tennessee Colony. Why can't we go back there and maybe find ours?"

Daniel grinned broadly. "You two have been thinking on this a long time, haven't you?"

"Yes, sir, we have," said Henry. "But you know how Mama is about schooling. You'd have to be the one to ask her if we could go."

"You know her answer will be no," Daniel stated flatly.

"That's why we want you to ask her. You have a way of saying things to her to make her listen," added Willie earnestly.

Daniel laughed out loud at that statement. "I did try once to make her listen," he said thinking of the failed trail drive many years before. "I promised myself I'd never do that again. Nearly cost me my marriage," he said under his breath. "No. I can't make her listen." He looked at the boys' fallen faces. "But if I can work it into the conversation at the right time, I'll approach her about it. It's a good thing you boys started early on this project. It may take a long while to get a yes out of your mama."

Just then the screen door opened and Mary Anna appeared with a tray of lemonade and glasses. "I thought I heard you boys out here with your father. You look real serious. Is anything wrong?"

"No, ma'am," they chorused.

"We were just talking about the weather. About how we need the rain," Henry added.

"You looked pretty worried about it from inside the house," she said as she handed out the cold glasses of pale yellow lemonade.

"Believe me, it's something to worry about," Daniel said casually.

The boys drank their lemonade quickly and made excuses to leave.

Their feet had barely left the porch when Mary Anna said, "And what did those two want? It must be something pretty big for them to come to you behind my back." Her eyes narrowed as she tried to guess what they were up to.

"Oh, you know boys," Daniel said noncommittally.

"I know those two. Now what did they want?"

Daniel grinned. "You don't give up, do you?"

"That's how I got you."

He joined in her teasing laughter. "I believe it was the other way around. Funny how your memory fails you when you want it to," he smiled.

"And?" she persisted.

"They want to go back to Tennessee Colony."

"Well, I never would have guessed that one," said Mary Anna calmly. "What for?"

"Well, first it was to seek their fortunes, then it was adventure, and lastly it was to look for a wife because that's where I found you and you're the best there is, so there surely should be some fine young women for them."

"Hmm."

He watched her in surprise. "I thought you'd be mad."

"Oh, all the women's magazines advise that women keep their men guessing in order to keep their marriages from getting boring. I don't want to be predictable all the time," she said sweetly. Too sweetly.

"You're mad," he said.

"Not exactly mad. But puzzled. Whatever gave them the idea to go back to our roots? They've heard a lot of stories of us living there, but I didn't think those old tales would inspire the boys to want to go back. We probably don't have anyone there who even remembers us."

Daniel's eyes sparkled wickedly. "Maybe Amos Strong is still there preaching."

Mary Anna colored slightly. "I haven't thought of him in years and years. He wouldn't remember me even if he were there," she insisted.

"I think he would," Daniel said. "I don't think he'll ever forget you."

"Now, Daniel, you know there was never anything between Amos Strong and me!"

"Don't get your Irish up. I know there wasn't anything from your side. But I am certain if I hadn't come back from the war, he would have asked you to marry him. And I think you would have done it. He was a fine man." He paused a moment and added impishly, "How long were you prepared to wait for me?"

"About one more day," she said teasingly. "Good thing you made it." She turned serious. "When do the boys want to go, and how long do they plan to stay?"

"I don't think they got that far with the plan yet. The first move was to get around you."

"Let me think about it. Don't tell them I know yet.

"I didn't say I was letting them go. I said I wanted to think about it."

That night at supper Mary Anna watched the two boys covertly. They were handsome in different ways. Henry was tall and broad-shouldered like his father. He had Daniel's coloring, too. Willie was more like her. His hair was dark auburn like hers, but he had grey eyes and sprinkles of freckles along the bridge of his patrician nose. *How did they grow up to be men in such a short while? I can't bear the thought of them going off so far, but if I don't let them, how can they grow like we did? I know some of the girls are sweet on these two. They're too handsome not to have somebody flirting with them. I'll speak to Elizabeth about it right away. Surely there is someone in town for them.*

After supper Mary Anna broached the subject with her daughter while they did the dishes.

"Why, yes, all four of the older boys have at least a couple girls with crushes on them. In fact, I'd say they were pretty much the catch of the day around Stephenville. Why?"

When Mary Anna explained about the boys' trip, Elizabeth said, "Looks like it's time to have some parties around here if you want to keep them home. Matchmaking time," she grinned. "You'll have to make up your mind, Mama, if you're going to choose the wives for your seven sons or if you're going to let it happen. Kate, Annah, and I will choose our own, thank you."

"Tump is already in love with Molly, and Peter is stuck on Parcinda. Arthur and Oscar and Little Dan are too young to worry about yet. It's just Henry and Willie I need to worry about right now." She turned and looked at Elizabeth. "And you? Is Henry C. Wylie coming to call for your hand any time soon?"

"Mama! How do you know all these things?"

"I can read minds. All mothers can. It comes to you when you hold your first baby in your arms. It sure saves a lot of time," she grinned. Then she looked serious. "The house will seem very empty without you, and I know it won't be long before you become a bride. I think Henry Wylie is a fine man. He'll take good care of you."

Elizabeth looked in her mother's steady eyes. "Thank you, Mama. I love him very much. We plan to stay right here in Erath County."

"I'll bet your father might have a little land for your dowry that won't be too far away," she smiled.

That night, as they often did, Mary Anna and Daniel talked long into the early hours of the morning. By dawn the unsuspecting boys were given their chance for adventure with their mother's blessing. Henry and Willie were stunned by the news.

"I don't have to tell you the most important thing is for you to get there and back safely," Daniel warned. "And you must be back by Thanksgiving."

A few days later, Mary Anna hugged each one in turn. "I'm leaving your safety in God's hands, but don't do anything stupid to tempt Him." She was sober and dry eyed as they climbed into their saddles with a map of Texas to guide them.

The dazed young men were suddenly on their way and wild with the joy and anticipation of such a dream coming true. They carried their mother's letter to Amos Strong, if he was still there, asking him to watch over her boys.

The trip itself turned out not to be very exciting. But when they got to Tennessee Colony, they immediately stopped by the hotel their grandfather had once owned and where their mother had cooked.

"Oh, yes, I remember the Garland family," said the present owner. "Good people," he added. And yes, Reverend Strong could be found down at the church he pointed out.

When Amos answered the door, Henry said, "Sir, we're Henry and Willie Thornton, Mary Anna and Daniel's boys. Our folks wanted us to look you up if you were still here."

Amos was so surprised to see them, he almost forgot to invite them in. "I think I would have known you two. You're both very like your parents." He offered them food while he read Mary Anna's letter. He chuckled in a few places. It was a friendly letter, and the last part asked him to keep a watchful eye on her boys. He took on that task gladly, for the reason he had never remarried was his love for Mary Anna. He had never found anyone quite like her.

The boys went to church on Sunday. It was the proper way to meet girls, and it wasn't long until the boys met the Kenny girls. From the moment Henry met Florence Bell Kenny, he was a lost soul. He beheld her as the embodiment of everything feminine of which he had dreamed. Her saucy ways and ready wit drew him like the proverbial moth to a flame. In all his twenty long years of living, no one had ever smitten him the way she did.

She had a younger sister named Jackie, and Willie felt she was the jewel in the queen's crown. Something funny happened to his stomach every time she smiled at him, which was frequently. In many ways she was more beautiful than her older sister, and Willie couldn't believe she thought him more than a country bumpkin. Words seemed to cleave to the roof of his mouth every time he tried to say something clever to her. He was sure she thought him a perfect donkey. The two young men were granted permission to call on the young ladies. They were terrified.

"Do you think her father likes us?" Willie worried.

"We come from a good family that's well known," Henry replied.

"I hope they're well known in this part of the country, too." Willie looked up into the heavens. "Oh, thank you, Mama, that you made us go to school and learn to be gentlemen."

"That's a big plus, all right," agreed Henry. "A lot of good it does me, though. Half the time around her, I bump into furniture and spill my cup of tea in the saucer," he said sadly.

"I didn't think that being in love could make me feel so—so, awkward," sighed Willie.

"I've always felt real slick around girls. Cocky. But when I looked into Miss Florence's eyes, I turned into a cow-eyed dope."

They presented themselves to the Kenny home at precisely three o'clock. They followed the prescribed rituals of courtship, careful never to do anything that would offend the young ladies or their parents, who were always in attendance.

After they had spent countless agonizing hours of small talk and short walks, Henry and Willie decided to ask for the girls' hands in marriage at the same time. Both were total wrecks as the hour of their meeting with Mr. Kenny approached.

"I can't say this comes as a surprise to us," Mr. Kenny assured them. "However, we were surprised at the quickness of your offers of marriage."

Mr. Kenny helped himself to a careful bite of oatmeal cookie. Both young men refused his offer, for they knew they would never be able to get the cookies down their constricted throats. They tried to read his actions or his face for some sort of hint as to what his answer would be. Henry decided in his mind that Mr. Kenny would make one great poker player, for nothing was visible on his chubby face. He crossed his legs and looked at them. "Mr. Thornton," he said to Willie, "my wife and I feel Miss Jackie is much too young to even consider a marriage proposal at this time. And to take her away to Erath County, well, I'm sure you can appreciate our position."

Willie felt the ground fall away from his feet.

"And as for your request, Mr. Thornton," he said to Henry, "we feel you are perhaps, shall we say, a little too happy-go-lucky in your attitude toward life." His eyebrows rose with his statement.

The words cascaded over Henry like scalding tea. Happy-go-lucky! Those certainly were not words he attached to himself. But the words were hanging like a sword over his dream of marriage, and it neatly severed it.

"But, sir," Henry tried to say.

"We are, of course, flattered you should want to join our family."

"And our family would be overjoyed at having these two wonderful young women join ours," Henry said a little heatedly at the implication. "Our father and mother are prominent citizens of Stephenville. You can ask Reverend Strong."

"Yes, yes, I'm sure they're important in their own little town. However," he rose, leading the way to the door, "our final answer is no. Thank you for coming."

The boys were standing in a daze on the front porch with the door being firmly shut in their faces.

As they walked silently back to the hotel, Amos intercepted them. "You two look like you've been ridden hard and put away wet." And then he remembered their errand. "Oh," he said carefully. "You've been to see Mr. Kenny." He steered the boys to his home.

"I should have told you this before, but I've seen the way Miss Florence and Miss Jackie look at you. I thought maybe you'd have a chance. Many men have courted them, and all have been rejected out of hand. It isn't you. Mr. Kenny won't let them go until he finds rich men for them."

"We aren't exactly poor," Henry said.

"But they love us. I know they do!" Willie said desperately.

"If they love you, and you love them, then I say you should press your suit with Mr. Kenny. Don't give up. And don't let him get you down." He stood in front of them. "Are you willing to fight for your true loves?"

"Yes," said Henry, nearly in tears.

"Yes," added Willie heartily.

"Get jobs. Stay here. Go to every church social. Even if you're not their escorts, you must take every opportunity to be with them. Let Mr. Kenny see how much you care." It was good advice, and they followed it.

Finally, Henry could stand it no longer. He and Willie decided to ask the two young women to elope with them.

"Miss Jackie won't do it, I'm sure," Willie said sadly.

But Henry was hopeful. He got his chance at a social at the church. He and Florence were sitting at the edge of the gazebo listening to the laughter coming from the river where boaters were lazing down the ebony water.

"I have to talk to you. You haunt my dreams every night. All I think of the whole day is you." The sharp intake of her breath made him hope she felt the same way, too. He pushed on. "Do you miss me?"

She dropped her gaze so that her lashes feathered against her soft cheeks. "Of course I miss you. We've had such fun together."

"You know what I mean. Miss Florence, I love you, and I want to marry you," he said recklessly.

"Hush! Do you want someone to hear you?" But the words weren't angry. He took heart.

"Do you love me?" His eyes were wide with hope.

Once again she avoided his direct look. "Yes," she said softly, "I do. But there is nothing to be done about it now."

"I'll wait forever," he promised. His heart was pounding in a counterpoint to the waltz coming from the community building. *She said she loves me*, it beat out crazily.

"They'll never let us marry," she said miserably.

"If you could, would you marry me?" His whole future rested on the next few words, and he held his breath in order to hear each one clearly.

"Yes." She looked into his eyes. "Yes, I would."

Henry took a deep breath to steady himself. "Would you elope with me?"

"Why, Henry, that's the most romantic thing I ever heard of! Yes, yes, yes!" Her eyes gleamed with excitement.

"Tomorrow night. Reverend Strong will marry us. Oh, Florence, I love you with all my heart."

"Henry, you're the most romantic man I've ever met. I'll arrange to stay with a friend tomorrow night. Then I'll wear a red bonnet and hide in the bushes at the edge of town. I'll leave Mama and Papa a note so they won't worry."

Willie's face showed the desperation and the despair at the answer Miss Jackie gave him. "I'm going to die without her," he told his brother.

Amos could see the love in Henry's eyes, but he was against an elopement.

"If you won't marry us, we'll elope and we'll get married on the way," Henry said firmly. He looked at Amos with big eyes. "I'd rather you be the one to marry us."

Amos caved in. "Somehow or another I'm sure to get blamed for this whole thing," Amos said. "My hide won't be worth a nickel when Kenny gets through with me. I may as well go with you. I never thought I'd get caught up in a triangle like this."

Amos told everyone he was going back with the Thorntons, and the Kennys sighed in relief that the young men had given up their foolish suits.

Amos's wagon was packed in the daylight where everyone could see it. At the edge of town that night, Henry nervously scanned the bushes. At last he spotted the bright red bonnet, and the lovers were reunited. Amos wouldn't stop until they were far away.

Their church was an arbor of trees beside a glittering stream. Florence carried wildflowers and wore her big red bonnet. Willie served as best man and father of the bride. The birds sang in notes almost too sweet for human ears. Amos read their vows, and Henry claimed his bride.

"I'll buy you the prettiest ring I can when we get home," Henry promised.

"The ring doesn't matter," Florence whispered. "My heart is wed to yours, ring or no ring," and she offered her lips for him to kiss again.

The four hurried to the wagon and continued their trip to the safety of Barton Springs.

While the newlyweds talked softly to one another in the back of the wagon, Willie talked with Amos for comfort. Willie poured out his broken heart to him.

"If you love her that much, don't give up on marrying her. Jacob had to marry Leah before he was able to win Rachel. And that took seven years."

That didn't comfort Willie much. "I can't wait that long."

As they neared the ranch, Willie took his horse and rode on ahead.

Mary Ann wrapped her arms around his neck and almost choked him with her joy. "Where's Henry?" Alarm in her voice hurried Willie to tell the story of the elopement.

"Eloped! Her parents didn't approve?" The very idea that someone wouldn't approve of one of her children sparked Mary Anna's Irish temper to the fullest. But she was happy if Henry was. "Married a Tennessee Colony girl. Daniel, did you hear that? He's bringing back a bride." Mary Anna saw the pain in Willie's eyes. "And you?"

"I found her, but her parents said she's too young to marry, and I couldn't convince her to elope with me."

"I'm sorry, son," Daniel said.

And then the happy couple, with Amos driving, came in view.

Mary Anna gave the nervous bride a warm hug. "Welcome home, child," she said. "You're Henry's wife, and we love you already for that. I'm sure we'll love you even more as we get to know you better."

Florence cried in Mary Anna's arms. "Thank you. I was so afraid. . .well, you know."

"I do think you should write your folks a letter. You owe that to them."

"I left a note with my friend."

"Nevertheless, you write." Mary Anna's voice was motherly. "Now let me hug this fine man standing next to you. Henry, you did well, She's lovely."

Then she walked to Amos and silently enfolded him in a warm embrace. "Hello, Amos. It's a joy to see you again. You look well. You must have traded reading your Bible for *Romeo and Juliet*."

He grinned broadly. "Your son is hard to say no to. A real Thornton." He walked over to Daniel. "Hello, old friend. Your boys have told me of your successes. They're very proud of you."

Daniel pulled him into a warm bear hug. "Thank you, Amos. Looks like you've taken care of my family once again. Let's go in and celebrate!"

Amos said with admiration, "I don't think I've ever been in a house this grand."

"It's home," Mary Anna said. They sat in the more relaxed atmosphere of the second parlor, and Mary Anna served refreshments. "Are you here to stay?" she asked Amos.

"It appears that I'm a fugitive. I sure can't go back to Tennessee Colony."

Mary Anna smiled. "We need a minister for our church. The circuit rider doesn't get here often enough for most of us.

Daniel cleared his throat officially. "I happen to be on the pulpit committee.

I think I can guarantee you a job, Amos." He looked levelly at Amos. "I'm glad you're here. And you're welcome in our home anytime."

Later that night up in their bedroom, Mary Anna was pondering over all the events of the day. She thought it a shame that a nice man like Amos had never remarried. He'd make such a good husband and father. *Maybe he'll find his love here in Stephenville.* The thought made her happy.

"What are you thinking about?" Daniel asked. "You look sad and happy at the same time."

A slight blush highlighted her cheeks. "I was thinking about Amos," she admitted. "I was wondering why he never married again after his wife and children were killed by the Comanche. That was so many years ago."

Daniel came to her and took her in his arms, looking deeply into her eyes. "I think we both know the reason." He kissed her. "It's because I was the lucky one."

She nestled against him. "I love you, Daniel."

"I know." And he placed his lips softly against hers again.

# Chapter 9

Fall began to sprinkle a few colors about the trees, changing greens into vivid reds, deep purples, and flaming oranges. The nights became cool again, and everyone slept better.

Daniel went into town for his monthly lodge meeting. Mary Anna went with him, and he dropped her off at the white-planked church for her weekly quilting.

She enjoyed the company and made quick, neat little stitches as she joined the lively conversation. It was a relaxing time of harmless gossip, recipe and remedy exchanges, and good-natured complaining. They were working on a Texas Star quilt.

In the course of the morning's news, Annie Frank happily announced, "I planted flowers around the back of the church today."

"Well, they won't be there tomorrow," said gray-haired Gertrude Jones. "The way the town lets the pigs run around loose is a crime. As soon as they find those flowers, they'll root them right up." Her lips were set in a firm angry line.

"She's right," piped a small birdlike woman appropriately named Dovie. "I've planted flowers before, and that's exactly what happened. What we need is a fence to keep the pigs out."

"What we need is to keep the pigs in the pens where they should be," Gertrude said sharply.

"That'll be the day," mocked a stout lady with a florid face. "If that ever happens, I'd think civilization had finally come to Stephenville."

"Then why don't we just put up the fence?" Mary Anna asked reasonably.

"We still don't have the money to put up a fence," said Gertrude tartly, "or we would have done it a long time ago." There was rebuke at Mary Anna's stupidity in her voice, but Mary Anna was not offended. Gertrude was known for her pessimistic view of life, and Mary Anna often wondered what had happened to give her such a sour disposition and the will to express it at every opportunity.

"We could sell quilts and have bake sales to raise money, I suppose," said Dovie.

"We'd be the ones to buy the quilts and baked goods," said Gertrude. "Might as well just dig up the money out of our own pockets."

"Morning, ladies," a cheerful voice called out. It was Gertrude's husband, come to fetch her.

Mary Anna was glad to see him, for a small pinch of Gertrude's outlook on life went a long way.

"We were just talking about you men," his wife said in a complaining voice.

"I'll just bet you were, my dear," he said amiably.

*How has he lived with her all these years and stayed so happy?* Mary Anna wondered.

"We're going to raise money to build a fence to keep out the pigs so we can have flowers to beautify the church," said stout Pearl Harrison.

The women all looked at Gertrude to see if she would allow Pearl to overrule her assessment of how to get the money.

Gertrude's husband, Walter, was a rotund man, and he stood there with his hat in his hand, stroking his walrus mustache. He was dressed as a prosperous man and always gave the appearance of good humor. "I'll tell you what, ladies. I know all about what goes on at these quilting meetings. I'll give you fifty dollars for your fence." He smiled beatifically.

"What!" they chorused.

"If," he said smiling broadly and confidently, "you women can sit here for the whole day and quilt without saying so much as one word."

Heads swiveled from one lady to another. "Well, I never," began one lady.

"Wait," said Pearl to Mr. Jones. "I think that's a wonderful idea. We'll take you up on your most generous offer," she said graciously, inclining her head toward him.

"But. . . ," began the nervous Dovie.

"Thank you for getting us a fence built," said Pearl. She winked at the ladies around the quilting frame.

Mr. Jones was a bit taken back by her confidence. "I'll send my freedman over to sit with you next week," he said. "We surely want to do this fairly," he added with a smile.

Mary Anna could tell by his attitude that he felt sure his offer was safe.

On the appointed day, Mr. Jones came by the church with his freedman and entered the room where the women were already busily working. He burst into loud, raucous laughter. He laughed so hard, tears rolled down his ample cheeks. The ladies were sitting around the frame quilting steadily. Each one had a gag tied firmly over her mouth.

The fence was promptly built and new flowers lovingly—and permanently—planted for the enjoyment of the entire community.

Mary Anna couldn't wait to tell Daniel how they had outsmarted Mr. Jones. He thoroughly enjoyed the story, and it became a favorite tale told around town for years.

The next day Mary Anna and Daniel were having coffee out on the shady side of the big porch. A big table had been put out there for breakfast. Mary Anna looked around the table, marveling at the swift passing of time.

Tump was married and had come to stay overnight with his wife on their way into town. Molly was a lovely girl, and Mary Anna enjoyed watching the young couple bill and coo. Tump was very much like his father, and Mary Anna had a sense of déjà vu as she watched them.

Peter had become a fine young man and would be a good rancher. He was sweet on Parcinda. There would be a wedding soon. Elizabeth, too, would marry soon. Mary Anna was proud of her daughter and her many musical accomplishments. Henry and Florence were on their own place now. Willie was still pining for Miss Jackie. Oscar and Arthur were gangly colts. And then there was Annah, Mary Anna's reflection. Little Dan had taken over the care of Kate.

Mary Anna smiled at Daniel. "We're going to need more than one table this year for our Christmas feast."

Daniel felt every inch the patriarch of the clan. "The Lord is good." He took a bit of fluffy biscuit dripping with plum jam. "Did you think it would turn out like this?"

She looked at her husband. He had grown a beard and mustache. They were streaked with gray, but his eyes were still periwinkle blue like her own. He was lean from his constant time in the saddle, but only a small spread across his girth spoke of his wealth.

"No," she admitted. "I never thought this far ahead. I spent most of my time worrying about what was going on right then. In the time I've had for reflection now, I am surprised to find myself no longer young. It seems like only yesterday I was eighteen, but when I look in the mirror or see our children, I still can't understand where the time has gone."

Oscar grinned hugely. "Arthur and I will be sixteen at the end of September."

"It's only August," she retorted fondly. "And don't get your hopes up about that big party. It isn't going to happen."

"Ah, Mama, we know about it already. You know how you like to show off your two handsome sons." He elbowed Arthur. "Maybe Rose will be there, huh?" Arthur turned scarlet. "I don't care if she is or not," he said loudly.

They scuffled a bit at the table until Daniel settled them down with a stern look. The boys were perfect halves of a whole. They had some sort of communication system between them no one could understand.

"I want you boys to ride the fences today," Daniel ordered them. "Take your pliers and tools to repair any breaks."

"Yes, sir."

"And watch for rattlers up on that rocky place. It's been a bad year for snakes.

Take your rifles." Without a smile he added, "And if you kill any, don't bring home any skins. You boys don't need new belts."

The entire table broke out in laughter, and Henry turned the color of a beet. "Ah, Papa," he protested. "I was little then."

Mary Anna sent them out with a lunch big enough for three grown men. The day was oppressively hot, but riding pushed a cooling breeze across their tanned faces. They stopped at a place where the fence was down.

"Willie and Henry's trip to Anderson County sure was an adventure," said Arthur. "I wish I could have an adventure."

"Me, too. I wish I was going somewhere." Oscar sighed. "I love to hear the cowboys talk about the days when they made those drives."

"They're still doing the drives," Arthur said.

"Not the old way on this ranch. Papa has everything up to date." He looked at his twin. "Besides, we have to go to Huckabee Academy in the fall."

"I know. Mama and her schooling. But when we get out, let's go somewhere exciting. Maybe we could go to Anderson County."

"That doesn't sound exciting to me," Oscar said with disgust. "I'd rather go farther out west. Maybe to California. Now that would be an adventure."

One of the horses gave a frightened snort and a fast side step. Arthur grabbed the rifle and walked quickly toward the animals. He spotted the coiled rattler at once and shot his head off with a clean shot. "Nuisances. Worse than flies and mosquitoes."

"I hate those things," Oscar said with a shudder. "Papa said there was a man on the drive that used to eat them. Ugh."

They caught the jittery horses and moved on down the fence. Arthur looked up into the cloudless sky. "Sure is hot." He grinned. "There's a pool of water not too far from here. Maybe we ought to take a dip. Remember what Mama said about being careful. We might take a heatstroke out here in this hot sun. In fact, I feel one about to come on right now. We'd better cool off."

"Art, you're bad," said his brother with a grin.

After their romp, they crawled onto the edge of the pool and lay back in the cool mud with their feet still in the water.

"You hungry, Art? I'm starving." Oscar walked to the horses and took their lunch out of the saddlebags. They ate and agreed they should get on with their work. "I don't want a skinning by Papa," said Oscar.

Arthur grinned mischievously. "You know I'd never do anything to get us into trouble with him."

"Only every day of our lives," sighed Oscar.

They killed two more snakes that afternoon. The horses were jumpy.

"Papa was right. The snakes are bad this year," Oscar said in a worried voice.

"Be real careful where you put your feet," he ordered his brother.

"We'd better put on our chaps, too. Mine are so tough that no snake alive could get his fangs through that leather."

Oscar felt safer with his chaps on. He pulled on some work gloves, too. "I don't like snakes," he shot at his brother's unspoken remark.

"Did I say anything?" Arthur asked innocently.

"You didn't have to," Oscar answered. "I know you too well."

"I bet you don't know I stole a kiss from Jenny."

"Do, too. It was at the church picnic."

They laughed together, the two boys that knew each other's souls.

Suddenly Oscar's horse reared in panic. Oscar had been riding easy in the saddle with only the tips of his boots in the stirrup. The lunging movement of his horse threw him completely off the animal.

In a flash Arthur had his rifle out and killed the rattler coiled to strike. He ran over to his brother. "It's okay. I got him. You all right?"

Oscar didn't respond, and Arthur saw he'd been knocked unconscious by the fall. "Oscar! Oscar! Wake up! I got the snake." He put his hand under his brother's head and tried to raise it.

Oscar's eyes were wide open in surprise, but he didn't answer his brother's frantic plea.

"Oh, dear God, let him wake up. Mama'll kill me if you get hurt." He began crying and looking about him for help. "Help me, somebody, my brother's been hurt!" His voice echoed eerily across the land. He pulled Oscar up against him, cradling his head. "Oscar, say something to me! Please!"

Oscar's eyes stared at the scalding sky above. Arthur wept uncontrollably and rocked his brother's body. "Help," he whispered. "Help."

The sun was beginning to slide over to the west when he finally accepted the fact that no one could help him or Oscar. Awkwardly he draped Oscar's body over the saddle and led the horse at a slow walk toward home. "Oscar," he said, "you can't leave me. We have so much adventure planned. There's all those girls to kiss and the trips we want to make." He wiped at the dirty tears that stained his face with his hand. "I can't go home and tell Mama that you're dead. It'll kill her for sure. What am I going to do without you?" he wailed loudly to the silent sky.

Mary Anna was looking for the boys. Supper would be ready soon. It always irritated her when anyone was late for supper. She went outside and pounded loudly on the heavy iron triangle that was used to summon the men from the fields. "That ought to bring them fast enough," she said in an irate voice.

In the distance she could just make out two horses. "It's about time." But when she looked carefully, there was something wrong with the picture in her eyes. There was only one upright rider. "Daniel, come quick! One of the twins has been hurt!"

Daniel hurried out of the house. He saw Oscar across his saddle. "Get some water ready, Mary Anna."

She stood rooted to the spot. Her heart was pounding. *Don't let it be bad, God.* But when she saw the limp arms bumping against the side of the horse, her worst fears surfaced. She ran toward the boys with Daniel right behind her.

"It was a rattler, Mama! I killed him, but Oscar's hurt bad." Arthur said wildly.

Mary Anna helped Daniel lay the boy on the ground. As soon as she saw the wide-open eyes staring at nothing, she felt faint. She cradled Oscar's head in her lap. Arthur was babbling about the snake and how it had spooked the horses, but that he had killed the snake. Oscar should be all right.

Silently Daniel closed his dead son's eyes.

"Did the snake bite him?" Mary Anna asked as her eyes scanned all his protective gear.

"No, I told you, I killed the snake. The fall knocked him unconscious. Make him wake up, Mama!" He was crying so hard Mary Anna had to listen carefully to understand him.

Oscar's head rolled unnaturally over her arm. Quietly she said, "His neck is broken." Blackness settled around her, clothing her in numbness. "Take him in the house, Daniel." She leaned back as Daniel put his hands underneath the boy's inert form.

Mary Anna stood up and put her arms around Arthur. "He's not going to wake up, Arthur. He's dead. Come inside with me."

Arthur wept uncontrollably. "I tried to take care of him, Mama. I killed the snake. Killed a lot of them all afternoon. I tried so hard to make him wake up. I did the best I could."

Mary Anna led the weeping boy into the house. "I know you did, son, I know you did. You did fine," she said in a soothing voice. "You did everything you could. It's not your fault. It's going to be all right." She crooned softly to him as she had when he was a nursing baby and led him to the sofa in the front parlor. She sat beside him, holding him in her arms and rocking him.

Daniel came in quietly. His face was gray and strained. Tears had formed back behind his eyes, but they hadn't found a way out. He sat down heavily in a big rocking chair.

"What'll I do without him, Mama? We've never even spent the night apart. He's always been there, just like half of me. What am I going to do?" Arthur sobbed. "I let my brother die. It was my fault. He was afraid of snakes. I should have seen it. I couldn't get him to wake up."

"Listen carefully, Arthur," said Mary Anna. "It wasn't your fault. It was an accident. You couldn't see the snake. The horse threw Oscar and broke his neck. There was no way you could wake him up. You did all the right things. It wasn't your fault," she repeated in a firm voice.

Annah, Little Dan, and Kate peered with fearful eyes around the door frame. "Come sit here with your brother," Mary Anna instructed them. "I'll be back in a minute." She left them sitting on either side of Arthur. Kate was holding his hand, and Little Dan was patting his arm. Annah was in his lap nestled against him.

Mary Anna went up the stairs, pulling herself along the railing. She steeled herself for the next ordeal. Oscar was lying on his bed, looking for all the world as if he were sleeping quietly. She sat down on the edge of the bed and brushed back the hair on his forehead. He was cool to her touch. "My poor baby," she whispered. She took up his limp hand and held it in her own.

"Arthur is going to be only half a person for a long time until he gets used to your being gone," she told him. "I know you're with the Lord now, and that's a comfort for me." She felt the tears come unbidden and slide hotly down her face. She couldn't believe he was dead. None of her children had died after infancy. She had always kept death away with her nursing skills and the help of the Lord. She wanted to beg the Lord to give him back, to make a deal with Him for Oscar's life.

The sound of boots on the staircase made her turn to see Tump and Peter, white faced and red eyed. She rose to accept their sad embraces.

"Oh, Mama, we're so sorry. For all of us." It was all Tump was able to get out. Peter was crying softly.

He took a deep breath and said, "I never thought it would be like this. I thought we'd all live and get old together."

Mary Anna nodded, but she said, "It's called life. The good times and the bad. You boys do your sorrowing for Oscar, but it's the living who need taking care of. Arthur is the one hurting the most. He's lost half of himself." She turned to look again on Oscar's face. "I want you to help me make him understand that it wasn't his fault. You must do this for me."

"We will, Mama, we promise," Peter said for both of them.

"Now go downstairs and stay with Arthur and send Elizabeth up here." Sadly she turned away to look again at Oscar. Elizabeth found her mother talking softly to Oscar. She choked back a sob. While Coleman and Rabbit made a coffin in the barn, Mary Anna and Elizabeth prepared Oscar's body for burial.

Molly and Parcinda made the house ready for the many visitors who were sure to start coming as the word spread. When Mary Anna entered the big parlor and saw Oscar laid out in his coffin, she felt a pain so overwhelming it almost knocked her to her knees. The ritual was so familiar: the coffin, the flowers, the quiet voices, the muffled sobbing. Food and friends began appearing, lavishing comfort and soft words.

*My son is dead.* She had to keep reminding herself of that fact. Everything was so unreal. But she knew her pain was equaled by Arthur's. She would need all her strength to get him through this ordeal. And Daniel needed her, too. He looked so old. Old and broken. He had always been so strong, but she knew this time she would have to be the strong one.

Daniel leaned heavily on her as men from the town carried Oscar out to the cemetery, but he read the burial service with a strong voice. "A time for all things," she heard him say. "Today you shall be with me in paradise." The "ashes to ashes and dust to dust" made her heart hammer. She couldn't put a handful of soil on his coffin. She wouldn't. Before the men began to lower her son's coffin into the earth, Mary Anna abruptly turned around and headed for the house. "It's too much to bear," she cried as Daniel caught up with her.

Daniel's distraught face came close to hers, and through the mourning veil, she heard him say, "This is the other side of the dream. We can't expect to have only the sweet. You've told me that. You've been afraid of losing one of the children. Now we have. But we can make it through this together. Even Jesus felt forsaken at one point. God will not make it all go away, but He will give us each day in which to recover. We haven't lost our whole family. We've unwillingly given Oscar back to his Maker. We can do this together with God's help. Hold on to me, Mary Anna. Hold on to me," he begged.

Mary Anna tried to look ahead. With a sudden, heart-wrenching realization, she knew that there could be others to bury unless she died in her footsteps right now. The ebb and flow of life, living, birthing, and dying undulated like the waves on the seashore. It was natural and normal. "But parents shouldn't have to bury their children," she whispered.

During the long days following the funeral, the entire family stayed together, never far from each other. They comforted and loved one another, suddenly aware of their own mortality. Life had become a precious thing, not something to be lightly frittered away.

Even Little Dan and Kate matured. Sometimes Mary Anna longed for them to fight and shout at each other. The peace and quiet of the house was not normal, and she wanted to hear the sounds of boots on the floors and doors banging and children talking loudly to each other.

Arthur was the one she watched. Even sleep held only nightmares of snakes and Oscar calling to him. Mary Anna moved him in with Willie. Gradually the paleness began to leave his face, and once in a while a small smile crossed his face.

The first milestone came at the end of September on the twin's birthdays. Mary Anna baked a coconut cake, the boys' favorite. She prepared their favorite meal: chicken fried steak and mashed potatoes with gravy. And she set a plate for Oscar in his usual place.

That night in the soft light, the family made an effort to celebrate Arthur's birthday. It was a strain on everyone.

Finally, Arthur said, "I want to thank you for the good birthday. I know that Oscar is here with us tonight. He always loved a party." There was muffled laughter. "Mama and Papa, thank you for taking such good care of me and helping me to understand that it was an accident. I know that for sure now. I don't know why God took my brother, but I know he's okay and happy. I can feel it in my heart. And you know how Oscar and I always knew what the other was thinking." There was nodding and smiling.

"I'm glad Mama set a place for Oscar tonight. He will be with us, at least me, all the time. And I think it's time for all of us to quit being sad all the time. Life is like a river, and it's time for us to jump in and get scrubbed up for tomorrow. Tomorrow could be a wonderful day if we let it. Okay?" His young face begged for release from his sorrow and another chance to make things happy.

Mary Anna was openly crying, and Daniel had his napkin stuffed in his mouth. With glistening eyes the rest of the family smiled and gave Arthur the birthday present he really needed.

That night in the privacy of their big bed, Daniel said, "I was so proud of Arthur tonight."

Mary Anna nodded in agreement. "He's right, you know. We do need to get on with life. I doubt a thousand deaths would make any one of our children's any easier, but I am peaceful about Oscar. He is with the Lord." She paused thoughtfully. "I wonder if the babies were there to welcome him."

"Probably." Daniel pulled her a little closer to him as they cuddled under the covers. "Living out the dream did get hard there for a while. But you aren't sorry about us building a life out here, are you?"

"No. The story will be told no matter where we live. Are you sorry?"

"No," he admitted slowly. "I do wish I had the power to make nothing but good things happen, though."

"You wouldn't be happy with that arrangement, I'm sure," Mary Anna said firmly. "Life is a subtle blend of all shades of things. We've been so blessed so many times, I blush to think of all the good things the Lord has done for us. Oh, I ache to see Oscar come riding in with Arthur sometimes. But the pain is getting duller. And I look at the other children with different eyes now. I know they're not mine to keep. I can only take care of them and try to get them ready for their lives, whatever that may be."

She smiled. "That's been a bit of a relief, because I always thought it was up to me to keep them healthy and well and alive. Now I know I do the best I can, but I can't protect them from what I've been through. They would be only shells that would crumble at the first adversity. Our hard times have made us what we are. Their hard times will have to shape them, too."

And with those words, Mary Anna wrapped herself in her husband's embrace and was comforted.

# Chapter 10

Of all Mary Anna's children, Annah was the most openly affectionate. It had been Annah who had done everything in her power to ease her mother's sorrow at Oscar's death. Annah had become the child of Mary Anna's heart.

She loved the same things Mary Anna did—the tender springtime, soft furry animals, babies—and she seemed to have an uncanny ability to sense the hidden thoughts and feelings of those around her.

Mary Anna was weeding the garden that went up the middle of the double walkways to the front door. The flowers were beginning to look beautiful, and it made her happy to see them flourish as her children had after Oscar's death a year ago.

Annah came out and helped her in the garden for a while. Carefully she pulled the weeds from the young plants. She had forgotten to bring her bonnet.

Mary Anna was tempted to order her seventeen-year-old daughter to put on a bonnet to keep her skin white, but she seemed so happy in the sunlight that Mary Anna was reluctant to spoil the time by mothering Annah. And her auburn hair looked alive and glowing. She was a beautiful young girl.

The mockingbird who lived in the oak trees close by sang his multiple songs of theft. The cicadas were whirring, and the horses neighed in the meadow. A bee buzzed Mary Anna's flowered bonnet on his way to the meadow flowers. As the rich smell of earth assailed her nose and she dug her hands into it's dampness, Mary Anna realized she had seldom felt such peace.

"Mama, will I fall in love?" Annah asked. "When I see Henry acting so dumb with Miss Florence, I wonder if that's love. Does love make you silly?"

Mary Anna laughed. "Sometimes I'm afraid it does."

"I don't want to fall in love then."

"I said sometimes. But love is a powerful force. Sometimes it makes people do things they never thought they could. I don't think dumb or silly is its main definition."

"Did Papa make you feel silly?" She tried to see her mother's face up under her bonnet.

"No, but I did feel giddy when he was around. Sort of breathless sometimes. His just being there could make me tremble inside." Mary Anna's eyes turned inward as she remembered her short, intense courtship and early marriage.

"He must have been very handsome," Annah remarked.

"I think he still is. He's different but still handsome."

"You're still pretty," Annah said candidly.

"Why, thank you, child. You know all the stories about knights in shining armor riding up to pretty maidens?" Mary Anna asked. "The thing I don't like about those stories is that happiness always comes at the end. The end of the story is only the beginning of the real, deep happiness. There's so much to learn about being married after the last page of those stories."

"Like what?"

"Like learning new things about each other even after you've been married for a long time. How to make each other happy. When to fight and when to walk away. What kind of father he'll be."

Annah paused in her digging and played with a long earthworm that was trying to get away from the bright sunlight. "I like the stories about the knights in shining armor, but I'm glad to know the story has a lot more to it. I never thought about what happens after they ride away together."

"Maybe to some people the married part is not as romantic as the courtship. And for some I guess it isn't."

"But it has been for you and Papa. I can tell by your face." They exchanged broad smiles.

"I don't feel giddy around him now, but I still get a breathless feeling if he's been gone awhile and I suddenly see him."

"I'll have to choose carefully and get a man like Papa."

"I doubt you could do much better," her mother agreed.

"I think I'd like to be married and have babies. When I see you and Papa together, sometimes when you don't think I'm looking, I see a special look pass between you. A secret look I've never seen you give anyone else."

"It's a married look, I suspect." She was surprised Annah could be so observant.

"If a man ever looks at me like that, I'll know he's the right one." Annah seemed to have decided on the answer to her own question.

They moved to the new rose garden that was Mary Anna's pride and joy. The flowers were fully blooming and gave unstintingly of their fragrance. Annah buried her face in one of the blooms and sighed deeply. "Nothing in the world smells as good as a rose," she said happily.

"And nothing is quite as thorny," her mother replied as she sucked her pricked finger.

"When I have a house, I'm going to have millions of roses all around it, so that no matter which way the wind blows, there will always be the smell of roses in the house."

"Some people take rose petals and glaze them with sugar."

"To eat?"

"It's supposed to be quite tasty. Maybe we should try it."

Annah pulled a petal from a deep red rose and nibbled on it. "It does have a sweet taste, but I don't think I'd like to eat very many of them. No," she decided, "roses belong in the garden, not on a table to be eaten."

Mary Anna clipped a few stems to put on the supper table. "I don't really like to cut the flowers. They live so much longer if you leave them on the bushes. But I do love to smell them. Once I had a little rose bead necklace. My mother made it for me. I haven't thought of that in years. She picked lots and lots of petals and put them in a black skillet with some spices and water. Then she rolled the mushed petals into little balls and put a pin through them until they dried. The balls were black, and she strung them on a string for me." Mary Anna fingered the roses she had cut. "I was so proud of that necklace. I wonder what happened to it? Funny how you can love something so much, and then it just disappears out of your life."

When they went in to cook supper, Annah took the roses from her mother, put them in a tall vase, and placed them on the table. "Roses mean happiness to me. They give so much of themselves, and they live only for our enjoyment."

Mary Anna put her arms around the girl and kissed the top of her head. "Some people are like that, too, my darling."

Annah smiled softly and hugged her mother back.

After supper Mary Anna hummed as she set her kitchen in order. It pleased her to have such luxury in which to work. Life had become as gentle as it could be on the frontier. She was just putting the freshly washed Blue Willow dishes back in their cupboard when Annah came in. She was limping.

"What's the matter, darling?"

"I stepped on an old nail out in the barn."

"Why weren't you wearing your shoes?" she fussed. "Let me see."

Obediently Annah sat down and put her injured foot up for Mary Anna's inspection. She wiped the bleeding surface clean. Annah winced as Mary Anna probed the wound with her finger.

"It looks deep. You say the nail was old?"

"Yes, real old. I know because it had rust on it."

Mary Anna's heart quickened in alarm, but she kept her face composed. "I'll need to clean it very carefully." She got out a basin and washed the wound with soap. Annah tried to be brave when she put the foot in a basin a second time to soak it in the strongest disinfectant Mary Anna had.

"It burns," she complained.

"I'm sorry, but we must get it as clean as possible." She smiled faintly. "Wouldn't do much good to fuss at you for being so careless at this point."

Annah wrinkled up her nose. "No, I really wasn't being careless, Mama. I was playing with the little kids. We were chasing each other, and I jumped over this old lumber. Part of it fell off just as I stepped down. It was stacked right beside Old Molly's stall." Her glance scurried up to her mother's face in apology.

"Can't unspill the milk. But you just sit there awhile until it's good and clean."

Mary Anna returned to her work with less joy in her heart. People could get very sick from wounds made by rusty nails—even die. Impatiently, she pushed the thought away.

Mary Anna silently inventoried her medicines. She watched Annah all evening for signs of fever and hid her worry from the girl. When Daniel came in to get a glass of buttermilk, she shared her anxiety with him out of Annah's hearing.

"You cleaned it well. She should be all right," he tried to reassure her, but she saw the worry in his eyes, too.

By the third day, the puncture was showing signs of swelling and the area was red despite soakings each morning and evening.

By lunch Annah was feverish and grumpy. Mary Anna mixed up a tea of willow root to break the fever and applied cool, damp cloths to Annah's forehead.

In the days that followed, Annah's foot grew progressively worse. Her entire leg was swollen and red streaked. Mary Anna continued cleaning the wound, but she knew it wasn't making Annah better. Her fever stayed high no matter what Mary Anna did.

In the night Daniel cradled Mary Anna in his arms. "Do you want to send to Fort Worth for a doctor?"

"It would take too long, and she's too sick to take her there." Stark fear colored her next words. "I don't think he could help her anyway." She knew there was no cure for the thing called lockjaw, and she cried herself into a short sleep. When she awoke, she spent long hours on her knees begging God to cure Annah. But the young girl continued her downward spiral.

Daniel stood in the doorway watching Mary Anna fight the desperate war against death. Her shoulders were stooped with fatigue as she bent over Annah to change the cloth. He could just hear the soft conversation between mother and daughter.

"Mama, am I going to die?" Annah's lips were dry and her voice raspy.

When Mary Anna didn't answer right away, she added, "I'm not afraid, Mama. You always said people go to heaven when they die if they love Jesus."

"That's true." Mary Anna sat on the edge of the bed and took Annah's hand. She was encouraged by Annah's lucid conversation, but she had never lied to any of her children about anything. It was time to face the possibility. Mary Anna owed candid answers to Annah's question, to prepare her daughter for death.

"You are very sick, but I think you just need time to get well. It is also possible you may. . ." She couldn't bring herself to say the word die, so she said, "not get well."

"I always thought it would probably hurt to *die*. I don't hurt anywhere," she smiled. "Not even my foot."

"That's good." Mary Anna smoothed a confusion of curls from Annah's forehead, and the young girl gave her a wan smile.

"It's odd, but I'm not afraid I'll die at night. It's when I see the sun peeking up over the windowsill that I'm scared. Like the sun is coming to get me. But if I can make it until noon, I've made it another day. And each day means one more to get well in." She sighed. "Look outside, Mama. The sun is still climbing." She grasped Mary Anna's hand more tightly. "It isn't twelve yet, is it?" she asked hopefully.

"Not yet, my love, but soon." Mary Anna wanted to throw herself over her daughter, hold on tightly, and scream out against this thing that was taking her child away a day at a time. She would help Annah hold off the morning by sheer will. Her strength would flow through Annah's hands, and together they would defeat the raid of the morning sun.

She held Annah's hand firmly in her own and silently promised herself that every morning before dawn, she would come and help Annah. Together they could win. She held her tears in check as she begged the Ruler of the universe not to let Annah die. She didn't make foolish promises; she just begged.

"Mama, I feel better. Is it noon yet?"

Mary Anna looked back at Daniel, who nodded yes. "Yes, it's noon." She steadied her voice. "You've made it another day, my sweet."

"Keep holding my hands. I feel so strong when you hold them." She closed her eyes, sighing, "What time is it?"

Daniel walked to the bedside, holding out his pocket watch for Mary Anna to see. "It's twelve-twenty. You made it, Annah."

Annah smiled a long, slow smile. "Yes, I did. Twelve-twenty." Her head fell gently to the side as she let out her last breath.

"No!" cried Mary Anna. "No! Annah! It's twelve-twenty! You made it!" She looked helplessly at Daniel, who stood with tears running freely down his face to nestle in his soft beard. He knelt down beside the bed and sobbed into the colorful quilt.

"No, no," Mary Anna whispered numbly. "It's twelve-twenty." The refrain echoed in her head, rolling like a moan in a ghostly fog.

Daniel raised his head to look on the peaceful face of his dead child. "Oh, Annah," he whispered brokenly, "my sweet Annah." He leaned against Mary Anna and wrapped his arms around her, rocking her for both their comfort.

Mary Anna looked at her white-knuckled hands still holding tightly to her daughter's limp fingers.

Elizabeth appeared at the door. One glance told the story. White faced with grief, she went to her parents. "Come away. I'll take care of her. Come away." She took her mother's hand from Annah's and got both her parents on their feet, guiding them downstairs. "Rest now. I'll take care of everything."

Daniel took Mary Anna to their bedroom and helped her stretch out on their bed. She was dazed, and her hands were like ice. He spread the double wedding ring quilt over her and sat down in the rocking chair where he could watch. Her face was composed, but tears ran unabated from her blue eyes onto her pillow.

He rocked until she closed her eyes, checked her carefully, and then sat back down in the rocker. Unreality was his shield from the pain that had first washed over him. *Elizabeth will take care of Annah,* he thought. And he rocked.

Molly helped Elizabeth bathe and dress Annah's body. Both women wept silently as they put her in her best white dress and combed her hair. Then Elizabeth used a pair of scissors to clip some of Annah's hair in the back where it wouldn't show. Later it would be woven into a lovely flower shape and framed.

Tump and Peter, in silent shock, sent for the neighbors. In a short time, men were fashioning a wooden coffin in the barn, and solemn-faced women were bringing in food. It had been only fourteen months since they had done this for Oscar's funeral.

The casket was lined with white cloth placed over a bedding of wooden shavings, and the outside was draped with black cloth to cover the unfinished wood. Wooden sawhorses were set up in the main room and the casket placed on them. The sawhorses were hidden with more black cloth.

Tenderly Annah was carried downstairs by Tump and placed inside the coffin. Elizabeth put a fresh rosebud in her sister's clasped hands. A tear fell from Elizabeth's face and watered the fragrant flower.

The family took turns sitting with Annah's body through the long night.

In the morning Mary Anna, dressed in a stark black dress, hat, and mourning veil, was led by Daniel to view Annah's body, but it was apparent to all that she had retreated to a place where her pain and grief couldn't reach her. She sat where they put her, never uttering a sound. Only the tears that ran down her drawn face were alive. The rest of her benumbed body was as dead as Annah's.

Later that morning the family joined their neighbors at the small church. Mary Anna sat in the front pew beside Daniel. Her heart lurched in painful awareness as she saw the coffin a few feet from where she sat. For a moment she thought the blackness would engulf her again as she smelled the heavy perfume of the roses that surrounded the coffin. Annah lay with an expression of peacefulness, one red rosebud placed in her white hands.

Mary Anna felt faint, and a clammy sweat broke out on her forehead. Daniel was squeezing her hand hard. Annah looked so calm that for one insane moment Mary Anna was positive she would sit up from her sleep and smile, wondering what all the fuss was about.

Mary Anna longed to take away the heavy black veil from her face. There was little air in the room, and she felt faint again. Her mind wandered around, helpless to focus on the real reason for her being here. Muffled sobs rippled through the small building, and she tried to remember why someone would be crying. Annah couldn't possibly be dead. *Why, just look at her. She's just sleeping.* She heard a male voice say that very thing and felt Daniel shudder with his grief. The voice rolled on and on, saying things that didn't register in her mind. All she could feel was the awful blackness waiting at the edge of her consciousness to enfold her in its arms and the smell of roses hanging heavily in the hot summer air.

And then she was walking, Daniel supporting her wavering steps toward the cemetery. She saw the raw hole in the earth and realized they were going to put Annah in that hole. *No, no,* her heart screamed, *don't cover her up like that. She'll smother!*

But it was done, and the roses spread in a colorful shroud over the dark earth. Mary Anna held one of the roses in her hand and looked in surprise where the thorn had dug into her hand and blood was staining her black glove. But she couldn't unclasp her hand to stop it. Nothing in her body was working properly. Strange hands had taken away her child and put her in the earth. Now strange hands were guiding her away from that earth.

Vaguely she heard Virginia say something to her. Mary Anna could see her lips moving, but the words made no sense. Daniel said something to her, but he seemed to be speaking from the bottom of a well. She tried to concentrate. He was saying something important. His face looked lined and old. *He's so sad. What has happened to make him so sad? It must be terrible.* And then the smell of roses threw her back into the blackness. Annah was dead. That's why he looked so sad. She longed to reach out and embrace him, to comfort him, but her arms were like dead sticks. Something hard and white hot had risen in her chest. The ache was almost unbearable, and to her surprise, she found tears falling on the rose still clutched in her hand. Someone tried to take the rose, but she held on tightly. It was her only hold on life now. The only thing that was real in this upside-down world. Desperately she tried to form the words that would send a prayer to the Lord, but her mind remained blank.

It was getting dark. Someone had removed her mourning veil, and she heard soft footsteps and hushed voices around her. The bitter taste of a medicinal tea burned her lips. She pushed the glass away and felt hands leading her to her bedroom.

She was so tired. So tired. As she stretched out on the soft mattress, the feathers cradled her gently. Then she remembered Annah sleeping on the soft mattress of death. There was no sound, but Mary Anna felt the hot tears rushing down the side of her face into her hair and pillow. It was hot outside, but she felt as cold as ice. Fatigue pulled at her, and the blackness beckoned, inviting and painless. She gave herself up to its greedy arms with only the smell of roses to accompany her down its ebony path.

Every now and then she surfaced to a level just below reality. She was aware of people and voices, Daniel's most of the time. But even her deep love for him couldn't coax her to give up this new love that kept her. It was her friend and lover, stroking and caressing her in its arms of forgetfulness. It whispered to her to stay away from the light. The light brought only pain and sorrow, and she embraced the blackness, giving herself to it completely.

She was dreaming of being with Annah in a garden tending the roses. Annah was beautiful and happy. But from beyond the garden someone was crying and calling to Mary Anna.

"Mama, please don't die! Please come back to me!" It was the voice of a small child. She looked at Annah, but Annah was smiling. Mary Anna let herself go toward the light carefully. When she opened her eyes, Kate was standing beside her bed crying.

The child's face was frightened and sad. Mary Anna looked back at Anna and saw her smile gently. Then Annah raised her hand in a slow wave of farewell. She looked so radiant that Mary Anna didn't mind leaving the garden for a moment to take care of the crying child.

Kate crawled up into bed with Mary Anna and lay with her head on her mother's breasts. Mary Anna took the child in her arms and stroked her hair. Annah was still smiling and waving at her, but she seemed to be moving away from Mary Anna.

"What's the matter, Kate? Do you want to play in the garden with Annah, too? You'd better hurry."

The child cried harder, and Mary Anna knew this was not what Kate wanted. She pulled the child closer and kissed her wet cheeks. "What do you want, darling?"

"Don't go away from me," she sobbed. "I need you."

"I'm right here. I won't leave you." She felt the soft texture of Kate's hair underneath her stroking hand.

"Hold me, Mama. Hold me."

Big blue eyes, freshly washed with tears, pleaded with Mary Anna. Thunder cracked across the sky. "Don't be afraid of the storm," Mary Anna soothed her young daughter. "It won't hurt you. Come on, we'll get some milk and cookies.

That always makes you feel better." Slowly she sat up and led the child into the kitchen, feeling the small hand clutching her own.

Kate sat down obediently at the table. "I'll get both of us some cookies and milk, and we'll listen to the angels bowl." Mary Anna sat down at the table and shared the food with Kate. "That's what my father said was happening when it thundered," she reassured the child. "The angels were bowling."

Daniel came hurrying into the kitchen.

"Do you want some milk and cookies, too?" asked Mary Anna. She accepted his embrace and the soft kiss on her forehead.

"Yes, I'd like some. I'm glad to see you up," he said carefully.

"I've been asleep a long time, I think."

"Yes," he agreed. "It's been a long time. I've missed you."

She was surprised to see tears in his eyes. "It must have been a long while. You've gotten quite gray, my dear. I will be careful not to sleep that long again."

One by one the family members joined the big table and had the offered milk and cookies. They were watching her carefully.

And then she remembered the dream. "I was just in the garden with Annah. As I woke up, she was waving good-bye to me." She looked levelly at Daniel. "Annah is dead, isn't she? That's why I slept so long."

"Yes," he answered in a choked voice. "Annah is dead. But the rest of us are still here, and we love and need you."

"I'll be all right now. I saw her in the garden and she was very happy. I can leave her now. She's happy."

As she grew stronger, Mary Anna accepted Annah's death, and the tearing pain lessened. Only the smell of roses occasionally made her gasp. And then she went with Daniel down to put roses on Oscar's and Annah's graves. She was calm, for she had seen with her own eyes how radiant Annah was, and she tried to comfort Daniel with her knowledge. She seldom went to the grave as the days faded into the winter months. There was no need. Annah wasn't there.

Mary Anna looked at each of her children with new eyes as she had after Oscar's death. Their life was a slender golden thread suspended between heaven and earth. The thread could be broken at any moment, and she counted precious the days that she could have them. Yet she took comfort in knowing exactly where they would go if the time came again to give up one of them.

*Daniel is not the only one who is gray haired*, she noted as she brushed her long hair. With sorrow and wisdom had come the confirming streaks of gray. She twisted her hair into a soft knot on the top of her head with fingers made deft from years of practice. Her clothes were too large for her, but her appetite had returned.

She heard the gentle squeak of the front porch swing and went outside to join

Daniel. "It's still beautiful weather for October, isn't it?" he said.

"Yes. I love looking at the trees in their fall finery."

They spoke of soft, gentle things, edging their way back to one another.

Mary Anna looked at Daniel with careful eyes. They were still young in their hearts and minds, but Mary Anna was fifty-one and Daniel was already fifty-five years old. God willing, there would be many more years left for them together.

She laid her hand on Daniel's strong brown one, resting in his lap. Turning slightly, she looked at his face with great love and deep affection. "Remember when we were talking about living out the dream, and I told you I was afraid of it sometimes?"

"Yes." He patted her hand and then lovingly placed a kiss on its palm.

"These were the times I was afraid of. We were living in an impossibly happy time when everything was going right. I knew it couldn't always be that way. Money can't protect you from the realities of life. But God can get you through those times of sorrow." Softly she added, "I wouldn't have left you, you know. I was tempted because the pain was so great," she admitted.

"I wasn't sure if you would come back to me. I know that Annah was the child of your heart, a miniature of you in every way. It's all right that you loved her the best of our children. I was only praying you didn't love her more than you loved me."

She smiled sadly at that. "No, I could never love the children more than I love you. I needed time to heal. And my need was so great that only God could be of comfort to me at the time. Maybe that's why I had to give her back to the Lord. It won't be my ultimate test, Daniel. With clear eyes I can see what it will be like to lose you if you die before I do." Her voice was strong and controlled. "I may have to walk through that darkness again, but I know I can do it." She dropped her gaze to the floor of the porch, embarrassed to admit the next thought to him. "I'm selfish, for I hope I die before you do. I don't want to have to face life without you."

"We have eight living children of the fourteen you've borne, grandchildren, a good reputation, a beautiful ranch and farm, and each other. We have survived almost everything together building the dream. And we're still living the dream. God has given us these years in which to hold the dream in our hands, realize it, live it, and pass it on to our children. No man or woman could ask for more."

She leaned against him as the slow rhythm of the swing rocked them. "No matter what happens from now on, I won't be afraid. I've seen that dream fulfilled. And I see many more years of it yet to come. Thank You, Lord," she whispered. "Thank You."

# Epilogue

O n May 7, 1977, a historical marker, duly authorized by the Texas Congress, was erected in the cemetery where Daniel and Mary Anna are buried.

Daniel Robert Thornton (1833–1911) and Mary Anna (Garland) Thornton (1837–1906). D. R. Thornton from Mississippi married Mary Anna, daughter of frontier fighter, Peter Garland, in Anderson County, Texas, in 1853. The Thorntons settled here in 1857 as cattle raisers and helped make this frontier safe for less hardy settlers. The couple reared eight children. Thornton, a confederate soldier in the Civil War (1860s), served as a county commissioner (1876–78) and gave land for the local school (1882). Hannibal Cemetery stands on the donated land (1976). The cemetery is located eighteen miles northwest of Stephenville, two miles off SH108 on County Road. Barton Springs was renamed Hannibal.

On that hot May day, Thornton descendants from all over Texas assembled to pay homage to their forebearers. My mother, Fern Thornton Tinian, had the honor of unveiling the historical marker.

At the close of the ceremony, someone casually mentioned that the old log cabin was still standing. I was astonished, for I thought of that cabin as being a thousand years old and long destroyed.

It wasn't in the best of shape, but it still stood, solidly built and gaping here and there where a log was gone. I touched the weathered logs in an effort to feel the words they had stored, conversations of long ago captured by time.

Mary Anna and Daniel had built and lived in this very cabin. Incredible! When I walked around to the back, I could see a faint path still leading to a small stream.

I had gone to the dedication service more to please my parents than from a sense of honoring Daniel and Mary Anna. I knew nothing about them. When Mother spoke fondly of "Steamville," it stirred no memories in me. But now I stood with my hand touching the past. The cabin was slowly being bumped down by the cattle that pastured there. Ironic that it would be the cattle, not the Indians, that destroyed it.

I saw the cabin disappearing forever and couldn't bear the thought. My husband, Mel, didn't argue when I begged him to put one of the smaller loose logs in our car. I pulled out a heavy pink-tinted slab of limestone from the foundation.

344

He did balk when I said I wanted the door to make a table. "We only have a station wagon—and four kids," he reminded me. I think he envisioned the entire cabin being loaded by nightfall. Today the log is a long stool, thanks to my friend Jim Deal. On it sits a framed picture of the 1904 Thornton family portrait and underneath it, the foundation stone.

It has been a joyful labor of love to get to know Mary Anna and Daniel and to share their lives. Many years have passed since my fingers touched that building, sealing me forever into the lives of my great-great-grandparents. I'm eternally grateful for the memories they left behind.

# Song of Captivity

*To Perry, who led me through my captivity.*

# Chapter 1

*Summer 1925—Galveston Beach*

She was twenty that summer. Curled up under the beach umbrella, she watched him from beneath the small hat pulled down over her ebony hair. The harsh glare of the sun caused her to squint, and she raised her hand to shade her eyes.

He was laughing, trying to duck his male companion under the gentle swell of the waves. His muscles gleamed as the water streamed off his lithe body. Then as his friend lost his footing, he threw back his head in a jubilant guffaw, and a strand of dark hair fell into his eyes. He lifted a careless hand to brush it away from his face. Pausing a moment, he glanced toward the shore, as if he felt her watching him. At that moment his friend came up, gasping for air, shouting threats and lunging for him in retaliation.

"Ooo, he's divine," breathed her friend Mattie.

Cleo smiled a slow, secretive smile and nodded.

"Do you know him?" Mattie shifted on the blanket, careful to stay out of the sun's rays.

"Not yet," Cleo replied in her low voice.

"You aren't going to try to arrange a meeting, are you?" Distaste colored Mattie's tone. "That's so common." She checked her pale skin for signs of reddening.

"You know me better than that!" There was an air of injured dignity in Cleo's tone. "I've never picked up a man in my life."

"I know that you play with fire and skirt the rules whenever you can," snorted Mattie.

"Don't be such a bluenose." Cleo didn't contest her friend's statement. Her innocent antics were what made her life bearable, helped her endure her parents' tiresome moral and social code. But their status in the community was firm, and they wouldn't tolerate serious misbehavior on the part of their only daughter.

For Cleo, however, Christianity was a set of outdated rules, a moralistic code that seemed Victorian to her. She prayed erratically, and then usually only to plead to be excused from the wages of her sins.

As Cleo watched the man at play in the water with his friend, something deep inside contracted with excitement. A distant ache. A silent fluttering. He was most handsome, and the dark woolen bathing costume enhanced his well-proportioned physique.

Mattie eyed the sun, inching toward the westward horizon in sedate summer fashion. "We need to think about going back to Houston. It will be dinnertime soon." She arched her thinly penciled eyebrows. "Are you listening to me, Cleo Seachrist?"

"Hmmm." Cleo didn't take her eyes off the figure of the man. "What do you suppose it's like to really be in love?"

Mattie's gaze followed Cleo's out to the swelling waves. "That sort of man always looks dangerous to me. I want to wear white to my wedding and have it mean something." She looked again at her friend reclining gracefully on the sand. "Don't you?"

Cleo was thoughtful. "I suppose. But what I really want is to be madly in love." Her deep blue eyes glittered with intensity. "Think how exciting it would be. How romantic. To love someone enough to. . .to give yourself to him."

Mattie's mouth circled in a surprised O.

"Don't you want to love someone like that?" Cleo asked.

"Yes, of course, but my conscience wouldn't let me," Mattie assured her. "It would be wrong."

Cleo smiled ruefully at the warning note she had heard so often from her mother. "Let's go home. I've heard that sermon before."

Mattie got up huffily, dusting off the sand from her bathing costume. "Honestly, Cleo, sometimes you make me so mad." She looked down at her best friend, who was gathering up the umbrella. "And frankly, sometimes you worry me," she added, wrinkling her brow.

Cleo's laugh was husky. "Oh, don't worry. I'm not going to run away with a stranger. I've got a family, too." She threw one last longing look over her shoulder and sighed.

The two young women didn't go back to Galveston Beach that week, for the early spring weather turned cool and rainy. But Cleo had an idea. One that made Mattie's mouth circle in the astonished O once more. It took some persuading, but Cleo had always been good at that, and soon even Mattie was caught up in the spirit of adventure. Still, Mother would probably need her smelling salts when she found out about this escapade!

❧

Cleo felt a rush of excitement as she and Mattie stood in line at the public bathhouse on Galveston Beach waiting to rent a swimming costume. When her turn at the window came, she spoke clearly and distinctly. "A man's swimsuit, please." With a delicious flutter of anticipation, she noted the look of shocked disapproval on the clerk's face and heard a slight gasp of surprise from someone in the line behind her. She paid her money and accepted the suit, then stood aside for Mattie to step up to the window. Cleo gave Mattie a conspiratorial look as her friend made the identical request.

Ignoring the stares that followed their departure, they entered one of the small dressing rooms.

"You aren't going to back out on me, are you?" Cleo asked as she shucked off her dress.

"I don't think so, but my heart is beating ninety miles an hour. Did you see those shocked faces? Cleo, are you sure. . . ?"

A throaty laugh accompanied Cleo's delighted smile. "Just wait 'til we parade around in the Bathing Beauty Review!" She smoothed down the fabric of the swimsuit and struck an exaggerated pose, hands on her boyish hips, one knee cocked upward slightly, head tipped to the side. "How do I look?"

"Smashing, of course." A frown creased Mattie's smooth brow. "Do you think we'll get arrested?"

Cleo laughed her husky laugh once more. "Are you crazy? Only our arms are exposed. Besides, this is 1925, not the gay '90s. And it's Galveston Splash Day, the first day of the summer season. Everyone will be wearing these cute suits. Come on, Mattie, they don't enforce that old law about being covered from elbow to knees anymore. This is the twentieth century."

"Yeah, you'd better hope the police know what year it is," Mattie said darkly. She smoothed the close-fitting cloche over her fiery red hair, while Cleo put on the ankle-high shoes that were designed for the bathing costumes.

That familiar tingle of daring rippled through Cleo again, and she winked at Mattie.

"What now?"

"I was thinking how embarrassed my dear sainted mother would be if she could see her only child now." Unconsciously her hand went to the scooped neckline of the garment, tugging it upward a little.

Mattie pulled the mid-thigh legs of her brightly striped suit. "I'll probably get sunburned. Redheads never tan."

Cleo wrapped an emerald green headband around her coal black bob and inspected her own milky complexion in the dressing room mirror. "Oh, fiddlesticks! We can rent an umbrella." She sighed. "Well, this is it."

Firmly she pushed open the door, which made an alarmingly loud thud as it crashed into a very attractive young man standing just outside. "Oh, I'm so sorry!" she apologized quickly.

"No problem, ma'am," he drawled, his eyes large pools of chocolate brown. "Such a pretty young lady can run me down anytime." Even his grin was lazy, curling full lips above very white teeth.

She recognized him as the man she had seen playing in the waves several weeks earlier. "How very gallant," she murmured, acknowledging his grin with a coy look.

He nodded and passed by. If he had been wearing a hat, he would have tipped it, Cleo thought, easily imagining him in a gray Stetson.

"He's gorgeous!" exploded Mattie as they watched his muscular frame disappear in the direction of the beach. "He's the one, isn't he? The one we saw last time?"

Cleo nodded. "And he's even more handsome up close. Come on." She started in the same direction he had just taken.

"Cleo, for pity sakes! You can't follow him!"

"Don't be silly. We have to go this way to enter the contest." But there was a predatory gleam in the dark blue eyes that did not escape Mattie's notice. "How very fortunate," she murmured.

Cleo had been partially right. There were a few women dressed as they were, but the vast majority of them still wore the modest addition of skirt and stockings.

"Ohhh," Mattie groaned, "why ever did I let you talk me into this?"

"Isn't this fun?" purred Cleo softly as they lined up to get their sashes for the contest. Scanning the bevy of hopefuls, she decided that there was only one other girl who might be real competition.

So Cleo wasn't surprised when she won first place. She had been exclaimed over from the cradle, pampered and catered to from infancy. She accepted the little crown and the photographer's plea for one more shot for the *Galveston Daily News*.

"Your mother's going to kill us when she sees this in the paper," Mattie fretted. "I should have known this would get us into trouble. My mother will know right away that I was with you. Ohhh, Cleo, did you have to win first place?"

"I doubt very seriously that the Houston paper will run a story on Galveston's Splash Day," said Cleo. "There's too much competition between the two cities. Houston isn't going to advertise for Galveston. Come on, Mattie, where's your sense of adventure?"

"Probably on the front page," she answered gloomily.

"Come on, old girl, let's go get something cool to drink."

"Only if you take off that crown. You look like a deposed monarch advertising for a job."

Cleo laughed and accommodated her friend.

There were plenty of opportunities for discreet flirtations. The recent notoriety of their participation in the beauty contest had people pointing them out and young men making attempts to catch their attention. They kept the men at arm's length with practiced ease.

For the rest of the afternoon, the two young women played at the edge of the water, dodging the greedy waves licking at their shoes, and then settled in the shade at the base of the seventeen-foot-high seawall with their iced drinks.

"You're getting a bit pink," observed Cleo.

"So are you. Hmmm, this shade feels nice. We should have found it an hour ago. I'll probably peel like a molting lobster."

"Don't look now, but that good-looking cowboy is heading this way." Cleo shifted a little on the sand, adjusting her bathing costume modestly.

He stopped at their umbrella and peered under. "Congratulations," he said to Cleo.

"Thank you. Aren't you the young man I crashed into at the bathhouse?"

"I'm honored, ma'am, that the reigning beauty queen remembers me." He offered his hand. "I'm Tom Kinney."

She took his strong hand in her own, "Cleo Seachrist, and this is my friend Mattie Meyers."

Mattie and Tom exchanged nods, and Tom added, "Pleased to meet you, too, ma'am. I'm sure the judges had a hard time making up their minds."

Mattie laughed out loud. "This one's a keeper, Cleo!"

Tom turned his attention back to Cleo. "Are you from Galveston, Miss Seachrist?"

She could smell the salt water coming from his wet suit. His hair was damp and hung in careless waves, combed by the ocean breezes. "Ah, no. We're both from Houston and go to the university in Austin."

His eyes held hers, closing out the rest of the world. "I never got to go to college," he confessed. "I joined up for the war instead, and when I got out, I got a job as a ship's mechanic here on the wharves." He was not unaware of her assessing gaze traveling over his well-muscled frame, however covert it might be.

"Was it exciting, Mr. Kinney. . .the war, I mean?" she asked.

"Sometimes. Mostly it was scary or boring. So I wasn't too concerned when I got gassed with mustard gas. . .just enough to be sent home."

Mattie intruded into their private conversation. "It must have been wonderful seeing all those foreign countries."

He turned slightly, giving Cleo a view of his profile. "Not *that* way."

"I guess it would be a little different from going as a tourist," Mattie admitted.

"I'd like to go back to visit England someday."

"Cleo and I will be going to England in August."

"Is that so, Miss Seachrist?" The man's lazy Texas drawl was in perfect cadence with the casual glance he sent her way.

Cleo felt herself responding to his attention. "Yes. My father has business there. Perhaps we'll see you." Her frank look told him she'd like that.

He shrugged. "I doubt it. It'll take me a long time to save enough for a trip like that. Maybe someday. I do get to Houston to see my aunt once in a while, though," he added. "Would you mind if I called on you? We could have dinner."

"By all means." Her smile was genuine.

" 'Til then, ladies." Tom rose and waved as he walked toward the bathhouses.

"Your mother will go into cardiac arrest," Mattie said flatly as soon as he was out of earshot. "There's no way she's going to let you go out with a ship's mechanic."

"Mattie, you know I'm world class in getting my way with my parents. You just have to know which buttons to push." Cleo watched Tom's disappearing form. "Isn't he something? All those beautiful muscles. And that face. Even Mother will be impressed."

Mattie's face registered total disbelief at that statement. "Your mother knows rhinestones from diamonds, sweetie. You'd better hope he doesn't come calling in jeans and a cowboy hat."

"Hmmm," said Cleo, imagining the effect.

Mattie frowned. "Are you getting in over your head again, Cleo? I thought you'd learned your lesson with that down-and-out artist you dragged home to meet your folks."

Cleo stuck out her tongue. "This one will be worth the effort," she assured her friend. "Mark my words."

Mattie touched her fair skin with a tentative finger. "I need to get out of this sun. I'm burning for sure. Even an umbrella can't help me now. Come on, Juliet, let's get dressed."

The two women ignored the looks of disapproval cast by the modestly dressed women on the beach and made their way back to the bathhouses.

As they changed, Cleo practiced the story she would tell her mother and father about entering the contest.

"Honestly, Cleo, you spend more time covering your tracks than a renegade Indian," Mattie complained. "Why do you do these things?"

"Because I hate sameness, you old stick-in-the-mud! Where is your daring? Are you going to be bored out of your mind until they put you in the ground?"

"Not with you around. But I'll probably wind up in prison. . .or worse, disinherited by my folks!" Mattie laughed in spite of herself. With Cleo she never lacked for excitement. "You're not a bad girl, but you do seem to have a knack for living on the edge."

Cleo gave her friend a loving look. "You know me pretty well, don't you? Why do you put up with me?"

"Because I was appointed by God to be your guardian angel. That's the only reason I stay around. . .because I know He'll call me to account if I don't!" She heaved an overdone sigh. "I only hope I pass the test."

"Me, too," Cleo agreed.

They returned their damp suits and found Cleo's smart little Model A Ford parked on top of the seawall. Soon they were crossing the narrow causeway over Galveston Bay and watching the boats bob around in the smooth green water as they made their way back to Houston. It was already dusk, and Cleo pushed the car as fast as it would go. The salty air on her forehead was soothing.

"I do intend to see him again, you know," she told Mattie.

"I know." Mattie's eyes mirrored her concern. "Just don't do anything stupid. Please?"

Cleo smiled. She was replaying the moment of their first meeting, seeing the young man's strong features. Once again that familiar feeling stirred. Something unfulfilled, untasted. Each time she met an attractive man, it was the same. Was this the one who would satisfy her girlhood longings? Was this the man she would marry?

"I recognize that smile," Mattie said.

"Do you?"

"Of course. It's your someday-my-prince-will-come smile. Cleo," Mattie said, turning a solemn look in her friend's direction, "God will send you the right man. . .in His good time. Maybe even soon. And it will be someone you can take home without a problem." Her eyes lit up. "What's wrong with Bob? He's crazy about you."

Cleo dismissed the suggestion with a wave of her hand. "Bob is a bore. . .so immature." Then she spoke more hesitantly. "Mattie. . .do you really believe that God still does things for people? I mean, don't you think He more or less just sets things in motion and sits back and watches us run around trying to find the answers?"

Mattie sighed, this time with genuine concern. "I think He still takes care of us, and you wouldn't feel so insecure if you believed it, too. Why don't you just wait till God sends the right person? Maybe you'll even meet him in England. Wouldn't that be something?" she asked dreamily. "He might even have a title. . .Lord Somebody, not a nobody like that ship's mechanic."

Cleo shrugged. "You may be right, but I don't think even you could miss the totally masculine aura about Tom Kinney." She shivered in the hot, humid air as she braked to a stop in front of the well-tended grounds of Mattie's mansion.

"All I want is for you to be happy," Mattie said as she pulled her duffel bag from the backseat, her pink face screwed up with concern. "But I'm afraid this Tom Kinney is not going to give you what you're looking for."

"You worry too much," Cleo said with a laugh. "All I'm going to do is have dinner with him, *if* he calls."

"Oh, he'll call. He can spot a winner when he sees one." Mattie grinned reluctantly. "Speaking of winners, do you know what you're going to tell your family about the contest?"

"I do. And it's completely plausible. You?"

"I'll tell my folks you drugged me and I didn't know what I was doing!"

"And I'll tell mine," Cleo mused, "that you talked me into it and I went along to protect you from nefarious fortune hunters."

"*I* talked *you* into it?! You rat!" Mattie rolled her eyes. "No wonder your mother frowns when I come for tea. What must she think of me?"

"Oh, she'll only be mad for a day or two. Then she'll be proud that I won a beauty contest. She loves me, you know."

"Yes, I know." Mattie nodded solemnly.

"Now I gotta get out of here. See you tomorrow."

"What are we going to do? Rob a bank?"

"I was thinking of going back to the beach. . . ," Cleo began, staring off into the distance.

"You aren't serious! I couldn't! I'd be burned to a crisp!"

"No, I'm not serious. I was really thinking we could go shopping and spend some of my father's hard-earned money. I'll need some clothes for the trip."

When Mattie thought of all the clothes crammed into Cleo's closets, she laughed. But it would be fun to shop together. At least she wouldn't have to worry about her friend running into that man in the department store.

At dinner that night in the family dining room, Cleo told her version of the contest, careful to give it a humorous slant to placate her mother's fears.

As the servants cleared the table, Mrs. Seachrist spoke up. "I trust you will not find it necessary to repeat this. . .escapade to any of our friends."

"Now, Mother," her distinguished husband spoke up, "it was only a girlish lark. No one need know."

"Unless it comes out in the paper," Cleo added impishly.

A well-manicured hand clutching an Irish linen napkin fluttered to Mrs. Seachrist's bosom. "The paper! Oh, surely not! You don't really think it will be in the paper!"

"Probably only in the Galveston paper, Mother," Cleo soothed. "With the picture."

Her mother closed her eyes as if in a swoon. "Oh, dear Lord in heaven," she prayed.

"Calm yourself, Mother," Mr. Seachrist put in. "The Houston paper isn't going to print some silly article. Not when there's real news to report."

*Typical,* thought Cleo. Her father would not consider anything that happened in the provincial hamlet of Galveston worthy of mention in a Houston newspaper. For all their sakes, she sincerely hoped he was right!

Cleo quickly cast about for a more appealing topic of conversation. "Mattie and I are going shopping tomorrow. Would you like to come along, Mother?"

Her mother seemed genuinely regretful when she had to decline. "I'd love to, dear, but I have another commitment. The Garden Club is giving its spring tea. But you and Mattie run along. I'm sure you'll find some lovely things to wear in England when we see your father's business friends. One never knows whom one might meet." She arched one eyebrow in a meaningful way.

It occurred to Cleo that for her mother, this little trip might be an all-out husband-hunting expedition, but she couldn't honestly say she was displeased with the notion. How romantic to marry an English gentleman and live in his castle. "May I be excused now, Mother? I'm a little tired."

"Of course, darling. And, Cleo," Mrs. Seachrist added, "do find something to put on your skin. You're going to look like a field hand if you get one of those awful suntans. You must take good care of your complexion, you know."

"Yes, Mother, I'll take care of it. I want it to look as marvelous as yours when I'm your age."

Mollified, Mrs. Seachrist accepted the soft kiss Cleo dropped on her forehead.

In her room Cleo scattered her clothes in her dressing room for the maid to put away and walked into her bathroom. As she bathed, she decided that getting her parents to see Tom Kinney would be a little more difficult than she had led Mattie to believe it would be, especially if her mother discovered they had met on the beach without a proper introduction or chaperone. *Maybe a double date with Mattie and J.J.*, she mused. That would be much easier to arrange.

She crawled into bed with a half-formed plan simmering in her mind and a short prayer that God would approve. *It can't hurt,* she thought. *Besides, Mattie might be right. Maybe God does answer prayers.* In any case, she wanted to cover all her bases.

## Chapter 2

When Tom called a week later, Cleo was pleased but not surprised. On the phone his conversation sounded real and down-to-earth rather than the contrived small talk she was accustomed to hearing from the boys she usually dated.

"Dinner? I'd love it," she agreed heartily the instant he mentioned seeing her again.

"What's your favorite restaurant?"

It crossed her mind that her favorite, Chez André, was quite expensive, surely beyond his means. "Why don't you suggest a place," she stalled.

"Is there any reason you might not want to be seen with me?" he said with a trace of unexplained anger in his voice.

"Don't be silly! I'd love to eat at Chez André with you." The fact that she knew the headwaiter might come in handy, too, she thought.

"Then I'll be by for you around eight." The timbre in his voice promised an exciting evening.

"I'm looking forward to it," she purred, hoping he hadn't guessed just how much.

She gave him the address and immediately called Mattie as soon as she had hung up.

"Thus begins the drama," sighed her best friend. "What are you going to tell your folks about what he does for a living? I think all the shipping magnates are accounted for."

"Very funny, Mattie," Cleo observed wryily. "I'll introduce him and whisk him away before Mother has time to check out his portfolio."

"Good luck. The Lord knows you're going to need it. Where are you going?"

"Chez André."

Mattie laughed. "I can scarcely imagine a ship's mechanic in that place. So you're going to put him to the test right away, huh?" Her voice grew serious. "I do hope you know what you're doing, Cleo. He'll probably make a complete idiot out of himself, and if he does, he won't like you for that."

"I'm not testing him, Mattie," Cleo protested. "Not exactly, that is. Let's just say I'm giving him an opportunity to put his best foot forward."

"Well, it will certainly be an interesting evening. I hope *that* story doesn't wind up on the front page of the Houston paper."

"There's just one more tiny detail I neglected to mention," Cleo began hesitantly. "I need you and J.J. to go with us. You know I'll have a better chance with Mother if there's another couple along."

"Here we go again." Mattie couldn't resist toying with her friend. "The food is pretty good, but I don't know if J.J. is up to palling around with a ship's mechanic for an entire evening."

"So don't tell him until everything is set. Please?"

The unaccustomed plea in Cleo's voice was the clincher. "Oh, all right," Mattie relented. "Let's just hope this doesn't turn out to be a last supper for both of us!"

⌇

Cleo was ready at the stroke of eight. As if the Lord had orchestrated the plan, her father left minutes before Tom's arrival. Now she had only her mother to contend with.

When the door chimes sounded, Cleo hurried downstairs. No need to risk putting Tom through a family inquisition at the front door! She stepped back to allow the butler to open it, then offered her hand to Tom, drawing him inside.

"Hello," she greeted him, taking in the dark business suit, the expensive cowboy boots, and the light-colored Stetson hat in his hand.

"Hello, yourself," he returned in a deep voice.

Hesitantly, she led him to the formal drawing room where her mother was entertaining a friend. "Mother, may I present Mr. Tom Kinney. Mr. Kinney, my mother, Mrs. Seachrist."

"Evening, ma'am." He nodded. "It's very nice to meet you." Cleo was surprised to see that his manner was calm and easy.

Her mother gave him a long appraising look. "Good evening, Mr. Kinney. And this is my dear friend, Mrs. Amalie Long."

"We're going out to dinner, Mother," Cleo said breathlessly. "I won't be late." She ignored her mother's quirked brow and turned to leave.

"It was nice to have met you, ladies," Tom said politely as he followed her out.

He helped Cleo into an older version of her sleek little Ford and grinned his irresistible grin. "You look absolutely smashing this evening, Miss Seachrist."

She grinned back. "So do you."

He settled himself in the driver's seat and turned the ignition key, while she noted his strong hands on the steering wheel. "I hope you won't mind," Cleo began apologetically, "but I took the liberty of asking Mattie and J.J. to join us. They'll be at her house around the corner."

"Fine with me."

She was immensely relieved. "It will be better this way, since my parents don't know you or your family."

"I wondered about that," he said, turning to her with a frown. "Perhaps we should have spent a little more time visiting with your mother and Mrs. Long," he answered smoothly.

She gave him a weak smile but offered no explanation. "Turn here."

They went together to the door of Mattie's imposing brick home. When she and J.J. came out, Tom offered his hand to the other young man. "Tom Kinney."

"Joshua John Sagerton III here. Known and loved by all as J.J.," he laughingly replied. "It's good to meet you."

When they entered the restaurant, Cleo did not miss the admiring looks from some of her friends as they followed Tom's progress through the crowded dining room. His manners were correct and pleasant, she observed, and he didn't appear at all out of place among them. At dinner he sat back and let J.J. take the lead in the conversation, adding now and then a humorous anecdote of his own. Cleo thought him utterly charming.

When they excused themselves to go to the ladies' room, Mattie began to fire questions at her. "What a man! Cleo, that's no ship's mechanic! He's too smooth. Are you sure he isn't a millionaire's son in disguise? What do you know about him? Where is his home? And don't tell me Galveston. I know better than that."

"I don't know," Cleo confessed. "I haven't had a chance to talk to him alone." She wagged her finger in her friend's face. "And don't you ask him in front of everyone. I'll find out later."

When dinner was over and Mattie and J.J. had been returned to her house, Tom and Cleo drove up in front of Cleo's door. "It's still early," she said with a smile. "And it's a lovely night. Would you like to walk a little in the garden?"

"That sounds nice."

They wandered around to the back of the house where formal paths meandered through the lush rose garden.

"Did I pass muster?" Tom asked at last, breaking their companionable silence.

"Wh–what?" Cleo was startled at his perception.

There was a knowing smile on his handsome face. "Oh, you know. . .the right clothes, the proper etiquette. . ."

She had the grace to blush lightly in the moonlight. "Why, of course, you did."

He was the one who was amused now. "But you didn't expect me to, did you? I think you should know that I wasn't always a ship's mechanic."

"Oh?" She leaned near to hear what he had to say.

"No, I grew up on a ranch in West Texas, but my mom was big on manners and polish, so I was sent away to school. Good old Mom."

"Where is your mother now?"

"Still out on the ranch. My dad died several years ago, but she won't give up ranching." He sighed. "She would have enjoyed going to dinner with us tonight.

She's always loved the good life, but there's been very little of that these last few years."

"I'd like to meet her." The comment was made as a polite rejoinder, but Cleo was surprised to find that she really meant it.

"Maybe you will. I hope to get to know yours better," he added pointedly.

Again her cheeks colored in the warm night. "And *you* should know that Mother has a rather warped yardstick by which she measures people, Mr. Kinney."

"Call me Tom, and I'll call you Cleo. It's time we dropped the formality, don't you think?" Seeing her hand on the low garden wall, he covered it with his own.

"All right. . .Tom," she agreed, tasting his name in the night.

"Cleo." He lifted her hand and pressed a kiss in the palm.

A tingling sensation started in her feet and raced through her, exploding in her head as she felt his lips on her hand. Quickly regaining her composure, she withdrew it. "About my mother. . . ," she began.

"You didn't want her to know what I do for a living. Right?"

"Yes, otherwise I might not have gotten the chance to know you at all." The statement was simple and truthful. "She's not a snob, but she is inclined to be over-protective where her only daughter is concerned. Father is worse." She laughed nervously.

"And so they should be with their only treasure." He leaned back against the wall, his arms crossed casually, and observed her. "What will you do next time?"

"Next time?" She felt the tingling again.

"I hope there will be a next time," he said, looking deeply into her eyes.

In anticipation of his kiss, she leaned forward and closed her eyes. But he sidestepped her waiting lips and placed a brotherly peck on her forehead.

"I'd better get you in. No point in making your folks mad at me before they get to know me."

Her eyes flew open. And, feeling like a complete idiot, she could only nod dumbly. *I never should have allowed him to kiss me at all,* she groaned.

Walking her to the door, Tom shook her hand properly. "I'll call you again soon," he promised.

"Please do. I had a lovely evening." Dreamily, Cleo closed the door and leaned against it. "The loveliest evening ever."

Usually she called Mattie after her dates and they discussed in detail the events of the evening. But not this time. Cleo wanted to keep her feelings to herself, to sort them out, to ponder them. She fell asleep with a smile on her face.

⌖

The ringing of the phone stirred Cleo from a delicious dream, and she pulled the intrusive instrument onto the pillow. Without cracking an eyelid, she spoke into the receiver, her voice husky with sleep. "Not now, Mattie, I'm not awake yet."

A low chuckle rumbled through the wire. "This isn't Mattie. It's Tom."

Instantly alert, she sat up in bed. "Oh, good morning!"

"I called to tell you what a wonderful time I had last night. And to see if you wanted to picnic on the beach today. Uh," he added hastily, "why don't you ask Miss Meyers and J.J. to come along, too."

It was a perfect solution to her dilemma, of course. Her mother would never permit a second encounter with this stranger without a formal meeting to check out his credentials. But as long as Cleo could say he was a friend of Mattie's and J.J.'s. . .well, seeing Tom at the beach would be a good way to avoid a confrontation with her parents before she was ready.

"Why don't we meet you at the seawall at one?" she suggested.

"Swell! I'll bring the picnic. See you later, then."

When Cleo hung up the phone, she bolted out of bed and danced around the room, giddy with excitement. It occurred to her that either the Lord was answering her prayers or she was getting herself into a terrible mess! *Either way,* she thought, *I get to see Tom Kinney again.* Then, throwing herself on the bed, she called Mattie's number.

It was impossible to keep the tremor from her voice when she had Mattie on the line. "He called again! I knew he would but not this soon!" Cleo was bouncing on the edge of the bed, not even trying to stem her elation.

"And?"

"And we're going on a picnic today at the beach."

"You can't do that, Cleo. You're going too far this time," warned Mattie.

"Oh, it will be more or less proper. . .since you and J.J. are going with us." When there was nothing but silence on the other end, Cleo resorted to pleading. "Just one more time, Mattie. You know I never ask you for favors."

"Is it really worth all this to see him again?" Mattie hedged.

"Oh, yes! There's something about him. . . I don't know what it is, but it's never been like this with anyone before. Please. . ."

"Oh, all right. Just once more. Then you're going to have to do this the right way."

"I will. I promise! Oh, thank you, Mattie! Thank you a thousand times!"

Mattie sighed forlornly. "I hope the day doesn't come when you curse me a thousand times for aiding and abetting this insanity."

✺

The bell at First Lutheran Church was already tolling one o'clock when they parked the car and hurried to the bathhouses. As they strolled the beach, Cleo tried not to appear to be scanning the crowd as she looked for Tom. When she finally caught sight of him, his rugged masculinity struck her again with full force. Was it the thrill of sneaking around to see him, or was he that attractive?

A little of both, she truthfully decided.

"Hello," she said with studied casualness when they found him at last.

"Hello, yourself," he said with an admiring glance at the bathing costume she had just rented. He shook hands with J.J. and acknowledged Mattie with a nod. "Miss Meyers. Nice to see you again. I have an umbrella down the beach so we can eat in the shade."

They chatted about the weather and the water as is customary when people don't know each other very well. But when they reached his chosen spot, they all settled on the blanket he had spread out on the sand.

"I'm starved! Hope the rest of you are, too." He opened the large wicker basket and passed out sandwiches and cold drinks.

"Did you make these yourself?" Mattie asked, helping Cleo place them on plates Tom had packed in the basket.

"No, there's a little place that makes great roast beef sandwiches not far from where I work. I do the barbecuing at the ranch. But outside of that, I'm not much of a cook."

While Tom distributed cold bottles of pop, Cleo searched for some lively topic of conversation to ease the awkwardness between them. Shading her eyes with her hand, she gazed out to sea. "Is that a shark out there?" she asked playfully, enjoying the sudden look of alarm on Mattie's face.

"No," said J.J. "I think it's dolphins playing. Must be six or eight of them." Then, entering into the mood, he baited Mattie. "But I heard they pulled in a two-hundred pounder around the wharves last week."

"Had half a man's body in its stomach, so they say," said Tom with a twinkle in his eye.

Mattie's hand paused in midair, her sandwich halfway to her mouth. "You *are* just kidding. . .aren't you?"

"Yes," agreed Cleo, "they only found the man's arms."

All three laughed while Mattie shuddered. "That's not one bit funny, Cleo!" she charged. "You know that I'm deathly afraid of sharks. And I don't think any of you know a shark from a dolphin, so I have no intention of setting foot in water more than ankle deep!"

"Then you'd better watch out for the Portuguese man-of-war," Tom offered solemnly. "I saw several of them while I was waiting for you."

Mattie stuck out her lip in a charming pout. "You all make the beach such a delightful place to visit."

J.J. laughed. "Don't worry, Mattie. Scientists have proven that no living fish can abide a bad-tempered redhead."

She wanted to be mad but found it impossible with her companions smiling fondly at her. And in spite of her reservations, she joined the others as they romped in the surf, but stayed as close to the shore as the tugging waves would permit.

Cleo and Tom allowed the waves to carry them out to the first sandbar. Cleo found the strength of the tide surprising as the undertow pushed and pulled her, tossing her about like a rag doll. Tom made a grab for her as she lost her footing and a wave smacked her down. He helped her to her feet as she came up gasping for air.

They stood there, the warm water lapping at their knees, his strong arms still holding her. "The ocean plays rough," he said huskily. His eyes were intense as they searched hers.

"Yes," she whispered, hoping he wouldn't let go. She felt a tug as unmistakable as the surf. Should she move closer. . .or farther away?

Tom sensed her indecision. "Cold?"

"A little," she admitted. They struggled in the knee-deep water toward the beach, where their umbrellas and picnic things were waiting, and she allowed him to wrap her in the sandy blanket as they sat down. The sun was making a watery descent, and the wind had picked up a bit.

"I could build a fire if you like," he offered.

"That would be nice." She shivered, uncertain as to whether the source of her chill was her wet suit or this disturbing man beside her.

Tom left her to pick up pieces of driftwood along the dunes, then laid a small fire in the shelter of the long salt grasses springing from the sand dune. He sat down beside her and put his arms around her lightly. She sighed as she leaned against him.

"This is nice," he said.

The moon was rising over the lacy waves, casting a path of mellow light across the water. Seagulls, still circling above, cried to the sandpipers, who moved in a prissy walk at the water's edge, looking for a late supper. The sound of the water lapping against the shore had a hypnotic effect, and Cleo found herself relaxing.

"I love the water," Tom said. "Living inland, I didn't see much of it until I was in the army and was shipped overseas. But I loved it right away." He laughed softly. "I know this sounds kind of crazy, but it reminds me of the endless grassy plains I grew up with. The grass moves with the wind the same way the water does. And it makes a swishing sound as the blades rub together, a little like the sound of the waves."

"Do you have sharks, too?" she teased gently.

"Something just as deadly. Rattlesnakes."

"Oh." She shivered.

"There's some kind of danger wherever you choose to live," he reminded her.

"Life is like that, you know."

Cleo pondered his words, then brightened. "I love your comparison of the ocean and the plains. I'd never thought of that. Of course, I've never seen West Texas," she admitted.

Tom shrugged. "Some people love it, some hate it. There were even stories in the early days of folks losing their minds from loneliness out on those isolated ranches."

"Is it lonely on your ranch. . .for your mother, I mean?"

"My brother Robert lives with her. And it's not that far to town."

"It must be fascinating," Cleo said, giving him a sidelong look. "I've always lived in Houston. And when we travel, we visit the large cities—Dallas. . . Austin. . .New Orleans. And I'm looking forward to spending some time in England with my family. Everyone says it's so 'civilized,' whatever that means." She laughed her low, throaty laugh. "I only know it's full of history and that it will be fun to see the places I've only read about. My father says there's even a chance we may be presented at court."

Tom frowned in thought. "That wouldn't be my choice. I'd go to the museums and art galleries. Maybe to the palace to see the changing of the guard. But I'm afraid I'd have a problem with the language."

Cleo stared in disbelief. "The language?"

"Yes. The English people I met during the war couldn't understand my West Texas twang, and I had all kinds of trouble understanding theirs. They sounded like they had a mouth full of cotton."

Cleo laughed again, liking Tom more with every new revelation.

"I hope you're not leaving anytime soon. We're just getting acquainted." His dark eyes glowed, reflecting the firelight.

"Yes, I know." She reached for his hand. "Friends?"

"Friends," he echoed solemnly. Then realizing the time, he sprang to his feet. "Hey, we'd better get back! J.J. and Mattie will be wondering where we are."

Mattie's giggle wafted across the water as they swam back to the beach and approached the fire J.J. had built to hold the gathering darkness at bay. "Hey! Is anybody home?"

"Here we are!" J.J. called cheerfully. "Come on and get warm by the fire."

Mattie gave Cleo a searching look. "We wondered if you two had sailed off the edge of the world."

"Guess we lost track of time," Cleo confessed, grateful that the night disguised her burning cheeks.

Tom dropped down beside her. "Any sandwiches left?"

"Plenty," Mattie said, fishing for them in the basket. They made short work of them, then sat enjoying the wide sweep of moonlit beach.

"This is a swell place," J.J. said. "I'd love to have a weekend cottage out here."

Cleo chortled. "Nobody lives on the west end of the island. It's too remote."

"Oh, I don't know," said Tom reflectively. "I'd like to build a house over there so I could watch the sun go down on the water."

"Cowboys don't live on the ocean," Mattie spoke up.

Tom and Cleo exchanged knowing looks. "*This* cowboy might. I've lived long enough in the dust."

"That's what you say, but I think you must miss it sometimes," Cleo added.

"What I do miss are the rodeos. I've won a few events," he said modestly.

"Where do you find the nerve to get up on one of those wild horses?" asked J.J. "That's taking your life in your hands, old man."

"Oh, J.J., *you're* scared of buildings over four stories!" scoffed Mattie.

Tom ignored her friendly jab. "I do it real carefully," he explained. "I don't mind the broncs so much, but the brahma bulls do give me the sweats. Saw a man stomped once, and I see that in my mind every time I climb aboard one. The trick is not so much staying on as getting off in one piece."

"Do you plan to work as a ship's mechanic or go back to your ranch?" J.J. wanted to know.

"Oh, I suppose I'll go back someday. Mama has things under control for now, and my brother works there since my dad died. Grinding out my days on a ranch hasn't seemed too appealing since I've had a chance to travel with the service. It looks more like a place to *finish* things than to *begin* them."

"Most of the cattlemen who are friends of my father's have begun to look at this new oil business," J.J. said.

Tom looked thoughtful. "I've heard about it. They've found oil south of us at Pecos and Fort Stockton. A lot of money to be made, I guess, *and* to be lost. But I still hang on to my dad's old conviction: Oil and cattle don't mix."

"Well, it just may be the thing to supplement cattle and cotton here in Texas. My father's a banker, and it's his business to keep up with the trends. He's already making a few loans for wildcatting," J.J. concluded.

"Got to *have* money to *make* money," Tom intoned the old saying with a grin.

"Say, Tom," J.J. said, "it might be something for you and me to consider. I wouldn't mind making a few million dollars, and you don't strike me as a man who's afraid to take a chance."

"You and me. . .wildcat together?"

J.J. shrugged and poked up the fire. "It was just a thought. Tuck it away. There may come a time we're both ready."

Tom looked directly into the young man's eyes. He was dead serious. "Yeah, I will," he replied wonderingly.

"Just like men! Always talking business!" Cleo interrupted, getting to her feet.

"Anyone for an evening swim?"

"Not me," said Mattie, speaking from within the curve of J.J.'s arm. "I'm finally warm and dry."

"Besides," said Tom, "I've heard the sharks are much worse at night." He ducked Mattie's swing and followed Cleo into the moonlit surf.

# *Chapter 3*

Mattie peered at Cleo over her morning cup of coffee. "I'm worried about you." The statement was made calmly enough, but the expression on her face told a different story.

Carelessly Cleo twisted the china cup in her hands. "Why?" she asked, knowing the answer and the probable lecture that would follow Mattie's innocent-sounding words.

"I think you know." Mattie leaned closer to speak privately in the posh restaurant where she had met her friend for breakfast. "You've been seeing Tom for a month now, and you just can't keep sneaking around like this."

Cleo was hotly defensive. "I'm not sneaking around! We see each other openly. You ought to know! You're usually there!"

"But your parents aren't," Mattie hissed. "Why don't you take him home so they can get to know him?"

"*You* know why," moaned Cleo. "Mother would get that look on her face the minute she found out what he does for a living. And then she'd grill him on his family background. It would be awful!"

"My stars, Cleo, you've fallen for him, haven't you?" Mattie's pale blue eyes flew wide at the sudden insight. "What on earth were you thinking?"

Cleo nodded. "I love him, Mattie. I've tried not to. I've tried to tell myself that he was just another boy. But there's something about him. . .well, I can't help myself," she finished miserably.

Mattie felt a flicker of alarm. "Surely he hasn't. . .that is, you didn't. . .let him take liberties. . . ?"

Cleo blushed. "No, of course not. In fact, he's been a perfect gentleman." She laughed her throaty laugh. "Maybe that's one reason I fell for him." Her eyes took on a misty, dreamy quality. "He's so kind and thoughtful. He brought me a dozen red roses last week. . . ."

"What's new about that?" Mattie asked flatly. "Lots of boys have brought you roses."

"Yes, but Tom can't afford them. Don't you see?" Her eyes pleaded for understanding, but she didn't find it in Mattie's stony face.

"Drop him!" Mattie insisted. "Do it right away. Cut it off cleanly and forever."

"Oh, Mattie, I can't. I've tried, but I can't. I've never felt this way before."

Mattie's sigh was born of futility. "Then you have no choice but to take him home."

"If I do, Mother and Father will forbid me to see him again."

"That's because he's wrong for you," Mattie insisted.

Cleo started to protest. "He's only wrong for me by *their* standards. If he had money, everything would be all right. But I love him anyway. I'd follow him anywhere just to be with him." A tear threatened to spill down her cheek.

Mattie gritted her teeth. "You'll just have to get over it. It'll never work, and you know it. You'd be miserable. Your family would never accept him. Your father might even disinherit you! It'll never work," she repeated, then saw determination flare in Cleo's eyes. "Cleo. . . ," she warned.

"Mattie, I'm not going to give him up. But you're right. I must take Tom home. They'll have to accept him. I'm their only child. Besides, they've never denied me anything I really wanted."

"Humph! You've never made such a bad choice before," Mattie reminded her mildly.

Cleo's eyes narrowed dangerously. "He's not a bad choice. He's a good and decent man. He just doesn't happen to have money. You sound like my mother!" She was shaking with anger.

"Take it easy. I only meant that socially this relationship isn't going to make anyone happy. Perhaps not even Tom," she added kindly.

"Then we'll go live somewhere else, where people will accept him for what he is."

"You'd give up everything for this man?" Mattie's eyes drilled into hers.

Cleo didn't blink. "Yes, I love him that much."

Mattie breathed a sigh of defeat. "You're either the craziest or the luckiest person I ever met. *I've* never loved anyone enough to buck my family."

Hope brightened Cleo's face. "Then you'll help me?"

"What else can I do?" wailed Mattie. "You're my best friend. But I'm sure the Lord's going to get me for this one." In spite of her protests, Mattie was intrigued by the romantic notion of Cleo's forbidden love.

"I'll invite him over, but you and J.J. must come, too. J.J. likes Tom. Maybe that would give us a bit of an edge."

"And now you're bringing J.J. into this! Why should your parents care what he thinks of Tom?" she asked with a trace of sarcasm.

But Cleo was adamant. "I'm *not* going to let Tom get away," she said serenely. "He's the finest man I ever met."

Mattie rolled her eyes helplessly.

❧

Cleo wiped her damp hands on a crumpled handkerchief and smoothed her hair once more. The mirror reflected a well-dressed young woman waiting for her beau to call. It failed to show how shaky that young woman felt on the inside.

Glancing at the clock, she hurried it with her eyes. *God, if you're really there, help me!*

She had prepared her parents for the meeting only by mentioning that she had invited three of her friends for tea, and that one of them was a young man. Now Henry Seachrist was reading the paper in his study, and Madeline was upstairs getting dressed. Her mother's eyebrows had risen slightly at the news, but she'd asked no further questions. After all, it was not unusual for Cleo to bring young men home for tea. It was just that this young man was not like any other she'd ever brought before, and everything depended upon the events of the next hour or so.

Wringing her hands, Cleo peered through the lacy curtains that lay beneath the heavy damask at the tall windows. Soon she saw Tom's Ford pull up in the circular drive and stop at the front door. As he stepped out, he smoothed his dark hair, and Cleo's heart gave a happy little leap.

She stepped quickly to the massive double doors as the butler opened them. "Hello, Tom. I'm so glad you could come," she said formally, her joy in seeing him mirrored in her eyes.

He took her hand. "Thank you for inviting me." He glanced over his shoulder as a second car pulled up, bringing J.J. and Mattie.

Some of the tension lifted as the four of them moved to the formal living room and chose chairs, chatting companionably. But the tension returned as her father entered the room.

The foursome rose, and Cleo hurried over to greet him. Then, linking her arm through his, she led him back to the little group. "Father, I believe you know J.J. and Mattie." The two men shook hands, and Henry nodded to Mattie with a smile. But his smile faded a bit when he turned to regard Tom.

Cleo drew a deep breath. "And this is Tom Kinney."

"Happy to meet you, son." There was a wary look in Henry Seachrist's eyes as they traveled up and down the young man standing before him as if trying to place him. *Or to measure him,* Cleo thought. "I don't believe I've had the pleasure of meeting you. Is your family new to Houston, Mr. Kinney?" He moved easily to a chair and sat back, like a judge waiting to pass sentence.

"I don't live in Houston, sir. I live in Galveston."

Mr. Seachrist's eyes clouded a bit. "Oh," he said, quickly recovering his composure and continuing to make polite conversation. "Must be nice to live near the water."

"Yes, sir." Tom sat down again in the seat opposite his host.

At that moment Cleo's mother made a grand entrance, and the men stood as she took her place at the head of the tea table.

"You are from Galveston, Mr. Kinney? It must be dreadfully hot down there this time of year. Oh, my, and the mosquitoes!"

"What does your father do, son?" asked Mr. Seachrist as he accepted a cup of tea from his wife.

"My father is dead, sir, and my mother is back in West Texas on our ranch."

Cleo felt her stomach tighten, and her hand shook slightly as she passed the cups her mother handed her.

"A ranch," mused her mother. "How nice." Then she took on a quizzical air. "If you are a rancher, then what are you doing in Galveston?"

Cleo's throat closed. *Here it comes,* she thought.

"I work for International Shipping."

Cleo saw her mother's brow pucker slightly, and her father cleared his throat.

"In their offices?" her mother asked hopefully.

"No, ma'am. I'm a ship's mechanic." Tom sat erect, his gaze calm and direct as he dropped the bomb.

Madeline stifled a slight gasp. "How nice," she repeated.

J.J. stepped in. "Mr. Kinney and I have become quite good friends." He regretted the comment the instant he uttered it, for it implied that they had been together frequently. Quickly he regrouped. "Yes, he's been quite helpful in getting Father's boat repaired. Why, we never would have figured out what was wrong with it if it hadn't been for Mr. Kinney." He glanced around the room to see if he had redeemed himself.

Cleo could see the questions still written on her father's face and took a steadying breath. "Mr. Kinney is a good friend of mine, too, Father."

Taking this as his cue, Tom stood and spoke clearly and distinctly, "Sir, ma'am, I'd like your permission to call on your daughter."

Mr. Seachrist's flinty gaze did not waver, and his voice was cool as he replied, "I don't think that would be a good idea, Mr. Kinney."

"Sir, I can see you don't approve of me, but I'm an honest man and a hardworking one. I don't intend to be working the shipyards all my life."

"Good day, Mr. Kinney. It was kind of you to call." Henry's tone carried an unmistakable air of dismissal.

Tom remained standing, his dark eyes searching Cleo's. "Sir, I realize I have not known your daughter very long, but I love her and I think she cares for me, too. I'd like the chance to win her hand."

Cleo's heart lurched with joy. *He loves me!* It was all she heard, all that mattered.

"I'm sure you would," Mr. Seachrist replied icily. "But that won't be possible as long as I'm alive. Good day, sir."

Cleo turned a pleading look on her mother. There was only shock and disapproval on the frozen face. "Father," she began, but he interrupted her appeal.

"You will leave now, Mr. Kinney. And you will never see my daughter again. Do you understand?" The tone he used now had subdued many a business competitor.

"I'm not going to stand here and argue with you, sir. But if Cleo will see me, I'm not going to let you keep us apart." Tom's lips thinned with determination.

Mr. Seachrist stood with his fists clenched at his sides, perhaps in an effort to keep from striking the young upstart who had defied him. Not since he was a very young man himself had anyone successfully opposed him. It was a point of pride with him that he had made his way from a position as a lowly office boy to that of the president of an international company. Yes, he had to admire the firm-jawed young man standing across the room from him, but this was different. This man had come to take his daughter away, and it was clear he was not good enough for her.

Henry's next words were as hard and cold as the iron he manufactured and shipped. "Never, never try to see my daughter again." With that, he turned on his heel and strode out of the room. Mrs. Seachrist cast a baleful eye at her daughter and followed her husband, leaving utter silence in her wake.

Cleo was almost afraid to look at Tom, but what she read in his loving gaze caused her to run to his side. He took both her hands in his. "I meant what I said to your father, Cleo. I love you, and I want to marry you." When she opened her mouth to reply, he put a silencing finger over her lips. "No, don't answer me now. Don't say anything yet. You need time to think."

"But I already know my answer, Tom," she insisted breathlessly. "I love you, too, and more than anything else in the world, I want to be your wife. I can change their minds. I know I can!"

Mattie was sobbing openly, her handkerchief stuffed against her mouth. J.J., considerably paler himself, patted her shoulder awkwardly. "Come on," he said, eager to take action. "Surely the four of us can think of something."

Mattie sighed. "Oh, J.J., you're so romantic."

❧

The four met at the park soon after their hurried exit from the Seachrist mansion. J.J. spread out a lap rug for them to sit on, and they leaned against the ancient trees and took comfort from their shade.

Tom held Cleo's hand. "Well, you're in the soup now." His eyes searched her face for traces of regret. There was only love.

"I know. It's not the first time." She sighed heavily and glanced over at Mattie's red-rimmed eyes. "What were you bawling about back there?"

Her friend turned scarlet. "It was all so romantic the way Tom asked for your hand and then stood up to your father. Just like in the romance novels."

Tom gave a ghost of a smile. "And what would the romance novels suggest we do now?"

"We could elope," Cleo said shyly.

"No," said Tom quickly. "I think we should give your folks a little time to get over the shock. We did take them by surprise, you know."

Cleo laughed up at him. "Even *I* was surprised!" She plucked idly at his sleeve. "But I think you're right. I'll talk with them tomorrow. When they find out that I intend to marry you—with or without their blessing—they'll come around," she said confidently.

Tom laughed out loud. "Oh, you think so, do you? Are you so accustomed to having your own way? If so, I can see we have a rocky road ahead of us."

She pretended to pout. "What I meant was that when they see how much I love you, they'll give in." She reached up and, in front of J.J. and Mattie, sealed it with a kiss.

⤙⤚

Henry and Madeline Seachrist sat in the master bedroom, each busy with thoughts too big to share. Rising, Henry paced the room angrily.

"For heaven's sake, sit down, dear." Madeline patted the satin-covered settee beside her, and he obliged.

"What do we do now?" he asked. "She left with him. She's gone."

Madeline was surprised to see the welling of tears in her husband's eyes. "She's not gone from us, Henry. She'll be back."

"Married to that fortune hunter, no doubt," he said bitterly.

"And if the boy really loves her?"

Henry sighed. "Even if he does, how can he possibly take care of her? He's destitute—no family to speak of, no inheritance, I'll wager, and no prospects."

"We weren't rich when we got married, Henry," his wife reminded him, "and *we* managed."

"Yes, but we weren't used to all this." His sweeping gesture encompassed the luxurious room. "Cleo is. She'll be miserable with him."

"Now you can't know that, Henry. Love can compensate for many things. I *know*."

"She knows nothing of the real world out there. She's been so protected." Right before Madeline's face, grief aged his face.

She rushed to comfort him. "But what are our choices, Henry? We can never see her again, or we can accept this young man and have her back. It's possible that if she believed we would not interfere, she would drop him. You know how stubborn she is, dear. . .like her father."

A tiny light of hope crept into Henry's eyes. "You may be right. Perhaps the whole thing will die down." He stood, charged with excitement. "She'll come to her senses. If not, maybe I can give him a little incentive. There's nothing like money to change a man's mind, if that's what he's after."

"And if he loves her?"

"Oh, I have no doubt that he'll duck out when the going gets tough. Yes, Madeline, it's only a matter of time. I'll give them the biggest wedding this town has ever seen and a honeymoon in England. Then I'll offer him the job he's probably angling for anyway." He beamed, and the years fell away. "I'll scare the stuffings out of him with our way of life. He'll see he can never fit in. Yes, my dear, I believe it'll work!" He bent down and kissed his wife's forehead absentmindedly as he made plans.

&

It would be a wedding Houston would talk about for years. Mr. and Mrs. Seachrist opened their purse strings and dug deep. Nothing was too good for their only daughter and her new husband-to-be.

Mrs. Seachrist was in a state of near collapse by the time the day arrived, for Cleo and Tom wanted to be married as soon as possible. "Before Mother and Father change their minds!" she told Tom.

Mr. Seachrist was a bit disappointed when Tom declined his offer to work with his company, but he didn't push. Nor did he offer Tom money to call the whole thing off. No, it was increasingly apparent that the young man loved his daughter. Furthermore, where Cleo was concerned, Henry would strain all his resources to guarantee her happiness. And if this made her happy, so be it. He could wait.

For Tom, the three months before the wedding were a nightmare of social niceties and obligations. He had asked his boss for some time off, and with a wink of understanding, the boss had granted it. It was a good thing, for Cleo had crammed his days full of fittings at the tailor, parties and dinners with her friends, and a sundry other nonessentials. He took all the activity surrounding the wedding with consternation and a little awe. He had never seen anyone spend as much money as quickly as his bride-to-be! But she dismissed his concerns with an airy wave of her hand. "Oh, my parents want to do it, Tom, darling. Don't deprive them."

As for Cleo, she felt that when she and Tom returned from their honeymoon, he would join her father's firm and they would buy a house not too far away. Life would go on as before, but with the addition of a handsome new husband with whom to share her bliss. It was a fairy tale come true at last. Only one thing marred her joy. She suspected that her parents' dramatic change of heart about her marriage was not due to Tom's overpowering personality, but to their love for her. She had gotten what she wanted, after all, just as she had boasted to Tom she would.

It was not altogether a comfortable thought, and her conscience pricked her.

Cleo was more than a little nervous at the thought of meeting Tom's family—especially his mother. When she confessed this to Mattie, her friend only laughed. "Oh, I'm sure it's quite the other way around. She's probably terrified of meeting *you*. After all, she's only a rancher's wife. Besides, why wouldn't she love you?"

But when Mrs. Kinney arrived for the wedding, her other son in tow, she and Cleo struck sparks on sight. A tall woman, pared down to the bone, the woman appeared to have been chiseled out of the sallow land from which she came. Under her hat, her iron-gray hair was pulled back in a severe bun. She wore no makeup and only a single gold band on her left hand.

When Cleo and her mother came downstairs, they were met by the thin-lipped woman standing ramrod straight in their beautiful receiving room, her son slightly behind her. It was clear that he was wearing a new suit and that he was not yet comfortable in it.

Mrs. Seachrist moved gracefully to receive her guests and to put them both at ease. "Hello, Mrs. Kinney. And this must be Robert. Welcome to our home."

"Where is my son?" were the unfortunate first words from Mrs. Kinney's lips.

Madeline Seachrist ignored the tactless question and looked questioningly at her daughter. "Why, I believe he had a fitting for his morning suit, didn't he, dear?"

"Yes. He said he'd join us as soon as he was through at the tailor's."

At this, Mrs. Kinney fixed her sharp gaze on Cleo, who began to feel like a mare at auction under her future mother-in-law's intense scrutiny.

"Please sit down, and I'll ring for tea," Madeline Seachrist said pleasantly, hoping to ease the awkward moments. Rarely had she met anyone with whom she couldn't form a reasonably happy relationship, no matter how brief. For Cleo's sake, she would exert all her charms on this rather unpleasant woman.

As Madeline chatted with Mrs. Kinney and her son, she made a rapid inventory of Tom's relatives. Though his mother was not dressed in style according to Houston dictates and in spite of her rude entrance, she seemed completely at ease in the opulent room. And she handled her teacup with an elegance and grace that belied her crude background. She began to wonder if Tom had not told them the entire truth about his family background. Perhaps Cleo hadn't made a mistake, after all. Good breeding always shows.

But when she and Cleo filled Mrs. Kinney in on plans for the wedding and European honeymoon, she seemed singularly unimpressed. "Waste of good money if you ask me." Still, Madeline refused to be goaded into any kind of unpleasantness with this woman, so she chose to ignore the tart remark.

Cleo wanted very much to like Mrs. Kinney, for Tom's sake, if not for her own. *But she isn't making this any easier,* Cleo decided. And watching her mother graciously handle the difficult situation filled her with new admiration.

In spite of Mrs. Seachrist's skillful maneuvering through the rough sea of conversation, Mrs. Kinney's eyes made many a pointed reference to the gilded clock on the mantel.

"I do think Tom will be here any minute," said Cleo at last.

"I should certainly hope so," retorted Mrs. Kinney.

As if on command, Tom's handsome self appeared at the door. "Ma, Robert! It's so good to see you." He went quickly to embrace his mother and to clap Robert on the back.

"Tea, Tom?" asked Mrs. Seachrist.

"Thank you, ma'am." He accepted the delicate china teacup and, balancing it carefully, walked over to Cleo's chair. "Hello, darling, you're looking beautiful today," he greeted her, bending over to drop a kiss on her upturned mouth.

"Thank you. All done at the tailor's?"

"All done. And ready for a wedding." He grinned.

"Since you obviously intend to go through with this, son," said Mrs. Kinney who had been sullenly observing this little tableau, "I have a gift for you and your bride." With a hint of a smile hovering on her tight lips, she dug into the small bag on her lap and produced a ring. "It's my husband's grandmother's. All the Kinney men have given it to their brides. It's my wish that you wear it, Miss Seachrist." She handed the ring to Tom, who seemed perplexed, but accepted it.

"I—I don't know what to say, Mrs. Kinney," stammered Cleo when Tom had placed the ring on her finger. And truly she didn't. It was a fairly large diamond in the ugliest setting she had ever seen. She hated it, but what could she do but wear it? Swallowing her dismay, she looked up and said sweetly, "Thank you very much for the. . .ring."

Something akin to triumph glittered in the woman's eyes, but she acknowledged the comment with a nod.

When the chauffeur had at long last taken Tom and his family to the hotel and she was alone with her mother, Cleo burst into tears. "She hates me! I've never known anyone to be so mean! And just look at this ring! It's awful! Oh, Mother, how can I possibly show this thing to my friends?"

"There, there, my sweet," comforted Mrs. Seachrist, "she doesn't hate you. She doesn't even know you. Give her time." Her mother laughed softly. "You don't have to live with her. Be nice to her for the time she's here. As for the ring, we can have it reset. The stone is rather nice, and it seemed to give her great joy to give it to you. Think of it as a love gift and cherish it for that reason."

Cleo lifted her tearstained face. "How can you be so cheerful about all this, Mother? You didn't want me to marry Tom in the first place."

"All your father and I want is your happiness, darling. I believe Tom loves you and that you love him. We can manage to do whatever else is necessary. . ." Mrs. Seachrist gave her daughter a dazzling smile, "even if it means being nice to that old battle-ax for the entire week!"

Cleo smiled through her tears. "How could someone as nice as Tom have a mother like that?" She shuddered. "At least, after the wedding she'll go home and leave us in peace. But what have I done to make her dislike me so?"

Madeline slanted an appraising look at her daughter. "Could be she's jealous. After all, she's no longer the only woman in Tom's life."

"Were you and Father jealous, too?"

"Maybe a little, at first." She paused. "I hesitate to say this, Cleo, but if. . .well, if things don't work out the way you thought, you can always come home. Promise me you'll do that."

"I promise, Mother. But don't worry. My life with Tom will be perfect. Just wait and see."

But later, when Madeline Seachrist slipped between her satin sheets, she was deeply troubled. No matter how one looked at it, it was an unfortunate beginning.

# Chapter 4

With the fairy-tale wedding and honeymoon in England only a beautiful memory, the newlyweds came home to a round of parties to welcome them to their new place in Houston society. If not a native-born son, Tom was now related to the Seachrists by marriage and therefore entitled to their civility, if not their full acceptance.

Tom went to work for Henry, the young couple found a nice old house near the Seachrists, and they settled down to begin their married life in earnest. Tom, however, was constantly amazed at the amount of money flowing out of his small bank account. He was reluctant to accept money from his in-laws but had no choice if he was to make Cleo happy, for it was soon apparent that she had no concept of the value of a dollar. But she was happy and she made him happy, and Cleo and her parents never dreamed how often he compromised his honor to keep things that way.

Tom and Cleo spent a great deal of time with J.J. and Mattie, who were soon to be married. He liked J.J., who wasn't the typical spoiled rich man's son, but knew what it was to earn a living. His father had seen to it that he started at the bottom of the business and worked his way up. Mattie, too, was a true friend to both of them. Life was sweet. . .until the telegram.

It was from his brother Robert. "Come home immediately. Ma's very sick."

Tom walked up the stairs with a heavy tread to break the news to Cleo.

"Oh, Tom, how sick is she? Is she going to die?" Cleo's eyes filled with tears of compassion. Though she had gotten off to a poor start with Tom's mother, she knew he loved her dearly.

"I have no idea. I can't remember my mother being sick a day in her life." He looked at Cleo sadly. "I have to go to her, you know."

"Then we'll go together." Her voice was firm, despite the momentary twinge of dread.

"I can't ask you to do that. I don't know how long I might be gone."

"That's exactly why I'm going with you," she said, her tone deliberately light-hearted. "I don't want some good-looking rancher's daughter stealing you away from me!"

"But your parents. . ."

"You come first, Tom. They'll understand. And we'll be back before you know it. . .just as soon as your mother is well again."

The train rocked and swayed, clacking briskly across the endless miles. An unusually cold November had banished any vestige of green from the barren landscape, and as Cleo looked out the window, she watched in dismay as the lushness gave way to sandy desert. Stunted mesquite stood guard over tufts of buffalo grass dried by the ceaseless wind.

*Maybe this is what people mean by* godforsaken, she thought. She hoped not, because for the first time in her life, she had the feeling she was going to need a lot of divine guidance.

"Doesn't look much like Houston, does it?" Tom glanced at her with a worried frown, acutely aware of the radical differences she would soon encounter.

Her eyes were a bit too bright when she answered him. "It's prettier in the spring, I'm sure."

"Some years," he confessed honestly. " 'Course, with no rain, it's hard to tell what will happen come spring. It's been dry for nearly four years." He lifted her hand and kissed it. "I just hope you'll be happy here."

Heavy on his mind was the scene at the station. Her parents had stood, tight-lipped and mute, as Cleo had quipped about pioneering on the prairie and then kissed them good-bye with a certain bravado.

Tom had tried to prepare her for her new life, but she had remained determinedly optimistic and cheerful and simply continued to believe that "it wouldn't be for long." At her cavalier attitude, he had had grave misgivings. But he couldn't bear the thought of leaving her behind and so was grateful for her youthful ignorance.

"Did you sleep well last night?" Tom asked.

She smiled back at him. "Like a baby. I'm so happy. . .a little scared, too. But I'm with the man I love. Whatever happens out here is the stuff family yarns are made of. We'll share it with our children." She pulled her coat more tightly around her. It was the full-length mink her parents had given her last year for her coming-out party.

Tom felt the sleek fur brush against him and remembered how he had tried to talk Cleo out of bringing it. Nothing on earth could be more inappropriate attire for life on a ranch! He feared ridicule for her. Things would be hard enough without her estranging herself from folks before they got to know her.

The coat was a vivid reminder of the first argument they'd had in their short married life, and Cleo stirred uneasily at his pointed glance. To divert his attention, she asked, "Will it be long?"

He sighed and turned to look out the window. "No. We should pull up at Monaghan's Wells soon. Robert will meet us there with the wagon. Couldn't use the buggy because you brought too much stuff." His teasing tone brought the memory of another tiff. The atmosphere had been tense as they packed for their enforced farewell to civilization.

"You'll be glad I brought all that stuff someday. Just wait and see. If I hadn't brought it, you'd have had to buy it for me after I got out here," Cleo said smugly.

Tom arched a dark brow. "When we hit that sand, you'll know why the settlers littered the trails with their castoffs all the way to California!"

Cleo regarded her husband with wondering eyes. There was much she had yet to discover about him. Memories to make together. He was like a big book she had yet to read, a new page to be explored each day. The prospect was thrilling.

Every ten miles or so, they passed a section house belonging to the railroad. These were all identically painted in yellow with black trim. The Texas and Pacific Railroad had made settlement possible in this lonely area, Tom explained. Thousands of Chinese had chopped the dry ground back and laid the rails, pushing the telegraph lines ahead of it. Wells had been dug and houses built along the double steel fingers reaching for the coast of California. The railroad was the lifeline of West Texas, a metal umbilical cord.

"Tom! What's that?" Cleo leaned closer to the open window.

"Those are the Sand Hills. Pretty, aren't they? Everyone comes out here for picnics and celebrations."

Cleo's gaze traveled over the huge shifting sand dunes, pale yellow in the late afternoon sun. The watery light revealed stubby bushes and little else. "What an odd place to party."

"What's really odd is that there are water wells all over it. Only have to dig down eighteen inches to hit the sweetest water you ever tasted. Back a ways there's a big seep pond with tall willow trees all around it. Indians have used it for no telling how long. As a boy I found plenty of arrowheads there." His eyes took on a faraway look. "Used to picnic there, slide down the dunes, chase the rabbits. It was great fun. I'll take you there first chance we get. . .when it's warmer, of course."

"Sounds a little like the beach," Cleo offered.

"Better than the beach. No sharks!" He grinned, carefully refraining from mentioning the rattlesnakes.

The train was slowing for its stop at Monaghan's Wells, and they began to collect their things to get off. When they walked onto the platform, the sun was already falling behind the horizon.

"Over here!" Robert shouted. Stepping up to greet them, he embraced his brother and tipped his hat formally to his sister-in-law. "Welcome home."

Tom pounded him on the back. "It's good to see you. How's Ma?"

Robert avoided Tom's direct gaze. "Okay, I guess. She's still poorly. Hasn't left her bed for two weeks. Still don't know what's wrong with her. She won't let me get the doctor."

While the men loaded the wagon, Cleo became aware of an unbelievable stench. Robert explained that it was the holding pens, where a restless herd of cattle was confined a short distance from the platform. The cold wind carrying the foul odor had reached her nostrils, and now she felt nauseous.

"You all right?" Tom asked solicitously as he took her arm to guide her to the wagon. "You look a little pale."

"Ugh!" Cleo wrinkled her nose. "I think I was just introduced to a dose of prairie perfume. A little overwhelming, but I'm fine."

Tom grinned at her and helped her into the wagon while Robert climbed in the back to steady the boxes of supplies they had brought. "It won't be long now, honey. Can't wait to show you off to some of my friends in Kermit."

The wagon seat was not so friendly. Even with the padding of her coat, Cleo felt every jolt. The road between Monaghan's Wells and Kermit, if it could be called a road, was deep sand and unexpected holes. Periodically the men got out and used shovels and hoes to dig out the sunken wheels, putting bear grass down for traction. And then there were the wire gates. Thirteen of them to open and close behind them as the horses struggled to pull the wagon through the cloying sand.

In the outskirts of Kermit, they turned off, moving in a westerly direction toward the ranch. The road there wasn't any better. In fact, it was worse, for it wasn't traveled as often.

"You're a real trouper, honey," Tom said admiringly, looking over at Cleo. "I haven't heard a word of complaint out of you the whole trip. Now, just watch for the light of the lantern."

In the growing darkness, Cleo couldn't make out much of the countryside, but she could see the stars. The entire sky was ablaze with the reflection of a jillion tiny suns. "Oh, Tom, I've never seen so many stars in my whole life! And they seem so close! I do believe I could reach up and touch them. Makes me think maybe there has to be a God up there."

"Most everybody out here believes in God. Have to. We need all the help we can get just to survive."

Strange that they had never discussed it before. "Do *you*. . .believe in God, I mean?" It was suddenly very important that she know.

Tom shrugged. "I'm not much of a churchgoing man. I like to do my meditating in the saddle. But when I'm out riding and see how everything's laid out, well, I guess we'd have to be crazy not to believe in Somebody bigger than us. Robert here's the churchgoer though."

"There's a church out here?" she asked, unaware until now that her brother-in-law had moved up to join them.

"Yes, ma'am. Meets every time the circuit rider comes. We have a service, singing, and dinner on the grounds." Sheepishly he added, "I look at God a different way from Tom. I believe He's there all the time, not just in an emergency."

"I'll admit He gives us the good things. But who do we blame for the bad things that happen?" Tom challenged.

"The rain falls on the good and the evil equally, the Bible says. Guess we won't know all the answers 'til we get to heaven."

Tom snorted. "I won't need them then."

"All I really know," Robert continued softly, "is that Jesus is my Savior and that He's waitin' for you to come into the flock, too, brother."

"Now, you know how I feel about sheepherders, Robert," Tom teased.

Hearing Tom's lighthearted rejoinder, Cleo felt distinctly uneasy. This whole conversation had taken a strange turn. Though she was anything but a dedicated Christian, she did have a certain respect for those who claimed to be. And now, riding underneath the canopy of brilliant stars spangling the black velvet sky like diamonds in a jeweler's case, she was reminded that she really ought to give the matter serious consideration. . .someday.

As the wagon rolled past several windmills, the breeze playing upon their giant blades, she seized upon a safer topic of conversation. "That's a spooky sound."

"It's the sound of life out here, honey. Windmills made it possible to live in this place. I'd forgotten how quiet it can be. Guess I still have the noise of the city ringing in my ears. If you listen real carefully, you may even hear a coyote singing of a lost love."

She glanced about, her eyes wide. "There really are coyotes out here? I thought that was just in western stories."

"Honey, that's where you are," Tom explained patiently. "The West. The frontier. Oh, someday we'll catch up with the rest of the world. We just need a little time."

"And rain," Robert put in. "Haven't had a good rain in so long the rattlers have been knockin' on the door for a drink."

"You are joking, aren't you?" Cleo shivered as she tried to read her new brother-in-law's expression in the starlight.

"No point in scaring her to death before she gets there, Robert," Tom said mildly.

"Sorry, Cleo," said Robert. "Don't worry, rattlers sleep in the winter. You won't have to watch out for them. . .except on warm days. . .'til spring."

She grinned at Tom weakly. "I *think* that makes me feel a lot better."

Despite the bumping of the wagon, Cleo found herself drowsing against Tom's shoulder. So she had no sense of how much time had passed when he finally roused her. "Wake up, Cleo. There it is."

She opened her eyes but saw nothing except the darkness, thick as a quilt, stretching before them. "Where?"

"See that little light over there? That's the lantern on the windmill. Tom must've hung it out."

In the pale starlight, Cleo could see the outline of a tall windmill standing like a sentinel over a small house. The lantern's unblinking eye guided their approach.

Cleo fought off the feeling of despair as she made out the contours of a tiny house. As they neared, the door opened and a small figure stood silhouetted in the light that spilled out into the night.

"There's Ma," Robert said. "She must be feeling better."

Cleo was cheered by this news. Maybe their visit would be even shorter than she'd hoped.

They pulled up in front of the house, and Tom helped Cleo down. He took off his Stetson as he embraced his mother. "Hello, Ma."

"Hello, son. I'm glad you're home. We been needin' ya around here."

Cleo saw Robert duck his head and turn away. Since no one seemed inclined to acknowledge her presence, Cleo stepped up to greet her mother-in-law, who was in her nightclothes, a large shawl pulled around her frail figure. "Hello again."

The woman made no attempt to embrace her daughter-in-law but merely nodded. Her voice was firm and tinged with a heavier rural accent than Cleo remembered as she said, "Hope your trip wasn't too hard on ya."

"No, it was quite pleasant. An adventure, really."

"Well, come on in. The boys can git your things." She led the way into the house. "Robert, fetch the lantern off the windmill."

Buttery soft lamplight softened the austerity of the room, half of which served as a kitchen and the other half as living quarters. Cleo lowered herself onto a well-worn sofa and looked around. It was a practical room, with odd touches of culture. A leather-bound set of the classics, obviously handled by many loving hands, stood in the bookcase.

"Would you like a cup of coffee, or do you just want to go on to bed?"

Not knowing whom Mrs. Kinney was addressing, Cleo turned to Tom for guidance.

"I think we'll go on to bed, Ma," he said, "We're all beat. There'll be time to talk in the morning."

As Mrs. Kinney turned for her bedroom, she said, "You can have your old room, Tom. Robert can sleep in here."

Cleo felt a twinge of guilt, knowing they had pushed Robert out of his room, and tried to communicate her appreciation with a smile. But she was too exhausted to argue. Obediently she followed Tom to their new bedroom.

"This is it," he said, seeing the spartan surroundings through Cleo's eyes. "You all right, honey? You look a little pale."

"I'm tired, that's all." She smiled at the worried look on his face. "I'll be fine after a good night's sleep."

When she surveyed the sagging bed with its patchwork quilt, even that prospect seemed doubtful. And long after Tom lay sleeping, she was still awake, pondering the enormity of this change in her life. As much as she loved her husband, would she be able to adjust to his world? The thought was heavy on her mind as she slipped into a troubled sleep.

～

The aroma of frying bacon and hot coffee beckoned Cleo from the warmth of her nest beside Tom.

"Morning, sleepyhead," he said softly and pulled her back against him. His face looked relaxed and loving in the morning light.

"I'll cuddle later. Right now I need to step into the bathroom," she said with modesty.

He grinned wickedly. "Then you'd better wear that fur coat. The privy is down by the barn."

"Oh, no! Tom, are you serious?"

"Never more serious. It's at the back of the house," he said and ducked the pillow strategically aimed at his head.

Cleo threw him a dirty look and wrapped a warm, fluffy robe about her, then hurried down the outside path. "Now this is ridiculous," she mumbled to herself as she opened the wooden door and peered in. Never having seen a privy in her life, she was amused at the quaint single hole carved into the wooden bench. But the iciness of the seat sent a shock wave up her spine.

She thought of her luxurious quarters back home—the spacious bedroom with private bath—and gritted her teeth. *It'll only be for a little while,* she reminded herself.

Cleo had almost made it back to the house when she ran into Robert. Unable to hide her embarrassment, she blushed furiously. "Oh, good morning!"

Robert's own ruddy complexion deepened when he spotted Cleo in her nightclothes, and he did the only thing a Texas gentleman could do under the circumstances. He tipped his hat and moved on silently.

Tom was pulling on a pair of well-worn boots when Cleo returned. "Why don't you get dressed, honey, and after breakfast we'll go riding and I'll show you around."

"Do I have time for a quick bath first?" She was eager to remove the grime from the train ride the day before and had noticed a metal tub standing in a small cubicle at the rear of the house when she'd passed by on her way to the privy.

"A very quick one. But," he paused, hesitating to tell her this news, "you need to know. . ."

"Yes, Tom?" She turned to him with a bright smile.

"There isn't any running hot water. It'll have to be heated. But I can put on a kettle if you like."

The idea that he was joking died quickly. "I'll help you. Guess I'd better learn everything right away," she said on a positive note.

As they entered the kitchen, Mrs. Kinney was busy at the stove. She made no comment when Tom got out the two big pots, filled them with water at the kitchen sink, and put them on the back burners of the wood-burning stove. "Mornin'," she said not looking up.

"Good morning," Cleo replied and beat a hasty retreat to the privacy of their bedroom, not quite ready to begin the day with Mrs. Kinney.

When at last the tub was half filled, she added some cold water from the tap and stepped in gingerly. Opening her little travel bag, she got out the soap she had brought, eyeing with horror the lye soap on the little shelf over the tub.

When she drained the tub after her bath, she saw a fine netting of red sand left in the bottom. *I could have scrubbed myself without the soap,* she thought.

Hastily she put on a split skirt, a silk blouse, and her English riding boots, feeling more like herself than at any time since she'd left home. *Funny how a night's sleep and a good bath changes one's perspective,* she thought, combing her hair and pulling on the black derby hat she always wore when riding. With a final satisfied look in the mirror, she made her way back to the kitchen.

"Good morning again," she said cheerfully as she paused at the door. "The bacon and coffee smell divine."

Tom was frankly admiring her as she took her place beside him at the table. "You look as fresh as a prairie dawn," he said.

She *felt* more like a prize mare at a stock show as the three of them stared at her. Mrs. Kinney was dressed in a faded cotton skirt that reached her ankles. An apron covered most of her front. Cleo knew at once that she herself was overdressed, but these were the most casual riding clothes she owned. She smiled her thanks at her husband, then accepted the mug of hot coffee Mrs. Kinney handed her.

Cleo's gaze traveled around the plain room. In the daylight she could more clearly see the wooden cupboards, some missing their knobs, gaping open above the worn cabinets. An old cookie jar, shaped like a fat man, stood on the side of the cabinet next to the wood-burning stove. At least, Cleo thought, the room was clean and felt homey. She began to relax.

"How do you want your eggs?" Mrs. Kinney asked.

"However you're preparing them will be fine." Cleo had vowed to do everything possible to get along with this strange woman while she was under her roof, but she did hate eggs with runny centers.

The pale yellow yolks quivered as Mrs. Kinney set the plate in front of her, but Cleo bravely tasted the fare. "Mmm, these eggs are wonderful," she said truthfully. Tom put a dab of preserves on a piece of toast for her.

Tom glanced at her with a grin. "We get the plums from a thicket in the Sand Hills every summer. It's a big family affair, and most everybody joins in. Of course, Ma makes the best preserves in the county."

"You always did have a sweet tongue, Tom," Mrs. Kinney protested, but she couldn't hide the pleasure in her voice.

She had prepared a huge breakfast of bacon, eggs, biscuits, gravy, small beef steaks, and coffee. "You boys eat hearty now," she urged, "there's a lot of work to be done today. It's good to have you home, son. We've missed ya."

Mrs. Kinney sat down at the table but ate sparingly of the meal. "Need to check on the stock out in the east pasture. They may need some extra feed. No rain, no grass, so they're gettin' mighty hungry by now. There's cottonseed cakes in the barn, Tom. You and Robert can load the wagon."

She was preparing to list the rest of the chores when Tom cut in. "Wait, Ma. I want to know what's going on here." He leveled her a penetrating look. "First, I hear you're deathly sick. Then I come home to find you on your feet. Just why *did* you call for me?"

"Druther not talk family business right now," she said testily, eyeing Cleo.

Tom bridled. "Cleo is my wife, Ma. That makes her part of the family. And she's entitled to your courtesy as well as your hospitality."

There was stunned silence around the table before Mrs. Kinney replied. " 'Course she is, son," she said in a conciliatory tone. "Just didn't think her first meal was the time to be talkin' about hard times, that's all."

Tom considered her answer, studying her expression. He couldn't tell if she was patronizing him or not. Rarely had he been able to read his mother's face, for she had always kept her emotions carefully hidden away from prying eyes.

"I came home to find out what's going on," he said quietly. "I left a good paying job, my new home, and our way of life. If I'm not needed here, then I'll get back to that life."

"All right, son. I'll lay it out for ya," said Mrs. Kinney. "We're late with the payments on the ranch, and the bank is trying to foreclose on us."

Tom let out a long whistle. "Land rich and cash poor. The code of the rancher," he said grimly.

"Yep." A sad smile barely reached Mrs. Kinney's eyes.

"What's the bank going to do with all this land? Things are so bad there's no way they can sell it."

Mrs. Kinney took a sip of her coffee. "Seems like they've discovered oil down by Pecos. Old Kirby's got the itch. Buyin' up all the land he can get his hands on."

"But Pecos is seventy-five miles away. What does that have to do with us?"

"They struck in Ranger, too, and we're sittin' smack-dab between."

"There's no oil out here, Ma," Tom insisted. "People have already looked for it. Kirby's just whistling 'Dixie.' Why, there's barely a rise for fifty miles. How can there be oil?"

"Probably isn't, but Kirby is buyin' up the land anyway. And leasin' what he can't buy. That's not our problem. Money is." Cleo looked at Tom's stricken face and kept silent.

"I'll go talk to him tomorrow. Maybe I can get an extension." He smiled wanly. "Meanwhile, we'll knock out some of the work that's been piling up around here. How many hands you got working now, Ma?"

"Just three. They're hard workers, but they don't know a whole lot about ranching. They need a strong hand behind them."

Robert blushed deeply.

"I know you do your best, son," said Mrs. Kinney, noting her younger son's embarrassment, "but they need someone who won't be timid about tellin' them what to do and when to do it. With things so bad, I don't have the heart to fire 'em. They have families, too."

Cleo could see the new resolve as Tom flexed his jaw. "Robert and I will see to things, Ma. Don't worry."

"Just so you know. I *have* been sick. Sick at heart, I guess. I've been through this so many times. . .don't think I've got the strength to fight it again. Not without your pa."

Tom placed his hand over his mother's work-worn one.

There was a hint of tears in the woman's eyes. "We'll make out, son, now that you're here. Now get out of here and get to work."

Tom rose from the table and squared his shoulders. "Come on, Cleo. You can find out what a real cowboy does on a ranch."

"Better put on something warm to wear over them clothes," counseled Mrs. Kinney. "But not that mink coat. It would set us back a ways if the banker was to see it."

Cleo felt the sting of the waspish tongue, and Tom answered instead. "Now, Ma, don't you go trying to sell that coat while we're gone. Or wear it, either," he said in an attempt to lighten the mood of the past few moments.

"Humph" was her only reply to his needling.

As they walked to the corral, Cleo thought about the diamond ring Mrs. Kinney had given her. Her mother-in-law could have sold that ring and used the money to pay off the mortgage on the ranch. Suddenly it took on new value for Cleo. She'd keep the ring and never have it reset. It was a family heirloom she meant to pass on to her children, along with the story of their grandmother's sacrifice.

"What are you going to do now, Tom?" she asked softly as he saddled the horses.

"Work today. Talk tomorrow." He held her horse as she swung up into the saddle. "Let's just take one day at a time."

She nodded meekly. She wanted to talk about money. Her father's money. But it could wait. . .until tomorrow.

# Chapter 5

In the space of a morning's ride, Cleo was alternately shocked, dismayed, enthralled, and disappointed in the Texas landscape. The trackless land rolled on for miles, broken only by an occasional rise. Stunted mesquite trees, cold-shocked cactus, and patches of dried grass ran haphazardly across the vast prairie.

From Tom, Cleo learned that the land had been carved out by only two elements—the constant wind and extreme temperatures—for water had not touched this desolate stretch of country in a very long time. In places, the wind had eroded a corner of a rise, exposing the red earth under the ratted prairie grass that competed for breathing space. The surface was truly red. The varicolored layers of earth beneath could be seen like the layers of a cake.

"Does it ever snow out here?" Cleo asked, huddling into the heavy leather jacket Tom had brought out for her. Behind them, Robert rattled along in the wagon that held cottonseed cakes for the cows.

"Once a year. In February." Tom squinted from beneath his hat as he scanned the horizon. What he saw—the vast nothingness—was a balm to his spirit. Houston and Galveston bustled with busyness, with people rushing about madly, hurrying to work, hurrying to have fun. Here all was relatively serene.

The furrow returned to his brow when he thought about his mother's revelation at breakfast. There was never enough cash to go around. What little came in from cattle sales had to be plowed back into improving the herd or making needed repairs around the place. Land was sacred to a rancher, something to be worked and held on to at all costs. Tom's optimism had been intended to encourage his mother, but the truth was that he was as worried about the money as she. Losing the ranch would finish her off, would end his dreams, too. The ranch was everything—their roots, their inheritance to be passed on to their children and grandchildren. He had dreamed of building an empire like his father before him. He had temporarily abandoned the dream in a young man's pursuit of adventure, only to return and find it more precious than he ever could have imagined.

Well, Tom Kinney was back, and he intended to fight for his dream. He had a lovely young woman by his side, one who loved him more than he deserved. Their months in Houston had been a shallow sojourn, a way of life he knew now he never could have truly embraced. Now, for the first time in years, he felt a vital

389

new excitement throbbing in his veins.

He shifted in the saddle and turned to Cleo. Seeing her in the bright November sunlight only heightened his joy and his resolve. He would save the ranch, not just for his mother, but for Cleo. . .and their children!

"Beautiful, isn't it?" he exulted, caught up in the grandeur of his vision.

"It—it's so. . .*big*," she breathed, trying hard to find the beauty he was seeing. "Where are the cattle?"

"Out in the east section. There's better grass there. . .what there is of it. Before I left, it was pretty decent. Now things are looking mighty dry."

"Is there a lake or something out there?"

Tom laughed. "No, something more dependable. Windmills, remember? That old Eclipse near the house has been pumping water forever. Pa had it brought in when he first claimed this land. The water isn't far down. Just have to find it. Indians knew all the natural wells, but we've made our own. When people travel on horseback, they keep their bearings by using the windmills as landmarks. Each one is as individual as a horse with its own peculiar sound."

"How do you know where to look for the water?"

"Found ours by using a peach branch fork." He laughed at the look of disbelief on her face. "Amazing thing."

"Maybe you could find oil that way, too."

Tom's face clouded. "I don't want to find oil. We don't need that stuff out here. This is cattle country."

"I'm sorry. I only meant to make a joke," she apologized lamely.

He flashed her a grin. "Guess you hit a nerve. Just remember to keep your priorities straight. Out here, cows come first."

"Ahead of people?"

Tom flexed a muscle in his jaw. "A man can only hope he never has to make that choice."

They rode in silence for a time until the tension eased while Cleo tried to bridge the distance between them. Just then she spotted the cattle, moving like a colony of insects across an endless ocean of space. As they neared, the animals ambled toward them, anticipating the food. The men scattered the seedcakes from the wagon, dropping them in a long line to string out the hungry cows.

"Oh, Tom, they're beautiful. They're the same color as the dirt, all red rust. And their little white faces. . ." Cleo watched as the cattle began to eat, lowing in contentment. But she was grateful that the wind was blowing in the opposite direction.

A dream spider wound a silken web of unreality around her as she looked on. Could she really be here in this place, seeing these things with her own eyes? Her husband—a cattleman? Only a short while ago, she had thought him some rich man's son on holiday as she'd watched him at play in the blue waters of the Gulf.

Was she also poor now that she was married to a poor man? She still had all her family's resources at her fingertips, but if she lived on what her new husband could provide for her, wouldn't that make her poor? A quick stab of disloyalty pierced her. *I love him, no matter what,* she thought stubbornly. And though everything was still new, she had the feeling she had belonged to Tom all her life and that eternity was just beginning.

❧

That night in the privacy of their bedroom, Cleo tried to approach Tom about their financial plight. She had thought about it off and on all day as they rode around the ranch. Instinctively she knew that his male pride was involved, and she tried to be tactful.

"Darling, I know how much the ranch means to you, especially now that I've seen it for myself." She trailed a caressing finger across his cheek as they lay in bed. "Please let me write to Father. . ."

But that was as far as she got before he turned on her in fury. "This is *my* world! Your father's money has nothing to do with my ranch." Seeing the shock on her face, he relented. "I'm sorry, honey, I didn't mean to yell at you, but out here I'm my own man," he continued with great earnestness. "Your family has been good to me—the wedding, the house, the job—but we both know they did it for you. Out here I have to do things my way. I can't depend on your father's money to help me out of every problem I face from now on. Do you understand what I'm saying?"

She was trying to. "Has it been that difficult for you?" Her words were tinged with anger and hurt.

"Sometimes," he admitted. "But I wanted you to be happy, and I knew I couldn't give you all those things. Not right away." He sighed. "Things are different now, Cleo. Now you live in my world. It's not what you've been used to, but it's mine, it's what I have to give. I hope it's enough."

He wrapped his arms around her, pulling her close and inhaling the fragrance of her hair against his face. "I love you, and I promise you'll never do without the most important things. I may not be able to give you luxuries, but I can make you happy. Trust me. Let me do it my way. At my own pace. In a few years, this ranch could be one of the best in the state. I know it."

Cleo was still, absorbing the impact of his words. "You're saying it would spoil things if I got the money for you?"

"Something like that. All I'm asking for is a little more time. Can you give it to me?"

At the look of pleading in his eyes, there was nothing to do but go along with him. "All right," she agreed quietly. "We'll do it your way. But if the time ever comes. . ." The rest of her words were closed off by the pressure of his lips on hers. *This is all I really need,* she thought. *His love is enough. Everything else can wait.*

⟿

The next morning Cleo endured the ritual of a lukewarm bath in a cold room, for this was the day they were going to town to see the banker.

Before breakfast she dressed with care, putting on a kelly green morning dress from her trousseau and adjusting her stockings. Pulling on a green cloche over her dark hair, she took a final look in the mirror and smiled at her reflection. This outfit always made her feel attractive and feminine.

Hurrying into the other room, where Tom and the others were already seated, Cleo took her place at the table. "Good morning."

There were mumbled greetings and a great deal of shuffling around the table. Cleo looked up in surprise. "Is something wrong?"

"Honey," began Tom in a strained voice, "you can't go to the bank dressed like that. They'd laugh in my face."

"On the contrary. You know what Father always said: It takes money to make money. Bankers don't want to lend money to people who don't look as if they can pay them back, do they?" She arched her thin brows.

The brothers exchanged a look of confusion. "Maybe not in Houston," Tom spoke up, "but out here it makes the bankers feel righteous to give money to down-and-outers."

"Hey, Tom," said Robert slowly, "why not give 'em the Houston treatment? It just might work."

Tom chewed on a biscuit as he turned it over in his mind. "It just might," he echoed, grinning. "I'll change and be right with you, honey."

Cleo tried to make small talk with Mrs. Kinney and Robert while she waited, but it all sounded so silly. She was enormously relieved when Tom came back dressed in his best suit and his good boots. "You look mighty handsome, sir," she said, noting that the boots and the Stetson were a perfect complement to his rugged good looks.

"Why thank ya, ma'am," he drawled in an exaggerated voice.

Cleo had noted the distinction between Tom's softer speech and his family's country dialect, believing that it could be attributed to his time in the service and the desire to wash away the sand of the ranch. Since being home, however, he had occasionally lapsed into that familiar dialect. Right now, for example, she found it charming.

"Ready?" he asked as he pulled on the soft gray hat.

Cleo gathered up her purse and gloves. "Ready."

"Don't forget the coat" was Mrs. Kinney's only parting remark.

Tom helped Cleo into the mink. "If this doesn't impress them, nothing will."

He eyed the strand of pearls around her neck. "You don't have a big chunk of diamonds stashed away somewhere, do you?"

She smiled up at him and flashed the diamond ring his mother had given her. "Will this do?" She was moved to see a sheen of tears in the woman's eyes.

⟿

On the way to town, Tom had to stop several times to dig the carriage wheels out of the sand. Cleo sat on the seat, feeling the tug of unreality once more, and her mind wandered. *Here I am,* she thought, *in the middle of nowhere, stuck in the sand with a man I didn't even know six months ago, riding in a buggy to see a banker who can take away a ranch I don't care about from a woman who has been less than friendly to me. What am I doing here?*

But when Tom climbed in beside her again, she knew. "We'll get there," he assured her. " 'Course it might be next year."

She reached for his arm, tucking her hand through it, and snuggled close. His nearness, the familiar musky smell of him, was reassuring. She smiled at him, and they rolled on for several miles in companionable silence.

At last Cleo broke the silence. "What am I going to do about your mother?" she asked softly.

Tom clenched his jaw. "Just. . .wait. She'll come around. No one could resist you for very long."

But Cleo was not convinced. "I don't think I ever met anyone who disliked me so much and let me know it. At least the people in Houston are more subtle." She smiled sadly. "She won't even give me a chance."

"I know Ma. She'll come around." Tom forced a hearty tone, then he frowned. "She acted so nice at the wedding. I honestly thought things were going to be all right. Guess she had me fooled. Ma is strange. Living out here alone can do that to a person." He slipped his arm around her and squeezed hard. "You're more woman than she's used to coping with. Give her time."

*But how much time?* Cleo wondered. She had hoped to be back home in Houston to see the first daffodils. But now it appeared that Tom had other ideas.

She fought off the biting cold and eyed the desolation that stretched endlessly before them. Though they were traveling down the same road that had brought them here only a few days ago, everything looked strangely unfamiliar. It was disconcerting to see the same scenery over and over with nothing distinctive to mark its passage. "Tom, how on earth do the cows survive out here?"

He shrugged. "They're tough. It takes a lot of land to support one cow. That's why we need so much of it. But in the spring this prairie will green out, and if we get some rain, there will be plenty of grass. We'll round up the cattle and see who survived the cold and the coyotes. Brand the new calves. Save the best and move some to market for cash to operate on. It's not a bad life, really."

"Sounds like you sit back while the cows and bulls do all the work."

Tom flicked the reins to encourage the horse over a deep rut. "Come roundup time, you'll see. It's the hardest job I've ever done. And I've done some hard labor in my time." His eyes took on a faraway look. "It's a sight to behold. Men yelling and whistling. Cows calling to their calves, and the calves bellowing when the hot iron hits them. Bulls objecting to the slice of the knife. And sand. By gum, I think half my body is made up of sand!"

Cleo could not resist his little-boy look of pleasure. "And you love every minute of it! It's written all over your face." She felt herself longing to share more of his life, to understand his love for this land. A roundup sounded like fun. "Maybe we could have a barbecue in the spring after the roundup and invite Mattie and J.J. and my parents. . . ."

Spring. It sounded like forever. But maybe she could make it that long. Besides, she was confident Tom would be ready to get back to civilization as soon as he was sure the ranch was safe and operating in the black again.

"Let's take one thing at a time," he said, looking grim. "First, we go to the bank to do battle with the money-grubbing ogre who wants to cancel the whole deal."

Tom had no idea what the bank's reaction would be, for no one in the county had seen anyone like Cleo. But then the element of surprise was always useful during a fight, he thought with satisfaction.

"There it is—Wink," Tom said, gazing off into the distance. "Now don't expect too much," he warned.

Spread out ahead was the little town of Wink—all six buildings!

"There's the bank, of course," Tom pointed out as they rumbled into town. "The post office is in the general store, owned and operated by Mr. Blankenship and his wife. Slick Slattery owns the machine shop in town. And Mrs. Court has a house and lets out a room to Slick." He gestured toward a barn. "That's the livery stable over there. Blankenship's son takes care of it when there's any business. And down there is old Kirby's house." It was a nice home, with flowers planted and carefully tended in front of the little white picket fence. He shrugged. "That's all there is."

Cleo could feel Tom's tension as he pointed out the landmarks. Whether it was brought on by dread over their errand or by his desire that she approve, Cleo could not decide. "It's all so. . .quaint. You have everything you need here." She couldn't lie, but she didn't want to hurt his feelings either, and she thought she saw worry cloud his eyes as they made their way down the heavily rutted dirt street toward the bank.

It was not an impressive building, but it appeared solid. Built of red brick, the bank was fronted by a small porch supported by white columns.

Cleo took Tom's hand as she stepped from the carriage. A chill wind fanned her cheeks and ruffled her hair, and she pulled the coat more snugly around her.

Tom smiled down at her. "Ready?"

She took a steadying breath. "I think so."

The big smile she flashed him bolstered his courage, and Tom squared his shoulders to face the man who could wipe him out and end all their dreams.

He chose not to remove his gray Stetson inside the building, feeling that to do so would lessen his stature. He simply couldn't enter the bank, hat in hand. He needed an edge. His manner, along with his expensively dressed wife, just might get him the money he so desperately needed.

"Hello, Leaf," he greeted the young woman sitting at the front desk.

She was petite and attractive, Cleo thought, and could have been beautiful if she had known how to use the many beauty aids Cleo had packed in her little traveling bag. Cleo liked her immediately but felt a bit of pity for this young person trapped in this little spot in the road. She gave Leaf her warmest smile.

"Leaf, this is my wife, Cleo."

Leaf studied her openly, visually caressing Cleo's mink coat and fine clothes. "Why, I'd heard you got married, Tom." Not taking her eyes off Cleo, she rose gracefully and walked toward them, extending her hand. "Hello. Welcome to Wink."

Her eyes were a bit too bright and the smile held a note of falsity, but Cleo took her hand. "It's very nice to meet you. I could use a new friend so far from home."

"It does get a little lonely out here sometimes," admitted Leaf before she turned a warm smile on Tom. "I know Papa will be glad to see you, Tom. He talks about you a lot."

Tom laughed. "I'll just bet he does! Probably talks about me behind my back for leaving the ranch, doesn't he?"

Leaf laughed, a high tinkling sound. "Matter of fact, he does. He never did understand about that. But some of us did."

At the look Leaf gave Tom—hungry, sad, defeated—Cleo knew. Leaf was in love with her husband! The thought struck her like a bolt of lightning, and for a brief second, she was frightened.

But in the next instant, she had all the reassurance she needed.

"My wife and I would like to see your father, please," Tom said pointedly, taking Cleo's hand and tucking it possessively through his arm.

*So he knows Leaf is in love with him,* thought Cleo. There was no time to dwell on this discovery before she and Tom were ushered into Mr. Kirby's office.

The room was small by Texas standards and sparsely furnished. But there was no mistaking the Western decor. A stuffed longhorn cow's head hung on one wall, and the other walls appeared to have been marked with various brands, perhaps burned into the wood with branding irons, Cleo guessed. But it was the glass case standing on a table that made her blood run cold. On display was a live rattlesnake, coiled inside a cow's skull.

"You're safe, madam. Felix is sealed up real tight."

The room was pungent with cigar smoke that hovered in a visible cloud around the speaker. The man had stood to his feet and was moving briskly to greet them, dangling his cigar in one hand and extending the other for Tom's handshake.

The portly executive was wearing a suit, Cleo noted right away, the fine material stretched taut across an impressive bay window where a watch chain swung importantly. He had a full head of very white hair, and his eyebrows were wild and free as they roamed fiercely across his forehead. Sharp, snapping eyes took in every detail of Cleo's expensive attire as the banker took her hand and led her to an overstuffed chair opposite his desk.

Here was a man to be reckoned with, Cleo thought. She'd met his kind before, though never in a business transaction, of course. She listened carefully as the two men observed the rituals of greeting.

"Heard you'd got hitched, Tom. Appears you did quite well for yourself. She's a looker."

Cleo felt an undeniable spark of anger. This was the second time she had heard herself referred to as if she were not even in the room. It rankled her.

"Yeh, heard you married a Houston girl. Bet she finds West Texas a big surprise. Your ma doin' better?"

"She's still a bit off her feed, but she'll be good as new in no time." Tom sat down beside Cleo, and Mr. Kirby eased his ample girth into the chair behind his desk.

"Guess I know why you're here, Tom. Sorry about your financial embarrassment. Sorry, too, about the ranch. . . ."

Cleo had never heard such a lie! The cold blue eyes, in stark contrast to the thin-lipped remark, registered not one whit of sympathy.

"No need to feel sorry. We're here to settle that matter right now," Tom said smoothly. "Of course, my money is back in Houston, so if you'll let me sign a personal note until I can liquidate some of my holdings back there, we'll be in business."

Cleo was fascinated. Tom had never mentioned any "holdings." They'd tried to live on his salary, but when that hadn't covered her expenditures, her father had picked up the bills. She blushed, realizing the burden she must have been.

"What kind of holdings are we talkin' 'bout?" Kirby's narrow-eyed gaze reminded Cleo of a dangerous animal who had been cornered but not yet captured.

"Real estate mostly," Tom replied with a bland expression on his face. "Of course, there's my wife's jewelry, our home, the cars we left behind. . . ."

Admiration and fear charged through Cleo. Would the banker be impressed?

Kirby chewed on this information briefly, then conceded defeat. "You've done good for yourself, Tom. 'Course, I'll accept your word and arrange the loan. It's been nice doin' bidness with you." Kirby seemed gracious enough, but Cleo knew he'd always be around, waiting for a chance to gobble up another ranch. He was not a man to be trifled with, and she hoped they wouldn't have to do "bidness" with him again.

"Nice to meet you, Mrs. Kinney. I'll draw up the papers right away, Tom. You can pick 'em up before you leave town."

Tom nodded. "We'll be at the general store, buying a few things we need." He rose and shook the flabby hand again.

"You were very convincing back there, Tom," Cleo said outside the bank as they were climbing into the buggy.

He grinned broadly. "You weren't bad yourself, Mrs. Kinney." The name still sounded strange in her ears. "But I learned something today. I learned that you can do what you set your mind to. Imagine me, walking in there to old Kirby and coming out with the money I need." His countenance was glowing. "You're the best collateral I ever had, honey." Then he sobered. "Now all I have to do is get the money to pay off Kirby and keep him off my back."

"What will you do when the loan comes due?" she ventured.

"Whatever I have to," he said grimly. "My grandpa fought Indians, my Pa fought the drought and squatters, and now I'll take on old Kirby to keep this land."

The intensity of Tom's declaration frightened Cleo, for it sounded like he anticipated a long, drawn-out battle. Her thoughts roiled. *Tom is so happy here. He's his own boss, not Father's son-in-law. But if we stay much longer, we'll never get out of here!* Her mind spun, seeking an answer to her dilemma. Would she ever be able to persuade her husband to return to Houston?

*Please, God, don't leave me out here in this strange land,* she prayed. *Help us get home. And show me how to make Tom happy.*

There was no one else to whom she could turn. Maybe this wasn't a forsaken land, after all. Maybe God would hear her cry for help. But time would tell if He heard prayers, even in West Texas.

## Chapter 6

C leo stood out in the cold air behind the privy, throwing up as quietly and delicately as possible. As she leaned against the rough wood frame, she blamed her husband and then she blamed herself for this carelessness. She took a deep breath of the cool air to settle her stomach, but the acrid smell hit her nostrils instead, and she threw up again as she clung to the little house for support.

She had been replaying this scene for a whole week, so there was no doubt in Cleo's mind that she was pregnant. But the thought of having a baby out here without her parents to help her struck terror in her heart. She longed for her mother's sheltering arms and her father's assurances that everything would be fine.

Instead, she had a mother-in-law who was barely civil and a husband who expected her to drop the baby as easily as the cows out in the pasture. He, of course, was absolutely delighted. Proof of his masculinity and prowess, she thought bitterly. She felt every inch the victim.

When her stomach calmed down enough for her to return to the house, Cleo walked back to the bedroom and stretched out on the bed, fully clothed. She heard the door open softly.

"Feeling better?" Tom asked hopefully, feeling a little guilty that she was so sick. She looked so fragile and pale lying there. "Can I get you anything?"

"A little weak tea would be nice. And a piece of dry toast," she mumbled.

Tom's mother was in the kitchen when he went in to heat the water. He stuck a few more pieces of mesquite in the stove.

"Is she still feeling poorly?" Mrs. Kinney wanted to know.

"Yes."

"I know how she feels, believe me. But," she said a bit smugly, "*my* husband didn't wait on *me*. We were too busy trying to make a go of this place. I just toughed it out by myself. And that's when there was still Indian trouble in these parts."

"Ma, you know the Indians hadn't raided for years before you were expecting me," Tom chided.

"Now, son, you don't know what you're talking about. There were still a few renegades about." She gave him a challenging look and shoved a roast in the hot oven.

Tom refused to be drawn into another argument with his mother. As time went by, she seemed to grow harder and more unyielding, but he must not let Cleo bear the brunt of her discontent. He'd have to find a way, somehow, to change things.

He made the weak tea and toast in silence and took it back to the bedroom. Thinking of this woman who was to bear his child caused a surge of love and warmth to well up in his heart. He'd protect Cleo from unnecessary pain, even if it was inflicted by his own mother!

≈

As the days and weeks rolled by, Cleo moved into the next stage of her pregnancy, far more comfortable than the first. She began to round out nicely and felt wonderfully alive and serene. There was a doctor homesteading to the north, and her mother-in-law had told her rather tartly of several midwives in the area. But Tom had promised to move her to Pecos or Midland before the baby came so she could go to the lying-in clinic.

In letters to her parents, Cleo wrote glowingly of her life on the ranch, discouraging them from making a trip to see her since she would be bringing their grandchild to Houston as soon as possible after the baby was born. It was not that she didn't want to see them. The truth was that she was ashamed for her parents to know about her living conditions and the dreadful impasse with her mother-in-law.

In December her father had a mild heart attack. That solved the problem of keeping her parents at bay, but his illness wasn't serious enough to merit a visit from Cleo. Life rocked along as she waited for the baby. And except for the constant subtle friction with her mother-in-law, she was happy.

A few weeks later, a brief warming trend brought an invitation to a social to be held on a ranch to the east of them. Cleo was more than ready for some entertainment to break the long monotony of her existence. Even Mrs. Kinney was excited. Dances were held on a more or less regular basis, depending on the weather, and everyone in the county was invited.

The ranch they approached was much like the one they had left many hours ago, with the mandatory windmill and tank. But the yard was filled with every type of conveyance and a large assortment of children of all ages. Though it was early evening, the sun hovered on the horizon, an orange pumpkin bobbing toward the stark black line of earth below.

The lively beat of country music, led by a whining violin, rolled out to greet them, and the sound of thumping feet invited them to join in. They were met at the door by their host and hostess, who shouted a welcome over the din.

C.J. "Crook" O'Tool was nicknamed for his back, not for his profession. As a young man, he had been stomped by a horse, leaving him slightly stooped. Now he was in his late forties. His face was like a map of the country, reddish with white patches and sunspots, and there was a white line on his forehead where his hat never let the sun touch his skin. Perched on his beaked nose were wire-rimmed glasses. It was a kindly face, filled with humor and goodwill.

"Howdy, y'all come right in." He stuck out a big rough paw to the men and nodded formally to the two women. "Y'all know my wife, Ina Mae, don't ya?"

Ina Mae ushered them toward a table filled to overflowing with venison, antelope, wild hog, rabbit, and beef cooked in a dozen different recipes. There was a large complement of vegetables and desserts, too. "Hep yourselves, and be sure to save room for the real dessert, y'all hear? We've got iced tea for now and 'nilla ice cream for later. C.J. got three hunderd pounds of ice, so don't be bashful. The boys are out turnin' the dasher right now." She smiled up at Tom. "You shore got yourself a purty one, Tom. Guess she was worth waitin' for, huh?" She jabbed her sharp elbow into his ribs and laughed a big barrel laugh that filled her thin frame and shook her graying pompadour.

"Why, thank you, Mrs. O'Tool. She's a doozie, all right," Tom replied.

Cleo cringed a little, hearing the pure Texas drawl come out of her husband's mouth. She wasn't accustomed to it yet, though he seemed to be able to fit in with any audience. She smiled, accepting her hostess's compliment.

They ate heartily, and Cleo especially enjoyed the iced tea. There was even lemon to go in it. Though it was late winter, the promise of spring was in the air, and inside the crowded house, it was already as hot as the Fourth of July. She fanned her flushed face with one of Ina Mae's fancy napkins.

All the furniture in the big front room had been moved out, except for a line of chairs rimming the room. The men providing the music were playing a fiddle, a guitar, a harmonica, and a big upright piano, and they performed with enthusiasm, if not skill.

Cleo spotted Leaf Kirby and her family. The owner of the general store and his wife smiled and waved, but outside of these few, she didn't recognize anyone. Much of the evening was spent in introductions to her "neighbors," the friendly folk who lived on the outlying ranches.

She and Tom danced together often. Especially the waltzes. Tom was an expert. "Gets it from his pa," Mrs. Kinney informed her.

As she sat out a dance to catch her breath, Cleo spotted Tom dancing with Leaf Kirby during one of the square dances. But he was soon spinning back to Cleo and swept her into his arms with such enthusiasm that all her doubts faded away.

Even the children danced with any willing partner. But as the hour grew later, the younger ones began to disappear. And when Cleo peeked into the adjoining rooms, she found some of the children already asleep on pallets spread out everywhere. They had eaten their ice cream and had gone to sleep with smiles on their faces. She closed the door softly and returned to her seat.

While Tom danced with his mother, Cleo became aware of the woman sitting beside her. The woman's face was strong featured, and a warm smile lighted her steel gray eyes as she introduced herself. "I'm Tante Olga. Everyvun calls me that," she said in a heavy German accent. "Velcome to Vest Texas. I hope you vill be happy here. I see you are expecting a kinder. I am midvife, if you need me. I bring many kinder into the volrd."

"Wh–why, that's very kind of you, Tante Olga," Cleo said, not knowing quite how to reply. "I'm planning to go to Midland or Pecos when my time comes. But if I need you, it's nice to know you're there."

Tante Olga nodded sagely. "Sometimes first kinder aren't so eager to come into the vorld. Sometimes they come too early. You are strong and young, but doctors are far away. I am near. You send for me, and I vill come."

Cleo was mesmerized by the great strength and kindness she saw in the woman's eyes. Here was someone to lean on. She felt tiny shards of tears splinter in her own eyes. "Thank you, Tante Olga. I'll call you if I need you." Something in Olga reminded Cleo of her own mother, a faint chord of memory plucked softly. And then Tom was back to dance her around the floor and introduce her to yet another group of latecomers.

At first the other men had been shy about asking Cleo to dance, until her host glided her around the room in a dignified waltz. Crook spun her away from him, still holding her hand, then brought her back to him. He covered a lot of ground with his long legs, showing her off with his twirls and spins, and then gallantly returned her to Tom with a slight bow. "Your little wife's a mighty fine dancer, young man. Yes, sir, a mighty fine dancer."

Tom was about to agree when suddenly a shot rang out. The room fell instantly silent as several of the men sprinted for the door to see what had happened. But before they could investigate, a boy of around twelve staggered inside, holding a smoking pistol.

"I got 'im, Pa. I got 'im," he gasped, and collapsed on the floor.

His mother cradled her son's head in her lap, while his father ripped his shirt open. There, on the boy's neck, was a neat set of fang marks. The father patted his shoulder awkwardly as the mother rocked him, crooning pitifully.

"I'm so sorry, Hardy, I'm so sorry," said Crook, realizing that the child's life had already been snuffed out.

"Boy should have knowed better than to sleep on the ground this time of year," replied Hardy huskily, tears filling his eyes. "Snake probably crawled up into the blanket with him. At least it was quick, for I'd a hated to see him die by inches."

The couple was clearly stunned, barely able to take in the tragedy that had befallen them. Crook handed Hardy a mug of strong black coffee, and Ina Mae gave one to his wife.

"W—would you wantta bury him out here?" Crook asked hesitantly. "It would save the folks some travel time, and we can lay him out just as easy. We'd be honored to do it if you give the word." He paused. "Circuit rider ain't goin' to be around for a spell, so I'll read the service myself. . .iffen you're not up to it."

Mr. Hardy glanced over at his wife. With quiet tears streaming down her face, she nodded her consent. "Thank'ee kindly. I'm prayin' we'll never have to return the favor," she said in a strangled voice. She allowed the boy's body to be removed, and the Hardys were led into another room.

Cleo's face was ashen. "We'll spend the night here?" she whispered to Tom.

"Yes, we can sleep in the wagon. There's plenty of room and blankets."

Her skin prickled in horror. "But that boy was sleeping outside," she protested.

"He was sleeping on the ground," Tom reminded her. "We'll be up in the wagon, safe and sound. Snakes don't climb wagon wheels." When he saw the real terror in her eyes, he put his arms around her. "Don't worry. We'll be as safe as if we were in our bed at home."

But despite the warmth of her husband's embrace and his vow that he wouldn't leave her for a moment, Cleo slept little that night and was limp with exhaustion the next morning, when the sun appeared over the barren plain.

At breakfast, cooked over a campfire built by one of the men, there was time to get better acquainted with Ina Mae O'Tool, who had brought out enough provisions to feed all who had stayed for the funeral.

"We come in nineteen and ten," Ina Mae said in answer to Cleo's question. "Set up housekeepin' in two half tents. They was floored and walled up for three feet." She lifted her head proudly. "I put down my best Brussels carpet. Figgered the sand might ruin it, but I wasn't gonna live like a savage even if I did have to live in the sand." Her gaze sobered. " 'Course the sand did chew it up some. Guess you noticed the bare floor last night. Finally had to put that rug away. That near broke my heart. But I've learned to live with the land, not agin it. The time will come when I'll put down my fancy rug agin. Just as soon as we git rain and the market goes back up, we'll be sittin' purty. J.C. is a hard worker. We've never gone hungry." She grinned. "Sometimes it wasn't what we wanted to eat, but we always had somethin'. Some folks ain't so lucky. J.C. says the Smithtons are leavin'. Jest can't hang on no more. He's gonna try and find work in Midland. Land's for sale. Thank heavens we don't have no ready cash, or J.C. would buy it fer sure!"

"You don't want more land?" Cleo was puzzled.

"Honey, what'd we do with more land? Got thousands of acres right now. Got more land than sense. J.C. has it in his brain that he wants to own this half of Texas. Don't know why. It's jest all that much more work, if you ask me."

Cleo thought of what Tom had said about owning the land. Must be something men felt. She shrugged Tom's leather jacket closer around her.

Ina Mae smiled at Cleo. "Law me! I've done all the talkin'. When is that baby of yours due, and are you goin' to the laying-in sanitarium at Tante Olga's or are you goin' to Midland or Pecos to have that little cowboy?"

"Tom said he'd move me into town." Cleo dropped her eyes. "It's my first one, so I'd like a regular doctor to deliver it." Quickly she added, "Nothing against Tante Olga, of course."

" 'Course not. I 'spect I'd feel the same way if I'd had any choices. But if you do need her, she's the best in the whole state. She jest kinda naturally has this healin' touch. . .gift of God I'd call it. 'Course no one got a chance to do anything for the boy last night."

"Are there other children?" Cleo asked.

Ina Mae sighed. "All they have left are those three litte girls. They lost another boy a couple of years back. It'll be hard on him. He's gonna have to hire out all his work with no sons to help him. The girls may be able to help some, but it takes a man to do ranchin'. You'll find that out all too soon. Boys make the difference whether a man can make a go of a place or not."

Cleo considered what Ina Mae had told her as she rode with Tom over to the burial place. Tom had left his ranch, and now it was in bad shape. Was it his fault, or Robert's? Panic overtook her at the thought of Tom being tied to the land for years instead of only months.

During the short funeral service, where the mother sat trancelike, there was more time to think. Though Cleo had never spent much time dwelling on God outside of the mandatory Sunday school classes and church attendance with her family, she was beginning to believe that the only way to cope with this fearsome wilderness was to beseech the Almighty for His protection. *Dear Lord,* she prayed sincerely. *Comfort this family in their sorrow. And keep Tom and the baby and me safe.*

By the time they got home, Cleo was sleeping soundly against Tom's shoulder. She roused when the wagon pulled to a stop and, over her protests, he carried her into the house and tucked her into bed. "You rest for a while. A nap will do you good. Ma can take care of the cooking. Sleep, honey." She didn't argue, but snuggled into the feather pillows and nodded off again.

⤙⤚

"Well, well," clucked Mrs. Kinney as Cleo entered the kitchen the next morning. "Finally finished your beauty nap, I see."

Cleo wanted nothing more than some good hot coffee to clear her head. She poured a cup and ignored the sarcastic remark, determined not to be goaded into an argument with her mother-in-law. "Good morning. Where's Tom?"

"Out where he's supposed to be. Robert, too. Workin' and gettin' things lined out for the roundup. Someone has to do the chores around here."

Cleo flushed at the implication. "What can I do to help?"

Mrs. Kinney eyed her blossoming figure. "Not much in your condition. 'Course, I was plowin' a truck garden when I was as far along as you, but you bein' so delicate, I don't think you should help me plant the potatoes."

"I can plant," Cleo insisted. "I'll be careful. Actually, I'm very strong and healthy. It's just that I want to do everything right for this baby," she said somewhat defensively.

Mrs. Kinney cleared her throat pointedly. "Heard you're trying to move off to Midland or Pecos to have that baby." She turned from her soapy dishwater. "Just where do you think we're goin' to get the money for you to live in town?" She shook her head. "We don't have no money to be wastin'." She looked accusingly at Cleo. "You think you're the first woman to ever have a baby out here? I had four. Yes, four. Two dead before they ever got to their first birthdays. But nowadays, women think they got to go live in Midland to have a baby. Pshaw!"

This was the first time Mrs. Kinney had leveled an open attack on Cleo. She gasped under the force of the stinging rebuke. But now, words she had been storing in the reservoirs of her heart welled up, begging to be spoken. Cleo set her cup unsteadily on the table in front of her and took a deep breath.

"Mrs. Kinney, it wasn't my idea that Tom and I move out here. I hadn't planned to have a baby yet, either. And if I'd looked the world over, I'd never have chosen *you* for a mother-in-law. You've done nothing but bait me the entire time I've been here. You've even used silence to keep distance between us. . .you, who should know better than anyone what a treasure it is to have another woman to talk to in this lonely place!"

Cleo's rage was building. "Just know that I love your son with all my heart. And he chose me as his wife. . .for the rest of our lives! You'll just have to learn to accept that fact or—" here she paused significantly, her voice softening ominously— "risk losing him."

"Well, you do have some spunk in you, after all." Mrs. Kinney was deadly calm, but her icy eyes shot sparks. "You're right about some of the things you said. But I'll never be satisfied that you're the one for my son until you prove to me that you can do somethin' for him besides sit around in fancy duds!"

"Give me some time, and I can make a *real* home for him," Cleo challenged. "I've got the money and the taste to do it."

Mrs. Kinney turned white. "This is my home, and I'll thank you to keep a civil tongue in your head."

"You don't want to be friends," Cleo continued with a wondering tone. "You want a contest for Tom's love." A sudden thought dawned on her. "And you weren't sick. At least not with anything a doctor could cure." Cleo's eyes narrowed as if seeing Mrs. Kinney for the first time. "You couldn't stand the thought of Tom and me living the good life in Houston while you and Robert scratched out a living in the sand. You were *jealous*," she breathed. "All this time I thought *I* needed to do something to win your approval. But it's *you*. *You* have the problem."

Mrs. Kinney had slumped against the cabinet, clutching a wet tea towel against her chest. "How dare you speak to me like that!" she hissed. "And in my own home. Get out, and take all your things with you! Get out!"

Cleo eyed her coolly. "And if I do, who do you think will follow me? Who will leave you with only Robert to help with the ranch?" Steady hands picked up the cup and refilled it. "You'd better think twice before issuing an ultimatum like that. I can shut down this little family business just by walking out that door."

Mrs. Kinney straightened and drew a deep breath. "Yes, I suppose you could. You're a cold, heartless woman, Cleo. . .Kinney. . .but I'm glad to see that Tom didn't marry a spineless little rabbit. He'll need a strong wife out here." There was a flicker of admiration in the pale eyes.

The two women had made no peace pact nor negotiated any terms. But Cleo knew she had won something this day. With a heady rush of power, she watched the woman go outside to feed her chickens. Never in her life had she spoken to anyone the way she had just now. The sensation of euphoria quickly subsided, replaced by panic as she wondered if Mrs. Kinney would say anything to Tom and just as quickly decided she probably would not wish to betray her own defeat. She knew the rivalry was not over. Nor the silences. Only the snide little remarks and catty digs.

As the day wore on, Cleo continued to feel a niggling doubt about the wisdom of her outburst. Up until now she had buried her own feelings of hostility toward her mother-in-law. Then something had snapped and she had said things that should have been left unsaid. She couldn't really be sure Mrs. Kinney wouldn't tell Tom. What if he sided with his mother?

In desperation, Cleo prayed, *Lord, please get me out of this mess!* Then she felt a flush of defiance. *But I won't apologize. What I said was true. Just please don't let her tell Tom, and I'll promise never to lose my temper with her again.* At least she would try not to.

She and Tom had to get away from here. They needed a house of their own, or even one room. She would have to speak to Tom about it tonight.

<sub>∞</sub>

"Honey, you know there's no money to build a house," Tom said with a sigh of defeat. He was propped on his elbow in bed, leaning over to stroke Cleo's small rounded belly through the quilt.

She looked up sorrowfully. "You know what's going on in this house between your mother and me, don't you?" She tried to read the truth in his eyes. Did he know about the fight she'd had with his mother this morning? She didn't think so.

He lay back on the pillows, hands behind his head. "Yes, I know. Maybe if I speak to her. . ."

"No," she said quickly, "there's no need to talk to her. Just do something. Your mother loves you, Tom, and she doesn't want to share you. Think about it. She's all alone. But if we don't get some distance between us soon, one of us is in big trouble." The warning tone in her voice left no doubt about that.

"You can complain until the cows come home, but there's no money to build another house." A slow grin crossed his face. "Let's find her a husband instead."

Cleo sat up straight. "What?"

"I meant it as a joke."

"But. . .maybe it's a good idea," she mused. "She'd have somebody else to help with the ranch besides you and Robert."

Tom shrugged. "Well, I'm not so sure I'd want any of the bachelors around here to marry my mama. That could lead to problems of another kind. But," he began, his eyes brightening, "maybe we could build on a little section to the back of the house. We could share the kitchen. I could dogtrot it so there'd be a little space between the house and the room," he said thoughtfully.

"Oh, that would be wonderful! I could fix it up and make a place for the three of us. . .a real retreat. Oh, Tom, how soon can we start?"

"You know the roundup has to come first right now. It'll take two or three weeks to get the cattle gathered and branded. Then I'll have to drive some of them to Monaghans for shipping." He kissed her sweetly. "But we'll get around to the building as soon as possible," he promised. "I'm sure I can get some of the men to work with me after roundup. Ranchers are used to helping each other out."

Cleo wasn't especially thrilled to hear Tom speak of himself as part of the brotherhood of ranchers, but she knew he'd keep his promise. That room would ease the strain of living in this wilderness with a woman who seemed to hate her.

She snuffed out the light, gave a deep sigh, and snuggled into the pillows. *But how long, Lord, how long?* She looked toward the heavens, but she didn't expect an answer.

# Chapter 7

Though every tortured muscle in his body was complaining, Tom was exhilarated from his physical labor. The roundup was going well. He and his fellow ranchers had driven the scattered cattle into a a pasture for holding, and he was pleased with the number of calves that had been added to his herd. Still, there was always the worry about having to buy more fodder to feed them, he fretted silently. A rancher's curse. He wanted more—more cattle, more land. But times were hard, and he couldn't afford to buy any more, so he was determined not to let one acre slip through his fingers. More and more people were moving into the area, and more and more land was being bought up, land he wanted. *If I can just hold on until the drought breaks,* he thought, *I can expand.*

Ever since returning to the ranch, the obsession to acquire more land had gripped him. He was sure that in time, especially now that he had promised Cleo a little place of her own, he would be able to convince her to stay. He was deeply contented working the land again, with his wife at his side and a baby on the way. It would be a fitting legacy to pass on to the next generation of Kinneys.

The only rock in his bed was the relationship between Cleo and his mother. Tom had looked on from the beginning and knew things were not easy for Cleo. His mother hadn't cut her any slack, but at least there were fewer barbed remarks, and he took this as a good sign.

The smell of scorching hair and flesh assailed his senses, and Tom reined in his wandering thoughts to address the task at hand. He had a good horse, a cow pony who knew how to work the cattle, thus saving the rider a lot of work. Today he was cutting out calves for branding, castrating, and earmarking. Yesterday he had worked on the ground, and his back was sore from the strenuous bending and stretching. It felt good to lean back in the saddle while the horse pulled the rope tight.

They broke for lunch, and wearily he accepted the inevitable beans and sowbelly and a mug of hot coffee that singed the hair off his tongue.

"Don't you have any iced tea?" he complained to the cook.

A wave of laughter broke out among the cowboys sitting under the mesquite trees. "Go soak your head in the stock tank iffen you want to cool off, Tom," advised Crook.

Tom sank down in the scant shade next to Crook and Robert, and the three of them ate in silence for a few moments, each lost in his own world. Conversation was never a prerequisite for friendship on the range, and each man respected the others' right to contemplation.

It was Crook who shattered the silence when he spoke up, pointing with his knife at a figure riding into camp. "Well, look who's here, Tom! The little lady!"

Tom jumped up to help Cleo down off the mare. "What are you doing out here?" The displeasure in his voice was undisguised.

Cleo, not expecting a reprimand, pouted prettily. "Why, I wanted to see what a roundup was all about, darling. I need to know about your work, Tom." She walked under a mesquite, pulling off her hat and fanning herself.

"Women don't belong out here. It's too dangerous," he said flatly. "Not only that, you shouldn't be bouncing around on a horse right now."

She gave Tom a withering look. "I'm a very good rider. Besides, I walked the mare part of the way."

"And if she'd gotten spooked, you might have lost the baby."

"She didn't, and I didn't." Cleo tried a dazzling smile to charm him out of his foul mood. "Could I have a little something to eat? I'm famished."

Reluctantly he brought her a plate of food and a cup of coffee. "Sit here and don't get in anybody's way. We've got work to do."

Cleo couldn't swallow over the large lump of anger and tears knotted in her throat, but she sipped at her coffee, hoping the scalding brew would help. With the branding fire only a short distance from where she sat, she found herself with a front-row seat to a calf roping. Or was it? The men were so deft with the knife that at first she couldn't be sure what they were doing. A swift slice, the sudden bawl of the calf, and then she knew. For one awful moment, she thought she was going to gag. Quickly she got to her feet, putting the chuck wagon between herself and the activity around the fire.

Just at that moment, an enormous man came from around the tailgate. "Would you like something to settle your stomach, missus?" he asked kindly.

Though not much taller than she, the man had to weigh close to three hundred pounds, she thought. He was wearing a clean white starched shirt and a big apron over his clothes. With garters on his sleeves to hold up the cuffs, he looked more like a bartender or a gambler than a cowboy.

"Yes, thank you." Gratefully she accepted the cup he offered her.

"Peppermint tea. Best thing for an upset stomach. Always keep some handy. Use it myself sometimes when the smell out here gets to me," he said apologetically. He tipped his hat to her. "Smallwood's the name, though everone here 'bouts calls me Fatty."

"The tea does help, uh. . .Mr. Smallwood." She couldn't bring herself to call him by the nickname. "Is your ranch around here?"

"Oh, no, ma'am. No self-respectin' horse'd let me on his back. I have a café in Midland, and I run a chuck wagon for the ranchers at spring roundup time. But my daddy used to go on the long trail drives. This here's his very own wagon." He lovingly caressed the wood on the wagon bed.

"I've never seen a real chuck wagon."

"Then come around back, ma'am. Here's the best part." He showed her how the tailgate acted as a small two-legged table and how a cabinet had been built in the back of the wagon with drawers and compartments to hold the staples and cooking gear. It was quite ingenious and compact. "Cook also acts as a doc, especially on a drive. I enjoy comin' out here in the spring, but I'd never survive a real drive. 'Course, ain't many of those no more. Fartherest I've ever been was to Pecos and Monaghans." He pulled his hat down more firmly on his big ears. "Yes, sir, times have changed."

Cleo glanced in the direction of her working husband. Apparently Tom had no intention of spending any more time with her. Besides, she was furious at him for treating her with such indifference.

As if reading her thoughts, Fatty cleared his throat. "Ah, ma'am, I was plannin' on goin' back in, since I don't feed the men their supper. If you'd care to ride along with me, I'll swing by your place." He all but stubbed his toe in the dirt in his embarrassment at being so bold as to ask to accompany her home.

Cleo favored him with a bright smile. "Why, that would be lovely, Mr. Smallwood." She started for the wagon.

"Ma'am, you'd do better ridin' that sweet mare. This here seat bounces like an unbroke bronc. But you stick close by the wagon. Snakes is bad this time of year, and I noticed you ain't carryin' no gun."

She looked around with concern. "I didn't see any on the ride out, though my horse did shy a few times. Do you suppose. . ." She left the sentence unfinished but felt the finger of fear prod her spine at the thought.

Riding home, Cleo gradually relaxed. Fatty had keen eyesight and a ready rifle and fired at regular intervals. . ."jest to make sure."

As he told her, "Rattlers is the curse of the land, not the sand."

"Don't the cattle ever get bitten?" she inquired.

"Oh, sometimes, but you put a snake in a herd of cattle, and he's most likely to get hisself stomped to death before he can make up his mind who to bite first."

Cleo laughed out loud. "Have *you* ever been bitten?"

"Well, no ma'am. Guess they figger I'm too big, but I was almost *licked* to death by one onct," he replied with a wide grin.

She laughed again as she envisioned that scene.

"It's a real pleasure to see a fine-lookin' woman enjoyin' herself," Fatty observed. "That Tom is as lucky as a dog with two tongues."

Cleo could not hide another smile. "Are you married, Mr. Smallwood?" she asked with interest.

Fatty positively blushed. "Why, no, ma'am. No gal would ever take me serious, I reckon. Had an endurin' friendship with a lady of the evenin' until she moved to the big city, though. Right purty thing, she was. You put me in mind of her, your black hair and all." Quickly he added, "No offense intended. It's just that I've always been a fancier of beautiful women. Like to watch 'em and all their dainty ways."

"Why, I'm not offended. I'm flattered." She looked at him from under the brim of her hat. "I've seldom met a man as honest and forthright as you, Mr. Smallwood. I hope we'll be friends."

"My ma always said there wasn't nothin' between my brain and my mouth, so the words just ran out." He laughed. "It's got me in a heap o' trouble a few times."

"I understand how easy that can be," she confessed, "getting oneself in trouble, I mean." Then she told him about the bathing beauty escapade.

They shared the telling of the tale with mutual good humor, and then Fatty said, "I can see how come you'd think it was all right to be out here on the roundup, then. Tom didn't know he'd got hisself a live one, I reckon. You'll be good for him, I expect. He's a careful man, Tom is. He could use a little livenin' up. And his mama is a good woman and a hard worker, but she's about as much fun as eatin' chili with a burnt tongue."

Cleo laughed her agreement. "Humor is not her strong suit. But I think we're coming to an understanding." For the remainder of the trip, Cleo found herself telling Fatty all sorts of private things, things she had never dreamed she would confide to anyone but Mattie. He was a sympathetic listener. And he didn't offer advice. He merely listened, nodding and grinning on occasion. She was disappointed when she saw the ranch house come into view, for the ride was almost over, and there would be only the dour Mrs. Kinney waiting for her there.

Cleo moved her horse closer to the wagon and put out her hand. "Thank you for seeing me home, Mr. Smallwood. I truly had a wonderful time and hope we'll meet again soon."

"Just one more thing, ma'am. Would you call me Fatty? It would make me mighty happy."

She smiled. "Only if you call me Cleo." And they sealed their new friendship with a handshake.

Fatty was clattering off as Cleo opened the door to the house. Needing a cool drink of water from the gravity flow tap, she went into the kitchen where she found Mrs. Kinney cutting up one of her nonlaying hens for supper.

"Could have told you not to go. Tom was mad, wasn't he?" her mother-in-law muttered. And not waiting for an answer, she hurried on. "Women don't belong at a roundup." Softly she added, "Everyone knows that." There was no mistaking the satisfaction behind the words.

Cleo's chin lifted defiantly. "Yes, he was mad, but I'm still glad I went. First, I now feel that I understand my husband's work a little better. And secondly, I got to meet Mr. Smallwood. I was very impressed."

Mrs. Kinney shrugged. "Doesn't take much to impress you, I guess. Fatty is just. . .Fatty."

For one crazy moment, Cleo wondered if they could marry her mother-in-law off to the man. Maybe some of his kindness would rub off and melt the crust of bitterness Tom's mother had built up around herself. Cleo giggled a little at the notion. And when Mrs. Kinney turned to stare, she explained inanely, "He made me laugh."

Unaccountably, the woman looked off at the rolling prairie framed by the kitchen window and began to share. "Fatty came to call once when I was a young girl livin' in Midland. He was as irresponsible then as he is now. Playin' cowboy the way he does. Why, by now he should have built that little café into a fine big restaurant."

Cleo darted a sidelong glance at her mother-in-law. "Maybe he would have. . .if he'd had a good wife to help him."

"Humph," she grunted. "Man's a dreamer, not a doer. He'd of never made it out here on a ranch. Good thing he stayed in town."

Cleo gave up. She wasn't about to change Mrs. Kinney's mind so easily, and she deplored hearing Fatty ridiculed. So she went to her room to get out of her riding togs and into something more comfortable. Looking up, she was surprised to see her mother-in-law standing in the doorway.

"Changin' clothes again? I declare, I never knew anyone who wore as many duds in a week as you do, but then I never had that many myself," Mrs. Kinney commented, her lips thinned in disapproval. "Just came by to tell ya one of the men left some buildin' lumber out back. What's it for?"

Cleo finished buttoning her blouse and turned to look the woman directly in the eye. "It's for the new room Tom's adding on for the two of us and the baby." She waited, but there was no reply, only a crumpling of the blanched face. The woman left without a word, and Cleo smiled a tiny smile of triumph.

The smile faded when she heard Tom's booted tread on the porch. She hurried to meet him, eager to make things right between them. Despite his dust-covered clothing and the stench of the corral, she hugged him close and mumbled her apology into the warmth of his shoulder.

He patted her awkwardly. "It's all right, honey. I was just surprised to see you, and I was tired and hot. But," he warned, "I don't want you out there again. . .not until after the baby is born."

She breathed a sigh of relief over this swift absolution and gave him her promise. And later before she slept, she thanked God for Tom's love. *Please don't ever let him stop loving me,* she prayed, vaguely aware that prayer was becoming a vital part of her everyday life.

～

Cleo was gradually becoming accustomed to the inconveniences of living on a ranch. Though she did not relish the chores, keeping busy with the cooking, cleaning, and washing did help to prevent those painful confrontations with her mother-in-law. And she enjoyed the outdoor gardening tasks. Still, fresh vegetables in turn required canning and storing, and Cleo hated canning days.

The kitchen was like an inferno, and she felt faint and limp when it was over. She did nothing she thought would hurt the baby, but she took grim satisfaction in being able to keep up with Mrs. Kinney. No one could say she wasn't doing her share of the work.

Her one real joy was caring for her rosebushes. When Mrs. Smithington left, she had given the bushes to Ina Mae, who in turn had passed them on to Cleo, with lots of advice on how to raise them. Cleo had listened carefully, then had planted them in a sheltered area under the bedroom window, where she would be able to enjoy them all summer long. No matter how tired she was, she tended them daily. They were budding now, with the promise of heavenly blooms very soon.

True to his word, Tom had enlisted the aid of some of the ranchers, and they had come to help him frame up the new room. It was about half finished now, and Cleo was wild with the desire to go to town to purchase the things they'd need.

Knowing how scarce money was, Tom had tried to hold her down. Being a fair carpenter, he could trade for the wood and build some of the furnishings himself. But she was dead set on recreating a room she'd seen in one of those ladies' magazines, and she wouldn't be satisfied with homemade furniture or hand-me-downs. And she wanted one of those fancy baby beds—a cast-iron one, painted white, all fluff and frills.

When Tom had been less than enthusiastic, Cleo had pouted. Men didn't understand such things, she fumed inwardly. They were so doggedly practical! Anyway, she'd planned to use her own money to furnish the room. Though she had left the bulk of her dowry in the bank in Houston, she had a hundred dollars secreted in her big traveling trunk. Tom wouldn't want her to use it. But since it hadn't been enough to save the ranch—and after his last impassioned speech about his manly need to fix things by himself, she wouldn't have risked damaging his ego by offering it—she'd kept quiet about it.

Now she had a use for that money, one she could justify, since it would be used for Tom and the baby as well as for herself. And mentally planning how she would decorate their room had kept her sane in all the long hours she'd spent under Mrs. Kinney's roof.

Cleo was working with her roses when she noticed that the day was growing sultry, an oddity in this dry country. While the sun was baking the earth as it did every day, something did not feel quite right, and she remarked about it to Mrs. Kinney.

"Storm's probably on the way. I noticed thunderheads buildin'."

When Cleo scanned the horizon, she could see only a tiny cloud that appeared no larger than her hand. "You mean it might rain?"

"Maybe. Might just storm. We've had dry storms before."

The preoccupation with the weather that was peculiar to West Texas annoyed Cleo. In Houston a cloudy day usually signaled rain with occasional rolling thunder. But, hurricane weather excepted, it was an uneventful thing.

Here every cloud was examined and commented on, every sign observed and attached to the story of some former storm, or lack of. The wind was constantly monitored and any change noted. Since the wind blew every day from some direction, it was an unflagging topic of conversation.

Cleo had endured Texas bragging all her life, but never had she lived where it was hotter, drier, or windier. It remained to be seen if it could be wetter, too. And seeing that the clouds had spread along the horizon in a thin black line, she decided that they might be about to get some rain, after all.

At that moment Tom came wheeling in on his horse. "Get everything battened down! Get the chickens in the barn! Everything, inside!"

"But, Tom, the clouds are so far away," she protested.

"Honey, those aren't rain clouds. That's a black duster, and it's headed this way as sure as sunrise. Now get going! I'll put the horses in the barn."

The look on his face frightened her. "Sand? Is that all?"

"Sometimes behind the sand is a big storm. I don't like the looks of this one. We're likely to have cattle in the next state before it's all over. Now go, and then get into the house. Quick!"

It was as if a giant blanket was being pulled slowly over them from the ground. Cleo watched from the porch as the boiling black sand moved inexorably toward them. And with the approach of the storm came a gentle twilight as the sand blocked out the sun.

She leaned closer to Tom when he joined her, shucking off his sweat-stained hat. "It really is a black sandstorm, isn't it? It's getting as dark as night."

He nodded, frowning. "Seems like we can't have a few clouds gather and drop a little rain on us. To get rain we have to have a major storm, and then we may not get anything at all but mud falling out of the sky."

Cleo was puzzled. "Mud?"

"Just enough rain to wet down the sand. When it falls, it's mud."

She sighed. "I shouldn't be surprised, I suppose. Apparently anything can happen in this part of Texas. Now I believe some of the tales I've been hearing." She moved closer to Tom as the darkness deepened and the edges of the storm approached. He took her inside and shut the door. A big piece of wood was dropped into metal slots on each side of the door and the four of them.

Robert and his mother came in from the barn, and the four of them gathered in the kitchen, by common agreement the safest place. Shutters had been closed over the few windows of the house, and they began to jiggle and bang in their confinement as the wind picked up.

Mrs. Kinney lit the lamp, and they sat around the table listening. The wind howled, hurling sand against the house with giant fingers. At first the grains made a pinging sound, but it was soon swalllowed up in the fierceness of the storm. It was awesome to be trapped inside the house in the eerie darkness.

"Tom," Robert said softly. "Do you hear it?"

Tom's face looked suddenly drawn and haggard. "I hear it. Under the table, everyone."

Everyone except Cleo sprang into action. Robert sprinted to the bedrooms, dragged blankets off the beds, and brought them back. Mrs. Kinney blew out the lamp. Tom covered Cleo with a blanket.

"What is it, Tom?" Cleo was pale with fright.

"A cyclone, most likely. With any luck, though, it'll miss us."

"Sounds like the train coming into Monaghans," Robert observed.

The wind changed from a howl to a shriek, rattling the windows and shaking the very foundations of the house. This was followed by a soft plunking sound that gained in intensity. Faster and faster.

"Hail," said Mrs. Kinney. "We're in for it now. It always hails before a cyclone." She closed her eyes in prayer, and her lips moved as she begged the Almighty for His mercy.

In her fright Cleo prayed, too, a childish litany of entreaty. *Dear Lord Jesus, don't let it hit us, please! Keep us safe. Please, Lord, don't let it hit us. Keep us safe. Help us, Lord. Please, dear God, don't let us die.*

Robert was praying out loud, and Tom mumbled under his breath.

The roar grew louder, and the entire house quaked as if aware of what was coming. The groaning of boards and hinges was almost human, and then the monster wind began chewing its way over them, snapping and tearing in a frenzy of destruction.

For one awful moment Cleo thought she might faint, so terrifying was the sound. She could feel Tom's arms around her, holding her tightly, and she was aware of her heart beating beneath the scratchy woolen blanket he had pulled over her. The table danced a macabre dance over their heads. And then it was as still as death.

Cleo wondered if the storm had left her deaf until she heard Tom let out his breath. "It's over."

He crawled out from under the table and walked to the door. Cleo wanted to beg him not to open the door. The monster that had raged outside might still be out there. But he raised the heavy board and pushed away the sand that had piled up against the door. The sky beyond was cloudless and impossibly blue.

Cleo scrambled out, nearly losing her footing on the thin layer of grit that covered the kitchen floor. When she straightened her rumpled clothing and licked her dry lips, she felt as if she had been dipped in water and then carefully rolled across the beach. Everything she touched on her way to the back door was coated with sand.

"No rain," Tom said.

"No room," said Robert with rare dry wit as he looked around to the side of the house.

Sure enough, all the careful building of the past few weeks was completely gone. Not a trace of it remained. Cleo was too shocked to cry. She could only stare stupidly.

"Barn roof is gone, too," Mrs. Kinney clucked her tongue sadly. "Wonder if the animals are all right? Oh, there's the tin roof. . .over there in the pasture." Obediently, they looked in the direction of her pointed finger. "But where is the chicken coop?"

It was found some hundred yards away, perched atop a mesquite tree, all the chickens safe inside, but without a feather left on any of their frightened bodies.

Mrs. Kinney laughed in relief. "Poor things look pitiful, don't they? But at least they're alive."

Robert came back with a report on the barn animals. "They're okay. Ranger kicked down most of his stall, but he ain't hurt."

Further inspection of the property revealed that the blades of the windmill next to the house were gone, too. It was easy to follow the path of the twister, where the tail had dipped down into the pasture and taken mesquite and grass with it. "Made us a road," said Robert.

"Yeah." Tom gave a short laugh. "But to where?"

Robert scratched his head. "Wherever you want it to lead to, I reckon."

"You saddle up and check on the cattle close around," Tom told his brother. "I'll go out to the far east pasture and check there. We may be having a big barbecue soon. And while I'm at it, I'll see if anyone else had any damage. After I see to our stock, I'll ride over to the O'Tools."

Cleo was turning to go into the house when she remembered her roses. With a heavy heart, she walked around to the sheltered side of the house. To her surprise, she found that while the canes looked a bit beaten up, the roses were still intact. She laughed out loud with relief. "Thank you, Lord, for keeping us safe from the storm! Thank you, thank you, thank you," she whispered into the blue sky as she fingered the buds tenderly.

Just beyond the roses, she saw a piece of hail the size of an apple. How odd to see ice lying on the sunbaked earth. But in this heat, it would be quickly gone. The chilled air was warming, and things would soon be back to normal.

It had all happened so fast that it seemed like a dream. A very bad dream. But they were all safe. She and Tom and the baby. Robert. Even her mother-in-law. Cleo took one last look at the roses and hurried inside.

# Chapter 8

There was very little damage to any of the other spreads, so the ranchers and their wives turned out to make a day of reroofing the Kinneys' barn and putting up the frame for the additional bedroom. One of the cows that had broken its neck during the storm was barbecued, and the front room was cleared for dancing. It turned out to be a very festive occasion, and Cleo enjoyed it immensely, realizing again how fragile life is and how valuable one's friends. Robert, Tom, and Crook continued to work on the room for the next week, adding a little breezeway between the two structures, where they hung a porch swing for Cleo to enjoy the evening coolness.

It had taken tears, arguments, and compromise, but she had finally talked Tom into letting her use a little of the money she had put away to furnish the new room. She was thrilled that she would soon have a place to call her own.

From the Sears and Roebuck catalog, she ordered an ornate brass bed for them and the fancy baby crib she had wanted. With freight, the amount came to twenty-five dollars. She also ordered some floral printed fabric for curtains and a bedspread. Of course, Mrs. Kinney was scandalized at the "waste of money," but she made very few ripples in their pool of happiness.

When the room was finished and the beds from Sears had been dragged through the sucking sand to the ranch, Cleo stood in the doorway and drank it all in. Soft lamplight glowed from the table beside the bed. The brass headboard shone, and the colorful bedspread looked inviting. The Smithingtons' big chifforobe, contracted for by Tom when they moved out, stood to one side, and the baby bed waited serenely on the other wall. She smiled softly. It was worth everything she had endured.

"Someday I'll have a real home for you to live in," she said to her child. "Maybe not like the one I grew up in, but much nicer and bigger than this." She patted her stomach. "You come from good stock. Your grandparents in Houston are quite well-to-do. And someday your father will have this ranch on its feet. You wait and see." Tears gathered in her eyes. "But you'll never go hungry or ragged, I promise you. You'll always have the best I can give you."

❦

The summer days were like the forged links in an overheated chain, too hot to touch, and they sizzled to an end, one by one.

In June the garden was at its height, and canning went on all day. Cleo was sure she had sweated every ounce of fluid from her body by lunchtime each day. The men slaughtered a cow, and the thin strips of meat were hung over the barbed-wire fence to dry in the merciless sun. The meat could then be boiled or fried for a tasty dish in the winter.

Cleo stood beneath the lone tree in the front yard and gazed out over the trackless land. Heat waves shimmered above the ground, and a steady, drying wind sucked the sweat from her clothes. The sky was a turquoise blue without a suggestion of a cloud. The prickly grass rustled in the slight breeze, and she could hear the cattle lowing distantly. At her feet was Old Jack, the mixed-breed dog, panting and heaving in the heat. In the house she could hear the clinking of hot glass jars as they were released from their boiling bath, and she imagined the blistering steam rising from the vessel.

Cleo had let her hair grow out, and she lifted its heavy weight from the nape of her neck to catch whatever breeze was about. Well into her pregnancy, she felt the baby kick hard. "What are *you* complaining about," she asked grumpily. "You're perfectly comfortable. You should feel it out here." As if to make a point, the baby kicked her again.

Cleo closed her eyes and tried to will herself back to that day on the beach when she had first seen Tom. She tried to recreate the damp, salty sea breeze and the sound of the waves teasing the shore rhythmically. It was a hazy imagining, and with it came a distinctly painful ache. She opened her eyes. "From sand and salt water to more sand and scarce water." She shrugged her shoulders helplessly. What was, was. She had a husband and a baby on the way. She had her own little retreat. It wasn't much, but it was everything.

She purposefully blocked the thought of her lovely Houston home and the friends there. She simply couldn't deal with that right now. She could only live in the present, one day at a time, for whenever she allowed herself to dwell on the fact that she might be stuck here for years, she was overwhelmed with hopelessness.

It had been more than nine months since she had seen her parents. Mail service from town was sporadic at best, for though it normally came in every two weeks, someone had to ride in to get it, and lately they hadn't been able to spare the time. But a trip to the post office always rewarded Cleo with letters from her mother. She would sit on the bed and arrange them by dates, savoring each one, carefully splitting the tops of the envelopes with a small pen knife, and then putting them in order in a little box. In between times she would reread them.

Her mother's letters, filled with news of home—social events, her father's health, and assurances of her love—always gave Cleo a lift. Sometimes she cried as she read, overcome by such love for her parents that it spilled from her eyes. And then the homesickness would threaten to drown her, until she thought of

Tom and the baby. It was as if she were caught between two worlds—one in Houston with her parents and one here on the ranch with Tom.

Cleo tried to keep her own letters light, hoping the sadness didn't creep in between the lines. "I'm hoping to bring the baby to you at Christmas," she wrote. "Tomorrow we're going on a picnic. My first visit to the famous Sand Hills. A picnic in the sand sounds a lot like home, doesn't it?"

With the anticipated outing, it was a little easier to get to sleep, thinking of the welcome break in their dull routine.

～

"Hand me up that big basket, and mind you be careful—it's full of pies," ordered Mrs. Kinney as she stood in the back of the wagon. Cleo was carrying out old quilts for them to sit on in the dunes, while Robert and Tom dutifully loaded the mountain of food that had been prepared.

There had been a short discussion about the propriety of Cleo's appearing in public so late in her pregnancy. A very short discussion.

"If you think I'm ashamed of my condition, you're flat-dab crazy!" she said loudly enough for Mrs. Kinney to hear. "And I'm not going to miss the biggest party of the year because I stick out in front. That lump is *your child*, and I'm not ashamed of it. And you shouldn't. . ."

"Wait, wait. I give," Tom said laughingly, holding up his hands in mock surrender. "You win. I just thought, well, never mind what I thought." He kissed her tenderly, and she wore a loose-fitting smock that looked quite attractive on her. He was careful to tell her how pretty she looked.

The sun had barely rubbed the sleep out of its eyes when they were underway to the Sand Hills to celebrate the Fourth of July. But it seemed like more than half a day's travel before they reached the dunes and found the other revelers.

A huge tarp had been secured as a shelter underneath the trees at the largest water hole toward the back of the dunes. Sawhorses had been set up and planks laid to make a table that was already groaning with food.

The sand was so bright from the blistering sun that Cleo had to squint to see where she was going as she helped carry their food to the makeshift table. It was awkward walking in the deep, shifting sand, and her balance was impaired by both her pregnancy and the big basket of fried chicken she carried.

"Here, let me help you with that."

Still squinting, Cleo saw only a set of dazzling white teeth and then dark blue eyes, crinkling with good humor and sunlight, laughing out from under the brim of a Stetson.

She surrendered the basket to her rescuer. "Oh, thank you."

"I'm Delmore Albert Lennon, but everyone calls me Dal."

He took her elbow to steady her in the sand as they walked. "I know who *you* are. You're the talk of the county." He flashed that smile again, his long legs propelling them quickly to the table, where he helped himself to one of the crispy pieces of chicken he had set down. "The spoils of battle," he declared as he bit deeply into a leg.

"Do you live on a ranch around here?"

"Yes, we have the spread west of yours, but your fame and beauty have spread even to the ends of the earth, otherwise known as the Rocking L Ranch."

"You look like a rancher," she said surveying his jeans and the bandana tucked into his shirt, "but you sure don't talk like one."

"Much to my papa's dismay, I've left the ranch behind me for now." The confident smile appeared once more. "I'm an oil promoter. I've been working down in Fort Stockton, but I've moved up here for now." His eyes scanned the horizon. "Someday this is going to be a rich oil country, in spite of what some folks say. There's oil under these big old pastures. I've been buying, selling, and holding some of the leases."

Cleo frowned. "You speculate, then."

"Yes, ma'am. Me and my partner have made some good money, too. We lease some land, dig a well, and pay the rancher and everyone else who put something in the pot."

"You make it sound so simple," she said, intrigued in spite of herself.

"Well, it is, when the oil comes in. The only problem is when it doesn't." The tall stranger laughed.

Looking up, Cleo saw Tom walking toward them with a scowl on his face. "Do you know my husband, Tom?" she asked when he had reached them.

"From when we was pups. How are you, Tom? Been getting to know your wife, here. Hope to be so lucky myself someday." His gaze was frankly admiring.

"You still selling those leases?" The way Tom pronounced the word, he might have been saying *rattlers.*

"Yep, wheeling and dealing all the time. You'd do well to consider leasing me some of your land." The man's eyes were as steady as a poker player calling a bluff.

Tom bristled. "Even if there was oil under my land, that's where I want it to stay. I'm a rancher."

"I won't give up on you, but I'll let you be. . .for now." Dal slapped him on the back. "Let's just celebrate the holiday." He tipped his hat to Cleo and wandered off to greet another group of men.

"Stay away from that snake-oil salesman," Tom said softly as he watched Dal make his pitch.

*The very idea!* Cleo fumed to herself. Why should Tom forbid her to talk to this charming man? But she sensed his jealousy and didn't argue.

It was an enjoyable day, an opportunity to spend time with her new friends.

Tante Olga studied Cleo's ripening figure. "You carry your baby high." She smiled. "A nice, fat little girl for you." Noting the sudden frown on Cleo's face, she was immediately solicitous. "You feel all right? You look tired."

"It's all the canning we've been doing in the heat, Tante Olga. I need a little rest, that's all."

Olga nodded in agreement. "I have a tonic that vill help you get your strength. You need to be strong for your delivery."

Cleo had a lot of questions to ask Olga, things she normally would have asked her own mother but would never have considered sharing with Mrs. Kinney. And as Olga answered, Cleo found herself growing impatient for the miracle to occur.

"Who could not believe in Gott when they see a newborn kinder? From the love of a man and woman comes a new life." Olga's face was soft with love. "And it is up to you and that man to love that little one and care for her. To teach her about Gott's love for her."

Cleo flushed, thinking of her own fragile faith. "I'm afraid I only call on Him when I'm in trouble," she confessed.

"It's a beginning. Now you can start to practice thanking Him, too. When it comes to raising kinder, I don't know vhat vomen who don't pray do. Ve can't control life around us. All ve can do is ask the Lord's mercy."

Cleo thought of the boy who had been bitten by the rattlesnake. Had his mother failed to pray for his safety?

"Read the Scriptures every day for the strength and courage to be happy in this hard land." Olga patted Cleo's hand. "And pray."

On impulse, Cleo seized her hand. "I want you to be there when the baby comes."

"I vill be there," Olga promised. Looking up, she shaded her eyes. "There is Miss Lemmon and her nephew. I think someone say he fall off his horse."

"Then you're needed. I'll talk with you later." Cleo's eyes glistened. "Thank you, Tante Olga."

Olga nodded and turned her attention to the boy.

Cleo helped herself to some iced tea, then found a seat under the shade of the big willows. It was a relief to be off her feet. The great, restless dunes around her radiated heat, and she was certain an egg could be cooked on the surface quickly.

Tom came and sat beside her on the blanket to polish off a big slab of chocolate cake.

"I can't believe there's water right here in the middle of all this sand," Cleo observed, seeing the great still pool, reeds lacing its face and willows swaying around the perimeter. "And those willows. They aren't like the weeping willows at home, and they're so large."

"Been used for years by Indians and people moving west," Tom said. "And over there is where a man claimed he found some mastodon bones. You can still see where the Indians made camp. See those smoky stones over there in a circle? A cooking fire."

Cleo's gaze followed his pointing finger, thinking of all the history built into this region. Then she sighed. "It feels sad here."

"Sad? With all this festivity going on around us? What's sad about it?"

"Because it's a place of survival. I can see people and animals dying out there because they didn't know water was close by. Or people traveling so far from home and barely making it to the pools. I don't know. . .it just feels sad to me."

A somber refrain from her days in church floated murkily to Cleo's mind: *"By the waters of Babylon, there we sat down and wept."* She couldn't remember the rest of the poem, but she thought it was a psalm. Something about willow trees and harps. *I'll look it up in that little Bible I carried on my wedding day,* she thought.

All day long the older boys had chased each other with firecrackers, and their irritating pops were constant. But at sundown the real fireworks began, spectacular against the blackness of the great vaulted sky.

It was late when the events of the day wound down. Some would be going to town to spend the night, while others—like the Kinneys—had planned to camp out among the willows and start back for their homes in the morning.

Cleo lay awake on her quilt under the starry heavens long after Tom was snoring beside her. Funny how these same stars were shining over Houston just as they were here. The same God she had learned about in Sunday school had made them. But the stars seemed brighter out here, bigger, almost close enough to touch. God, too, seemed nearer. . .almost close enough to touch, she thought just before she drifted off into a dreamless sleep.

# Chapter 9

A few days later, noticing Tom's restlessness and irritability, Cleo questioned him about it.

"It's time for the loan to come due," he said with a defeated sigh. "I'm so tired of scratching out a living on this place. If only it would rain, things would ease up. Joneses are leaving. They can't make it."

She held her breath. "Are you thinking of leaving, too?"

"Not until I don't have any other choices."

"Tom, it doesn't have to be this hard," she said quietly. "I have money. Father has money. There's no shame in letting someone help you." She snuggled against him in their feather bed. "Consider it a loan. You could pay it back in time."

He looked down into the deep pools of her smoky blue eyes. "You should know me well enough by now to know I can't do that."

She was careful with her next question. "Tom, would you let me and the baby suffer because of your pride?"

He recoiled. "Are you suffering? I thought you were happy here with me."

"Of course, I am!" she reassured him. "And I'm not really suffering. It *is* hard, but that's because I've never known what it was to work for a living. Father always had money, but I never saw him earn it. The point is, if you'd let me help you, we could have a nice home out here. Be comfortable. Have the things we needed. You could concentrate on building, not just holding things together."

Recognizing the wisdom of her words, he didn't answer her right away. She was right. He shouldn't be scraping and clawing; he should be improving the ranch. But if he took the money, his manhood would be in question. He had to prove—at least to himself—that he could make it on his own the way his father had, and his father before him.

As if reading his thoughts, Cleo spoke up. "I don't think people would look down on you. Your father and grandfather had their own ways of making money. If by marrying me, you came into some, then that's just another way of making it. And heaven knows, being married to me, you've earned every cent of it!"

He chuckled and pulled her even closer. "Let me think it over, honey. I've never been one to jump on the first train."

"You jumped quickly enough on my train."

"Yeah, but I could see it was first class all the way."

423

Their laughter drained away the tension from between them, and curled together, they slept like innocent children.

~

Cleo didn't speak of the money to Tom for the next few days, but she could tell he was thinking about the matter.

Once again, waiting until they were snuggled in their bed after the others had retired for the night, he broached the subject. "I've given a lot of thought to what you said." He sighed deeply and with a hint of resignation. "I guess my pride will have to take a backseat to my common sense. I can't stand by and see you work so hard. And I don't want to lose the ranch. So I'll take you up on your offer to use your money. But I promise you, you'll get it back, with interest!"

It was all Cleo could do to restrain her squeal of delight. "Oh, Tom, you won't regret this! But you do realize that this makes me part owner in the ranch, don't you?"

"I guess it does. Well, partner, if you agree, I'd like to begin by paying off the mortgage on the ranch so we can own our place, free and clear. Then we'll see where we are."

She grinned at him broadly. "There's something else I haven't told you."

He eyed her with suspicion. "And that is. . . ?"

"When I'm twenty-five, I come into my trust fund." She paused to give him time to think. "That's about a million and some change." She laughed loudly at the astonishment on his face.

His gasp of astonishment let her know that she had taken him completely by surprise.

"I didn't tell you, because I was afraid I'd scare you off."

"And you never said a word." He shook his head, still not believing his ears. "I knew you'd get something when your father died, but I never dreamed about any kind of trust fund. No wonder he was so protective." His mind was reeling with all the possibilities of her disclosure. "I never dreamed," he breathed again.

A tiny breath of frosty fear stirred in Cleo's heart as her husband's delight grew. She moved against him, seeking reassurance, as the fears of her childhood echoed in her mind. "This doesn't change anything. We're still the same people. Money is just money."

Tom heard the raw need in her voice. "Honey, if I had known about your money before I knew you, it might have changed things between us," he said gently. "But I knew the real you. I love the real you. The money means that things will be easier for us, that's all." And his kiss sealed the bargain.

But in spite of his reassurances, for the next few days, Cleo watched Tom for signs of change. She thought she noticed subtle differences—maybe he was a little too quick to pull out a chair for her, or he took her arm a bit too readily—and then was ashamed of her suspicions.

She wrote to her family, asking her father to transfer the remainder of her bank account to the bank in Wink, telling him that she wanted to pay off the loan on the ranch. It was a cheerful letter, describing the picnic on the dunes and her meeting with an oil speculator. Once again she mentioned the plan to come for a visit after her child was born. "If it is a girl, I want to call her Claire," she wrote, "but her full name would be Madeline Claire, for you, Mother."

⌒

The Seachrists had been spending more and more time in their sitting room off the bedroom, lounging before the fireplace, which was now filled with potted plants for the summer. The deepening wrinkles on Madeline's face bore mute testimony to the worries she had endured since her daughter's marriage. And Henry looked much thinner, almost frail. He was grateful to be alive but deeply grieved by the letter he was holding in his hand.

"It's starting, Henry, just as we feared," Madeline said softly.

"Now, Mother, it may not be as bad as we think." He tried to comfort her. "The rest of her letter is quite cheerful."

Madeline's concern thrust her from the chair into a restless pacing. "Our daughter is married to a man we don't know, is living in the wilderness, and is going to have her first child! Now we learn that she has obviously not been telling us everything that's going on. Why does she need the money?"

Scanning the letter over the glasses perched on the end of his nose, he looked up. "She says it's to pay off the loan on the ranch. Doesn't sound as if she's going hungry to me. Sounds like a firm business deal."

While Madeline fretted about Cleo's latest revelation, Henry was trying to decide how to tell his family that things weren't going too well for him financially. With his ill health, he hadn't been able to oversee his business. The market was in a slump, and several of his deals had gone sour. If things continued on this track, it was possible that he wouldn't be able to support their current lifestyle for long, unless he borrowed on his life insurance.

He was still thinking about it later that night as he eased to the edge of sleep in the sumptuous bedroom, though he didn't pray about it. Prayer was reserved for the dignity of the stately church service on Sunday morning. Intelligent men knew God didn't interfere in the business world. That world was a dice throw. Henry wondered how long his luck would last. And if it would get better. . .or worse.

⌒

The letter Cleo held in her hand was rather brief and straightforward. Her father had laid it on the line. He was unable to send the money she requested, vaguely alluding to some "problems" with the business. He recommended she come home immediately, with no apology for failing to grant her request. Cleo was utterly confused. What about her bank account? Her house? Obviously her father didn't want to share any of this with her yet. But why?

She turned her shocked face to a tight-lipped Tom. "I don't understand. What shall I do?"

"*I* get it," he said through clenched teeth. "Your father doesn't trust me. He thinks all I ever wanted from you was your money. . .and his. This is his way of making sure I don't get my hands on any of it." Tom's face, bronzed from the sun, was now flushed with anger.

Cleo kept silent, wondering whether she should try to defend her father, and the tiny doubt about Tom's love for her coiled and rattled in the corner of her mind. Hearing no denial of his accusations, Tom stomped from the house to the barn, where he saddled his horse and rode off into the darkness to cool off.

Mrs. Kinney came out of her bedroom. From the look of condemnation on her face, it was clear that she had heard the entire conversation. Without a word to Cleo, she lit the kerosene lantern and walked outside to hang it high on the windmill next to the house, lighting her son's way back.

But Tom didn't return until well after dawn. And when Cleo came in for breakfast, Tom was sitting at the table with a cup of steaming coffee in his hand, his mother stirring a pan of grits.

"Tom, can we talk about this in private?" Cleo asked quietly. She heard a soft "Hrumph!" from the vicinity of the stove but ignored it. Tom took his coffee and headed out the back door for the shade of the old mulberry tree. Then, leaning with his back against it, he waited for her to speak.

"What do you want me to do?" she asked.

"What do you want to do?" he countered. "I don't think going back there will help anything. But it's obviously where he wants you. . .away from me. Maybe he's right." Tom peered into the endless prairie as if to read the future. "Maybe you'd better get out while you still can. It's obvious I can't take care of you like your daddy can."

Her silent tears traced a path down her cheeks. "Tom, I don't want to leave you. I love you and my place is here with you. I'm sorry I got your hopes up for the ranch. I honestly thought I could help." She walked over and eased her bulk beside him, leaning into the broadness of his chest. "Please tell me you don't want me to leave." Her smoky blue eyes were enormous in her pinched face.

Tom leaned down and gently placed his lips over hers. "Stay with me," he then whispered into her hair. "I don't ever want you to leave me. You know I need you, with or without your money." He smoothed back her hair, and they sealed their pledges to one another with another kiss while Mrs. Kinney watched shamelessly from the kitchen window.

In the next few days, Cleo gave a great deal of thought to the letter she was writing to her parents. She was working on the final draft when Robert burst into the kitchen where she was sitting at the table. "Wire for you, Cleo!"

With hands that trembled, she reached for the envelope, opened it, and read silently. "Oh, no. . .no!" she cried brokenly. Telegram dangling from her hand, she walked out to their bedroom in the new wing and sat down on the bed.

Mrs. Kinney wasn't far behind. "Bad news?" she asked, wiping her hands on her damp apron.

"Where's Tom?" Cleo said dully, ignoring her mother-in-law's question. "I want Tom."

"Robert, go get Tom and bring him here." Mrs. Kinney took one look at Cleo's ashen face and hurried to get her a glass of water. Clumsily she pushed the water into Cleo's numb hand and guided the glass to her lips. Then she retreated to the living room to wait for her son. She could hear her daughter-in-law's soft sobs, but she made no attempt to go comfort the girl. That was her son's job.

Tom rushed into the house and headed straight for his weeping wife. "What is it, honey?"

"Oh, Tom, he's dead! Father's dead! Why didn't they tell me he was so sick? I didn't know. The letter must have been his way of asking me to come home before it was too late. Oh, why didn't I go?"

Tom made soothing noises and stroked her hair, holding her close while she wailed her guilt and remorse.

There was no discussing whether she would go back home for her father's funeral. She started packing right away. Pregnant or not, she was needed at home. And she needed to be there. However, it was decided that Tom would not make the trip with her.

Traveling over the sand was a trial, but it was the easy part of the journey. The train ride seemed to take forever, and its constant lurching and swaying made Cleo sick. In her car she tried to breathe through thick cigar fumes, plotting revenge on the insensitive old goat who alternately smoked and chewed the awful weed.

Her mother met her at the station, and the familiar ritual began to unfold.

The funeral was orchestrated to bring comfort to the grieving family, with many of Houston's most prominent families attending. In public her mother was stalwart and strong. But it was only after all the mourners had left at last and the maid had cleared the huge dining room table of the food brought in by friends that Madeline invited her daughter up to her room to talk privately.

"It was a lovely service, don't you think, dear? I love the way the Reverend Kohl preaches. And so many people. My, I knew we had a lot of friends, but I never realized how many until I saw the full church today. It's quite a tribute to your father." Madeline sipped a cup of coffee and threaded her way carefully through the first acknowledged day of her widowhood.

Cleo recognized the reddened eyes, faded mirrors of her own, and replied with the correct responses to her mother's monologue.

"And the reading of the will tomorrow, of course. I don't think there will be many surprises." Madeline Seachrist took another sip of coffee and leaned back in her chaise lounge, running her fingers lightly around the rim of the bone china cup. Time seemed to be softening the edges of her immediate grief and taking her back to the happy days.

Cleo listened to her mother reminisce and watched with some concern as she let down her guard. But Cleo's attention was jerked sharply into focus at her mother's next words.

"I should say that there won't be any surprises for *me* tomorrow. . .but I must prepare you. . ." Madeline paused and watched Cleo anxiously. "I think it's all gone. . .the money, I mean. Henry would never tell me the whole truth. When he refused to send you the money you asked for, I knew something was wrong, for he has never denied you anything. When I questioned him, he admitted to some trouble with the cash flow, but I could tell that things were worse than he was letting on."

She shook her head and laughed sadly. "Men are so silly about not wanting to worry us, and then they die and we have to put everything together again." She walked over to the mantel, fingering the ornately carved molding. "I think I'll sell the house and move into something. . .cozier. Without Henry"—Madeline broke off, her eyes filling with quick tears—"this place will feel so empty."

She turned to regard Cleo sadly. "It was all for you, anyway. You were the only reason we needed money. I wanted to give you everything. To make you happy. To give you the kind of life you deserved."

Cleo made soft protests, but her mother continued. "I loved you from the first moment I thought of you. I was so happy we would have our little girl."

"And how could you be so sure I would be a girl?" Cleo asked curiously.

Her mother paused only a moment, then drew up her shoulders with resolution. "A long time before I met your father, I was in love with a man. . .a boy, really." She sighed. "I was young and ignorant, and I thought he loved me, too. When he found out about the baby, he took the first road out of town. My parents sent me back East to stay with my aunt until the child came." She began to weep as Cleo's face crumpled in disbelief. "Don't hate me, darling. Please don't hate me."

"What happened to. . .that baby?" Cleo's voice was strangled with emotion.

"I gave it up. My aunt took her to an orphanage." She looked pitifully into Cleo's eyes. "I couldn't take care of a child, darling. I had no choice."

Cleo heard her mother's confession with horror. Horror at the deception her mother had revealed to her, pity for the ordeal she had endured. Carefully and lovingly she gathered her weeping mother into her arms. "You didn't have to tell me this now, Mother. It makes no difference."

"But there's more." Madeline Kinney moved away to compose herself. Then, looking at the daughter she loved so desperately, she drew a deep breath, knowing that her next words would change Cleo's life forever.

# Chapter 10

I never got over the guilt of giving my little girl away," Madeline went on. "I never stopped thinking of her. Your father was a kind and loving man, but I never tested his love by telling him about my child. Her birth was difficult, and when we wanted to have children, I wasn't able to conceive. When it appeared that we could not have children of our own, I decided to help someone else's child, the way I hoped someone had helped mine. It wasn't hard to talk your father into an adoption."

Cleo felt fear tighten her stomach and a denial sprang to her lips, though she did not utter it. *No, no, don't tell me this! I don't want to hear it!*

"I read in the papers that New York City was crowded with children of all ages. They were to be loaded on trains and sent throughout the rural parts of the country."

"You mean the orphan trains?" Cleo was horrified.

"Yes." Madeline smoothed her dressing gown. "The same baby trains we have today."

Cleo could feel the room beginning to spin.

Her mother quietly continued her story. "Oh, I didn't do as some did—wait until the train stopped and the children were lined up on the depot platform. I wrote to the same orphanage where I had left my child and asked specifically for a baby girl. For *you*." Her eyes filled with unshed tears. "Your father and I ordered you. . .like a doll from a catalog."

Cleo could see her mother leave the present as she relived the past. "I got a reply from the orphanage very quickly. You were a newborn—black hair, blue eyes, of course, and the most exquisite skin. White like milk. And a baby bud of a mouth." She turned and looked at Cleo. "I'm sure your father would have preferred a son, but I was so insistent on a daughter that he didn't have the heart to oppose me. And I loved you from the moment I sent off the letter.

"The day the train was due, I thought we would never get to the station. We knew you would be accompanied by a woman from the orphanage, so we looked for her." Sadness strained Madeline's face as she remembered the scene. "It was awful. Children and babies everywhere—crying, confused, being inspected like cattle at an auction. Some would choose a child, separating him from his brothers and sisters. Farmers selected the oldest and strongest ones to work on their farms. Others, like you, were chosen in love.

"When I found you at last, tagged with our name, I thought I would die of happiness. You were my little girl come back to me."

Cleo knew of the baby trains, but they were seldom mentioned in polite company. An open secret that no one wanted to acknowledge. The idea had seemed like a good one at first, but it had grown ugly over the years. And now her own mother was telling her that she was one of those orphans! *This is a nightmare,* she decided. Maybe she would wake up.

But when she opened her eyes, her mother was standing before her, tears raining down her cheeks, washing away the years of guilt, and in her confession, destroying forever the security Cleo had always known.

Cleo couldn't bear any more revelations. "Come, let me put you down to sleep now, Mother. You'll feel better after you rest."

Madeline didn't resist but willingly allowed Cleo to tuck her into bed. And in the stillness of her girlhood bedroom, Cleo tried to deal with all that she had learned. It was too much to comprehend. Grief over the loss of her father and her mother's admission rolled over her like a huge green ocean wave, drowning her in its depths.

⤖

Cleo's child woke her in the morning with a rollicking bounce. It was a now familiar sensation, but when she opened her eyes and looked around, she knew she was not in her bed at the ranch.

A giant fist slammed into her middle as she remembered the events of the day before, and she felt as if she were choking. *I'm not really their daughter. I'm not part of them. It was all a charade.* And she wept tears of desolation. She had lost her father who wasn't really her father, and her mother had picked her out of an orphanage. *Who am I?* she cried.

Exhausted from her restless night, Cleo went into the luxurious bathroom and ran a tub of hot water. Easing her bulk down into the fragrant bubbles, she soaked for a long time, thinking of the news she had heard.

Still feeling numb, she toweled herself dry, dressed, and went downstairs to the dining room to face her mother who wasn't really her mother.

When Cleo entered the room, Madeline rose and enfolded her in a warm embrace. "I wasn't sure you'd come down today, darling." Cleo lost no time in getting to the point as she took her seat at the table, feeling the warming rays of sunlight streaming through the tall English windows. "Mother, why did you tell me? Why now?"

"The timing may not have been best," Madeline admitted, "but I felt you had the right to know the truth. It's possible someday you would have found out anyway, and I would rather you hear it from me."

They nibbled their toast in silence, each absorbing the finality of recent events. "Have you ever wondered what happened to your. . .other daughter?" Cleo asked at last.

Madeline smiled sadly. "I think of her every year on her birthday. But it would serve no useful purpose for me to intrude on her life now. Besides, I have you. She's a closed chapter in my life." She hesitated. "But what about you. . .do you want to know about your real mother?"

Cleo put down her coffee cup and stared at her. "You *are* my real mother!" she decided on the spot and swiped at her eyes. "And you know, Mother, you're an amazing woman. It took a lot of courage to tell me your story. I doubt that many women would have taken that risk."

Madeline sighed deeply. "The most important part of that story is that your father loved you and I love you. When you hold your child in your arms, you'll understand. But I've often thought that when one deliberately seeks out a child, perhaps it is even more precious."

Without another word, Cleo rose from her chair and enfolded the seated woman holding out her arms. They wept silently together, resealing their relationship on a new level. They had chosen one another. There was no need to return to yesterday.

"What time is the lawyer coming?" Cleo asked as she refilled their coffee cups.

"Around ten. I expect a few long-lost cousins, too," her mother said wryly. "I think they will be in for an unhappy surprise."

"It's gone? All of it?"

"I can't be sure, but I know I will have to make some major changes in my life. As you know, Henry didn't want to trouble me with his worries. Consequently, I worried alone. Men are such ninnies about their wives, don't you think?"

Cleo felt a new surge of understanding between them. "Sometimes I think I've married a little boy," she agreed. "Will you be all right here?"

"Of course, dear. Believe it or not, I am quite strong and self-sufficient." She gave her daughter a penetrating look. "And you? Tell me about life in West Texas."

Cleo made no further attempt to withhold anything from her mother. Her words rushed out in a torrent. "I love Tom desperately, but I can't abide his mother. We're poor as church mice and likely to lose the ranch. I hate the dreary West Texas weather. But most of all I hate the sand. And I miss you terribly." Her eyes filled with tears as she concluded her grim recital.

"Then stay with me," Madeline said quickly. "Write Tom and tell him to come back here. He can find a job again. Let the old biddy run her sandy kingdom."

"I wish it were that easy." Cleo shifted uncomfortably in her chair. "I'm sure Tom loves me, but to tell the truth, I'm not sure how much. The ranch means more to him than I realized. It seems to be all tied up with his male ego. And you know how big that is!" she added humorously.

"We'll work on this problem at tea time. I'll think about it, and by then we'll know for sure what our financial picture is. As my mother used to say, 'It'll all come out in the wash.' " Madeline patted Cleo's hand and rose to face her new world.

❧

Later that day, in the ornate room where Tom had asked for Cleo's hand, Madeline served the tea as gracefully as she had for the past thirty-five years. Her hand was steady and her voice clear and firm. "Now," she said as she settled back into the deep cushion of her chair with her own cup, "let's make some plans. I've already arranged with the lawyer to put this house on the market. And the realtor is searching for an appropriate apartment or small house for me. I've given the servants their notice." She paused, looking out the richly hung window, "You know, I'm rather looking forward to starting a new life in a new place. I think staying here would be harder for me with all its memories. I've arranged my life. Now, what shall we do about yours?"

"I can see only two options. Go or stay," Cleo said miserably. She looked toward her mother hopefully.

"Oh, no, my darling, you have to make this decision on your own. The only thing I can tell you is that nothing is forever. You can make a decision for now and, as things change, you can alter your plans. Just listen to your heart."

Cleo thought about that. It sounded like something Tante Olga might have said, though her mother had not mentioned God or prayer. Suddenly an overwhelming desire to run into Tom's arms swept over her. All else paled next to her need to be with him.

Her mother smiled. "I can see by the expression on your face what you've decided. I'll help you pack." She embraced Cleo. "I think you've made a good choice. And after I'm settled and feeling up to it, I may even come out west and give that old witch a run for her money."

Cleo's accompanying laugh was the happiest sound Madeline had heard in a long while.

As Cleo was putting her things in the traveling cases, she heard the phone ring and ran to answer it.

"Cleo!" came a familiar voice. "J.J. and I just got back from Bermuda. I'm just devastated about your father's death. I'm so sorry I wasn't there when you needed me. Are you all right? Can I come over now?" Mattie ran on, not pausing for breath.

"I'm fine, and yes, I'd love to see you right this minute."

"I'm on my way!"

❧

It was like old times. The laughing and crying were pitched high and girlish, though the hugging was a little more long distance with Cleo's child between them.

"I'm jealous," Mattie admitted as they went into Cleo's bedroom. "J.J. and I would love to have a baby, too."

Cleo wrinkled her nose. "It's not what it's cracked up to be," she warned, "especially the first few weeks."

"Going back already?" Mattie asked when she saw the open suitcases.

"Yes. Tom is expecting me tomorrow."

They pushed the cases off the bed and curled up as they had in earlier, more carefree days. Cleo told Mattie the whole story while Mattie listened with astonishment, scarcely breathing throughout the entire monologue.

"Well?" Cleo demanded when she had come to the end of her tale. "Aren't you going to say something?"

"I—I don't know what to say," Mattie sputtered. "For the first time in my life, I'm speechless." Her lashes were laced with tears. "All I know is that you're still the dearest friend I have in the world. I've missed you and didn't know how much until I saw you again today. Do you really have to leave tomorrow?"

Cleo nodded firmly. "Things were very tense when I left. I want to go back and make sure Tom knows I love him and want to be with him." On impulse, she gave Mattie a conspiratorial glance. "Come with me."

"What?" Mattie was aghast. "I can't come with you! I'm a married lady now. J.J. would have a fit." She paused. "For how long?"

"As long or as short a visit as you like."

"Would I have to share a room with Mrs. Kinney?"

Cleo went along with the mischievous look in her friend's eyes. "No, you can sleep out in the barn where it's safe."

Mattie sobered. "Are you serious. . .about my coming, I mean? Since it isn't your house. . ."

Cleo drew herself up importantly. "Remember, we've just built an addition to the house. I can invite anybody I please. Besides," she went on, suddenly serious, "I need you, Mattie. It would mean a lot to me to have you there when the baby comes, especially since Mother can't come out until the estate is settled."

"Well, J.J. *is* working on an oil deal night and day. That's one reason we went to Bermuda. Maybe he'd appreciate my being out of his hair for a while." The sparkle in Mattie's eyes matched Cleo's.

❧

On the train the next day, the two women talked all the way. Cleo tried to prepare Mattie for the experience. "You know we live on a real working ranch," she explained. "It's nothing fancy. No indoor plumbing. . .no running hot water. . .that sort of thing."

Mattie sighed. "Oh, I know you've said it's rustic, but it all sounds so terribly romantic."

"You won't think it's so romantic when you have to use the privy in the middle of the night. Did I mention to be careful of the black widow spiders that like to hide under the seat?"

"Oh, Cleo," Mattie wailed, "now you'll have to go with me!" And Cleo laughed as Tom had laughed at her introduction to ranch life.

They spoke of the coming baby and the small layette Cleo had assembled. Privately Mattie planned what she might do to make Cleo's life easier. But the more she heard about her friend's spartan existence, the more she disliked Tom Kinney. It was all his fault that Cleo was suffering! And she deliberately refused to think about Mrs. Kinney until she was forced to deal with Cleo's mother-in-law face-to-face.

Cleo had wired Tom to meet her but had not mentioned that Mattie would be coming, too. She noticed with relief that he covered his shock well, and she concentrated on demonstrating to him how much she had missed him.

Tom, on the other hand, was quietly resentful. His greeting to Mattie was cordial but restrained. *That's all I need now,* he thought, *reinforcements for her side.* But he knew alienating Mattie wouldn't help his cause, so he was carefully deferential.

Mattie amused them with her naive remarks as they jounced along the road to the ranch. Both Tom and Cleo were happy to postpone the exchange of any serious news and pointed out the landmarks along the way.

At the ranch Robert gallantly gave up his room, and even Mrs. Kinney was civil to her houseguest, though her sharp eyes were taking in every detail of Mattie's attire. In those faded eyes, Cleo could read the same disapproval she herself had received from her those months ago.

After Mattie was settled, Cleo went back to her own retreat where she knew Tom would be waiting for her.

Silently he took her in his arms. "I missed you like crazy," he breathed against her mouth. "Promise me you won't ever go away again."

She pulled away to look up into his dark eyes. "I was afraid you'd never speak to me again. You were so formal at the train depot."

"I was surprised to see Mattie, that's all. I thought maybe you had brought her in for reinforcements." He smiled a lazy smile. "But when you wouldn't let go of my hand all the way home, I knew you weren't mad at me." To demonstrate how glad he was to see her, he kissed her long and lovingly.

"Guess we were both wrong." Cleo gently disengaged herself from his embrace and began taking off her traveling clothes. "I have so much to tell you. So very much."

Pulling on a wrapper, she perched on their bed and considered how best to break the news. "First of all, there isn't any money. I'm sorry. Father wasn't being mean; he was just broke. And Mother is selling the house and moving into an apartment. She'll have only enough money to take care of herself." She looked intently into her husband's face. "What are we going to do?"

Tom plowed his hands through his hair, taking time to assimilate the information. "I don't know, but I'll think of something. I hadn't counted on your money to begin with, you know."

She wanted to tell him about the orphan train, but he seemed so distracted that she didn't have the heart to dump any more on him. What could he do about it anyway? It didn't change things between them. Or did it? She wasn't ready to find out.

"I'm planning to ship some cattle. Maybe I'll ship more than I planned." He looked at her rounded figure lovingly. "Don't you worry, honey. You just take care of that baby of ours."

She took him at his word. With the baby coming, there was a lot to think about. And if Tom lost the ranch, would that really be such a tragedy? After all, it would mean that they could go back to Houston. And after seeing "civilization" again, West Texas now looked like the end of the world. She began to have serious doubts about having a baby in this forsaken place. *What if something goes wrong?*

The thought persisted over the next few days, and each kick of the baby was a reminder of her fear. And then she remembered what Tante Olga had said about depending on God each day and began to pray. *Lord, I don't have any control over what happens to me and the baby. Please keep us both safe. And thank You for Mattie. I know she's an answer to my prayers. I haven't always been faithful to You, and I've been careless with all the blessings You've given me. But as I grow older and wiser and live in this land, I know I can't make it without You.* A lump had risen in her throat at her confession of her need for the Lord, and she knew that she had come a long way since her Sunday school days. Her prayers were no longer girlish babble, but the deep heart cries of a grown woman.

❧

Mattie never complained about the lack of amenities on the ranch, but it was plain that each day was a surprise to her. And when they took her to a dance over at Crook's place, she chatted with everyone there and danced the night away, while Cleo sat on the sidelines and drank gallons of tea.

On the way home in the stillness of the night, she told Cleo, "I don't think I ever met a nicer bunch of people. Quaint, but nice. Living out here sure changes one's point of view, doesn't it?"

Cleo laughed. "Yes. Life seems completely different out here. Sometimes I hate it," she said softly so Tom couldn't hear her, "but the people make it bearable."

"*Most* of them anyway," whispered Mattie, and she cut her eyes to the dour Mrs. Kinney as they both suppressed a soft giggle.

# Chapter 11

Tom made the next mortgage payment with a large shipment of cattle. It was a disappointment to see his herd growing smaller, but there was nothing else to be done. Once, when Mattie tried to approach him about the wildcatting J.J. was doing, he cut her off with a surly retort before she could finish her sentence.

Near the end of Cleo's pregnancy, the two women were sitting under the tree in the backyard, sipping lemonade and enjoying the cooling fall breeze.

Cleo watched Mattie scanning the horizon. "You're getting bored, aren't you." It was more statement than question.

Her friend turned to her with a sigh. "A little, though being with you is rarely boring. But I do miss J.J."

"And parties and restaurants and plays and. . .life," added Cleo lightly. "So do I."

"You'll soon have your hands full with your little one."

"The sooner the better. I'm so uncomfortable I'd walk barefoot through hot coals to get this lump off my front."

"I still think you should move into Midland. If it's a matter of money, I'd like to. . . ," Mattie began carefully.

A sudden look of alarm crossed Cleo's face. "Oh, Mattie, I think it may be too late to go anywhere. I think the baby is coming. . .now!"

Mattie helped her into the house and called Mrs. Kinney and Tom.

"Cleo, honey, what do you want me to do?" he asked.

"Go get Tante Olga. She promised she'd come. I need her, Tom."

"I'll get her, honey. Don't worry." Tom glared at his mother. "I know you can take care of things while I'm gone, Ma."

She nodded silently and went into the kitchen to put on the coffeepot.

When Olga arrived, she found Cleo dressed primly in a white cotton gown and tucked into bed. Tom was sent away to occupy himself with chores while the women got down to work.

As her labor progressed, Cleo said, "I wish I were at home." This escalated to "I wish I'd never married that man!" Finally, her wail blossomed to "I never should have come to this place with that man!"

"I know how you feel," observed Tante Olga.

"Not unless you've had a baby, you don't!" Cleo shot back tartly.

"I've had six." She wiped Cleo's forehead. "Vhen I first come to America, I vas so frightened. I don't speak the language even. Den I marry and come here and vas *really* frightened!" She laughed. "I remember a psalm. I read it many times:

> By the rivers of Babylon we sat and wept
>> when we remembered Zion.
> There on the willow trees
>> we hung our harps,
> for there our captors asked us for songs,
>> our tormentors demanded songs of joy;
> How can we sing the songs of the Lord
>> while in a foreign land?

"Dis out here is, for sure, a foreign land." She fussed around Cleo. "But soon you vill think of it as your home, not a foreign land. And you vill love your husband again. More than ever." Her eyes twinkled with good humor.

As another contraction hit Cleo, she had the gravest of doubts. "And where is my loving husband now?" she moaned.

"Soon. He vill be here soon," crooned Tante Olga.

Tom and Mattie were keeping vigil outside, but the sounds of Cleo's deepening labor could be clearly heard. They comforted one another with assurances neither fully believed.

Mattie moved between Tom and Cleo as the time drew nearer for their child to be delivered. So it was her good fortune to announce to Tom the arrival of his baby daughter. "Hale and hearty, with blue eyes like her mother and hair like yours!" she cried delightedly.

～

Cleo named the baby for her mother as she had promised, and the days went by in a blur as she cared for the infant. Each day she thanked the Lord for her beautiful daughter. And Tom, being a dutiful father, hid any disappointment he might have felt in not having a son.

He also hid their deepening financial pit. He had ridiculed Mattie's suggestions about drilling for oil on his land, but with news of a big oil strike in Pecos again, he found himself reconsidering. It would mean quick money if he hit oil. *If.*

A few days later, Robert came riding up to the ranch yelling for Tom. His mount was hard ridden and Robert's eyes were glassy with wonder. "They did it! Old man Hendricks has struck it rich! The whole town's gone wild. The place is crawlin' with men and machines. Promoters, drillers, tool dressers, gamblers, and ladies of the night! It's like a circus. Money is flowin' like water!"

"Whoa. Slow down. You mean in Kermit?"

"You wouldn't even recognize the place," Robert told him. "Tent houses have sprouted like mushrooms in a good rain. Buildings made of anythin' people can get their hands on!"

Tom shook his head and tried to picture sleepy little Kermit as Robert had described it. "I've got to see for myself."

Tom and Robert could hear the ruckus long before they rode into town. In a very short time, the place had been overrun with blocks and blocks of hastily constructed shops. It seemed all the trades and services were represented. Tom didn't like the looks of some of the men he saw scurrying by. And there were attractive women whose eyes were not shy when they looked at a man.

It was in the midst of this hullabaloo that he spotted Leaf entering a brand-new mercantile. It had been a long time since they had chatted, and he hurried to catch up with her.

"Leaf!" he called, seeing her pause along a planked wood counter. "Leaf, it's been a long time." When she turned to face him, he was shocked to see the change in her appearance. It seemed that she was wearing too much makeup, and her dress was cut so low that he willed himself to keep his gaze glued to her face.

"Hi, Tom. What do you think of our new town? Exciting, isn't it?" Her eyes held an unmistakable challenge.

"And I see you've changed your style to fit the big city."

She shrugged. "I got tired of cowboys who never had time for anything but cows. The men here are very interesting."

"What does your father have to say about that?"

"I wouldn't know. I have my own place now. I share it with another girl."

"Do you have a job?" he asked, hoping he was wrong in his suspicions.

Her chin went up defiantly. "You might say that. The shop owners aren't too thrilled with me, but they take my money. And I have quite a lot of it. It's an easy job, and I make my own hours."

Tom's eyes dropped to the tips of his boots. "Leaf. . ."

"Don't say anything, Tom. I think I was meant for this kind of life. It sure beats being a secretary for my father. I like the money. I like the freedom. And I meet some really nice men." She regarded him steadily. "But I hope I can still talk to some of my old friends."

"We go back a long way."

"*Too* long. That was one of the problems." She laughed again. "I see Robert over there. Say hello to him for me. Guess he's too shy to talk to me right now."

"Be happy," Tom said softly, and tipped his hat to her.

"Is she all right?" Robert asked when Tom rejoined him.

"*She* thinks so. How long has she been. . .in town?"

"How should I know?" Robert spread his hands innocently.

"I think you know more than you let on. What else have you been finding out in town?"

Robert was belligerent. "Talking to some promoters."

"About what?" Tom asked through clenched teeth.

"Leasing our land. For drilling. They'd make us a real good deal, Tom. And if they hit oil, we'd be rich!"

Tom could hear the greed in his brother's voice, but with the idea of quick money staring him in the face, he would be stupid not to hear more. His ranch was still in danger.

When they picked up the mail, there was a letter from J.J. to Mattie, and that reminded Tom of J.J.'s offer to stake him in a business venture. Oil was swirling all around in his brain, but he couldn't shake the feeling he was betraying all his ranching heritage if he succumbed. Could he use the one to support the other? If he got oil-rich, he could make the ranch into the dream he had for it. He shook his head to clear his mind. But the idea wouldn't die as he rode back to the ranch.

Robert was sullen and silent, still chafing from his brother's rebuke, as they rode along in the soft sand. Tom's eyes wandered across the vastness of the range to the blue horizon. *What should I do, Lord?* he asked. *You gave us all this land for the cattle. Is this oil thing Your way of helping me get the ranch going again? Tell me what to do.* He sighed as he walked his horse toward the barn and waited for an answer.

Mattie met the letter from J.J. with a delighted squeal and retreated to her bedroom to read it privately. In a few minutes, she let out a loud "Whoopee!" and came tearing out of the room waving the letter. "J.J.'s coming! He'll be here in less than a week. Seems news of the strike has reached all the way to Houston." Her eyes danced with happiness.

⤙⤚

J.J.'s arrival was cause for a celebration. There was a lot of catching up on news, the baby to admire, and the local boom to discuss. Robert was full of information, and Tom listened. Later during a lull, Tom and J.J. drifted to the backyard.

"So, how will all this affect your ranching, Tom?" asked J.J., looking prosperous and up-to-date. Tom felt like a handyman beside him.

"Depends," he replied noncommittally.

"Up to you, you know, whether you cash in on it or not." J.J. took a deep drag on his expensive cigar. The smoke ring rose around his head, and he stroked his newly grown mustache with a well-manicured hand.

"I know you love your wife, J.J., but I have the feeling this is really a business trip." Tom laughed softly.

"You are an astute man. Are you as good a businessman?"

"How do we do this?"

"I put up the capital; you provide the land. And labor, of course. I'd want you to be there to supervise the whole thing."

"I don't know the first thing about drilling an oil well."

"You'll learn quickly. And we'll hire good men." He took another puff. "Before you know it, we'll both be oil men." He winked happily.

"Just that easy?"

"Yep. I've seen it happen many times before."

Tom was skeptical. "Hmm. What happens if there isn't any oil on this land?"

"There's oil in Pecos and there's oil on the Hendricks's ranch, and you're sitting squarely in between. How can we miss?"

"It's tempting. But I swore I'd never drill on my land."

"It takes a smart man to change his mind when the facts change," J.J. said smoothly. "Besides, what alternatives do you have?"

"None I can think of." Tom chuckled. "But I don't want to go into this thing by default."

"Not by default, my friend. By choice. You'll choose to make us both very rich." He smiled a wide smile at Tom. "Deal?"

Tom matched J.J.'s firm handshake. "Deal." He shook his head. "But I'm not sure what I'm getting myself into."

J.J. clapped him on the back. "A brand-new world, my friend, a brand-new world."

⌦

J.J. went into town the next day with Tom as a very silent partner. J.J. did all the wheeling and dealing. He hired men for a drilling crew while Tom nodded an affirmative once in a while on his choice of workers.

The most important decision they had to make was where to drill. Using a map, J.J. drew a line straight from Pecos to the Hendricks strike. He pointed, grinning, to where it crossed Tom's land. "That's the honey hole."

With the help of a man who claimed to be a geologist, the spot was confirmed and they were ready to drill.

The news had been met by Mrs. Kinney first with rage, then with grudging acceptance. She retreated more and more from the family, muttering dire predictions under her breath. Had they not all been so busy—Cleo with the baby and Tom with his new venture—they would have noticed that she was fading from the world. But everyone was too busy to take time for a bitter old woman.

Tom was out at the drilling site day and night, taking two "towers" a day, as the shifts were called. Robert made himself a camp on the site, and J.J. often stayed in town to oversee the business end of things.

"I thought this was going to be good for all of us," complained Cleo to Mattie.

"Did I forget to mention what it's like to be married to a hotshot business-man?" she said with a wry look. "That's one of the reasons I knew J.J. wouldn't miss me too much if I came out here."

"Well, as soon as they hit the oil, things will change," Cleo consoled herself.

"Sure they will. Then they'll start on the second well so they can be twice as rich. You don't understand that this is a sickness. And it only gets worse."

"Then I hope they don't strike," Cleo said adamantly.

Mattie laughed. "Oh, that won't change anything. Once the fever takes hold of a man, he's hooked. We'll be oil widows no matter what."

Cleo felt a tingle of alarm. "I hope you're wrong. After all, Tom does have a family," she said hopefully.

"Maybe Tom will be different," suggested Mattie. "But you can thank God every day you have little Claire."

To her prayers for her child, Cleo added some for Tom's new obsession. *Please don't let it change Tom,* she pleaded. *Help him keep his balance and let us be a happy family.*

The first well came in a duster. Cleo had never seen anyone as disappointed as Tom when he came in to tell her. But when she tried to console him, he pushed her away.

"I'm disappointed, of course, Cleo, but there's oil out there. I'm positive of it. You know when they were going to drill on the Hendricks's ranch, they chose the place and then tried to drag the drilling sled there. It got stuck in the deep sand before they ever reached the drill site, so they decided to drill right there. And that's where they hit it! If they'd drilled in the original place, they might have missed it altogether. That's the oil game. Exciting as all get-out." He took off his grimy shirt and pumped water into the kitchen sink, splashing it all over his head and upper body.

It had been too long since she'd snuggled next to that firm body. Drilling had taken her place in his heart for now. Every moment was dedicated to bringing in the oil. She turned away sadly.

Tom and J.J. sat up late and worked their way through the new drilling plans. J.J.'s father would put up the money for the next test well. But, he had warned, he'd go with only one well. If they hit another duster, they'd have to find other ways of financing the next venture.

"We'll get her this time, old pal," J.J. assured Tom.

"To Number Two," Tom said, lifting his water glass. "Two has always been my lucky number."

Mattie and Cleo went to their respective beds and listened to their men bragging and patting each other on the back until they fell asleep to its boring repetition.

～❦～

On their husbands' orders, Mattie and Cleo hadn't ventured into town. "A boom-town is no place for a lady," they had told their wives, which only made Cleo and Mattie more determined to see what they were missing. With the two men away so much and Mrs. Kinney keeping to herself in her room, they decided that they deserved a day out. Cleo had asked Tante Olga to keep Claire, and she and Mattie were like the young girls back in Galveston, getting ready for the adventure of Splash Day.

Cleo regarded her long dark hair in the mirror. "It looks so shaggy and so. . . well. . .country." She turned slowly and studied her image. "What happened to the chic society girl?"

Mattie laughed. "Oh, she's still there, somewhere under all that sand and hair."

Cleo's eyes widened. "Oh, Mattie, I just remembered a dream I had last night. I was standing outside this shanty overlooking the prairie with a baby in my arms and one dragging on my skirt, and I was pregnant with another child. I woke up crying because I knew we were all hungry." She turned to Mattie. "It won't be like that, will it? Tell me it won't!"

"Never." She hugged Cleo and said, "Hurry up and get dressed. We're going to be 'beautified' today. My treat," she added firmly.

Cleo walked to the chifforobe and reached deep in the back. "I still have a little money of my own."

"Hmm, just think what damage the two of us can do!" laughed Mattie.

～❦～

Cleo gasped when she saw Kermit in the distance. "This isn't a little town any-more. Look at all the people!"

"It looks more like Houston. . .the other side of the tracks, that is," Mattie said through gritted teeth as the buggy bounced over the ruts in the road. "Where did all those cars come from. . .and trucks. . .and isn't that an electrical line overhead?"

People were swarming all over the town like ants on a hill. Buying and selling of every sort was going on on every street corner, and the noise was like downtown Houston at rush hour. For a moment, Cleo thought she was dreaming.

"Where do you want to go first?" Mattie asked, jolting her out of her reverie.

"The beauty shop. Then a dress shop."

"What about this one?" Mattie said, eyeing a woman who had walked out of one little shop patting her fresh coiffeur.

Inside, a beautician indicated a vacant chair. "I have room for one of you. Now, dearie, what can I do for you today?" she asked Cleo as she tied a large towel around her neck. Seeing Cleo's look of surprise as another patron—a flamboyantly dressed young woman—left the shop, she hastened to reassure her. "Oh, don't worry, we don't have too many of *that* kind in here. Besides, she's a pretty nice person, but I can't say much for her business practices, if you know what I mean. Oh, I can't afford to turn them away. They have most of the money in this town, you know, and they tip good. . . . Now, what's for you today?" She ran her hands through Cleo's ebony hair, lifting its weight from her neck.

"I want it cut in the latest fashion. . .whatever that is."

The operator laughed at Cleo's look of puzzlement. "Just leave it to me." And for the next hour, Cleo put herself in the woman's hands while Mattie received a full beauty treatment in the adjoining chair.

Their ears grew bigger as they listened to the two beauty operators talk in lowered tones. "The one who was just in here. . .you know? I hear Slim's taken a liking to her. Keeps his stooges off her back. She don't have to pay him no kickbacks as long as she keeps seein' him," said the one named Thelma.

"Yeah," Helen replied, "he's got this town locked up. Slim bein' the mayor and the police chief his partner, what sweeter deal could there be?"

They continued gossiping, giving away many of the town secrets to the two young women who sat immobile in their chairs. And by the time they left the shop, Cleo and Mattie were well informed about the local news.

"Mattie," Cleo whispered outside the shop, "I wanted my hair done, but I'm glad I didn't spend any money on a permanent. Those stories curled my hair!"

Mattie glanced around nervously. "I had no idea all this was going on. No wonder the men didn't want us to come to town. Let's get our shopping over and get home."

On the way home at last, they welcomed the vast slab of land that curved out of sight before them, broken only by a few mesquite trees and stubby grass. At least it was peaceful here. And then she heard it. A slow and steady thudding.

Cleo put one hand over her ear. "One of the things that bothered me when I first came out here was the quiet. Now that sound is driving me crazy!"

Mattie nodded. "The drilling. J.J. would say that's the sound of money."

"Maybe it's the sound of a marriage cracking up," Cleo said softly.

"Oh, come on, you're tougher than that. At least he's not out with another woman. He's just trying to make you rich."

"No, he's trying to save the ranch."

"Maybe you're looking at things with too narrow a view." She laughed lightly. "Besides, I've heard this isn't unusual for women after their babies are born. Buck up, old girl. You've got a new hairdo and a smashing new dress. Tom will *have* to notice!"

Cleo's smile was melancholy. "I wonder when Tom will ever be home to see these wondrous new changes in me."

～

Fay's name belied his gender and stature. He was an enormous man with a tightly muscled body and drilling expertise to match. He was Tom's number one man on the rig, but he was shaking his head in a way that made Tom's stomach knot up.

"I'm afraid that's about it, Tom!" Fay shouted.

"Can't we go down any deeper?" Tom's desperation was evident.

"No. I've played this one out as far as a man can. I'm sorry. I know how much this means to you." He shrugged his massive shoulders. "It's another duster."

Tom fought back tears of anger and disappointment. He was grimy from head to foot, and he could smell his own foulness. "Wait ten more minutes, and then shut her down," he shouted to Fay. And for the next ten minutes, he prayed harder than he had ever prayed in his life. The ten minutes passed, and Fay called to the men to shut down well number two.

The sudden quiet was hurtful to Tom's ears. "Tell the men to take today and tomorrow off, and then check back with me."

Climbing up on a wagon loaded with pipe, he sat down and tried to decide what to do next. There was no thought of not drilling again. The only question was where? With a sigh that came up from the soles of his working boots, Tom heaved himself up and started for the ranch house.

Both Mattie and Cleo were instantly aware of the sudden silence and exchanged worried looks.

"Maybe it came in," Mattie said hopefully.

"Maybe." Cleo felt a thrill of hope. Everything would be all right again. They could do so much with the ranch and all that money.

But from the set of Tom's shoulders as he trudged to the house, she knew the news was bad, and she put on a falsely cheerful front for him. "Hello, darling," she said lightly. "Would you like a cup of coffee?"

At his nod, she poured one and put it on the table in front of his slumped figure.

It sloshed crazily as he slammed his fist down on the table. The baby began to cry from the other room, and his mother came in from her room. Robert stood in the door frame, but there was no need to explain anything to anyone.

When J.J. rode up from town, the three men held counsel out under the tree in the backyard.

"I told you up front my dad would only go for one well. I staked us to the second one, but I have no more money to offer, or believe me I would." His gaze was transparent. "But I know there's oil out there. I know it."

"Well, there's no money in this family," Tom sighed.

"And none in Cleo's either, I understand," J.J. said.

"I know where we can get the money," Robert offered quietly.

"The banks aren't going to give us a dime," Tom reminded him angrily.

"Not the bank. Leaf."

Tom spun around to stare his brother full in the face. "What are you saying?"

"Those. . .uh. . .ladies have the money, I hear. They hold money for a lot of the men 'cause they don't trust the banks. And the ladies make loans with interest and everything, just like the banks."

Tom and J.J. exchanged a look of hope.

"You know one of these women?" J.J. asked Robert.

"*Tom* does. She's been in love with him for years. I bet she'd loan him the money."

Tom's chuckle gave rise to a full-fledged, heart-lifting belly laugh and caused the women to look out the window to see what was going on. "Robert, my boy," he said as he swiped at his eyes with the back of his hand, "there have been times when I thought you didn't know when to get in out of the rain, but when you get a good idea, you get a doozie!" He hugged his embarrassed brother in a rough, playful embrace and clapped him on the back. "It's worth a try, son."

The men fended off the women's questions with assurances that they had one more "banker" to see. "A new one in town," Tom told Cleo truthfully.

"I'll bet that doesn't make Leaf's father happy," said Cleo, who wondered why Tom's laughter seemed a bit too hearty for her little joke.

When they were in bed, Cleo asked, "Are we going to do the Houston bank scene?"

"No, honey, this is a new banking world. I don't think it would help the cause this time. But thank you, my love, for the offer," Tom said, and he fell asleep with dreams of riches supplied by the "businesswoman" daughter of the local banker.

# Chapter 12

Tom groomed himself carefully, but he didn't put on his suit to wear to the "bank."

As he rode into town that afternoon, he rehearsed several possible scenarios, talking things over with his horse. "If Robert's right, and Leaf loved me once, maybe she'll give me the money for old time's sake. Or maybe she'll hate me for marrying Cleo. On the other hand, if she's a good businesswoman, she'll see an opportunity to make more money. Maybe that's what she's looking for. . .a way out of her present condition."

He did not allow himself to ponder the possibility that she might *prefer* her "fallen" life, nor what Cleo would say if she knew his plans. Besides, it was strictly business.

He gazed across the endless land and began to pour out his heart to God. "Lord, I'm way past a rock and a hard place. Maybe my motives for wanting the ranch are wrong. But I know deep in my heart that I want to make a good place for Cleo and the baby. I want to be able to hold my head up and take my place in life. Ma and Robert need taking care of, too, Lord, and this part of West Texas needs to be settled. I want to be part of all that, Lord. I realize I'm going to see a woman who isn't living a very good life right now. But she's been a friend of mine for a long time, and I don't think of her as a. . .You know. . .'businesswoman.' I'm going to her as a friend who has the money I need to save my ranch and make a good life for my family. Please help me, Lord. Please."

It wasn't hard to find Leaf's little house. But his pulse raced unnaturally as he lifted his hand to knock.

Wearing a fetching silk kimono trimmed in white maribou feathers, and matching mules, she looked quite lovely in the harsh afternoon sun as she opened the door. "Well, well, well. Do come in, Mr. Kinney. This is an unexpected pleasure." She led him to the fashionable couch across the room. "Drink?"

"Coffee, thanks." Tom had always felt fully in charge in Leaf's presence. With their roles reversed, he was a little off balance. He sat down on the couch and crossed his knees, putting his hat on them.

Leaf sat down beside him and handed him the coffee. "I think I'm supposed to ask you if this is business or pleasure." Her laugh was throaty and relaxed.

Tom took a sip of the hot coffee to unlock his partially paralyzed vocal cords.

"It's always a pleasure to see you, Leaf."

She smiled knowingly. "I don't think so, or we would have gotten married, dear Tom, but it's nice of you to say so. Do you have a business proposition for me? Don't look so startled. Men come to me for more than my good looks, you know."

Tom blushed faintly at her candor. "I may have made a mistake about you," he said honestly. "You are lovely, and to top it off, you have a good mind."

"Water under the bridge. I'm happy for now." She refilled his cup. "You need money?"

"Yes. Enough to drill one more hole."

Leaf gave Tom a coy glance. "This is the part I like best. A man in your position will do anything to get the money. Make no mistake. I have the money to loan. But if I have any old debts I want paid off, here is the time to call them in, wouldn't you say?" She leaned closer to Tom. "I always dreamed of a time you might need me. . .back in the old days when I sat behind that desk."

Tom could smell her perfume, could feel the softness of her shoulder as she leaned against him. Her hair fell loose and brushed his face with the softness of a cloud.

"You'd be in some kind of trouble, and I'd help you, and you'd be so grateful that you'd fall in love with me and marry me," she murmured as she moved closer. "I thought you were the most wonderful man I'd ever known. My heart used to jump right out of my chest when I'd see you. And it died every time you played dead."

"Leaf, I had no idea. . . ." Beads of perspiration popped out on Tom's brow. "If only things had been different, Leaf."

"They *are* different, Tom. *I* hold all the aces." She sighed. "It feels delicious. I wouldn't trade places with any woman in the world right now." She sat back. "How far are you willing to go to get the money, Tom?" Her smile was predatory and there was a gleam in her eye.

Tom's gaze locked with hers. "I guess I'm willing to do. . .whatever it takes."

"I thought so." She positively purred with possibilities. She rose and walked over to a small desk where she pulled out a long sheet of legal paper. "There isn't any small print here, Tom. It's all very up front. The interest rate and my cut of the royalties. Standard."

Tom reeled. "That's all?" Then he felt a little let down. She didn't want him at all. Just his money.

"Don't be disappointed, Tom. If I force you to love me, it doesn't count. I only want you if you want me. Maybe that day will come, but it isn't today." Leaf smiled at him. "I love seeing that confusion on your face. It's been a wonderful experience knowing I could shake you up a little." She laughed in delight. "You didn't know whether to run or jump into the fire with both feet."

With great chagrin, he chuckled. "You're right. I'd already considered my options on the way over here. But after I got here, it didn't seem to be too large a sacrifice, after all." His grin was still an embarrassed one. " 'Course I hadn't planned on being the one to get turned down." He reached for the pen she offered and signed his name without reading the paper. "There's no need to read it. I'll go along with whatever you've got laid out for me. I'm dead out of options."

She went to the other room and returned with a wad of bills. They exchanged paper for money, and Tom started for the door.

Leaf was close on his heels and plucked at his sleeve. "There is something you can do for me, though. You were always so distant, Tom. How about one kiss to remember you by?"

It was a sweet kiss, the kind he had given Cleo on their first date, and she sighed. "Don't be too hard on yourself, Tom. You made the right choice with Cleo. She's good people."

Riding out of town, Tom fingered the wad of money. "Lord, I hadn't planned on a lesson in humility quite so severe. I found out I was willing to cheat on my wife to get the money for the ranch." His face burned with shame. "And I found out that Leaf's morals were better than mine." Tears began to stream down his face. "I don't deserve this money. I don't deserve the wonderful wife I have, nor Leaf's friendship. But most of all I'm sorry, Lord, that I failed Your test. And I promise You that I'll use this money, remembering Your mercy and goodness to me in spite of my sinfulness. Thank You, Lord, thank You."

He was glad it was a long ride to the ranch, for it gave him time to compose himself and to come to terms with his humanness and the overwhelming grandeur of God's love.

It was close to supper time when he rode in. He took a deep breath of the sweet air and looked at the land he owned. The Lord had given all of it to him. He would have the money to take care of Cleo and the ranch. He could give her back all she had lost when she married him. He knew how unhappy she had been here in the wilderness. And he loved her all the more for her sacrifice.

There was oil out there. He could smell it. He had the money now to find it. He had kept his marriage vows, though it was not to his credit, and he could look Cleo in the face without deceit. "God, please show me now where to look for the oil. I know all this is in Your plan for my life, or You wouldn't have given me another chance. Show me. Lead me."

The women assumed that he had acquired the money from a legitimate bank, and the men didn't let on. And when Cleo asked Tom about it later that night, he could only tell her that the Lord had provided.

The very next day, Tom's crew came back together again with the geologist.

Everyone felt he had the right to put in his two cents' worth, for all of them had worked in the fields in some capacity and had seen these men find oil.

Tom felt serene as they finally came to one accord on the exact place. He knew it would be the right one, and as the drill began to pound away at the earth, it echoed each beat of his heart. Everything would be all right now. God was on his side.

~

"That pounding is killing me!" Cleo muttered irritably as she poured Mattie another cup of coffee. "It'll probably wake the baby, too."

"I think she's used to it by now," Mattie consoled her. "Maybe you could use a little break. Why don't we go back to Houston and see your mother? It would do us all good to get away for a while. Your mom wanted to see little Claire so badly."

Cleo winced. "I guess Tom wouldn't even know if I was gone. There's just one thing in his life right now. Oil. I'll write Mother today."

In the privacy of their bedroom that night, Tom protested loudly. "But you can't leave now. I'm just about to strike oil!"

"That's what you've told me twice before." She faced him squarely. "Why don't you stop this foolishness? There's no oil on this ranch. There's nothing but rattlesnakes and sand! And the few cattle we have left are only here by dumb luck!

"Stop and think, Tom. Even if you do hit oil, do you expect me to raise our daughter in this solitude? No children to play with. No decent school. Nothing but loneliness. Let's go back to Houston," she begged. "You could get a good job. J.J. could surely find you something. We'd be able to give Claire all the things she's entitled to. Do you remember how lonely it was out here for you growing up? And you had Robert." Her eyes pleaded with him.

"We can have more children," he said stupidly, grabbing at anything to keep her from leaving.

She regarded him as if he had lost his mind. "Do you expect me to populate the area by myself?"

"Of course not, but now with the boom, the town will grow and there will be lots of people."

She began to pace angrily. "And I just can't wait for Claire to be best friends with all that riffraff. They have so much to offer her." Bitterness spewed out of Cleo's mouth, and words better left unsaid, were spoken. "I despise it out here in this place. Mattie is the only reason I've stayed this long. If I stay here any longer, I'll look just like your mother. Have you noticed her lately? She looks like one of those mesquites in wintertime. Is that what you want for me?

The look she turned on him was cold and unyielding. "Tom, you're responsible for two people in this world—Claire and me. How do you plan to take care of us?"

He was stung by her sharp words, and like the mesquite thorn, they immediately began to fester in his mind. "I'm doing the best I can for both of you," he protested. "And for the rest of my family. Right now I'm breaking my back to bring in this well. Then we'll be as rich as you want to be and can do whatever you please." He wrapped his arms around her slender frame, but he could feel her resistance. "Please, honey. You know how much I love you."

She shook off his embrace and stepped away. "And you think if you tell me you love me, all our problems will melt away? Not this time. I'm thinking of Claire as much as myself. Obviously, *you* can't." She dragged out her big traveling trunk and began to pack.

Tom couldn't think of another thing to say, his anger building at her recriminations. "Women!" he spat out as he stomped from the house.

Mattie appeared at her door. "Guess I'd better get some things together. Looks like we're going home."

"And the sooner, the better," Cleo replied huffily.

"J.J. will understand if I go back with you and wait for him there," Mattie said softly. "But maybe you'd like to give yourself a day or two before we leave. . .in case something changes."

But the look on Cleo's face told her that her mind was made up. There would be no delays. She was going. . .home to Houston.

# Chapter 13

Cleo stood on the porch of the little house her mother had bought and knocked. The baby was fussy and she herself felt the accumulated layers of travel dust and grime.

"My goodness, come in, come in!" Madeline took the fretful baby and soothed while welcoming Cleo with a smile. "My girls are home," she cooed to her namesake. Tactfully she didn't ask about Tom.

With the baby asleep and Cleo bathed and changed, the two women sat down in the small living room with a glass of iced tea.

"This was a special treat at the ranch," Cleo said, taking a sip. "It was saved for dances or parties." She rolled the damp glass across her forehead and sighed. "It's been like living with a foot in two different worlds."

"And to what do I owe this visit to our world?" her mother asked. "I wanted to see the baby, but I didn't think you'd be able to bring her this soon."

Cleo fought the tears that formed in her eyes. "I'm not as good a wife as you were. I couldn't take it anymore."

"Don't nominate me for sainthood, my dear. I took my own little 'vacations' away from your father now and again. I think that may have been one of the reasons we stayed married for so long." Madeline smiled. "Sometimes couples can have too much time together. Everyone needs to have a little breathing space occasionally."

Cleo abruptly changed the subject. "Mother, you look wonderful. And content. I've missed you. Now tell me everything that's going on."

Madeline beamed. "Well, I feel very well, I'm learning to live by myself, and as you can see, there is very little maintenance to this small home. I cook simple meals, shop a little, play too much bridge, and see a few old friends." She patted Cleo's hand. "It is a fact of life that when one is widowed, one doesn't receive the invitations one used to receive. I'm an odd number at a dinner party. And, you know, I do think some of those women act as though I'm after their husbands now that I'm not married." She laughed. "As if one of those old goats could ever replace your father!"

Cleo laughed delightedly. "You could give them a run for their money, Mother. You're still very beautiful. You'd be quite a catch."

"Oh, everything changes, dear," Madeline said, sobering. "People and situations don't remain the same. I want to warn you that you should be prepared to find things different, too. At this late date, I'm just finding out who my real friends are."

Cleo shrugged. "Well, dear old Mattie never changes. We had the most wonderful time together. . .almost like the old days. With the men away so much, we sort of relived the past. Oh, Mother, let me tell you about the oil boom in Kermit!" And she regaled her mother with anecdotes.

As the laughter subsided, Cleo hesitantly told about her fight with Tom.

"Oh, my darling, I wish I had a magic wand to wave and make everything perfect for you. This little vacation will give you time to think things out. I'm sorry it took this for us to be together, but I'm thrilled to see the little one. She's beautiful. She reminds me so much of you as a baby." Love shone brightly from her face.

Taking her cue, Cleo filled her mother in on Claire's birth and Tante Olga's loving care. And there were stories of other kindnesses from the West Texas folks. But Cleo's happy face sobered as she approached the next part of her story.

"I don't think I can say this without sounding like a snob, but I think you'll understand, Mother. The people out there are kind. But it's not the place I want Claire to grow up in. I want her to have polish like you, knowledge of good books and music. Manners that will take her anywhere. Clothes and friends. A good college."

"You want her to be like you, my sweet. You are all those things." Madeline smiled gently.

"If I am, it's because you gave them to me. I want no less for my own daughter." She fingered the wedding ring on her hand. "Tom doesn't understand."

"So you feel you must choose between your husband and your daughter?"

"I hadn't thought of it that way, but. . .I'm afraid so."

A frown of distress furrowed Madeline's brow. "There's an old saying about not throwing away the baby with the bathwater. Perhaps if you think in terms of compromise, you won't have to choose one or the other. Let me remind you of one thing: You promised on your wedding day in front of God to cling to Tom in sickness and in health. . .in good times *and* in bad. . . ." She put her arm around Cleo. "Darling, I've seen Tom look at you. I've seen the things he endured here to make you happy. He's a good man, Cleo. I don't think you'd ever find anyone who loves you more. Maybe he's not on track right now. Maybe he's put you second place in his life. But that's no reason to throw away what you have together."

She sat back against the soft cushions. "I've found that life is like a roller coaster. Sometimes you're up and sometimes you're down. But the roller coaster keeps moving. Life keeps moving. You weather the bad times and savor the good. And as you learn to live together, there is steadily more good than bad. Until near the end of your time together, it's so good that it's almost unbearable when one leaves the other. . . ." Tears spilled down her cheeks.

"Oh, Mother, I'm so sorry!" Cleo threw her arms around her mother and hugged her hard.

Madeline dabbed her eyes with her hanky. "No, don't feel sorry for me. I've had a wonderful life. And I plan to go on having a full life.

"Cleo, perhaps the one thing I regret is not speaking more often to your father about God. He was such a reserved man. So private. I felt as though he had put God in some sort of compartment. It was something we just didn't speak of. Now I wish I knew how he felt about dying. Was he frightened? Did he think he was going to heaven? Cleo, don't make that mistake with Tom. Share your faith with him. Talk to him. Invite God into your home. We gave you everything. . . except the most important thing. . .a mother and father who prayed openly and sought God's direction."

Madeline's eyes glowed with conviction. "How odd that this late in my life my faith is beginning to flower. Imagine. . .an old lady like me in the flush of an awakening. I am preparing now for my own death, and it's not frightening at all. I'm at peace now. I want that for you long before you get to be my age." She looked into her daughter's eyes. "You live in an uncertain land. You need God to help you through the years ahead."

Cleo nodded, but in her room later, she couldn't help wondering if the strain of her father's death had caused a true spiritual awakening or if her mother was grasping at religion to shore up her faltering spirits. Still, the things she had shared with Cleo were true. Things she needed to think about seriously. God had become much more important to Cleo since her move to West Texas. She found herself praying without formality over the smallest things.

But she blushed to think she hadn't prayed at all about this enormous rift with Tom. *I'm sorry, Lord. I was so mad I didn't think. I just acted. But I need time to think all this out, Lord. Both Tom and I are going to have to make some changes in our lives. Help me to be wise. I do love him, but he makes me so mad! Lead me, Lord. And keep Tom safe until we can work all this out.*

⤳

The next day Cleo called Mattie and they set up a luncheon at one of their favorite restaurants with some of their old friends. Cleo felt like a girl again as she dressed carefully.

"Hey, I like that dress," Mattie said smilingly when she slipped into the passenger seat of Madeline's little Ford. "Did you get that here?"

"Of course not, dahling," Cleo said in the exaggerated dialect of the very rich, "I bought it in the most expensive store in all of West Texas. You wouldn't know it. It's much too exclusive for the Houston set."

Mattie giggled. "I don't think you've changed at all, dahling."

They walked into the restaurant. "It feels wonderful to be dining in a lovely place again. I've missed all this," Cleo told Mattie.

Mattie wrinkled her nose. "That's funny. I never noticed you can almost smell money in the air here. And talk about class!" She glanced around. "I don't remember feeling this way about this place before."

Cleo didn't wait to hear Mattie's remarks. Her mind was on the good time ahead. "Don't be silly. Oh, there are the girls over there."

The conversation swirled about the table as the friends caught up on the latest news. Talk of horses and men and trips to Europe and clothes and parties. Muted references as to who was misbehaving with whom, accompanied by giggles. It was all too stimulating for Cleo.

During a lull, she told her ranch tales, shading them to sound like a great adventure, or even a safari to a foreign land. Once she caught sight of Mattie's puckered brow, but she staunchly refused to tell her friends the real story.

As they left to go home, Mattie shot her a look of disgust. "Now *that* was an uplifting experience."

Cleo bridled. "Well, I had a wonderful time. It was great to hear about all the things that are going on."

Mattie shook her head. "I never noticed before, but what I heard today was a lot of tripe."

"Mattie! It was just girl talk."

"We're not girls anymore, Cleo. If you took all the gossip we heard in the beauty shop in Kermit, tied it up in fancy wrappings, and dropped it in the middle of that high-class café, you'd have exactly the same thing."

Cleo was shocked. "How can you say that! They were talking about Europe and concerts and glamorous parties!"

"They were talking about *people*, not cathedrals or paintings or music. Except for her correct grammar, Betty St. James sounded just like those two beauticians."

"Mattie, you've become the ultimate snob!" Cleo accused.

Mattie caught Cleo's arm and jerked her around to face her. "I met some nice people out there. They were honest and real and they had goals in their lives. They were building something worth dying for. Those 'girls' in there are just that—girls. And it makes me sick to think I sounded like that myself not too long ago. Thank you for inviting me to the land of the real. And if you had one ounce of sense, you'd catch the next train back to the ranch, get down on your knees, and beg Tom to forgive you and take you back!"

Cleo felt as if she had been slapped hard in the face. "Mattie, what's gotten into you?"

"I think maybe one of us has finally grown up." Her eyes reflected a deep understanding. "And I think it's me."

There was little else to say on the way home, but when Cleo let Mattie out in front of her house, Mattie said, "You think hard on what I said about Tom. There isn't a better man around. You're a dope if you let him slip out of your life because of some silly set of values you learned as a kid."

To say that Cleo's sleep was fitful that night would be an understatement. Her head felt like a giant mixing bowl, with thoughts and voices tossing and tumbling inside. But when she awoke in the morning, her decision had jelled. She loved Tom. And no matter what, she wanted to live with him. Instead of being fatigued, she felt renewed and energetic, eager to get back to the hub of her world.

Cleo kissed her mother and Mattie good-bye at the train depot. This time the tears were happy ones.

"I'm going to miss little Claire," Madeline said. "And you, too, my darling. But I know you're happy, and that's all that matters."

"Mother, it's easy to get on a train and come to see us. I promise you an exciting and unique experience." Cleo smiled. "And my Mattie. What would I have done without you?" She hugged her red-haired friend tightly as her mother held the baby one last time.

Mattie only shrugged. "Oh, you'd have figured it out eventually. I just gave you a shortcut," she said with false modesty. Then she whispered in Cleo's ear, "Don't forget what I told you. You have the best guy I ever met. Don't let anyone or anything come between you. And invite me back to the ranch soon. I'm hankering to dance with old Crook!" Mattie was crying openly as Cleo mounted the steps to the train.

And after the baby was asleep, Cleo leaned against the window of the train, feeling the hypnotic rocking of the train as it swayed its way over the tracks back to Tom.

Cleo had put on a brave front with those two. But now she wondered what was waiting for her at home. What if Tom didn't want her back? What if she had gone too far? She moaned silently as she recalled all the hurtful things she had slung at him the night she had left.

*Father,* she prayed silently, *please help me. I want Tom's love back...and our home and family. I have no idea what to do next, but when I look back at my life, somehow I feel You've been there all along, guiding me and making things happen. How else could Tom and I have met? I'm at the bottom of the cup, Lord. I won't make deals with You, but I will promise that if I get the chance, I will be what You want me to be. But I can't do it without Your help.* There wasn't any outward sign that God had heard her prayers, but she added another petition. *And help me to love Tom's mother, even if she seems impossible.*

Cleo fell asleep against the window, feeling a measure of relief that she was no longer alone. God would help her set everything straight.

⤐

Despite her prayer on the train and the restful nap, Cleo's stomach was in knots when she reached the sandy dunes outside Monaghan's Wells. She was in a foreign land again. And her harp was still on the willow. It would be until she knew Tom still loved her and wanted her.

The town looked busier than it had the last time she saw it. Spillover from the Kermit boom, I guess. "Well, Baby Claire," she said, nuzzling the child's downy head, "all we have to do is find someone to take us to the ranch."

Glancing across the street, she noticed the Holman House, a restaurant that seemed to be enjoying a thriving business. She was starving to death. Leaving her luggage, she walked over for a good meal and a chance to inquire whether someone might be going her way. She could always hire someone, if worse came to worst.

Inside, she heard a familiar voice coming from the dining room. Fattie Smallwood, napkin tucked neatly under his chin and covering his ample chest, stood immediately as she entered.

"Why, Mrs. Kinney, er, Cleo! What a wonderful surprise!" He offered her an empty chair beside him and took the baby from her arms, cooing softly to the child.

"Always room for one more," Mrs. Holman called out from the kitchen.

"Fattie, is there any chance you might be going out toward the ranch?" Cleo asked.

"Why, ma'am, even if I wasn't, I'd make a special trip just for you," Fattie said gallantly.

He was much too kind, Cleo knew, to ask any more personal questions, such as, What was she doing getting off a train by herself with no one to meet her?

❧

Fattie loaded Cleo's things in the wagon and clucked the mules to an easy gait, swaying over the sand like a boat gliding, if somewhat roughly, over an earth-toned sea.

"Beautiful country, ain't it?" he observed with a smile of satisfaction.

With great surprise, Cleo realized that it was. "I don't think I ever considered it so before. But I suppose it is beautiful in its own way."

"You know, ma'am, beauty is a funny thing. I've met up with some women so homely they'd have to rub their faces with barbecue sauce to get the dogs to lick 'em. And I've seen women near as beautiful as you." Cleo smiled at his compliment. "But you know as well as I do that unless there's a reason to love the inside of that woman, neither one of 'em is appealing."

He looked around. "Now take this country out here. It's sort of the homely one, some say. I like to think of her beauty bein' in her spareness. There ain't nothing extra on her. She's lean and clean. There ain't a lot of stuff to take my mind off o' lovin' her for jest what she is. Restful. Oh, I know it takes a heap o' work to make a livin' out here, but after it's done, she's restful to be with."

Cleo's eyes scanned the endless horizon and thought of the busyness of Houston's streets. There was so much to love about Houston, so many happy memories, and some sad ones. And she loved that city. But with clearing eyes she saw what Fattie was talking about. And she thought about what Mattie had said. *They are building something out there. Something worth dying for.* Cleo felt her pulse quicken with a new beat. "Thank you, Fattie."

"Ahh, I was just ramblin', ma'am. I oughta pay ya to listen."

They rolled on past the China Springs windmill, and Cleo remembered the first time she had seen it with Tom. "How come this one is named China Springs?"

"Some say it's because one woman went crazy when they camped beside it and broke every dish she had in the wagon against its base." He joined her in a chuckle.

"I can understand how she felt," Cleo admitted.

"Funny thing about windmills," Fattie observed. "They all have their own sounds, you know. Jest like people's voices. Some of 'em sound lonesome and some of 'em have a comforting sound, like a mama croonin' to her baby."

Cleo shivered in the warm air.

"No need to feel spooked, ma'am. Them windmills all look like a tree of life to me."

It was nearly dusk, that time in the West when the sand creates an odd alchemy of nature that can be duplicated nowhere else on earth. Cleo saw it now. The rays of the setting sun, sifting through the sand and molded into unbelievably gorgeous hues of red, orange, yellow, pinks, and purples, splashed against a canvas of fluffy white clouds just above the horizon. It was truly breathtaking.

"What a wonderful homecoming," she breathed, as much to God as to Fattie on the wagon seat beside her.

As they neared the ranch, sounds of music could be heard and lights twinkled on in the coming darkness.

"Looks like they're havin' a git-together at your place," Fattie said.

As they drew closer, Cleo could see that a full-fledged party was in progress. "Must be our turn to host the dance."

She could pick out Tom's broad-shouldered frame in the distance as he mingled with the guests under the string of lanterns. He was heartbreakingly handsome. As if feeling her eyes on him, he turned and saw her coming.

He loped to meet her, his face flushed, a big grin spread from ear to ear. "Cleo! Cleo! You're back!" He swung her down from the wagon as Fattie climbed down and took the baby out of the little nest he had made for her in the back.

"My darling, Cleo," Tom whispered against her hair.

"I'm sorry, Tom. . ."

"Not now, Cleo. Not ever. Honey, we're rich! We've struck oil!"

"Tom, put me down! Hold me close." Her mind as well as her body was spinning. "You really did strike oil?"

He nodded. "And we're having a party to celebrate." He led her into the yard, where Cleo was welcomed as if she had only been on a short trip to town to buy supplies.

Her mouth fell open in surprise when she saw Mrs. Kinney dancing and laughing and looking fifteen years younger.

"Sometimes it only takes the rain to make the cactus bloom," said Tom happily.

Catching Cleo's eye, Mrs. Kinney abandoned her partner and came to greet her. "Welcome, home, Cleo! And where's my granddaughter? I need to see how much she's grown!"

All the noise and confusion awakened Claire, but she went into Mrs. Kinney's arms without a whimper, eyes round with wonder. "Now you dance with your husband, child. I'm a good hand with babies, if I do say so. Besides, I need to catch up on things with Hiram. . .uh. . .Fattie." And she gave Tom a meaningful look.

Everyone was there. Crook asked Cleo for a waltz, and if she had been on a ballroom floor in Paris, she couldn't have had a better partner. "Cowboys are the best dancers in the world," she told him.

"Yes, ma'am," Crook agreed, "it's from stayin' on horses and tiptoein' over trouble."

And then, while the fiddle music swirled the women's skirts and lifted the men's boots, she was back in Tom's arms. His arms felt so good around her. His smell was familiar, as was the contour of his body. She snuggled against him, cherishing the knowledge of him. "Tom, the Lord has brought all this about, I know it. I've learned I can't live my life without His guidance and care."

"You're not the only one who's learned a few things," he confessed. "If you only knew how many times I've prayed lately, most of all, that He would send you back to me. He's given us everything, Cleo."

She smiled up into his eyes. "Everything. So much that, even if we hadn't struck oil, we'd be rich!" She thought of the psalm Tante Olga had quoted to her when Claire was born, and she laughed. "I want to go out to the Sand Hills, out by the big water seep."

Tom pulled away to look down into her radiant face. "Whatever for, my dearest?"

"I want to take down my harp from the willow tree. I can sing the Lord's song in a foreign land. No more regrets. No more doubts. I'm home."

# A Letter to Our Readers

Dear Readers:

In order that we might better contribute to your reading enjoyment, we would appreciate your taking a few minutes to respond to the following questions. When completed, please return to the following: Fiction Editor, Barbour Publishing, Inc., P.O. Box 719, Uhrichsville, OH 44683.

1. Did you enjoy reading *Texas Dreams*?
   ❑ Very much—I would like to see more books like this.
   ❑ Moderately—I would have enjoyed it more if _____
   _____
   _____

2. What influenced your decision to purchase this book?
   (Check those that apply.)
   ❑ Cover          ❑ Back cover copy          ❑ Title          ❑ Price
   ❑ Friends        ❑ Publicity                ❑ Other

3. Which story was your favorite?
   ❑ *Dreams of the Pioneers*     ❑ *Dreams Fulfilled*
   ❑ *Dreams of Glory*            ❑ *Song of Captivity*

4. Please check your age range:
   ❑ Under 18          ❑ 18–24          ❑ 25–34
   ❑ 35–45             ❑ 46–55          ❑ Over 55

5. How many hours per week do you read? _____

Name _____

Occupation _____

Address _____

City _____ State _____ Zip _____

E-mail _____